SADIE'S MONTANA

TRILOGY

Three Bestselling Novels in One

LINDA BYLER

SADIE'S MONTANA

TRILOGY

Three Bestselling Novels in One

WILD HORSES

KEEPING SECRETS

THE DISAPPEARANCES

THREE SPIRITED NOVELS *by the* BESTSELLING AMISH AUTHOR

Good Books

New York, New York

Copyright © 2016 by Linda Byler

Good Books books may be purchased in bulk at special discounts for sales
promotion, corporate gifts, fund-raising, or educational purposes. Special
editions can also be created to specifications. For details, contact the Special
Sales Department, Good Books, 307 West 36th Street, 11th Floor, New
York, NY 10018 or info@skyhorsepublishing.com.

Good Books is an imprint of Skyhorse Publishing, Inc.®, a Delaware
corporation.

Visit our website at www.goodbooks.com.

10 9 8 7 6 5 4 3 2

Library of Congress Cataloging-in-Publication Data is available on file.

Cover design by Koechel Peterson & Associates, Inc.

Print ISBN: 978-1-68099-123-9
Ebook ISBN: 978-1-68099-134-5

Printed in Canada

Table of Contents

LINDA BYLER

WILD HORSES

SADIE'S MONTANA
Book 1

Chapter 1

It was easier to love a horse than it was to love people. Horses understood. Oh, Sadie knew her sisters rolled their eyes about that philosophy, but that was all right. It meant they didn't understand, same as Mam and Dat. Especially Dat.

He was the one who made her finally part with Paris, her old, beloved, palomino riding horse. Paris wasn't really her own horse. Her uncle had kind of loaned her to Sadie to see if she could do anything with the unruly monster who bit, bucked, and even attacked men—especially small men who were assertive in their way of handling her.

Sadie understood Paris. Underneath all that bucking and kicking was a timid spirit—perhaps too timid—and that's why she bucked and kicked. It was hard to explain, but Paris was afraid of being controlled by someone she could not trust completely.

Paris was beautiful, but she hadn't always been that way. When Uncle Emanuel brought her in a silver horse trailer, Sadie was shocked at the sight of the pathetic creature that was coaxed out of the trailer's squeaking door.

The truck driver, a tall, skinny youth with a wad of snuff as large as a walnut stuck in his lower lip, refused to help at all. Paris terrified him, there was no doubt about that.

Sadie crossed her arms tightly across her stomach, watching every move Uncle Emanuel made, urging, talking, threatening, and pulling on the dirty halter. First she heard an awful commotion—dull, thudding clicks against the side of the trailer and yelling from Uncle Emanuel. Then he came skidding down the manure-encrusted ramp, his eyes rolling behind his thick glasses, his straw hat clumped down on his head of riotous red curls.

"Yikes!" he shouted, grinning at Sadie.

Sadie smiled and said nothing. Her stomach hurt so badly, she couldn't utter a word. She was afraid, too. She didn't have much experience with horses, other than with their fat, black, little Shetland pony named Chocolate that they had when she was barely six years old.

She had always wanted a horse of her own—one she could name and brush, a horse whose mane and tail she could braid. She'd give the horse its very own saddle and bridle and pretty saddle blanket with a zebra design on it, and she'd put pretty pink ribbons at the end of the braids.

She was almost 15-years-old when she heard Mam tell her sister Leah about being at sisters' day. Uncle Emanuel's wife, Hannah, had related the story of this palomino horse he bought, saying, "She was a pure danger, that one. Emanuel was scared of her, that was all there was to it." Mam was laughing, thinking of her brother and his quick, funny ways.

Sadie had been standing at the refrigerator, peering inside for a stalk of celery to load up with peanut butter. She was so hungry after having spent the afternoon with her cousin, Eva, who lived down the road.

Slowly, as if in a dream, she closed the refrigerator door, completely forgetting about her hunger, the celery, and the peanut butter.

"What?" she uttered dreamily.

"Oh, my brother Emanuel. Can you imagine him with a horse he can't handle?"

Mam laughed again and plopped another peeled potato into her stainless steel pot.

"What kind of horse? I mean, did he buy her or him? Is it a driving horse for the buggy or a riding horse?"

"I think a rider. He bought her for his son, who I'm sure is not old enough to ride a full-grown horse."

"Mam!"

Mam's knife stopped slicing through the potato as she turned, giving her full attention to Sadie, her oldest daughter.

"What, Sadie? My, you are serious!"

"Mam, listen to me. Could I... Would I be able to... Do you suppose Dat would let me try to...?"

Sadie swiped nervously at the stray brown hair coming loose from behind the *dichly* she wore for everyday work. A *dichly* is a triangle of cotton fabric, usually a men's handkerchief cut in half and hemmed, worn by Amish women and girls when they do yard work or anything strenuous.

Sadie's coverings were always a disaster, Mam said, so she only wore one to go away on Sundays, or to quiltings, or sisters' day, or to go to town.

"Ach, now, Sadie."

That was all Mam said, and the way she said it was not promising in the least.

Her hope of ever having a horse of her own stood

before her again like an insurmountable cliff. There was no getting over it or around it. It was just there, looming high and large, giving her a huge lump in her throat. No one understood. No one knew about this huge, gray and brown cliff ahead of her which had no handholds or any steps or easy ways to climb up and over. And if she told anyone, they would think there was something seriously wrong with her.

She wanted a horse. That was all.

Dat didn't particularly like horses. He was a bit different in this area than other Amish men. He hitched up his big, brown, standard-bred road horse to the freshly washed and sparkling carriage every two weeks to go to church and on the rare occasion they went visiting someone on the *in-between* Sundays. But mostly, Jacob Miller's horse had a life of leisure.

Sadie had knelt by her bed every evening for weeks, folded her hands, bent her head, closed her eyes, and prayed to God to somehow, some way soften her father's heart. As she prayed, she could feel some little crevices in her cliff—just tiny little cracks you could stick one foot in.

The Bible said that if you had faith as small as a grain of mustard seed, you could move a mountain, which, as far as Sadie could tell, no one had ever done. Surely if someone had done it in the past, they would have written about it and stashed it away as very significant history.

But that mustard seed verse is why she decided that it was worth a try. Dat's big, brown horse had no company in the barn except a few rabbits and the cackling hens. He had always said horses do better when there are two or three together in one barn.

Her opening argument came when Dat asked her to help move the rabbit hutch to the other end of the barn beside the chicken coop. She tugged and lifted mightily, pulling her share, glad she had a good, strong back and arms.

"There," Dat said, "that's better. More room for Charlie to get his drink."

Sadie lifted her big, blue eyes to her father's which were a mirror of her own.

"Dat?"

He was already lifting bales of hay, making room for the straw he had ordered.

"Hmm?"

"Dat? Eva got a new white pony. Well, it's a horse, actually. A small one. She can ride well. Bareback, too. She doesn't like saddles."

"Mm-hmm."

"Does Charlie like it here by himself?"

There was no answer. Dat had moved too far away, hanging up the strings that held the bales of hay together.

Sadie waited. She arranged her *dichly*, smoothed her blue-green apron across her stomach, scuffed the hay with the toe of her black sneaker, and wished with all her heart her dat would like horses.

When he returned, she started again.

"Dat? If someone gave me a horse to train, would you allow it?"

Dat looked at her a bit sharply.

"You can't ride. You never had a horse. And I'm not feeding two horses. No."

"I'll pay for the feed."

"No."

Sadie walked away, hot tears stinging her long, dark lashes. Just plain no. Flat out no. He could have at least tried to be kind about it. Every crevice in her cliff disappeared, and the mountain became higher, darker, and more dangerous than ever. There was no getting around it or over it anymore. There was no use. Dat said no.

Sadie knew that a basic Amish rule of child-rearing was being taught to give up your own will at a young age. Even when they prayed, they were taught to say, "Not my will, but Thine be done."

She knew very well that both Mam and Dat thought that was the solid base, the foundation of producing good, productive adults, but why did it always need to be so hard? She wanted a horse. And now Eva had one.

But the good thing about Eva having a horse was that Sadie learned to ride, and ride well. The girls roamed the fields and woods of the rural Ohio countryside, sharing the small white horse named Spirit. They wore their dresses, which were a hassle, but there was no other way. They would never be allowed to ride in English clothes, although they each wore a pair of trousers beneath their dresses. It was just not ladylike to have their skirts flapping about when they galloped across the fields. Even so, their mothers, who were sisters, frowned on these Amish girls doing all that horse-back riding.

Then, when Sadie had given up and the cliff had faded a bit, church services were held at Uncle Emanuel's house. Only Dat and Mam had gone because it was a long way to their house in another district.

Dat and Emanuel had walked to the pasture. Dat looked at this long-haired, diseased, wreck-of-a-horse, and he thought of Sadie. It might be a good thing.

He didn't tell Sadie until the morning before the horse arrived. Sadie was so excited, she couldn't eat a thing all day, except to nibble on the crust of a grilled cheese sandwich at lunch. That's why her stomach hurt so badly when Paris arrived.

She had often told Eva that if she ever owned a horse of her own, she would name it Paris, because Paris was a faraway, fancy city that meant love. Paris was a place of dreams for an Amish girl. She knew she could never go there because Amish people don't fly in big airplanes, and they don't cross the ocean in big ships because they'd have to have their pictures taken. So they were pretty much stuck in the United States. She guessed when they came over from Germany in the 1700s, they didn't need their pictures taken. That, or else cameras had not been invented yet.

So Paris was a place of dreams. And Paris, once Sadie's dream, had now become her horse.

The truck driver grinned around his wad of snuff.

"Havin' problems, are you?"

"Hey, this thing means business!" Emanuel shouted, tucking his shirttail into his denim broadfall pants.

Sadie stepped forward.

"Can I look at her?" she asked timidly.

"You can look, but you better stay out of the trailer."

Sadie moved swiftly up the ramp, only to be met by a bony rear end and a tangled, dirty tail swishing about menacingly.

Uh-oh, she thought.

A tail swishing back and forth without any pesky flies hovering about meant the horse was most definitely unhappy. It was the same signal as ears flattened against a head, or teeth bared, so Sadie stood quietly and said, "Hello, Paris."

The bony hips sidled against the trailer's side, and the tangled tail swished back and forth furiously.

Sadie peeked around the steel side of the trailer. Paris looked back, glaring at her through a long, unkempt forelock stuck with burrs, bits of twigs, and dirt.

"Poor baby," Sadie murmured.

Their eyes met then, Sadie declared to her sister Anna, and Paris sort of stood aside and her tail stopped swishing. A trust was born between Sadie and Paris, a very small one, of course, but it was born nevertheless.

Sadie didn't try to ride Paris for three weeks. She brushed her and bathed her with a bucket of warm, soapy water. She bought equine shampoo at the local harness shop, a new halter, a rope, and brushes.

When she wasn't with Paris, Sadie mowed grass, raked the leaves, watered flowers, worked in the neighbors' yard—anything to earn five dollars. Then she was finally able to buy a nice brown saddle, secondhand, of course, but a saddle was a wonderful thing to own, no matter how used. She put the new green saddle blanket on Paris, whose coat was now sleek and pretty. Her ribs were still quite prominent, though, but they would take time to fill out.

When the day finally arrived when she could put the real saddle on Paris' back, Sadie's heart pounded so loudly, her ears thudded with a dull, spongy, bonging sound.

She didn't tell anyone she was riding Paris. Not Mam or Dat, and especially not her pesky little brother Reuben, or any of her sisters. It was better to be alone, unhurried, quiet, able to talk to Paris in her own language which everyone else would probably think was silly.

She would never forget the thrill of trusting Paris. Oh, the horse danced sideways awhile, even tried to scrape her off, but Sadie sat firmly, talking, telling Paris all the things she'd like to hear.

It seemed that Paris loved it when Sadie told her she was beautiful and her best friend. Her eyes turned soft and liquidy, and Sadie knew she lowered her lashes, those gorgeous, silky, dark brushes surrounding her eyes.

Sadie and Eva spent many days galloping across the rolling farmlands of Ohio. Eva never used a saddle, so Sadie learned to ride without one as well. They walked their horses, they talked, they rode to the creek on hot summer days with a container of shampoo, swam with their horses, washed them—and their own hair—with the soapy liquid. This was their favorite activity when the August heat flattened the leaves against the trees, the sky grew brassy yellow-blue with heat, and crickets, grasshoppers, and ants found cool leaves to creep under. Sometimes storms would come up in the northeast and drive them home, dripping wet and clean and filled with the joy of their youth, their girlhoods, their innocence.

They raced their horses in freshly-mowed alfalfa fields. Sometimes they became competitive—and a bit miffed—when one thought the other got an unfair start to a race. They asked Reuben to call "Go!" then, but he was too busy playing with his Matchbox cars in the dirt under the silver maple tree where the grass didn't grow well. He pushed the dirt with his tiny bulldozer and backhoe for hours on end. The girls and their horses bored him completely, and he told them so, glaring up at them under his strubbly bangs, his shirt collar rimmed with dust, his hands black from the fertile soil around the base of the tree.

It was a wonderful summer for two 15-year-old girls.

Then, one night, when the whole house was settling down with a creaky sort of sigh, the way houses do when darkness falls and the air cools and the old siding expands and contracts, Sadie heard her parents' voices rising and falling, rising and falling. Their sounds kept her awake far into the night. She plumped her pillow, tossed the covers, turned to a more comfortable position, and finally put the pillow over her head to shut out her parents' voices.

The next day, they made the announcement.

Dat and Mam asked Sadie, Leah, Rebekah, and Anna to come sit in the living room with them. They looked extremely sober. Reuben was still out under the maple tree with his Matchbox toys, but they let him there undisturbed.

Sadie remembered hearing his faint "Brrr-rrrm, Brr-rm," as Dat cleared his throat and dropped the bomb, as she thought of it ever after.

They were moving. To Montana. Sadie felt like she was being pulled along by a huge, sticky, rubber band made of voices, and she had no scissors to cut it and get out from under its relentless power.

Montana. An Amish settlement. Too many people. The youth misbehaving. Sadie soon 16.

Mam looked happy, even excited. How could she? How could she be swept along, happily putting her hand in Dat's and agreeing?

The rubber band's power increased as Anna clapped her hands, Leah's blue eyes shone, Rebekah squealed, and Dat grinned broadly.

David Troyers would be going, too. And Dan Detweilers. Sadie sat back on the sofa, creasing the ruffle on the homemade pillow top over and over. The noise around her made no sense, especially when Leah shrieked with pure excitement about a train ride.

What train?

"You mean, we're traveling to Montana on a train?"

Sadie managed to croak, her mouth dry with fear. "What about Paris?"

It was all a blur after that. Sadie couldn't remember anything clearly except the pain behind her eyes that carried her out of the living room and up the stairs and onto her bed. Sadie dissolved into great gulping sobs, trying to release the pain near her heart.

She could not part with Paris.

But she would have to. Dat said she had to. That was that. There was no livestock being moved all those miles.

"Livestock?" Where in the world did he find a word like that to describe two horses, eight rabbits, and a bunch of silly hens? Paris was no "livestock."

The only consolation Sadie had was that Uncle Emanuel found a home for Paris on the local veterinarian's farm. The vet's daughter, Megan, an English girl who loved horses as much as Sadie, was ecstatic, Sadie could clearly tell.

Sadie spent the last evening with Eva and Paris, crying nearly the whole time. Sometimes—between tears—she and Eva became hysterical, laughing and crying at the same time. But even when laughing, Sadie cried inside.

At the end of the evening, Sadie and Paris clattered into the barn and Sadie slid off her beloved horse's back, that golden, rounded, beautiful back. She threw her arms around Paris' neck, and held on. She hugged her horse for every time they played in the creek, for every time Sadie braided her mane, for every ribbon she tied in it, for every apple Paris had ever crunched out of her hand, for every nuzzle Sadie had received on her shoulder, and for every aching hour she would never have with Paris ever again.

Sadie did not watch them take Paris away in the big, fancy trailer. She set her shoulders squarely and went for a walk all by herself, knowing that it would be a long time until she would ever love another horse.

But Paris would live on in her heart. That's why she was named Paris—she was a dream. And love.

Chapter 2

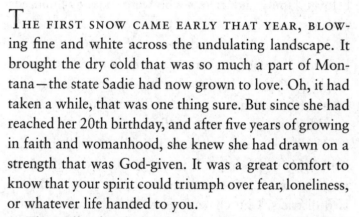

THE FIRST SNOW CAME EARLY THAT YEAR, BLOW-
ing fine and white across the undulating landscape. It
brought the dry cold that was so much a part of Montana—the state Sadie had now grown to love. Oh, it had
taken a while, that was one thing sure. But since she had
reached her 20th birthday, and after five years of growing
in faith and womanhood, she knew she had drawn on a
strength that was God-given. It was a great comfort to
know that your spirit could triumph over fear, loneliness,
or whatever life handed to you.

The Miller family lived high on a ridge overlooking
the Aspendale Valley, where a mixture of sturdy pines,
aspen, and hearty oak trees protected them from much
of the frigid winter winds. Dat had remodeled parts of
the old log house, built a barn large enough to accommodate the horse and cattle they owned, and surrounded
the pasture with a split-rail fence.

It was an idyllic setting overlooking the valley dotted with homesteads, ranches, and dwellings where the
Amish community had settled and thrived.

Dat was no farmer or rancher. His love was not in

horses or cattle, although he owned both—enough to keep the pasture clipped and to transport his family to church on Sunday.

Instead, he built log homes and established a good reputation as an honest, hardworking carpenter. He left his customers happy with their sturdy houses made from the finest quality material and precise workmanship.

Their life in Montana was blessed, Mam said. She was very happy most of the time, although Sadie sometimes found her wiping a stray tear directly related to her homesickness. It was a constant thing, this missing dearly beloved family and friends who were so many hundreds of miles away.

Mam wrote letters and went to the phone out by the barn to talk to her mother and sisters. Sometimes she was laughing when she came back to the house and sometimes crying. It was all a part of Sadie's life now but more manageable than it had been that first year.

The surrounding valley, and on into the hills beyond, held 33 Amish families. It was a good-sized community, which meant it was soon time to divide the church into two districts. Church services were held in the homes. When the house became too crowded, dividing the church became a necessity.

There was a group of 20 or 30 youth, which Sadie had always been grateful for. They had been her friends for quite a few years, good friends with whom she could share her feelings and also Sunday afternoons and evenings playing volleyball and having supper together, often with a hymn-singing afterward. Sometimes the youth went camping or riding or shopping in a faraway location, which was something Sadie always anticipated.

The winters were long here in Montana. Months of

cold wind swept down from the distant mountain ranges, which were always covered with snow. The snow on the tips of the mountains never ceased to amaze her, especially when the sun warmed her back or she felt a gentle summer breeze in her face. But in winter, everything was white and cold, and the whole world felt like the tops of the mountains.

Sadie sat at the table in the dining room watching the snow swirling across the wooden patio floor. Little eddies of it tried to accumulate in the corners of the panes in the French doors but were swept away by the howling wind.

"It's always windy here, Mam."

Mam looked up from the cookbook she was leafing through, took a sip of coffee from the brown stoneware mug, and nodded her head.

"It's Montana."

Sadie sliced half a banana into her dish of thick, honeyed oatmeal, adding a handful of dark, sticky raisins, and nodded.

"I know."

Mam glanced at the clock.

"Jim's late."

"Probably because of the snow."

She finished pouring the rich, creamy milk onto the raisins, stirred, and spooned a large amount into her mouth. She closed her eyes.

"Mmmm. Oatmeal with honey."

Mam smiled.

"What do we want for Christmas dinner this year?"

Sadie looked at Mam, surprised

"Christmas is two months away."

"I can still plan ahead."

Sadie nodded, grimacing as the battered truck pulled

up to the French doors—a dark intruder into the lovely, pristine whiteness outside.

"Oh, here I go."

"You haven't finished your breakfast."

"It's all right."

She put her arms into the sleeves of her black, wool coat, threw a white scarf around her head, and was out the door to the tune of Mam's usual, "Have a good day!"

The whirling bits of snow made her bend her head to avoid the worst of the sharp little stings against her bare face. She pulled quickly on the door handle, bounced up into the torn vinyl of the pickup seat, and flashed a warm smile at the occupant behind the steering wheel.

"How you, Missy?"

"Good. Good, Jim."

Jim put the truck in reverse, a smile of pleasure lighting his pale blue eyes, the dark weathered lines of his face all changing direction. His long, graying mustache spread and widened with the lines, and he touched the brim of his stained Stetson more out of habit than anything else.

Jim Sevarr was of the old western line of hard-working, hard-driving range riders who lived with horses and cattle, dogs and sheep, and were more comfortable on the back of a horse than behind the wheel of a truck. His jeans were perpetually soiled, his boots half worn out, and his plaid shirttail was hanging out of his belt on one side, with the other side tucked securely beneath it.

He ground the gears of the pickup, frowned, and uttered an annoyance under his breath.

"These gears are never where they're supposed to be."

Sadie smiled to herself, knowing the gears were right where they needed to be. It was the hand that was more adept with a horse's bridle that was the problem.

"Twelve inches," he said, shifting the toothpick to the other side of his mustache.

"What?"

"Of snow."

"Really?"

"Yep."

Sadie knew the cold and snow meant more work for her down in the valley at Aspen East Ranch. She was one of the girls who helped prepare vast amounts of food each day for the 20 ranch hands, give or take a few. There were always newcomers, or someone moving on, but the number of men never varied much.

Sadie kept the lovely old ranch house clean as well. There was always something that needed to be cleaned after the food was prepared.

The furniture was rustic, the seating made of genuine leather. Valuable sculptures were placed carefully to complement the costly artwork on the wall behind them. The lighting was muted, casting a warm, yellow glow from the expensive lamps. Candles flickered and glowed in little alcoves built into the rooms. Sadie especially loved to clean the rooms filled with art, expensive objects bought from foreign countries, and the fine rugs on the wide plank floors which were all aged and worn to smooth perfection.

Aspen East Ranch was owned by a man named Richard Caldwell who came from a long line of wealthy cattlemen from the west. He was a man of great height and massive build. His stentorian voice rolled across the rooms like a freight train. Once, Sadie almost knocked an expensive item off a shelf while dusting with a chamois cloth and a can of Pledge Furniture Polish, her body automatically recoiling at his first booming yell.

Everyone snapped to attention when Richard Caldwell's voice was heard rolling and bouncing through the house, and they tried to produce exactly the response he demanded. Patience was not one of his virtues. If the poor, hapless creature he needed was out of earshot at the moment he opened his mouth, woe to that unlucky person. It felt, as Jim once said, like being "dragged across coals."

Richard Caldwell frightened Sadie, but only at first. After the can of Pledge almost went flying out of her nerveless fingers, her initial shock was over. Sadie's eyes stopped bulging and returned to their normal size, and her heartbeat stopped pounding and slowed considerably when that enormous man entered the room. Now she could face him with some semblance of composure.

But she still always felt as if her covering was unbalanced, that her breakfast was clinging to the corner of her mouth, or that there was something seriously wrong with her dress whenever Richard Caldwell appeared. His piercing gaze shot straight through her, and she felt as though she never quite passed his intimidating inspection.

Sadie had been helping at the ranch for almost three years and he could still unnerve her, although she had glimpsed a kindly heart on more then one occasion.

He teased her sometimes, mostly humorous jabs at the Amish ways. Then he would watch her like an eagle, observing her struggle to keep her composure yet answer in the way she knew was right.

"That thing on your head," he would say, "What's it for?"

Sadie blushed furiously at first, appalled as the heat rose in her cheeks, knowing her face was showing her discomfort. After stumbling clumsily and muttering a few words about her mother wearing one too, she asked Mam what she should say if he kept up his relentless questioning.

One day, when almost nothing had gone right and she was completely sick of all the menial tasks, Richard Caldwell's booming questions irritated her. When he pulled on the strings of her covering and asked again why she wore that white thing on her head, she swiped at an annoying lock of brown hair, breathed out, straightened up, and looked Richard Caldwell straight in the eye.

"Because we are committed to the ways in which the Bible says we should live. God has an order. God is the head, then man, and after that his wife is subject to her husband. This covering is an outward sign of submission."

Richard's eyes turned into narrow slits of thought. "Hmmm."

That was all he said, and it was the last time he mentioned "that thing on her head." Sadie had been a bit shaky after that outburst of self-defense, but he always treated her a bit more respectfully than he had previously. Her fear shifted to confidence, making her job less nerve-wracking.

Richard Caldwell's wife, Barbara, on the other hand, was a formidable figure in Sadie's life—a person to be feared. It wasn't her voice as much as the sheer disapproval that emanated from her cold presence.

Her clothes were impeccable; the drape of the expensive fabric hiding the well-endowed figure, making her appear regal. Scary to Sadie.

She did not accept Sadie, so she knew it was Richard Caldwell who hired her, not Barbara. She was only tolerating Sadie for her husband's sake.

It was always a humbling experience to be with the Lady of the House. Whether she was cleaning, dusting, or running the vacuum, it was always the same. Sadie felt violated, silly even, knowing Barbara held only derision for the Amish and their strange ways.

Sadie always thought that if there was a true version of a woman of the world, Barbara was it: no children, no interest in cooking or cleaning, no need to care for anyone but herself.

Much of her time she spent either buying clothes or arranging them in her enormous walk-in closet. Shoes, hats, jewelry, it was all at her fingertips to be tried on, shown off to her friends, given away, or sent back if things weren't quite up to her taste.

But Sadie knew it was not up to her to judge Barbara or condemn her. She was just being Barbara, the wife of a wealthy ranch owner. Sadie simply did her best to stay out of the way.

She loved her job, she really did. She always felt fortunate to have the beautiful old ranch house to clean and admire, and she liked being a part of the atmosphere—the hubbub and constantly-changing, colorful world that was Aspen East Ranch.

Amish children were not educated beyond eighth grade, spending their eight years in a one-room parochial school, learning the basics of arithmetic, spelling, reading, and English. They also learned German. Their first language was Pennsylvania Dutch, a dialect related to German with a sprinkling of English that kept changing through the years.

So for the short time between age 15 and marriage, most girls took jobs, normally cleaning, cooking, babysitting, quilting, or sewing. They handed the money they earned over to their parents, except for a small allowance.

When a young woman married, her parents provided most of the young couple's housekeeping necessities—furniture, bedding, towels, dishes, and almost everything else. The gifts from the wedding completed their household needs.

Sadie often wondered how it would be to put her entire check in the bank and then have money of her own to do anything she wanted. She understood, having this knowledge instilled in her at a young age, that money, and the earthly possessions it could buy, was not what brought true happiness to any person. Rather, money was the root of all evil if you let it control your life.

No, she did not want a lot of money, just enough to buy another horse like Paris. But she had to admit to herself that she had never connected with another horse in the same way, not even close. She could never figure out why.

Horses were everywhere here in Montana; on the hills, in trailers, in barns, being ridden. Everywhere Sadie looked, there were horses of all colors, shapes, and sizes, but not one of them interested her.

Dat bought a riding horse for the girls, but in Sadie's heart, he was just the same as a driving horse. She treated him well, fed him, patted his coarse forelock, and stroked the smooth, velvety skin beneath his mane, but she never wanted to bathe him or braid his tail and put silky, pink ribbons in it.

She still harbored that longing for just the right horse. Once, she had watched a black and white paint being led from a trailer. He bounced and lifted his beautiful head and something—she didn't know what—stirred in her heart but only for a moment. It wasn't Paris, and it wasn't

Ohio with Eva and the creek and the alfalfa fields.

Mam said it was because Paris was a part of her youth, and she'd never be able to recapture that youthful emotion that bound her to the palomino. It was time for Sadie to grow up and stop being dreamy-eyed about a horse named Paris. Whoever heard of a horse named Paris anyway, she said. But that was how Mam was, and Sadie still knew, at the age of 20, that Mam just didn't understand.

Mam and Dat didn't understand about breaking up with Ezra, either.

Ezra was a fixture in the Montana community. He was 26 years old, a member of the church, and concerned about keeping the Amish *Ordnung* and not being swept up into the worldly drift. A too-small covering, a fancy house, pride in the amount of money one made—those kinds of things seriously worried him.

Worried him and those around him until Sadie felt her head beginning to bow and her eyebrows elevating with these exact same worries. Her life stretched before her in one long, tedious blend of worries, concerns, cannots, and do nots, until she felt like screaming and jumping up and down and rebelling. She wanted to tell Ezra that there was *not* a black cloud hanging over every little thing—that God made roses bright red and daisies white and yellow instead of gray and black.

She did not mean to be irreverent, she really didn't. She just hated the feeling of having a wet blanket thrown over her head and suffocating her freedom and her breathing whenever she spent time in his company.

Being Amish was not hard, and certainly it was no burden. It was a way of life that was secure and happy. When Richard Caldwell asked her if she'd like to take his new Jeep out for a spin in that semi-mocking manner of his, she could truthfully say no. If you don't know any better and are taught to be content, nothing is a hardship—nothing within reason—and Sadie didn't feel that her life was squashed down, flat, heavy, or drained of happiness.

The teachings of her parents were a precious heritage handed down for generations and a firm foundation that allowed for happy freedom of spirit. Honoring her parents and respecting their wishes brought peace and a secure, cuddly feeling like a warm, fuzzy shawl you wrapped up with in the wintertime.

Sadie often thought about this. What if she would have rebelled and refused to accompany her parents to Montana? It would have been unthinkable, but still... So far, no husband and no horse. She wasn't sure which one she longed for more. Probably a horse.

Every husband was apparently a little like Ezra. Sadie sometimes caught Mam compressing her lips into a thin, straight line when Dat said something was too fancy. Like French doors. Mam had her heart set on them so she could look at the awesome, gently rolling, wooded hillside while she ate at the dining-room table. Dat had snorted, saying he didn't know what kind of fancy notion she got herself into now. French doors were too English. But in the end, Dat smiled and agreed, saying Amish houses could have French doors, he guessed. Mam had laughed and her eyes shone and Sadie could tell she was very happy.

So husbands could be a bit intimidating, especially if they were too weird about a lot of different subjects. Horses were easier. If only she could find one.

Jim gripped the steering wheel and slammed on the brakes, hard, drawing Sadie back to the present. She grabbed at the dash, nearly slamming against it, a scream rising in her throat.

"What the...?" Jim yelled.

Sadie struggled to regain her seat, her eyes wide with fear. Through the swirling whiteness outside, a dim, shadowy form leapt in front of the truck, slid, and went down—way down—as Jim struggled to keep control of the careening vehicle. Sadie screamed again as the tires hit the form on the road and bumped to a stop.

Her hands crossed her heart as if to contain the beating, and her eyes searched Jim's, wild with questions.

"I'll be danged if it ain't a cow," he muttered, jerking on the door handle.

"Sh...should I..." Sadie asked, her voice hoarse.

"Come on out. We'll see what we got."

Chapter 3

SADIE GRABBED FOR THE DOOR HANDLE, THEN hesitated. A cold blast of air from the opposite side of the truck caught her head scarf, and she was shaken to reality.

What had they done?

Struggling to stay on her feet in the ice and snow, Sadie held on to the side of the truck, straining to see what had gone down, what had been so big, so unexpected, what had so suddenly disappeared in front of the truck.

She heard Jim's low whistle. In the same instant, she saw the thick, heavy hairs of...

"Well, it ain't a cow."

Sadie stood and stared. She had never seen a horse as thin and gaunt as this. In fact, she had never seen *any* animal as thin as this—a skeleton covered with hide and a shaggy black and white coat.

"Skinniest horse I ever laid eyes on."

"Is he...hurt?" Sadie ventured.

"Dunno."

"He's... just lying there. Do you think he's dead?"

"Well, no. We didn't hit him very hard. He sort of slid

and went down before we hit him."

"He's likely starving. He could be dying right here."

"Dunno."

Jim knelt in the swirling snow, bent low, and laid a hand on the horse's cheekbone. Sadie stood, holding her arms tightly against her waist, and wondered how a horse's face could be thinner than normal.

Horses don't have a lot of flesh on their faces. The softest part is the smooth, velvety nose, always whooshing warm, sweet breath into your face. Horses don't have bad breath like humans. That's because they eat clean hay, oats, corn, and fresh, sweet grass in pastures. They don't eat greasy bacon and aged cheese and Twinkies and whoopie pies and potato chips that leave their stomachs sour and make gas rise to the top, and then cause them to belch the way people do.

This horse's face was thinner than most, its large eyes sunk into huge cavities. He looked like a skeleton with a head much too large for the scrawny, protruding neck, almost like the drawings prehistoric men etched on cave walls.

The snow kept coming from the sky, a whirling, grayish-white filled with icy little pings which stung Sadie's face. She watched as Jim felt along the horse's painfully thin neck, then down to its shoulder, before touching its pitiful ripples of bone and hide that was its side.

"He's breathin'."

"He is?"

Sadie knelt in the snow by the horse's head, watching for a flicker—any sign of life—from this poor, starved creature. Slowly she reached out to touch the unkempt forelock, still very thick and heavy in spite of his weakened state. She lifted it, letting the heavy hair run through her fingers, and murmured, "Poor, poor baby. Whatever happened to you?"

Jim rose a bit stiffly, then reached in his coat pocket for his cell phone. Sadie stayed by the horse's head, speaking soft endearments, willing this emaciated creature to life.

Jim was muttering to himself, clumsily pressing buttons too small for his large, calloused finger, repeatedly pushing the wrong one, growling over and over before finally stoping, his eys narrowing.

"Hey. Yeah, Jim here. I'm bringin' the Amish girl to the ranch. A half-dead horse jumped out in front of us. He's down. Ain't responding."

There was a pause.

"Huh-uh. No. Dunno. Just... No! Somebody bring a trailer. What? Up on Butte Road. Where? So there's no trailer?"

Jim paced, went to the truck for a pair of gloves, still talking, listening, talking.

"Listen. I ain't stayin' here all day. Either Jeff brings a trailer or I'm callin' the boss."

Jim hung up angrily. Sadie hesitated, then stood up and faced Jim.

"You go get the trailer. I'll stay here."

"No you ain't."

"Yes, I'm not afraid of this horse. I'll stay here. Just go. Hurry."

"Listen, little girl. You ain't stayin' here by yerself."

"Yes, I am. I will. No one will go by here that's dangerous. We can't let this poor, sick horse lying in the middle of the road. Someone else will hit him. I'll be fine. Just go."

Jim stared at Sadie, then shook his head.

"All right. I'll go fast. Be back soon. But..."

"No, Jim. Just hurry."

The truck roared to life, eased carefully onto the road, and disappeared around an outcropping of overhanging rock. The snow kept falling around Sadie and the horse. Little swirls piled up in the strangest places, as if the snow was trying to wake up the inert form on the cold ground. It settled into crevices in the animal's ears, which were so soft and lifeless, and formed tiny drifts in the soft, black hairs. The long, sweeping eyelashes even held tiny clumps of cold particles, making the horse appear to have no spark of life. It looked completely dead.

Sadie shivered, then knelt again.

"Come on, come, boy. Wake up. Don't die now."

She kept talking, more to instill confidence in herself than to elicit a response from this bony, wasted form. Even if he was still breathing, he was indeed a very sick horse—probably too sick for anyone to try and revive.

She straightened as she heard the unmistakable sound of a vehicle, though muffled, the way vehicles sound in the snow. Probably someone I know, Sadie assured herself in spite of her thudding heart.

A large, red cattle truck came plowing around the bend, much too fast on road conditions like this.

Irritation replaced fear, and Sadie stayed in the exact same spot, knowing the truck's occupants would see her much better than one thin horse half covered with snow.

Suddenly it registered in her brain that the road was icy, and she might very easily be hit. She began flailing her arms, screaming without being aware that she was, jumping, and shouting. She was in danger of being swallowed by this monstrous red cattle truck.

Suddenly, the driver saw her but applied the brakes too hard. The truck slowed, skidded, zigzagged, righted itself, and came to a lopsided halt with its two left tires in a ditch by the side of the road.

Everything went quiet except for the jays screaming in the treetops and the sighing of the cold wind in the alders. The truck door slammed and a very irate person plodded in front of it, his beefy, red face supporting his battered Stetson, which he pushed back before yanking it forward over his face again.

"And just what do you think you're doing, young lady? Don't you know this is a very good way to get killed?"

Sadie met his angry gaze, then lowered her eyes.

"I'm sorry. I...well... Look."

She waved her arms helplessly, gesturing toward the still form on the road, now almost covered with snow.

"What the..."

He smashed his Stetson down harder until Sadie thought his hat would hide his whole head completely and just sit on his shoulders. But somehow she guessed he could see because he said the same thing again.

"What the...?"

He bent lower and asked, "What's wrong with him? He ain't dead, is he?"

"I think he's dying."

"How are you going to get him off the road?"

"I don't know."

She explained what happened, about Jim leaving, and assured him he'd soon be back for her and the horse. The beefy man whistled, then motioned to the truck, moving his arm to indicate that he wanted the rest of the occupants out.

"Mark, get over here."

Sadie watched a tall person jump down from the

truck. Not really jump, more like bounce, or pounce like a cat. He was huge—tall and wide with denims and very dark skin. His steps were long and lively, and he reminded Sadie of a horse one of her uncles owned in Ohio. He seemed to be on springs and hardly ever held still long enough to... well, hold still.

She thought he was Mexican, except Latinos generally were not this tall. She wondered if he was Italian with that dark skin. Or Indian. Or maybe white but just spent a lot of time in the sun.

He didn't smile or say hello or even notice her. He just stood there beside the beefy man and said nothing. He was wearing a navy blue stocking hat. Everyone wore Stetsons or leather, wide-brimmed hats of some sort here in Montana. The English did, anyway. English is what the Amish people called other people who were non-Amish. This was because they spoke English.

His clothes were neat and very clean—too clean to be an ordinary cowpuncher. But why was he wearing a stocking hat?

"What do you think, Mark?"

Mark still said nothing but lowered his huge frame easily and felt along the horse's neck, flanks, and ribs. He lifted the soft muzzle and checked his teeth, then rubbed his ears.

"Did you call a vet?"

He straightened as he said this, then turned to look down at Sadie with eyes so brown they were almost black and fringed with the thickest, blackest lashes she had ever seen. His cheekbones were high, his nose perfect, and his mouth made her knees turn to jello, so that she lost her voice completely.

Oh, it was sinful. It was awful. She felt deeply ashamed.

She also felt as incapable of changing one thing about her emotions as a seagull feather trying to change direction as it hovered on the restless waves of the ocean. Then to her horror, she felt the color rise in her face. She was sure it was noticeable to both men.

Sadie adjusted her head scarf, lowered her eyes, then raised them to his, summoning all her courage to keep his gaze.

"I..."

She was so flustered she couldn't speak, so she brushed miserably at a stray lock of hair before lifting her eyes again.

Then he smiled.

Oh, he smiled the most wonderful smile. His white teeth turned her knees straight back into the shakiest sort of jello—the kind you got out of the refrigerator before it was fully set, and which Dat laughingly dubbed "nervous pudding."

"I guess you don't have a cell phone, seeing you're Amish and all."

Sadie shook her head.

There was a whooshing, snorting sort of sound. Mark whirled, the heavy-set man exclaimed, and a soft cry escaped Sadie's lips. They all turned, but Sadie was the first one to reach the horse's head. She knelt in the snow murmuring, running her hands along the smooth planes of his face. There was another whooshing sound, and he tried to raise his head before letting it fall back weakly.

"Let's get him up."

Sadie looked up, questioningly.

"How?"

Mark didn't answer. He just kept looking at Sadie with the strangest expression in his eyes, almost as if he was about to cry. Sort of. Not really, though. More like his eyes softened, and he caught his breath before she asked the same question.

"How?"

"Just… Okay, Fred. You help lift his hind end. You…," His eyes questioned her.

"Sadie."

"Okay, Sadie. You stay at his head. Keep talking. Are you used to horses?"

"I live here. Yes."

"Here we go."

The horse was black and white with black lashes circling deep blue eyes, now filled with a strange sort of despair and terror. His eyes opened wider, and he lifted his head again, making soft grunting sounds as he reached forward, trying to get his hooves beneath him.

"Come on, sweetie pie. Come on, you can do it."

Sadie was completely unaware of the fact that she was speaking in her accustomed Pennsylvania Dutch dialect.

"*Doo kannsht. Komm on. Komm. Vidda. Vidda.*"

Mark lifted at the shoulders, urging, pushing. Fred lifted, strained, and fussed as his face grew more and more red. Sadie watched as the horse lay back down, completely at the end of his strength. She shuddered as he laid his head down in the snow and closed his beautiful eyes.

Sadie forgot her shyness, her thoughts focused only on this horse and the fact that she wanted him to live. She had always wanted a paint. Maybe, just maybe, she could have this one if she could get him to survive.

"If we just let him lie down, he's going to die!"

"Whose horse is he?" Fred asked.

"I have no clue."

"I don't know if he's gonna make it," Fred announced.

"Well, we can't just stand here and let him die," Sadie said, her voice conveying her desperation.

"We need a vet."

Mark said this bluntly but quite meaningfully. It was just a fact and had to be carried out.

Fred got out his cell phone and, with nimble fingers for a man his size, called one of the local veterinarians. Then he snapped his phone shut and, grumbling, returned to the truck.

Mark put his hands in his pockets, turned to Sadie, and was about to speak, when a vehicle came rattling from the opposite direction. It was Jim, pushing the old truck to the limit.

He slowed, rolled down the window, and yelled to Sadie.

"Get in."

Sadie's eyes opened wide.

"The boss is all up in the air. Bunch o' extra men and not enough help in the kitchen. Said I'm supposed to get you down there straightaway and let this bag of bones die. Probably some diseased old mustang from out on the range."

He swung his grizzled head.

"Get in."

A lump rose in Sadie's throat. She wanted to stay so badly, just like when she was a little girl and had to leave the playground because the bell rang just when it was her turn to go down the slide.

"Jim, please. I can't go and leave this horse."

"You better if you want your job."

Her shoulders slumped dejectedly, her upbringing stirring her conscience. She knew her family needed the weekly paycheck she brought home from Aspen East, but she couldn't walk away from this horse either. Indecision made her feet falter, until she turned back to the horse without thinking. Quickly, anything, please, please, please let's do something for this horse.

"I...I don't know who you are and I may be asking too much, but if this horse survives, would you let me know? We're Amish, so you'll have to leave a message on our phone, but... Oh, I'm sorry, do you have a pen and paper?"

"I do."

Mark produced his wallet, extracted a business card and a pen, and she said, breathlessly, "761-4969."

He wrote down the number and looked up.

"Just...if it's not too much bother, let me know."

"All right."

With one last glance at the broken form on the ground, Sadie hurried to Jim's old truck, got in, and slammed the door. She didn't look back.

"Who's that?"

"I don't know."

"City slicker, that one. Beanie. Humph."

Jim had no use for anyone covering their ears in cold weather, Sadie knew. She didn't care who wore a beanie and who wore a Stetson or Amish straw hat or whatever, she was sick in her heart about that horse.

Why was it always the same? If she felt any connection at all with a horse, it was taken away. She would never see or hear from that Mark person, and like Paris, this sick animal would disappear and that would be that. It was just the way life was.

Oh, my, but that Mark.

Just wait 'til I tell Leah.

It was a secret the girls shared, knowing Dat would snort and Mam would rebuke them. They talked about who was good-looking, who was available for marriage, who they would accept, and who they wouldn't. Amish or not, all girls talked and giggled about this subject. Sadie and Leah endlessly tried to figure out what Mam meant when she said, "You don't go by looks."

Of course you went by looks. They never told Mam this, but it was a universal truth. The way a courtship began was with physical attraction. Even birds chose just the right one by the beautifully-colored plumage or the best song or the most intricate dance. It was the same way with katydids and bats and frogs and squirrels and every living thing on God's earth.

That was the way it was.

But Sadie wasn't sure if she would tell Leah about Mark after all. She wanted to laugh and giggle and talk and dream, but, somehow, this was not like the other times. This seemed to be something more dangerous. Also more embarrassing. And more hopeless. It was truly horrible. Whoever heard of one's knees becoming weak from looking at another person?

Oh, it was awful.

She glanced over at Jim, almost sure he could tell what she was thinking. Instead, he was frowning, shifting his wad of chewing tobacco from one cheek to another, which always made Sadie swallow hard.

So she looked out the window to her right and watched the snow swirling and the trees and the hillside being converted from dull browns and earthy sage-green to a pristine winter wonderland.

Sadie truly loved Montana. The scenery was absolutely breathtaking almost the whole year-round. Her favorite season was the long winter because of the skiing, sledding, and snowboarding. Another favorite pastime for the youth in Montana was piling on a huge inner tube from a tractor and being pulled with a sturdy rope attached to the saddle of a horse. A good horse lunged through deep snow, easily pulling a person on an inner tube until they were completely covered with snow, like a peanut butter cracker dipped in chocolate—only it was white. And there was nothing that quite matched the exhilaration of riding a horse on an endless sweep of sparkling snow, especially if the horse had been bored from standing in his box stall and was aching to run.

Sadie's thoughts returned to the day as they approached the magnificent entrance to Aspen East.

Elaborate brick pillars rose on both sides of the wide driveway with scrolls of beautiful ironwork across the top. Bronze statues of cattle were cemented into the brickwork—truly a testimony to a local artist's talents. Heavy trees bordered the driveway, bent with the weight of the snow, and the long, low ranch house came into view.

It was built with the finest logs and the shingles resembled old, gray Shaker ones, although they were only replicas. Huge windows and doors completed the look of the house, and the wonderful scenery enhanced the matching barns, stables, and sheds. There were also fences, gates, paddocks, bunkhouses, and garages. Everything was kept in fine form by the many employees that worked around the clock to keep this vast enterprise running efficiently.

The truck stopped, Jim grinned, and Sadie hopped down.

"Try and have a good day."

"Jim, if you find out one thing about the horse, would you let me know?"

"Sure thing, little girl."

Sadie was comforted by his words. Jim was such a good man. He surely deserved to be treated well in return.

The resounding voice of Jim's wife greeted her before she pulled on the door latch.

"...where she got to! Ain't never seed nothin' like it. You get ten extra hands for breakfast, and that Sadie don't show up. Them Amish havin' no phones in their houses is the dumbest rule of 'em all."

Sadie walked in amidst this tirade and grinned cheekily at the tiny buxom woman.

"Here I am!"

"Sadie! Now you heard me yellin' about ya!"

"It's okay. You love me."

"I do sometimes."

"I'm hungry."

"Go get your apron on. How come you're late?"

"If I told you, you wouldn't believe me."

"Try."

"Huh-uh. We don't have time, Dottie."

"Don't Dottie me."

Sadie slid an arm across Dottie's shoulders and whispered, "Good Morning, Dottie."

"Hmmpfhh."

Chapter 4

SADIE IMMEDIATELY FELT THE PRESSURES OF HER job, which were unusually demanding today. Dorothy had not arrived at her usual early morning hour because of the snow, which meant there were no potatoes cooked for hash browns, no sausage gravy, and no biscuits made for a count of 44 men.

Sadie grabbed a few tissues from the gold box by the food warmer, blew her nose because of the cold, windy morning, and turned to wash her hands with antibacterial soap from the dispenser mounted on the wall. Then she rolled up the sleeves of her green dress and compressed her lips, ready to start in.

She was starving, having skipped supper the evening before. Mam had made fresh shoofly pie yesterday morning, and when Sadie came home from work a bit early, ravenous as usual, she had eaten two slices. She doused them in fresh, creamy milk from the doe-eyed Guernsey in the barn—completely spoiling her supper.

Shoofly drowned in milk was simply the best, most comforting taste in all the world no matter whether you lived in Montana or Ohio. Mam made huge, heavy pies piled high with rich, moist cake, then covered with sweet, crumbly topping. The brown sugar, molasses, and egg mixture on the bottom complemented the top. Eaten in one perfect bite, all three layers combined to give you the most…well…perfect taste. It was wonderful.

Mam's pie crusts were so good you could eat them without the filling. She always made some *schecka hauslin* when she made pies, and Sadie thought they were better than the pies themselves.

Schecka hauslin were "snail houses"—little bits of pie dough rolled around brown sugar and butter, then popped in a hot oven for a few minutes. Sadie always burned the tips of her fingers and her tongue tasting them, but it was all worth it.

"What do you want me to do first, Dottie?"

"I'm Dorothy. Now don't you go Dottie'n me all morning."

That voice came from the interior of the vast, stainless steel refrigerator, and Sadie turned to see Dorothy's backside protruding from it.

Sadie never ceased to be amazed by the size of this little person and her stamina. She practically ran around the huge kitchen on short, heavy legs clad in the "good expensive" shoes she knew Dorothy had purchased at the Dollar General in town.

"They only cost $29.99!" she had told Sadie proudly. "Them shoes is expensive but they're worth it. Good arch support."

She had them worn down on one side in a few months but still bustled about the kitchen, never tiring, saying it was all because she wore "them good shoes."

Dorothy turned, her face red from bending down.

"Go ahead and make that sausage gravy. I'll tend to

the biscuits."

Sadie smiled to herself, knowing Dorothy would never allow anyone else to make the biscuits. She never measured the ingredients—just threw flour, shortening, and other ingredients into a huge, stainless steel bowl, her short, heavy arms flapping, working the dough as if her life depended on the texture of it. She talked to herself, whistled, sang bits of a song, and pounded away ferociously at the biscuit dough as if each new batch she made had to be the best.

And it always was! Dorothy's biscuits were light, yet textured with a velvety solidity. They were unlike anything Sadie had ever tasted. They were good with butter and jam or honey or loaded with gravy or, like Jim did, eaten cold with two thick slices of roast beef and spicy mustard.

Sadie reached up to the rack suspended from the log beam above, grabbed the 12-quart stockpot and set it on the front burner of the commercial stove. Reaching into the refrigerator, she unwrapped a stick of butter, deposited it into the pot, and turned on the burner beneath it. After it had browned nicely, she scattered an ample amount of fresh, loose sausage into the pot. The handle of the long wooden spoon went round and round, keeping the sausage from sticking to the flour and butter. Her thoughts kept time.

Surely the horse was someone's pet. Why was it out there in the deserted forests and vast empty acreage if it couldn't feed itself? Was there simply nothing there for it to feed on, or was it too sick to search for food? Was it neglected at the home it had come from? Why was it loose and alone?

Wild horses were not uncommon in the west, though

they were centered mostly in Wyoming. Bands of them roamed free, but the government kept them from becoming a threat or nuisance to the ranchers and farmers in the area. Helicopters would herd them into man-made ravines and corrals, always met with outrage by the animal-rights activists. But to Sadie's way of thinking, it was a necessary evil. You couldn't let wild horse herds grow too large. They could do lots of damage or graze areas meant for cattle, which was almost everyone's livelihood here.

But, oh, horses were so beautiful! There was no other animal on earth that Sadie could relate to quite as well. She could lay her cheek against a horse's, kiss its nose, smooth that velvety skin beneath the heavy waterfall of mane, and never grow tired of any of it. They smelled good, were intelligent, and came in all different shapes and colors. There were cute, cuddly ponies and tall, big-boned road horses, as the Amish referred to them.

The steady, brown or black, Standardbred driving horses were the backbone of the Amish community. They obediently stood in forebays of barns while heavy, leather harnesses were flung across their backs and then attached to thick, heavy collars around their muscular necks and shoulders. A horse allowed itself to be led to a carriage, backed into the shafts, and attached to the buggy. They waited patiently while family members clambered into the buggy, then trotted off faithfully, pulling them uphill and downhill in all sorts of weather.

The most amazing part of hitching up a horse was the fact that these docile creatures allowed that hideous steel bit to be placed in their mouths. This is the part that goes between their teeth and attaches to the bridle that goes up over their ears. Good, responsible horses never seemed to mind, lowering their heads so the bit could easily slide into their mouths.

There were some horses, of course, who were cranky and disobedient, but Sadie always felt sorry for them. Very likely, at some point in their lives, these horses had been whipped or kicked or jerked around simply because they were born with a stubborn nature and made their owners' tempers flare like sticks of dynamite. This destroyed the trust and any thread of confidence they had once acquired.

Usually, a calm, obedient horse had a calm, quiet owner and vice versa. Horses didn't require much of their owners: a quiet stall and a bit of pasture, decent feed and hay, water, and enough attention to know they were cared for and appreciated.

Sadie browned the sausage until it was coated all over with the butter and flour mixture. Then she went to the refrigerator for a gallon of milk, which she poured slowly into the sizzling sausage, stirring and stirring after this addition. She added the usual salt and pepper, then reached up to the rack again for the huge cast-iron skillet.

"Watcha gettin' that for?" Dorothy asked.

That woman has eyes in the back of her head. Seriously, Sadie thought.

"Hash browns."

"Them potatoes ain't even cooked. How you gonna make hash browns? That's what happens when young girls moon about boys and stuff."

Sadie suppressed a giggle. She knew Dorothy always got a tiny bit miffed when the pressure was on. She never failed to let Sadie know when she did something wrong, implying that Sadie's misstep was the reason for the pressure to begin with.

After working with Dorothy for almost three years, Sadie knew she had the best heart and kindest demeanor of anyone she had ever met. Her scoldings were sort of soft and harmless beneath all that fuss, and Sadie often suppressed her laughter when Dorothy was bustling and talking and scolding.

"Oh, I forgot."

"You forgot. Moonin' around, that's what."

Dorothy went to the pantry, which contained 50-pound bags of potatoes, lugged one out to the sink, and proceeded to throw the potatoes in by the handfuls. Grabbing a sharp paring knife, she set to work, the peels falling into the sink in rapid succession. Sadie joined her.

"I'm hungry," Sadie announced for the second time that morning.

"Make some toast. Didn't you have breakfast? You need to get up earlier. Set your alarm 15 minutes earlier."

"No, thanks."

"Hmmpfhh. Then be hungry."

She slid a pan of perfectly-rounded, precisely-cut biscuits into the oven, and Sadie hid another grin.

The kitchen door banged open, and Jim hurried in, a box under his arm. Snow clung to his greasy Stetson, and he took it off, clapping it against his legs. Snow sprayed in every direction.

"Jim Sevarr! You borned in a sawmill? Whatsa matter with you? Gettin' my kitchen soakin' wet. I'll fall on them puddles. Now, git! Git!"

She waved both arms, then her apron, as if her husband was a huge cat that needed to be chased away from her work area.

"Don't you want a doughnut?"

Immediately Dorothy's expression changed, like the

sun breaking through clouds, spreading warmth through the kitchen.

"Now, Jim, you know if there's any one thing I can't resist, it's them doughnuts. You got 'em at the Sunoco station?"

"Sure did. Coffee on?"

"Sadie, come on. Take two minutes to eat a doughnut. There's only one way to eat 'em—big bites with the cream filling squishing out the side."

Sadie laid down her knife, wiped her hands on her apron, and smiled as she selected a powdered, cream-filled doughnut from the box Jim held out to her.

"Mmmmm," she said, rolling her eyes as the first soft sweetness of the confectioners sugar met the taste buds on her tongue.

"No news of the horse?" she asked, wiping the corners of her mouth. Jim's mouth was full of doughnut, so he shook his head.

"May as well have the vet put 'im down. Sorriest bag of bones I ever laid eyes on," he said after chewing and swallowing.

Sadie said nothing.

"What horse?" Dorothy asked, slurping a mouthful of coffee, then grimacing and shaking her head at the heat.

Jim related the morning's events, his heavy mustache wagging like a squirrel's tail across his upper lip. His lower face was a dark brownish-red, etched with lines from the sun and wind, but it never failed to amuse Sadie the way his complexion lightened as it met his hat or the shade from the brim. The top of his balding head was creamy white with thatches of graying hair sticking out the way a hat causes hair to stick.

He'd look a lot better if he took off that Stetson

sometimes, Sadie thought. At least long enough to tan that pearly, white head.

Jim slouched on a chair, and Dorothy moved over to pat the top of his head.

"Thanks, hon. That was so nice of you."

Sadie felt quick tears spring to her eyes. The sight of those work-roughened, cracked hands so tenderly touching the bald head of her husband was a sight she wished she could portray on paper. They had been married at least 40 years, and Sadie had seen them at their best. She smiled as she watched the slow, easy grin spread across Jim's creviced face.

"You better get that breakfast on. There's a bunch of hungry men out there."

"Jim, do you... do you think they'll all agree to put him down?" Sadie broke in.

"What? Who?"

"The horse."

"Ain't none of their business."

"Well, whose business is it? Who's going to say what gets done with him?"

"I dunno, missy. Likely the boss."

Sadie turned back to peeling potatoes, her shoulders sagging a bit. She stiffened as she felt Jim's hand on her shoulder.

"Listen. That there horse is gonna die, okay? He's on his last breath. Don't even think about him 'cause he ain't gonna live."

"He wants to live, Jim. I saw it in his eyes."

Jim shrugged. Dorothy caught his eye and shook her head, and the conversation was over.

Sadie put the potatoes on to cook, then began breaking dozens of eggs into a large glass bowl. She added milk, salt, and pepper, then set the mixer on low, preparing the huge amount of scrambled eggs. Great loaves of home-made wheat bread were sliced and put into the toasters, slabs of butter spread thickly across the bread, melting into the crusty slices. The grill was loaded with bacon siz-zling into curled, darkened, salty goodness. Dorothy kept forking finished pieces onto a serving platter and replen-ishing the grill with more long, limp slices of raw bacon.

They worked quietly now, both concentrating on finishing all the food at approximately the right time. This was all routine work. Today there was just a larger amount.

The dining room was majestic. At least Sadie always thought of it as majestic. There was simply no other word to describe it. The ceilings were vaulted and the beams exposed with great chandeliers hanging from the lofty height on long, thick chains. The windows were huge, allowing a view that was one of the most beautiful Sadie had ever seen.

She never tired of cleaning up after the hungry cow-hands had eaten. Just being in that room made her happy. But she hardly ever ventured in while the men were there eating, being strictly warned by her mother not to be gallivanting about while that room was filled with those cowboy "wannabes."

Sometimes when Mam spoke in that derisive tone, Sadie could tell that she thoroughly disliked some aspects of the West, but her pride and her upbringing would not allow her to say it directly. When Sadie mentioned it to Leah, she was met with stony opposition.

Of course Mam loved the West. She loved her house and Dat, and why in the world would Sadie come up with something like that? Sometimes she was just disappointed in Mam, that was what.

Sadie carried the square, stainless steel pans filled with scrambled eggs, biscuits, sausage gravy, and all the food they had prepared that morning. She dropped them expertly between the grids of the ornate steam table, an oak table with lights above it and hot water beneath the shining, stainless steel pans to keep the food piping hot.

She checked the number of heavy, white stoneware plates, the utensils wrapped in cloth napkins, and the mugs turned upside down beside the huge amount of coffee in shining urns.

The long pine tables were cleaned and polished to perfection with long benches on either side. The floor was wide with heavy planks, worn smooth and glistening from the many coats of polyurethane varnish that had been applied years ago.

Two massive glass doors stood at the end of the dining room, and Sadie's heart skipped, stumbled, and kept going as she spotted a white pickup pulling a large gray trailer through the blowing snow.

Could it be? Would Mark... No, they were in a red cattle truck. It would be months before she heard anything, if ever. Jim was probably right.

She retreated when she heard the voice of Richard Caldwell in even louder tones than was normal, leading his men to breakfast.

"Never heard anything like it!"

Someone answered in quieter tones. Then, "But a whole herd? How are you ever going to make off with a whole herd at one time? I mean, yeah, years ago when the range was wide open, but now people are going to notice a bunch of horses together. Come on!"

Sadie couldn't go back to the kitchen. Not now. She

had to hear this. She turned her back, which was much the same as not being in the room at all. A herd of horses stolen? She agreed with Richard Caldwell. Not in this day and age.

She cringed inwardly as the huge doors opened and the men began to file in. She busied herself folding napkin and replenishing the ice bin, being quiet and straining her ears to hear what the men were saying. She hardly breathed when she realized the conversation was very serious. The men never stood around like this when there was breakfast to be eaten, especially at this late hour.

"Did you watch it?"

"Nah. Don't watch TV."

"Well you should watch the news."

"Bah!"

"Yeah, but listen," Richard Caldwell's voice was heard above the din. "This guy in Hill County is wealthy. His horses are worth thousands of dollars. Thousands and thousands. I mean, he has a very distinguished bloodline going on there. He's been breeding horses for years and years. All of a sudden, this guy goes out to the stables, and 'Poof!' his horses are no longer there. It's unheard of."

"The work of some extremely smart men."

"Terrorists."

"Arabs."

"Oh, stop it. Those people wouldn't bother with our ordinary horses."

"I can't think of one single person in a thousand-mile radius that would be brilliant enough to carry this off. Not a one."

The conversation became more animated, each acquaintance contributing his voice, until it was hard to comprehend what they were really discussing. And they thought women at a quilting were bad! They couldn't be much more talkative than this.

Now she heard Jim's voice.

"Yeah, it's weird. But hardly much weirder than a starved and dyin' horse jumping down a bank out of the woods smack in front of my truck bringin' the Amish girl this morning. That thing appeared outta nowhere. Hit the brakes and skidded 'fore we hit 'im."

"Did you kill 'im?"

"No. I got 'er stopped in time. But don't think the horse'll make it. Skinniest thing I ever seed. Ever."

There was a murmur among the men, nods of agreement as each contemplated the scene in his own imagination.

Sadie knew Jim was well-liked and highly esteemed among the men. The few times he gave his opinion, the men considered, talked about, and respected it.

"Easy for a horse to git pretty skinny in this weather."

"He weren't just skinny. He was pretty bad."

"What happened to him?"

"That Fred Skinner came along in his cattle truck. City guy with him was gonna call the vet."

The snorts were unanimous.

"Spend a couple hundred for the vet when the poor miserable creature'll go the way of nature anyhow."

"Yep."

"Them city people."

"Looks as if breakfast is ready."

Sadie slipped through the swinging doors into the kitchen, unnoticed.

Now that bit of news was something to think about. And...well, she may as well give it all up. Maybe that horse lying on the road was really just like a mirage to a person dying of thirst and walking in a desert. You thought what you wanted was there, but it never really was, despite the fact that you were absolutely convinced of its existence. Maybe instead of a look in a horse's beautiful eyes, it was only her own emotions—all a fleeting mirage, her imagination run wild.

It was probably the same with Mark. Whoever he was. Of course, any girl would react to someone as good-looking as him. What did Mam say? Don't go by looks. So there you go. It wasn't real attraction.

Sadie tackled the pans, scraping their residue into tall garbage cans lined with heavyweight garbage bags, getting them ready for the commercial dishwasher. Thankfully, today she would not encounter "Her Royal Highness, the lofty Barbara Caldwell," as Sadie was prone to thinking of her.

Sadie had long decided some people were wealthy and you would never know by their attitude. Only their clothes, the cars they drove, or their homes revealed their monetary value. And some people... Well, Barbara was a piece of work. If she could, she would clean the floor with a Lysol disinfectant wipe after Sadie walked on it. She had no use for those pious, bearded people, even refusing to speak the name "Amish." Sadie had found it extremely hard at first, cringing whenever Barbara approached, but, after three years, Barbara actually addressed Sadie, though only on rare occasions.

One of her favorite put-downs was asking Sadie to pick up the dry cleaning in town. Then she would wave her long, jeweled fingers and say, "Oh yes, I keep forgetting. You don't have your license."

Each time, Sadie ground her teeth in an effort not to tell Barbara that if she did have her license, she wouldn't pick up her dry cleaning anyway. In fact, she wanted to say to Barbara that she could just heave herself and all her excess poundage off to the dry cleaners and pick it up herself. But her upbringing, of course, denied her that wonderful luxury.

Jim said Barbara wasn't like that when he was around. But Dorothy heartily disagreed and told him so.

"You can't be peaches and cream at one person's table, then turn around and be sauerkraut at the next."

Sadie never said much, if anything at all. She was taught at home not to speak ill of anyone, and Sadie knew without a doubt that was one of the hardest things for human nature to overcome. How could you respect someone who so obviously viewed you with only contempt?

Chapter 5

Sadie was always happy to return to her home in the evening. She just wished Jim would push that old truck a bit faster and never failed to be amazed at how slowly he navigated the winding, uphill drive to the house. Tonight, though, the snow made the hill treacherous, so she was glad he didn't accelerate around the bend.

The warm, golden square windows of home were welcoming beacons through the grayish-white evening light, and Sadie could almost smell the good supper Mam had already prepared.

"See ya!" Sadie said, hopping lightly out of the old pickup.

"Mm-hm," Jim grunted.

Sadie swung open the door to the kitchen, which was awash in the bright glow of the propane gas lamps set into the ornate wooden cabinet next to the kitchen cupboards.

"I'm home!" she sang out.

There was no answer, no supper on the stove, no table set by the French doors.

"Hey! I'm home!"

Leah came quietly into the kitchen, making no sound at all, her face pale, but smiling a welcome in the way sisters grin at one another after an absence.

Sisters were like that. A grin, a look, a soul connection, a mutual knowing that one was just as glad to see the other, an understanding of "Oh, goody, you're home!" but with no words.

Leah was only two years younger than Sadie, and, at 18, one of the prettiest of the sisters. Blonde-haired, with the same blue eyes as Sadie, Leah was always light-hearted, happy, and upbeat about any situation. Mam said Leah was the sunshine of the family.

But today there was a soft, gray cloud over her sister's blue eyes, and Sadie raised an eyebrow.

"What?"

"It's Mam."

"What?"

"I don't know. She's…" Leah shrugged her shoulders.

"She's what?" Sadie asked, feeling a sickness rise in her stomach like the feeling she used to have in school before the Christmas program.

Leah shrugged again.

"I don't know."

Sadie faced her sister squarely, the sick feeling in her stomach launching an angry panic. She wanted to hit Leah to make her tell her what was wrong with Mam.

"Is she sick? Why do you act so dumb about this?"

Sadie fought to keep her voice level, to keep a rein on her sick panic so it wouldn't make her cry or scream. She would do anything to stop Leah from looking like that.

"Sadie, stop."

Leah turned her back, holding her shoulders stiffly erect as if to ward off Sadie's obvious fear.

"Leah, is something wrong? Seriously. With our Mam?"

Leah stayed in that stiff position, and Sadie's heart sank so low, she fought for breath. The lower your heart went, the harder it was to breathe, and breathing was definitely essential. It wasn't that your heart literally sank. It was more like the sensation you had whenever something really, really scared you.

Sadie sat down hard, weak now, struggling to push back the looming fear. Sadie put her head in her hands, her thoughts flooding out any ability to speak rationally to her sister.

Nothing was wrong. Not really. Leah, can't you see? Mam is okay. I haven't noticed anything out of the ordinary. You haven't either. She's just tired. She's weary of working. She loves us. She loves Dat. She has to. She loves Montana. She has to do that, too. Dat loves our mother, too. He has to. There is nothing wrong in this family. Turn around, Leah. Turn around and say it with me: There is nothing wrong in our family.

Leah turned quietly, as if any swift or sudden movement would enable the fear to grip them both.

"Sadie."

Sadie lifted her head, meeting Leah's eyes, and in that instant recognized with a heart-stopping knowledge that Leah knew, too.

Leah knew Mam had been...well...weird. She had been acting strangely, but not so strange that any of her daughters dared bring up the subject, ever.

They all loved Mam, and if she changed in some obvious ways, well, it was just Mam—just how some people became older. Mam had always been meticulous. Her housekeeping was her pride and joy. Her garden was tended lovingly.

Mam was always hoeing, mulching, or spraying, and her vegetable garden produced accordingly, which kept them busy canning and freezing all summer long.

One of Mam's secrets to gardening was how she kept the weeds at bay. She attacked them with vengeance, using old, moldy mulch hay. She brought it in and spread it until the weeds had no chance of maturing or taking over everything.

Sadie could still feel the slimy hay in her arms, the outer layer scratching her legs as they lugged the gruesome stuff from the wagon to the corn rows. The cucumbers and zucchini squash grew in long, velvety spirals over thick chunks of "old hay," as Mam called it. The old hay kept the plants moist. So they produced abundantly, as did all Mam's vegetables even though the growing season was short in Montana.

Lime was absolutely necessary, Mam said. Pulverized lime was like talcum powder in a bag, and so smooth and cool, it was fun to bury your hands deep into the middle of it.

The strawberry patch was weeded, mulched with clean, yellow straw, and sprayed so it produced great, red succulent berries every year. There was nothing in the whole world better than sitting in the straw beside a plant loaded down with heavy, red berries and pinching off the green top before popping the berry into your mouth.

They grew their peas on great lengths of chicken wire, held up by wooden stakes that Dat pounded into the thawed soil in the spring when the stalks were still tiny. As the rain and sunshine urged them to grow, the peas climbed the chicken wire, and little white flowers bloomed with vigor. Later they would turn into long, green pods, heavy with little green peas.

Picking peas was not the girls' favorite job, but sitting beneath the spreading maple trees on lawn chairs with bowls and buckets of peas to shell definitely was. They would spend all afternoon shelling them—pressing on one side with their thumbs and raking out all the little, green peas from inside the pods.

They talked and laughed and got silly, Mam being one of the silliest of all. And they would make great big sausage sandwiches with fresh new onions and radishes from the garden along with a gallon of grape Kool-Aid that was all purple and sugary and artificial and not one bit good for you, Mam said.

After the pea crop was over, they all had to help with the most hateful job in the garden. Taking down the pea wire and stripping off all those tangled vines was the slowest, most maddening task, and every one of the sisters thoroughly disliked it.

They always fought at one time or another. Often the sun got too hot, and no one was particularly happy, so they argued and sat down and refused to work and tattled accordingly.

Mam was always busy and…well…so very normal. Canning cucumbers, making strawberry jam, canning those little red beets that smelled like the wet earth when she cooked them soft in stainless steel stockpots. She would cook them, cool them, cut them into bite-sized pieces, and cover them with a pickling brew. Oh, they were so good in the wintertime with thick, cheesy, oniony, potato chowder.

All this went through Sadie's mind as her eyes met Leah's. Then Sadie turned her head to look away, out over the valley.

"We didn't have red beets for a long time," she whispered.

Leah nodded.

"It's the little things: dust under the hutch in the dining room, unfinished quilts, the pills, the endless row of different homeopathic remedies…"

"But Sadie, she's still all right, isn't she?"

"Yes. She's just changing. Getting older."

"Hey! Why is there no supper?"

"Well…" Leah began.

Then she looked down, bending her head as great, tearing sobs tore at her throat. Sadie's horror rose, a giant dragon waiting to consume her, maybe even slay her.

How could she? How could Mam be like this?

Hot tears pricked her own eyes, and she sat quietly, waiting until Leah's tears subsided.

"Sadie, I think it's pretty bad. For a few months now, I've watched Mam when she thinks she's alone. She hoards things and…and…oh, I mean it, Sadie, it's too painful to talk about. She keeps certain things like combs and dollar bills and…and hairpins in a certain drawer, and as long as that drawer is undisturbed, she appears… well…she is fairly normal. She works, she talks, and no one notices anything different."

"I do."

"You do?" Leah lifted her head, wiping at her eyes with the back of her hand.

"Well, she's…I don't know. Like this morning, she was leafing through a cookbook asking what we want for our Christmas menu. Christmas is over a month away. Almost two months. It's as if…almost as if she isn't really here. Here in this house. With us and Dat."

Leah sat up, bringing her fist down on the table, startling Sadie.

"She *isn't* here. Her heart and soul are still in Ohio."

"But Leah, by all outward appearances, she wanted to come. She held Dat's hand, her eyes sparkled, she was so excited. I can still see her sitting in the living room with Dat. Oh, I remember. I felt as if she was deserting me. I was so heartbroken about Paris. I felt as if she didn't care about me or Paris, she was so completely with Dat."

"She's not with Dat anymore. Sadie, there's a lot going on that can easily escape us. Dat and Mam are just keeping on for pride's sake. It's...not the way it should be."

"Like...how?"

"Oh, just different ways. When did we last have Dat's favorite supper? Huh?"

There was silence as the conversation fizzled. Was it all in their imaginations? Were they imagining the worst? Maybe it was normal for mothers to change after they turned 46.

"Where are Dat and Mam now?"

"They... argued, fought."

"About what?"

"I don't want to tell you. They didn't know I overheard. I'd feel like a traitor if I spread it around."

Suddenly anger consumed Sadie, sending its fiery tentacles around her body until she thought she would suffocate.

"All right, be that way—all your lofty pride intact, walking around with a serene expression when you know something is wrong—way wrong—with our mother. We have to face it. We can't just sweep it under the carpet and then go around acting as if we are one perfect, happy family, when we know it isn't true because it's not."

Leah sighed.

"Sit down and stop that. All right, Mam told Dat she wasn't feeling good, but she refused to go get help. They...well, it wasn't pretty. She finally agreed to go to the chiropractor in town."

"As if a chiropractor is going to help."

"Well, it's something."

"Pffff!"

Rebekah appeared, straight pins stuck in the front of her dress, thread stuck to her sleeve, an anxious expression in her eyes.

"What's for supper? Where's Mam and Dat?"

Reuben and Anna followed Rebekah into the room, laughing about something. Sadie could tell they had been in the basement playing their endlessly competitive games of ping-pong. Reuben was 10 years old now, old enough to let Anna know that his ping-pong game was worth worrying about.

Sadie groaned inwardly. Oh, they were so precious. So innocent and sweet and dear and good. Why couldn't things just remain the way they used to be?

Sadie walked over to Reuben, wrapped her arms around him, and pulled him close, kissing the top of his thick, blonde hair. She got as far as "How are you...?" before he pulled away from her, straining at her arms, pounding them with his fists, twisting his head, shouting, "Get away from me!" His eyes squinted to a mocking glare, but his mouth was smiling, although he tried desperately to hide that fact.

Ten-year-old brothers had a serious aversion to hugs.

Leah sat up then, bolstering a new-found courage, and said brightly, "Who's hungry?"

"We all are," Anna said.

"Everybody vote. Grilled cheese and tomato soup?"

"Ewww!"

"Hamburgers?"

"Had that last night!"

"Hot dogs?"

"No way. Not for supper."

Sadie watched Leah summoning more strength, a wide smile appearing, as she said, "Eggs-in-a-nest? With home-made ketchup?"

"Pancakes!" Reuben yelled.

"Pancakes!" Anna echoed.

"All right, pancakes and eggs-in-a-nest it shall be."

Leah marched resolutely to the kitchen cupboard, Rebekah at her heels, and Sadie slipped away, gratefully unnoticed.

Bless Leah's heart. I don't know if I could do that right now. I'm tired, I'm worried, and I'm going to my room.

Wearily, Sadie slowly climbed the stairs, supporting herself with the handrail. She entered the bathroom, lit the kerosene lamp suspended from the wall on a heavy hanger, and braced herself against the vanity top with her hands. Her hair looked horrible, her covering crooked, and there was a greasy sheen on her forehead. Her eyes were puffy and frightened, her whole face a mess.

Well, it's been quite a day, she thought, turning away from the mirror and going to her bedroom.

She felt a strong sense of homecoming, rest, and peace as she entered the cool, beige room with its two large windows facing the west. Heavy, white curtains were parted on each side, held back with sand-colored tiebacks to match the bedspread. Her furniture was fairly new; a matching oak bedroom suite made by her Uncle John from the Ohio district where they had once lived. She had collected some pottery that was handmade in Brentwood, which was her pride and joy. White and beige candles and pictures in subdued hues completed the room.

There was a beige-colored sofa by the windows piled with darker beige pillows, and she sank gratefully into one corner, letting her head fall back as she closed her eyes.

Dear God, if you can hear me in my rattled, frightened way, please, please, look down on us and help us all. What should I do? Should I confront Mam? Talk to Dat?

Suddenly she realized that was her first priority—talking to Dat. He was good and steady and sensible. He would explain the situation, they would find some plausible solution, and this would all be over.

It had to be over. She couldn't bear to think of Mam spiraling out of control, or worse. There had been so much strange behavior lately, but always Mam's good behavior was dominant and erased the questionable times for Sadie and, evidently, for Leah, too. She wondered how much 16-year-old Rebekah knew? Or Anna and Reuben?

Oh, dear God, keep them innocent and safe from worry.

The time Mam insisted there were ladybugs in the pepper shaker was the first Sadie had ever noticed anything amiss, other than her usual lack of energy. Usual is what it had finally come to be. Mam was not the same and hadn't been for a few years now. This became increasingly obvious to Sadie after she and Leah had finally confronted the truth.

First, Mam no longer wanted a garden. Mam not have a garden? It was unthinkable. How could you live without a garden? The growing season was too short, she said, and then the soil was too thin, her back bothered her, and it was easier to just buy frozen or canned vegetables at the supermarket in Brentwood.

Dat's irritation flickered in his eyes, but he appeased his wife, saying if she no longer had an interest in gardening, then he supposed they could survive without one. Smiles then, but a bit like a clown's, painted on.

After Mam stopped gardening, her fear of bugs began, but only jokingly. If you laughed about it and said Montana didn't have very many bugs, she laughed with you and dropped the subject.

Ach, Mam. My Mam. My rock in my youth. In Ohio she was the best, most supportive, most nurturing mother anyone could possible ask for. Sadie had always felt lucky to have one of the best. And that first year in Montana had been so good, building the barn and remodeling the house.

Sadie sighed. It was all downhill from there.

She needed to think of something else—something less burdensome. Oh, she should check messages. Perhaps Mark remembered to leave one to let her know how the horse was doing. Or how dead he was.

She ran downstairs, grabbed a coat, swung the door open, and stepped into the clean, cold, whirling snow. No one had bothered to shovel the driveway or path to the barn, that was sure. She wondered who Mam and Dat's driver was. He'd have to be pretty brave to be out on a night like this.

She yanked on the door to the phone shanty, clicked her flashlight on, picked up the telephone receiver, and punched numbers to check messages.

There were three.

The first one from the blacksmith who would be there on the 14th. The second from Mommy Yoder, who said her cat died the night before and her chimney caught fire, but the Lord had been with her. The cat was buried and the fire put out without the fire company having to come. She had tried to tell Ammon the wood was too green, but Ammon was still the same as he always was and didn't dry his wood properly and if their house didn't burn down someday she'd be surprised…

Dear, dear fussy Mommy Yoder. She ate tomato sauce with dippy eggs for breakfast, and called oatmeal "oohts," and was round and soft and cuddly. She was a treasure, talking nonstop in her eccentricity. She always had a story to tell, like the first time she went into the drive-thru at the bank and that round canister went flying up the pipe. She just knew the end of the world was near.

As the third message came on, headlights wound their way slowly up the drive.

Her heart took a nose dive and fear enveloped her. She hung onto the phone shelf, lowered her head, and prayed for help. She knew she must confront her father.

"Hey," a deep voice said, "this is Mark Peight."

She bit down hard on her lip, holding the receiver against her ear as tightly as possible.

"The horse was seen by a vet. He has a chance. He's at Richard Caldwell's stables. I'll be by to check up on him."

That was it. No good-bye, no wishing anyone a good day, still no information on whose horse he was or why he was there or anything—just a few clipped sentences. Definitely Mark.

But the horse had a chance!

A chance!

Oh, praise God!

Tomorrow morning could not come soon enough. But first, she needed to talk to her father. Things didn't seem quite as hopeless as they had before her heart was filled with joy about the message. Surely if there was hope for the dying horse, there was hope for all kinds of situations—Mam's included.

As Sadie walked out into the snow, Dat was paying the driver and Mam was stepping carefully onto the sidewalk. Sadie hesitated until Mam closed the kitchen door before calling to Dat. She had startled him, she could tell, but he found his way through the snow to Sadie's side.

"Sadie."

"Dat. I was checking messages, but...I really need to talk to you about Mam."

"Why?"

Instantly Dat was alert, defensive.

"She's...she's...there's something wrong with her, right?"

"What do you mean?"

"She's...she's acting strangely, Dat."

There was a slight pause before he stepped close, thrusting his face into hers, only the thin, swirling snow between them.

"Sadie, if I ever catch you saying anything like that to anyone in this community...I...I...don't know what I'm going to do. Never, ever, mention Mam to anyone, do you hear me? There's nothing wrong with her. She's just tired."

"But...but Leah heard you arguing."

"Leah didn't hear anything. Do you hear me?"

His large hand clamped like a vice on her forearm, and he shook her slightly.

"You do hear me, don't you?"

Sadie nodded dumbly, her feet like dead weights in the snow, her body shivering as a chill swept through her. As Dat turned on his heel and walked away, Sadie leaned against the rough boards of the barn and thought her heart would break in two.

Chapter 6

M<small>AM WAS IN THE KITCHEN AT SIX O'CLOCK THE</small> following morning, frying bacon in her good Lifetime pan, her hair neatly in place beneath her covering, a fresh white apron tied around her waist. Dat sat at his desk in the adjoining room, his gray head bent over a few papers spread before him.

So normal. A fresh start. Last night was all a bad dream which would soon evaporate like a mist, Sadie thought.

"Good morning!" she said.

Dat returned the greeting, avoiding her eyes, and Mam turned, the spatula dripping bacon grease, and smiled.

"Good morning, Sadie."

Sadie sliced the heavy loaf of whole wheat bread, then spread the thick slices in the broiler part of the gas oven to make toast as Mam broke eggs into another pan.

The ordinary silence was deafening this morning, taut with undiagnosed worries and fears. Sadie desperately wanted to chatter needlessly, the way families do, comfortably knowing their words are accepted, considered worth something of importance. Not until now had she ever thought of the pure luxury of such simple things.

But they had the snow, the heat from the great wood-stove, the smell of bacon—the usual parts of their lives that bound them together.

She cleared her throat.

"I...guess you heard about the horse, huh?"

"What horse?" Mam asked without turning.

Sadie told them of the previous day's excitement, but her words banged against the wall, slid down, faded into the hardwood floor, and became nothing at all.

Dat was still poring over his papers, and Mam made a sort of clucking sound with her tongue, which could mean a series of warnings or wonderment or amazement. Or she may have done it completely out of habit from listening to four daughters and their views of life in general.

Sadie tried again to part the curtain of indifference.

"Did the chiropractor help you, Mam?"

"Yes."

"Good."

Sadie poured the rich, purple grape juice into short, heavy glasses and then sat down. She pulled her chair up to the table, and Dat, Mam, and Sadie bowed their heads, their hands folded in their laps, for a silent prayer before they began eating their breakfast.

Dat lifted his head, looked questioningly at Sadie, and lifted one eyebrow.

"Where's Leah?"

"Asleep, I guess. She has off today."

"The reason I ask, I saw someone walking down the driveway at one o'clock last night. Was it you? Do you know anything about it? Definitely a dark coat, scarf, and a skirt. The snow had stopped before then, but I still couldn't see clearly enough to tell who it was."

"It wasn't me," said Sadie. "And why would Leah be walking in the snow at that hour? That's creepy. Are you sure?"

"Sure I'm sure." His tone was brusque, his manner brushing off her question like bothersome dust.

Mam bowed her head, shoveling bacon onto her plate with studied movements. Suddenly she raised her head. Sadie noticed the grayish pallor, the dark circles, the shadows beneath her eyes that made her appear so sad, so... almost pitiful.

"It was me. I...sometimes when I wake at night, my thoughts seem like real voices, and they all cram into a tiny space, and I can't quite sort them out the way I should. So I thought perhaps my head would clear if I walked in the snow for awhile, Jacob."

"But I thought you were there in the bed beside me."

"Oh, I just propped up a few pillows so it looked like I was there so you wouldn't worry."

Dat frowned. Mam turned to Sadie.

"You'll probably think there's something wrong with me, but, Sadie, I saw something in the faint light of the half-moon and the stars. The snow wasn't blowing anymore, and over on Atkin's Ridge, just about at the tree line, there were animals sort of milling about in and out of the trees. At first I thought they were elk, then long-horned cattle, then... I'm not sure if they were horses or not, but it was something."

Sadie looked into her mother's eyes. There was an earnestness and sincerity—no reason for her to doubt what Mam saw.

"Wow, Mam! Weren't you afraid?"

"I turned back," she said with a soft laugh.

Sadie hesitated, then dove headfirst into the unknown

waters, realizing the danger but hurtling in nevertheless.

"Mam, why are your thoughts so crammed together? Is there anything anyone could do to help sort them out? Would you like to talk about it?"

"No."

"But, Mam, we... Leah and I...

There she was, diving deeper, lungs straining, desperately needing strength to accomplish this tiny, if not insignificant, step toward finding out how Mam felt.

"Leah and I are worried."

"I'm fine."

"She's fine. You and Leah keep to yourselves. Mam is fine."

Sadie bowed her head, rose to the surface, gulped air, and came up with absolutely nothing. She nodded. Mission not accomplished.

"Well," she said, falsely cheerful, "Jim will soon be here."

Mam got up and went to the corner cabinet to begin taking down her countless bottles of ginseng, St. John's Wort, brewer's yeast, Lifespan supplements, and liquid Body Balance—her usual morning ritual of bolstering her faith with those hopeful little bottles.

Sadie turned away, wanting to flee.

Hurry up, Jim.

✿ ✡ ✿

Down at the ranch, things were normal. Dorothy bustled about, shaking her head at the pools of water gathered on her spotless kitchen floor. Why couldn't the men have enough common sense to dry their feet when they came barreling inside?

Sadie had barely hung her coat on the hook before the kitchen door swung open and Richard Caldwell entered, thumping his hat against his legs.

"Sadie!" he thundered.

Please help me, God.

She finished hanging her scarf over her coat collar, fought to calm herself properly, then smoothed her apron over her hips and turned to face him.

"Yes?"

"Somebody told me you want that horse they brought in yesterday."

"The...the dying one?"

"They didn't bring in any other one."

"Is he still breathing?" Sadie clasped her hands, her eyes shining, her feet refusing to stay on the floor as she stood on her tiptoes.

"I really don't know. But if you want him, you'll have to take him out of here."

"But...I don't know if my father will allow it. I'm sure there will be medical, I mean, veterinary bills to pay, and my...father doesn't like horses much."

Why did Richard Caldwell always do this to her? Why did she stumble over words and flounder about like a half-dead fish and say stupid things that made no sense at all when he was around?

"Well, if you want that horse, it's yours. I don't want him. I have no idea where he came from, and I sure don't want to become involved. That old Fred Skinner has a way with words, or he wouldn't have dumped that horse off in my stables."

Sadie bounced a bit, her eyes still shining bright blue.

"That's very nice of you, Mr. Caldwell. And I do thank you. I just need to get permission from my father."

"Come with me and we'll go see the horse."

Sadie fairly danced over to the hook to get her coat, trying to conceal the excitement that kept bubbling over.

Dorothy confronted her then, like a ruffled, banty hen, her eyes flashing, hands on hips.

"And just where do you think you're prancing off to with all this breakfast to be done, young lady?"

Richard Caldwell's booming laugh rolled across the kitchen, bringing a giggle to Sadie's throat, which she suppressed just in time when she saw how upset Dorothy became. Her eyes popped some serious sparks as she turned and wagged a short finger beneath Richard Caldwell's face.

"Now don't you laugh, Richard Caldwell. It's not funny. I ain't young anymore. I got all these hands to feed and yer gonna go gallivanting all over creation with my best help. I ain't puttin' up with it!"

Sadie knew no one ever spoke to Richard Caldwell like that, except feisty little Dorothy. Sadie hid a wide grin, then ducked her head as she unsuccessfully tried to hold back a joyous bubble of laughter.

"Now, Dorothy. Now, now. We're just going to the barn to see this horse. We'll be back in two shakes."

Dorothy harrumphed disdainfully, turning away to mutter to herself as Richard Caldwell held the door for Sadie.

The fresh, cold air smacked Sadie's face, and the wide, blue sky with its white, brassy sunshine filled her heart with its sheer beauty. She flung out her arms and skipped like a small child.

Snow was like that. It was so cold and so white that even the sun and the blue sky blended together to make everything more cold and white and awesome. She wanted to fling herself on her back and make snow angels the way she used to back home in Ohio, but she knew better. She couldn't do that—she was walking to the stables with her boss, Richard Caldwell.

She stiffened when she felt his big hand touch her shoulder and stay there.

"Sadie, you're a good girl. I appreciate your work here at Aspen East. This horse is a gift, and I hope you have many happy days together."

Sadie was speechless. She could not have spoken one word to save her life, so she stopped walking and turned to face him, hoping to convey her thanks somehow.

Richard Caldwell was not a man given to flowery compliments or words of praise. It just wasn't his way. But there was something about this girl's dutiful demeanor, her faithfulness, that touched a chord in his heart.

✿ ✡ ✿

With hairbrush stopped in mid-air, Barbara Caldwell parted the curtains for a better view. Her breathing grew rapid, and her steely, gray eyes flattened into lines of hatred. Then she flung the gilded hairbrush against the wall, creating a slight dent in the scrolled wallpaper before the brush hit the carpeted floor.

Barbara watched her husband open the stable door for Sadie and disappear inside. She threw the matching, gilded hand mirror against the same wall, creating a larger dent than the first.

So that's what Richard Caldwell is up to, she thought bitterly.

She remembered the sleepless night she had recently alone in the huge, canopied brass bed, wondering what had happened to her husband. Did marriages deteriorate on their own?

That sweet-faced, serene-looking little hypocrite! How could she? Weren't these odd people who drove around in their horses and buggies supposed to be different? Better?

Barbara snorted, a sound of frustration and aggravation, followed by a feeling of helplessness and fear.

She never knew Richard Caldwell to be so cold and distant. He never wanted to go out with her anymore or share an intimate conversation. She wouldn't think of trying to hug her husband—or touch him in any way—as many women did naturally throughout the day. There was an unseen barrier, a frightening, cold, barbed wire fence surrounding him, leaving her completely unsure of herself. So she hid behind an armor of dignity, of cruelty. Or she thought she did.

Sliding the stool over to the vanity, Barbara turned up the lights. She leaned forward, turning her face this way, then that.

She needed more Botox. Her wrinkles were becoming too prominent around her eyes.

As she lifted her thick, blonde hair, a plan formed in her mind, turning her eyes into a narrow line, a calculating thinness.

She would talk to Richard. She had her ways. Sadie would pay for this.

✧ ✪ ✧

The dim interior of the stables was a contrast to the brightness outside, but the warm, wonderful smells enveloped Sadie. She breathed in, savoring the smell of the hay and oats, the saddle soap and leather, the straw and disinfectant—all odors pertaining to the creature she adored most on earth, the horse.

The stable was not an ordinary barn like the place where Amish people kept their horses. This stable was luxurious, housing fine horses with good bloodlines that cost thousands of dollars.

There was a long, wide walkway down the center of the barn with large box stalls on either side. The stalls were built of wood and finished to a glossy sheen. Throughout the barn, black and shiny iron grids were built into the wood. Large airy windows, ceiling fans, and regulated temperatures kept the place comfortable, no matter the weather.

Sadie had been in these stables before, but she had never actually walked along the center walkway. Her eyes roamed the walls, the ceiling, the texture of the floor, marveling at the unbelievable amount of time and expense that went into something as simple as a horse barn. Richard Caldwell must have more money than she could even imagine.

"Over here," he said suddenly in his loud voice, and Sadie instantly clutched at the lapels of her coat, compressing her lips to hide her nervousness.

He slid back a bolt and swung open a heavy gate.

Sadie blinked.

He was standing up! On his own four feet!

She didn't realize that a soft sound escaped her compressed lips. She didn't know she had lovingly reached out to touch the horse. She just knew she had never felt such aching pity for any other creature.

He was bigger than Sadie thought, remembering his still form lying in the snow. He didn't seem that big then. His two front legs were splayed, as if placing them farther apart would enable him to stay upright longer. His breathing was shallow and much too fast. His tender nostrils changed their shape with every breath as he struggled to stay on his feet, to stay alive. But his neck! Oh, it was so horribly thin! His head was much too big!

How could a horse stay alive looking like this? How could he keep from dying? Sadie looked questioningly at Richard Caldwell, who nodded his head knowingly, though she didn't say a word.

Slowly Sadie advanced, not even breathing. Her hand slid under the long, black forelock and stayed there. Up came his head then, the long, black eyelashes sweeping over his blue eyes. And he looked, really looked, at Sadie.

He whinnied. But not really a whinny. More like a soft nicker or a long, shaky breath. But Sadie felt it, she heard it, and she put her hands on each side of this poor broken horse's head and gathered it against her coat. She squeezed her eyes shut, bit so hard on her lower lip that she tasted blood, and still a sob rose up from the depth of her being.

Poor, poor thing. Who did this to you? Where do you come from?

She turned her back to Richard Caldwell, not wanting him to know how emotional she was. She bent her head and murmured, telling the horse how much she loved him, how much she wanted him to be strong, to be better, get well, and be healthy, and did he know that she might be allowed to keep him? She still had to ask Dat, though.

Richard Caldwell blinked his eyes, looked away, cleared his throat, tapped his toes, then yanked angrily at his collar. He never cried. He was never touched by any old, sick horse, and he sure wasn't planning on starting now. But when the horse tried to nicker, and out came only a rumpled breath, he had to swallow hard, fighting back feelings of tenderness and pity. And when Sadie bent her head and murmured to the horse, he was horrified to feel the hot sting of genuine tears, an emotion he had not experienced for so long, he hardly knew he was capable of it.

The sun's morning rays found their way through the glass, highlighting Sadie's shining brown hair, the circle of her dark lashes on her perfect cheek, and the glistening mane and forelock of this black and white horse. The picture rooted Richard Caldwell to the floor of the stall.

Suddenly he could smell earth, dripping leaves, a sort of fishy, wormy wet coolness where he had found the dying dog. It was a stray dog—a matted, dirty, thin dog down by the wet mud of the creek.

He could still feel the holes in the knees of his jeans and the way the frayed denim stretched across them, almost hurting if he bent too far. He had used his old t-shirt to lift the dog. He strained and slid but whispered the whole time to the frightened animal.

You poor, poor thing. Come on. I'll take you home. What happened to you? Poor baby.

Now he felt his father's wrath. He felt the words he said, the finger he pointed.

"Get that flea-infested mongrel away from me, and don't even think of keeping him. The only thing good enough for that dog is a shot of lead. Get away. Get away!"

Oh, he got away, both ears stopped with muddy, shaking fingers. But it was not soon enough or far enough to erase the single, mind-shattering slam of his father's shotgun.

He ran then, blindly, through grass almost as tall as he was—the tops of it raking his wet cheeks, slapping his moist forehead as he fell to the ground. He lay there for hours, shaking and crying.

His revenge had been burying the dog. When the alarm clock on his tattered nightstand showed 1:26 a.m., he crept down from his bedroom with a pink towel from the bathroom. He remembered the touch of the soft towel, how sacred it seemed, and how clean.

He was amazed at how loose a dead dog felt. There were a lot of bones and skin and not much to hold him together. His cheeks were wet as he tenderly folded the jumbled limbs, then covered the dog neatly, making sure the towel was straight.

He crept to the shed for a shovel, then dug a hole behind the lumber pile where the ground was low and soft. He carried the dog, laid him carefully into the shallow grave, and wondered what a preacher would say. Shouldn't God be involved somehow?

"God, I need you to look after this dog. If you care about dogs, I named him Sparky. So there you go, God. Be good to him. He has a pink towel."

Richard Caldwell blinked again, then cleared his throat. He had believed in God that night. He had. If he had ever felt the presence of God in the times in between that childhood memory and now, it had never been as real as this. Sadie looked like an angel administering her magic to this lovely creature.

"Look!" Sadie whispered.

Richard Caldwell came closer and bent to look.

"It's a hammer!"

He could see it, too. Beneath the black mane, the shape of the black hair was much like a hammer, depending which way you viewed it.

Sadie stroked and stroked, beaming, her face illuminated by the morning sun.

At that moment, Richard Caldwell promised to himself that this horse would receive the best medical attention from his trusted veterinarian, and Sadie would never know. He would never tell her. He could not bear to think of this horse dying and that angelic face bearing the disappointment.

"Can I...I mean...do you think he'll live? Do you want him moved? Is he a bother? In your way? I don't know what my father will say..."

Sadie broke off, miserable. Richard Caldwell was a hard man. How many times had she heard Dorothy say, "If the boss don't see no profit in it, out it goes."

Richard Caldwell knew he could not put a price tag on this feeling. It was a kind of redemption, a chance to prove himself a better man, a moment to show he was not his father.

"Dad, can I keep him? He won't eat much."

The blast of the shotgun.

He cleared his throat to relieve his tightening emotions.

"Let's give him a couple of days. He'll be in no one's way here. If you want, you can come out and talk to him on your dinner break. Probably be best if you came to see him often, but you know Dorothy."

Richard Caldwell smiled, almost warmly, and Sadie could hardly believe the softness it created in his eyes.

"Thank you!" she said quietly.

"You think your Dad will let you have him?"

"I don't know." Sadie shrugged her shoulders.

"Strict, is he?"

"No. Not really. He's just not much of a horse person."

"And he's Amish?"

Sadie grinned, "I know, strange, isn't it?"

"He drives his horse and buggy though?"

"Yes. But, he calls horses 'livestock.'"

Richard Caldwell laughed genuinely. "They're not livestock?"

"No."

She didn't know why she did it, but as she stroked the horse's neck, she began talking to Richard Caldwell—of all people—about Paris. She never mentioned Paris to anyone, not even her sisters. But Richard Caldwell listened as Sadie's story unfolded. When she finished, a bit hesitantly, he looked out over the snowy landscape for a long time, then bent his head to look at her.

"Sadie, I know how it feels. We'll get this horse better. What will you name him?"

Sadie's intake of breath was all the reward he needed.

"Nevaeh."

"Nevaeh?"

"It's 'heaven,' backwards."

"Sounds like a girl's name."

"Maybe...but this horse is just so...perfect...and... well...the name just seems to fit."

Richard Caldwell turned away, opened the box stall door, and said, "Nevaeh it is."

It was too gruff, but a man couldn't get emotional now, could he?

✿ ✪ ✿

A few evenings later, Richard and Barbara Caldwell sat in their private dining room, the oak table seeming incongruous as it stretched out far past the two large people seated at one end.

Barbara was dressed in red, her husband's favorite color, her hair and make-up perfect. She had spent hours in town at the hair salon as she hatched the perfect plan for revenge.

Sadie Miller would have to go.

Richard Caldwell's favorite dishes were served: crusty baked potato and filet mignon with horseradish and dill. The wine was perfect. Her husband was in a jovial mood.

"So, what was going on at the barn today that the Kitchen Help needed your assistance there?" she asked, heavily emphasizing "Kitchen Help."

Richard stopped chewing and slowly laid down his fork. He picked up the monogrammed napkin and wiped his mouth before he cleared his throat.

Their eyes met. Clashed.

"Jim Sevarr almost hit a horse. Sadie was with him. The horse is in our barn and Sadie wants to keep him, but her father won't let her."

Barbara stabbed at her meat as her lips compressed.

"I thought Amish daughters are expected to obey their fathers. Why wouldn't you respect that?"

"I am. That's why the horse is here."

"I see."

The words were cold, hard pellets stinging Richard Caldwell's mind. She was making him as uncomfortable as only cunning Barbara could. When she looked up, Richard Caldwell checked a mental urge to shake his wife. Malice glittered in the hard eyes he once thought beautiful. He shuddered and stopped himself, thinking of the look in Sadie's eyes as she knelt by the failing horse— eyes so unlike his wife's eyes.

"So does that mean she needs you to escort her to the barn?"

"Barbara. Stop. Of course not."

"Well, I'm letting her go. She isn't capable in the kitchen. We need a better helper for Dorothy Sevarr."

"You will do no such thing. I hired Sadie Miller, and I say whether she stays or goes."

"She's been stealing food."

Barbara's breath was coming fast, her agitation rising, as she sensed her husband's unwillingness to cooperate and his loyalty to Sadie Miller. Fear goaded her now, her words making very little sense as they hammered her husband.

"She…she took two biscuits. And ground beef. And…and tomato sauce. She…picked up the dry cleaning and kept $20. She…oh, I know now what she did. She broke my mother's heirloom watch. She also broke her vase. On purpose."

Richard Caldwell's head went from side to side, like an angry bull pawing the ground.

"Barbara, you have no idea. I could never even imagine anything—any wrong notion—with her. She's too good with that horse. She's too pure. Firing her is out of the question. Sadie Miller and her horse are staying. I… need to see this, to see what happens."

Barbara's mouth fell open in astonishment as she watched the change in her husband's eyes, his voice. He kept his voice low and even, but there was no doubt in his wife's mind that he did not believe her. He never would.

And if she wanted to feed her own sick jealousy, she could go right ahead.

Defeat wilted Barbara. She faded before her husband's quiet anger in disbelief.

They ate dessert in silence, the edge of the room in darkness.

Chapter 7

Dat was in a jovial, if not downright silly, mood. He was singing snatches of "Old Dan Sevarr" when he washed his hands at the small sink in the laundry room, which made Sadie wince. Why did that make her cringe, she wondered? Maybe because she was still smarting from his rough words the evening before. Now she wished he'd just stop that silly tune.

The Miller family sat together for the evening meal as usual. The ordinary, everyday, white Correlle plates with the mismatched silverware and clear plastic tumblers sat a bit haphazardly on the old, serviceable knit tablecloth. The tan and beige-colored Melmac serving dishes holding the steaming food were homey and comforting, bolstering Sadie's courage.

Dat reached for the bowl of mashed potatoes, piled high with the usual little stream of browned butter coming from the small well on top. As a child, Sadie loved the taste of the dark browned butter, but now she knew that if she wanted to stay thin, she needed to work the serving spoon around it.

The chunks of seared beef, which had simmered in rich gravy as the potatoes cooked, were passed around the table followed by green beans liberally dotted with little bits of bacon and onion cooked just long enough to soften them.

"I was going to toss a salad," Mam said, "but the price of tomatoes was just too high at the IGA in town."

She looked apologetically in Dat's direction, but Dat never looked at Mam or gave any indication that he heard. He just bent his head over his plate and ate fast and methodically. He was no longer being silly.

"It's okay Mam. We don't always need a salad," said Sadie hurriedly to ease the uncomfortable moment.

"I hate salads," Reuben said loudly, with no pretense. "They're not good."

"Tomatoes aren't," Anna agreed, always a staunch supporter of Reuben and his views.

"I love tomatoes," Rebekah said smiling.

"Mmm. So do I," agreed Leah.

"Not when they're $4.99 a pound," Mam said shaking her head. "I never heard of prices like that 'til we moved here."

Dat looked up and sighed.

"Pass the potatoes," he said brusquely.

Plates were scraped, dishes passed, forks lifted to mouths, everyone chewing and swallowing silently. Mam got up to refill water glasses, and a soft fog descended over the supper table, a fog that you didn't see unless you knew Mam and noticed the change in her. The change was subtle, but it was there, just like fog that swirled and hovered.

Sadie pushed back her plate and said too quickly and loudly, "I'm full."

"Don't you want dessert?" Mam asked, her eyes blinking rapidly.

"What do we have?"

"Well, I guess just canned peaches from the IGA. I was going to bake a chocolate cake but sort of...got side-tracked. I...couldn't find the recipe."

Sadie looked at Mam, her mouth hanging open, stupidly.

"But, Mam...," she began.

Mam's eyes stopped Sadie. They were brimming with terror. Mam was afraid—frightened of her own inability to bake a chocolate cake without a recipe. Mam never used a recipe. Never. Not for chocolate cakes or chocolate chip cookies or even for pie crusts. It was all written in her mind, emerging the minute the big Tupperware bowl of flour hit the countertop.

"It's all right, Mam."

"I want ice cream!"

"We don't have any."

"We do. I saw it in the freezer."

Reuben got up, walked to the freezer, and yanked the door open dramatically.

"See? There it is!"

Anna swung her legs across the top of the bench in one little-girl movement and dashed over to peer around the freezer door.

"You're right, Reuben."

Reuben bounced back to the table, the ice cream clutched firmly in his hands.

"Chocolate marshmallow!"

Dat leaned back in his chair, grinned at Reuben, and said, "Guess who bought it?"

"You did!"

"I did. That's my favorite and Mam forgets to buy it."

Sadie winced. Come on, Dat. Did you have to say that?

As Dat helped himself to a large portion of chocolate marshmallow ice cream, Sadie's mind drifted to something more pleasant. Her horse. She knew she had to ask Dat, and now was a good a time as ever. She had to do it. Dat was kind and good to them all. He was. Surely he would allow it this time. He had said no to Paris and then relented later. So he wanted her to have a horse, right? Surely.

She cleared her throat.

"Dat?"

He lifted his head, swallowed, and acknowledged her question.

"You know the horse? The one...that one I told you about? The one that was dying?"

"Mm-hmm."

Firmly pleating the knit tablecloth beneath the table, she plunged in.

"I...he's down at Richard Caldwell's stable. He's alive. Breathing on his own. He's standing up. Can you imagine? He's barely able to, but he's standing. He's so skinny. His neck is pitiful. Richard Caldwell doesn't want him, and he said I can...can have him. Keep him."

Reuben stopped eating ice cream, watching Sadie with calculating eyes.

"Whose horse is he?" asked Dat.

Sadie relaxed, then launched into recounting the whole story to the family.

"Wow!" Anna said slowly, her mouth forming a perfect "O" around the word.

"It has to be someone's horse. What if you keep him and the owner shows up? It happens all the time. People rescue dogs, fall in love with them, name them, and one day the owner appears at their door."

"Yeah. What are you gonna do then?" Reuben asked, returning to his pile of ice cream, which was entirely too much for one 10-year-old to consume by himself.

Anna looked at him, her eyes narrowing before helping herself to a large spoonful from his bowl.

"Hey!"

"You don't need all that ice cream. It's already melting."

"Children!" Dat's voice was firm, his frown a significant indicator of their less-than-perfect behavior.

They both bent to their own bowls, but Reuben's elbow found Anna's side, fast and smooth, bringing smiles to both of their faces beneath their demure, downcast eyes.

"So?" Sadie began.

"What? You're telling me you want this stray horse kept in our barn?"

"Well..." Sadie lifted her hands and shoulders, then lowered them, along with her expectations.

"Where else would we keep him?" she asked respectfully.

Dat breathed through his nose, hard, the way he often did when he felt strongly about something. It wasn't a snort. It was more of a whoosh of air, but it meant the same as a snort.

"For starters, I think the whole deal is odd. We don't want a stray horse. How can we prove we didn't steal him when the owner comes looking for him? He wouldn't believe our story."

"Dat! You know there are acres and acres of government land without a single soul around for miles!" Sadie burst out. "The horse could have wandered from there."

"Why didn't this horse seek shelter in someone's barn? Or on someone's ranch? Something's fishy."

"But, Dat, the horse is sick! He's not just starved, he's sick!"

"Well, then, we don't want him for sure. Charlie will catch whatever this horse has.

"Please, Dat. Just let me have a box stall. Just one. You won't have to do a thing with him. Not feed him, not water him. Nothing."

"I've heard that before."

Sadie's shoulders slumped, defeat settling in. She wasn't going to beg or whine or grovel at Dat's feet. If he said no, then no it was. She had expected it all along, in a way, like an underlying riptide in the ocean that you suspected was there but didn't know for sure until it carried you out to sea. And here she was being flung about, pulled steadily along.

But she had to try one more time.

"But I'll never have another horse. Not like this one. He's so much like Paris."

"We don't have room," Dat said firmly.

Afterward, Sadie didn't know what had possessed her to give vent to her despair. Leah told her, quite seriously, it was because she was stubborn and would never give up. That thought scared her.

She had leapt up, talked loudly and forcefully, and told her father he was being selfish. Why couldn't she have a horse of her own? She had given up Paris for him and now this one, too. Why? Why?

She remembered Mam's white face, Dat's disbelief, Leah's shock, but she had been beyond caring. She had gripped the table's edge until her fingers were white and told Dat exactly what she thought. Then she turned and fled to the refuge of her room.

She had tried to pray, she really had. But her prayers hit the ceiling and bounced back down, not appearing to reach heaven at all. So she lay across her bed, too angry and upset to cry. She knew she should be remorseful, at least a little bit sorry, but she wasn't. She was glad she had told Dat all that stuff. She was.

He had no right. He had no right to keep that horse from her. There were two empty box stalls in the barn, but his excuse was always the same: If every stall was full, then where would visitors tie their horses?

How often did they have visitors? And if company did show up, they could always tie their horses in the forebay. They could even tie Charlie and put the company's horse in the same stall. There were options

Dat was cruel. He had no sympathy for horses or anyone who loved horses. He said horses didn't have stable manners, kicking against a good, strong wall for no reason at all, and they were always looking for a chance to run away. Well, maybe his horses did, and no small wonder. She would run away, too, if she was Dat's horse. He didn't like horses, just sort of put up with them, and the horses knew it. Why didn't he just go Mennonite and get a car? Or a bike?

Angry thoughts swirled around and around inside Sadie's head, bringing only a weariness of body and mind and no peace. She felt old and tired, her future uncertain. With no horse, what did she have to look forward to? Just work at the ranch and give Dat her paycheck, on and on and on. Go with the youth on the weekends, same old supper crowd and hymn-singings. On and on and on.

There weren't even any interesting boys. Not one Amish guy in all of Montana caught her eye. Not one. They were all too young—not old enough to date—or too old—too set in their ways, too much like a bachelor. It was all so annoying, She bet, too, that behind Dat's refusal was his own unspoken feelings about Sadie and his expectations of her. He thought she was being childish and that young Amish women shouldn't ride horses anymore. Why couldn't she grow up and get married the way other Amish girls did at her age?

Sadie guaranteed that Mam thought the same thing. She just didn't say it quite as readily as Dat. Well, what was she supposed to do? Marry someone English? They'd have a fit about that.

There had been Ezra. They had been on a few dates—dated quite awhile, actually. But it didn't last. Ezra was too…too…well…strict. He lived by the law—acting prideful and judgmental of others—and he expected as much from her. It was suffocating. So they broke up, much to the chagrin of Dat, Mam, and what seemed like the rest of the Amish community.

Sadie sat up, kicked off her shoes, then flung herself back on the pillows. She was hungry now, especially since her supper remained mostly uneaten, but she wasn't about to go down there now.

"Sadie! Phone!"

The voice calling for her sounded urgent—that same rushed tone that occurred whenever someone was on the line. The telephone was out in the phone shanty by the shop, and the person who had called was fortunate if someone heard the phone and could answer its insistent ringing. Otherwise, they would need to leave a message and wait for a return call.

Sadie leapt up, stuck her feet into her shoes, and without bothering to tie them, raced down the stairs. She grabbed her coat and went out into the starry night.

"Hello?" she said, lifting the receiver.

There was no answer.

Bewildered, she repeated, "Hello?"

Silence.

Annoyed now, she fitted the receiver back on its base and pushed the door open to leave. So much for that interesting caller.

Back in the kitchen, Sadie hung up her coat, then went to the refrigerator in search of something to eat. The kitchen was dimly lit, the gas light in the living room the only source of light. Usually, after dishes, the light in the kitchen was turned off, the one in the living room was turned on, and everyone gathered there to read or write.

She found some lunch meat, which seemed less than fresh, and a pack of Swiss cheese. Montana Swiss cheese was so tasteless, not at all like the Swiss cheese in Ohio. Mam was right; this cheese tasted a lot like the packet it came in.

She yawned, then pulled out the produce drawer. There were two green peppers and a big sweet onion. Mmm. She would make a sandwich.

Finding a soft sandwich roll, she spread it liberally with home-churned butter, and then put sliced peppers and onions on top. She sprinkled it well with salt and pepper and closed the lid.

She was just about to enjoy a big bite when the kitchen door was flung open and Dat stuck his head in.

"Phone!"

"For who?"

"You."

Grabbing her coat, the sandwich forgotten, Sadie dashed back to the phone shanty. What was going on?

Lifting the receiver, she said, "Hello?"

"How are you, Sadie?"

Sadie's heart sank. Ezra!

"I'm doing well, thank you. And you?"

"Fine, fine. I'm fine."

There was a long, awkward pause.

"Sadie, there is a practice hymn-singing at Owen Miller's tomorrow evening. You haven't been attending them, and I called to inquire why."

Sadie swallowed her annoyance.

"I... I've been busy."

"Doing what?"

None of your business, she thought, instantly on guard.

"I work full-time at the ranch now. I guess that's most of it."

There was a long pause.

"Well, tell me if I'm being impertinent, but I'm surprised your parents continue to allow you to work there."

"Oh. Why is that?"

"It's a worldly place. The way I understand it, quite a few men work for that Caldwell."

"Yes."

"Are you... Do you meet up with any of them? Do you work with them?"

"No. No, I work in the kitchen with Dorothy, an older English lady. Her husband, Jim, takes me to and from work."

"I see. Is that all you do?'

"No. I clean. I keep the big house in order—or most of it."

"I see. Do the ranch hands come in while you clean?"

"Oh, no. Never. They're working outside."

"Uh-huh."

Sadie doodled on a Post-it note with a pen.

"Do you speak to Richard Caldwell or his wife?"

"Sometimes."

"Is he trustworthy?"

"Who? Richard Caldwell?"

"Yes."

"Certainly. He's very kind to me now."

"The right sort of kindness, I would hope."

"Ezra, I…"

"Sadie, I worry about you working there. No good can come of it. You are not well-versed in the Bible, and you always did have an inclination toward rebellion."

Anger swelled up in Sadie. How dare he speak so boldly to her. He had a few faults of his own, too. She wanted to scream at him—tell him to mind his own business—but that would never do. It would be disrespectful, and she would only have to apologize later.

Sadie took a deep breath, "I appreciate your concern, Ezra. That's kind of you."

"May I pick you up tomorrow evening to take you along to the practice singing?"

Sadie's heart sank. No, no, no, she whispered silently.

"Leah, too?" she ventured, looking for a way to avoid another one-on-one date with him.

"If she wants. But it would be more appropriate if you and I went alone."

"Why would it be more appropriate?"

"I have a question to ask you."

Oh, help! Just say no. Say it. She did not want to ride all the way to Owen Miller's with Ezra. It was just unthinkable.

Then she almost pitied him. He was so good and he tried so hard to do what was right—even if he didn't always have much tact. She couldn't bring herself to say no, imagining his pleasant, open, sincere face. Why couldn't she go with Ezra?

"All right."

A pleased sigh.

"Good. Oh, Sadie, we'll have a lovely time. All the memories we share. Thank you, Sadie. Are your parents well?"

"Yes, they are."

"Give them a hello from me."

"I will."

"Good-night, Sadie."

"Good-night."

Slowly, she replaced the receiver, then sagged against the wall.

No, Ezra, we're not all well. Mam is going crazy and Dat is a stubborn mule. I don't like him much. I don't like you either. I don't want to live the way I do—working at the ranch with no hope of a future. I want a horse I'm not allowed to have.

So I'm inclined toward rebellion, am I? Am I? Is that what's wrong with me? Give up the horse the way good, obedient girls do and marry Ezra instead? Maybe if I learned to give up, I could learn to love Ezra.

She touched her eyebrows. She knew they were already elevated into that "holier-than-thou" Ezra attitude.

Sadie began walking toward the house. What should she do? Mam probably did not want to hear all this, and she wasn't going to tell Dat. He'd start planning her wedding that same hour.

"Who was that?" Mam asked the minute she entered the living room. Thankfully Dat wasn't around.

"No one."

"Now, Sadie!" Mam chided.

"Ezra Troyer."

"What did he want?"

"There's a practice singing at Owen Miller's tomorrow evening. He wants to take me."

"Are you going with him?"

"Yes."

"I'm surprised."

Reuben looked up from his drawing pad. He brushed the hair out of his eyes, then said bluntly, "I thought you didn't like Ezra?"

"You need a haircut, Reuben."

"Mam won't give me one."

"Mam, don't you think Reuben needs a haircut?"

"Yes, he does. But I'm afraid I can't cut his hair straight. It's hard for me to do that job right—the way it should be done, I mean. His hair is so straight, and... well, Dat said I should do it better."

To Sadie's horror, Mam began to cry. Not soft crying, not wiping a stray tear here or there, but huge, gulping, little-girl sobs. Sadie instantly tried to stop them by rushing over and holding her mother's shoulders firmly, murmuring, "Don't, Mam. *Do net.*"

Still her mother cried on.

"*Do net heila, Mam.*"

Anna and Reuben looked up. Rebekah laid down her book, coming to Mam's side in one long, fluid movement.

"I just...feel so dumb. Things I used to enjoy are like a big mountain now. Jacob—Dat—is so terribly unhappy with me. I just don't seem to be able to do some things I used to."

Sadie sat on the sofa beside her mother, holding her hands.

"Mam, I think you are depressed. I think you need to see a medical doctor and let him diagnose you. They can give you something to help you cope with the worst of this."

Mam sat up, her eyes alert, cunning even.

"You mean drugs?"

"Yes."

"No. I won't take medical drugs. They're poison to my system. You know that. Dat feels very strongly about that. So do I. I am taking natural pills—building up my body—to cope with these new and strange wanderings. Sadie...my mind will be fine, won't it?"

Sadie sighed.

"No, Mam. I don't think it will."

"Here comes Dat!" Mam hissed, returning to her book, the afghan thrown hastily across her lap.

Sadie turned to look as Dat hung his hat on the hook. He washed his hands, then came into the living room, surveyed it, and said, "Bedtime, Reuben."

"I'm not done drawing this."

"What is it?"

"Sadie's horse."

Dat bent to look, then he straightened, laughing uproariously.

"I doubt if Sadie's horse looks like a giraffe!"

Reuben swallowed, attempting to keep his face a mask of indifference. Slowly he closed the drawing pad, put his pencil and eraser in the coiled springs on the side, and got to his feet.

Dat was still chuckling as Sadie rose, pulled Reuben close with one arm, and together, went up the stairs to bed.

Chapter 8

Sadie winced as she dragged the brush through her thick, heavy mass of brown hair. Her thoughts were tumbling through her head, so the uncomfortable chore of brushing her hair was a welcome diversion.

Why had she promised Ezra she'd go? She seriously did not know. Maybe life was like that. You didn't know why you said or did certain things, but it was all a part of God's great and wonderful plan for your life. Maybe God's will just happened no matter what.

Dat and Mam thought Ezra was truly a special young man who would make a terrific husband for her. But why do parents think they know better than you do? They just didn't understand. There was not one other person in this community of Amish families for whom she could even try and summon some kind of love.

She often wished she could express her true feelings to Mam. And she wanted to ask questions, too, especially, how deep should the feelings of love be before you know you are fully committed and ready to marry? How could you know if you were ready to spend the rest of your days here on earth with this one other person?

The Amish were expected to date for a few years before getting married. They were also expected to not touch each other while dating. Not hold hands, not hug, not kiss, not have any other physical contact. The couple would be blessed by God if they entered into a sacred union in purity.

Sadie always thought that this was all well and good. But if she was really, really honest, she wondered how you could tell if you wanted to marry someone if you never touched him. What if you were pronounced man and wife and then discovered that his touch repulsed you? Wouldn't that be a fine kettle of fish, as Daddy Keim used to say. She didn't believe every couple stuck to that hands-off policy anyway.

Sadie clasped her hair into a barrette and firmly gathered the heavy mass on the back of her head, fastening it securely with hair pins. Her new covering followed, and she turned her head first one way and then the other, adjusting the covering more securely as she did so.

Some girls spent close to an hour arranging and rearranging their hair and coverings, which always drove Sadie to distraction. If you didn't get it right that first or second time, you sure weren't going to get it any better the seventh or eighth round, that was one thing sure.

She was glad she had a new dress and that it was a soft shade of light pink. She supposed it was a bit daring, but Mam had allowed it, though grudgingly. Grudgingly or gladly, it was pretty. The fabric hung in soft folds, the sleeves falling delicately to her wrists. It made her feel very feminine and, if she admitted it to herself, more attractive than usual.

She wondered vaguely how the person who was driving the buggy to take her away to the hymn-singing would feel about the dress. When she thought about it, she was glad she would wear the black coat, as Ezra would never approve of the soft, pink shade she was wearing.

Why did she wear it? She wanted to, that was why—and not for Ezra either. Maybe that was the whole reason after all. She wanted to be who she was—not who Ezra wanted her to be.

Nothing like real old-fashioned honesty with oneself, she thought wryly.

Sadie parted the white curtains in her room. Darkness had already enveloped the Montana mountainside. But the night sky was so brilliant, it seemed only a dimmer version of daylight. The starlight blended with the moon and snow to create a stark, contrasting portrait of the landscape, as if painted black, white, and gray.

Sadie watched for the lights she knew would come slowly up the driveway. Ezra was very kind to his horse. Wasn't there an old saying—The way a man treats his horse is the way he will treat his wife.

The moon was full. It made the stars seem tiny and insignificant, like afterthoughts. Each one twinkled bravely in spite of being outdone by the moon.

The pines on the ridge seemed so dark, they were black and ominous-looking. Sadie thought they were beautiful in the sunlight, each dark bough harboring glints of light woven with deeper shadows. She loved the smell of pines, the sticky, pungent sap that seeped from their rough trunks, and the soft carpet of needles that covered the ground beneath them.

The lulling sound of the wind through pine branches was like a low, musical wonder—like a song. There was no other sound on earth quite like it. It was haunting and inspiring and filled Sadie with a deep, quiet longing for something, but she never understood what. Perhaps the song was God—his spirit sighing in the pine branches, his love for what he had created crying out and touching a chord in Sadie's heart.

From earth we are created, and to earth we return, she thought. She supposed it was a melancholy kind of thought, but it felt comforting and protective. But the sound of wind in the pines reminded her that life is also full of unseen and unknown forces.

> *Down in the valley, valley so low,*
> *Hang your head over, hear the wind blow.*
> *Hear the wind blow, dear, hear the wind blow,*
> *Hang your head over, hear the wind blow.*

It was an old folk song that Sadie often heard Mam humming to herself as she went about her daily chores. It was a kind of spiritual for Mam. She always said she felt the same passion her "foremothers" felt in that song. Women were like that. They heard many beautiful songs in the wind that no one else could comprehend. Subject to their husbands, women often hung their heads low. Many of them—Mam included—had to. It was just the way of it.

So, that's what's wrong with me. I go off wearing a light pink dress, yearning for a horse of my own, not submitting to kind, conservative Ezra because I can't hang my head low.

Sadie caught her breath. She pushed the curtain back farther with unsteady fingers, then leaned into the windowpane. It seemed as if the pines became alive and did a kind of undulating dance, but only the lower branches.

What was that? What was running, no, merely appearing and disappearing on the opposite ridge?

Sadie strained her eyes, her nerves as taut as a guitar string.

Wolves! There were wolves in the pines. But wait. Wolves were not as big as…as whatever…that was.

Sadie gasped audibly and her hand came to her mouth to stifle a scream as the dark shadows emerged.

Horses! Dark, flowing horses!

Like one body, the horses broke free of the pines that held them back, and in one fluid movement, streamed across the snowy field, disappearing again in a matter of seconds.

Whose horses were loose? Who owned so many? It was like a band of wild horses. And yet… Had she really seen them? Or was it a mirage of wishful thinking?

As if to bring her back to earth, the yellow glow of two headlights came slowly around the bend in the driveway, making steady progress up the hill.

Ezra.

I cannot imagine what possessed me to try this again, she thought, suddenly face-to-face with reality.

Her eyes turned back to the black and white serenity of the moonlit ridge. There wasn't a trail or dent, not even a shadow, in the snowy hillside to show her if what she had seen was actually real. Tomorrow! Tomorrow she would climb the ridge and see if she could find anything.

Tonight, however, belonged to Ezra.

Sighing, she shrugged her shoulders into her black, wool coat, grabbed a pair of warm gloves and her purse, and went slowly down the stairs.

"Ooooo!" sighed Rebekah, clasping her hands.

"Pink!" Anna yelled.

Reuben looked up from his book and grinned toothily. "Pink! For Ezra!"

Sadie wrapped a cream-colored scarf around her neck, adjusting it just so.

"It's not a date!" Sadie hissed at Reuben.

"What else is it?" Reuben called from his perch on the brown recliner.

"I'm going to clip your ears!" Sadie shouted.

Reuben howled with glee, slapping his knee, and Sadie ground her teeth in frustration. Little brothers were the most bothersome things anyone had ever endured, like lice or cold sores, and worth about as much, too.

She didn't say good-bye to anyone, just let herself out the sturdy, oak door into the glare of Ezra's buggy lights.

"Hello, Sadie."

"How are you, Ezra?"

"I'm good, I'm doing well. And you?"

"I'm fine."

He came over to the buggy steps, immediately holding out his hand to assist her. She had forgotten how tall he was.

"Thank you."

Sadie settled herself on the buggy seat, sliding over against the side as far as she could, hoping his leg and the side of his coat would not touch her at all.

She blinked rapidly when he stepped into the buggy and his large frame filled three-fourths of the seat, his upper arm secure against her shrinking shoulder, his thigh firmly against her coat. His gloved hand reached down and pulled on the buggy robe, tucking her securely against him, protecting her from the cold. Sweet Ezra—kind and thoughtful as always.

"All right then. Here we go. Comfortable?"

"Y—yes, yes, I am."

She was suddenly aware of how really close one person sat to another in a buggy. It was so...so intimate, especially in winter with both people covered by the same lap robe. She wondered, fleetingly, how you could keep a good and proper courtship for two years while tucked cozily together under a buggy robe like this.

"We've got quite a few miles to go, so I thought I'd be on time."

"I was ready."

"Yes. I remember that about you, Sadie. You never made me wait very long."

"Mmm-hmm."

Sadie shrank against the side of the buggy, the close proximity strangling her or suffocating her or maybe just making it hard to breathe. She wanted to yank open the window, gulp great, deep draughts of cold, winter air so she could survive.

Calm down, Sadie, she told herself. It's just Ezra. He can bring up all the "remembers" he wants, but you still have a choice.

They talked then, easily and as comfortably as possible, but only after Sadie calmed herself and prepared for his reminiscing of the time they dated.

Ezra actually seemed more relaxed and jovial than Sadie remembered. He was not so black and white, not as strict and overbearing as he once was. She actually found herself enjoying the conversation. He and Sadie talked about horses and, yes, he had heard about the theft of the horses in another county. They talked about that being a coincidence, but agreed that it was highly improbable that there could be a connection.

Sadie kept the subject of Nevaeh to herself. It just

seemed too emotional, too intimate to think of sharing the whole story with Ezra. Besides, it might open the subject of Richard Caldwell and her job, both of which he disapproved of so strongly. Better to let that one lie, she thought. No use saying anything.

As if on cue, Ezra blurted out, "So, how's work down at the fancy ranch?"

Sadie cringed.

"Good."

"I heard you had quite a scare with that horse jumping out in front of the truck."

Sadie jerked her head in his direction.

"How ... how do you know about that?"

"What does it matter?"

"Oh, nothing. It's all right, of course."

Ezra's eyes narrowed.

"You ain't hiding anything are you?"

"No, no. Of course not."

"Guess the horse didn't make it, huh?"

"Yes, he did."

"He did? Found the owner yet?"

"No."

"Where is he?"

"At ... at the Caldwell ranch."

"Really?"

Oh, just hush up now. Let it go, she pleaded silently. But Ezra was tenacious, hanging onto a subject like a bulldog with his teeth sunk into his prey.

"Bet old Richard Caldwell wasn't happy."

"No."

"Can't believe he kept him."

"Yes."

"You don't really want to talk about this, do you?"

"No."

"Why not?"

"I don't know."

"You always wanted a horse, so here's your chance."

"Yes."

Ezra laughed. "Yes. No. Yes. No."

Sadie laughed with him.

"Not exactly an exciting person, am I?"

To her complete horror, Ezra stopped the horse, making sure he came to a complete stop before dropping the reins and turning to face her squarely.

"Sadie, nothing could be farther from the truth. You are on my mind, in my thoughts, constantly. I still love you with all my heart."

Sadie went numb with disbelief as his large, gloved hands wrapped themselves tenderly around the wool fabric of her shoulders.

"If I was not an Amish person who takes his vows seriously I would crush you to my heart, Sadie, and kiss you senseless. I would. Just like in romance books. But I want to serve God first, deny myself, and pray about us and His perfect will for my life. I feel I owe that to God and to Jesus Christ who has died for me. It is the only thing that keeps me going. The Christian life, the narrow path."

Sadie had never been so shocked in all her life. Ezra! To think he was capable of such speech, of such emotions, of such...such tenderness and...love and of shameful thought...of desire.

"Now I've said too much, right?"

His hands fell away and reached for the reins while a thousand words and feelings crashed through Sadie's senses. Was this Ezra? Was Ezra able to voice these kinds of feelings?

"I've ruined it now, the little thread we were hanging onto. Or I was. You probably let go a long time ago."

Sadie was still speechless, although she managed to put a hand on his arm. For what? For reassurance? For conveying regret? She didn't know.

"Ezra, it's quite all right. It really is. I just...didn't know."

"I've had a lot of spiritual struggles. When we dated, I was obsessed with perfection according to the *Ordnung*, to our walk in life. I can see so clearly why you broke up with me."

But you're still like that.

Sadie couldn't keep the thought back, although she said nothing. She was more than happy to ride the remaining miles in silence. It was not entirely uncomfortable. She felt as if they had reached a truce. For now.

When they turned in the Owen Miller drive, Ezra began again.

"I'm sorry, Sadie, for that bit of..."

He laughed nervously, ashamedly.

"I guess I'm sorry for what happened between us. But a lot has happened since we broke up, and I've let go of my iron resolve to be the perfect Christian man. You know there is no such thing. I am a weak person and you are my weakness—my undoing. And that is the truth. I used to imagine that the more I walked perfectly with God, the more he would bless me for that and give you to me. You are all I wanted in life."

He shook his head ruefully.

"Selfish, aren't I? Do you know how stupid that is? I'll be good if you give me what I want. But don't we all sort of bargain with God in a way?"

Sadie was in disbelief again.

Ezra! Talking this way! It was mind-boggling.

"Well, here we are. I'll be ready to take you home after the singing."

He smiled down at her. From the light of the head-lights, Sadie could see his genuine, broad smile containing more honesty than she could have ever imagined from him. Tenderly, he laid the back of his hand on her cheek, then let her go. She thought she heard him say, "So perfect." But perhaps it was only her imagination.

Her mind reeling, Sadie made her way dizzily into the *kessle-haus*, or laundry room, the part of the house most families used as a catch-all for coats, boots, umbrellas, and laundry, for mixing calf starter, warming baby chicks, canning garden vegetables, or like now, for containing a gaggle of fussing girls. They were dispensing coats and scarves, giggling, leaning into mirrors to adjust coverings, swiping at stray hair, sharing secrets, and squealing with glee at the sight of a close friend too long unseen.

"Sadie! Oh, it's been too long! Missed you terribly!"

Lydiann grasped Sadie's gloved hands.

"What's wrong with you? You look as if you've seen a ghost!"

Sadie laughed nervously, waving it off with one hand.

"No! You're overworked imagination is seeing things as usual, Lydiann!"

"Come with me to the bathroom! Come on!"

Lydiann pulled her along, and Sadie was profoundly grateful to be in the small bathroom with only one person until she could gain a semblance of normalcy. Her hands were shaking so that she could barely fix her hair or adjust her covering. Lydiann prattled on about Johnny, her current crush, while Sadie nodded, smiled, said yes or no at the right times, and, in plain words, acted like a zombie.

"What in the world is up with you?"

Lydiann stopped prattling, stood squarely in front of her friend, put her hands on her hips, and eyed Sadie shrewdly.

"Who brought you?"

Sadie said nothing, just looked down at the toe of her shoe, rearranging the brown shag of the carpet.

"Who?"

"The man in the moon, that's who!" Sadie said finally, laughing.

"Oh, he did, did he? I bet he's a real nice guy!"

They burst out laughing together.

"Seriously, Sadie, who brought you?"

"I told you."

"Stop it, Sadie. It's not funny."

"How did you get here?"

"All right. Ezra."

"Ezra?"

"Yes. Ezra. So what's wrong with that? Huh? Can you tell me? What's wrong with Ezra bringing me to the singing? We used to date, you know."

Lydiann's mouth hung open, her eyes wide.

"You can close your mouth any time now," Sadie said as she flung open the bathroom door and walked out, Lydiann on her heels.

The girls filed into the Miller living room, greeting the parents that were seated on folding chairs along the wall. Furniture had been pushed back to accommodate the long table in the middle of the room. The gleaming, varnished church benches sat on each side of the table. The brown hymn books were placed along the table in neat piles, waiting for the youth to open them and begin the singing.

At a hymn sing, the youth sang the old songs of their forefathers in German, although they sang some classic English tunes and choruses as well. The singing was a fine blend of youthful voices, and the evening was meant for fellowship in each other's company, while practicing new songs to replenish the old.

The girls sat on one side of the table, the boys on the other. When the boys slid into place on the smooth bench opposite the girls, Sadie looked up and straight into brown eyes that seemed strangely familiar.

Mark!

His look of recognition mirrored her own. Cheeks blazing, she looked at the only safe place—down at her hands in her lap. Her first thought was, what is an English person doing here at our hymn-singing? I wonder what the parents will think?

"Sadie? *Vee bisht doo?*"

Bravely, she looked up and calmly said, "*Gut.*"

He smiled then, relaxed and at ease. Opening the hymn book, he talked to Nathan Keim beside him and acted like a total veteran of hymn singings—as if he'd been attending them all his life.

How did he get here—and him not being Amish? He had nerve. He probably picked up that "*Vee bisht doo*" thing tonight. Imagine. He would not get away with this, that was one thing sure.

Her head lowered, Sadie stole glances, watching Mark when he was not looking.

The singing began in earnest then, leaving Sadie completely nonplussed again. Mark joined in the singing! He knew the verses. He knew the words. He knew German perfectly. But how could he? He was not Amish! His hair wasn't even Amish. It was cut close to his head.

She bet the Miller parents were silently having a fit. This would be the talk for months—that brazen, English person who came to the singing.

And he knew the German.

Likely, he came from Germany. With a name like Peight.

Chapter 9

A FEW WEEKS LATER, SADIE OPENED THE STABLE door, catching her breath after her fast sprint from the ranch kitchen. Warm smells swirled around her, sharp pungent hay and sticky, sweet molasses mixed with the nutty odor of oats and shelled corn.

Gomez, one of the stable hands, nodded, averting his eyes shyly and ducking his head beneath the bill of his cap as he pushed the wide broom back and forth across the aisle between the stables.

"Good morning!"

Sadie jumped.

"Oh, it's you! Good morning to you, too!"

Richard Caldwell was standing at the door of Nevaeh's stall, shaking his head back and forth. As he turned to look at her, Sadie saw a soft gleam in his eyes, a sort of excitement, a different light than she had ever seen in him.

"Sadie Miller, I think we have us a winner here!"

Sadie stood, surveying the dim interior of Nevaeh's stall. He lifted his head, his nostrils quivering with soft, little breaths. It was a movement of recognition and of gladness the moment he spied Sadie. Immediately, the horse made his way through the sawdust and straw to stand before Sadie. She slipped past Richard Caldwell and slid her arms around Nevaeh's neck, bending her head, murmuring her greeting in Dutch.

It was a sight that never failed to bring a tightening to Richard Caldwell's throat. The connection between the girl and this horse was amazing. That horse knew Sadie as sure as shooting, and he would do anything Sadie asked of him.

"Yep! We got us a winner!" he said, in his normal, much-too-loud kind of voice.

"You mean...?" Sadie asked.

"This horse is no ordinary one. You can tell by the lines of his shoulders, the way he holds his head, the deep chest. The more he's gaining, the easier I can tell. He's no wild mustang, this one. He's someone's horse with outstanding bloodlines running in them veins of his."

Sadie's heart sank at his words.

"Then, he's someone's horse?"

"He has to be."

"So why are we bothering to spend all this money? All these veterinary bills? The feed?"

Richard Caldwell looked out the window of Nevaeh's stall.

"It doesn't mean the owner will be here to reclaim him," he said flatly.

"But...it's not our...your horse," she insisted.

"Sadie, I told you, this horse is yours. I give him to you. I gave him to you a few weeks ago. He's getting better—improving much faster then I thought possible. Your visits, the grooming, the apples and carrots and sugar cubes you take from the kitchen..."

"I'm sorry."

Sadie was deeply ashamed. She hadn't meant to steal, just figured Richard Caldwell wouldn't mind the few treats from the kitchen.

"Don't worry about it. You can feed this horse a bushel of my apples if you choose. You're doing something right."

"How long until I can try to ride him?" Sadie asked, bolder now by his words of praise.

"You want to try this afternoon?"

Sadie clasped her hands, sighing, before she said, "Thank you! Oh I'm so glad! I think he'll do just fine. I won't gallop him—just walk him. He's still not very strong. Do you have a saddle and bridle I could use? I still have Paris' tack, but it's stored away and likely all cracked and dusty. Did you know I could ride Paris without a sadle? I never told you that, did I? Eva and I both did. Her horse's name was Spirit, but he listened to anything we wanted him to do. Spirit was a unique horse; small, but very muscular. Paris was the beauty, though. Her color was exactly the shade of honey—you know, the good kind that is done right, not that darker, brownish stuff in the grocery store."

Suddenly, realizing she was rambling and allowing her stern boss to see her with her guard down, she stopped. She was just being herself, but she felt embarrassed about her open display of emotions. She looked down and kicked gently at Nevaeh's hoof with the toe of her boot.

Richard Caldwell's eyes crinkled at the corners, and he smiled from the heart.

"You really loved that Paris, didn't you?"

Sadie nodded.

"And that dad of yours still won't allow you to have a horse?"

"I guess not. I tried."

Sadie shrugged her shoulders helplessly.

"Well, if that's how he feels, we'll just keep him here. You can ride in the afternoon or stay an hour later—whatever you decide. If that fearsome Dottie allows it."

"Don't call her Dottie," Sadie said grinning.

✿ ✡ ✿

Dorothy fussed up a storm when Sadie told her she was allowed to ride for an hour each afternoon. Forgetting the ham and beans on the stove, Dorothy waved the wooden spoon she was using in irritation. Her eyes sparked and her hair bounced around for emphasis.

"And who, young lady, is going to help me out? Who? Barbara Caldwell? Gomez? Harry? I can't cook these gigantic meals myself! At my age? It's too much! If I didn't have this good pair of shoes on my feet, there's no way I'd be here now. No way."

She returned to the pot of beans, stirring, muttering, shaking her head about the young generation, while Sadie hastily began loading the dishwasher. Guilt swirled around her heart. Maybe riding Nevaeh and caring for him here at the ranch was not a good idea. Dat didn't approve of the horse, and now Dottie was upset. Perhaps she should just tell Richard Caldwell to allow the horse to finish his journey back to good health and then sell him, or better yet, search for his owner.

Isn't that what computers were for? Couldn't Richard Caldwell go on-line or post something about a lost horse, perhaps a stolen horse, and the owner would see it? She'd have to ask him.

Another thing—it would probably be best if she never rode him at all. Once the bond between horse and rider started, there was no turning back. Not for her, anyway. She'd just become attached to this horse, and like Paris, would have to give him up in the end.

But she had to try, just once, just this afternoon.

✿ ✡ ✿

Sadie glanced at the clock then back to Dorothy. It was two o'clock, and Dorothy was having her afternoon rest, which was a nice way of saying she sat down in the soft rocking chair in the corner of the huge kitchen and fell asleep so soundly, her glasses slid down her nose, her mouth gave way to gravity, and loud snores erupted at regular intervals from her dilating nostrils. But it was not a nap. "No, siree, I never take a nap," she'd say, "Just rest my eyes, just rest my eyes. Need to go to the optical place and get my lenses changed."

What a dear person! Sadie wanted to be exactly like Dorothy when she grew old. Like Dorothy and Jim, a love and commitment eternal.

But for now, it was out to the barn.

The everyday coat Sadie wore to work was perfect—warm and loose-fitting, leaving room for her shoulders and arms to move. She wore an extra pair of socks, riding boots, her well-worn pair of jeans beneath her dress, and a warm, white scarf on her head.

Her breath came in little gasps, short puffs of nervous energy. She fully admitted to herself that she was afraid—only a little—but scared nevertheless. Who could know what might happen when she swung herself up on Nevaeh's back? Horses could be the most docile creatures until the minute someone sat on their back, and then, WHAM!

Sadie went to the tack room, which held all the saddles, bridles, harnesses, brushes, combs, polishes, waxes, and anything else a person—or horse, for that matter—could need or want. She stood hesitantly beside the door, not entirely sure what she should do. There was a dizzying array of saddles in all colors, sizes, and shapes. She wasn't sure which were to use and which were for display.

Maybe she should have asked Richard Caldwell to accompany her this first time to the tack room. She had wondered if Richard Caldwell would be here to help her, but she knew his business, the many hands he managed on the ranch, and numerous other ventures kept him extremely busy. She supposed Nevaeh was only a small blip on the screen of his life.

What to do? She looked past the cabinets to the row of gleaming, leather bridles, then walked over quietly, her hand reaching out for the one closest to her. It looked like an average size, and it had buckles along the side so she could adjust it. Well, she had to start somewhere.

The opposite end of the room sprang to life when the door burst open, and a small man charged through it. He had a huge, black mustache, a greasy, filthy coat, and a slouched leather hat.

"Hey, girl, whatcha doin' in here?"

Sadie put her hands behind her back, the color seeping from her face.

"Ain't you s'posed to be in that there kitchen helpin' the old lady?"

"N-not now. I have an hour to ride Nevaeh, the black and white paint."

"Richard Caldwell, the boss, know this?"

"Yes. He...he is the one who wants me to ride him."

"Yer gonna need a saddle then."

Sadie's eyes narrowed as she picked up courage.

"And a bridle. And a blanket."

The black mustache lifted from its long, droopy shape to a higher, friendlier look, and a massive brown hand went out.

"Lothario Bean! Master of the Tack Room."

Large white teeth flashed below the mustache, looking for all the world like a giant Oreo cookie. His skin was the color of a Brach's Milk Maid caramel that Mam used when she made a turtle cake.

Sadie shook hands, wincing as her sturdy, white one was crushed in the huge hand of Lothario Bean.

"Ain't you the prettiest thing? You remind me of m' daughters, only whiter. Got five daughters. 'Fore every one was borned, thought sure God give me a son. Never was. All daughters. All five of 'em. Felida, Rosita, Carmelita, Frances, and Jean Elizabeth."

He ticked them off on thick brown fingers, his beady, brown eyes polished with love and pride.

"All girls. Love of my life."

Sadie smiled warmly, instantly liking this individual with his thick Latino accent.

"Jean Elizabeth, you know? She named that to break up Jean Bean!"

He laughed uproariously, slapping his leather chaps so hard, Sadie felt sure his hand stung afterward.

She laughed genuinely. Poor Jean Bean.

Lothario squinted at Sadie, cocking his head to one side like a large, overgrown bird.

"You know Christmas is coming? You celebrate Christmas? Your religion believe in Jesus' birth?"

"Of course."

"Good. Good. So do we, so do we."

"You know Christmas is coming. Me and my darling Lita, we is planning a huge surprise—a huge one! No presents this year, none. A trip! We gon' take a long trip back to the ol' country!"

He spread his arms, joy crossing his face, and the Oreo cookie became bigger and wider as he told Sadie the wonders of returning to South America.

Sadie finally glanced apprehensively at the large clock on the wall of the tack room. Twenty minutes had already gone by, and she hadn't even seen Nevaeh yet.

"I must go, please. I have only one hour."

"Oh, oh, oh, I am please to be excused. Forgive me fer keeping ya here. Here. Here. This is your bridle, and this? No, this? This one? This is your saddle."

Moving as swiftly as he talked, he pulled off a saddle, snatched a bridle, and collected a blanket. Keeping up a constant chatter pertaining to his mother's corn tortillas, Lothario swept through the door and into the stable, released the latch of Nevaeh's stall, then stepped back. He bowed deeply, one arm across his back, in a manner so genteel, it warmed Sadie's heart.

"Thank you, Mr. Bean. Thank you so much!" she said smiling.

"No, no Mr. Bean. Lothario. Lothario. Just like the romantic hero in the book!"

Sadie laughed, then went into Nevaeh's stall as Lothario Bean hurried off to do what masters of tack rooms did.

She was still smiling as she led Nevaeh out and began brushing his coat—which was still not as glossy and smooth as Sadie hoped it would be by this time.

Nevaeh was a perfect gentleman for grooming. He stood quietly, allowing Sadie to brush every inch of him, down to his grayish-brown hooves. He never pranced away or refused to budge, the way Paris had always done.

Sadie slid the horse blanket gently over Nevaeh's back, lifting and settling it down a few times to let him get used to the feel of it. His head lifted, ears flickered back, then forward, and Sadie knew he would readily accept the saddle if that was all he had to say about the blanket. Standing on tiptoe, she threw the beautiful brown saddle up and over his back. Nevaeh still stood quietly, ears flickering.

"Good boy. What a *braufa gaul*. Good boy."

Sadie kept up the soft speech while she stroked and patted, adjusted straps, and tightened the cinch strap beneath his stomach. Sliding her hand between the strap and the stomach, she checked to see if it was too loose or too tight.

Nevaeh seemed comfortable, keeping a good-natured stance. He lowered, then raised his head, but in a calm manner so that Sadie felt more relaxed, her erratic heartbeat becoming more normal.

When she introduced the bit, he clamped his teeth and lifted his head to avoid it, but Sadie gently coaxed him to cooperate. She had to remove the bit to adjust the leather straps on the side of his head, but the second introduction to the bit didn't seem to bother him too much.

Taking a deep breath, Sadie took the reins and spoke to her horse.

"*Bisht* all right, Nevaeh? *Doo gehn myeh*."

She lifted the reins, tugged, and Nevaeh followed. She rolled open the door. Nevaeh stood quietly, then followed her outside into the brilliant, white world.

They stood together, surveying the ranch before them. Nevaeh's head came up and his ears pricked forward as he stood at attention, waiting to see what Sadie would do.

Sadie cupped his nose in her gloved hand, murmured, stroked his silky neck beneath the heavy mane, and told him what a wonderful, big, handsome horse he was. Then she swung into the saddle, as light and gentle as ever.

"Good, good boy, Nevaeh."

✿ ✡ ✿

In the garage where the black Hummer and the cream-colored Mercedes were kept, Richard Caldwell stood, feeling more foolish than he had ever felt in his life — at least since he was in sixth grade and had thrown up in math class.

He wanted to see how Sadie would handle a horse, yet knew it was probably best not to let her know this. He knew she'd do better on her own. He was also curious about what this modestly dressed young woman would do with her skirt, and he did not want to embarrass her by asking silly questions.

What was it about Sadie that brought on these emotions, these feelings he had long forgotten? He was in awe of her — if any such thing was possible for the great Richard Caldwell. Could it be that this is how fathers felt when they had grown-up daughters? How would he know? He and Barbara never had children. She never wanted them.

Shortly after they were married, he knew. She had no time for babies. They cried, took up all your time, and in this day and age, who knew if they would even turn out all right?

Parenting was hard. Barbara thought it would hardly be worth the effort, even with one child.

He didn't know how he felt about having children. He guessed he always figured there would be an heir to his ranch, an acquisition he had obtained in his 30s. And now, almost 20 years later, he was old. His wife was much younger, but just not the type to have children.

He shrugged, passed a hand across the sleek surface of the Mercedes, and thought about having a son. He would teach him to ride and buy him a miniature horse.

Richard Caldwell laughed, covering his weariness with humor. What else could he do?

Surely he was not in love with Sadie. Falling in love? No. Flat out no. Sadie was too pure, too good, almost angelic. Besides, how could he defile something that reminded him of home? Somehow she gave him that same cozy feeling he had from a snowy, white tablecloth set on a cheap, wooden table that held his mother's breakfast of homemade pancakes—a stack of three, dribbling melted butter and sweet, sticky home-cooked syrup. No, Sadie was not the type of girl that brought the wrong kind of emotions to his head. Not at all.

He just wanted to see if she could handle this Nevaeh. He was afraid he would come to regret letting her try to ride. He doubted the whole situation—and the outcome.

Sliding his huge frame over a bit, he peered through the glass. Well, she was up. Looked as if she had a bit of a problem now, though. Didn't that Nevaeh just stand there now? Refused to budge. Typical horse with no brains. Should have let him die.

He slid back from the window when Sadie's gaze swept the house and garage. Still she sat, relaxed, looking around. The horse pawed the snowy ground with one forefoot.

Richard gasped.

Now he was going to throw her! She had better get off.

He had to restrain himself from leaving the garage, walking out and grabbing that stubborn horse's bridle. The beast was going to hurt Sadie.

The forefoot pawed again. The head lowered, then flung up. Sadie leaned forward, loosening the reins when he lowered his head, gently gathering them when he raised it.

Still she sat.

Now she leaned forward again, patting, stroking, playing with the coarse hair of the mane, talking. On and on, until the tension in Richard Caldwell's back caused him to swing one shoulder forward painfully.

Now Nevaeh was prancing—a sideways dance that could have easily unseated a lesser rider. He saw the leg of the jeans. The boots. The skirt adjusted in a modest manner. So that was how she rode.

Nevaeh's two forefeet came up in a light buck. Sadie leaned forward, still talking, still relaxed.

Now he was definitely going to throw her. She'd be hurt.

Richard Caldwell sagged against the silver bumper on the Hummer and clenched his fists. Why didn't she get that stubborn piece of horseflesh moving?

Now they stood quietly again.

Nevaeh shook his head back and forth. He snorted. He dug the snow with one foot, sending a fine spray back against the stable wall. He shook his head and snorted again.

Oh, great. Just great. He was a balker, culled from the herd for his stubborn behavior ... running loose. No one could handle his obstinate conduct.

Just when Richard Caldwell thought he would pop a vein in his head, the horse stepped out. He was cautious, but he stepped out, the beginning of a walk.

And so they walked. They moved around the circular driveway twice. Nevaeh was still prancing sideways, still snorting, but moving along.

Now Sadie was turning the reins against the side of Nevaeh's neck, first one way and then the other, testing her beloved horse's response to the rein.

Perfect.

Richard breathed again.

Sadie's head came up, her back straightened, and she nudged Nevaeh ever so slightly. Then she leaned back into the saddle, relaxed, prepared. Nevaeh broke into a slow trot, followed immediately by a slow canter, a sure-footed, springy, graceful motion that took Richard Caldwell's breath away.

What a horse! Unbelievable! Still too thin, the hair still coarse in spots, but, like an unfinished painting, emerging beauty.

The horse and rider disappeared behind the barn, and Richard Caldwell slowly made his way out of the garage and into the kitchen, looking for his wife, Barbara. He didn't typically share with others—often keeping feelings to himself—but this time he just had to talk to someone about this remarkable Sadie and her horse.

He encountered Dorothy waving a soiled apron and yelling for her poor, hapless husband, Jim, while black smoke poured from the broiler pan of the huge commercial oven. Carefully, Richard Caldwell backed out, knowing it was up to Jim to quench that volcanic outburst. He backed into his wife and expertly steered her away from Dorothy's angry screeches and into the safety of the living room.

They sat together on the leather sofa and he told her, with eyes shining, about Sadie and Nevaeh.

He stopped when he saw the icy, cold glint in her eyes.

"You have no business monkeying around out in the stables with that pious little Amish do-gooder. On the outside, that's what she looks like, but on the inside, she is no different from any other 20-year-old looking for a husband with money," she told her husband.

On and on her voice grated, hurling selfish words, hurting, imagining the worst.

The powerful emotions that welled up in Richard while watching Sadie with that horse contrasted greatly with Barbara's sordid accusation. They were vile, worldly, dirty, and horrible—words that were as untrue as they possibly could be.

Springing up, Richard Caldwell restrained his wife.

"Stop!" he thundered.

She stopped. She cowered. She had never heard her husband speak to her in that tone, ever.

Then, he softened and opened up. He told her many things he should have spoken before, how both of them had no idea what goodness was, or purity or selfless-ness.

"She's like a daughter. I think I believe in some sort of God when I watch her with Nevaeh."

Barbara's mouth hung open in a ghastly way as she listened to her big, rough husband. She didn't know he was capable of talking like this. What had gotten into him?

"And, Barbara, why did we choose not to have children?" he finished, his eyes soft, the crows-feet at the corners smoothing out the way they sometimes did.

"You chose," Barbara whispered.

"I thought it was you," Richard Caldwell said, quietly, calmly.

"It wasn't."

The sun slipped below the barn, casting shadows across the opulent living room, and still they talked. They rang for coffee, for a light dinner. They turned on lamps and continued talking.

Later, when Dorothy came to the living room to remove the dishes, she saw a most unusual sight—Barbara's hand resting on her husband's shoulder, his arm around hers.

"Well, I'll be dinged. Lord have mercy. A miracle has occurred," she whispered, stepping back lightly in her Dollar General shoes.

Chapter 10

Sadie tucked the lap robe securely around her knees, shivering in the buggy, her breath visible in small puffs of steam.

Glancing sideways, she checked Ezra's profile. Hmm. Not bad.

He had asked to take her to the hymn-singing again on Wednesday evening, which was a source of some discomfort—like a cut on your finger. It annoyed you if you bumped it or got salt in it or put it under hot water.

The thing was, she liked Ezra—especially the new and improved version of Ezra. He was a good friend, and she was comfortable with him. She had absolutely no reason at all not to go back to him, date him regularly, and succumb to the love she felt sure God was already supplying.

Love was a strange thing. It could be elusive, like the wildflowers in spring that grew in great clumps on the ridges, turning into purple, yellow, and white splendor. All you wanted to do was be there among the flowers, spreading your arms and running to them through the soft, spring winds. Then you would fling yourself down on the soft hillside, your senses soaked with the smell of those beautiful flowers.

But often when Sadie climbed the ridge to pick great armfuls of wildflowers, the earth was still slick and wet with patches of snow hidden among sharp thistles. The black flies, mosquitoes, and a thousand other flying creatures either bit or sat or buzzed or zoomed toward her, causing her to flail her arms wildly between grabbing handfuls of columbine. The flowers were never nearly as beautiful as they were from a distance.

The thought of Ezra was better than Ezra himself, which was awful to admit even if it was true. He was so pleasant, attractive, a good Christian, and had oh, so many other good qualities. Her parents silently pleaded with her to accept him, marry him, and be a good wife, fitting of their culture.

Aah, why? What kept her from doing just that?

"Sure is getting colder."

The sound of Ezra's voice jerked Sadie back to reality.

"Yes, it is. It'll be snowing again soon."

"That's one nice thing about Montana—we always have a white Christmas."

"Always!" Sadie agreed joyously.

Christmas was a special time in Amish homes and had always been as long as Sadie could remember. It was filled with gifts, shopping, and wrapping packages. Christmas-dinner tables were loaded with all sorts of good food from old recipes, handed down from generation to generation.

There were hymn-singings, too, where voices blended in a crescendo of praise to their Heavenly Father for the gift of his Son born in the lowly manger. The songs of old, printed hundreds of years ago in the old land and in the German dialect, were still sung together with thankful hearts.

When Sadie turned 16 and was allowed to go to the youth's singings, the songs were never as meaningful as they were now. Youthful hearts were like that. They were more interested in who sat opposite, which boy was most handsome, who started the songs, and whether the snack served at the close of the singing was tasty or just some stale pretzels and leftover pies from church that day.

Sadie suddenly realized that Ezra was having a hard time holding his horse to a trot. His arms were held out in front of him, rigid, a muscle playing on the side of his face. The buggy was lurching and swaying a tiny bit, the way it did when the horse is running faster than normal.

Sadie watched Ezra, aware of his arms pulling back, his gloved hands holding the reins more firmly.

"Don't know what's getting into Captain. He better conserve his energy. We've got a long way to go."

Captain's head was up, his ears forward. He was not just running for the joy of it. He was wary. Scared.

"Ezra, I think Captain senses something."

Ezra's jaw was clenched now. With a quick flick of his wrist, he wrapped the reins around his hands to be able to exert more pressure on them without clenching his fists.

"Nah, he's just frisky."

Sadie said nothing, but watched Captain's ears and the way he held his head in the white-blue light from the buggy. Captain's ears flickered back, and the muscles on his haunches rippled, flattened, as he leaned into the collar.

Ezra shook his head.

"Guess he's getting too many minerals. There's a hill up ahead, that'll slow him down some."

"Are we... Are we on Sloam's Ridge?"

"Starting up."

Now Sadie watched the roadside. The pines and the bare branches of the aspen and oak were laden with snow—picture-perfect. Shadow and light played across them in the moonlight and highlighted the steep embankments on either side.

Captain was slowing his gait, the long pull up the ridge winding him. Ezra unwrapped the reins from around his hands, shook one and then the other, took off the glove, flexed his fingers, and laughed.

"He sure wants to run!"

Then she saw them. She swallowed her fear, said nothing, and leaned forward. Was it her imagination? Straining her eyes, she searched the pines. There! There was a dark, moving shadow.

There. Another!

"Ezra!"

"Hmmm?"

"I think...we're... We might be followed."

"What?"

"There!"

Sadie pointed a gloved finger, her mouth drying out with the certain realization of what had caused Captain to run.

"In the woods. Up that bank. Horses are there."

Her heart pounded, her breath came in gasps.

"Captain knows it."

"I don't see anything," Ezra said quite calmly.

"I think it would be safer for us to stop the buggy, get out, and try to hold Captain. We think...my mother saw...and I think I did, too...a herd of horses here on the ridge two weeks ago. Well, not this one—on the one they call Atkin's Ridge. It's the one closer to our home."

"There are no wild horses in this area. Here among the Amish? Someone would capture them."

Sadie opened her mouth to reply but had no chance to utter a word. Captain lunged and her body flew back as the seat tipped, then settled forward again. Sadie grabbed the lap robe, stifled a scream, and opened the buggy door on her side to see better.

Here was a figure! A crashing sound! There, oh my!

"Ezra!" she screamed. "We must stop Captain! We're almost at the top of the ridge. These horses are following us. He'll break! He'll panic! Ezra, please stop."

Ezra was holding onto the reins, staying calm.

"He won't run away. He has more sense than that."

"The top of the ridge is just ahead. There's a wide bend, then straight down. The embankment to the left is hundreds of feet down. Please Ezra!"

She had to physically restrain herself from reaching over, grabbing those reins, and making him listen. If those horses emerged from the woods, if there was a stallion among them...

Sadie felt the hot bile in her throat. Her eyes watered and her nose burned, but she had no sensation of crying. It was raw fear.

The top of the ridge! Oh, dear God.

Despair as Sadie had never known sliced down her spine, like the ice water with which Reuben loved to attack his sisters. Now she was crying, begging, pleading with Ezra, but they kept traveling around that long bend, straight toward the dreaded embankment.

A horse! The clear, dark form of a large, black horse appeared beside the buggy. Two! They were on each side of them, streaming down from the woods with hooves clattering, manes whipping in the moonlight. Horses everywhere—black species of danger. Light in color to deep black—a whirl of hooves, wild eyes, lifted heads. They pounded on.

Now they surrounded the buggy.

Ezra yelled out as he lost control. Captain broke into a frenzy, lunging, rearing, coming down, and galloping on. The buggy was swaying, bouncing, careening left, then right.

The black horse in the lead was so close, Sadie could have touched him.

"Ezra!" she gasped. "Just try to stay…"

Her words were torn from her mouth as she felt the buggy whipping to the right. Captain was running neck and neck with the huge black horse, downhill now, completely out of control.

Sadie felt a certain pity for Captain, but inside she felt terror and a horrible fear as the black horse came closer, his mane whipping, his long forelock flying, his mouth open, reaching, reaching.

It wasn't fair. Captain didn't stand a chance. He was at a severe disadvantage with the blinders on each side of his head and with being hitched to the cumbersome buggy. He strained into the collar and gave everything he had, every ounce of sense and power he owned, but it was not enough. He was so loyal, and it made Sadie sad, this knowledge of how far a good horse would go to protect his beloved master.

The black horse reached out, his long, yellow teeth extended. His jaws reached the top of Captain's mane and he bit.

Sadie's world exploded as Captain went down. There was a sickening, ripping sound as the shafts broke, parting with the buggy, and they were thrown to the left.

She remembered Ezra's yell of disbelief, her own hoarse screams, the buggy beginning to fall, and then she was hurled into a cold, white world filled with jagged pain.

Glass was sharp; rocks cruelly insensitive to human forms thrown against them. There was a roaring in Sadie's ears, and she felt as if her head was severed from her shoulders. She screamed and screamed and screamed. The pain was excruciating, but she remained conscious.

The buggy! Oh, Lord have mercy! It rolled and crashed and tumbled.

Ezra!

Mercifully, then, everything went gray. A white, hot explosion inside her head turned her knowing into a blessed nothingness. She guessed she was dying now. So peaceful.

Something hurt. It was annoying. Why didn't it stop?

Then she slipped into that softness again. It was so peaceful there, reminding her of the memory foam pillows her mother loved so much and told everyone about. If you laid your head on Mam's pillow, it was firm and soft and supportive all at the same time. It seemed impossible, but wasn't. Sadie's whole body was made of memory foam. That was nice.

Ouch.

Shoot! It hurts. Stop that, Reuben. That ice is cold.

Reuben wasn't made of memory foam. Just her. At least, her legs were made of memory foam. That was nice. Nothing hurt there.

Oh, it was so cold. She needed to stop Reuben from pouring that ice on her neck. Why was her voice so quiet? She was suffocating now. Great swells of horrible, dark ink enveloped her, wrapping her in murky, stinking arms.

Get away from me. I can't breathe! Get away.

Fight, Sadie. You have to fight this.

She was stuck on the bottom, held tight by the inky, black mud. She was clawing, clawing, gasping, using all her strength. Memory foam was better.

Just let go. Let it go. You don't have to breathe. Just lay back.

A great and terrible nausea gripped her. She clawed, swam, up, up, her lungs like a balloon with too much air. They would surely pop.

Someone smacked an icy rag against her face.

Stop smacking me, please. I have to throw up. Don't smack me like that.

She burst to the top, retching, her face hitting the side of the cold gray rock. She tried gasping for great, deep, breaths of pure air to banish the black ink forever, but the horrible retching completely overwhelmed her.

Blood!

She tried sitting up, raising herself a bit. Where was all that blood coming from? If she could only stop heaving, throwing up, but her body wanted to rid itself of all its stomach's contents.

All right. Think now.

She regained consciousness, of this she was certain. She just couldn't see anything but blood. The ink was still there.

Raising one hand, she slowly brought up her arm. One arm. Okay. She touched her face, then recoiled in horror. The ink was everywhere. No, it wasn't ink. She wiped weakly at her eyes now. Over and over, tiredly, back and forth, back and forth.

Clear the ink.

Grayish light was her reward.

Keep working.

Painfully blinking.

Why was a blink so excruciating?

Aah, now she could see white. And black. Stones. Rocks. Snow. Snow everywhere.

She reached to the top of her head with a shaking hand. It was still sticky from the ink that had stayed on her head when she burst through it. She brought her fingers down.

Red! Blood. It was coming from her head, falling into her eyes. She had a gash in her head. Oh, it was so cold.

Where were her legs? She better check.

Reaching down, she found one. The other. Was that her foot? Way out here? Turned like that? She better fix it.

Willing her foot to move, she felt a stab of pain unlike anything she had ever known. A scream escaped her, only it wasn't really a scream, more like a hoarse moan, as she laid her head against the gray, cold stone and fought to stay out of that horrible hole—that place she had been and clawed her way out.

Breathe now. Slowly. You can do this. Count. Just count and bear the pain.

Women were created to bear children, so pain was not unfamiliar or unbearable. It was certainly not going to put her back into the ink. She was afraid if she went there, she would never be able to claw her way to the top again. It had taken every ounce of life and energy she could muster to get out, so she had better focus on staying conscious.

That was important.

All right. Leg broken, yes. Gash in head, yes. Nausea, yes. Might have a smashed stomach.

It was very cold. She might die.

How long did people live in the cold? And survive? She tried to think of books she had read. No clue. She guessed as long as one breath followed another, she would live.

She thought of Mam, Dat, Leah, Rebekah, Anna, and Reuben, all at home, all happy and secure in the knowledge that she was being taken to the singing by the beloved Ezra.

Where was he?

Where was Captain?

A shiver of fear.

The horses? Where were they? Oh, that black stallion—as dark and sinister as the devil himself. But still, he was a stallion. Protecting his mares. Keeping his turf.

Dear God in heaven, my leg hurts so terribly. Please help me. Send someone to find me. I'll die out here. Wolves will smell my blood. Or mountain lions. I heard they introduced the wolves back into the wilds of Montana to manage the elk herds. Smart. Unlucky for ranchers.

Her thoughts wandered away from her prayer.

Where was the buggy? Was she at the bottom of the embankment? Or halfway down?

Leaning away from the gray rock, she tried to assess her surroundings.

Oh, that blood in my eyes. I have to stop it somehow.

Her breathing stopped completely, but her heart beat on as the howl of a wolf split the air in two with that mournful, undulating wail of the wild. One clear howl brought chills and fear of the awesome creatures into Sadie's world of pain.

Momentarily, she surrendered.

Okay, this is it. Tumbled down a cliff, half dead, and wolves will finish me. No one will ever know what happened. Posters tacked on telephone poles in town—at the post office, the IGA. Missing. No picture. She was Amish. Just information.

No, they would find her. They would!

Another howl hit a high note, joined by more voices now and more long, drawn-out calls of the wolves.

I must get out of here. I have to try.

She leaned forward, her hands clawing the snow, searching for a handhold, anything to propel herself forward. Blood spurted, a fresh, warm stream flowed down her forehead and into her eyes.

I must stop this bleeding first. With what?

Reaching up, she touched her covering, still dangling on the back of her head. Gratefully, she pulled it off and rolled it into a type of tourniquet. Her hands shook. They were too stiff.

I can't do this.

Slumping against the gray rock, she bowed her head as hot tears ran down her face. Tears and seeping blood mixed together and dripped into the snow.

It was hopeless. Maybe it would be easier to just let go now. She could go to the memory foam.

I would just let go—but I'm afraid of the ink or whatever that horrible stuff was. Why was it like that?

She looked up.

Where was the road?

She couldn't have fallen very far off the road. She heard a car but saw no lights.

Oh, yes. The buggy fell. Ezra must have fallen along with it. Captain ran away, attached to the shafts. So no one on the road at night would have any idea of the accident.

Oh, Mam.

Dat.

Somebody come find me.

She could feel her strength ebbing, going out like the tide. They had been at the beach once, along the bay, and she watched the tide come and go. Piers that were almost submerged at one point in the day stuck way out of the water later that same day. Reuben said—he always knew these things—that it was because the world tilted on an angle and spun as fast as it could go, and the water tilted back and forth with the moon's force. Amazing.

Well, the tide was slipping out for her, and she didn't know if it would come back.

So tired.

She closed her eyes.

Just for a minute, I'll rest.

The wolves aren't close yet.

No ink this time. That was a relief.

Just a white light. So white. So bright.

Stop yelling at me.

No. I said, no.

Mark Peight. Go away.

But wait, Mark was a small boy. That was odd. His hair was not cut close to his head like the English. So innocent. So…so pathetic?

She reached out her arms.

Come, Mark Peight.

But wait.

Behind Mark Peight—a large, rotund man. He was smiling, talking, persuading. He had a whip. A real whip. Not a quirt.

Come, Mark.

That bright light was so annoying.

"Sadie! Sadie! Can you hear me? Wiggle your toes. Lift your finger."

Well, forget that. Duh, people. I can't do that.

"I think she's hearing us, but she doesn't seem to be able to do what we're asking."

"Sadie! Sadie!"

What in the world was Mam doing here on Sloam's Ridge by the gray rock? She had better get up to the road. She'd fall and hurt herself. And now she was crying, rocking herself back and forth, back and forth, moaning, mumbling.

"*Schtup sell*, Mam. *Do net.*"

"We're going to inject a solution into her veins. If she is close to being conscious, this will completely revive her within 30 seconds. If it doesn't work, she will sleep much longer."

Who was that?

The lights were too bright. She couldn't open her eyes. She wanted to leave them closed. The lights reminded her of summer daisies when the sun hit them just so in the morning when the dew was still on them.

So beautiful, daisies. You are so beautiful.

Chapter 11

THE FIRST THING SADIE REMEMBERED SEEING WAS the brilliance of the green and red in the large Christmas wreath on the wall—the shining, white wall. The Christmas wreath was much too bright. It made her eyes hurt.

Was it Christmas?

"Sadie! Sadie!"

Dat was crying. Dat never cried. Why was he crying?

She rested her eyes again, closing them gently, succumbing to the all-consuming sense of total exhaustion. Nothing had ever felt better than closing her eyelids and letting her body sink into the soft, soft mattress, the soft, soft pillow.

"Sadie, can you hear me?"

Whoa, better answer. Someone's at the door.

She willed herself to go to the door but was much too tired.

"Sadie, lift your hand if you hear me."

Of course I can lift my hand. I'm coming to answer the door. I'm walking to the door. Can't you see?

She lifted her hand. Then she opened her eyes, looked

around, and saw the Christmas wreath again, the window with the blinds pulled, the flowers on the wide sill.

She saw Mam, Dat, a doctor, two more doctors, a very large nurse, and another person with a chart. There were hums and beeps and clicks and whirs and a clear plastic bag hanging from a clean, silver pole.

"Hello, Sadie."

She tried to smile and say "Hello," but her eyelids wanted to fall down again, completely on their own.

"Hi," Sadie croaked, then fell into a deep, peaceful sleep.

✿ ✡ ✿

Sadie woke on her own, no one calling her. It was nighttime and the room was dark. There were still clicks and buzzes, whirs and hums, but except for these machines, it was all very quiet.

She tried turning her head to the right to see what was beside her. That worked okay. There was a night stand and a pitcher—a plastic one, covered with Styrofoam.

Hmm.

She turned her head to the left and closed her eyes as great spasms of pain shot through her temple. She sucked in her breath, squeezed her eyes shut to bear the pain, and cautiously opened them again.

Wow! That hurt.

Gingerly then, her hands traveled across her body. Shoulders intact, face weird, bandage on head, hand wrapped in bandage, waist and hips hurting but tolerable.

Whoops. That leg.

Opening her eyes wide, she saw her right leg held upward at an angle, encased in a heavy cast, wrapped with that white stuff where people could sign their names.

Oh, boy. She was really banged up.

She pieced together the remnants of what happened as best she could, although there was very little she actually remembered.

Snow.

Cold.

And that was about it.

Sighing, she lay back. She was in the hospital being taken care of by competent people—competent, trained personnel who knew how to operate the machines that clicked and hummed around her, she thought wryly.

She wondered vaguely whether Mam and Dat had gone home and she was here alone, or if someone from her family was here sleeping at the hospital.

She thanked God for the fact that she was alive. Her heart was beating, battered, but alive.

Himmlichser Vater, Ich danke dich.

"You awake, Honey?"

Sadie started, smiled, then nodded slowly.

"You are! Welcome aboard, Sweetie! Good to see you awake."

The nurse wore a flowered top. Her round arms turned machines, released the rail on the side of the bed, and checked the IV drip in swift, fluid motions, confident and sure.

"You in pain?"

Sadie winced.

"My back."

The nurse clucked.

"Let me tell you, Honey. We've got you as comfortable as possible, but you'll be experiencing some discomfort, 'til it's all said and done. You are one fortunate cookie, you are."

"Am I?" Sadie asked, her voice hoarse.

"Indeedy. If it's all true what they say."

"Is…my family here?"

"No. They went home to get some sleep. You'll be fine. How badly are you hurting, Sweetie? From 1 to 10?

Sadie grimaced.

"Eleven."

The nurse laughed.

"You're awake, Sadie."

She pushed a few buttons, wrote on a chart, asked if she needed another blanket, pulled up the sheet, patted her shoulder, and was barely out of the room before Sadie drifted into a wonderful, cushioned sleep.

☆ ☆ ☆

The heavy blinds were yanked open, the sun streamed through the window, the nurse trilled a good morning, and Sadie turned her head away, moaning.

Everything hurt. Everything. Even her fingers and toes. She groaned.

"We're getting you out of bed this morning!" the nurse chirped.

There was no way. Absolutely not. They can't. I can't, she thought.

"My leg is…uh…sort of attached!" Sadie said.

"Oh, we'll get you a pair of crutches. See how you'll do."

"I'll pass out."

"Oh, no! No, you won't."

And she didn't.

They sat her up, and she thought her head would explode. They held her, prodded her, stuck crutches under her arms, held the heavy cast, and watched her wobble down the hallway. The nurses talked and encouraged her, and Sadie gritted her teeth in determination. Her forehead seeped perspiration, but the heroic effort she made was evident to the hospital staff.

When they finally reached the bed, Sadie sank onto the edge of it. She felt as if she had run a marathon, which they assured her she had.

After a bath, clean sheets, and a clean gown, she was exhausted. Hungry, too, although she was too shy to ask about breakfast. Maybe they allowed only juice or ice water.

A rumbling in the hallway and a jolly voice calling out made Sadie listen eagerly. She hoped it was some sort of food. Even a package of saltines would take that dull ache away from her stomach. She wondered if this was how the poor, starving children in Africa felt. Innocent victims of civil war, suffering and dying, so hungry.

Sadie grimaced, then turned her head to watch eagerly as a small, stout woman bustled into the room. Her head was covered with an aqua-colored cap that closely resembled what Mommy Yoder wore to take a shower if she didn't want to wash her hair. The woman balanced a dish covered with a plastic lid.

"Breakfast!" she called out gaily.

Sweeter words I have never heard, Sadie thought, smiling to herself.

The woman hurried to Sadie's bedside, pulled up the tray on wheels, and plunked down the dish.

"There you go. Piping hot. Have a wonderful day!" She bustled back out, the aqua shower cap bobbing with each step.

Sadie lifted her right hand quickly, eager to lift the lid and peek underneath. Stopping, she looked at the bandage in dismay. But then she shrugged. Food could be conveyed to your mouth with your left hand if that was what needed to be done.

Removing the plastic lid was relatively easy, but unwrapping the utensils from the napkin was not.

The food looked all right—scrambled eggs, a few pieces of bacon, and an orange slice arranged on dark, curly lettuce—a bit wilted, but still inviting. Buttered wedges of whole wheat toast, juice, and milk completed the meal.

She lifted a slice of toast, eating half of it in one big bite.

Mmmm. Delicious.

She remembered to bow her head and thank God for the buttered toast in a silent prayer of gratitude. The fact that she was alive and able to eat brought tears of gratefulness—and completely renewed thanks.

The toast was a bit squishy and thin. Sort of flat. It was not the thick, heavy, whole wheat toast her mother made in the broiler in the gas oven at home

Reuben told her once that the cheap, whole wheat bread they bought in the store in town wasn't one bit whole wheat. It had artificial coloring so it looked like whole wheat. It was the same as white bread, but because it was the color of whole wheat, people felt they made a healthy choice.

He probably learned that around the same time he learned about the earth being tilted and spinning as fast as it could go, causing the tide to go in and out.

Sadie realized that she had not known these things before he told her, but she would never, ever tell him—that little know-it-all.

Quite suddenly, then, she was overcome with love for Reuben, for that sweet little troublemaker. Oh, she hoped he would be allowed into the hospital to see her.

She was filled with light, a joyous light of love for her family. She could hardly wait to see all of them! Mam, Dat, her dear sisters—everyone—even annoying Anna who always stuck up for Reuben.

Quite a bit of the scrambled eggs landed on the tray or in her lap, but she could eat enough to feel comfortable. The orange juice created a certain nausea—like a summer virus when you knew it was not going to be a good day for your stomach—so she pushed the tray away and lay back on the pillow, turning her head and closing her eyes.

Her head felt as if it was twice its normal size, but she supposed that was because of the bandage around it. I hope I'll be normal again soon, she thought.

And then the room was filled with her family. All of them.

Dat was there, and Mam. They cried, hugged her carefully, held her hand, exclaimed quietly, talked in their Dutch dialect, and asked questions. Tears streamed down Sadie's face as she nodded or shook her head. She smiled in between the tears and was grateful.

Reuben hung back, clearly not wanting to be there. Sadie called out his name. The rest of the family stood aside, Mam prodded his shoulder, and he came reluctantly to stand by her bed—self-conscious and obviously uncomfortable.

"Reuben!"

"Hey, Sadie."

"What do you have in your hand?"

Instantly, a wrapped package was thrust into her lap. "Here."

"A package! Thank you, Reuben!"

She struggled with her left hand, trying to undo the Scotch tape, until he stepped forward saying, "I'll do it."

Sadie peered into the cardboard box, then gasped.

"Nevaeh! My... The horse! Reuben, where in the world did you get a picture of Nevaeh?"

"Jim."

"Jim? He gave this to you?"

Reuben nodded.

"I made the frame."

"It's gorgeous, Reuben!"

Anna stepped up proudly.

"I sanded and varnished it. Three coats. Dat said to do it that way."

Sadie looked questioningly at her father and was rewarded with a look of such tenderness, so much love, it took her breath away. Dat never expressed his feelings in such a way. He shuffled uncomfortably.

"You... I just thought you may as well bring the horse home if he's yours."

"Oh, Dat!"

That was all Sadie could say, but it was enough.

Rebekah cried, grabbed a few tissues, and hid her face in the white softness she held to her nose. Leah smiled a crooked smile, then gave in and cried with Rebekah.

"We cleaned the box stall and put down three wheel-barrow loads of sawdust," Anna chirped proudly.

"I'm so glad. Did you really? Someone had to work hard to clean that box stall."

"We did!" Reuben announced triumphantly. "Me and Anna!"

Sadie laughed, her throat swelling with emotion. Her dear, dear family.

Mam stepped up then, took Sadie's hand, and asked her how much of the accident she remembered. Sadie shook her head and lowered her eyes from Mam's gaze. Her hand grabbed the sheet, pleating it over and over.

"Do you remember being picked up at our house? With Ezra?" she asked, very gently.

Sadie was puzzled.

"Well, he ... took me to a singing once."

"Yes. But do you remember this time — the second time?"

Sadie shook her head, her brow furrowed as she tried to remember. Then she shook her head again.

"Well, we need to tell you if you feel strong enough to hear everything. Do you?"

Sadie nodded.

With Dat leading, her family pieced the story together, like sewing scraps of fabric for a quilt. They told her about the ride, the unexplained slide down the side of the steep embankment, the long wait when she did not come home, the hours of agony for her parents. They knew she had gone to the singing with Ezra, but she never returned that night. When daylight arrived, they hired a driver and went to Amish homes asking questions. No, they had not been to the hymn-singing. No, Ezra's horse and buggy were not at home.

They found Ezra's parents in the same state of anxiety. They searched the roads between homes. Word spread fast and more men came to help. The local police were contacted—English people coming to help.

Then, they found Captain. He was hurt and bleeding, and his harness was partially torn. There were parts of the shafts, too. It was worse then, in those hours when they knew there had been an accident, but they still hadn't found the buggy.

Jesse Troyer found it first. The buggy was in pieces, smashed on the overhanging rocks. Ezra was nearby.

"Life had fled," Dat said quietly.

"What do you mean, 'life had fled'?" Sadie asked, bewildered.

"Ezra is gone. He was killed. The autopsy showed his neck was snapped. They think he died instantly and didn't suffer."

"But...but...how could he die? It wasn't that far down the cliff, was it?"

"Oh, it was, Sadie! We've been back to the site, and it was only the hand of God that kept you alive. You were in that snow for almost 20 hours. You were, Sadie," Mam said, the fear and agony of those hours threading through her words.

Ezra gone. He died. But how could he?

She would have dated him. Married him. She and Ezra and Captain and Nevaeh would have lived together in a new log home, the home of Ezra's dreams. He already owned a large tract of timber on Timmon's Ridge, and he had spoken of his dreams to her. He may have told her in an off-hand manner, but still, he couldn't have made solid plans that included her without knowing how she felt in her heart. Towards him. About being his wife.

Great walls of black guilt washed over Sadie. She lifted agonized eyes to Mam.

"I would have married him, Mam! I would have. I was planning on dating him. That night. I would have. And now he is dead, and he never knew that. I would have come to love him. God would have provided that love for me," she said, sobs shaking Sadie's battered body.

Then Dat spoke, his roughened carpenter's hands gently, clumsily, stroking her hair.

"But, Sadie, you must come to understand. The love you would have had with Ezra is only a drop compared to the love of our *Himmlischer Vater im Himmel.* We mortals will never fully grasp a love that great, joyous, and all-consuming. Ezra will be much, much, better off in his heavenly home than he could ever hope to be here, even if it meant having the love of his life.

"Marriage here on earth is good, and every mortal longs for that certain person to share his life, but it is only peanuts compared to the love of God. Remember that, Sadie. Ezra is in a much better place now, and you can be thankful he enjoyed those last few buggy rides with you. I'm sure he passed on a happy person because of it."

Sadie nodded, silent.

"Don't carry any guilt, please. God's ways are not our ways, and his thoughts so high above ours that we can't figure these things out. You still have a purpose here on earth."

"Yes, Dat. I do understand that. I do."

Rebekah stepped forward.

"You've been sleeping a long time, Sadie."

"How long?"

"Four days."

"What?"

Rebekah nodded.

Sadie slowly shook her head.

"Then… Ezra… the funeral…"

"Yes, he is buried in the new cemetery beneath the trees. It was a large funeral. There were many vans and buses from out of state. It's very sad. His family is struggling to accept this. They want to say 'Thy will be done,' but it's very hard to do that for one who died at such a young age."

"It had to be sad."

"It was, Sadie. I'm almost glad you weren't there."

The remainder of the visit went by as a blur, Sadie only half-listening, struggling to remember.

Why? Why had they gone down over that embankment?

Nurses came and went, but they continued talking about that night. Leah told her part of the story, her eyes still wide with the horror of it.

The doctor arrived and asked the family to step outside. He removed the bandage on her head, and Sadie lay back as he redressed the cut. Then she asked how severely she had been wounded.

"You have a very deep cut with 22 stitches. I suppose the cold saved your life, and the fact that your blood clotted easily."

"My hair?" she asked.

"Lets just say a significant amount was removed," the doctor said smiling.

Sadie wrinkled her nose.

"Bald?"

"Just on one side. Don't worry. It'll grow back."

Sadie touched the new bandage tentatively, then turned her head and closed her eyes. She wondered how long this all-consuming weariness would stay in her bones. She heard Mam's favorite expression ring in her ears. After a day of back-breaking labor, she would say, "I feel as if a dump truck rolled over me." It was a gross exaggeration, but fitting.

If anyone feels like she was flattened, it's me, she mused. That accident must have been severe.

The doctor finished jotting on a chart, spoke tersely to the nurses, then probed Sadie's stomach to check for more internal injuries. He asked questions, patted her abdomen, spoke to the nurses again, and was gone before Sadie thought to ask how long she would need to stay.

Her family streamed in to say good-bye and that they'd all be back that evening. Reuben gave her a bag of M&M's, a Reese's Peanut Butter Cup, and a small package of salted peanuts.

"You can eat these while you watch TV," he announced importantly.

Sadie laughed, then gasped, grabbing her stomach as pain rolled across it.

"Oh, I just hurt everywhere," she breathed.

Anna patted her arm.

"You'll be okay, Sadie. Hey, you know why Reuben got you all those snacks? Because he loves putting quarters in vending machines and pushing the buttons. He has a whole stash of candy, and not one of us has any quarters left in our wallets."

Reuben punched her arm, Mam herded them out, and Dat winked at her as the door closed softly behind them.

Sighing, she snuggled against the pillows and closed her eyes.

Ezra. Dear, dear Ezra.

She was suddenly very, very glad she had consented to go with him to the hymn-singing. It was a consolation — a sort of closure — pathetic as it seemed. Dat was right. Ezra had been a fine young man — a devout Christian, baptized, trying to do what was right, listening to his conscience.

Sadie fell asleep, peaceful.

Chapter 12

THE BUGGIES STREAMED TO THE JACOB MILLER home. There were brown horses, black ones, beautiful sorrels, and saddlebreds hitched to the surreys and smaller buggies. Some of them plodded up the curving drive beside the group of trees, others trotted fast, their shining coats dark with sweat, turning into lather where the harness bounced and chafed on their bodies.

The buggies were filled with smiling occupants, friendly members of the Montana Old Order Amish coming to visit the Miller family to see how Sadie was doing. They brought casseroles, pies, home-baked raisin bread, cupcakes, and heavy stoneware pots of baked beans wrapped in clean towels to keep the warmth inside.

They grasped Sadie's hand and asked questions. Kindly faces smiled shakily, eyes filled with tears of compassion. Rotund grandmothers clucked and shook their heads, saying surely the end of the world was near; God was calling loudly, wasn't he?

Shy children peeped from behind their mothers' skirts, their eyes round with wonder. This was that Sadie—Jacob Miller's Sadie—who almost died on that snowy hill. They had heard it all—around oil-clothed kitchen tables and as they played in the snow and dirt outside the phone shanties, listening while their mams were busy talking.

Most of them had been taken to the viewing of Ezra Troyer at his parents' home. Viewing the deceased was part of life, death, birth, a heaven, and a hell. The children were not kept from life's tragedies and sometimes brutal truths; it was all instilled in them at a young age.

Parents explained gently about death and what happens after someone dies. There was very little mystery. They made it all simple, uncomplicated, a concept any child could grasp. It was enough to soothe them, comfort them when they questioned with serious eyes while mulling things over in their childish minds. Then they ran out to play, forgetting, as children do.

Jacob watched his wife as her face became troubled, her countenance high with anxiety. He was afraid this whole incident would prove to be too much for her, although he didn't speak of it to anyone. Sometimes, he believed, if you hid your feelings and fears and worries, they all disappeared and no one ever knew. This left your pride and sense of well-being intact.

But still he watched her.

He was drawn into conversation when it turned to gossip at the local feed store in town. Simon Gregory, the feed-truck driver saw it on the news, but everyone knew that Simon stretched "news" to the limit. There was real news and "Simon news" at the feed mill, and everyone grinned and raised their eyebrows when Simon related another new item.

This time it was "them wild horses roamin' them ridges and pastures. They's there. I seen 'em. They said on th' news, they's stealin' horses all over th' place. No one's safe. You Amish better padlock yer barns. They don't care if you wear suspenders and a straw hat, or a Stetson and a belt, all's they want is yer horse."

"No one's horse was actually stolen," Levi Hershberger stated, sipping his coffee and grimacing at the heat. He stroked his beard. Heads shook back and forth.

"No one had any horses taken in this community," Alvin Wenger agreed.

Men nodded, drank coffee.

"How about that Simon down at the feed mill? Isn't he the character?"

There were chuckles all around.

"But you couldn't find a guy with a bigger heart. He'd do anything for anyone. Remember the first winter we were here? How many driveways did he open that year? Not a penny would he take," Alvin said, reaching for a cookie.

"Elsie baked him many a pie that winter."

Calvin Yutzy, a young man with a louder than normal voice, chimed in. "Yeah, you know what he says now? He says those wild horses could have caused that accident. He claims they're running loose up there on Sloam's Ridge."

"Nah!"

"Sounds just like him."

"I know, but if there's a stallion, and he's territorial, a buggy at night..."

Sadie was listening half-heartedly, laying her head against the cushioned back of the recliner, willing herself to keep the weariness at bay.

If there's a stallion...

He was black! He was so large.

Why did she know this?

She sat up, her mouth dry, her breath coming in short jerks. Somewhere, she had seen that black horse. She knew he was powerful. He was dangerous. How did she know?

She remembered Captain, that faithful, dutiful creature. She remembered his loyalty that night.

It would have been too bold to break in on the men's conversation, so Sadie sat up and listened, her face pale, her heart hammering, every nerve aware of what the men were saying.

"I dunno."

"Sounds a bit far-out."

Calvin leaned forward, his excitement lending more power to his voice, "A stallion will kill another horse if he's protecting his mares."

"Ah, I wouldn't say that," Levi shook his head.

"In books, maybe," old Eli Miller said, smiling, his eyes twinkling.

"All I'm saying is, it could have happened the way Simon said. What else caused that buggy to go down over?"

Sadie put down the footrest of the brown recliner. Instantly Mam was on her feet, going to her, reaching out like a nervous little hen always expecting the worst. Frankly, this drove Sadie's endurance and patience to the limit.

"I'm all right, Mam. Just go sit down."

The men's conversation slowed, then stopped as heads turned to look.

No doubt about it, Jacob's Sadie was a beautiful girl. Almost too beautiful—if there was such a thing. No one meant to stare, but they did just for a moment, perhaps. Beauty was appreciated among them.

It was God-given, this thing called beauty. A face in perfect symmetry with large, blue eyes, a small, straight nose, clear complexion, and a smile that dazzled was appreciated and admired. Who could help it?

But the women knew that beauty could be a curse as well. The girl may become completely self-absorbed, loving only herself. She may turn down many suitors, because she could marry anyone she wished. Plain girls, on the other hand, knew they were fortunate to be "asked," and they made good wives—thankful, obedient, loving to their husbands, glad to be married.

This mostly held out, but not always.

Most admitted that Sadie Miller was a mystery. She was soon of age—nearly at that 21st birthday when she would be allowed to keep her money and everything she earned. She could open a savings account at the local bank and be on her own financially, although still living with her parents.

When a girl like Sadie turned 21, eyebrows rose. Knowing she was past the age when girls dated and were betrothed, everyone wondered why she was not.

She must be too picky, they thought.

Independent, that one, they said.

She has it too nice with that good job down at the ranch. I wouldn't let my girls work there. Mark my words, she'll fall for an "English one."

No, not her, they said.

And now Ezra was gone, so what would Sadie do?

Sadie reached out to the arm of the recliner to steady herself. She lifted blue eyes to the men and addressed them quietly.

"I…was listening to your conversation. And…," she hesitated and then shook her head.

Everyone waited, the room hushed.

"You know I don't remember much, if anything, about the night the … the … buggy … you know. Well, you mentioned the wild horses."

Suddenly she sat up straight and began to talk.

"That night, there was a huge, black horse. I don't know why I remember this. I don't really. All I know is that a really big, black horse was running beside the buggy. I could have reached out and touched him. He was so powerful, so wild-eyed, and angry. Like the devil. He reminded me of an evil force in the Bible story book when I was a child.

"And I remember, or I think so… I remember Captain, Ezra's horse, trying so hard. He was so loyal. Oh, he was running—running so desperately."

The men leaned forward. Coffee cups were set on the table, forgotten. Sadie fought her emotions, her chest heaving. Mam came to her side, her hands fluttering like a helpless bird.

"I wanted Ezra to stop. I … we would have been safer out of the buggy."

Dat sat up, then got to his feet.

"Sadie, you don't have to put yourself through this."

"I'm all right, Dat. Really."

Calvin Yutzy was on his feet.

"Hey, if this stuff is true, we have got to do something. Simon may be on to something."

"Sit down," Dat said smiling.

Calvin's wife, Rachel, holding her newborn son, smiled with Dat.

"Sounds like some real western excitement to Calvin," she said.

Old Eli Miller shook his head.

"Sounds a bit mysterious to me."

He turned to Sadie.

"Not that I'm doubting your word—I think you do remember some of what happened—but if there are horses out there, whose are they?"

"Where do they come from?" Calvin asked, almost yelping with excitement.

Everyone laughed. It was the easy laughter of a close-knit community, a comfortable kinship. It was the kind of laughter where you know everyone else will chuckle along with you, savoring the little moments of knowing each other well.

"Mam and I both saw them a few weeks ago."

"Seriously?" Calvin asked, his voice breaking.

Laughter rippled across the room. Men winked, women cast knowing glances as comfortable and good as warm apple pie.

"Sadie, tell them about the … your horse."

"Go ahead, Dat. You tell them."

Immediately Dat launched into a colorful account of her ride to work with Jim Sevarr, the snow and cold and the black and white paint. He described how Richard Caldwell kept him at the stable and what an unbelievable horse he would be, if he regained his health.

Calvin sat on the edge of his chair, chewing his lip.

"I bet you anything this horse of Sadie's is connected."

"Huh-uh."

"Aw, no."

Sadie sat back then, the room whirling as a wave of nausea gripped her. It was time to return to her bedroom, although she didn't want to. The weakness she felt was a constant bother, and she still faced weeks of recovery.

Rebekah and Leah helped her to her bath and finally

to bed as the buggies slowly returned down the drive. Anna and Reuben would be helping their mother clean and wash dishes while Dat went outside to sweep the forebay where the horses had been tied.

Lights blinked through the trees, good-nights echoing across the moonlit landscape accompanied by the dull "think-thunk" of horse's hooves on snow.

And now Christmas was a week away.

✡ ✡ ✡

Sadie sat at the breakfast table, her foot and cumbersome cast propped on a folding chair. The bandage was gone from her head, leaving a bald spot showing beneath the kerchief she wore, although, if you looked close enough, new growth of brown hair was already evident. Her eyes were no longer black and blue, but the discoloration remained and cast shadows around them.

It was Saturday, and Rebekah and Leah were both at home, a list spread between them on the table top.

"Where's Mam?" Sadie asked.

"Still in bed."

Leah rolled her eyes.

Rebekah sighed.

"Are we just going to go on this way? Just putting up with Mam?" Sadie asked. "I could spank her. She acts like a spoiled child at times."

"Sadie!"

"Seriously. She's been driving me nuts since the accident. She's not even close to being the mother we remember back in Ohio. She does almost nothing in a day. Just talks to herself. She irritates me. I just want to slap her—wake her up."

"It's Dat's fault."

"Her own, too."

"Why won't they get help? Sadie, it wasn't even funny the way she caused a scene at the hospital when you got hurt."

"Someone should have admitted her then."

"How?"

"I know. The rules are so frustrating. As long as Dat and Mam insist there's nothing wrong, and she doesn't hurt anyone or herself, we can't do anything."

"In the meantime, we have Christmas coming," Leah said, helping herself to another slice of buttered toast and spreading it liberally with peanut butter and grape jelly.

"I hate store-bought grape jelly."

Leah nodded. "Remember the strawberry freezer jam Mam used to make! Mmm."

"I have a notion to get married and make my own jelly if Mam's going to be like this," Rebekah said slowly.

Sadie howled with laughter until tears ran down her cheeks. Her face became discolored and she gasped for breath.

"And, who, may I ask, will you marry?" she asked finally, still giggling.

Leah and Rebekah laughed, knowing the choice was a bit narrow.

It was a Saturday morning made for sisters. Snow swirled outside, Dat and Reuben were gone, Anna was working on her scrapbooks in her room, the kitchen smelled of coffee and bacon and eggs, the cleaning was done, and laundry could wait until Monday.

They were still in their pajamas and robes, their hair in cheerful disarray, all of them feeling well rested after sleeping late. Rebekah was trying to think of things they could buy for Reuben and Anna and the person she got in the name exchange at school.

"Gifts, gifts, gifts. How in the world are we ever going to get ready for Christmas if Mam isn't in working order?" Rebekah groaned.

"Well, she needs to shape up," Leah snorted.

"And, then, here I am, leg in cast...," Sadie began.

"You're going to get fat."

"Another slice of toast! Did you guys eat all that bacon?"

"Well, you're not getting more."

"I'm not fat!" Sadie finally said, quite forcefully.

"You will be. You don't do a thing."

Sadie threw a spoon, Leah ducked, and Rebekah squealed.

"Watch it!"

They were all laughing when Mam emerged from the bedroom down the hallway. Her mouth was twitching as she talked to herself in hurried tones, her voice rising and falling. Her hair was unwashed, greasy even, and she had lost enough weight to make her face appear sallow and a bit sunken. She walked into the kitchen as if in a dream, her eyes glazed and unseeing as she continued the serious conversation.

Sadie felt a stab of impatience, then guilt. Poor Mam. After the initial shock of accepting their Mam as less than perfect—realizing she was unwell, depressed, whatever a doctor would call it—the girls had all decided to do their best, especially if Dat was too stubborn to do anything.

"Mind bother" was not something anyone wanted in their family. It was whispered about, secretly talked of in low tones. It was discussed in close circles, a never-ceasing debate. Was it always chemical? An imbalance?

Or had the person done it to herself by refusing to bend her will, living in frustration all her days? Who knew? In any case, it was looked on as a shameful thing. It was a despised subject.

Sadie had spent a few sleepless nights mulling over the subject. She read everything she could get her hands on. She even asked a friend, Marta Clancy, the owner of the small drugstore in town, to print information from her computer at home.

Old myths about "mind bother," suicide, and other unexplainable troubles were like a wedge in Sadie's mind. Prescription drugs probably wouldn't make a difference if it was a spiritual problem, so it had to be a chemical imbalance. So what unbalanced the chemicals? And round and round went Sadie's troubled thoughts and her frustrations.

She could never fully settle the matter within herself, so she decided it was not something she could figure out on her own. She would have to let all that up to the Almighty God who created human beings and knew everything, right up to each tiny molecule and cell and atom.

But why must we live this way?

Mam could be so normal. When Sadie was hurt and Mam forgot herself, thinking only of Sadie, she almost seemed like the Mam of old. But now that Sadie was recuperating, Mam was worse than ever, and this morning it was annoying.

Sadie ricocheted off walls of impatience, battling to keep her voice low and well-modulated. She felt like shaking some sense into Mam, then quickly realized how hard and uncaring she was being. Mental illness, depression, whatever you called it, was like a leech. It just sucked the vitality out of your life.

It was almost Christmas, and Sadie was determined to make it as normal as possible, especially for Reuben. But always, always, Mam and her condition were in the background.

Ignoring Mam, Sadie turned to Leah.

"Okay, Miss Leah. 'Christmas is coming, the goose is getting fat...'"

Rebekah chimed in, and they sang together.

"'Please put a penny in the old man's hat.'"

Sadie glanced at Mam, who was smiling.

"It is Christmas, isn't it?" she said, her voice like gravel.

"What's wrong with your voice, Mam? Does your throat hurt?" Sadie asked, concerned about the roughness, the rawness in her mother's words.

"A bit, yes. I should have dressed warmer last night. I was out walking." She shook her head from side to side. "I just wish I could get a good night's sleep. Maybe the voices in my head would stop."

Rebekah turned, stood by her mother, and said gently, "Mam, won't you go to a doctor if we take you? Dat doesn't need to know. The doctor could give you a correct diagnosis, give you the proper medication, and soon you would feel so much better."

"No! Drugs are bad for us!"

She turned her back, opened the cupboard door, and proceeded to take down the many bottles of vitamins and minerals she so urgently depended on. She insisted they were what sustained her.

A determination, a sort of desperation, expanded in Sadie's chest.

All right. If this was how it was going to be, then they would rise above it. Like a hot air balloon in a cloudless sky, they would soar. They would have Christmas, and they would have a good Christmas in spite of the many obstacles set in their way. There was the accident, the thousands of dollars in hospital and medical bills that needed to be paid, and Mam's ever-worsening condition, but no matter, they would figure out a way to have a happy Christmas.

"Rebekah, let's make a list of gifts we want to buy. Then we can talk to Dat and arrange to go shopping today. We'll see how much money we can have, then shop accordingly, okay?"

"Sure thing," Rebekah chirped, sliding down the bench toward her.

"First, Reuben and Anna."

Immediately, they were faced with a huge decision. Reuben was 10 years old. He was too old for most toys and too young for serious guns and hunting things. He had a bike, two BB guns, and a pellet gun, but no hunting knives.

"Not a knife," Sadie said. "It's too dangerous."

Anna was mixing Nesquik into scalding hot milk, adding a teaspoon of sugar and a handful of miniature marshmallows. She stirred, sipped, and lifted her shoulders, a smile of pleasure lighting her young face.

"Taste this, Rebekah!"

"Is it good?"

"It's so good I'm going to make a cup for each of you after mine is all gone," she said, grinning cheekily.

"Anna, what can we get Reuben for Christmas?" Sadie asked, toying with the crust of her toast.

"A puppy."

"We can't. Mam and Dat will never let us get another dog."

"He wants a puppy."

Sadie wrote "puppy" on the list, dutifully.

"What else?"

"A football and a new baseball bat."

Sadie bent her head and wrote it down.

Leah helped, and with Rebekah's common sense, they had a list that was actually attainable. After checking the money they could use, which was, in fact, a decent amount, the idea of Christmas settled over them like a warm, fuzzy blanket, comforting and joyous, the way Christmas had always been.

"Hot chocolate's ready!" Anna called.

"You better let up on the hot chocolate-making, Anna. We're going shopping at the mall!"

Anna squealed and jumped up and down, rattling the cups on the counter.

"The mall? The real mall?"

"Yes! Let's all wear the same color... Something Christmasy!"

"We have to push Gramma Sadie on her wheelchair!"

"Let's rent a wagon—make her sit on the wagon!"

"Let's do!"

Mam watched the girls' joy, then turned her head, sighing. She couldn't remember the last time she felt that way.

Chapter 13

Rebekah stomped in from the phone shanty after calling a driver, her eyes sparkling. Leah washed dishes and Sadie watched. She longed to go to the barn to see Nevaeh and talk to him, but she knew it was best to remain in the house. The upcoming trip to the mall would be about all she could handle.

There was a general hubbub of activity as each one returned upstairs to shower, dress, and comb her hair. The ironing board was set up in front of the gas stove, a sad iron heating on the round, blue flame. Last minute ironing of coverings was always a necessary part of the routine.

After she was ready, Sadie sat on her chair and watched her mother. She was lying on the recliner, hair uncombed, no covering, her face turned to the wall. Mam's breathing was even and regular—she was so relaxed, she seemed to be asleep. Sadie decided to try again, just one more time.

"Mam?"

"Hmmm?"

"You sure you don't want to come with us? You know how much you enjoy Christmas shopping."

"We don't have any money."

"Now, Mam, you know that's not true."

Mam sat up very suddenly, her face a mask of anger and despair.

"It is true. Can you even imagine how much your hospital bill was? And there you go, traipsing off to the mall to spend money on Christmas gifts that should be used to pay that bill. And then there's that useless horse standing idle in the barn, eating up our hay and feed—but no, you don't think about things like that. You're all wrapped up in yourself and your own broken foot, and everyone pities you because poor Ezra died."

Sadie was stunned, speechless. Never had she heard her mother speak with such anger.

"Mam, won't you please see a doctor? You are not well. You would never have spoken like this before. We'll even put off the shopping trip to take you."

But Mam had turned her face to the wall and would not respond no matter how Sadie pleaded. It was like rolling a large rock uphill. You couldn't do it. You budged it an inch, and it always rolled back.

Mam had become so much worse since the accident. Her rapid decline was especially evident to Sadie, who spent most of her time in the house with Mam. She no longer did her small duties, like washing the dishes, dusting, even reading her Bible in the morning. The largest part of her days was spent lying on the recliner, her face turned to the wall.

Even her thought patterns had changed. She became obsessed with one subject at a time. The amount of money they owed the hospital weighed heavily on her, as did the cost of feeding Nevaeh. She seemed to resent the black and white horse, of this Sadie was quite certain.

She sighed and looked out across the snowy landscape as the other girls came rushing down the stairs.

Clattering! Sadie thought. What a bunch of noisemakers!

"Driver's here! He's coming up the lane!" Anna yelled.

"Where's my coat?"

"Did someone see my big leather purse with the two handles?"

"I can hardly keep track of my own purse in this house, let alone yours," Sadie said laughing.

"'Bye, Mam!"

"'Bye!"

And they were out the door, Sadie hobbling along on her crutches, the girls helping her into the 15-passenger van.

Most people who drove the Amish owned a large van so a group of them could travel together. They divided the cost among themselves, which made for cheaper fare, even if they needed to exercise patience while making stops for the other passengers. The cost of traveling was roughly a dollar per mile, so they usually planned to go to town together.

Today, however, was Christmas shopping, a special treat that required no other passengers. They knew the driver, John Arnold, a retired farmer, well and were at ease in his presence.

"Good morning, my ladies!" he boomed. "How's Sadie coming along?"

"I'm doing much better, thank you!" Sadie answered, although she already felt a bit lightheaded after swinging between the crutches.

"So where we going?"

"To the mall in Critchfield!" they echoed as one.

John Arnold grinned, put the van in gear, and said, "Waiting time is $20 an hour!"

And they were off, down the winding drive and along country roads until they came to the state road leading to the populated town of Critchfield. Traffic was heavy this close to the holidays. The occupants of cars looked a bit harassed as they waited at red lights, made U-turns, and tried passing just to arrive a minute before anyone else on the road.

At the mall, a huge low-lying structure made of steel and bricks, the vast parking lot was filled with vehicles of every shape and size imaginable. Christmas music already filled their ears as the girls hopped out of the van.

"How long?" John Arnold asked. "All day till ten tonight?"

"No-o!" the girls chorused.

"'Til four or five?" Rebekah asked.

"Sounds good. I'll be back around four."

"Thank you!"

"Take care of your cripple here," he called.

The girls waved, the van moved slowly out of the parking lot, and they were on their own. What a wonderful feeling to be free and able to browse the stores completely at ease, spending all these hours Christmas shopping!

"Listen to that song!"

"Oh, it's so beautiful it gives me goose bumps!"

"I love, love, love to go Christmas shopping!"

"One love would have been enough! We get the point!"

Laughing, they entered the huge glass doors of the mall. Immediately, they were surrounded by sights and sounds that took their breaths away—bright electric lights, Christmas decorations, beautiful music wafting in the air, real Christmas trees lit with brilliant, multi-colored lights. The wonder of the season, coupled with the achingly beautiful music in the air, brought unexpected tears to Sadie's eyes.

Christmas music did that to you, especially the instrumental music the Amish were not accustomed to. It elicited emotions of pure joy, lifted your spirits, and elevated you in almost every way. It was enough to bring forth thanks, a gratitude as beautiful as new-fallen snow, for the wondrous gift of the baby Jesus. He was born so humble and poor, wrapped only in swaddling cloths, which Mam told them was a type of long diaper that served as clothing as well.

God was, indeed, very good.

Ezra's death was still painful, but it was accepted now, unquestioningly, in the way of the Amish. There was a reason for his death, and they bowed to God's will. So be it. Heartaches were borne stoically without complaint, as was the heartache of Mam's illness.

Dear, dear Mam, Sadie thought. Her heart filled with love as she listened to the swelling strains of the Christmas songs.

I wish you could be here with us and have your poor, battered spirits revived again.

With Reuben in mind, they entered a sports store and had too much fun dashing here to this gigantic display of skateboards, then there to the tower of footballs, then back again to the baseball section. Their red and green dresses swirled, faces flushed, voices chattered—brilliant birds with white coverings.

They chose an expensive football for Reuben. They discussed at length the merits of a skateboard, but decided against it, opting for a new set of ping-pong paddles to go with the football. Reuben had acquired a mean serve, Anna informed them, shaking her head with wisdom beyond her years.

Next stop was JC Penney where the girls oohed and aahed, fussing in Pennsylvania Dutch—the Ohio version, where they rolled their "r's" into a soft "burr." Giggling, they loaded up with a new sheet set in beautiful blue for Mam and good, heavy Egyptian cotton towels for their bathroom in blue and navy. They were sure this would please their mother.

They found a package of good, warm socks for Dat and two soft chamois shirts, one in dark brown and another one in forest green.

"Who's going to volunteer?" Rebekah asked slyly.

"Volunteer for what?"

"You know, remove these pockets."

Sadie groaned from her perch on the rented wheelchair.

"Probably me, since I sit here all the time."

"Why don't Amish men wear pockets on their shirts?" Anna asked.

"Dunno!"

"Some people just sew them shut."

"Not at Dat's age. The older men should be an example to the younger ones, so we need to take off these flaps over the pockets for sure."

"'We?' You mean, me!" Sadie said.

"Why do we have an *Ordnung*?" Rebekah asked. "The English people dress any way they want, and we have to sit with a razor blade and remove a stupid old pocket from a perfectly nice shirt."

"Rebekah! That is so disrespectful," Leah scolded, crossing off Dat's name on their list.

"The *Ordnung* is like anyone else's rules. The world has rules, too, and police officers enforce them. Our rules are according to Biblical principles—about dressing modestly and being old-fashioned in thoughts and attitudes. I would never want to be anywhere else but right here in the Amish church in Montana. I love our way of life," Sadie said.

"I know. I was just having a fleeting 'rebel moment,'" Rebekah said.

"We all have them, especially at a mall," Leah assured her, draping an arm across Rebekah's shoulders.

"Wonder what we'd look like in jeans and t-shirts, our hair done, makeup, the whole works!" Anna piped up.

"No!" Leah gasped.

"Want to?" Rebekah asked, laughing.

They all laughed together, knowing it was not a priority. It was a subject to wonder about but certainly not one that brought any amount of genuine longing. It was simply not their way.

They paid for their purchases and, with shopping bags in hand, began the long walk through the rest of the mall.

Sadie announced that she needed to go to the ladies' room, assuring everyone she would be fine on her own and that she'd find them later. Leah voiced her concern, but Sadie told her no, she was perfectly capable, and besides, she wanted to buy a few things for them, too.

As she wheeled herself down the wide center of the mall, her heart beat rapidly, and she slowed down.

What a weakling, she thought. I am just not worth two cents since this accident. I suppose it will take many more days of being patient, but it drives me crazy.

On the way back from the restroom, Sadie spied an Orange Julius booth. The frothy orange drink would definitely give her a shot of much needed energy. Besides, it was a drink she loved, having sampled it only a few times before.

She wheeled over, then hoisted herself up to order her drink, carefully settling her weight on one foot. When she had her drink, she turned to sit down again, but her wheelchair was gone!

Her eyes grew large with anxiety. She gripped her drink, then turned carefully, hopping on one foot, wincing as pain shot through her calf.

Where was her wheelchair? Who would take it? Maybe her sisters had found her and grabbed it to tease her.

Looking around, she saw a young boy pushing it around and around a display of calendars in the middle of the hall.

Where in the world is his mother? He could use a few lessons in proper behavior.

Perhaps if she yelled. But no, that would cause too much attention.

People streamed past her, no one really noticing her dilemma. They were all too intent on their own destination. An elderly lady, bent at the waist, smiled sweetly but went on her slow way. She thought of asking the server at the Orange Julius booth to dial the mall office when she heard someone say, "In trouble again?"

Irritated, she looked up and into the deep, brown eyes of Mark Peight.

He was watching her, eyes shining, causing her immediate discomfort.

She shook her head.

"No."

He pointed his chin toward her foot.

"No?"

"Well, I…was in a rented wheelchair. This kid took off with it!"

"No crutches?"

She shook her head, and as she did so, the floor tilted at a crazy angle, and she gasped, reaching out with one hand toward Mark—toward anything or anyone to hold on to.

Instantly, he grabbed her arm.

"Are you…?"

She shook her head, swaying. Instantly, his strong arm moved around her waist, supporting her.

"Can you lean on me enough to walk?"

She shook her head and whispered, "I…have to hop."

Mark looked around, then down at Sadie's face turning ghastly pale. The drink slowly turned in her hand.

"Give me the drink."

She shook her head again, and the mall swam in all sorts of crazy directions. She heard the orange drink slam against the tile and Mark say, "Hang on!" in his deep voice. With his other arm on the back of her knees, he lifted her, swung her helplessly up, up, against the rough, woolen fabric of his coat.

She wanted to say, "Put me down," but if she said anything, she'd be sick. She could not protest. She could not even speak. Great waves of nausea terrified her. She could certainly not be sick.

She heard his breathing. She heard him say, "She'll be okay."

People must be watching. Oh my! What would Mam say?

Then she was deposited gently on a wooden bench, his arm supporting her. She smelled Christmas smells—pine and some sort of spice that actually helped keep her awake.

"Are you all right, Sadie?" he asked.

She wanted to nod, but the nausea still threatened to make her lose her breakfast. She lay her head against his shoulder and could feel the perspiration pop out on her face as she struggled to overcome the embarrassing weakness.

A clean white handkerchief appeared, and Mark began gently wiping above her eyes and around her face with his large, brown hand.

"There. Feel any better?" he asked.

"I think so," she whispered.

A crowd had gathered, so she kept her head lowered. She heard Mark assuring them that she would be okay, saying emphatically that if someone spied a kid with a wheelchair, they'd appreciate having it back.

Tears formed in Sadie's eyes. Another sign of this all-consuming weakness, she thought, irritated at feeling humiliated.

She sat up, swayed a bit, then steadied herself as Mark's arm dropped away.

"Thank you," she said quietly and looked up at him.

She was unprepared for the look of tenderness in those deep brown eyes, or the length of time he kept looking at her.

"Sadie, believe me, it was my pleasure. I would gladly rescue you from awkward situations every day of my life."

"You shouldn't talk like that, seeing...that...I mean, Amish girls don't go out with English boys. You shouldn't come to our singings, either. It's going to cause a fuss," she finished breathlessly.

She was deeply embarrassed when he threw back his head and laughed, a sound of genuine happiness.

"I'm not English."

"Yes, you are."

"I am?"

She sat back, grabbing the arm of the wooden bench to steady herself.

"Your...your hair is cut English. You wear English clothes."

They stopped and turned as a harried, very overweight man appeared with Sadie's wheelchair. The small boy was in tow, his hair sticking up in many directions, a grin as wide as his face making him appear far friendlier than his father.

"I apologize," the man said breathlessly, his chins wobbling, making him appear a bit vulnerable. Sadie felt only sympathy for the overwhelmed parent and his energetic offspring and assured him it was quite all right. His relief at being forgiven was so endearing—the way he thanked her politely, but profusely.

"Eric is six years old and a bit of an adventuresome kid. I lost him at the food court!"

"I have a little brother at home," Sadie said, "and I know the stunts little boys can pull off at the drop of a hat."

They smiled, exchanged "Merry Christmas," and the overweight man shuffled back to the food court, his son firmly in hand.

"Would you like to get something to eat?" Mark asked.

Oh, my!

She wanted to go with this man. In fact, she wanted to stay with him always. That truth slammed into her with the force of a tidal wave. She knew her sisters would look for her, might worry about her, but oh! She wanted to go with Mark.

"Yes. I would," she announced firmly.

Mark pushed the wheelchair up to her, then extended his hand to help her sit in it. She placed her small hand into his firm, brown one and felt a touch of wonder, of complete and honest truth, of homecoming. How could a touch convey this message?

Mark pushed the wheelchair, and Sadie sat back, her eyes shining, her strength returning.

At the food court, they were fortunate to find a table. Mark pushed the wheelchair against it hurriedly, before some frantic, last-minute shopper grabbed it away from them.

"Just bring me whatever you're having," Sadie said, looking up at him.

"Okay."

He shouldered his way through the crowd, and Sadie relaxed. She smoothed her hair and straightened her covering, hoping she looked all right.

When she spied him carrying a tray, she marveled again at his height. He had to be over six feet tall.

Why did he claim to be Amish? He sure didn't look like an Amish person. Perhaps she shouldn't be here.

He set the tray carefully between them.

"Cheese steak for me, and one for you," he said grinning.

Sadie eyed the huge sandwich and laughed.

"I'll never eat that whole thing!"

They ate big bites of the fragrant, cheesy sandwiches as onions, peppers, and tomato sauce slid down their fingers and onto their plates. Mark brought more napkins. They laughed and talked about everyday things. Mark ate his whole sandwich and what remained of hers. Then he sat back and looked at her quite seriously.

"I am from the Amish, you know. I really am. My parents still live where I was born and raised—in Buffalo Valley, Pennsylvania."

Sadie looked up, questioningly.

"Why do you look English?"

He shrugged his shoulders, then a cloak of anger settled over his features. He looked away, out over the sea of people, his eyes completely empty of any feeling or emotion.

Finally, he turned back to her.

"I am Amish, Sadie. I was raised Amish. The strictest sect. I suppose I lost faith in any plain person, not just the Amish. In anyone who dresses in a pious manner and is…" He stopped, his fingers crumpling napkins restlessly.

"Ah well. I have no business being here with you. I know what I am. You are…like a beautiful flower, and for you to be with me…It just wouldn't be right."

He pushed back the tray, then gripped the table as if to leave.

"You know that time I went to the hymn-singing? I went just to find you. Seriously. I know I can't have you, but I…guess I get a kick out of tormenting myself by spending time with you."

"Why do you put yourself down like that? Why do you say such things?" Sadie lifted troubled eyes to him.

"Let's change the subject. Tell me about the horse."

Sadie knew she had lost him. That certain trust, as delicate as a drop of dew, was gone. So she told him about Nevaeh, and his eyes turned soft when she explained why she named him that.

"You must really like horses," Mark said.

"Oh, I do. Just certain ones, though. Like Paris."

"Who?"

"Paris. She was my other horse, back home in Ohio."

"Why 'Paris?'"

Sadie blushed, shrugged her shoulders, then surprised herself by telling him every detail of her days with Eva and Paris. He listened, his eyes watching her face. He took in her emotion, her perfect eyes, her exquisite features, filing the images away in his heart for future examination.

When she stopped, he said, "You still didn't tell me the reason for naming your horse Paris."

"Maybe someday I will, but you'll think I'm silly and sentimental."

His eyebrow arched.

"Someday?"

"I mean ... What?"

She was flustered now, embarrassed, floundering for something to say.

Why had she said that? Maybe because she wanted to see him again. Maybe because she wanted to be with him. And she wanted to tell him that. Oh, how she wanted to!

And then they were surrounded by three very worried and very excited sisters. There were shopping bags, ice cream cones, soft pretzels, and tacos. All talked and ate and admonished.

Mark stood up, smiled, acknowledged the introductions, and was gone through the crowd.

Sadie finished her Christmas shopping in a daze—exhausted, but so happy that she thought she might just float off the wheelchair.

He was not like other young Amish men. When would she ever see him again? And how?

Chapter 14

Early Christmas morning, the moon slid down below the tree line, making the silver-white and darkly shadowed landscape seem like night. In winter, there were very few night sounds at the Miller home—perhaps a falling icicle or the creak of the log house, wood falling a bit lower in the great wood stove or one of the horses stamping his feet or snorting.

The Miller family was sound asleep, even Reuben, who seemed to have endless energy on Christmas Eve. He had helped the girls wrap gifts, prepared food, ran in needless circles, bounced on the sofa, slammed the handle on the side of the recliner until he almost upset it, lost the Scotch tape, spilled the whole box of name tags, and was finally sent to bed long before he deemed it necessary.

At a very early hour, however, Reuben sat up. He sat straight up—his mouth dry, his heart pounding. He had heard a sound. It was not a usual night sound of little clunks or squeaks. It was a larger sound, a harder sound. Not a distant gunshot. Not snow sliding off the roof. It was the kind of sound that woke you right up and instantly made you afraid, although you hardly ever found out what it was.

He turned the little plastic Coleman lantern that was his alarm clock and peered at the illuminated numbers. Four-thirty. It was Christmas!

He wanted to get up but knew he'd be in big trouble with the girls. That was the whole thing about having only sisters. They were bossy and sometimes downright mean. Like that Sadie last night. Whoever heard of someone getting so mad about the Scotch tape?

Reuben lay back, listening and thinking. There were some seriously big packages on the drop-leaf table in the living room, and that thought kept him awake after hearing the rumble in the dark.

Whoa! There it was again!

Reuben rolled over, pulled the flannel patchwork quilt way up over his head, and burrowed deeply into his pillow. Maybe there was a cougar in the barn. Or a wolf. Or a coyote. Likely all three.

That was the end of Reuben's night. The nighttime sounds, along with the thoughts of the brightly wrapped and beribboned packages, kept him awake.

Finally, there was the sound of Dat lighting the gas lamp downstairs and filling the teakettle for the boiling, hot water he poured over his Taster's Choice coffee.

Reuben sat up, swung his legs across the bed, and without further hesitation, dashed out of his room. Slamming the door unnecessarily and pounding noisily down the stairs, Reuben slid into the kitchen and grinned up at Dat.

"Hey!"

"Is it Christmas yet?" Reuben asked, his hair tousled and bearing that famous bunched-up look in the back. If he'd only rinse his hair properly and not sleep on it wet.

Amish boys don't have their hair cut close to their heads the way English boys do. Their hair is longer and cut straight across the forehead, then bowl-shaped and a bit lower in the back. That is the *Ordnung*, and no one ever thought to cut their little boy's hair any different. It is just the way of it.

Reuben's hair, and that messed up bunch of it in the back, was the source of many battles between him and his sisters. Rebekah, the worst of them all, told him if he didn't start using conditioner and rinse his hair better, she was going to march right into the bathroom and rinse it for him. Reuben told her if she ever dared set foot in that bathroom while he was in it, he would pour bucket after bucket of hot, soapy water all over her. And he meant it. He knew she wouldn't think about the fact that there was no bucket in the bathroom.

Dat grinned down at Reuben.

"Yes, Reuben, it's Christmas, that is, if you can persuade your mother and sisters."

"Do we have to have breakfast and the Bible story before presents this year?"

"Oh, very likely. We always do."

"May I wake the girls?"

"At your own risk," Dat said, chuckling.

Reuben weighed his options. He could sit on the couch and think about the packages while watching the hands of the clock—which was torture—or he could go to his room again—which was worse than watching the clock or thinking about packages. Or, if he was really brave, he could knock on the girls' bedroom doors, but that would bring some serious consequences, now wouldn't it?

He sat back against the couch, rubbed the unruly hair on the back of his head, and sighed. Christmas shouldn't be this way. English kids woke up and opened their packages without breakfast and a Bible story. It wasn't fair.

Dat slurped his coffee in the kitchen, and Reuben sat on the couch watching the clock, estimating the size of the oblong package and listening for any sign of activity upstairs. Finally, when the suspense was no longer bearable—like a burn in his pant's leg—Reuben simply marched right up the stairs and knocked loudly on each sister's door.

There were muffled "Reuben!" sounds, but nothing very seriously angry, so he knew they were aware of Christmas morning as well as he was. They were just trying to act mature and not get too excited about it.

Eventually, they all straggled into the kitchen with their robes clutched around themselves and their hair looking a lot worse than his. Anna was the only happy one. Leah bent over the wood stove, shivering, and asked Dat why he didn't get this thing going. Rebekah yawned and stretched. Sadie just sat there. She didn't say anything at all. What a bunch of lazy girls!

After breakfast was eaten, everyone dressed faster than normal. Dat read the Bible story about the birth of Jesus, choking up the way he always did. Reuben knew the story of the angels, Joseph and Mary, the shepherds, and Baby Jesus. It was a good story and one he was taught to be very reverent about. This was a serious miracle, this *Chrisht Kindly* who grew up to be Jesus, the Savior of all mankind.

Reuben knew there was no Santa Claus. They weren't allowed to have pictures of Santa Claus in school, and no one thought Santa delivered their packages. Reuben knew Mam bought them and the girls wrapped them, and likely Dat paid for them. The reason they received gifts on Christmas day was to keep the tradition of the Wise Men who brought gifts to Baby Jesus.

Finally, the story was over. Dat wiped his nose, and Mam smiled as Reuben asked, "Now?" He said "*Denke*" to Mam as nicely as he could, hoping it conveyed all the love he felt at this moment. And then, he was allowed to open his packages—that wondrous moment he had been waiting on for much too long.

He tore off the wrapping paper of the first package and sighed with the wonder of it. Here was a full-sized, very expensive, grown-up-looking football that would impress all his friends at school. The ping-pong set was an added bonus he had not expected. He squealed, pounded the arm of the couch, and yelled to Anna to come here and look right this minute. Anna screeched, and they bent their heads to examine the new, heavy paddles very closely. Then, Mam handed him another package—the biggest one of all.

Reuben looked up, questioningly.

"Are you sure this is mine, Mam?"

"Yes, Reuben. It's for you. It was under my bed!"

Reuben's mouth fell open.

"But...I already have a football. And a ping-pong set."

"Open it!" Mam urged.

He couldn't remember ever having been speechless before. He simply couldn't think of anything to say, so he didn't say anything at all.

It was a skateboard.

A real one.

For bigger boys.

It had a heavy, gritty top and flames painted on the bottom. Bright orange wheels finished it off. The wheels were absolutely unreal. They spun like mad. It was twice as big as anything he had ever owned.

And then Anna got one just like it, except hers was fluorescent teal—a girl color.

The whole thing was unbelievable. Reuben felt so spoiled, so completely greedy with three big items for Christmas. It almost wasn't right.

"*Denke*, Mam!" he said, over and over, his voice thick with the emotion he felt. Anna echoed his thanks. Then they set their skateboards on the hardwood floor and tried them out through the ribbons and wrapping paper. Dat wiped his eyes again.

The girls started opening packages, but, to Reuben, it just seemed like girl things—fabric for new dresses, ice skates, dumb-looking candleholders, framed pictures that weren't a bit pretty. They giggled and fussed and yelled their high-pitched, silly girl sounds, but Reuben wasn't interested in all that useless stuff.

Sadie received a really nice saddle blanket, though. It was black and white, sort of like a zebra—the exact one she had always dreamed of for Paris. It would look sharp on Nevaeh.

Dat gave Mam a beautiful battery lamp for the bathroom, which made her smile a lot. Reuben wished Mam would smile the way she used to, but he figured when you got as old as Mam, you had to take a lot of pills to keep going. He guessed you were often tired and didn't feel like smiling.

✿ ✼ ✿

Later that morning, Sadie sat at the kitchen table chopping celery and onions, her leg propped up on a folding chair. Mam was peeling potatoes, Rebekah was putting together the date pudding, and Leah was mixing ginger ale and pineapple juice.

"Mmm! That ham smells heavenly!" Sadie sighed.

"Lets eat at eleven, instead of twelve!"

"Uncle Samuel's coming this afternoon?" Rebekah asked.

"Oh, yes. And Levi's."

"Oh, goody! I'm so glad. I love to sing with Samuel," Rebekah said.

Sadie smiled to herself, settling contentedly into the Christmas atmosphere. Thank God, Mam appeared so normal—making dinner and enthusiastic as always. For Reuben and Anna, it meant so much for this special day.

"When I get married, I want date pudding on my *eck* in a trifle bowl just like this one," Rebekah announced, putting the final layer of whipped cream on top. Standing back, she admired her date pudding.

"That bowl was on my *eck*," Mam said, putting down her paring knife to go to Rebekah's side.

"Really, Mam?"

"Yes, it was. It's beautiful, isn't it? And I was so in love," she sighed.

Date pudding was the best thing ever. Once you started eating it, you couldn't stop until you were quite miserable. That was true. First you baked a rich, moist cake filled with dates and walnuts. Then you cooked a sauce with butter and brown sugar and chilled it in the refrigerator overnight. The next day you assembled this sticky, sweet cake in layers with the sauce and whipped cream.

Next, you crumbled the cake in the bottom of the clear, glass trifle bowl. Then you carefully spooned the rich, brown sauce over it, spreading it evenly. This was followed by a generous layer of sweet whipped cream. Then the layers were repeated.

Some people used Cool Whip, which was all right, but Mam insisted on the real thing. Whipped cream was just better.

Sadie thought about her own *eck*—that highly-honored corner table where the bride and groom sat after they were married in the three-hour service beforehand. It was a wondrous thing, that *eck*.

The designated corner was the place where long tables, set hastily against two walls, met. The bride and groom sat on folding chairs with the two couples who were members of the bridal party. The bride's best table linens were used on the *eck*, as were her china, stemware, and silverware. These were gifts from the groom while they were dating. It was all color-coordinated, and each bride dreamed of her own *eck* as her teenage years went by.

Sadie was no different than any other young Amish girl. She thought about marriage, her wedding day, the guests, and the food, much the same as everyone else. There simply was no one for her to marry.

A career was out of the question. Being raised in an Amish home, she had only one choice, really. Well, no, two: to marry or not to marry. But being a wife and mother was the highest honor and the one goal in every young girl's life. If you didn't marry, you could teach school or get a job cooking or cleaning or working in a store or maybe caring for someone who was sick or disabled.

Sadie sighed as she dropped the small bits of celery and onion into a bowl.

"Here, Mam. This is ready for the stuffing," she said.

With the girls' help, the stuffing was made and put in the oven, and the potatoes were peeled and put on the gas burner to boil. Rebekah bent over to retrieve a head of cabbage from the crisper drawer in the refrigerator while Sadie sat tapping her fingers on the wooden table top, absentmindedly humming the same Christmas tune over and over.

"Stop that, Sadie. You're driving me nuts!" Leah warned.

"Testy, testy," Rebekah said.

"Hey, what am I supposed to do? I have to sit here or get around on crutches, which isn't real easy in a kitchen filled with three other people."

"You could get your wheelchair and set the table," Mam said.

So Sadie did. That wasn't easy either.

Someone had to get the plates from the hutch cupboard. Then she had to balance them on her lap as she wheeled into the dining area. She opened the oak chest containing the silverware that Dat had given Mam before they were married. She laid each piece carefully side by side on the tablecloth beside the china plates. The whole task took about twice as long as normal, leaving Sadie in no mood to seriously pitch in and help with the rest of Christmas dinner.

By eleven, the table was set with Mam's best tablecloth and her Christmas china, which had an outline of gold along the plates' rims with a circle of holly berries surrounding the center. They used the green stemware Mam had purchased at the Dollar General. It was exactly one dollar for one pretty glass tumbler. It was all very pretty and so grand and Christmasy, with the red and green napkins completing the picture.

The whole house smelled of the salty ham cooking in its own juices in the agate roaster in the oven of the gas stove. They mashed the potatoes with the hand-masher. Rebekah and Leah added lots of butter and salt, and then took turns pouring in hot milk until the potatoes reached the proper consistency.

Mam made the rich gravy with broth from the ham, adding a mixture of flour, cornstarch, and water. She whisked in the white liquid carefully until the gravy was thick and bubbly.

They took the pan of stuffing out of the oven and spooned it into a serving dish. The edges were brown, crisp, and salty with bits of onion and celery clinging to the sides. There was a dish of corn, yellow and succulent, with a square of butter melting so fast that no one was really sure it was there in the first place. They had grated the cabbage on a hand-held grater and mixed it with Miracle Whip, salt, sugar, and vinegar. They placed bits of red and green peppers on top for Christmas. A Tupperware container of fruit salad held maraschino cherries and kiwis, mixed in just for their colors.

The layered jello, called Christmas Salad, was made with lime green jello on the bottom, a mixture of cream cheese, milk, and Knox gelatin in the middle, and red jello on the top. It was the most perfect thing on the table—all red, green, and white and cut in shimmering squares. It looked so festive sitting on a small dish beside the green glasses.

Rebekah had baked a Christmas cake made of apples, nuts, raisins, and dates. The heavy cake, so rich and moist with a thick layer of cream cheese frosting, stood on Mam's cake stand with the heavy glass cover.

Mam had not baked the usual pecan pies, which no one seemed to notice, and certainly no one commented on if they did. She was doing as well as she could. Sadie knew she was using up all her reserve energy and determination to keep going, joining the Christmas spirit for Reuben's and Anna's sakes.

After everything was put on the table, they all gathered around, slid into their chairs, and bowed their heads for a silent prayer of thanksgiving for all the food and the gift of the Baby Jesus.

They ate with enormous appetites, enjoying the rich home-cooked food unreservedly. After all, Christmas came just once a year.

Dat proclaimed the meal the best ever. He said the ham was similar to the kind he ate as a child when they butchered their own hogs and cured their own meat. He couldn't believe this was from IGA. Mam beamed with satisfaction, her cheeks flushed with pleasure.

Reuben just grinned and grinned, eating so much it was alarming. Sadie asked him where all the food was going, and he shrugged his shoulders and grinned some more.

Reaching for his second whole wheat dinner roll, he spread it liberally with butter. Then he turned the plastic honey bear upside down and squeezed with both hands until a river of honey spread its golden stickiness across the snow-white tablecloth. That was no problem for Reuben who lowered his head to lick it off the tablecloth before being firmly reminded about good table manners. Dat's gray eyebrows lowered in that certain way that drew instant respect.

Sadie ate two squares of Christmas Salad, ran a finger inside the belt of her dress, then eyed the date pudding.

"Go ahead," Leah laughed, her blue eyes sparkling.

Sadie caught her eye, knowing Leah had seen that exploratory search for a measurement of her waistline.

They threw back their heads and had a good old, little-girl belly laugh, one that floated up through the region of their stomachs and felt as delicious as all the good food. It was truly Christmas, a time of celebration and joy, a special time of happiness when families remembered Christ's birth and were made glad, as in times of old.

They lingered around the table and made plans for the New Year festivities. That was the evening they had reserved for Richard Caldwell and his wife, Barbara. The Caldwells had asked for an invitation, never having visited an Amish home before. So the Miller family talked and planned ahead, knowing they would try and do their best in cooking and baking the old-fashioned way.

Reuben said Richard Caldwell was only a human being, same as everybody else, so why would you have to go to all that trouble?

Sadie wanted to invite Jim and Dorothy, too, but it was a bit questionable whether Dorothy would be comfortable with Richard Caldwell, him being the boss and all.

Finally, the dishes were done, leftovers were put away, and snacks were set out on the counter top for all the families coming to spend the afternoon singing the German Christmas hymns. There was Chex Mix, Rice Krispie Treats, chocolate-covered peanut butter crackers, homemade chocolate fudge, peanut butter fudge, and all kinds of fruit. Vegetables and dip were arranged in a colorful display.

They had just finished when the first buggy came up the driveway, the spirited horse spraying chunks of snow with his hooves. Smiling faces entered and were greeted warmly. Soon the German hymnbooks were brought out, and Uncle Samuel's beautiful, rich baritone filled the room with song. They sang *"Shtille Nacht, Heilige Nacht,"* the women's alto voices blending perfectly. They followed that with *"Freue Dich Velt."* When the volume increased, chills went up Sadie's arms.

What a wonderful old song! The words were a clear message of joy; the assurance the Lord had come and all heaven and earth were to rejoice. It was so real and so uplifting, Sadie rose above the worry about Mam, the sadness of Ezra's sudden death, the horror of the accident...just everything. God was in his heaven. Yes, he was! He loved all mankind enough to send the Christ Child, and for all lowly sinners, it was enough.

Sadie was ashamed of the tears that sprang to her eyes, so she got her crutches and left the room, her face turned away. They would think she was crying about Ezra, perhaps, or that she had "nerve trouble" since the accident, so it was best to keep the tears hidden.

The kitchen door banged open, depositing Reuben and three of his cousins in a wet, breathless, fast-moving, fast-talking bundle on the long, rectangular carpet inside.

"Sadie!"

She stopped, leaned on her crutches, and raised one eyebrow.

"Do you absolutely have to be so noisy?"

"Hey, Sadie! Did someone borrow Nevaeh? He's not in his stall! He's not in the pasture! Where is he? Did Richard Caldwell come to get him?"

Sadie leaned forward, looking sharply at Reuben.

"Reuben, stop it! It's not funny. Of course Nevaeh's out there somewhere. You know he is."

"He's not! Uncle Levi's and Samuel's horses are tied in his stall. Charlie is in his own. No horses were left in the pasture."

"Was his gate broken down? Does it look as if he got out?" Sadie asked, her voice rising to a shrill squeak.

Reuben shook his head, snow spraying from his dark blue beanie.

"No! He isn't around anywhere."

"Go ask Samuel and Levi if he was there when they arrived."

The singing soon stopped, and Sadie listened as she heard the boys relate their news. She heard Dat exclaim, "He was there this morning. I know he was!"

"Well, he's not now."

The men all trooped out to the kitchen, grabbed their coats and hats, pulled on heavy gloves and boots, and went to the barn. Sadie hobbled over to the kitchen door, her heart banging against her ribs, waiting, watching anxiously for the men's return.

They were gone for a very long time, an eternity it seemed. Then they appeared, talking and waving their arms toward the phone shanty.

Now what?

Dat came out, spoke a few words, then hurried to the house. Sadie stepped aside as the door was flung open.

"Get your coat on. There's a phone call for you. Think you can make it? It's a guy."

"What?"

"Hurry, Sadie. It's going to take you awhile. Reuben, you go with her, make sure she's okay"

Sadie looked up, "Nevaeh?"

"He's not around. We're going to search the pasture."

Rebekah and Leah looked on worriedly as they helped Sadie into her heavy, wool coat. They watched from the dining room window as she swung herself between the crutches through the ice and snow. They didn't relax until the door to the phone shanty was closed.

Sadie picked up the black receiver, "Hello?"

"Merry Christmas, Sadie."

All the air left her lungs when she heard the unmistakably masculine voice of Mark Peight.

Chapter 15

"I..." WHOOSH, HER BREATH LEFT HER COMPLETELY on its own accord.

"Are you there?" the deep voice queried.

"Yes, yes, I'm here. Just...catching my breath."

"Oh, that's right, you would have to go to the phone on your crutches."

"Yes."

Just "yes." Why couldn't she say something wittier, something a bit more knowledgeable, something smarter than just "yes"?

"I'm calling to see how you are doing. You sort of scared me there at the mall. Do you feel better?"

"Yes."

There I go again. Yes. Why can't I say something more?

Her heart was beating so hard and fast that there was the sound of the ocean in her ears.

"Did you know there's a skating party at Dan Detweilers? On Friday evening?"

"Leah told me, but I can't go with crutches."

"When does your cast come off?"

"At least another two weeks."

"I... what if I came to pick you up? You could stay in the buggy and watch for awhile. Your sisters could join us."

"Mark, seriously, do you even have a horse and buggy? Where do you live? And are you Amish? For real? I mean, I don't wish to sound ignorant, but suddenly you appear out of nowhere, not looking Amish like the rest of the young men in this area, and... well..."

She was floundering now, but she needed to know.

He laughed a deep, comfortable, rolling laugh.

Oh, she could imagine his face. She remembered every line, even the way little pleats appeared beside his brown, brown eyes when he smiled. And his teeth were so white and perfect. She could look at his face for a hundred years and never tire of it.

That thought struck her, slammed into her knowing, and she clutched the receiver tightly to steady herself. These thoughts were absolutely ridiculous.

He was talking again. She needed to hear what he was saying.

"Sadie, my life is a long story. I suppose to you, I'm a bit of a mystery."

He paused.

She pulled her coat down over her lap, shivered.

"All right, I'll tell you what I really want to say. I would love to sit somewhere with you and talk for a very long time. Sadie, I'm almost 30 years old. And to think of... well, I went to the hymn-singing just to see you."

Sadie watched the afternoon light on an icicle through the phone shanty window. She straightened her covering and cleared her throat.

"I mean, I don't really want to join the youth group.

I'm too old. I've been through too much to...I don't know." His voice fell away.

And now she could not think of a word to say. Not one word.

"I guess I'm sort of messing up this conversation, Sadie."

She loved the way he said "Sadie," sort of dragging out the "e." Her name became something fabulous when he said it, not just plain old Sadie.

"No, no, not at all. Are you really 30 years old?"

"Twenty-nine. I'll be 30 in May."

"Wow! That's old. A lot of young men have four or five children by that time."

He laughed again, that rolling, comfortable sound.

"Yeah. Well, not me."

"I guess not."

"How old are you?"

"Twenty."

"That's good. At least you're not 16."

"Yes."

"So...if I come by with my horse and buggy, which I happen to have, will you go with me to the skating party?"

Sadie searched frantically for the proper answer. Of course she would go! But what would people say? Who was he really? She hardly knew one thing about him, other than his astounding face. Well, not just that, everything about him was astounding. From the moment he had stepped out of Fred's truck, she had been speechless and dumb around him. How could she sit in a buggy with him? She'd prattle away like a child, or else have nothing to say. Just yes.

"I better not go."

"Why?"

"Well, I'm ... not well, really."

"Okay"

Don't hang up. Don't. She lurched into desperation.

"Mark, Nevaeh is missing. We ... our uncles are here and they put their horses in the barn, and now Nevaeh is not in his stall. We have no idea where he is. And Mark, have you heard of the wild horses—the ones that presumably are running the ridges? The state game lands? I'm just afraid, I mean, what could possibly have happened to Nevaeh? He was in his stall this morning. Dat said he was. There is no gate broken down, no sign of a scuffle, nothing. I'm so terribly worried."

"Do you want me to come over?"

"Well, where are you? What would Dat say? I mean..."

"I'll be over."

Click.

Sadie held the receiver away from her ear, panic rising in her throat.

Mark! No! You can't come here. Nobody knows you. You're English, sort of.

Sadie sat and stared out the window at the day's disappearing light. Her hair was a mess, her nose a shiny red, no doubt, and she had stuffed herself with all that food! Groaning inwardly she got up, swung herself through the snow, and wondered how long before he got there.

Yanking open the door to the house, she hobbled through, banged her crutches against the wall, and shrugged out of her coat without bothering to hang it up. Now if she could just get upstairs without anyone noticing, she'd be all right.

"Sadie! Who was on the phone?" This from Dat.

She kept going, hoping he wouldn't ask again.

"Sadie! Come here. Who was on the phone?"

Resignedly, her shoulders slumped, she turned obedi- ently into the living room.

"It was Mark Peight."

"Who?"

Her uncles stopped drinking their coffee, a chocolate- covered Ritz cracker held in midair.

"Just someone I know. He's coming over to help look for Nevaeh."

"He doesn't need to. We'll find him. We're going to head out soon."

"Well, he says he's coming over."

The men resumed their talking and she turned, grind- ing her teeth in frustration.

Parents! Nosey old things. Why did Dat have to act so *grosfeelich* in front of Samuel and Levi?

Panting, she reached the top of the stairs. Rebekah and Leah were in their rooms unpacking Christmas gifts. Sadie decided not to say anything—just go to her room and fix her hair.

Which dress?

Oh, my.

Just leave this one on? No, she spilled gravy on the front. Red? No, she had worn it at the mall. Blue? She had a gazillion blue dresses. Green? She looked ugly in green. Well, not the deep, deep forest green with nice sleeves. Anna said that color made her eyes look blue for sure and her skin a beautiful olive color. Anna was a bit dramatic. Whoever heard of olive skin? Well, forest green it was.

Her back ached and her arms slumped wearily as she put the final hairpin into her wrecked hair. She felt as if her strength would never return, sometimes being impa- tient with her lack of energy.

She had experienced trauma, she knew. Ezra was gone, and sometimes, at the oddest moments, she missed his kind face. Always she was glad she had planned on dating and marrying him. She would have. But in all things there is a reason. This is what she was taught.

God knew what he was doing from his throne on high. The ministers assured everyone in the congregation about this. God had a plan for each individual life and cared about each one. When things like the accident happened, you had to bow your head in true submission, saying, "Thy will be done." It afforded a certain peace in the end, if you could mean it.

Sadie had gone through moments of self-blame. She wondered if she was false-hearted and if she should not have gone with Ezra that fateful evening. Her sisters assured her those thoughts were the devil trying to destroy her, and she needed to be watchful. What would you do without sisters? They were, indeed, the most precious thing God had ever thought about creating.

When two heads appeared at her door and two more nosey questions were thrown into the room, Sadie grinned.

"Oh, someone's coming to help look for Nevaeh."

Rebekah came in and plunked herself on Sadie's bed.

"Let me guess. Mark Peight or Mark Peight or Mark Peight?"

Sadie whirled, throwing her hairbrush.

"Smarty!"

He showed up then, and in a horse and buggy, too. Sadie could tell it was not his team. It was an "old people's" horse and buggy. The difference was plain to see. The youth had sparkling, clean, new buggies with lots of reflectors and pretty things hung inside the windows.

There was brightly-colored upholstery on the walls and seats and matching carpet on the floor. The horse's harness was usually gaily decorated as well, with shining collar hames, a colorful collar pad, and a bridle studded with silver.

This horse and buggy looked exactly like the one her parents' had. It was clean but dull, with a black, traditional harness without silver or color—a very Amish team.

Just as English youth enjoy a nice car, so it was with the Amish buggies. Sadie often thought about that. Youth were youth, each one trying to be someone—nature's way of calling for a mate. Wasn't that true? She had never said that. It sounded too … well, sort of primitive or a bit vulgar perhaps, depending who heard you say it.

English people liked to think Amish people were elevated a bit or in a highly esteemed place, and so just a bit better than they were. Hopefully the Amish were good, although Sadie knew they were certainly also human. Sadie guessed, that some areas, their heritage was a God-given thing, a gift they had acquired at birth. She wondered if Mark truly had been born and raised in an Amish home.

Who knew?

He definitely was a mystery.

And then, he saw her standing hesitantly at the door. He waved and said he'd put his horse in the barn and be right back.

Sadie swung to the kitchen table and sat down a bit weakly, trying to appear calm and nonchalant—if that was even a possibility.

Oh, my!

Dat, Uncle Levi, and Uncle Samuel had the worst

timing in the world. How could they? The exact minute Mark appeared in the kitchen hallway, they all crowded in, all talking at once, trying to come up with a feasible plan to find the missing horse.

"What I cannot understand is how that horse got out in the first place," Dat was saying.

"Someone had to let him out," Uncle Levi said, setting down his coffee cup and reaching for a handful of Chex Mix. He chomped down on the salty mixture, scattering half of it across the clean linoleum floor.

Sadie sighed. Mark stood in the hallway. Then Samuel turned and caught sight of him.

"Hi, there!"

Too loudly. Too boisterously. Sadie despaired.

"Come on in. Make yourself at home, whoever you are. One of these bachelors that feel the pull of the West?"

Oh, no! Sadie wanted to disappear through the floor, down into the basement, and through that floor, too.

Mark grinned, and said quietly, "Yeah, I guess so."

"Dat? This is Mark Peight. Mark, my father and his brothers, Samuel and Levi.

"You all live around here?"

"Oh, yes. We do. Been here for five years, almost six."

Dat's eyes narrowed.

"How do you know Sadie?"

Sadie tried to salvage her pride by telling them Mark was the one who came upon her on the road with Nevaeh before Richard Caldwell had the veterinarian nurse him back to health.

"Mmmm," Uncle Samuel said, nodding his head in that certain way, his eyes twinkling.

Levi grinned outright. Sadie willed him to be quiet.

They talked loudly now about other horses who had

gotten away, the size of the pasture, if anyone believed there were actual horse thieves in this day and age, and whether there was a band of wild horses. The conversation turned to the night of the accident.

Sadie caught a movement behind the bathroom door. Mam!

What was she doing pressed between the door and the shower curtain? Listening? Why wouldn't she come to the kitchen?

"I know that horse was there this morning. I know it," Dat insisted.

"But if he was, someone had to let him out. Do you think there could be a horse thief in broad daylight?" Levi asked around his Chex Mix.

"Hey, they do anything these days."

"Let's go search the pasture."

They got into their coats, smashed their wool hats on their heads, stuck their feet into boots, pulled on gloves, and were gone.

Mark turned back, searching Sadie's eyes.

"We'll find him," he assured her.

"Oh, I hope," she whispered.

She held his gaze. Too long. The kitchen was filled with nothing at all. It all went away, except for the look in Mark's eyes. It was a look so consuming, she heard singing, sort of a tune in her mind, a speck of happiness in song she had never heard before in her life.

Was love a song? Sort of, she figured.

Boy, she was in dangerous territory now, letting that happen. But she could have no more looked away than she could have stopped breathing. It was so natural.

Oh, my.

She sat at the kitchen table, her head in her hands, turmoil in her heart.

An hour passed with Aunt Lydia and Aunt Rachel sitting in the kitchen with her. They drank coffee, sampled desserts, and talked of things women talk about—having babies, which laundry soap works best, how to secure towels to the wash line without the ceaseless wind tearing them off and away, whose teacher was strict, whose was incompetent, and so on.

Sadie was becoming very worried and uneasy. She tapped her nails on the tabletop. How long could it take to find a horse in a pasture? It wasn't that big.

Finally she heard voices and stamping feet.

Mark came in first, his face grim, followed by Dat, Levi, and Samuel. Their noses were red, eyes serious.

Sadie rose, standing on one leg. A hand went to her throat.

"What? Did you find him?"

Mark looked at Dat. Dat shook his head, saying nothing. Mark cleared his throat and looked away. Sadie knew, then, that something was wrong.

"What? Did you find him? Someone tell me."

They told her.

They got to the very lower end of the pasture where the alders and brush almost hid the fence. The fence was torn, even the post pulled out. Brush everywhere. Snow mixed with the dirt and brown winter grasses. Signs of a terrible struggle. Blood. Lots of blood.

The blood left a trail that was easy to follow. They found Nevaeh. He was down, a great gash torn in the tender part of his stomach. There was a pool of blood and he was holding his hind leg at a grotesque angle.

Mark's head was bent, one shoe pushing against the baseboard.

"But…" Sadie stammered.

It was not exactly clear what happened, what caused Nevaeh to become so frightened he became impaled on the fence post. Perhaps there was a cougar.

"But…how could he bleed to death?" Sadie whispered.

"He didn't…completely. His leg was broken, almost off. We…we had to put him down."

Sadie lifted agonized eyes to Dat, Levi, Samuel, and finally to Mark.

"Why?"

It was all she could think to say. Paris, then Ezra, and now Nevaeh. Would she be able to bow her head in submission one more time? What purpose was there in letting that beautiful horse die? There was no reason that made any sense. God was not cruel this way, was he?

Dat came over with Rebekah and Leah. They all touched her, trying to convey some sort of hope, sympathy, caring, but Sadie was past feeling anything. She was numb, completely numb.

"We'll get you another horse, Sadie," Dat said, so kindly.

"We have a hospital bill," Mam said sharply.

Everyone turned to stare at her, most of them in disbelief.

Dat straightened, said grimly, "I know we have a hospital bill. God will provide a way for us to pay it."

Rachel and Lydia exchanged glances as Mam turned, her eyes black with hatred, and…what else?

Sadie was afraid, shaken.

Dear God, help us all.

They had company now. She must brace up for Dat's sake.

Sadie squared her shoulders, took a deep breath, and willed the pool of tears to be contained for now.

"Well," she said, quietly. "He didn't suffer long."

Dat shook his head.

Mark said, "He was brave. That horse was..."

He stopped.

Sadie nodded, then said, "Well, it's Christmas. Why don't we make another pot of coffee?"

Everyone smiled in agreement, relieved at Sadie's strength. Lydia gave her shoulder a squeeze of reassurance, and Rachel smiled a shaky smile in her direction.

Reuben, Anna, and the gaggle of towheaded cousins clattered up from the basement. Dashing into the kitchen, they slid to a stop when they saw all the serious faces.

"Did you find Nevaeh?" Anna asked innocently, helping herself to a large dish of date pudding.

"Yes, we did," Dat answered.

"Good!"

Reuben grabbed three large squares of peanut butter fudge, was told to return two of them to the platter, and then he dashed out the door. The cousins followed, clumping back down the stairs to the basement.

"There's some serious ping-pong going on down there," Levi grinned.

Mark came over, stood by Sadie, and asked if she wanted to see Nevaeh.

"How would I?" she asked, gesturing to her cast.

"Do you have an express wagon?" he asked, looking around.

Dat brought the express wagon and Mark spread his buggy robe on it. Her sisters bundled Sadie up and deposited her unceremoniously on the wooden wagon. Then she and Mark were off.

They didn't talk. Mark focused on using his strength to pull the express wagon through the trampled snow, and Sadie had nothing to say. The whole afternoon had a sense of unreality and, now that the sun was casting a reddish glow behind Atkin's Ridge and creating the color of lavender on the snow, it all seemed like a fairy tale.

Sadie shivered, then smiled up at Mark when he looked back to ask how she was doing.

They came to the place where the fence was torn. The post hung by one strand of barbed wire. Its top was rough and not cut evenly, the way some western fences were built. Snow was mixed with dirt, grass flung about, bits of frozen ground clinging to the post as if reluctant to let go.

Mark showed her where Nevaeh had started bleeding, then began pulling her through the thick brush. She held up an arm to shield her face as snow showered her from the branches. She used the other arm to hold onto the wagon. She bent her head to avoid the whipping brush. Then the wagon stopped.

"Here he is."

That's all Mark said.

Sadie looked and saw the beautiful black and white coat—saw Nevaeh. It's strange how a horse's head looks so small and flat and vulnerable when it lies on its side. Its neck, too. Its body seems much too large for that small head. Dat told her once that horses don't lie flat like that for a long period of time; they have difficulty breathing.

Yes, Dat, I know. But Nevaeh is not having difficulty breathing. She's not even breathing. She's dead.

Sadie gathered her thoughts and remembered Mark.

She was not going to cry, not when she was with Mark.

She was always in some kind of stupid trouble when he was around, so no crying. Certainly not this time. Nevaeh was only a horse.

And then she lowered her face in her hands and cried hard. She sniffled and sobbed and needed a handkerchief. Her eyes became red and swollen, and so did her nose. Tears poured through her fingers, and she shook all over with the force of her sobs.

Mark made one swift, fluid movement, and he was on his knees at her side. His arms came around her, heavy and powerful, and he held her head to his shoulder the way a small child is comforted. He just held her until her sobs weakened and slowed, the way a thunderstorm fades away on a summer day. Tears, like rain, still fell, but the power of her grief was relieved.

"I'm sorry," she said finally, hiccuping.

"Sadie, Sadie."

That's all he said.

She didn't know how long they were there, Sadie seated on the wagon, Mark on his knees. She just knew she never, ever wanted him to go away. She wanted those strong, sure arms around her forever. Of this she was certain.

Besides, nothing else made any sense.

Finally he released her, leaned back, searched her eyes. "You okay?"

Meeting his eyes, Sadie nodded.

That was a mistake, was her first coherent thought, before his arms came around her again, crushing her to him. He held her so tightly, her ribs actually hurt a bit. Then he released her quite suddenly, stood up, cleared his throat, and went to pick up the wagon tongue. He trudged back to the house, not saying a word.

Sadie was stung, mortified. What had she done wrong? Had she offended him?

At the house, he declined her invitation to come in for coffee. Instead he hurriedly hitched his horse to the carriage and flew down the drive at a dangerous speed. It seemed he couldn't get out of there fast enough.

Sadie knew she had lost him again.

Chapter 16

After the cumbersome cast was removed, Sadie returned to the ranch.

It was wonderful to be back. Richard Caldwell welcomed her with his powerful voice bouncing off the cathedral ceilings. Jim told her, in his drawly, shy manner, that the place was not the same without her.

"Yer sorta like one o' them sunbeams that comes down out o' the gray skies, Sadie," he said, sliding the ever-present toothpick to the opposite side of his teeth.

"Why, thank you, Jim. That's a very nice compliment," Sadie told him.

Dorothy held nothing back. She wept, she hugged Sadie close, she stood back to look deep into Sadie's eyes, wiped her own eyes with a paper towel, honked her nose into it, then shook her head.

"In all my days, Sadie honey, I never seen nothin' like it. When I walked into that there hospital and seen you layin' there, I thought the hand o' God was hovering right above your head. God brought you through. Only God. Praise his Almighty Name, an' I mean it."

Dorothy paused for breath, plunked her ample little body onto a kitchen chair, reached for her half-empty coffee cup. She set it down, pulled at her skirt, and began rubbing her knee.

"You know there's a new store in town called Dollar Tree? Well, that's where I got you that china cross. The artificial flowers around that cross looked so real, I swear I coulda pulled 'em out o' my own flower patch. You liked that, didn't you?"

Sadie nodded enthusiastically.

"Oh, yes, I put it away with the rest of the things in my hope chest," she said carefully.

Dorothy's eyes brightened.

"You did? See? I knew you'd like that! Too pretty for your room, wasn't it? You had to put it away for your own house once you get married! Well, I always had good taste when it comes to gift-giving. Just have a knack there. I'll tell you what, on your weddin' day, I'll get you another one, an' you can have one on each side of your hutch cupboard." Dorothy slapped her knee with enthusiasm, watching Sadie's face like a small bird.

"Well you can, can't ya?"

"Of course, Dorothy. I will."

"Now that Dollar Tree, it's not quite like my Dollar General. They don't have them good shoes, mind you. Their Rice Krispies is two dollars a box, though. That ain't so dear."

Sadie nodded.

"Well, here I am runnin' my mouth about the price o' cereal and you didn't tell me how you're doin'."

Sadie took a deep breath, then poured herself a large mug of coffee.

"My leg and foot are still swollen and sore. I have to be careful how I walk on it. My hair..."

She reached up to brush back the unruly, short strands on one side of her head.

"Be glad you're alive. Just be glad!" Dorothy said, nodding her head for emphasis.

"Oh, I am, I am. I don't mind my hair so much, but it's hard not having the strength to be able to work the way I used to."

"Well, today yer gonna do the light dusting and run the vacuum. Then you can sit right here at this table and chop vegetables. I'm havin' vegetable soup with lots of ground beef and tomatoes, the way the boss likes it."

There was a knock on the kitchen door, a small tapping sound.

"Now, who'd be knockin'? No need to do that!" Dorothy said, her eyebrows lowered.

She lifted her head and yelled, "You don't need to knock!"

Sadie cringed when she saw Barbara Caldwell enter the kitchen, her long, white robe clutched around her middle. Her hair was disheveled, and without makeup she looked young and vulnerable. Her face was a ghastly color, so pale Sadie was afraid she'd fall over right there in the kitchen. Her voice trembled as she told them she'd been sick all morning, and was there anything Dorothy knew of that could help her digestive system?

Sadie held her breath, knowing Barbara was not Dorothy's favorite person on the ranch, but Dorothy was cordial. She clucked and stewed, fussing on and on about the merits of gingerroot tea and how she would put in plenty of sugar for strength.

Barbara Caldwell sank gratefully into a kitchen chair, then looked at Sadie and smiled.

"How are you, Sadie?"

Sadie could not believe the smile or the question, especially since she had refused to come to their house on New Year's Eve. Richard Caldwell had canceled at the last minute, apologizing profusely, and the whole family had eaten the delicious food all by themselves, shrugging their shoulders in resignation. Barbara was probably just too high-class to eat in an Amish home, they thought.

"I'm doing much better, thank you," Sadie said politely, ducking her head to hide her embarrassment.

"You've come through a lot. Richard tells me your horse was killed."

"He was put down, yes. His leg was broken."

"Must be hard."

"It is."

Dorothy bustled over with the tea, setting it daintily on the table at Barbara's elbow.

"There now. Try it."

Barbara sipped appreciatively, then grimaced at the heat.

"Taste good?" Dorothy asked hopefully.

Barbara nodded.

Sadie got up, went to the closet, and got down the Pledge furniture polish and a clean cloth. It would be good to dust the beloved house again. She'd do the upstairs first, working her way down. She left the kitchen then, letting Dorothy care for Barbara.

Humming, Sadie started in the den—the great oak-paneled room that housed all of Richard Caldwell's treasures. It was a massive room with great windows reaching to the height of the cathedral ceiling where fans moved quietly to ease the stuffiness of the baseboard heat.

She was whistling low under her breath, the way she always did when she dusted, enjoying the smell of the lemon furniture polish and the luster of the well made furniture under her hand.

"Hey! Sadie!"

Sadie jumped at Richard Caldwell's booming voice.

Calm. I will be calm, Sadie told herself, giving one last swipe to the tabletop and turning slowly to face him.

"It's real good to see you back, Sadie!"

"Thank you. It's good to be here."

"Sit down."

Sadie obeyed, pressing her knees together nervously, smoothing her gray skirt over them.

He came straight to the point.

"What happened to...to your horse?"

Sadie thought of the fact that he always called Nevaeh "your horse." Perhaps he wasn't comfortable pronouncing her name. Either that, or he thought it was a foolish name for a horse.

"He tried to jump the fence. He...suffered a lot."

Sadie stopped, the dreaded emotion rising in her throat.

"But why would he have the urge to try and jump the fence?"

Sadie shook her head, bit her lip.

Richard Caldwell got up, and in his abrupt way, grabbed the remote off the coffee table and pressed a button.

"I kept this for you."

The huge flat-screen TV flashed to life on the opposite wall. Sadie saw the newscaster finish the story of a local murder in Billings, then look straight into the camera before beginning the news item Richard Caldwell wanted her to hear.

"There is increasing concern in the Aspendale Valley east of Billings as ranchers and landowners report seeing wild horses. The fact that it is a fairly large group is reason for concern. Stories of an enormous black stallion are circulating."

The picture changed to a weather-beaten old rancher wearing a sweat-stained John Deere bill cap. He was in desperate need of a shave and a toothbrush.

"Yes, sir! They're runnin'! I seen 'em. Big black devil's the leader. They're dangerous to other horses. Keep yer's corralled or in the barn."

They interviewed another rancher, and then the camera returned to the spokesperson.

"The Amish buggy accident may have been caused by this band of horses running loose. In the meantime, Harold Ardwin of Hill Country is offering a $20,000 reward to the person who can find his missing herd of blue-blooded horses. Could there be a connection between these horse stories? Local ranchers say it's highly unlikely."

There was music, the picture changed to a map of the weather forecast, and Richard Caldwell pressed the button of the remote control device.

He turned to look down at her.

"What do you think?"

Sadie shook her head, her eyes wide.

"Do you think there was a herd of wild horses that night—the night the buggy went down over the ridge?"

Without hesitation, she said, "Yes, I do. As time goes on, I remember bits of . . . well, more. Captain was scared. He was running scared. . . He. . ."

"Who's Captain?"

"Our ... Ezra's horse—the horse that was hitched to the buggy. His ears were flicking back and forth, his head was up, his pace much too fast."

"Did you see the wild horses?" Richard Caldwell asked intently.

"Yes, I did. Well, at first I felt them. Do you know what I mean? I knew some animal or some person, just something, I guess, was running behind us."

She stopped.

"I'm not wording that very well, am I?"

"That's fine."

"A horse hitched to a buggy does not normally run uphill at breakneck speed, but Captain was doing exactly that."

She shuddered, remembering, then continued.

"He was there, beside us. He was."

"Who was?" Richard Caldwell sank back against his desk, crossed his arms over his chest, and watched her from beneath his shaggy eyebrows.

"The big, black one. The one the..."

She pointed to the television on the wall.

"You're sure about that?"

Sadie nodded.

The door opened quietly and Barbara Caldwell entered, still clutching her white robe against her body. Richard Caldwell instantly moved to go to her, putting his big hands on her shoulders. His voice lowered as he asked her how she felt, and she looked up into his face with an expression Sadie had never seen before.

What had happened between these two? It was amazing.

"I'm feeling much better. Dorothy fixed a cup of gingerroot tea for me and some dry toast."

He smiled down at her, and she held his gaze, returning his smile. They didn't notice Sadie at all, these two middle-aged people suddenly so happy in each other's presence.

Richard Caldwell turned, keeping his arm around his wife's shoulders.

"We were discussing what happened the night of Sadie's accident. On the news last evening, they talked about the band of wild horses. More and more ranchers are seeing them."

Barbara nodded, listening intently, watching Richard Caldwell's face.

Sadie got up, picked up the dust cloth, and was ready to finish her work when Richard Caldwell told her to sit down again.

Sadie sat.

"Your horse—the one you had to put down. Do you think there's a possibility of him becoming frightened by this same band of horses? Is your pasture very big? Is it isolated?" Richard Caldwell was very serious, his voice only a little less than booming.

What? Oh, it couldn't be. Poor Nevaeh. Was he terrified by that huge, black stallion? Was that why he tried to leap the fence? Had he felt threatened?

It was too much for Sadie to comprehend. Pity for her beloved horse welled up inside her until it became an object so painful, she felt physically sick.

What had that poor horse encountered in his life? First alone, sick, and starving. How had that all come about? Then his life ended much too soon by some foolhardy act of his own?

All these thoughts swirled in Sadie's mind until she

remembered that Richard Caldwell was waiting for an answer.

"Uh, yes. Yes, our pasture is at least 20, maybe 30, acres. And, yes, it is very isolated. The lower part anyway."

Richard Caldwell nodded.

"But," Sadie continued, "The biggest mystery about Nevaeh's death is why he was in that snowy pasture to begin with. Who left him out? Or how did he get out of his stall? We had visitors that day—on Christmas Day—and my uncles put their horses in Nevaeh's stall without knowing he belonged there. Dat...I mean, my father never lets him out in winter."

She stopped, wringing her hands on the gray fabric of her dress. Richard Caldwell held up his hand and said he didn't mean to upset her. She assured him she was fine. It was just hard sometimes to accept the fact that Nevaeh had to die in such a mysterious manner.

As she went about her work, Sadie kept thinking of a terrified Nevaeh all alone in the snow, and it was more than her heart could stand. She had to put that thought behind her and focus on other things, but that just led her into deeper, murkier water where she floundered helplessly.

She forgot the Tilex bathroom cleaner, lost the furniture polish, and couldn't find the crevice attachment for the sweeper. She was tired, her leg hurt, and it was high time to go to the kitchen and chop vegetables for Dorothy.

Then there was Mark.

If she really wanted to get off track and get all mixed up mentally, emotionally, and in her heart, or whichever term was used to describe feeling in your heart... See? She couldn't even think straight.

She was happy about one thing. He had held her in his arms. Twice. Well, the time at the mall had been a very necessary thing, of course. But would he really have had to carry her that short distance? It brought the color to her cheeks to think how his wool coat felt against her face. Mam would have a fit. Well, what Mam didn't know didn't hurt her.

Oh, my! Now she was a real rebel.

Could it be God's will for her life to love someone as good-looking as Mark? Could good looks—no, not just good looks—could downright the most handsome man she had ever seen fall into the same category as God's will?

If it was as depressing as Mam put it, every beautiful girl would be paired off with some homely little person. This was God's will, and the only form of true love, according to Mam. But that little homely man who got the good-looking wife didn't have to give up his own will at all. How could you figure that one out?

Truthfully, more than anything else, Sadie wanted God's guidance in finding the companion he wanted her to have. Ezra would have been the perfect one, according to Mam and Dat. But wasn't she always taught to believe death, too, was the will of our Lord? He giveth and he taketh away, and that was that. So, according to God's will, Ezra wasn't meant to be her husband.

Mark was so handsome, but he was hard to explain. His past, for one thing.

Sadie stopped, sniffed, held the bottle in her hand up to her face, and was horrified to discover she was dusting with the bathroom cleaner! Quickly, she hurried to the bathroom, procured a clean cloth, and washed the top of the dresser she was supposed to have been dusting with Pledge. Her heart pounding, she checked to see the results.

Whew! Looked all right. Hurriedly she sprayed a liberal amount of furniture polish onto the dresser and rubbed furiously with the cloth.

This had to stop.

Perhaps her brain had been injured in the accident and she couldn't think normally. No. More than likely she was falling in love, if there was such a thing.

Dusting finished, she hurried back to the kitchen, where a cloud of steam enveloped her. Dorothy was in a fine tizzy.

"Now what do y' know? Here comes Miss High-and-Mighty, telling me she's having her family tonight for a 'pahty.'"

She straightened, blinked her eyes, and fluttered her fingers beside them to accentuate the way Barbara Caldwell talked.

"Tonight!"

"What time?"

"Seven."

"Oh, well, that's plenty of time. What does she want to serve?"

"Pasta!" Dorothy fairly spat the word.

Sadie hid a smile. How well she knew the disdain Dorothy held for any food that was not plain, home-cooked, and old-fashioned.

Dorothy flopped a tea towel in the direction of the steam coming from the just-opened commercial dishwasher. Sadie went to the wall and flipped a switch. The great ceiling fans were activated, pulling up the steam and clearing the air as Dorothy hustled about, fussing and complaining as she fried ground beef.

"Never saw a woman put on so many airs. Now you know her family ain't that highfalutin. Pasta! Likely them kids don't even know what that olive oil coated stuff is. Fresh green peppers. That means Jim has to drive his truck to town, and fuel ain't cheap. I'll tell you what, it's goin' on my paper when I hand in my hours. I ain't payin' the gas outta my own pocket to get her green peppers for that smelly, slippery pasta dish. No way!"

She gave the ground beef a final stir, banged the wooden spoon on the edge of the frying pan, and slid the whole panful of sizzling meat into the large container of vegetable soup.

Sadie held her breath, hoping none of it would fall on Dorothy's dress front. She was so short and her arms were so heavy, it looked as if the pan was actually higher than her head.

"You better get started, Sadie," she snapped.

It was bad. When Dorothy talked to her in that tone of voice, Sadie knew she'd better buckle down, keep her head lowered, and work swiftly.

She had just reached for the great wooden cutting board when the door burst open so hard, it banged against the counter top. Jim came barging through, a hand going to his hat, clumping it down harder on his head as he sat down.

"Dorothy!"

"James Sevarr, you slow down this instant! If you don't pop a blood vessel in your head, I'll be surprised. What in the world is up with you?"

"I can't slow down now. You know them wild horses?" He reached up and grabbed his hat off his head, his head white in comparison to the rest of his face.

"Them horses, mind you! Hey, Sadie! You know the bend in the road where that horse of yours come charging across and fell that time?"

Sadie hurried over to the table, her hands gripping the edge. She felt the color drain from her face.

"Yes?"

"I was drivin' down through—almost exactly the same place—and here they come! They was scared, every last one. Skinny lookin' bunch. Long hair on 'em. There's definitely a big, black one in the lead. Looks wilder than a bunch of mustangs. I ain't never seen nothing like it in all my days."

He clasped his hat back on his head, shook his hands free of his gloves, and walked over to the stove to warm them, sniffing the pot of vegetable soup.

Dorothy rested her fists on her hips, her feet encased firmly in the shoes she bought at Dollar General in town.

"Jim, first off, decide if you're gonna wear that hat or if you're gonna take it off. Same thing with the gloves. And get away from my vegetable soup this instant. Yer breathin' down into it."

He brushed her off like a fly.

"And, Sadie, I'm havin' a meetin' with the men at the lunch table. We're getting' together with the fire company an' somethin's gonna be done. We're gonna round 'em up. At least go after 'em. They're here, ain't no doubt about it, an' they've racked up enough of mischief, 'n I mean it. You know that feller down by Hollingworth? Somethin' ripped into his fence—barb wire strung out all over the place. It's them horses."

Sadie was breathless with excitement.

"Oh, Jim! I wish I could go!"

"You can!"

Sadie laughed, her cheeks flushing.

"If I had Nevaeh, I would."

"Jim Sevarr, don't you take this here young girl out gallivantin' after some wild horses. Don't even think about it!"

The soup was bubbling over and a whole pile of vegetables needed to be chopped, but Sadie didn't even notice.

Oh, to have Nevaeh, Sadie thought. She knew her mother would never let her go with the men, but to ride Nevaeh like that was all she had dreamed about for weeks. Nevaeh had been like Paris—except in color. But now she would never know how beautiful Nevaeh could become—especially in the summer when he lost all his winter coat, leaving his soft, silky new coat shining in the spring sunshine.

The part of his death that was hardest to bear was the thought of all the rides they could never have. They would have traveled for miles and miles, enjoying the beauty of the Montana landscape which was breathtaking in the spring.

And now he was gone. The truck had bounced back through the snow, and they had winched his large, dead body onto it while the vultures circled overhead in the winter sunshine. Now everything seemed gray and dead and sad, even the sun.

She had ridden along with Dat. He hadn't wanted her to, but she did. She wanted to make sure that Nevaeh's leg really was broken as badly as they said. It was, and that gave her a measure of peace. Nothing is quite as final as a grotesquely bent limb on an animal as awesome-looking as Nevaeh. But it was severely broken, no matter if she wanted to see it or not, and he never could have lived a normal life with it.

They had looked for tracks, but the brush was too thick and the cows had trampled everything.

So there was no use thinking about riding with Jim and the men. Nevaeh was gone.

Chapter 17

THE MEN MADE THEIR PLANS AND RODE OUT, BUT they did not find a single horse. It was as if the horses were phantoms, dark winds, specters in the night. Maybe they were contrived only by people's imaginations.

"A *schpence*," Dat said.

"What's a *schpence*?" Reuben asked, looking up at his father as he lay on the rug in front of the wood stove. He was on his back, one leg propped on an upended knee, balancing a book precariously on top.

"A ghost," Dat replied.

Reuben grunted and returned to his book.

Sadie was curled up on the recliner, a warm throw over her shoulders. She still tired easily, and home was a welcome haven when she returned from the ranch.

Always the dutiful one, Rebekah was finishing the supper dishes. Leah was in the phone shanty, and Anna was doing the crossword puzzle in the *Daily Times*.

The clock on the wall ticked loudly, the pendulum swinging back and forth. A log fell in the wood stove, the propane gas lamp hissed comfortably, and Sadie's eyelids dropped as she felt herself falling into that state of bliss just before sleep overtook her.

She was rudely awakened by a clattering sound. The front door banged open, and she heard a resounding, "Sadie!"

Sadie tossed the cotton throw, sat up, and tried to remember where she was.

"There's a sledding party at Dan Detweilers! Want to go?"

Sadie groaned inwardly.

Hard as it was to admit to herself, she was no longer 16, and Sadie knew it was true, especially in moments like these. She no longer got excited by the same things as she did at 16—that time in your life when sledding parties, suppers, singings, and every event where a group of the youth had gathered, was a great deal.

Now at 20, she seriously had to weigh her options—the warm, cozy living room with the crackling fire versus the cold, snowy hillside where the wind penetrated your back no matter how many coats and sweaters you wore. There was always a bonfire, but that thoroughly roasted your face and your back was still cold.

Her hesitation brought a snort from Leah.

"What a spinster! You act like you're not even thrilled to hear about it!"

"I'm tired, Leah."

"Come on. This will likely be the last one of the season."

"How are you going?"

Leah glanced at Dat.

"Our horse and buggy?"

Dat frowned, then shook his head.

"Battery's dead."

"Our buggy battery is always dead. You never put it on the charger."

"I don't like you girls out on the dark roads with the horses. It's not safe."

Leah sputtered, and Sadie knew she was holding back a quick retort. She managed to ask Dat quite civilly if he had money for a driver since they weren't allowed to have the team.

Dat shifted his weight, searched his pockets for his wallet, and mumbled something about money melting away with a houseful of teenage daughters.

Leah took the money he handed over, thanked him, and said sweetly, "You know you could keep this if you let us have Charlie and the buggy."

"It might cost me a whole lot more than that if you had an accident."

It was Dat's favorite comeback, and Sadie giggled as Leah dashed upstairs, taking the steps two at a time.

Should she go? The only reason she would was for Leah's and Rebekah's sakes. It would be entirely different if she had any hope that Mark Peight would be there, but she had not seen or heard anything from him since that Christmas night. She had thoroughly messed up whatever friendship they might have had at one time. But what had she done? She didn't know. She guessed Mark was like that. He was like that band of wild horses—you could never quite figure him out.

Slowly, Sadie rose. She looked around and asked where Mam was. Dat looked up with pain, shame, indignation. What was it? It flickered in his eyes before he told Sadie Mam had gone to bed. She wasn't feeling well.

Mam had taken to her bed quite frequently of late, but it seemed as if she could do nothing else but sit on the recliner or lie on the sofa if she was awake. Her condition was deteriorating before their eyes, little by little. The girls were learning to live with it as best they could. Mam kept up the appearance of normalcy—going to church every two weeks and doing whatever duty was asked of her, but the girls knew Mam was suffering.

Sadie pushed thoughts of Mam from her mind. Maybe she should go sledding and clear her mind.

That Leah. Dashing up the stairs with the money clutched in her hand, she hadn't even bothered calling a driver.

When the driver finally pulled up to the door, the girls were eagerly waiting—except for Sadie, who was stifling huge yawns, trying to stay awake for the evening.

✣ ✪ ✣

Dan Detweiler's homestead was filled with buggies in the driveway and around the outbuildings. Boys milled about, putting their steaming horses in the barn.

The air was crisp and cold, but heavy. Every noise seemed magnified by the atmosphere which always seemed to amplify sound just before snow or rain. The stars hung low, twinkling as sharp and bright as ever, but Sadie figured storm clouds would likely cover them by morning.

The girls' breaths came in quick gasps as they climbed to the top of the long, sloping hill on the ridge in back of Dan's barn. There was nowhere else in the Amish settlement more suited for sledding.

You can't really call this a pasture, Sadie thought. It's too big. This whole place is more like Richard Caldwell's ranch than our home.

Aidan and Johnny were riding horses below them, pulling a tractor inner tube on a long rope attached to the saddle horn. The only bad thing about a ride in the tube was the snow kicked into your face by the flying hooves of the horse. You had to keep your head lowered or your eyes, nose, and mouth were soon packed with snow.

In spite of herself, Sadie grew more and more excited. She had had some thrilling rides on an inner tube in the snow before, so perhaps if the boys asked the girls, she would try it again.

Leah and Rebekah were already filling a toboggan with shrieking girls. A huge bonfire roaring at the bottom of the slope clearly showed the girls which way to steer the giant sled.

Of course they'd steer close enough to the boys to have their yells of alarm noticed, Sadie thought wryly.

Then she felt very old and very wise and suddenly wished she wasn't there. Her feet were already tingling with the cold, she was sleepy, the wind was definitely picking up, and she knew if she wanted to stay warm, she'd either have to start sledding or go sit by the fire. Neither option sounded overly appealing.

Her best friend, Lydiann, was already flying down the hill, shrieking in a high-pitched tone, which irritated Sadie.

Johnny will see you without that war whoop, she thought, then felt bad. Maybe she actually was turning into a "sour old singleton," as Rebekah put it.

Well, she had reason to be sour. Her leg ached as it did most every day and especially before a storm. She did her best to hide the discomfort from everyone in her family. She had to work. They needed the money to help with living expenses and to make payments on the large hospital bill.

Sadie shrugged, looked around her, and started downhill, dragging her feet to keep from sliding uncontrollably.

The group of girls on the toboggan was starting back up the hill, their noise punctuated by laughter and frequent looks in the direction of the boys who were by the bonfire. They were changing riders of the horses, both with inner tubes attached.

Another horse and rider came from the opposite direction. The horse was large, as was the rider, but Sadie could not distinguish the color of the horse or recognize the rider.

Cautiously, Sadie made her way down the slick slope. She heard someone call her name and turned to find Lydiann slipping haphazardly toward her.

"You need me to help you get down, Sadie?" she yelled panting.

Her hair was a mess, her scarf hanging completely off her head in a snowy loop about her neck. Sadie shivered as she thought of the trapped snow melting down Lydiann's back.

Sadie waved her hand in dismissal and said, "I'm all right."

"You sure?"

"Yes."

Without further ado, Lydiann charged back up the hill, her arms waving as she struggled to keep her balance.

How old is she? Three? Sadie muttered to herself.

Wasn't that just how life was? If you were tired and grouchy, people that were overly enthused and much too happy about everything only made you grouchier.

Especially Lydiann. If she wasn't so excited about the prospect of Johnny Schlabach talking to her, maybe she could calm down and act normal.

When she reached the bonfire, Sadie plopped down on a bale of straw and held her hands out toward its warmth. She felt someone standing close by, and she turned to find tall, quiet Mark Peight beside her.

She blinked, then bent her head. A spray of sparks erupted from the largest log falling inward, fanning the flames higher.

"Hello, Sadie."

Oh, his voice! The way he said her name with the drawn out "e." Her knees felt weak, but she managed a polite, soft-spoken, "Hello, Mark."

She still didn't look at him. He asked if there was room on the bale of straw and she said there was. The whole bale filled with him when he sat down. Her heart hammered against the many layers of clothes she wore. He turned his head.

"How are you?"

She gazed steadily into the fire, then nodded her head. He said nothing.

Then, "So, does that up and down movement mean, yes or you're okay or what?"

Sadie smiled.

"It means I'm okay."

"Back to work?"

She nodded again.

"Can I... May I talk to you?"

Sadie shifted away from him.

"You are talking to me, so why would you ask?"

"Can I talk to you alone, I mean? Away from all of this?"

"What for?"

"Just...ask you some questions."

"Everybody will see us walk away. Then they'll talk."

"Do you care?"

"Not really."

He stood up, waiting.

She didn't want to go with him. There would only be more disappointment. He would just tell her he was going back east or wherever it was he came from. She had no reason to hope he wanted anything more than to explain his sudden departure and tell her good-bye.

"You need help?"

"Let's go back to the farm. We can talk on the way, and then you can leave me at the house. I'll wait there until the girls are ready to leave. My leg is bothering me this evening," she said curtly.

"All right. Do you want up on Chester since your leg is hurting?" he asked politely.

"Chester?"

"My horse."

It would be nice, she considered. She was wearing fleece-lined pants beneath her skirt so modesty would not be a problem. Yes, she would ride. It had been so long since she had been up on Nevaeh.

"Okay."

He walked off, said a few words to some of the boys who were taking turns riding and flying along on the inner tube, then grabbed Chester's reins and brought him back to Sadie.

Chester was a huge boy—built solidly and in top shape. His mane and tail glistened in the light of the fire, and his ears pricked forward intelligently as he approached her. Sadie watched his soft, brown eyes and the way he lowered his head. She forgot Mark, the youth's calls, the bonfire—everything—as her hands went out to cradle the soft, velvety nose.

"Hi there, big boy," she whispered.

Chester nuzzled his mouth into her mittened hands, and she stroked the side of his head over and over, murmuring softly as she did so. She told him how big and beautiful he was in a horse language all her own. The lengthy absence of Nevaeh brought a lump to her throat, and she lowered her head so Mark would not see the emotion she was feeling.

Mark stood aside, watching Sadie. He knew she missed her horse, so he stood quietly, letting her have a few moments with Chester. He listened to every whisper, marveling at her way with a horse. It was uncanny, this sincere rapport she had with these huge creatures. There was no fear, no hesitation, just this loving trust, this connection she had so naturally with each and every horse.

Finally, Mark said, "He likes you."

"He does!"

Sadie looked up at him, completely transformed. She was laughing happily, her somber mood dispelled.

"You ready to get in the saddle?"

"I can get up by myself."

"I know."

He stood back, watching as Sadie gathered up the reins and slid her gloved hand along Chester's neck beneath the mane, talking as she did so. Chester acted as meek as a lamb, which was not his usual way. He was always sidestepping and prancing and doing everything to make Mark's leap into the saddle challenging.

Sadie stopped.

"Oh," she said in a small voice.

Mark stepped forward, listening.

"I forgot. My foot probably won't hold me. It's the one I would put in the stirrup."

"Well…" Mark began.

"I'll walk him," she said quickly, gathering the reins and starting off at a brisk pace.

There was nothing for Mark to do but follow.

They walked through the snow in silence except for the soft, swishing sound of snow crunching beneath their feet. The snow was silver in the starlight, though the stars were slowly being blotted out, as if an eraser was sweeping across the night sky. The air was still heavy with the approaching storm so every night sound was clear. The tree line along the ridge was almost black, the tops of the trees swaying softly as if they sighed at night when the world rested. The young people's noise slowly faded as they walked, the light of the fire gone.

"Sadie," Mark said, then reached for her arm to stop her.

She stopped, and Chester came to a halt behind her, his ears pricked forward.

"I said I wanted to talk to you," he began in his low vice, the sound she loved.

"I want to apologize about Christmas evening. I'm sorry."

"It's okay," Sadie began, but he lifted a hand.

"No, it's not okay. I need to be a man and tell you about my life. I would like to come see you next Saturday evening, if I may. We'll not plan anything. I just need to have a quiet place to tell you things about me, and then you can decide whether it's worth it for you to try … well, to get to know me better. After you hear the truth, you may not want to. Then I'll go back to Pennsylvania."

"But…why would you go back home to Pennsylvania?"

"Because I don't want to live in Montana if I can't have you."

The music in her heart began then. It was as full and soaring as the music Barbara Caldwell listened to, taking her along to the heights of joy. It was an emotion that lifted her above the snow, the hills, the trees, and the cold. She could not speak, because if she did the music would stop. And she couldn't bear to part with that sound.

"Sadie…"

She blinked, lifted her head, faced him.

"Yes, Mark. We'll sit in the living room after my parents are in bed. I would be glad to hear what you…" She broke off, watching Chester.

His head went up, his ears forward and turned slightly toward the tree line. Mark stiffened, watching. An icy chill went up Sadie's spine, and she turned her eyes, straining. Chester stood stock still. Sadie's hand went to his neck.

"Mark?" Sadie whispered.

"Shhh."

She felt them before she saw them. The wind picked up, there was a sense of rushing, and the ground vibrated beneath her boots with a shuffling of snow.

"Mark!"

She stifled a scream as a line of dark shadows moved along the tree line. It was as if the trees were swaying along the ground in an up and down movement in a mixture of colors and shadows, and yet there was not one horse, or even a band of horses, in sight.

"Mark! Mark! It's them! It's… It's… They're in there!" she screamed in a hoarse, terrified cry.

"Get up! Now! Sadie, you have to listen to me. Let me put you up. Whoa, Chester! Good boy! Hang on!"

She was picked up firmly and dumped unceremoniously on the leather saddle. Chester was prancing frantically beneath her and she hung on, grateful for all the skills she remembered. In a flash, Mark was behind her, turning Chester, goading him back the way they had come.

Sadie leaned forward, the wind nipping her scarf, her hair. The air was frigid. She felt Mark's solid form behind her, felt his breath.

The line of horses was moving with them. They weren't visible except as undulating shadows among the trees. Chester was galloping steadily, his powerful strides covering the slopes easily. Sadie turned her head and screamed as she saw the dark forms emerging from the tree line. Mark saw them at the same moment and called to Chester.

"C'mon, boy! C'mon!"

Chester responded with a gathering of great, powerful leaps. Sadie's mind turned to the night with Ezra. She fought off the panic and fear from the accident.

The black leader called his terrible stallion challenge, a scream of territorial rights. It lent wings to Chester's feet, goading him across the snow. Speed was their only chance, and Mark urged his horse on.

The bonfire!

Brightly it blazed, like a beacon of rest, of safety. Sadie could see the two horses, the youth seated around the blazing light. Sadie felt Chester relax, loosen his gait. She saw the youth scatter, calling in alarm as they slid up to the fire.

Mark was down before Chester stopped, and he lifted Sadie off in a blink.

"Get the horses and stay by the fire!" Mark yelled in an awful voice.

The girls screamed, their hands going to their mouths, their eyes wide with fear. Aidan and Johnny grabbed the reigns of the horses, and they all huddled around the blazing fire. They watched in disbelief as the band of horses streamed past. Chester stood between the youth and the horses, his nostrils flaring as his sides heaved with exertion.

The great black leader shook his head, reared, and pawed the air as if to warn them. They were in plain sight, the firelight identifying the colors, the heads, whipping manes, streaming tails. The snow obscured the feet and legs, but as one body they galloped in perfect rhythm.

Sadie watched in wonder.

The horses were not any old, scraggly, wild mustangs. They were not the usual stock that were a nuisance to all the ranchers in the area. These horses were different. Sadie had caught the wild-eyed look on a small mare. She was afraid. These horses were running scared and they were very thin.

Something was not right.

And, oh, that black stallion! His cry! She would always remember the sound in her worst dreams and nightmares of that night.

After the last hoof beat faded, a general babble of voices broke out. The boys began talking at once. The girls came running to Sadie, asking a dozen questions. She sank weakly onto a bale of straw.

"Now I'm telling you, this is the real thing! No one can even pretend these wild horses aren't around!" Marvin Keim was yelling.

"Good thing we had this fire!"

"I mean, they were running!"

"Did you see that big, black one?"

A somber mood enveloped them. They knew they were extremely fortunate to have been by the blazing fire, all of them together. The sledding was over. No one felt like straying very far from the bonfire.

Mark reached out to Chester and said they'd better stay as a group and all return to the Detweiler farm together.

The walk back was quiet, the girls casting fearful glances in the direction of the trees.

Mark walked beside Sadie and held her gloved hand in his. She was grateful and let her hand rest inside his strong one.

"I'll see you next Saturday evening."

"Oh, yes," she breathed happily. "But try to get to my house fairly late."

"Why?"

"Well, Reuben is... He'll never go to bed if he knows you'll be there. He'll lie flat on the floor upstairs with his ear pressed against the floor and listen to every word we say."

Mark laughed his deep rolling laugh that Sadie loved to hear. It would be a very long time until Saturday evening.

Chapter 18

After the sledding party, the Amish community in Montana buzzed with the news of the wild horses. The women sat in their phone shanties and had long conversations about what had actually happened that evening. Mugs of coffee at the men's elbows turned cold as they talked, visualized, and tried to come up with a feasible plan.

Before church, when the men stood in the forebay of Jesse Troyer's barn, the topic was wild horses. And after services, around the long dinner table spread with traditional church food—pie, homemade bread, jam, pickles, red beets, homemade deer bologna, and slices of cheese, all washed down with cups of steaming coffee—the talk was wild horses.

Of course it was the Lord's day, and the sermon was not about wild horses, but instead a good, solid lecture on forgiveness and the wonders of allowing ourselves to be freed from any grudges or ill feeling toward others. Still, no one could keep their minds from the events of the youth bonfire.

Mothers shook their heads, children listened wide-eyed. It was not safe to be on the road after dark, especially alone with a horse and buggy.

There was an undercurrent of gossip about that Jacob Miller's Sadie as well. That girl had better slow down. What was she doing riding a horse with that stranger from Pennsylvania? Someone told Katie Schwartz that he had been raised Amish but that his parents were English. They clucked their tongues and shook their heads, saying nothing good could come of it, that Jacob and Annie better rein in their Sadie. She almost died in that accident. Her Ezra was gone, bless his soul, and here she was gallivanting about with this other man already.

That's what happens when someone is too pretty for her own good. Look at Aunt Lisbet. She ran off with the butcher from Clarksville, and if she hadn't been so pretty, it likely never would have happened. But then, her mother hadn't been very stable either so...

Mary Miller shrugged her shoulders and said Jacob Miller didn't look like himself these days. Someone mentioned Annie wasn't doing so well, but she looked all right to her.

They watched Annie as she brought more pies to the table, lowered them, then stooped to talk to little Clara Amstutz, patting her head and smiling so nicely. Nothing much wrong with her.

Sadie stood against the counter in the *kessle-haus* and listened halfheartedly as Lydiann and Leah talked endlessly about the wild horses. She was hungry, tired of the restless chatter, and wished those fussy older women would hurry up and eat so they could have their turn.

She skipped breakfast that morning, having overslept. She had tried to pull off looking tired and grouchy, although inside she was anything but that. She had lain awake, giddy with the thought of Mark Peight coming to see her. But her giddiness turned to concern when she thought of all the things that could go wrong between them.

What did he want to tell her? Was it something so terrible that there was no possible way they could begin dating, let alone get married?

She had slid out of bed, wrapped her warm robe around her, then stood at the window looking out over the snowy landscape with the stars scattered all over the night sky and prayed.

She always prayed at her window, standing. She knew the proper way was to kneel beside her bed and clasp her hands, but somehow she couldn't find God in the way she could when she stood by her window and saw the night sky, the stars, the whole wide world. She imagined God was just beyond those twinkling little lights, and he could see her from up there where he was. And so she prayed.

She asked God to direct her heart and to help her remain a sacrifice so she could discern his will for her life. She already knew without a doubt that she wanted Mark Peight for her husband someday. She wanted to be with him, listen to him talk, watch his deep, brown eyes crinkle at the corners when he laughed. She had been amazed at the depth of her own emotions the first time they met, but she had tried to hold him at a distance. She had felt good when she was in his presence. He had been so kind, so sincere, and that was something.

She would have married Ezra. She had planned on dating him. But God took him away. There was still a special part of her heart that was Ezra's, but there was another part—a bigger part—that belonged to Mark.

She ended her prayer.

Thank you, God, for Mark.

She had let the curtains fall, but caught them again when she saw a dark form moving slowly down the driveway. Surely it wasn't Mam on a frigid night like this?

The dark form continued forward, the head bent. Yes, it was Mam. Should she get dressed and go to her?

Sadie's heart beat rapidly as she struggled to suppress her fear of the unknown, wondering why Mam would roam the roads alone at night. Was she so troubled in her spirit that the freedom of the outdoors soothed her?

Sadie had remained by the window, watching until her mother returned, still plodding quietly, head still bent.

It was a pitiful sight. Love for her mother welled up in Sadie's heart like the fizz from a glass of soda. Dear Mam. She had always been the best Mam in the world. It was just now ... she was only a silent shadow. She went about doing mundane little tasks, but the bulk of the work fell on the girls' shoulders.

Sadie breathed a sigh of relief when the laundry room door creaked quietly, and she could be sure Mam had safely returned.

✡ ✡ ✡

At work on Monday morning, Sadie divulged her plans for Saturday evening. Dorothy's spirits soared.

"You got a honest-to-goodness date?" she yelled above the high, insistent whine of the hand-held mixer.

Sadie glanced at her happily. Dorothy clicked it off and tapped the beater against the bowl, streams of frothy egg running off.

"Well, do ya or don't cha?"

"Yes, I do. He's coming to our house," Sadie answered as she sliced oranges, popping a section into her mouth.

"Well, what are you gonna do? You don't have a television set to watch an' you can't go to the movies. So how are ya gonna entertain this young man?"

Sadie smiled.

"First, I have to think of some kind of brownies or bars or cookies to make. I have to have a snack, of course."

Dorothy's eyes lit up, her smile wide.

"I can sure help you out on that one!"

Dorothy turned to her eggs, poured them into a greased baking pan, and then got out the vicious looking chef's knife. She held it like a professor about to begin a lecture with his wooden pointer.

Sadie raised her eyebrows.

"We played Parcheesi!"

"What?"

"Parcheesi! It's the most fun game ya ever saw. I'll bring my game of Parcheesi, and you and yer feller can play. Aw, that's so sweet. Just like me and Jim. Now my Jim, he's different from other rough cowboys. He's a good man, my Jim. If he wasn't so stuck on riding those horses and working at this ranch, we'd have more money. But then, ya know, Sadie, he wouldn't be happy, an' what's money compared to being a purely contented soul? Huh? Tell me that. The whole world is moving faster and faster and faster tryin' to make more money, and it ain't bringin' nobody no happiness. Jes' look at my Jim settin' on the back of a horse, his chaw stuck in his cheek, and his old hat covering his bald head. Why he's happier 'n a coon in a fish pond. An' me? I like it right here in Richard Caldwell's kitchen cookin' up a storm."

She paused for breath, threw a handful of mushrooms

into the beaten eggs, and surveyed her breakfast casserole. Sadie looked over her shoulder.

"That's not very much food."

"This ain't for the cowhands. It's Barbara's. Richard Caldwell's taken to eatin' with her upstairs in her bedroom in the morning. He says she's feeling sickly. Well, it don't hurt that woman to lose a few pounds, let me tell you. You done with them oranges?"

Sadie nodded.

"You didn't tell me which recipe to make for Saturday night, yet."

"Give me time, give me time."

✿ ✡ ✿

After breakfast was over, Sadie and Dorothy sat down together at the great oak table with a stack of dog-eared, greasy cookbooks. Dorothy wet her thumb and began flipping pages.

"Okay, now. You gonna make these at home, or can I help you here?"

Sadie looked at Dorothy.

"Well, we're getting paid by the hour, so it wouldn't be very honest to bake something here and take it home. We'd be using their ingredients, and..."

Dorothy snorted.

"So what? Richard Caldwell don't care."

"I know, but..."

"You Amish is strange ducks. Now whoever heard of being so painfully honest, you can't even bake a brownie or two with a wealthy guy's ingredients? Huh? Never heard such a thing in my life."

"But I'd feel guilty. Should I ask him first?"

"Naw. He don't care."

Sadie decided it would be condescending, perhaps even a bit self-righteous, to insist that such a minor thing be done her way. After all, Dorothy was the boss in the kitchen.

"Okay, Dottie, if you say so."

A profound whack on her backside with the large rubber spatula was her answer.

"Now, don't you go Dottie'n me again! It's just plain disrespectful."

"Okay, Dottie, if you say so."

They had a hearty laugh together, the kind of laugh that binds your heart to another person with pure good humor and friendship, the kind that keeps a smile on your face for a long time afterwards.

They flipped through the cookie and brownie sections, finally settling on a chocolate bar swirled with cream cheese. Dorothy assured Sadie they were so moist and delicious that you couldn't eat just one.

"What else are you servin' this guy?"

"Oh, coffee likely. And something salty. I thought of making those ham and cheese thingys that you roll up in a tortilla."

Dorothy wrinkled her nose.

"You Easterners don't know how to make a tortilla."

They flipped pages, searching for more recipes, and the subject of the wild horses came up. Dorothy shook her head wisely.

"They ain't no mystery. If any of these highfalutin men had a lick o' common sense, they'd know this band o' horses ain't wild. It's them stolen ones. Poor babies. They's runnin' so scared, it ain't even funny. Imagine now, Sadie. They lived in a warm barn, blanketed, fed, exercised, brushed, among trainers and people that treated 'em like kings and queens, and suddenly they're exposed to the wild world, and they can hardly survive. I told Jim they ain't gettin' them horses until they build a corral and round 'em up with them new-fangled helicopters. You know what he said? 'Pshaw!' But I don't care what my Jim says, they won't get 'em."

Sadie nodded.

"If Nevaeh had lived, he'd be a grand horse by now. He was no ordinary horse."

Dorothy nodded in agreement. "That he wasn't, that he wasn't."

There was a knock on the kitchen door, and Sadie hurried to open it, wiping her hands on her clean, white apron.

Dat!

Sadie blinked in surprise.

"Why, Dat! What brings you here?"

Dat's face was pale, his eyes somber.

"You need to come home, Sadie. Your mother is missing."

"Missing? You mean, you don't know where she is?"

Dat shook his head, searching Sadie's face.

What was it in Dat's eyes? Humiliation, pride, fear, self-loathing, shame? It was all there. She knew this would be very hard for him if the Amish community found out.

"But…she…she can't have gone far. She walks a lot. She's likely close by."

Turning, she told Dorothy she had to leave, getting her coat and scarf off the hook as she did so. Dorothy waved her hand, and Sadie followed Dat out to the car. He had hired a driver, so he must have been very concerned.

The ride home seemed like 30 miles instead of the usual eight. Dat said very little, and Sadie's heart pounded with fear as she thought of all the things that could have happened to Mam. She was so fragile, that was the thing. Her mind, her nerves—whatever they were—were like a banner in a stiff breeze attached to a solid anchor, but with a frayed rope. As long as Dat would not admit she needed help, who could keep the rope from snapping?

"Oh, dear God, please stay with her," Sadie prayed. "Wherever she is, just stay with her."

When they arrived home, Dat gathered his three daughters around him at the kitchen table. Anna and Reuben were still in school, but Leah and Rebekah had been summoned from their cleaning jobs.

Sadie looked at her sisters, their eyes welling with tears.

"Sadie, you know Mam better than any of us. Where could she have gone? And why?" Rebekah asked shakily.

Sadie took a deep breath, squared her shoulders, and looked directly into Dat's eyes. His fell beneath her gaze.

"Well, first, we need to have a long-overdue, honest, all-out talk about our mother. She is not well. She is having issues related to her mind. In plain words, she is mentally ill. And, Dat, you will not admit that. And as long as you don't, Mam cannot get better."

Dat shook his head back and forth, vehemently.

"No, she's not."

"Then what's wrong with her?" Sadie spoke quickly, forcefully.

"Don't speak to your father that way."

Sadie was on her feet, then, her hands palm down on the table. She leaned forward, her eyes boring into his.

"Dat! If it means putting some sense into your head,

I'm going to disobey you. Mam is more sick than any of us realize. She's living in an agony of depression and fear. She hears voices at night and sees things that aren't really there. She's hoarding stupid little things like hand-kerchiefs and barrettes. She's not working. She's much worse than any of us are even allowed to think she is. And it's all your fault, Dat! Your dumb pride!"

Leah and Rebekah looked on, horrified. No one talked to their father that way. Not ever.

"Sadie!" Dat spoke in a terrible voice, rising from his chair.

Sadie remained standing.

"I'm sorry, Dat," she said, her heart pounding. "I don't want to speak to you in this manner, but you are not God. You cannot make Mam better. We have to let our pride go, Dat!"

At this, she broke down, sobs engulfing her, racking her body.

"Mam is so sick, Dat! Please allow her to go to the hospital for help. I think she'd go!"

Rebekah and Leah were crying. Dat stood over them, his face grim, his eyes blazing. His daughters bent their heads.

"She's not as bad as you say, Sadie."

"Yes, she is! I will not back down. You need to let go of what people will say. Mental illness is no shame. She can't help it."

Dat sagged into his chair, his eyes weary.

"Well, what will they do at the hospital?" he asked.

"Evaluate her. Talk to her. Get her on the right medi-cation. They'll explain it to her. To you. Please, Dat."

"If you don't give up, I'm afraid Mam will do harm to herself—if she hasn't already," Rebekah said firmly.

Dat's head came up. His eyes opened wide with fear. "No!"

"You're seeing in Mam what you want to see, Dat, and not what's actually there. She's a courageous woman, and she's doing her best to appear normal for your sake— she is—but she's so pitiful," Leah wailed.

Sadie could see fear grasp her father. His breath came in gasps, and he stood up.

"We need a plan to look for her now!" he ground out.

"We'll search our farm, first, the house, pasture, barn, the woods. Everywhere," Sadie said.

"But what if she's not here?" Dat asked.

A great wave of pity rose in Sadie. He knew. He knew it was true, the things they told him.

"Then we'll call the police."

"But...everyone will know."

"Exactly. And they'll help us look for her," Sadie said firmly.

They got into their coats, boots, and scarves, their faces pale, their hands shaking as they pulled on their gloves. They opened the door and stepped out into the brilliant sunshine. Somehow the sunlight was reassuring, as if God was providing plenty of light for them to find Mam. She couldn't have gone far, surely.

Dat searched the pasture, Leah went down the driveway calling Mam's name, Rebekah went to the buggy shed, and Sadie walked off to begin searching the barn.

Charlie, the driving horse, nickered softly when she opened the door. The barn cats came running to her, wanting to be fed. She looked behind every bale of hay and in Nevaeh's empty stall, calling Mam's name over and over. She climbed the stairs to the hayloft, searching it thoroughly.

Fear dried her mouth, made her breath come in gasps. Oh, Mam. We neglected you too long.

Remorse washed over her. They hadn't done enough soon enough. Where was she?

Sadie fought down the panic that threatened to engulf her, making her want to run and scream Mam's name. She had to remain calm, stay within reason. They would find her. Dat had probably found her already. He had to.

As the forenoon wore on and there was no sign of Mam, their fear and worry deepened. There was simply nowhere else to look, unless they walked the roads or called a driver to go looking for her. That was a bit uncommon and likely would not help at all.

"Before we call the police, we need to bring Anna and Reuben home from school. If they see policemen up here, they'll be beside themselves. Besides, they'll find out anyway," Sadie said.

The little parochial school was situated just below the Millers' driveway, nestled in a grove of pine and cedar trees, but in plain view of their house. The school was picturesque, covered in cedar shingles, stone laid carefully on the porch, two swinging doors and neat windows on either side, a split-rail fence surrounding it.

Rebekah offered to walk down and bring Anna and Reuben home. Dat took to wringing his hands, pacing, muttering to himself. Leah cried quietly.

Sadie stood on the porch not knowing what to do next. What did a person do when their mother was missing? She had prayed, was still praying.

Yet the sun shone on as brightly as ever, the snow sparkled, the branches waved in the midday breeze. The day went on as if all was as normal as ever. But a sense of unreality pervaded Sadie's senses. Suddenly it seemed as if this was not happening at all. Surely Mam would come walking out of the bedroom or up from the basement, bustling about like usual, her hair combed neatly, her white covering pinned to her graying hair, the pleats in her dress hanging just right the way they always did.

Mam, please, where are you? she cried, silently.

Rebekah came panting up the driveway, Anna and Reuben beside her, lunch buckets in tow. Anna was crying. Reuben was wide-eyed and grim, bravely battling his tears.

So she had told them.

They all went into the kitchen, trying to reason among themselves.

Now what?

Call the police?

Certainly.

Suddenly, Anna sat upright and, without a word, walked swiftly to her parent's bedroom. They heard the closet doors open, close quietly, then open again.

"Sadie, come here," she called.

Sadie looked questioningly at her sisters, then went to her parent's room. She found Anna standing, looking up at the top closet shelf.

"It's gone, Sadie!"

"What? What's gone?"

"Her suitcase. Their suitcase. The big one."

Sadie's heart sank as she joined Anna at the closet door.

"Oh, Anna. It is."

"Sadie, I heard her. I was working on my English at the kitchen table about a week ago, and she was puttering around the way she does and talking to herself. She kept saying over and over, *"Ya vell. Tzell home gay. Tzell."*

"Why didn't you tell us, Anna?"

"She often talks to herself and no one pays attention."

"Oh, I know. I know."

They hurried to the kitchen, telling the rest what Anna had said.

The news was Dat's undoing. He bent his head, shook it back and forth. No one spoke as Dat fought with his own thoughts. It seemed as if they could see his spirit breaking before them, a thin, glass vase shattering beneath the weight of a heavy object, ground to a thousand pieces, shattered with the knowledge of what he had always known. He had put his will before his wife's. He had loved his own life instead of giving it for her. He had not loved his wife as Christ loved the church.

He had wanted to move to Montana so badly. He had. And they had all honored his wishes as happily and contentedly as possible.

But was it right?

When he broke down in great, awful sobs, five pairs of arms encircled him, held him up. They were the arms of angels for Jacob Miller.

Chapter 19

It was an unusual thing, an Amish girl hugging her father. In an Amish home, love was an unspoken attitude, as common and as comfortable as the air you breathed or the clothes you wore. No one said "I love you" or hugged you, but there was no need. Home, church, school, it was all an atmosphere of safety. Because of this love and safety, everyone had a place and belonged. There was no need to find oneself. Your parents had already found you on the day you were born into the well-structured Amish heritage.

But seeing Dat's bent head and his heaving shoulders was more than any of them could bear, so surrounding him with their arms seemed the most natural thing in the world.

When they stepped back a bit self-consciously, Dat kept his head lowered. Digging into his worn, denim trouser pockets, he procured his wrinkled, red handkerchief, shook it, and blew his nose. Then he removed his glasses and wiped his eyes.

"Ach, my," he sighed.

The girls stood silently surrounding him, supporting him with their quiet presence. Reuben marched to the cupboard, swiping viciously at his eyes. The set of his shoulders said how shameful it was for a big guy like him to be crying. He opened the cupboard door, yanked at a glass, and went to the refrigerator to pour himself a glass of milk.

He sat down at the table, took a sip, then said angrily, "Well, I guess if Mam went so far as to take a suitcase, we better call the police."

Dat looked at Reuben, unseeing.

"Somebody better go out to the phone shanty and dial 911."

Did they actually have to?

Sadie took a deep breath to steady herself.

"Well?"

"If the police arrive, we all need to make sense. We have to tell the whole truth, Dat. She's mentally unstable and has been for…"

"Longer than any of you know," Dat groaned, holding his head in his hands.

Leah raised her eyebrows and looked at Rebekah.

"I…I persuaded her for much, much too long to carry on for her children's sake. I kept telling her there was nothing wrong—that it was all in her head. I told her to swallow all the pills she wanted, but to keep it from all of you, the church, and our community. No one needed to know."

He stopped, averted his eyes.

"This is my fault. She cried during the night. She cried a lot. She wanted to go back home to Ohio. I thought she'd get over it. It's worse in the wintertime."

Sadie was horrified.

"Dat! Why didn't you tell us? Why?"

He sighed. "Because I was afraid you would all want to return to Ohio with her."

"Well, we're here now," Sadie ground out. "I'm going to the phone."

She could never remember feeling such anger, such a gripping disgust that she actually felt like vomiting. What horrible pride controlled Dat? Why had Mam been so passive? What caused a person to slowly tilt outward and move toward the edge of reasoning? Was it all because, if it boiled right down to it, Mam refused to give up her own will and submit to Dat's will?

She yanked open the phone-shanty door, punched 911, and briskly told the dispatcher what she needed to know.

No sirens, please, she begged silently. The school children will go home and tell their parents there was a policeman at Jacob Millers' and tongues will wag. Well, it couldn't be helped. There was no time for her own foolish pride now.

The crunch of gravel heralded the policemen's arrival. Two of them stepped out of the unmarked vehicle. Sadie's heart beat loudly, and for a second she was glad it was a car that was not the usual kind the police drove with flashing blue lights and "Police" written across it in big letters.

The two men strode purposefully to the door, knocked, and stood aside politely when Dat opened it. They were kind but firm, writing on clipboards, searching the room with their eyes, speaking in short but professional tones.

The Millers answered truthfully. Dat spoke and the girls answered when they were asked. Reuben was white-faced, silent, frightened out of his wits. He slouched in his chair at the kitchen table, trying to appear brave, even nonchalant, but his huge blue eyes completely gave him away.

When Dat described Mam to the men, Anna stifled a sob, and Sadie's arms were instantly around her shoulders. She slid her face against Sadie, struggling to conceal her emotions.

The policemen's radios crackled, their badges and holsters gleamed. It all seemed like one big, awful dream that would come to a welcome halt the minute Sadie woke up.

One policeman went to the car while the remaining one told them he was alerting every radio station, television news channel, and airport.

"Why an airport?" Sadie blurted out. "She would never fly. We don't go... I mean, our beliefs forbid us to fly in an airplane. She wouldn't be in an airport. Perhaps a bus station? A train station? An Amish driver?"

"Amish driver? I thought you don't drive cars?" Mr. Connelly, the elder of the two, inquired.

"No, I mean, she would have called a person who provides transportation for us."

They made phone calls to every driver and neighbor on the list, but to absolutely no avail. Trucks and more troopers arrived, search parties sent to comb the entire region around the house and throughout the neighborhood.

Amish friends and relatives arrived, wide-eyed and in different stages of disbelief. Dat remained strong, his face a mixture of despair, agony, pride, shame, and finally, acceptance. There was nothing left to do as wailing sirens climbed the driveway, lights flashing, radios crackling messages.

Someone from the firehall set up a post inside the buggy shed with thermoses of hot coffee and sandwiches. Neighbors brought kettles of chili and vegetable soup, homemade rolls, smoked deer bologna, pies, and cookies. They comforted Dat, hugged the girls, whispered endearments.

Then darkness fell. With the darkness came a fresh despair, a sense of loss felt so deeply that Sadie thought she could not hold up against its crushing force. She cried with Anna. She went into the bathroom with Leah and sat on the edge of the bathtub and cried some more.

"Why? Why on earth did Dat let her go like this? How long has she been sick and we didn't know?"

Leah peered into the mirror and fixed a few stray blonde hairs. She shook her head in disgust at her swollen, red eyes.

"Well, I know one thing. Remember last year when we had church at our house? Sadie, I mean it, I honestly don't think we would have gotten ready without you. Mam got nothing accomplished all day. She just puttered around the way she does, you know.

Sadie sighed.

"There were lots of signs—if only we wouldn't have been so dense."

They sat for a few moments, Leah on the floor, Sadie on the edge of the bathtub.

"Do you think she became mentally ill from wanting to go back home?"

"Home?" Sadie's head jerked up in an angry motion. "Where is home?"

"For me, here. In Montana," Leah said flatly.

"Is it home to you?" Sadie asked.

"Of course."

Sadie said nothing.

There was a knock on the door. Richard Caldwell and his wife, Barbara, had come and wanted to speak to her. Surprised, Sadie went to the living room.

Sadie's boss and his wife sat uncomfortably, glancing at the softly hissing propane lamp. In spite of herself, Sadie hid a smile, knowing they had never set foot in an Amish home.

Despite their uneasiness, their concern was genuine, and their hugs bolstered Sadie's courage. Once again she was amazed at the change in Barbara, the tenderness in Richard Caldwell, and she was grateful.

"They'll find her, Sadie," Richard Caldwell boomed.

And then Dorothy came bustling into the living room, the soles of her inexpensive Dollar General shoes squeaking on the highly varnished hardwood, oak floor.

"Oh, my, oh, my!" she kept saying over and over as she gathered Sadie into her heavy arms. "You never let on! You never let on!" she kept saying.

Sadie knew that never again in their household would they take for granted the wonders of human sympathy. It was the genuine caring—that giving of oneself—that brought so much warmth to Sadie's heart. It was like an Olympic runner carrying the flaming torch, relaying hope from one person to the next.

How could one be crushed beneath despair when so many held them up? Rough cowhands, wealthy ranchers, plain Amish people, men of the law—they were all there, bound by the soft, gentle cord of caring. White-covered heads bobbed in conversation with permed and dyed heads, earrings twinkling beneath them, as tears flowed together.

Mam couldn't have gone far. She'd be okay.

Was there anything they could do?

Poor lady, she must have been in agony.

Sadie could almost see her father aging before her eyes. It was hard to look at him. Remorse is a terrible thing, she had read once. It's the hopelessness of wishing that you had not done things in the past, or that you could undo something you knew you couldn't.

That's where Jesus came in, Sadie thought. He died for pitiful creatures like us, people who make mistakes because of their human pride and wrongdoings.

Dear God, just stay with Dat. He didn't do it on purpose. He thought he was doing the right thing.

And then Mark came. Mark Peight. Would she ever tire of just thinking his name?

He was in the kitchen, taller than everyone else except Richard Caldwell. He was talking to Leroy Miller who was moving his hands to accompany his fiery red curls that flew about his head with every movement. His hair was plentiful, and it looked even more so the way he shook his head when he became agitated. His beard was as red as his curls, and it wagged up and down at an alarming rate.

Sadie wished they would all go home now and leave her with Mark. She knew that was quite selfish, but she wished it anyway. Finally she was able to catch his eye and almost swooned when he conveyed all his feelings in his direct look.

"Sadie, how are you?"

She turned into the waiting arms of Nancy Grayson, the taxi driver, as Leroy Miller broke into another passionate tirade, this time to Mark.

The clock's hands turned to ten o'clock, and still the Miller house was full of people who came to wish them well. Dat was becoming weary, his eyes drooping behind his glasses the way they did at the end of a long day. Reuben was curled up on the recliner covered with a blanket, his hands tucked beneath his cheek. He looked so young and so vulnerable, his usual tufts of hair on the back of his head sticking straight out, the way they always did when he hadn't brushed his hair completely.

Mark moved across the kitchen to stand by Sadie's side, being careful to keep an appropriate distance between them.

"Sadie, tell me what happened," he said quietly.

Tears immediately sprang to her eyes. It was the soft urging in his voice that showed how much he cared. She raised her eyes to his, then looked down as she saw Leroy Miller's flinty eyes watching their every move.

"Can you come upstairs with me?" she asked.

"You go first; I'll sneak away later," he said quietly.

Sadie went over to Reuben and took him upstairs to his bedroom, waiting outside his door until he had his pajamas on. Reuben would never change clothes in his sister's presence, properly locking the bathroom or bedroom door when any change of clothes or showering was necessary.

After the door was unlocked, she caught his shoulders and drew him against her. He did not pull back but laid his head against her shoulder as she held him, rocking him the way she did when he was two years old.

His hair smelled of shampoo and hay and little boy sweat and his hat. She could feel his thin shoulders shaking beneath his t-shirt as his breath caught in suppressed little sobs.

"Reuben. Listen. They'll find Mam. In this day and age, people don't disappear the way they used to. They have computers and video cameras and stuff we can't even imagine to track every traveler that moves through train or bus stations."

"But what if she's lying outside somewhere and she's cold?" Reuben asked, his breath catching on a sob of despair.

"Don't think that. Don't let yourself imagine such things. Remember to pray earnestly tonight, and God will watch over Mam and over you if you can't sleep, okay?"

Reuben nodded, crept into his bed, and pulled the covers up to his chin.

"You want the lamp on?" Sadie asked, brushing back a lock of hair.

"Nah."

Sadie blew out the steady, yellow flame that lit a room so cozily, then whispered, "Good-night."

She met Mark coming down the hallway uncertainly, never having been upstairs in the Miller household. It was not uncommon for a girl's friends to come upstairs to her bedroom on Sunday afternoons when church was over. All girls had chairs or loveseats in their bedrooms for that purpose.

Now, however, Sadie was uncertain. Should she ask Mark to come into her bedroom at a time like this? He might think her extremely bold, but where else could they go to talk about Mam?

"Is...is it all right to...go to my room?" she whispered.

"If you're okay with it."

She entered her room and lit the kerosene lamp with the lighter beside it, replaced the glass chimney, and turned it up to brighten the room.

Mark stood inside the door, waiting until Sadie asked him to sit down. His large frame seemed to fill the entire loveseat, so Sadie sat gingerly on the edge of the bed, her body tense, the pulse in her temples pounding. She pleated the fabric of her skirt over and over, her long, thin fingers never ceasing their movement. Her head bent, her voice barely audible, she related Mam's disappearance and the shameful, sad history of her parents' relationship.

"I think Mam is in a much more serious depression than any of us realized. The only person that had any idea was Dat, and he is much too stubborn or proud to admit anything is ever wrong in our family. As long as he can present a smiling group of good Christians to the Amish community, he thinks everything is just great."

Mark nodded. "Do all of you want to live here in Montana?" he asked after a respectful silence that was so typical of him.

"I have no choice, so this is home now. But if I was allowed to choose, I'd probably go back to Ohio."

"Why?"

"I miss family. I miss Eva most of all. We've been here for almost six years now, and I'm used to Montana. But..." she broke off, timidly.

"What?"

"Well, it's just that ever since the accident with Ezra and those wild horses, I sense a bad omen. It's as if fear is alive and haunting, and that black, devilish horse...and then Nevaeh...I don't know. Is there such a thing as an un-blessing? You know how the ministers say, an *unsayah*."

Mark was silent.

The small heart-shaped alarm clock ticked steadily. Only their breathing could be heard above it.

Then there was a great shout from the kitchen, followed by a hubbub of low voices, high ones, and everything in between.

Sadie jumped to her feet and dashed to the door. Mark following closely. As she pulled the door open, was it only her imagination, or did Mark place his hand on her waist, as if to steer her through the door like a gentleman?

Reuben's tousled head appeared.

And then Leah was pounding up the steps, calling her name, nearly colliding with all three of them.

"They found her! Oh, Sadie! She's been found!" Leah burst into sobs of relief.

"Where, Leah?"

"In an airport somewhere!" Leah said between her sobs.

"A what? Are you sure?"

They hurried down the stairs and into the crowd of people rejoicing and crying. So much relief. So much happiness. It was hard to grasp this joy when only moments before the despair had been so real.

Finally someone clapped their hands and the room grew silent. All heads turned to the aging, white-bearded gentleman who stood just inside the door. His eyes were kind but stern, and he was flanked by two policemen in heavy coats.

"Annie Miller has been found. She is extremely

disoriented and her speech is totally incomprehensible. We need Mr. Miller and any of the immediate family who wishes to accompany us."

Dat's sad eyes searched his daughters'.

"I'll go," Rebekah said immediately.

"I'll stay with Anna and Reuben," Leah volunteered.

"Come with us, Sadie," Dat said, a pleading note in his voice.

Sadie's heart melted. Forgiveness like a soothing balm ran joyously over her heart, coating it solidly with love for her father. He had only been doing what he felt was best for his family, regardless of how foolish it seemed now.

It was all surreal, the long ride through the night, the winding country roads turning onto the interstate highway, the kaleidoscope of bright lights, hissing tires, neon signs blinking. It seemed as if they had left the state of Montana.

Finally the car slowed onto an exit and circled the ramp to a red light. Turning left, they came onto a steady stream of vehicles and more red lights.

Sadie wondered what all these people were doing out in the middle of the night. She had no idea the world didn't sleep at night. How would they ever be able to get up and go to work the next morning? No wonder people were fired from their jobs. They should all be at home in bed getting their much needed eight hours of sleep.

The car slowed again and turned left into a huge parking area. The building ahead of them towered like the buildings in New York City. Well, almost.

Sadie counted eight stories.

Toshkoma Medical Center.

Mam was at a hospital!

Acceptance settled across Sadie's shoulders. It was a yoke to bear—a heavy, sad feeling—but it was coupled with joy. There was finally help available for poor, dear Mam.

They found Mam sitting on a chair in a large, blue waiting room. Her cumbersome luggage was by her side. Her head was bent, her hands twisting and turning in her lap. She was wearing her black bonnet and her Sunday coat with the new buttons she had sewed on herself. Her woolen shawl was folded neatly on top of her big suitcase. She was mumbling to herself and didn't see them until Dat stood close to her, touched her shoulder, and said, "Annie."

At first, Sadie thought she would not recognize them. Her eyes were so clouded and she seemed a million miles away. She was talking in mumbles, laughing hoarsely, then crying.

Cold chills crept up Sadie's spine, the icy feelings of fear and dread.

Mam! Have we lost you completely through our neglect?

White-coated doctors joined them. Psychiatrists, nurses, men in authority, talking, talking. They could not admit Mam without her consent.

Mam sat so bent, so hysterical. Now she was saying, "Sadie, Sadie."

"Which one is Sadie?"

The little man with the bald head and black mustache reached for her, escorted her toward her mother.

Blindly, Mam reached for Sadie's hand.

Sadie fought back panic for a moment. This is your mother. Relax. She's just sick. She's not wild or dangerous.

Just help her. Listen to her.

"Sadie, Sadie." It was all Mam could say, over and over.

Sadie bent her head to hear the garbled words. She tried to still her mother's restless hands, then bent closer. "What?"

Mam spoke in Pennsylvania Dutch.

"*Halt aw. Halt aw. Halt um gaduld aw. Gaduld.*"

The voice went on, jumbled, begging for patience.

"*Ich do, Mam, Ich do.*"

Then suddenly Mam lifted her head, looked at Sadie, and said in an articulate voice, "It was me that left Nevaeh out."

She began sobbing so heartbrokenly that Sadie was on her knees immediately, holding her mother as her shoulders heaved. Murmuring brokenly now, she told Sadie that she needed help.

Sadie stood up, nodded to the doctors, and told them Mam was willing to be admitted. Dat stood beside her uncomfortably, nodding his assent.

"Oh, yes. Yes. She most certainly will be admitted. Thank God. If that is what she wants."

Sadie nodded. Rebekah rushed to her mother. Together they guided her off the chair and into a waiting wheelchair. Dat grabbed the suitcase, and they all loaded into an elevator that clanged and pinged its way to the floor where Mam would be treated.

The doctors talked and asked so many questions that Sadie thought it must surely be morning when the last form was signed and completed. Dat turned hesitantly, not sure what he should do as they finally wheeled Mam to her room.

"Come, Dat. I think it's time you and Rebekah and I

had the largest sized coffee this hospital's snack bar has to offer. Everything is going to be all right now. They'll adjust Mam's medication until they get it right, and she'll soon be okay."

Only now did Sadie have a chance to absorb what Mam had said about letting Nevaeh out of the barn. In this moment, Sadie felt that her beloved horse was a small price to pay for the stability of her mother's mental health.

Chapter 20

Spring came late that year. It was always later than Ohio springtime, but this time it was almost the end of May until the last chilly winds died away.

Sadie climbed one of the steep ridges surrounding her home. She was alone. The house was suffocating her, even with the windows open a bit at the top to allow the sweet smell of the earth to circulate about the rooms. So she decided to go for a walk.

Her breath came in short gasps, the calves of her legs ached, and she could feel the soft fabric of her robin's-egg blue dress attach itself to her perspiring body. The sun was warmer than she thought it would be, and she realized with great joy that they could be planting the garden soon.

Another spring, another garden, and here I am alone in Montana, she thought wryly.

It was when she was alone, and especially on days like today, that she thought of Mark Peight most.

Why had he done that? For the thousandth time she asked the wind, and, like always, there was no reply.

Even with Mam hospitalized, she had planned for
that special date, that awaited Saturday evening when he
would open his heart and tell her his life's story. Instead,
a flat, white envelope had arrived in Friday's mail with
small, neat handwriting addressing the letter to "Miss
Sadie Miller."

Her life had not been the same since then. He had
written on a yellow legal pad and minced no words in
his flat, round script.

> *Dear Sadie,*
>
> *I'm going back to Pennsylvania. I can't write that
> I'm going home, because I don't necessarily have a
> home. I'm just going back.*
>
> *I simply can't be with you anymore without telling
> you the truth about myself. I apologize to you for
> being a coward. I'm not good enough for you and
> never will be.*
>
> *This is good-bye.*
>
> *Mark Peight*

That short letter literally rocked her world. It was as
abrasive as steel wool on a smooth surface. It had hurt as
badly as falling off a bike on a poorly paved road, tearing her skin into rough, raw patches. There was no way
around the desolation of that letter. But she just had to
give up and endure the pain without cringing or crying,
which she did during the day. At night, she cried.

Who was he? Why did he run without leaving as much
as an address or a phone number?

The wind had no answers. It caressed her warm face, played with the brown hair that straggled loose from her white covering, sighed in the branches of the pines, but had no answers for her as usual.

God was in nature, or so it seemed to Sadie. He spoke to her of his love when she saw twinkling stars, new wildflowers, fresh-fallen snow. Sometimes his voice in nature was soft and warm like today's gentle breeze. Other times it was strong and powerful like in thunder and torrents of rain. But always, God was there.

She had much to be thankful for. She knew that sounded like an old cliché, an overused Amish phrase, but it was true.

She was thankful for her mother first. Dear, dear Mam. She had made an amazing comeback, but the struggle had been heartrending to watch.

After the doctors had observed, adjusted medications, and counseled, Mam finally underwent extensive thyroid surgery.

Her problems had been real, not imagined. A serious chemical imbalance, coupled with a diseased thyroid gland, had taken a horrible toll on Mam's mind, on her well-being. She had become so confused and was hallucinating and hearing voices which were very real to her.

The final straw, the one thing that had pushed her over the edge, was the cost of Sadie's hospital stay. Somehow, in her poor, twisted mind, she had linked this with the cost of keeping Nevaeh. That pressure troubled her so much that she released the horse, believing this was the only thing she could do to help pay the cost of Sadie's bill.

After her confession and complete breakdown, she

began to heal with Dat's support. He had long conversations with the physicians and therapists, nodding his head, listening, observing, and being completely supportive of Mam's care. It was wondrous to behold.

Mam smiled now. She ate healthy meals. She cooked and baked.

Dat offered to move back to Ohio. He told her it wasn't right that he had dragged her out to Montana against her wishes. Mam had a faraway look on her face—an unveiled glimpse of her homesickness. Then she had turned to Dat.

"But, Jacob, I don't think I could go back. I don't know if I could be at home there. This is home."

And Sadie knew she meant it.

She had laid a hand on Dat's arm, and her eyes were pure and clear and honest without a trace of malice or ill will.

"I love Montana now, Jacob. I haven't always. Sometimes I miss the folks in Ohio, but you know, whithersoever thou goest I will go."

She had smiled such a beautiful smile, her gray hair shining exactly like a halo about her head, that all the girls agreed she looked like a middle-aged angel.

Sadie still loved her job at the ranch. It was the one thing that kept her grounded, kept her sane. She could always stay busy cooking, cleaning, and doing laundry. Sometimes she rode the fine horses from Richard Caldwell's stables. But she never connected with another horse like Nevaeh or Paris. Horses, like life, were too unpredictable, so it was safer to stay away and not lose your head or your heart to a horse or, for that matter, to handsome Mark Peight either. You just got hurt or bruised.

Sadie flopped down in a meadow of wildflowers, wiping an arm across her forehead to dry it.

Puffy, white clouds trailed across the blue sky as Sadie lay on the soft carpet of flowers. An eagle soared across the treetops, riding the current with a natural ease. His head was white against the dark color of his outstretched wings.

She wondered what had happened with the herd of wild horses. There had been a great public outcry with posters tacked to the wall of the post office, the bank, and the local grocery. It was the main subject on Sundays after church and when visitors came to see Mam, but no one had a solution. Helicopters were never brought in because no one could prove the horses had ever damaged anything. As Dat said, it didn't amount to a hill of beans. And then the subject died off and everyone moved on to other topics.

The horses had been responsible for Nevaeh's death, Sadie felt sure, although she never spoke of it, not even to Leah or Rebekah.

She could feel her body relaxing with each intake of the sweet smell of wildflowers. Her eyelids felt heavy. God was, indeed, so good. How could anyone ever doubt his presence lying on a flower-strewn hillside in May?

She wasn't sure if she heard something first, or if she only felt it. She just knew the earth vibrated a bit, the way the hardwood floor in the living room did when Dat walked across it in his big boots.

She stayed still, every nerve tense, listening.

There. That sound.

It wasn't a rushing, scurrying sound. It was a stumbling, sliding sound.

Should she be afraid?

Strangely, she felt no fear. Surely the band of wild horses had gone. No one ever spoke of them anymore. Oh, the men snorted and said how incompetent the law was, unable to solve a mystery that was quite obviously under their nose. But who were they to say?

Amish people were a peaceable lot, driving their horses and buggies at a slow trot on the winding, country roads of Montana, taking care of family and friends, loving their neighbors—for the most part. If the law chose to ignore the obvious, they were in authority, and the Amish abided by their rules. No use fighting. It wasn't their way.

So Sadie listened, her pulse quickening, but not with dry-mouthed, raw fear. Instead she had an inquisitive feeling.

There now. It had stopped, so likely she had imagined it in the first place.

A jay called from the pines. Another one answered. They screamed the way blue jays do when they're disturbed. Then she heard a tearing sound like when a cow wraps its tongue around a tuft of grass and pulls or bites. The grass makes a soft, breaking sound. Perhaps someone's cows wandered up here.

Sadie sat up slowly so she wouldn't spook the cattle. They were amiable creatures for the most part, so she wasn't afraid, although she didn't want to start a stampede if she could help it.

She blinked.

She ran the back of her hand across her eyes and blinked again.

A horse!

Three!

Her hand went to the front of her dress to still her beating heart. The horses had not seen her. Slowly she turned her head just enough so that she could see them out of the corner of her eyes.

Her mind could not fathom the sight of the black horse. She knew he was there grazing, but it seemed like a dream. He was so gorgeous and much bigger than any driving horse or any horse in Richard Caldwell's stables, that was sure.

Was she in danger?

She shivered.

To get up and run would only show fear, and she desperately wanted to observe them, if even for a second.

Along with the black stallion, there was a brown mare. She was small and compact with a beautifully arched neck. Her mane and tail had been luxurious at one time but were unkempt now. They were matted with burrs, and the forelock needed a trim.

And then...

Sadie didn't remember opening her mouth, she just knew it had been open for some time because her tongue felt dry when she closed it again.

Paris!

It was Paris!

It couldn't be Paris.

The horse was exactly the color of Paris after she had lost her winter coat. Paris was honey-colored then, a rich, amber color that was complemented by the beige of her mane and tail.

This horse was that same color, and it, too, was a mare. She moved behind the black horse as he grazed slowly, clipping the grass with a crunching sound. There was only one thing better than hearing a horse eat grass and that was to hear him eat oats and corn from a wooden feed box. Horses bit deep into the oats, then lifted their nose a bit and chewed. Most of the oats fell out of the side of a horse's mouth when he did that, but he chewed them later until the feed box was completely clean.

Slowly Sadie got to her feet.

The black horse lifted his head, his ears pricked forward, and he wheeled immediately, lunging back the way he had come. The brown mare looked at Sadie, then ran off with the palomino following.

Sadie stayed rooted to the spot.

Involuntarily her arm reached out toward them.

"Paris!" she whispered.

The black horse disappeared, but Sadie had a feeling the mares' return to the woods was halfhearted. They hadn't made an all-out dash for the trees the way the big black had done.

Yes, they ran, but they were curious, too, Sadie thought.

Slowly, with her arm extended and hand reaching toward the mares, she walked through the wildflowers. She was talking, telling them the things she told horses, even if she couldn't see them through the forest.

"Come, Paris. Come on, you big baby. Don't be afraid. I'm not going to hurt you. It's about time you returned to the fold and started living a decent life after all the mischief you've been up to. Come on. Come on. Just let me look at you."

But she could not coax them out. The horses stayed in the safety of the trees.

"Well, okay, stay away then, Paris. But I'll be here tomorrow. I'll bring you some oats and corn and molasses and I'll leave a salt block. You'll love that."

She kept talking to the unseen horses, which may have been silly, but it may not have been either, she reasoned.

Those mares were not terrified. Sadie was certain about that.

Adrenaline surged through her veins as she turned. Yes!

But Dat would never let her come up here alone. Never. Especially if he knew there were any wild horses within a mile of her.

She could tell her parents she was going on a hike to get back in shape. But that wouldn't work. Her sisters would want to join her, and Leah, she knew, would catch on faster than anyone.

It would have to remain her secret. She'd bring a salt block by herself somehow.

She was running down the hill, her knees bearing the impact which she knew was no good for her newly healed bones.

When she got home, she tried to act as carefree as when she left the house, but she knew her cheeks were flushed. If her eyes showed any of the excitement she felt—which they probably did—she'd be a dead give-away. So she went to the barn to make plans.

Sadie stood back, surveying the interior of the barn. That Dat. He would never change. He hardly ever swept the forebay. Cobwebs hung from the floor joists above her head, and empty feed bags were strewn beside the wooden feed box. Dusty scooters and bikes and children's riding toys that should have been discarded a long time ago were all piled in one corner.

Bales of hay lay where they landed when Dat threw them down the hole from the second floor. He never carried the bales of hay over against the wall and stacked them neatly. He just broke them apart and fed the hay to Charlie from the area where they had landed, which meant there was loose hay everywhere. It was embarrassing, the way this barn was always a mess.

Sadie sighed and got to work. At least this would keep her out of the house so she could hide her excitement about the horses and make her plans in secret.

☆ ✡ ☆

The following evening Sadie was in luck. She could not believe her good fortune. The whole family went to Dan Detweilers for the season's first cook-out, leaving before Sadie got home from work.

Sadie was ecstatic. It was too perfect.

She immediately changed into her oldest clothes and a pair of sturdy shoes. She grabbed Reuben's backpack, the biggest one he owned, and hurried out to the barn.

Good! The feed bin was almost full so Dat wouldn't notice if she took some of it up the mountain. He would just think Charlie had gotten hungry.

There was no extra block of salt, but she remembered to check Nevaeh's stall just in case.

Nostalgia enveloped her as she remembered that feeling of walking into the stall and being welcomed with Nevaeh's funny blowing of breath from her nose. It wasn't loud enough to be a nicker or whinny, just a soft rustling of her nostrils instead.

There was still part of a salt block, and Sadie grabbed it and put it in the bottom of her backpack. Opening a white, plastic Wal-Mart bag, she carefully scooped some of the sticky, pungent horse feed into it. She knotted the bag securely and slipped it into the backpack with the salt. She dashed back to the kitchen for a few apples and stuck them into the pack with the rest of the things.

She slipped one shoulder into the strap. She had to bend over and struggle to get the other strap in place, but determination goaded her. She had to see what those horses would do when confronted with food they were unaccustomed to having. Surely they would remember it and long for it.

In Sadie's mind, the wild horses had to be connected with that wealthy person who lost his horses—the one she had seen on the news that Richard Caldwell had shown her. As long as the horses weren't found, there was no proof they had been stolen, so rumors swirled through the valley continuously. That's all the talk amounted to. Rumors.

Sadie had never entered the conversation at the ranch, but she had listened plenty and formed her own opinions.

Her opinion was confirmed, especially after seeing the horses up close. They weren't ordinary horses. Wild, yes, and definitely scruffy-looking, but not as small or as mangy as many western mustangs she had seen.

Sadie walked rapidly at first, then slowed. She knew climbing the ridge with 10 or 15 pounds on her back would be a daunting task, but she'd have to try.

She wished she would have taken time to eat. She felt her stomach rumble and hoped the adrenaline rush would propel her up the incline, because there wasn't much food in her body.

For one thing, it had been Dorothy's day to make chili, and she sure had been heavy-handed with the ground chilis. The dish was so hot, Sadie gasped and ran for the sink when she innocently put a large spoonful to her mouth.

"Dorothy!"

Dorothy chuckled.

"You're not good western stock, Sadie! You're just an Ohio Dutchman raised on milk pudding and chicken corn soup. You don't know what good chili is."

Sadie drank water, spluttering, her face turning red. "That stuff is on fire!"

Dorothy laughed and went about her duties, knowing the cowhands would not think the chili was too hot. So Sadie had made a cold bologna sandwich for herself and hadn't bothered to sit down long enough to eat all of it.

She could hardly keep her secret from Jim and Dorothy. She had even considered talking to Jim about it on the way to work but then decided against it. She didn't want anyone to know she thought the wild horses were still in the area, mostly for fear of a group of men following her up the ridge to round them up.

Turning off the road, Sadie started across the field on her way to the ridge where the trees met the open grass. She could feel her heartbeat increasing from exertion, but she could climb surprisingly well with the weight distributed evenly on her back. The wind caught her covering, and she grabbed it just before it tore off her head.

Oh, dear, she had forgotten to pin it.

If an Amish girl went outside for a hike on a windy day, she had to put in a few extra straight pins or her covering would not stay put.

Stopping, Sadie tied the strings loosely beneath her chin and decided to let it blow off if it wanted to—which is precisely what it did. She walked on, her brown hair in disarray now and her covering flapping about her backpack. The wind tore at her navy blue skirt, whirling it about her legs, but she pushed it down impatiently and kept walking.

Glancing at the sky, she noticed a bank of dark clouds

building in the west.

Hmm.

She hoped this was no spring thunderstorm. She knew how quickly storms could come up at this time of year, becoming quite violent.

The wind bent the grasses, tossing the purple and yellow flowers relentlessly. Dry leaves, leftover from the winter snow, skidded down the hill, and still Sadie climbed, her breath coming in gasps.

She stopped, turned to look back, and as always was awed at the sight before her.

She was glad they had decided to stay in Montana. It was home to them now, and she couldn't imagine moving back to Ohio where the landscape was flat, the homes too close to each other, and the roads crowded with traffic.

She still missed Eva though. Letters and phone calls were not the same as being with someone. Eva was getting married in the fall, and she still had Spirit, her horse. Sadie wished Eva could be here with her now. She'd have a fit. She would just have to write her a letter when she got back.

She watched the bank of dark clouds. They were farther away than they appeared to be, she knew, but the thought of being caught here in a thunderstorm did not appeal to her.

Finally, her breath tearing at her chest, she reached the spot close to where she had been when the horses first appeared. Carefully she tore the grass away and spread the feed in clumps with the salt on one side, the apples on the other. Then she sat down to catch her breath and wait.

The wind moaned in the trees, its intensity picking up as the pine branches bent to its power. The grasses whipped about now, and Sadie knew she could not stay or she'd be caught in a storm. She watched the clouds moving and expanding, and then she shouldered her empty backpack and started down.

"Okay, Paris and company, enjoy your dinner. I'll be back." She hoped the horses would find their feed before the deer or squirrels or birds did. Likely the wild creatures would get some of it.

Thin streaks of lightning flashed out of the dark clouds now, and Sadie hurried down the hill, the backpack flopping and her covering whipping around every which way.

She'd better hurry. How would she explain a soaking wet dress and a ruined covering if she got caught in the rain?

As it was, she had to run the last half mile as huge drops of cold rain began pelting down on her bare head.

Chapter 21

IT WAS SUNDAY. NOT JUST AN ORDINARY SUNDAY, but one of those rare days when the breeze is cool, the sun is pleasantly warm, and there are so many puffy, white clouds in the sky that you can lie on your back and find all sorts of shapes and animals and maybe even one that looks like a person you know.

Sadie sat on the glossy, oak bench at the Daniel Bontrager home and tried not to tap her fingers on the windowsill beside her. She also tried not to gaze out the window too much, but instead keep her focus on the visiting minister and the sermon he was preaching.

He was a portly, older gentleman from somewhere in Pennsylvania, and his voice had a thin, squeaky quality that was sort of endearing. His short beard wagged methodically as he expounded upon the Scriptures, telling the congregation about the seriousness of this life here on earth and encouraging them to shoulder the cross and follow the Lord Jesus, even in their younger years.

Sadie gazed unseeingly, knowing deep inside that her very own personal cross to bear was none other than

Mark Peight's disappearance. It would not become any easier just yet.

She had been so sure that God had plopped Mark Peight straight down from heaven. She had been so in love—was still so in love. She remembered the way he walked, the depth of his brown eyes, and his quiet ways. He never talked much at all, but when he did, the sound of his voice was like music. She loved to hear him talk, hanging onto every word and being warmed by the sound of his voice.

She sighed. Some things weren't meant to be.

She supposed if she could catch Paris—if that was possible—she'd be happy to have a horse of her own again, which was, after all, something.

Rebekah leaned over and whispered, "I need a tissue."

Sadie lifted her apron and dug into her pocket.

"Don't have one," she whispered back.

The minister droned on.

A fly buzzed by and settled on the windowsill. Sadie watched it and wondered how some people could catch houseflies in their hands the way they did. She had often tried but only hurt the palm of her hand, and the fly flew off unscathed.

She hoped her family would go somewhere this evening. She had been to the ridge only once all week and had not seen a trace of any of the horses. The feed, apples, and salt had all disappeared—every speck of them—but did the horses eat it? She could be feeding horses, deer, elk, even bears, although that was unlikely.

She did not want to go to the supper that would be held for the youth later in the day. She had to come up with a good excuse not to go, one that would be believable to her sisters.

There was always the flu bug going around, which was a good reason for staying in her room feigning serious stomach ailments, but that hardly ever worked with Leah. She could let Reuben in on her secret and then give her sister a whole sad row about Reuben needing to spend more time with her. No, that would be risky.

She looked for Reuben across the room where the men and boys sat facing the women. He was between two larger boys and looked small and innocent. He also looked very, very bored.

She caught his eye and gave him the slightest wink. He grinned and ducked his head, embarrassed at the boldness of his sister.

Sadie smiled, then felt a rush of excitement. She would let him in on her secret after all. He would love every minute of their excursions. He always loved even the thought of an adventure.

After the strains of the last hymn died away, Sadie filed out with the rest of the girls. They crowded together in a corner of the kitchen, waiting until the tables were set up.

Men turned the benches into tables by setting them on legs built for that purpose. The women brought armloads of clean, white tablecloths and spread them on top of the tables. The girls helped carry trays of peanut butter spread, cheese, ham, pickles, spiced red beets, butter, and huge platters of thickly sliced homemade bread, whole wheat on one side and white on the other. They placed a saucer, coffee cup, tumbler, knife, and fork at each setting along the lengthy tables.

Pitchers of water appeared like magic and glasses were filled. Pies—peach, blueberry, raspberry, custard, pumpkin, even a few mince pies—all found their way to the middle of the table.

The men were called in by the person who lived in the home where church was held, and they filed in by their age, the ministers going first. The women sat at a long table next to the men. The ministers' wives sat down first. The rest of the women sat in order by age.

They bowed their heads in silent prayer. Servers offered coffee to each individual, the only hot item for the traditional dinner at church. It was all very organized, although an English person wouldn't be able to tell upon observing. The women were constantly moving, the children dodged in and out, and the noise of conversation was amplified by the sheer number of people assembled in one large room.

Sadie ate hungrily, slathering the thick, gooey peanut butter spread on a heavy slice of whole wheat bread, deciding once again that it was truly the best thing ever. If you sat on a hard bench for three hours straight without any breakfast, the lunch at church was simply the most delicious food.

Sadie chewed the rich, nutty-tasting whole wheat bread accompanied by the sticky sweetness of peanut butter, marshmallow cream, and molasses. Spicy little red beets, pickles, and ham on another slice of white bread, washed down with the fragrant, hot coffee, rounded out the meal. Now she was ready for the grand finale, which was pie, of course.

Of all the pies at church, Sadie always watched for pumpkin. It was her all-time favorite. Pumpkin pie was sweet and custardy and shivery all at the same time, with a spicy flavor that perfectly complemented her cup of hot, black coffee. At home when Mam made pumpkin pie, Sadie spooned Cool Whip on top, but at church there was no extra Cool Whip so she ate it without.

She was finished eating and was piling some soiled dishes in a large bowl when someone tapped her elbow. Turning, she found herself face to face with the visiting minister. He smiled at her, and Sadie put down the bowl of soiled dishes to shake his proffered hand.

"Are you one of Jacob Miller's daughters?" he asked, his eyes alight with genuine curiosity.

"Yes. I am."

"Well, we're from Abbottstown, Pennsylvania. We had a young man come to our community not too long ago—four, five weeks, maybe. We, and the other two families we're traveling with, got to talking about our planned trip to Montana, and he said he was out here on vacation not too long ago. I don't remember his name. Melvin something, I think."

Sadie raised her eyebrows, "Melvin?"

"Yes. He talked of Jacob Millers. That's your dat, right?"

"Yes."

"Something about wild horses you had running around out here."

Sadie nodded.

"You can't think of Melvin's last name, can you?" he asked.

"No, I'm sorry. So many young men come and go that we often lose track of who they are and how long they stay," Sadie answered politely.

"Yes, it would appear so. Well, I sure wish I could think of this young man's name. It wasn't Peachy, but…"

He paused. "Anyway, it was nice talking to you."

He wandered off, and Sadie shook her head ruefully.

Whatever, she thought, a bit irritated. Everyone wanted to know who you were, especially people on vacation checking out these Montana-ians.

They all think we're a bit odd to live so far away from our home settlement, but they're much too polite to say so, she thought, then chided herself for thinking like an old hermit.

✿ ✿ ✿

The buggy ride home was a pure joy with the side windows flung open and the back canvas flap rolled up and secured with leather straps. Sadie hung her arm out the back, whistling lightly under her breath. Reuben was close beside her and Anna on his other side. Leah and Rebekah had gone home with Verna and Magdalena Amstutz, two of their favorite friends.

Reuben shifted his weight toward Sadie, folded his arms across his chest, and mumbled to himself.

"What?" Sadie asked, grabbing his ear and pulling him over.

He yanked his head away.

"I can't see why you couldn't have gone with Leah and Rebekah.

"Because..." Sadie said, pausing to purse her lips importantly, "I have better things to do."

"Like what? It's not like you have a boyfriend the way normal girls do."

"Normal? I'm normal," Sadie said, her eyes dancing.

"No, you're not. You're a queer duck!"

Sadie howled with laughter, an unladylike squawk of pure humor that made Dat turn around in his seat to see what was so funny. Mam chuckled, Anna grinned, and Reuben scowled, looking straight ahead.

The driving horse, good old dependable Charlie, plodded on through the lovely Montana landscape, the harness flapping rhythmically on his well-padded haunches. Some of the hair beneath the britching strap was darker in color, showing signs of moisture.

"Dat, Charlie's sweating already. He's getting fat. You feed him too much grain," Sadie said.

"Well, if Charlie's sweating, get out and walk!" Reuben said forcefully.

"All right, I will. It's a bee-you-tiful day. Walk with me, Reuben."

"No!"

"Yes! Come on. We only have two or three miles."

"Not me. No way!" Anna said, shaking her head.

"Dat, stop. Let me off. Come on, Reuben, you little chicken."

The buggy stopped, and Sadie looked back over the way they had come to make sure no one could see her less than modest exit out the back window of the buggy. She quickly scrambled out and over the springs along the back. When her foot hit the road, she pulled on Reuben's sleeve and begged him one more time to accompany her. To her great surprise, he piled out of the back and onto the road beside her.

Perfect!

With a crunch of steel wheels on gravel and Dat's "Hup!" the buggy moved off. Sadie wasted no time coming straight to the point. Breathlessly she told Reuben what she meant by saying she had better things to do.

"And, Reuben," she concluded, "I'm running out of excuses to go on walks by myself. I honestly think Mam is getting suspicious, or at least wonders what I'm up to. If Mam and Dat find out, they will not let me do this. And that horse! I can't tell you how beautiful she is! It's... She's exactly like...Paris!"

Reuben plodded on, his hands in his pockets, his hat shoved down so hard his ears looked painfully cramped. He looked less than thrilled and was still upset they had to walk so far.

"Paris? Who's Paris?"

"You know. Don't you remember Paris? That yellow-ish palomino I raced against Eva's Spirit?"

"Eva's spirit? That sounds spooky... like Eva had a ghost or something."

Sadie slapped Reuben's shoulder.

"You know which horse I mean."

Reuben stopped, squinted, then bent down to examine the remnant of a stone. He picked it up, held it to the sun, rubbed it, and announced, "Arrowhead!"

"Is it? Let me see."

Sadie turned it over in her hand but could certainly not distinguish any outstanding features that made it come close to looking even vaguely like an arrowhead. But she knew that to stay on good terms with Reuben, she would have to pronounce it one.

"Yup, Reuben, I think it was an arrowhead at one time."

"Do you?"

His troubles forgotten, especially the length of the walk home, he became wildly enthusiastic about looking for arrowheads.

"Yeah, I'll go with you this afternoon. But you can watch for horses, and I'll look for more of these."

He pocketed the very ordinary stone, his future vast-ly improved. Sadie cringed, despairing of her ability to break the news that he would have to lie quietly in the tall grass and wildflowers to watch for the horses.

"Don't you want to see the horses?" she began, tongue in cheek.

"Aah, I guess."

"Course you do. So we'll have to sit quietly. Sort of hide."

"I ain't walking all the way up there to sit there all that time. If I want to see a horse, I can go out to the barn and look at Charlie."

Sadie ground her teeth in frustration.

"Reuben! You are just like Dat!"

"Well."

Sadie realized her luck was running out. Self-righteous little man! Oh, he made her so angry.

"Okay, Reuben, I'll make a deal. Every time you go with me, and at least act as if you want to go, I'll give you five dollars."

"Five whole bucks?"

Even his hat came up off his ears at the mention of money. He clamped it back down then, lifted his shoulders, and started planning what he would do with such untold wealth.

"I need a scope for my pellet gun. How many times is this gonna take until you catch her?" he asked, watching her face with calculating eyes.

"Who knows? She may never come back. But if I don't try, I'll never be able to forgive myself," she said, her voice becoming thick with emotion.

Reuben looked at Sadie sideways and thought she was, indeed, the queerest duck he had ever met.

✿ ✡ ✿

And so they developed a pattern. Reuben filled the backpack and shouldered it until they were out of sight. Their parents thought they were hiking to get Sadie back into better health, especially to strengthen the muscles in her legs. They thought Reuben tagged along to look for arrowheads, explaining the backpack.

After two days of the feed disappearing and no sign of horses, Reuben demanded his $10. Sadie was in despair and, on top of that, had to cope with a rash that appeared on the calves of her legs. It was red, ugly, and so itchy she thought she would go crazy trying not to scratch.

Reuben said it was a sign from God that they shouldn't be up there against their parent's wishes, and Sadie asked him when he became so worried about being good. He told her if she didn't watch it, he wouldn't go with her anymore. Sadie scratched the rash on her legs, fought tears of sudden anger, and said, "Good, I'll go all by myself then. Stay home."

But he did go the next Friday afternoon, albeit reluctantly. It was achingly beautiful, one of those early summer days when everything seems tinged with a golden glow. Even the laundry on the line seemed whiter and the grass a vivid shade of lime green. Wildflowers grew in so much profusion, it seemed a bit surreal to be surrounded by so many different colors bobbing and waving around.

They walked and walked, then climbed up the ridge as usual. Reuben flopped into the grass, rolled on his back, and flung an arm across his eyes.

Sadie took the backpack, unzipped it, and heard them before she had a chance to scatter the oats.

She froze, her breath ragged from the climb.

There! A dark shadow. Another.

"Sadie!" Reuben called.

"Shhh!" she hissed.

He sat up, blinked.

She lifted a finger to her lips and drew her eyebrows down. It was then that she saw the raw fear in Reuben's eyes. He was afraid! Why, of course. That was why he was so reluctant to accompany her on her trips up here. Reuben had always been frightened of horses when he was small, and still was, only he tried not to let anyone know. All other Amish boys liked horses, drove them at a young age, and never showed any fear at all. But not every little boy had a father who didn't like horses and showed no interest in them the way Dat did.

"Come, Reuben."

Reuben came over to stand by her, and she put a protective arm around his thin shoulders. He did not pull away.

"Watch, Reuben. There at the tree line."

The wind blew softly as the trees whispered among themselves, the way trees do when the leaves are newly formed and velvety and rustling against each other. The grasses moved like waves of the ocean, restless, always moving in one direction or another, brushed by the ceaseless wind.

Sadie and Reuben stood together, her brown skirt blowing across his blue denim trousers. He wore no hat, leaving his hair free to blow in the wind in all its dark blonde glory. His brilliantly blue eyes were wide with fear now.

Sadie stood sturdily, unafraid. She did not believe for one minute that these horses would harm them, even the big black one. Perhaps if they were sitting on horses, the black stallion would become territorial and menacing, but it was unlikely with two human beings standing together.

These horses had been trained at one time, Sadie always felt sure. Why, she didn't know. She just sensed in her spirit that they were not totally wild and untrained. Frightened, alone, learning to fend for themselves, but not wild.

So she stood, her features relaxed.

"They won't hurt us, Reuben. Just stay calm."

"But... Sadie! That big black one chased Ezra's horse."

"Yes. But we're not horses. He won't hurt us. Just stay calm, Reuben."

"I want to go back."

"No. Just stay. Watch."

Bending, she scooped a handful of oats and corn into the palm of her hand. Holding it out, she advanced slowly toward the tree line.

"Come, Paris. Come on. Be a real good girl. You can have these oats if you want. Come here, you big, beautiful, gorgeous horse. I'm going to name you Paris, did you know that?"

Reuben clung to her, too afraid to stay by himself, terrified to go with her.

The sun was turning the lovely day into an evening of burnished copper with streaks of gold where the rays escaped the confines of a few scudding clouds.

At first Sadie thought Paris' face was a ray of sunlight dancing on the tree trunks. But when the horse flicked her ears, Sadie could see the perfect outline of her eyes all blended into the golden evening.

"Oh, Paris!" she whispered, completely at a loss for any other words.

"Sadie, I want to go home," Reuben said hoarsely.

"Reuben, trust me, okay? If I thought these horses would harm us, we wouldn't be here. They won't hurt us. Paris is the most curious of them all. Now watch."

She shook the oats in her hand and dribbled some of them on the ground, enticing the horse with the smell of the feed. The molasses made it sticky and gave off a pungent odor, one she never tired of smelling.

Sadie took another step, then stopped. She continued talking in soft, begging tones. She held her breath as Paris stepped out, a vision of beauty to Sadie.

"Come on, girl. Come get your feed."

She watched in disbelief as Paris lowered her head, snuffled at the blowing grasses, then lifted her head in a graceful motion. Her mane blew as if it was part of the earth itself.

Now she looked at Sadie, really looked at her. Sadie held her gaze steadily, talking in low tones. Reuben stood beside her.

"Sadie!" he whispered, pointing.

Paris snorted, retreated a few steps.

Sadie looked and saw the brown mare stealthily moving out from the trees, followed by the black stallion.

Her heart leaped.

Still she stood steadily.

She began calling to Paris in coaxing tones. The horse's ears flicked forward, then swiveled back. She threw her head up, only to lower it. She pawed the ground. The brown mare watched from the safety of the edge of the tree line.

Paris had burrs in her mane and forelock. Sadie's hands ached to feel the sturdy comb raking through that wonderful, thick mane. What would be better in all the world but to stand beside this horse with a bucket of warm water, fragrant with shampoo, and wash that honey-colored coat? To feed her carrots and apples and peppermint candy? Paris always ate peppermint patties. She loved dark chocolate.

Now Sadie was close enough to see the dark veins in the whites of her eyes. She saw the little whirl of lighter hair on the upper part of her chest.

"Paris, you are going to be my horse. You just don't know it yet. Come on, taste this. It's really good. It's corn and molasses. Can you smell it?"

The horse's hunger overcame her fear then, and she took another step forward. Sadie held out her arm, steadily talking.

When the moment came, it was beyond description. How could a nose feel so much like the nose of her past? It was heavy and soft and velvety all at the same time. It was lighter than the touch of a blue jay's feather. When Paris moved her mouth to gather up the feed, Sadie felt that funny little pressure horses make against the palm of your hand.

Sadie could not stop the tears of joy that welled up in her eyes.

She would not reach out with her other hand to stroke that wonderful mane. She just let Paris lip all the feed. Then Sadie slowly lifted her hand along the side of Paris' mouth to see if she would allow her nose to be touched.

The black whinnied a loud nicker, a call to retrieve her. Her ears went back. Then she lifted her head and wheeled, trotting back to the security she knew.

"Good-bye, Paris," Sadie called.

Then she turned, grabbed Reuben's hands, and shouted to the golden evening around them, "I have a horse! I have a horse!"

Sadie hugged Reuben and went running down the slope, leaving him to get the backpack, close it, and run down after her.

When she could talk, she solemnly told Reuben that he was the best brother in the whole wide world, and she would give him 10 whole dollars for this evening.

Immediately he calculated his wealth at $20. He was sorry he thought his sister was sort of strange, because she really wasn't. She was one of the best sisters in the world, which was allowing some, because sisters didn't rank very high according to Reuben.

Chapter 22

She told Richard Caldwell then. She told Dorothy and Jim and anyone who came into the kitchen after that. The ranch was abuzz with the news of these horses and Sadie's ability to touch one of them.

But she still did not tell her parents and, as far as she knew, none of her sisters suspected anything unusual. They seemed to accept Sadie's determination to strengthen the muscles in her leg by hiking and Reuben's sudden interest in accompanying her.

Dorothy had a fit. She waved her long-handled wooden spoon. She spluttered and talked "a blue streak" in Mam's words. She became so agitated one morning that Sadie watched her snapping little eyes and the heightened color in her cheeks with dismay.

Small, plump, and clearly disturbed, Dorothy stepped back from the stove and retied her apron. Retying her apron always meant a serious lecture, one that did not allow for any joking or smiling from Sadie.

"It'll be the death of you, Sadie Miller, you mark my words. That big black one will attack you. You think you know something about horses, young lady, but you don't.

They're unpredictable, same as all wild creatures."

"But..." Sadie started. She was promptly cut off.

Closing her eyes self-righteously and lifting herself to her full height—which was still not very tall—Dorothy put both fists to her soft, round hips and snorted.

"Don't even start, young lady. Your parents need to know about this. Yer puttin' that little Reuben in danger as well. You simply ought to be ashamed of yourself."

They were harsh words, coming from Dorothy.

Oh, shoot, Sadie thought.

"It ain't right, Sadie."

"But, Dorothy, please listen. You have no idea how much I loved my horse, Paris. We don't have the money to buy a horse like her now. And this palomino is even prettier, or she will be. She's so perfect, and surely if I can tame her, she'll be mine."

"That there thinkin' is gonna get you in serious trouble. You don't know whose horses they are. And if they're wild, you got the government or the state of Montana or whatever to wrestle with. An' you know how weird you Amish are about stuff like that. Nonresistant and all. You don't stand a chance."

Sadie let her shoulders slump dejectedly. Perhaps she should listen to Dorothy and at least let her parents know what she was up to.

Dorothy turned, brushing back a stray hair, and began scraping the biscuit pan. She nodded her head toward the stack of breakfast dishes.

"Best get to 'em."

Sadie swallowed her defeat, fighting back tears. Dorothy meant what she said, and going ahead with this adventure was just being openly rebellious and not very wise at all.

Halfheartedly, Sadie began scraping the bits of food clinging to the breakfast plates. What a mess! Whoever cleared the table could have put the scraps in one bowl and stacked these plates cleanly.

Suddenly she became so angry, she turned, faced Dorothy, and said, "You could have scraped these leftovers at least."

"Hmmm. A bit hoity-toity now, are we?"

"Yes, we are. I mean...yes, I am!"

She whirled and flounced away from the kitchen, pushing open the swinging oak doors with so much force that there was a resounding whack and an earsplitting yell that could only have come from the boss, Richard Caldwell.

Sadie was horrified to find him leaning heavily against the wall, holding his prominent nose while tears began forming in his eyes.

"Oh!" Sadie's hand went to her mouth, her eyes wide as she realized what she had done. She had lost her temper so that she swung those doors hard enough to smack them into Richard Caldwell who was just about to walk through to the kitchen.

His nose was clearly smarting, his expression boding no good for the person who had pushed the doors open. Blinking, he extracted a blue man's handkerchief from his pocket and began dabbing tenderly at his battered nose.

"You! Of all people," he muttered.

"I'm sorry," Sadie whispered.

"I'm okay. What got you so riled that you came charging through like that?"

"Oh, nothing. It was just..."

Sadie lifted miserable eyes to Richard Caldwell's face. "Well, Dorothy made me mad."

Richard Caldwell snorted, wiped his nose tentatively, then stared down at her. "You aren't going to cry, are you?"

"No. I mean..." She had never fought so hard in all her life to keep her composure. Reuben said if you thought of jelly bread, potato soup, a washcloth, or any object, you wouldn't cry or laugh, whichever one you didn't want to do. He assured her it really worked, but it certainly did not work now. Sadie even thought of white bread with a golden crust slathered with fresh, soft butter and homemade grape jelly, but it did absolutely no good. She simply stood in front of her big, intimidating boss and began crying like a little girl having a bad day at school.

She felt his big hand on her shoulder, steering her into his office.

"Sit down," he said, too suddenly and too gruffly to be very kind.

"Is it all Dorothy?" Richard Caldwell asked.

Sadie couldn't talk. She couldn't say one word with her mouth twisting the way it did when she cried and her nose and eyes both running.

Richard Caldwell handed her a box of tissues from the desk, and she grasped at them, a simple act of redeeming her broken pride.

"Well, it's not really Dorothy, or is it? I don't know. She's been going on and on about the danger of taking Reuben to feed the wild horses. She says my parents need to know. And...if they find out, it'll be the end of my dream to have that palomino horse...to have...Paris."

Richard Caldwell sat behind his desk, leaning on his elbows. He studied her intently, a mixture of emotions playing across his face. He cleared his throat a few times, as if that would delay having to say what he would eventually need to tell her.

Finally he said, "Why are you so sure that horse can be yours?"

"I can tame her. I can."

Sadie said this so emphatically, her voice became deeper, rich with an unnamed emotion.

Richard Caldwell said nothing. He could still remember her standing in that stall. He could still hear that broken Pennsylvania Dutch as she talked softly to that poor wreck of a horse. And then she lost that pet, likely because of the wild horses.

"Sadie, I want you to have that horse. But I think you're going about getting her the wrong way."

"No! I'm not. I know what I'm doing. She is already taking feed out of my hand."

"No, what I mean is, do you really think those horses are wild?"

She slowly shook her head.

"If they're not wild, then you'd be taking someone else's horse."

"No, no. I wouldn't. No one knows whose horses they are or has any idea where they came from."

Sadie was ripping a tissue into dozens of tiny pieces, her hands never ceasing their nervous movement.

"Now, Sadie," Richard Caldwell began.

"What?"

"You remember the story I showed you from the news? It wasn't too terribly long ago. Here at the ranch we all think that these horses are the stolen ones from... Ah, where was it? Hill County? Someplace south of here. As long as we let those horses run, it's okay, but if you'd tame that palomino and someone discovered her, how could you prove you weren't the horse thief?"

"Do I look like a horse thief?" Sadie said tersely.

Richard Caldwell's booming laugh filled the office. He shook his head.

"Well, then," Sadie said.

"We need to get to the bottom of this. If you tame that horse, then we'll have to try and locate the person who had those horses stolen. It can be done."

"You mean, I can go ahead and try?"

"Only if you tell your parents."

Sadie was already shaking her head back and forth.

"I can't."

"You have to."

Sadie remained silent, her thoughts racing.

"Did I ever tell you the story about the first dog I ever had?"

Sadie shook her head. A faraway look fell across Richard Caldwell's weather-worn face as he told Sadie about the time he found the dirty, near-dead dog. He hid nothing—sharing how his father shot the dog before he could get away, and how he snuck out in the middle of the night to bury the thin body. He told about the sorrow, anger, guilt, and even forgiveness that eventually followed.

"And I never had another dog until I left home. My father hated dogs, so..."

"Now you have seven or eight."

Richard Caldwell smiled, his eyes moist. He marveled at the onslaught of emotion she evoked in him. He could smell the wet grass, feel the smooth wooden handle of that shovel, and he knew exactly what this young woman was going through.

"So I need to wait to have a horse until I leave home, or what are you...?"

"No, no. I just want you to level with your parents."

"If I level with them, as you say, there will be nothing to worry about. It will be over. My father does not like horses. He doesn't understand that bond, that true... I don't know." Sadie hung her head miserably.

"I need to warn you, Sadie. You know if you tamed that mare and actually did take her home, the first problem is being caught and accused of being a horse thief. The second is that if the black stallion is as aggressive as you say, and if you have another horse with this palomino, he'll kill him or wreck your whole barn trying."

Sadie looked up.

Of course. She had not thought of that.

Defeat confronted her, raised its impossibly heavy head, and her spirit wavered within her. Like an accordion folding, the last notes dying away in a high, thin wail, she felt the piercing sadness of losing yet another horse.

Ach, Paris, I would have loved you so much.

Richard Caldwell watched the display of emotion on Sadie's beautiful face, the drooping of her big blue eyes, the loosening of her perfect mouth.

She sighed, ran her fingers along the crease of the leather chair. Then she stood up abruptly, unexpectedly. Her chin lifted, her eyes darkened, and she spoke quietly.

"All right then, Mr. Caldwell. I will take your advice. I know you're right. I've been blind, my own will leading Reuben and me into danger. I'll go home and speak to my father, and if it's over, it's over. Thank you."

Slowly she turned, her skirts swinging gracefully. She opened the door and was gone as quietly as a midsummer's breeze.

Richard Caldwell cleared his throat. He stared unseeingly at the opposite wall. Overwhelming pity knocked on his heart. He picked up a gold pen and scribbled on a notepad. He crossed his hands behind his head, put his boots on his desk, and stared at the ceiling.

That was one courageous young woman.

How could she? Just like that, she gave up. It was the way these odd Amish people raised their children. Once the parents said no, the no was accepted. Perhaps not immediately, but … it was something.

Suddenly he lowered his feet, swiveled the great, black, leather chair, and clicked on the computer, straightening his back as light danced across the screen.

☆ ✡ ☆

Sadie opened the door to the kitchen. Without speaking, she went to the supply closet and found the vacuum bags.

Dorothy peered over her glasses.

"Whatcha doin', honey?"

"I'll start the upstairs."

"Where've you been?"

"Talking to Richard Caldwell."

"About what?"

"Oh, I'm getting a raise—$20 an hour more."

"Pooh! Get along with you!"

As Sadie passed the downstairs office, she saw Richard Caldwell bent intently, his fingers working the keyboard of his computer.

☆ ✡ ☆

That evening, the Miller supper lasted much longer than usual. After everyone had eaten their fill of Mam's delicious fried chicken and baked potatoes, Sadie started the conversation.

Reuben looked up, wild-eyed.

"It's okay, Reuben. My boss told me a few things so I'm going to tell Dat and Mam."

With that, Sadie launched into a vivid account of her hikes, carefully watching Dat's expression. Mam's eyes were round with fright, then alarm, until finally, she burst out.

"Why, Sadie! I'm surprised at you. How could you do this?"

"Mam, it's the age-old thing! Same as it always was!"

"What do you mean?"

"You never understood my love of horses. Never."

Leah, Rebekah, and Anna all began talking at once. They scolded, asked questions, answered themselves, and just raised the most awful fuss Sadie had ever heard. She reached for the chicken platter. She knew the chicken was fattening and not very healthy, but it was the best fried chicken in all the world.

Mam rolled the chicken in flour, fried it in real butter, salted and peppered it generously, and when it was golden brown, laid it carefully on a baking sheet and finished it in the oven.

It was crispy and salty and buttery and fell off the bone in succulent mouthfuls. It was so good that you could eat a leg or thigh and not believe you had already eaten the whole thing. So you sort of went into denial about how much you were eating and reached for another piece. And it was perfectly all right because in the morning, you would have only an orange for breakfast. Not even a piece of toast. Certainly no butter or strawberry jelly.

Sadie put her fork into the perfectly done chicken thigh and pulled it away. She closed her eyes as she savored the rich flavor.

"Mmmm."

"How can you sit there and eat as if nothing in all the world is wrong and after you went and pulled off this horrendous deed?" Rebekah asked.

Sadie put down her fork, leaned forward, her eyes alight.

"You want to know why? Because I gave up. I won't go anymore. No one thinks it's safe. And Paris—I mean, the palomino—will no longer come to the field of wildflowers for food if I'm not there to give it, and now I'm trying to relax. And if I cry into my pillow tonight, Rebekah, you are going to be the last to know!"

Dat watched his daughters without comment. He could see the unshed tears in Sadie's eyes.

"Hey!" Reuben shouted above the din.

Everyone quieted, staring at normally disinterested Reuben.

"Rebekah, you know what? You should just hush up. You weren't up there on that ridge with Sadie. I was. It's something to see."

"I would like to see it," Dat said, quietly.

"You … What?"

All eyes turned to Dat who was sitting back in his chair, his eyes twinkling, running a hand casually through his thick, gray beard.

"Like I said, I would like to see where Sadie goes. I would like to see these horses. They're as mysterious as a phantom or a ghost, so I would like to see for myself what is happening up there and whether the horses really are dangerous. They may not be a threat at all. The stallion wouldn't be as long as there are no other horses around."

Mam nodded in agreement, watching Dat's face.

"But, you mean…? You mean I'm allowed to go again?"

"Yes. I'll go with you."

"Oh, Dat," Sadie breathed.

It was all she could say.

Reuben bounced up and down, knocked his water glass over, then ran for a tea towel as Anna yelled and jumped out of the way when water dribbled onto her lap.

"Hurry, Reuben," Leah said dryly.

The supper table was a bit chaotic after that. Sadie was so excited at the sudden and unexpected prospect of seeing Paris again that she ate another piece of fried chicken and a pumpkin whoopie pie and three slices of canned peaches. She was so full, even her ears felt warm to the touch.

"Are my ears red?" she asked, laughing.

"Magenta! Purple!" Anna shouted.

Mam told them all to quiet down, to get the dishes done and the kitchen swept. She still had some ironing to do. When Mam gave these barking orders and proceeded to do something she hadn't done in years, Sadie remembered to thank God for the gift of her mother's health and well-being. God had been good to all of them. It could have been so much worse and they all knew that. They would never again take Mam's health for granted.

✿ ✡ ✿

At Aspen East Ranch, the perfect moon rose and began its steady journey across the night sky into the starlit heavens. Gates creaked as gates do when the night air cools them, and horses moved slowly behind the fencing, their tails swishing as softly as the grasses surrounding them. A lone owl hooted down by the bunk house as a star fell, leaving a bright streak in the ever-enduring constellation of stars.

Most of the windows were dark, but the great window on the second story of the ranch house was a beacon of warm, yellow light.

Inside, Richard Caldwell sat at his desk. His wife, Barbara, was by his side. They were both leaning forward, staring intently at the bluish-white light from the computer. Half-eaten plates of food were on the desk, tall glasses of ice water forgotten, forming small rings of moisture on the glossy desktop.

"There!" Barbara said, pointing. "That email address might be it."

"But we don't know if it's from Hill Country."

"It could be."

The night wore on, and finally a victorious shout came from Richard Caldwell. Barbara was exultant, embracing her husband warmly.

"You did it!"

"Looks like it!"

Then he turned, dialed quite a few digits on his desk phone, winked at Barbara, and waited for someone at the other end to pick up the phone.

"Hello?" Richard Caldwell's voice boomed across the room. "Yes. Richard Caldwell here of Aspen East Ranch in Tacoma County."

"Yes."

There was a pause.

"I am looking for a Mr. Harold Ardwin."

"All right, yes, sir."

"I have a question to ask you. Are you the guy who had those horses stolen, oh, maybe about nine, 10 months ago?"

There was a long pause.

Richard Caldwell turned, raising his eyes to his wife who was leaning forward to hear the voice speaking to her husband. Her hands were clenched in anticipation, her eyes bright with interest.

"Well, is that right? Seriously? Mm-hmm."

Another long pause.

"Well, my wife and I would like to meet with you, if it's possible."

"Oh, oh, you are? Well, then we'll wait until you get back. Can you let us know what would be a good time?"

The two men exchanged a few pleasantries, they set a definite date, and Richard Caldwell carefully replaced the phone.

"They're leaving on vacation for three weeks."

"Awww."

Barbara was clearly disappointed.

"It's all right. We'll not breathe a word to Sadie."

"For sure."

"Or that Dorothy and her husband!"

They sat quietly, companionably, watching the silver moon in the night sky. Barbara slipped her hand beneath Richard Caldwell's elbow, laid her head on his massive shoulder, and sighed dreamily.

"Now we have two secrets: one to keep from Sadie and one to keep from everybody!"

"How long until we announce it?" Richard Caldwell asked, softly stroking his wife's abundant hair.

"I'm so excited. Oh, Richard, do you think everything will be okay? At our age and all?"

"It will be. Remember, if it's a girl, we're naming her Sadie."

"Of course."

"And would to God she'd be half the girl that Sadie Miller is. What touches my...Well, I hate to sound like a softy, but she loves horses so much and has the most rotten luck I've ever seen. It's just not fair."

"But you know what they'd say, those Amish people: 'It's the will of God.'"

"Don't make fun of them, Barbara."

"Oh, Richard, I'm not. There was a time not long ago, I would have. But there has been such a great change in you that I have to believe she has brought goodness to the ranch. To us."

"She'll never know."

"That is God's way."

Chapter 23

AND SO BEGAN ONE OF THE BEST TIMES OF SADIE'S
young life.

That first week the whole family joined her and Reuben on their hike up to the wildflowers at the edge of the surrounding forest. They took a bag of pungent horse feed, three apples, a bag of carrots, and a few slices of salt off the brick that was in Charlie's feed box.

It was a warm evening with a gentle, swirling breeze, the kind that whirls around you, going first one way and then another. It was a teasing sort of wind that pulls at your covering so that you have to adjust the straight pins at the side to keep it on.

Dat was puffing heartily by the time they were halfway up the ridge, but Mam was surprisingly agile. Her cheeks were flushed, her graying hair escaping her covering in the twirling wind, but her eyes sparkled with excitement at the prospect of actually seeing these fearful creatures.

Reuben behaved badly. He was clearly beside himself with anxiety. He stretched everything he told his parents about the palomino and especially about the black stallion. When Sadie gently corrected him, he became angry and pouted, falling back so far that they all had to wait for him to catch up. When Anna slowed down to walk with him, his wild stories started all over again—hands waving, eyebrows dancing at a fearful pace, blonde hair tossing in the breeze.

Dat laughed and shrugged his shoulders. "He's excited about showing us the horses. Let him go."

"How much farther?" asked Leah, her breath coming in gasps.

"Not far," Sadie assured them.

When they reached the field of wildflowers, Mam threw up her hands in amazement. "Ach, my goodness, Sadie! How could you keep all of this a secret? Why, it's absolutely *himmlisch* up here!"

"I know, Mam. It's lovely."

Reuben was telling everyone to hide, to either sit down or lie down and hold very, very still. Dat said he'd be glad to oblige, sinking wearily onto the carpet of grass and flowers.

"Do the horses always come when you're here?" Rebekah asked.

"Not always. But more and more it's a usual thing to see them."

Reuben distributed the feed. The wind sighed in the pines. The family whispered among themselves. Anna became extremely restless, making faces and gesticulating silently, asking Sadie, "How long?"

Sadie shrugged her shoulders, biting nervously on her lower lip.

Come on, Paris, she thought.

She watched the tree line carefully for the moving shadows that turned into real horses. This was the expectant moment when she always held her breath, unable to grasp the fact that they had come one more time to eat the feed she had brought. The miracle was new each time.

The horses did not disappoint her.

Sadie's body tensed as she heard them moving through the trees. She held up one finger to quiet everyone, then pointed.

Paris was first, as usual.

She stepped out, her ears pricked forward, and nickered softly. Sadie stood in a swift, quiet movement, then proceeded forward, holding one hand out, palm upward. She spoke softly in Pennsylvania Dutch, saying the same words of endearment over and over.

Paris stretched her beautiful neck, her head lowered. Sadie's hand touched her nose, a movement as natural as the world around them. As sure as an apple falls from the tree at harvesttime, Sadie's hand caressed first the nose and then the neck of the honey-colored horse. She combed the unruly mane with her fingertips and removed burrs. She ran her hands along the rough coat where the winter hair still clung, stubbornly refusing to allow the honey color of the new, sleek growth to shine through.

"If only I had a comb and brush," she told Paris. "You need a bath in the creek with my Pantene shampoo," she chuckled.

She bent to lay her cheek against the horse's head, and Paris stayed completely still. They stood together, a bright picture against the backdrop of trees while Sadie's family watched in amazement. There were tears in Mam's eyes as she sought Dat's face. Dat looked at her, then smiled and shook his head. Reuben saw the look pass between them and was glad.

The brown mare stepped out then and walked easily over to Sadie who began talking to her, caressing her face and combing the mane with her fingertips, as she had done with Paris.

When the huge black walked hesitantly out behind the brown mare, Dat gasped. Mam looked at him questioningly. "Jacob, should we…?"

Dat shook his head.

Rebekah moved as if to stop Sadie, but Reuben held her back. "Let her go. She's okay. Watch."

Sadie appeared to ignore the black horse, but she kept him in her sight out of the corners of her eyes. He snorted, pawed the grass, tossed his head, and flicked his ears. He walked then, slowly and with a stiff gait, as if too proud to be beholden to anyone. He grabbed a mouthful of the feed hungrily. Then another.

The brown mare walked over, bent her head, and eagerly crunched an apple.

Slowly, Sadie reached out a hand to the black. He lifted his head, his nostrils flared, and his ears pricked steadily forward.

His coat was a mess, Sadie noted.

"Come here, boy. Come. Let me touch you. You were once used to it. *Sei brauf. Sei brauf.*"

Sadie kept one hand beneath Paris' chin, the other stretched out to the black. Talking quietly, she closed the gap between them until, like a feather drifting on a newly mowed field, she felt the soft dryness of the stallion's nose on her hand. He snorted and she removed her hand, but she did not move away.

Oh, the wonder of it!

The fearsome creature, the black phantom of the night that had created horrible dreams after Ezra's death, the snow, the pain—all of it gone. Here he was, standing in the golden light of the evening sun, and, in a different light, he was a different creature. There was nothing to be frightened about now.

Or was there?

She looked into the black's eyes so far above her head. He was huge. There were no whites of his eyes showing, but she could sense the wariness, the ability to whirl away and be gone in a few seconds.

Slowly she moved her hand up from his nose, stroking the long, broad face like a whisper. The hairs in his forelock were stuck together in a hopeless tangle of burrs, bits of leaves, and twigs, but they would have to remain there for now. No use pushing her luck. She had used up more than her fair share today.

When she turned to go, Paris followed her. Sadie's laughter rang out across the field, a sound of pure and unrestrained joy.

"Paris!"

The flowers nodded and sang "Paris!" with her. The clouds rolled and danced in jubilation. The trees joined in the symphony, bowed their heads for an encore, and sang "Paris!" in response. Sadie's heart overflowed with love, and she turned and threw her arms around Paris' neck, hugging her as tightly as possible.

"I have to let you go now. But I'm going to ride you yet. You watch, Paris. I will. Be good now until I come back."

When she joined her family on the trek down the hillside, she looked back and found Paris watching after her, her head lowered as if preparing to step down and follow her home if asked.

She asked Dat why she couldn't take Paris along home right then. Dat gave her the same wise answer Richard Caldwell had. Until they knew whose horses they were, it was best to let them roam wild.

❉ ✡ ❉

That evening when Sadie knelt by her bed, she thanked God for the wonderful way he had shown her family the horses. Her heart was full of gratitude, and she fell into bed tired, but so happy that she felt sure she would be smiling while she slept.

Despite her utter happiness, her mind turned to Mark Peight as it always did when she drifted off to sleep. The thought of him always brought a certain void, a question mark hanging in the air that never ceased to fill her with an unnamed longing, a particular kind of remorse.

Why? Why had he entered her life for so short a span? Why had he almost asked her for a date? But no. He had asked her, and she had said yes. Then Mam became ill, and he disappeared to Pennsylvania.

Was he still there? Would she ever see him again?

She truly did not know God's plan for her life as far as a husband was concerned. Ezra was taken from her, and she supposed Mark was very much a dream. Loving Mark had been much more than she had ever imagined, but he had also been taken.

Or...he just went.

It was maddening. It was also ridiculous. He was simply a great big chicken. Albeit, a good-looking chicken.

Sadie giggled, then buried her face in her pillow and cried great, fat tears of longing and frustration.

It would be different if she could do something about it, but she couldn't. Amish girls did not ask someone out or write a letter or try to find him or whatever a person could do. It was simply not done.

Girls were supposed to be shy and chaste, waiting

until someone asked them for a date, which happened for most of them. Sometimes a girl couldn't wait and went ahead and asked a guy out. But girls who did that were considered fast and didn't usually fare as well with guys, once they got serious about finding a wife.

Well, she wasn't going to hop on Amtrak or hire a driver or book a flight on an airliner to go traipsing off looking for Mark Peight.

She wondered who the Melvin Peachey was the visitng minister had talked about. He had known her family.

Melvin Peachy.

Mark Peight.

Suppose it had been him?

Sadie yawned, sleepiness settling over her like a warm blanket. She rolled onto her side, blinked at a twinkling star in the night sky, and thought drowsily, "I wish I may, I wish I might have Mark Peight here with me tonight."

It was a silly school-girl rhyme, but a sincere young girl's heart longing for the love of her life.

✿ ✡ ✿

Sadie made daily visits to the ridge now, sometimes accompanied by Reuben, sometimes by Anna, and some-times by her other sisters. She much preferred Reuben's company, for the simple reason that he now shared her love of horses. He had learned to stroke the horses, and they followed him willingly wherever he went with the feed.

Sadie and Reuben studied an old Indian book explain-ing the method of handling horses with a rope. Dat had told them very firmly that they were not allowed to put a halter or a bridle on any of them, figuring that would put a stop to any thought of riding them.

Sadie felt a wee bit guilty for riding when Dat hoped she wouldn't, sort of like sneaking a cookie out of the Tupperware container in the pantry an hour before suppertime. But it wasn't as if they galloped dangerously around the field. It was more like giving pony rides at a kiddie petting zoo.

One thing led to another after they pored over the old Indian book. They simply put the rope around the horse's neck. Stopping, starting, and going left or right was much like neck reining, which Sadie was already used to. She accomplished that with a mere shifting of her body.

It had been a memorable evening when Reuben helped her climb onto Paris' back. She was unaccustomed to the feeling of riding bareback, especially without a bridle, so she felt a bit at odds. Her knees shook and her breath came in short gasps, making her mouth feel dry.

She laughed nervously when Reuben told her to calm down, that Paris wasn't going anywhere.

It was quite unlike anything she had ever experienced, the dizzying height of the horse, along with the feeling of riding a horse with no bridle, and then Reuben walking along, assuring her that Paris wasn't going anywhere.

It was exhilarating, a freedom Sadie reveled in, a butterfly emerging from the stuffiness of its larva.

In time, Reuben rode the brown mare and Sadie rode Paris. Sometimes they walked and sometimes they trotted until they perfected the rope technique. In a month, there was no holding back. They raced through the wildflowers, the black stallion watching or sometimes running along beside them.

The days were long, and their evenings together remained the joy of their lives. Their faces turned brown and their hair lightened in the summer sun. They formed an unbreakable bond, their horses the tie that bound them.

One evening as they sat side by side, their horses grazing quietly, Sadie voiced her longing to have Paris in the barn.

Reuben wagged his head wisely.

"Can't do it, Sadie!"

"I know."

"It's too risky."

"Mm-hmm."

"One more ride?"

"Race ya!"

Sadie hopped up, ran over to Paris, grabbed a handful of her mane, and leaped up from the side, the way they had practiced over and over. Reuben was more agile, bounding up as if he had wings on his shoulder blades.

The horses lifted their heads, wheeled in the direction the riders' knees prodded, and were off flying through the long field of grass. Hooves pounded, and the grass made a funny sort of rustling noise, an insistent whisper like a weaving sound.

The wind rushed in Sadie's ears as she bent low over Paris' neck, urging her on. Reuben looked back, laughing as they completed the long circle, coming back up the slope as if their lives depended on being the first to arrive at the starting point.

They slid to a stop, laughing breathlessly, their horses panting.

"Forget it, Reuben. It was nose to nose."

"No way!"

"Yes, it was!"

"Paris isn't faster than mine, Sadie!"

"She beat her though."

"I don't think so."

"Give your horse a name, Reuben. You can't just call her 'the brown horse.'"

Reuben squared his shoulders and looked out across the valley, a serious expression stamped on his face.

"I can't."

"Why?"

"If I do, it'll be much harder to let go of her. You have to realize, Sadie, we can't always come up here on someone else's land and ride someone else's horses. I mean, come on. Duh!"

Sadie glanced sideways at him, shocked to find his eyes bright with unshed tears. He was very sure of himself in reprimanding her, but it was still hard for him to hide the feeling he had for the horse he had grown to love.

"I mean, what'll happen this winter? We can't come up here. You know that."

Sadie nodded.

"I guess you're right."

"Let's go home. Sun's sliding behind the mountain."

"Okay. See you, Paris."

Sadie turned, loosening the rope, stroking the honey-colored neck. The horses had been brushed over and over, their manes and forelocks trimmed, burrs removed from their tails. Still, they had never been bathed and shampooed the way Sadie would have liked. But it was something the way they were able to groom them at all, even the black.

Sadie stood by her horse's head murmuring, when she heard Reuben's short, "Shhh!"

She raised her head and froze when she saw two men standing close to the tree line watching them. Her hands dropped away and her arms went numb as she watched them approach. They were dressed in black, one much larger than the other.

"Sadie, let's run!" Reuben hissed.

Sadie shook her head. She blinked her eyes and squinted into the shadows.

Could it be?

Yes. It was.

Richard Caldwell.

She felt the tension leave her body, then smiled when he threw up a hand.

"Hey, Sadie."

Reuben came over to stand very close to her, and she welcomed his nearness.

"Richard Caldwell! This is a surprise! What brings you up here?"

Paris and the brown horse stood alert, their ears forward. The large black stallion was back farther, his head held high, his nostrils quivering, ready to bolt.

Richard Caldwell stopped, his hand indicating the smaller man at his side. Sadie watched warily as he stepped forward.

"I'm Harold Ardwin of Ardwin Stables."

"Yes?" Sadie was puzzled. She had never heard of this place, and why should she? What was he doing up here with Richard Caldwell? She thought she could trust Richard. Now he had blown her secret, and this would be the last evening of her life with Paris.

Richard Caldwell stepped forward.

"Harold Ardwin is the owner of the ranch where all the horses were stolen."

"Oh. So..."

"We've been watching you and your brother for close to an hour."

Sadie's face flushed, and she looked down at the toe of her boots, her long lashes sweeping her tanned cheeks.

Reuben coughed self-consciously.

No one spoke.

Harold Ardwin looked at the horses. He looked at Sadie and Reuben. He cleared his throat. "I believe I've found my horses."

Sadie kept her eyes on her boots and bit her lower lip. The bottoms of her denims were frayed and torn, her skirt dirty and dusty. She blinked hard. She swallowed. She tried to look up, but if she did, she knew the men would see her misery, so she kept her gaze on her boot tops.

She heard Harold move away, his highly polished boots with the intricate design moving through the grass with a soft rustle. His shoulders were powerful beneath the black shirt, his waist trim for a man she guessed to be close to 60 years old.

"This is Black Thunder of Ardwin Stables, the sire of our finest colts," he said firmly. The black stood as if carved in stone. He trembled, then turned and bolted, but only a short distance.

"Sadie, can you get him back?" asked Richard Caldwell.

Reuben nodded, and Sadie walked after the black. She touched his nose with her outstretched hand, then cupped his chin, murmuring as she did so.

Harold Ardwin blinked and blinked again. He sniffed, then cleared his throat. He watched in disbelief as Sadie came back, the black following, a faithful pet who was as obedient and helpless as a kitten.

"Come here, boy! Don't you know who I am?" Harold Ardwin asked, his voice thick, his eyes misty.

Black Thunder whinnied. He had found his owner.

You just couldn't deny the recognition between a man and a horse.

This was a different kind of relationship than Sadie had with the big, black stallion. The black horse knew and respected Harold Ardwin, but Sadie had a hunch there was a stable boy at Ardwin Stables who spent more time with the horse than the wealthy owner did.

"After all this time. This is amazing," Harold kept repeating.

Finally he turned to the remaining two horses. "Butterfly and Sasha," he said, nodding toward them.

Sadie's heart sank. She had been foolish beyond belief. She had known this time would come. Paris was never hers. Never had been.

She felt old and weary then, and she wanted to run down the hillside without saying one more polite word to anyone. She wanted to get away where she could hold her sorrow and loss all by herself, stoic, accepting, and dry-eyed.

Reuben scuffed his foot against her boot.

"Answer, Sadie."

She raised her head.

"I'm sorry. What?"

"I asked, had you named the horses?"

"Only one. The … the palomino."

"Sasha?"

Sadie could only nod.

"Your riding is impeccable. I have never seen such a display of trust between a horse and a rider."

"Thank you."

Reuben grinned and grinned until Sadie elbowed his ribs slightly.

Richard Caldwell saw every emotion as it took control of Sadie's features—the horrible despair upon learning these were Harold's horses, the blaming of herself for getting too attached to Paris, the courage she had tried to muster when answering Harold, and how she failed miserably. It was every emotion he remembered feeling as he wrapped the body of his beloved dog in the pink towel and laid it gently in the cool, wet hole in the earth.

Courage was admirable, but sometimes your heart was so crumpled by pain that you couldn't really hold all the fragments together. Sometimes a broken heart couldn't be helped.

But not this time. Not if he could help it.

"We'll pay a visit to your house this evening, Sadie," he said, too tersely even to his own ears.

She nodded. There was nothing else to say, and besides, talking just didn't work around a lump in your throat. So she turned and walked down the hillside, Reuben at her heels.

Chapter 24

SADIE STORMED INTO THE KITCHEN PERSPIRING, her hair a mess, her *dichly* falling off her head. She flung herself down on a kitchen chair, a layer of dust and bits of grass trailing after her. Reuben went to the laundry bathroom and stayed there.

Mam looked up from the bowl where she was sifting flour.

"My goodness, whatever happened to you?" she asked.

"Oh, Mam," Sadie wailed, then launched into the events of the afternoon, pouring out all the heartsickness that clogged every part of her being.

"And to make matters worse, they're coming here tonight. What for? Whatever in the world would they want here?"

Mam considered the situation for a moment, slowly wiping her hands over and over on the underside of her apron. "Well, whoever that Harold Arken..."

"Ardwin."

"...Ardwin is, he must be very wealthy. And now he is going to enter our humble dwelling. Richard Caldwell, too. If an important person arrives, we offer him the highest seat, and if a poor one enters, he always gets the lowest, but this is not good in Christ's eyes. So we'll not get flustered, and instead we'll light our propane lamp and serve them these apricot cookies and coffee, same as if Jack Entan arrived."

Sadie glanced at her mother, caught her glint of humor, and smiled wryly. Jack was the town's junk-hauler who lived in a less than appealing environment, in spite of everyone's best efforts to reform him.

"Mam!"

"I'm serious. They're only human beings, wealthy and important or not."

Sadie frowned. She straightened her legs, stared at her frayed denims and dusty boots, and stood up abruptly.

"I'm going to my room."

"Oh, there's a letter for you. It's on the hutch."

Mam returned to her baking, and Sadie went to the cupboard for the letter. She recognized the handwriting instantly.

Eva.

Oh good, she thought.

Sadie and Eva wrote constantly. Letters were their regular way of communicating. It was always a joyful day for Sadie when one of Eva's letters arrived.

Sometimes they would plan a time to be at their phone shanties and have a long conversation, but that had its drawbacks, especially in winter. Phone shanties were cold and uncomfortable, so telephone conversations were kept to a minimum. Sadie supposed the whole idea for having that church rule about phone shanties was because women were prone to gossip, and telephones were definitely an aid to that vice. Therefore, the less convenient a phone was, the less women would be gossiping on it.

Sadie ripped open the plain white envelope, unfolded the yellow legal pad paper, and eagerly devoured every word.

> *Dear Sadie,*
>
> *You will never guess what! My darling husband-to-be is allowing me to travel by train to spend a week with you. Are you sitting down? So I'm thinking of spending Christmas with you!!! Are there enough explanation points for that sentence?*
>
> *Our wedding is not until April, and he really wants me to do this before the wedding because he knows how close we are and that we haven't seen each other in years!*
>
> *Oh, Sadie! I am so excited. I won't be traveling alone because Dan Detweiler's parents are coming, too. Maybe if we can get enough people to come, we'll hire a van and won't need the train.*

Sadie chuckled at Eva's two sheets of questions about the trip. It was so typical of Eva and so dear. They shared everything, every little detail of their lives, including Mark Peight, the ranch, Dorothy, Richard Caldwell, Mam's mental illness. They held nothing back, which was why they had a continuing friendship that began when they were little first-graders in the one-room school they both attended.

Sadie sighed as she replaced the papers in the envelope. It was a long time to wait. Christmas seemed far away—another time, another world.

She heard Reuben unlock the bathroom door and walk into the kitchen to Mam.

"Why, Reuben, where were you? I had almost forgotten about you."

"In the bathroom," Reuben said in the gruffest, manliest voice he could possible muster.

"You've been in there awhile then."

"Yeah. You know we're getting company tonight?"

"Sadie told me."

"They shouldn't come here. All they want is our... those horses anyhow."

Mam nodded.

"We'll see, Reuben."

✿ ✪ ✿

Mam tidied the kitchen while Sadie and Reuben informed Dat about the company. Mam made a pot of coffee and arranged her famous apricot cookies on a plate. The cookies were not filled with apricots but with apricot jam mixed with other things. They were soft and sweet and crumbly and delicious, and no one made them the way Mam did.

Eventually a large silver SUV wound its way up their driveway. No one was very thrilled at the sound of its tires on crunching gravel, although no one said as much. It wouldn't be polite, and certainly not a Christian attitude to be inhospitable to company.

Dat greeted the two men at the door, invited them in, and introduced them to Mam. She shook hands with them, welcoming them into their home.

Richard Caldwell was even louder than usual, nervously talking nonstop, his face flushed, his eyes bearing a certain excitement. Harold Ardwin was very professional, smiling only enough to be polite. Mustaches did that to a person, though. A heavy mustache just sort of lifted up or settled back down, covering any smile that might be underneath it. An Amish man's beard wagged a lot when he talked, and his smile was bare and unhampered so you knew if he was sincere or not.

"Where are Sadie and Reuben?" Richard Caldwell thundered.

Sadie imagined Mam wincing, not being used to those decibels of sound.

Sadie moved out to the kitchen. She had showered, changed clothes, combed her hair neatly, and pinned her white covering perfectly in place. She had chosen a navy blue dress, which she fervently hoped would make her seem older.

"Hello," she said quietly.

"You clean up well, Sadie," Richard Caldwell said, laughing.

Harold Ardwin said nothing.

They talked about the weather, the price of beef, the logging industry, the carpentry trade, anything but the horses.

Dusk was bringing shadows into the room, so Sadie got up and flicked a lighter beneath the mantle of the propane gas light. With a soft pop, it ignited, casting the room into a bright, yellow light.

Richard Caldwell was impressed, telling Dat so, but Harold Ardwin watched the soft hissing mantles carefully. He was clearly uncomfortable with his first encounter in an Amish home without electricity. Sadie stifled a giggle as he moved his chair farther away from the oak stand that contained the light.

After the light was lit, Mam and the girls served coffee. Both men drank their coffee hot and black and ate a countless amount of Mam's cookies. Richard Caldwell was profuse in his praise of her.

Then, as suddenly as the light popped on, Harold Ardwin said, "We watched your son and daughter this evening—late afternoon, really—riding the wild horses, which…are mine."

Dat blinked, listening carefully.

"I'm sure you know plenty of the local people have always felt these horses weren't mustangs."

Dat nodded.

"Horse thieves are notorious in our region. We still don't have all the pieces of this jigsaw puzzle, but I do know that Richard Caldwell here contacted me, told me the story of your daughter and her wild horses, and led me to her. It's impressive, what she's done."

There was a pause. No one breathed, it seemed.

"So, as a reward to her—to all of you—for finding Black Thunder, I give Butterfly and Sasha to you. One is for Sadie, and one for Reuben."

Sadie wanted to say something but couldn't. She tried. She even opened her mouth, but it sort of closed on its own and not one word escaped. She was shaken back to reality by Reuben's very loud and very sincere, "Thanks a lot. Thank you!"

He looked at Sadie as if to say, "Come on. Duh."

Sadie opened her mouth, and it instantly turned into a shaky mass like jello. Her nose burned and tears swam to the surface. She swallowed hard, tried to smile, but could only bite her lip as those despised tears slid down her cheeks.

Richard Caldwell knew Sadie and saw it all. Quickly he was at her side, his arm around her shoulders.

"It's true, Sadie," he said gruffly, his voice thick with

emotion.

Sadie nodded, swiped at the moisture on her cheeks, and whispered, "Thank you."

Harold Ardwin smiled then, a smile even the mustache could not diminish. He watched Sadie's face, and a softening came to his eyes.

"You love those horses, don't you?"

"Oh, my!"

It was all Sadie could say.

"And the sum still stands for finding my horses— $20,000."

Mam put up both hands and Dat protested.

"That is *unfadiened gelt*—unearned money—and we cannot accept it. It wouldn't be right."

"Well, then, let Reuben have it," Harold Ardwin said.

✿ ✡ ✿

When the headlights of the silver SUV found its way back down the drive, the Miller household was in an uproar. Everyone talked; no one listened. Reuben leaped onto the recliner and tipped the whole thing backward. Mam scolded and Dat said, "Wasn't that a fine kettle of fish, feeding three horses!"

Sadie said the reward money would pay their hospital bills so who cared if they needed to feed three horses, and Reuben said he wished Sadie would get married so her husband would have to buy horse feed and straw and hay and then there would be more room for the brown horse.

Sadie told him that if he didn't stop talking about "the brown horse" she'd lose it, and Reuben said whoever in all the world heard of a horse named Butterfly, especially if a guy owned her. Anna shrieked and teased him about

being a guy if he had just turned 11, and Reuben's face
turned red and he ate three cookies.

✿ ✡ ✿

Sadie and Reuben helped load Black Thunder, as he
was known now, into the luxurious red and silver horse
trailer. Sadie brought him down from the field by the tree
line, followed by Paris and the brown horse.

It seemed as if the horses felt the homecoming and
welcomed it. Paris stood by Sadie as Harold Ardwin led
the black horse up the ramp. She was watching with her
ears pricked forward, but she remained quietly by Sadie's
side. Reuben sat on the brown horse, relaxed, his bare
feet dangling out of his too-short denim trousers, his hair
disheveled above his sun-browned face.

Black Thunder whinnied and rocked the trailer but,
for the most part, settled back into his former way of
traveling. It seemed as if he remembered everything and
was ready to go.

Harold Ardwin thanked them both, shook hands, said
he'd be back to visit his...their...two horses whenever he
could, and was gone.

Sadie stood with her hand on Paris' neck. She stroked
the horse absentmindedly, her thoughts completely at
peace. Finally, she had a horse—a real, honest to goodness horse of her own, fair and square, and a beautiful
one at that. The added bonus was getting to share everything with Reuben and his horse. The rides, the grooming, the companionship—it was all a gift, and God surely
had something to do with it.

Thank you, God, for Paris.

It was that simple for her, but heartfelt in a way she

had never experienced.

Turning, she smiled at Reuben.

"Ready?"

"Sure."

Sadie grabbed a handful of her horse's mane and leaped expertly onto her back, which was a signal for Reuben to turn the brown horse and start galloping home immediately.

✤ ✡ ✤

Mam was sitting at her sewing machine in front of the low double windows, working the treadle in a steady "thumpa, thumpa" sort of rhythm. It was the music of every Amish housewife's heart. It melded with the soul when accompanied by favorite hymns, which was "Amazing Grace" for her.

Mam steadily watched the presser foot as she hemmed a pair of blue denim work pants for Jacob. When she came to the end, she stopped, looked up, and reached for her scissors. Out of the corner of her eye she caught sight of a cloud of dust with two figures ahead of it.

The scissors clattered to the hardwood floor, her nervous hand knocking them off the sewing machine stand. The other hand wobbled to her chest and held her dress front in agitation.

"*Siss kenn Fashtant,*" she mouthed, "Sadie and Reuben!"

Oh, it wasn't safe. Their speed!

The horses were running neck and neck, coming up the winding drive faster than most cars. Reuben was bent low over the brown horse's neck. He was looking at Sadie and laughing, his blonde hair blowing across his face and mixing with the black hair from the horse's mane.

Sadie was bent double across the honey-colored horse, her blue dress tucked down in front but billowing out the side. Her *dichly* was attached only by one pin, danger-ously close to disappearing, but it was the last thing on Sadie's mind.

The horses weren't really galloping. They were lung-ing great, long leaps, their feet hunched beneath their powerful bodies to propel them up the sloping driveway. As they flew past the house, Mam laid her head wearily on her arms and sighed deeply to catch her breath. It would take patience and strength to watch her son and daughter with their prize horses.

✿ ✡ ✿

Sadie sat up, slid off Paris' back, and ran to open the barn door. Reuben was at her heels, running across the gravel driveway as if he had shoes on.

"Beat you!" Sadie said as she turned, her face red with exertion, her eyes stinging from the dust particles, her chest heaving.

"You did not either. Not for one second did you beat me!" Reuben yelled.

"I did, Reuben."

"You did not. Paris did!"

With that, Reuben threw back his head and laughed just the way Dat did when something struck him as being really funny.

Charlie whinnied, then put on quite a show for his two new friends. He tossed his head and did a funny version of a graceful pirouette in the confines of his box stall, as if to impress them both with his ability.

Sadie and Reuben looked at each other and laughed in a shared comradeship none of them had ever felt for the other.

They groomed their horses, brushed them, cut their manes to perfection, and then at long last were able to shampoo, scrub, and rinse them with the water hose.

Sadie was in awe of Paris after she was finished. Her mane and tail were much lighter, her coat rich and velvety with an amber color that shone in the sun. Her small head and perfectly formed ears were the most beautiful things about her. Accompanied by the arch in her muscular neck, the horse was just too good to really be true.

"Just look at her," Sadie said in a voice of amazement.

Reuben stepped back, eyed Paris, and nodded.

"You know what?"

"Hmm?"

"If your horse is named Paris, would it be stupid if I named mine something like that?"

"You mean, like 'London'?"

"No," Reuben said snorting. "I mean, do you think 'Paris' is so...well, you know," Reuben said, clearly embarrassed.

"What?"

"Well, I think Cody would be a nice name for my horse. You know, Cody, Wyoming."

"But Cody is a boy's name."

"I don't care. I want to name my horse Cody, for Cody, Wyoming. Besides, you had a horse named Nevaeh, and he was a boy!"

It was all Sadie could do to keep from laughing. He certainly had a point.

She assured Reuben that Cody would be fine. In fact, Cody was a unique name, and she bet him anything his brown mare was the only one in Montana with the name Cody.

Reuben gave her a grin worth remembering.

✿ ✛ ✿

At work in the ranch kitchen, Sadie sang loudly and twirled around the kitchen holding a wooden spoon until Dorothy told her—quite sourly—that it was all right to be happy, but surely a horse wasn't worth all that adoration.

Sadie came to a stop beside her and announced, "I'll calm down now and get to work, but I can hardly contain so much joy! And then, to simply make my cup run over, Reuben rides with me," she chortled.

Dorothy shook her head.

"You know what? You don't really fit the mold of what I thought an Amish girl would be like at your age. Aren't you supposed to be gittin' married? An' here you are, as single as the day is long and don't give two hoots about it."

Sadie held up a large, shining kettle and scraped the inside with a rubber spatula. Slowly she set it down, turned, and said quietly and honestly, "Dorothy, you know I would love to be married. I'm just as unlucky in love as I am...was...with a horse."

"Luck has nothing to do with it," Dorothy shot back.

"Really?"

"Really."

Sadie put the leftover chili in a large Tupperware bowl and glanced sideways at Dorothy just to check her rate of approval or disapproval.

"Explain it to me," she ventured, carefully.

Dorothy sat down with a tired sigh, taking the toe of

one shoe to dislodge the heel of the other. Then she kicked both her shoes under the table, stretched her short legs, flexed her toes inside the white, cotton Peds she wore, and wagged a short, square finger at Sadie.

"Mind you, they don't make these shoes the way they used to. I think the Dollar General is shifting too much of their work to China or Taiwan or Mexico or them other places. My feet hurt me awful. But they say they're puttin' in a new shoe store in town right next to the bank called 'Payless' or somethin'. Might try my next pair from there. Leastways if they have somethin' similar."

Sadie nodded sympathetically.

"Now, what was we talking about? Oh, luck or love."

Dorothy rubbed one knee.

"It's you pretty ones that have the biggest problems lots a' times. Too many fish in the sea, and you know you could snag every one of 'em if you wanted to. But yer too prissy. Too pertickler, so you are. Now me, I never had much in the way of looks and was right glad for Jim to come a' callin'. Told my Mom and Dad he ain't much to look at, but he's a decent, solid guy. Turned out I was right as rain, and he done me good for almost 50 years."

"That's all I want," Sadie nodded, soberly.

"Don't you have anyone at all?"

Sadie hesitated, then nodded.

"I do. His name is Mark."

"Well, are you dating him now? Is this the same one we looked up those recipes for?"

"Yes. But my mother was ill, and he went back to Pennsylvania. It was sudden…sort of mysterious."

"If it's meant to be, he'll be back."

Sadie nodded.

"Did I tell you Eva's coming for Christmas this year?"

"Naw! Go on!"

"Yes! She is!"

"Bless her heart."

"Time to start the laundry, Dottie, " Sadie said, glancing at the clock.

"Don't you 'Dottie' me!"

Chapter 25

Sadie brought the curry comb down across the honey-colored neck, finishing with an elaborate flourish. It was mostly to impress Reuben who was working on a tangle in Cody's tail, his eyebrows drawn down as he concentrated.

"There!" Sadie said with a bright smile.

Reuben yanked on Cody's tail before looking up, his eyebrows rising with the movement of his head. He gave a low whistle in a very grown up way, or so he hoped.

"She's a picture!"

"Isn't she?"

Reuben nodded, then voiced his exasperation. "Sadie, what do you do if a tangle just won't come out?"

Sadie walked over, lifted Cody's tail, and told Reuben to go get a pair of scissors from Mam.

"Make sure the scissors are old, not the expensive ones she uses to cut fabric, if you know what's good for you."

"You mean, you're going to chop her tail right off— that far up?" he yelled as he dashed out the door.

Sadie answered but knew Reuben didn't hear anyway,

at the rate of speed in which he catapulted through the doorway.

When he returned, Sadie cut expertly through the coarse, black hair. The tail was shorter, but sleek and straight, and the stubborn tangle lay on the concrete floor of the forebay.

Stepping back, she surveyed the brown mare, then told Reuben to throw the cut hair into Paris' stall.

"Oh, no, I'm not going to. This bunch of horse hair would be any bird's dream come true—all this strong horse hair to build a good solid nest. Imagine the possibilities! Birds aren't picky, you know. They use almost anything to build a nest."

Sadie grinned, then told him to throw it out in the barnyard where the birds would find it.

They cleaned their saddles with an old piece of t-shirt and good saddle soap. Then they shook the saddle blankets over and over until the dirt and hair flew across the forebay. They wiped down the brown leather bridles, then began saddling up.

Reuben grunted as he swung his saddle up on Cody who lowered herself, bracing for the weight to land on her back. It was easier for Sadie who was taller and more experienced, but she nodded encouragement to Reuben.

"We wouldn't have to use saddles," he lamented.

"I know, Reuben, but it feels safer if we're going to ride along the highway. What if a large rig would come flying around a corner, blow its horn, and terrify the horses? They haven't been around much traffic lately."

"Cody!" Reuben yelled, then turned to Sadie.

"Why does she do that when I want to tighten the cinch?"

Sadie laughed.

"How would you like to run with a tight band around your stomach? She gets smart and puffs her stomach out while you're tightening it so that it's not too tight when you let go."

"Yeah, but then the saddle slips sideways. I'd rather ride bareback."

"Not this time."

Sadie swung herself up, adjusted her skirt, pinned her covering securely, then spoke softly to Paris. The horse stepped out eagerly, raising her head the minute she was out the door.

Reuben followed on Cody, still mumbling about using a saddle. His blonde hair lifted and separated in the never ceasing, restless Montana wind.

Paris stepped sideways, tossed her head, pranced forward and backward, dipped her head, then shook it from side to side as if to let Sadie know she was displeased about the saddle. It was an unnecessary evil that pinched her sides and was much too tight around her stomach.

"All right, Paris, now settle down. Be a good girl. Come on, come on. This saddle isn't going to hurt you."

"Cody likes hers," Reuben told her happily.

"Looks as if she does."

It was Saturday afternoon, and they were riding their horses a long way to see if they might possibly be able to purchase an old buggy. They had watched the ads in the local paper until they found one that sounded promising.

Buckboard. Good condition. $500.
Call 786-3142

Sadie and Reuben had huddled nervously in the phone shanty as Sadie dialed the number, then whacked their palms together in a resounding high-five when she hung up. They had raced across the driveway and into the house to tell Mam.

Mam smiled as her eyes crinkled and she told them she hoped it was as good as they thought. Then she shook her head after they raced back out the door, the wooden screen door slapping its usual annoyance.

How could you expect that Sadie to grow up as long as she loved horses so much? She couldn't care less about finding a husband as far as Mam could tell. It got discouraging at times, the way she just skipped over the part of life she should be concerned about most. After all, at 21 years old, her best chances were gone, and if she didn't soon worry about starting a relationship with a decent young man, she may not have any chances, in Mam's opinion.

Mam sighed as she watched Sadie and Reuben ride down the driveway. She hoped they wouldn't encounter too many Amish people. Riding a horse wasn't as ladylike as Mam thought it should be. A horse-drawn buggy was much more appropriate for getting around.

Then the thought hit her, and she sat down weakly and began fanning herself with the hem of her apron. Sadie and Reuben were thinking of breaking Paris and Cody so the horses would pull that rattling, derelict old buggy they were planning to purchase.

And that is exactly what they planned to do.

Reuben said the only harm the two horses could do would be to run and kick if they were both hitched to the same singletree. Sadie said the old buggy couldn't be in very good shape for only $500, but she would not want to see it fly into a thousand pieces. This caused Reuben to throw his head back and howl with glee at the sheer thought of so much excitement.

When had the change in Reuben started, and where would it stop? The small, thin body that had trembled beside her as they stood on the ridge waiting for the horses to appear had been transformed into an adventure-loving youth who seemed to find no reason to be careful. He rode Cody like the wind, having very little thought, if any, of the chance of a mishap.

Cody was chomping at the bit, tossing her head, waiting for the signal to run. Sadie told Reuben to hold her back. They had a long ride ahead of them, and there was no use working the horses into a lather so soon.

They turned right on to a county road, holding their horses at a brisk walk. The wind carried the same sighing note Sadie never tired of, and meadowlarks flew up and whirred away on busy, brown wings. The side of the road was dotted with small, pink bitterroot, which grew rampantly. It always added a touch of color, as if an artist had painted the deep pink when the picture was completed, simply to add interest.

Sadie's dress was a deep blue, though worn and a bit snug. She admitted this grudgingly. Too many days of healing that busted leg, she knew. Too many days sitting around the kitchen table with freshly baked cookies and cups of steaming coffee, laughing and talking and unaware of the amount of cookies she was consuming.

Her brown hair pulled loose from her covering and she tugged at it impatiently. She should have worn a *dichly*, but Mam would never allow it when she was in public and going to do business with a stranger.

They rounded a bend in the road, then began the climb up the lower hills of Sloam's Ridge. The pines sighed in the breeze, making Sadie's heart dip with the sadness of it.

Would the memories always raise their heads, crying for attention like a child craving to be remembered and noticed? It was never easy crossing this ridge in a buggy or a vehicle. Riding on horseback in the open air made it all even more memorable than before.

Even Reuben rode somberly, his head bent slightly, the back of his neck exposed between his hair and brown shirt collar. Cody swished her tail, flailing at unseen flies, walking steadily while Paris followed, their heads bobbing in unison.

Sadie tried not to look down the side of the steep embankment, turning her head to watch the pines on the opposite side of the road, following Reuben as Cody made her way carefully down the other side.

Sadie loved riding and being suspended above the ground, her feet solidly encased in stirrups. It was a support she could trust. She loved the creaking of the leather, the rocking gait of a horse moving along, the thick mane moving in that peculiar rhythm—hair so heavy it moved the skin beneath it. She loved the heavy, leather reins giving her the satisfaction of being in control of the beloved horse that carried her.

They came to a crossroad, and Reuben turned to look at Sadie. "Which way?"

Sadie pursed her lips. "Hmm. Right, I think."

"You wanna gallop?"

"We can."

Reuben leaned forward, making the squirrelly sound he always did, and Cody leaped ahead. Paris quickly followed, eager to run. They loped along easily, content to watch the surrounding countryside and for any passing vehicles.

Sadie caught sight of a lone person on the roof of the

old, weathered barn next to the Oxford place where Dat had built one of his smallest log cabins.

Who in the world would even think of patching up that old barn roof? The whole thing looked as if it could go sailing into the wild blue yonder the minute a good strong wind hit it broadside.

She watched, jumping as a piece of rusty metal went sliding down along the rafters, falling to the ground below. As they neared, she could see that the roof was being dismantled, one piece of rusted steel at a time.

Reuben watched, then slowed Cody to a walk.

"Somebody's tearing down that barn."

"Wonder what for?" Sadie asked.

"Think the horses will get scared next time he tears a piece of steel loose?"

"Let's wait here a moment."

They watched as the man on the roof pried off another piece of steel before they urged the horses on. As they passed, Sadie thought something seemed familiar. It was the set of his shoulders or the way he raised his arms.

What was it? Why did the person on the roof seem so familiar, as if she had seen him before?

He turned, noticing them, and stopped working.

Sadie recognized him at the same time he saw her, or so it seemed. At first her mind grasped it, then her heart engulfed it—this wonderful, all-consuming knowledge of who was on the roof.

Then doubt and fear tore loose, a tornado so strong she felt it suck her breath away along with her heart— out and away, never to be recovered, torn away and destroyed. She felt like a person drowning as she gasped at the sight of the man on the roof.

It was Mark Peight.

His white teeth in that dark face! His smile! She had forgotten.

Her nerveless hands pulled on the reins, willing Paris to walk as slowly as she had ever walked before. He inclined his head in a sort of bow, an acknowledgment that he knew she was Sadie Miller, that he remembered her and was glad to see her.

Reuben looked up and then back at Sadie. His eyes showed the whites the whole way around, and he was completely at a loss for even one word for once in his young life.

He stopped Cody and Paris' nose bumped into Cody's rump.

"Is that...who I think it is? That Mark guy?" Reuben hissed.

Sadie didn't answer. She couldn't.

Her eyes were riveted on Mark's. He was so far away, but there was no space between them, no time, nothing but the great shower of light that appeared from somewhere to illuminate the distance between them.

Mark raised his hand, then called, "Hang on. I'll be down."

Sadie tried to fix the hair that had pulled loose from her covering, but it did no good so she let it go. Her fingers weren't working properly as it was, so she may as well not try.

Should she get down? Or stay up on Paris?

Better to dismount, fix her dress—her dress that was too old and too small. Why in the world hadn't she taken the time to change?

And then he stood before her, his hands reaching to her shoulders before looking at Reuben and dropping them to his sides.

"Sadie."

"Mark. Welcome back."

"Thank you. This is Reuben?"

Reuben nodded happily, his grin literally spreading from one side of his face to the other. All his teeth were shining visibly, his eyes crinkling to a thin line of pure delight.

"Why'd you come back to Montana? I thought you were going to stay in Pennsylvania," she asked slyly.

Mark laughed good-naturedly. It was a sound Sadie loved.

"Well, Pennsylvania is nice, but Montana is nicer."

Reuben smiled, and Sadie prayed he would keep his mouth closed.

He didn't, of course. "I bet! Sadie don't live in P.A.!"

Sadie cringed when he said "P.A." Oh, how common! How old-timer-like! He could have at least said "Pennsylvania."

Mark scuffed the toe of his work boot against a tuft of grass, averting his eyes. Those impossibly thick, black eyelashes swept his cheeks, and he didn't answer.

Sadie was humiliated to the point of tears. He probably hadn't come back for her at all, and here was Reuben blatantly throwing her at him, as if he was so sure of the fact that anyone would be glad to be dating his sister.

Mark raised his eyes which were crinkled at the corners, still good-natured, still kind.

"Well, now, Reuben, I don't know about that. Hey, you think the horses might be thirsty? It's a warm day. Come on down to the barn. Maybe you can give them a drink."

Reuben slid off his horse, bounding lightly on his feet, his thick hair lifting and falling.

"Where's your straw hat?" Mark asked, still grinning.

"Don't wear one. Can't. Blows off all the time."

"Fine by me. Can you take the horses, and I'll show your sister around my place?"

My place? My place. Oh, my. Mark Peight had bought this property?

Reuben grabbed the reins before Sadie could recover her senses and walked away jauntily, whistling under his breath.

They were alone.

Mark turned to her immediately. She couldn't breathe properly. It was this dress. It constricted her breathing. She was actually having irregular heartbeats, and there was a rushing sound in her ears.

"Hello."

That was all he said. She tried not to take a step forward, but she did. Her feet took steps of their own, and she closed the terrible distance between them.

He folded her soft form close to his heart and held her there for the space of a heartbeat, not nearly enough to assure her of his feelings for her.

Why did he pull away so quickly? He must not want her at all, or he would convey his love in the most natural way on earth, to have and to hold. Was she so repulsive to him that he could only hold her for the space of one heartbeat? The loss was too great to bear.

She steeled herself before meeting his brown eyes, willing herself to be strong even in his denial of her.

"You are still so beautiful—even more than I remember."

"Thank you," she whispered.

"I'm back. I bought this place, Sadie. I can't wait to get started remodeling and fixing it up."

He gestured toward the barn.

Sadie smiled then.

"It's actually yours?"

"Well, the bank's. I have a mortgage, of course. But, yes, it's mine. I will make my home here in Montana. I love it here, the wide open spaces, the clean air, but most of all, the work I do as a farrier. I get paid well for shoeing horses at these ranches. It's the opportunity of a lifetime. I do other things as well—trim hooves, float teeth... I'm sort of an overall horse guy who helps other people with their animals."

Sadie nodded, then looked around.

"Where is the house?"

Mark laughed.

"There isn't one."

"Where do you stay?"

"In the barn, but just for the summer. I'll probably have to winter over with my uncle."

"In...in the barn?"

"I fixed up a room. It's quite livable, actually."

There was a yell from the lower end of the barn, and Mark grinned down at Sadie.

"He found it."

He turned to her then and stepped very close, his hand touching her chin as light as a summer breeze.

"Sadie, before we go to be with Reuben, I have to talk to you. I'm back in Montana because of you. I can't be away from you—this much I know for sure. The rest...is painful. I need time. My life is a puzzle with most of the pieces lost. I never liked working on jigsaw puzzles with little ones around to lose all the pieces...but... Let's just say almost all my border pieces are lost. I'm not sure anything good can come of my determination to get you back, but if I don't try, my life stretches before me like a long, hard road without joy."

He paused, then gripped her shoulders.

"Please, Sadie."

What was that look in his brown eyes? So intense. So...

"Mark, I..."

"All I ask is your patience. I'll...I will learn to talk if you will listen. We can't date publicly for now. Can you agree to this for awhile, or am I asking too much?"

Sadie looked into his brown eyes, sure that she would follow him to the ends of the earth.

Whithersoever thou goest, I will go.

The words started as a high, keening note, a song that rolled down from the heavens on wings of angels. As clear as a windswept day after a storm, Sadie recognized her destiny and, smiling, took a step toward Mark, ready to at least begin on this path with him.

"Hey, guys! Where are you?"

Mark caught Sadie's hand, and they walked to the barn in the afternoon sunlight, the grasses and the bitter-root swaying by the driveway.

The End

LINDA BYLER

KEEPING SECRETS

SADIE'S MONTANA
Book 2

Chapter 1

Even when you have a firm grip on it, hope can be torn away by the sound of your mother's voice. That's another reason why it's easier to love a horse.

Horses are sympathetic. You can tell by the way they lower their faces, very still, unmoving, when your fingers comb the silky forelock of hair.

Driving horses don't have that forelock. Their Amish owners keep it cleanly cut so that it is easier to put on the bridle. A driving bridle has two bits that must be coaxed between the horse's teeth, and shiny, patent leather blinders attach to the side of it. When the top of the bridle goes up over the ears and the chin strap is secured, the horse looks neat, and, well, Amish.

Sadie Miller's thoughts moved with the steady *ca-chink ca-chink* of the hoe as she chopped resolutely at the stubborn crabgrass between the rows of string beans. The unceasing Montana wind moved the tender garden plants restlessly, their green leaves swaying and bending like funny, green dancers.

Her mother moved ahead of her, bending over to remove the weeds from around the new string-bean plants, her graying hair tossed in the breeze like the bean plants. Her *dichly*, that triangle of blue handkerchief cut diagonally and hemmed on the sewing machine, moved and flapped wildly at the wind's command.

Mam was not overweight. She was not thin, either. She was just right for 50 years old. Her sage green dress whirled around, lifting above her knees, and she grabbed at the pleated skirt impatiently.

"Ach! Will this wind never die down?" she asked Sadie.

Sadie didn't answer, simply because it felt good to let Mam know she was sulking unhappily.

Why? Why did Mam have to come down on her like that? It wasn't fair. She was 21 years old, and Mark was as good as forbidden.

Ah, Mark. That tall, impossibly dark-haired, dark-skinned youth of her dreams. Not really youth. A man, at 31 years old. He was the only person Sadie had ever truly wanted. And now this.

Sadie had opened the subject earlier. She was the only one in the garden with her mother, and she was glad to tell her about meeting Mark on the day when Reuben accompanied her on the quest for a buckboard they had seen advertised in the local paper.

Sadie had been riding Paris, her beloved palomino, while Reuben was on Cody, the small brown mare. They had first thought the horses were from a wild herd. Later they discovered that the animals had been stolen from a wealthy rancher in Hill County. Richard Caldwell, the owner of the ranch where Sadie worked, had contacted the owner of the stolen horses to make things right. Meanwhile, Sadie continued cooking in the huge, commercial kitchen for as many as 25 ranch hands with Dorothy

Sevarr. Dorothy was rotund, and she was aging, but she had a heart of gold despite her fiery personality. Kindness flowed from her in great, healing quantities.

Dorothy's husband, Jim Sevarr, still drove his ancient pickup truck back and forth from Sadie's house, providing her transportation to work. He was an old cowboy, much more comfortable on the back of a faithful horse than driving his cranky pickup, whose gears were never where they were supposed to be.

Sadie and her family lived on the side of a wooded ridge, thick with pines and aspen trees. Their log home had been built by Sadie's father, Jacob, a carpenter and builder.

They had moved to Montana from Ohio about five years earlier, the age-old lure of the west drawing Jacob Miller. The family had settled into the budding new church and community, which the Old Order Amish had started in the beauty of the Montana landscape.

The move, however, had taken its toll on Sadie's mother, Annie, who had slid down a despairing slope of depression, her condition steadily deteriorating into severe mental illness, which Jacob found difficult to acknowledge.

✿ ✿ ✿

Mam's continuing silence made the space between them an uncomfortable irritation that Sadie could not let go. Inside her, disobedience raged while rebellion infuriated her. Tears lodged in her throat.

Yet as Sadie watched her mother's nimble fingers tugging at the stubborn weeds, she did thank God again for the educated doctors and the hospital stay that had enabled Mam to begin her long climb out of the pit of misery that she endured so bravely and silently.

Still. How could she? Did mothers have a right to forbid their daughters from seeing someone?

Life with Mark, or more precisely, the hope of life with Mark, was unthinkable now. Her future rose before her, black, bleak, and windswept. She would turn into a spinster, no matter her beauty or her hair shining like a raven's wing. It shone black actually, depending which way the light settled on it. It nearly matched her blue, blue eyes fringed with thick, black lashes.

Sadie Miller was too pretty for her own good, the old ones said. Beauty could be a curse. Once it got into a young girl's head and puffed up her pride, it became a great, heavy mushroom of vanity that would inevitably take her down every time.

They watched Sadie in church and shook their heads. God was already moving in her life, they whispered. Look what had happened to Ezra. Killed when the buggy went down over the bank on Sloam's Ridge. Sadie almost losing her own life. Ezra would have been the perfect husband for Sadie—loyal, steady, conscientious.

She was just different, that one.

Jacob and Annie had her hands full with three more daughters, one as pretty as the next. Leah, Rebekah, and Anna were all as pleasing to the eye as their oldest sister, but Sadie was the only one gallivanting around on that horse, as far as they knew. She rode around on that palomino horse named Paris, which was downright unladylike. If Jacob and Annie knew what was right and proper, they would rein her in with a firm hand.

They clucked, wise in their years, but they also knew that Jacob Miller's daughters added spice to their lives, mixing some flavor into their work-focused existence.

None of them dating right now either. Not one. Robert Troyer's Junior would be a good one for Rebekah, now wouldn't he? Him being so tall and fair. They clasped their hands and mostly thought these things, but with an occasional slip of the tongue to each other, accompanied by a knowing twinkle in their eyes.

"Mam!"

Mam straightened her back at Reuben's call. She lifted a hand to shade her eyes, searching for her only son, her youngest child.

"Here we are, Reuben. In the garden."

"Can I have a popsicle?"

"How many are left?"

"A whole bunch."

"Okay."

Mam bent to her task, her back turned, and resumed weeding. Sadie cleared her throat, never breaking the hoe's rhythm. The dirt was loosening nicely, although it wasn't the fine loam they were used to in Ohio. The growing season was shorter here in Montana, and having a good, productive garden was much more challenging.

The evening sun began its rapid descent behind Atkin's Ridge. Sadie often thought the sun was like a drop sliding down a tumbler of water. It didn't move very quickly until it neared the base of the glass. Then, in a rush, it was gone. That's how the sun was.

So once it began its descent for the evening, you didn't have much time left in the garden, or to return from a ride, or whatever it was you were doing in the evening.

The silence stretched between the women, until Mam straightened her back, rubbed it with her fist, and groaned. There was no sound from Sadie. Mam turned, watched her eldest daughter's silent hoeing, then stood solidly, her hands on her hips, her eyes narrowing.

"Now Sadie, you can just quit your *poosing* this second. I told you how I feel, and that's the way it is. If you don't want to listen to your father and me, then I suppose you'll have to suffer the consequences."

Sadie stopped her steady hoeing and learned on the handle with the back of the hoe resting on the ground.

"You don't have to say it again, Mam. You already told me once."

Mam watched Sadie lower her eyes and shuffle the hoe back and forth with one hand on the handle.

"Come, Sadie. Let's go sit on the porch swing. Then we can talk. I'll listen awhile and promise to stay quiet this time."

Sadie looked up, blue fire in her eyes.

"What is there to say? If you and Dat forbid me to see Mark at all, then there's nothing to say."

"It would be different if we knew his background. He says he was raised Amish, but where? By whom? Who is his family, if they exist at all? What kind of name is 'Peight'?"

Sadie sighed and lifted her hoe, the skirt of her green dress swirling as she turned and walked decidedly out of the garden.

Mam watched her go, then slowly made her way to the house, her shoulders stooped with dejection.

Sadie put the hoe into the small, log garden shed. She picked up an empty bag that had contained black sunflower seeds for the bird feeders by the window in the dining room. She put it into the trash barrel and wondered why Reuben never picked up anything.

It was the same way with his clothes. He shed his

trousers and shirts beside his bed, both turned inside out. His socks, also turned inside out, remained where he conveniently peeled them off.

No shower for Reuben in the evening. He hated showering before he went to bed. He did it only in the morning, so his hair stayed straight and silky all day, swinging handsomely, the brown and blond strands throwing off the light so that no one knew what color his hair actually was.

Reuben wouldn't talk about girls. He thought they were an unhandy lot, especially in school, bossy know-it-alls who weren't worth a lick at baseball. The only one who came close to being normal was Alma Detweiler, who could bat a ball over the one-room schoolhouse, and often did, making a home run in the process, her long, thin legs churning with admirable speed as she rounded third base, her head turned to watch the ball.

He had taken to dabbing a bit of cologne on his shirt from the wee bottle of Stetson that Leah had given him for Christmas. The practice was a source of knowing winks from his older sisters, who of course never said a word to him.

It was hard enough being 13 and the only guy in the family.

Sadie closed the door, turning the latch firmly, then watched the sky change from blue to orange then lavender, and, finally, purple. The sunsets were nothing short of spectacular here in Montana, and she never tired of them, ever.

She wondered if Mark was seeing the sunset. Was he up on that old barn roof replacing the metal, or had he already finished the job? Was Wolf, his dog, lying at the foundation of the barn? Was Mark whistling under his breath, or was he quiet? More melancholy, morose even, when he was alone?

How did one go about forgetting a person? How could you ever get over the pounding beating of a heart in love?

He had held her against himself three times—once at the mall when she was fainting, spilling her drink all over the shining tile floor. Once at the death of Nevaeh, the beloved black and white paint she had helped nurture back to health at Richard Caldwell's ranch. Once more... When was it? A few weeks ago? A few years? It was hard to tell the difference now.

Mark had gone out of Sadie's life, back to Pennsylvania, after Nevaeh died, saying he was not good enough for her. He had asked to come see her, a genuine Saturday evening date, and then disappeared. Leaving a note saying only that he needed time to make peace with the past. To right wrongs.

What wrongs?

Then there was her dream. Mark as a small boy, a florid-faced man with a whip, the knowing when she woke up. Did she still know?

She thought Mark was her destiny, the man who should be her much sought-after will of God that Mam preached to her girls.

And now this.

Verboten. Forbidden. If she saw Mark, she would be *ungehorsam*, a kind of curse clearly understood among her people. Parents were to be honored and respected. Above all, children were required to be obedient.

But at her age? Wasn't she allowed to make her own choices now?

Her choice was Mark Peight, clear and defined. She loved him and would travel to the ends of the earth for him.

Sadie started when Dat came around the corner of the shed, almost bumping into her. He pushed back his straw hat, ran a hand through his graying beard, and smiled his slow, easy smile.

"Whatcha doin'?" he asked, mimicking Jim Sevarr.

"Oh, just standing here watching the colors change in the sky," she replied easily.

Dat was like that nowadays. Ever since his pride had taken a crushing blow because of his Annie's mental illness, he had only become a better father—more open, mellow, and slow to judge.

"You look a bit poorly around the eyes."

Sadie laughed. "I'm not."

"You sure?"

She poked at a small rock with the toe of her foot. "Well, maybe a bit. It's Mam."

The concern Dat carried in his heart instantly became visible. Sadie saw this look only when Dat's confidence in Mam's health and well-being slipped a bit off center.

"Is she...?"

"No. It's about... Remember Mark Peight?"

Jacob nodded, his mouth a firm line.

"Reuben told me he's back. Said he has a dog named Wolf."

"Yes."

Her father shook his head heavily, burdened, concern clouding his blue eyes.

"I don't know, Sadie. Mam and I talked, and..."

"I know what you talked about. She told me. Twice."

The anger started in her feet and propelled her forward, away from Dat. Then it spread. The tingling adrenaline lent wings to her bare feet, and she ran, racing past the house, down the long, sloping driveway, onto the dusty, country road. Her feet pounded the macadam, her hands pushing down the pleated skirt that flapped in the stiff, summer breeze, her breath coming in quick puffs.

Better to get away. Just run. Keep running.

She ran past the one-room, Amish schoolhouse, the split-rail fence around the schoolyard. She ran past the patch of pines that were forever swallowing the ball from softball games.

She once told Reuben that a dragon lived in those pines and ate the softballs for dessert.

Sadie smiled, thinking of Reuben's indignation and his lecture reminding her that Mam and Dat had taught them not to tell lies. Now here she was, 21 and an old maid. Well, dangerously close to one, anyway, and still telling lies. There was no such thing as dragons.

S'hut kenn dragons.

Sadie laughed out loud. Her laugh became a hiccup, the hiccup caught in her throat and became a sob, and still she ran.

When she saw the moon climbing in the sky, she stopped beside the road, her chest heaving as she caught her breath. That felt better.

The exercise cleared her head, driving the anger away for now, but she knew it would be a constant companion. Yes, Reuben, a dragon of sorts. She would need strength to overcome it.

The unfairness of the situation was staggering. She sank to her knees beside the roadside, plucked long stems of grass, and bent them over and over. Still her eyes remained dry.

She saw Reuben, then. He was running, fast and low, his eyes wild. He was calling her name, and Sadie could tell he was afraid by the whites of his eyes.

Instantly she was up on her feet, waving her hands.

"Here, Reuben, here I am."

Her brother slid to a stop, his fists clenched, his face white. His words tumbled over each other like gravel pouring out of a wheelbarrow.

"I mean it, Sadie. If you ever take off running like that again, I'm going to…going to…I don't know what!"

"I was just…"

"No, you weren't. You big baby. Dat is about nuts. Now get back to the house and stop acting like…"

A shrill, whining rang out. A distant, yet uncomfortably close crack of a rifle, the bullet emitting a deadly whine. Then another.

"Hmmm," Reuben raised an eyebrow, mirroring Sadie's wide eyes and lifted brow.

"Somebody must be practicing their aim."

"It's awfully close."

"Let's get back."

Another shot rang out. The sound was not unusual in the Montana countryside. Ranchers were always on the lookout for predators, or chasing unruly cattle by shooting, or practicing their shots from horseback. "Cowboying around," in Dat's words.

"It's sorta dark for ranchers to be after the coyotes."

"Maybe it's a lion," Sadie said.

Reuben instantly turned his head to search the deeper shadows of the pines, chewing the inside of his cheek the way he did when he was afraid. "Ain't any lions around."

"Jim says there are."

"He don't know everything."

"Almost."

They walked back in silence until they came to the schoolyard. Sadie pointed to the pine woods on the opposite side of the split-rail fence. "How many softballs do you think that woods contains?"

"A bunch." Reuben spoke quickly, his eyes darting from one side of the road to the other.

Suddenly, he turned to Sadie and told her in no uncertain terms that she better not try a stupid trick like this again. He knew it was all because Mark was back, and Mam and Dat didn't like it one tiny bit. Why couldn't she get over Mark and like a normal boy from around here instead?

Sadie nodded, her face devoid of expression. Better to let Reuben have his say. At his age, he didn't understand matters of the heart.

"And, Sadie, not just that. You know when you were up there talking to Mark that day we saw him on the roof? Well, I went down to the barn and let myself into his living place. It's sort of a room he built where he sleeps and eats. Well, that place is totally packed with guns and knives."

He lifted his arm, bringing it down in a swinging arc for emphasis, drawing out the "totally," putting plenty of effort into the word "packed." "I bet he has 50 guns. And 50 knives."

"Mmm," Sadie said, acknowledging this bit of information.

"I don't know about him. He has English clothes lying around. And I don't know what a whiskey bottle looks like, but he has some strange looking bottles in his little refrigerator."

Sadie gasped. "Reuben, why did you go snooping in his refrigerator? That's just awful bad manners."

"I know. I... Well, it bothers me, Sadie. Your eyes turn to... I don't know, stars... or something when he's around. And he isn't a real Amish person, I don't think. I'm afraid of him, sort of. Even his dog is kind of wild-looking, even if he's friendly as all get out. And, I don't know, Sadie, but suppose you would marry this guy against Mam and Dat's wishes, and he'd turn out to be somebody completely different than you think he is?"

There was no answer to this youthful bit of wisdom, spoken in the raw, innocent concern of a person not quite a child and not quite an adult. She knew his words were truthful, without malice or prejudice.

As they neared the house, they heard the sound of the porch swing, a high squeak that turned to a much lower one as the swing went back and forth.

Anna leaped up from the wooden porch rocker, slamming the back of it against the log wall of the house. "Where were you, Reuben?"

"Ask Sadie."

"What in the world got into you, Sadie, taking off down the driveway as if someone's house was on fire?" Anna asked, clearly perturbed.

"I needed the exercise."

Dat cleared his throat from the swing, and Sadie prepared herself for a lecture, but it did not come. The swing kept its steady creaking, Mam's feet sliding comfortably across the wooden floor of the porch.

"That's not why," Anna sputtered, intent on the truth.

"Let it go, Anna," Mam said quietly.

"Well, I will, but they need to know it's too dangerous to be traipsing all over the countryside this time of day. Hey, do we still have those Grandpa Cookies with coconut on the icing?"

"I put the last two in Reuben's lunchbox," Mam replied.

"Of course. Anything for Reuben," Anna said, huffily, sitting down in the rocker again, hard, slamming the back of it against the logs of the house again.

"Pull that rocking chair out from the wall, Anna. You'll knock all the paint off for sure," Dat said sternly.

Sadie sank into the remaining rocker. Maybe she should include Anna in her life more often. Ever since Reuben had learned to ride, Anna's jealousy had become so real, you could almost touch it. It was only natural. Reuben and Anna had been inseparable until he had accompanied Sadie to the ridge to tame the horses. They had tried to persuade Anna to ride, but she refused to even try to get up on a horse's back, flouncing off in a temper every time.

Reuben confided in Sadie a few weeks ago, saying the reason Anna acted like that about riding was because she thought she was fat, and thought she'd look like a big elephant if she went riding.

Reuben had hissed the last bit of information as Anna strolled into the barn, peeling the Saran Wrap from a chocolate whoopie pie. "See? She's always chewing or slurping something, and she's *chunky*."

Anna got up to pull the rocker away from the wall, and Sadie noticed the back of her dress stretched tightly across her shoulders.

"I'm hungry," Anna announced.

"Well, what could we eat?" Mam said softly.

"Those cookies," Anna said, the loss and sadness of not having them in her voice.

"I made fresh shoofly pies this morning."

"Don't like shoofly."

"Oh, that's right. I forgot. You don't. Well, what else could you eat?"

"I know!" Reuben shouted. "Lucky Charms!"

"Lucky Charms!" Anna echoed as she leaped from her chair, slamming it against the wall once more, causing Dat to grimace.

Sadie rocked, the chair's rhythm calming her agitation. She sighed, wishing she was the age when the thought of a dish of cereal accelerated your heartbeat. Her youngest siblings had no serious concerns, no pressing matters, other than achieving passing grades in school or dealing with Mam's refusal to allow you to do some very important thing.

The door to the phone shanty swung open. A small, dark form emerged and walked slowly across the driveway and up to the porch.

"Who were you talking to?" Mam asked.

"Do I have to tell you?" Leah asked, her voice swelling with emotion.

"Kevin Nissley or Kevin Nissley?" Dat asked, teasing, as Mam laughed softly.

Suddenly, Sadie felt very old and very tired, too tired to fight the jealously that reared its ugly head.

Chapter 2

When Jim Sevarr's rusty, old pickup wound its way up the drive, Sadie rose slowly from her kitchen chair, pushing back the untouched English muffin with peanut butter and strawberry jam. She forced herself to swallow a bit of grape juice, then went to the door when the truck stopped.

Mam looked up from the steaming wringer-washer as she lifted the clothes from the soapy water and fed them through the rollers of the wringer. The laundry room smelled of Tide and Downy, the detergent and fabric softener Mam always used. Piles of sorted laundry dotted the floor, Mam plopping them into the sudsy water one by one.

The compressed air, held in a large, round tank, was generated by the slow-running Lister diesel generator in the diesel shanty. When there was laundry to be done, Dat started the diesel so that Mam could fill the washing machine with the hose attached to spigots on the wall. Then she only needed to open the valve on the air line, and, instantly, the up-and-down rhythm of the air motor filled the house.

Some women still preferred a gas engine mounted on brackets beneath their washer, but Mam liked her air motor, so that's what her daughters were used to as well. It was home, it was their way, and it seemed right to use that wringer-washer when they were there.

Down at Aspen East Ranch, Sadie used a large, front-loading, automatic washer run by electricity. Using electricity was as normal as breathing for the Caldwell family. Everything turned on with a flip of a switch or the turn of a dial. Mixers whirred, lights flooded the rooms, dryers turned and blew heat that dried the tumbling clothes, dishwashers hissed and whirred quietly, depending on the cycle. Coffee was ground, brewed, and heated with the flip of a switch. Microwave ovens heated things in a few minutes while the food container stayed cool. There was just no end to the convenience.

But that was at the ranch. The Caldwells were English people, and that was how they lived. It was not wrong for them to use modern conveniences, being born and raised that way. Amish people lived and abided by their *ordnung*. They preferred to stay "behind the world," or to practice living the way they always had, allowing only minor changes in order to be able to compete in the business world.

Sadie loved her job at the large ranch, but she especially loved working with Dorothy Sevarr, Jim's short, buxom wife with a large personality.

Opening the stubborn door of the pickup truck, Sadie grinned her silent "good morning" to Jim, plopped on the seat, and pulled mightily so the rusty door shut completely.

She stopped trying to expect a "good morning" out of Jim shortly after he started picking her up for work.

If she did greet him, the words fell on unfertile ground and withered away, swept under the cracked, vinyl seat by Jim's uncompromising grunt. If she only smiled as she entered the truck instead, he just shifted his toothpick. Sometimes coughed or cleared his throat. But his blue eyes always lit up and the crow's feet at their corners deepened.

It was just Jim's way, and Sadie knew he'd turn the pickup around and begin to talk before they were down the driveway.

"Y' git that there buckboard yet?"

"Not yet."

"Why didn't ya git it?"

"I'm not sure it's worth $500.00."

"Whatsa matter with it?"

"I don't know. The wheels seem sturdy enough, but the floor is rotting through, and Dat will definitely need to build new seats for it."

"Five hundred ain't very much."

"It's enough."

The Montana countryside was green and gold and brown. Sunlight dappled everything so that even the dust shone gold. It was one of those days when the weather was warm but not too warm. It was windy too, but not so windy that it tore at your skirts and grabbed your white covering, pulling your hair horribly and tossing it relentlessly.

The wind never stopped in Montana. It just changed its pace the way horses did. Sometimes it walked, lifting the leaves and the grasses gently. Other times it trotted, swirling skirts and flapping laundry briskly. Still other times it galloped, tearing at your covering, making you bend your head and dash wherever you were going, knowing your skirt was above your knees and knowing it did no good to try and control it.

The wind just blew.

Sadie loved the wind. God was in the wind, she always thought. His power was so visible then. No one could make the wind. No one could start it or stop it. It was God's—that's why.

In church, the ministers spoke of a new birth, comparing it to the wind. Did any man know where the wind stopped or started? God made the wind.

Sadie thought everyone made an awful big fuss about the new birth. The ministers said that God gave people a new birth. The new birth was from God, like the wind was from God. The wind created dancing leaves and swaying branches. The Spirit created good people doing kind deeds. But Sadie knew that sometimes people did kind deeds to be seen by others and not from the genuine goodness coming from a heart flowing with God's love.

People were hard to figure out. Horses were easier to understand and much easier to talk to. Paris always knew how Sadie was feeling. Paris knew when she was silly or light-hearted or angry. Paris was quiet when Sadie was lonely or blue. She would trot over and put her cheek close to Sadie's head, her warm, sweet breath whooshing in and out close to Sadie's shoulder. Then Sadie would cup her hand beneath Paris' nose and tell her everything that caused a dark mood to settle down over her, this cloak of grayness that made her breathe heavily, evenly, not wanting to perish because of it, but feeling as if she might.

Why couldn't she let go of Mark Peight? Here he was again, having bought the small, tumbledown place on the other side of Atkin's Ridge, and there she went riding happily along with Reuben one sunny afternoon, not a care in the world. And who should be up on the roof of the old Zimmerman place but Mark Peight himself?

Then that dry-mouthed, heart-hammering nonsense started all over again simply by the mere sight of him on that roof—the breadth of his shoulders, the way he turned his head, his blue-black hair tousled by the wind, his deep brown eyes looking straight into her heart. Suddenly she couldn't find one word to say.

He came back to Montana because of her, but what good did it do? Dat and Mam stood together as immovable as a rock. A fortress of parents. Staunch, and side by side. She was not allowed to date this mysterious stranger.

Was he a stranger? He had lived within their community for quite a while. He attended church, went to the hymn-singings, and joined the youth. He said he was raised Amish back in Pennsylvania.

But was he raised Amish, really? Who could know if he was telling the truth?

He had a past, that was sure. He was a troubled man, had been troubled in his teen years. But why? He had come so close to telling her his life's story, but then left suddenly to return to Pennsylvania. He sent a brief note to her but with hardly any explanation inside.

Sadie sighed, looked out the dirty window, and wished Mark Peight would get out of her life. But she knew if he did, her world would be completely devoid of meaning, as gray and miserable as the surface of the moon.

She was pulled back to reality when the truck came to a stop.

"There ya go, little lady."

"Thanks, Jim. See you in a little while."

A shifting of the toothpick was her only answer, but

she knew he'd soon be in the kitchen to see Dorothy, the love of his life.

The long, low ranch house was as beautiful as ever that morning, the yellow glow of the morning sun casting it in gold. The yard was immaculate, the shrubs and perennials tended lovingly by the aging gardener, Bertie Orthman.

Bertie rounded the corner of the house, his shoulders sloped and stooped with age, his blue denim shirt hanging loosely on his sparse frame. His hair was as white as snow, and probably just as clean, his mustache trimmed just so, just like the shrubs he kept in perfect form. He stopped when he saw Sadie.

"Now, ain't that a sight for an ol' man's eyes?"

Sadie turned to look behind her.

"What?" she asked, her blue eyes two beautiful pools of innocence.

Bertie grinned, then shook his head.

"Sadie girl, you really are one different person. Don't anybody ever give you no compliment? I meant *you*. You look so pretty wearing that there bluish dress. Just reminds me o' my Matilda, God rest 'er soul."

"Why, thank you, Bertie. I thought you meant someone or something was behind me."

Bertie bent to pluck a weed, then tenderly ran a hand over the top of a boxwood.

"Watch this!"

Sadie watched as he showed her his technique for running the gas-powered trimmer. He was so precise that the shrubs looked like a horticulturist's dream.

"You're good, Bertie. You really are. You have this place looking wonderful."

"Yep, I do."

Bertie grew visibly taller at Sadie's compliment, straightening his shoulders, puffing out his thin chest.

Not much humility in that one, Sadie thought as she smiled at Bertie. Still, he was a dear old man who would never hurt a flea. She felt blessed to work with people who truly were the salt of the earth.

Sadie went around to the side of the house, stepped up on the porch, and let herself into the kitchen. This huge, commercial room was her work place; the room where large meals were planned, cooked, and served to the dozens of hungry ranch hands who worked for Richard Caldwell. Richard was a massive giant of a man with a voice that matched his size, never failing to give Sadie a start when he entered a room.

This morning, there was no one in the kitchen.

Hmm, that's strange, Sadie thought.

She sniffed the air. Biscuits baking. She turned to lift the lid on a large, cast-iron Dutch oven. Sausage on. She pulled on the stainless steel container that held the filter of coffee grounds and found it empty. No coffee made yet.

"Dorothy?" Sadie called tentatively.

There was no answer, the kitchen silent except for the hissing sausage in the Dutch oven.

She bent to retrieve the coffee can and filters from the cupboard below. Measuring a half cup of coffee grounds into the white filter, she placed it into the container and slid it into place. She pushed the "START" button, happy to hear the usual gurgle accompanied by a whirring of sound.

Where was Dorothy?

Sadie walked to the basement door, opened it, and called Dorothy's name again. She was just about to pull on the bathroom door handle when it flew open. A red-faced Dorothy stepped out, wiping her hands on two very wet, brown paper towels.

"Sadie! Can't ya give a person a rest? You just 'Dorothy! Dorothy!' all over this kitchen the minute you can't find me! Can't you just come in quiet-like and figger I'll be around? When nature calls, I have to heed its voice. Can't I get a moment's peace in the bathroom? No!"

"I'm sorry."

"Sorry ain't gonna getcha nowhere. From now on, if'n you come to work and I ain't around, nature has called, and I'm where I should be at such a time."

Sadie looked into the snapping blue eyes below hers, the round face red with exertion, the gray hair electric with fury, and burst out laughing. She laughed until she clung to the counter for support, until tears squeezed between her eyelids, until she gulped and giggled and hiccupped. She peeped at Dorothy sideways, and when she saw Dorothy was still huffy, sitting now on a kitchen chair and eyeing her testily, she laughed some more.

"Ach, my. Oh, my."

Sadie straightened her back and grabbed a paper towel from the roll on the wall to wipe her eyes, apologizing as she did so.

"Dorothy, I won't do it again. I am truly sorry."

Dorothy slurped from her big mug of tea, licked her lips, and eyed Sadie levelly.

"It ain't funny. When you get to be my age, the constitution of your body is an important part of your life. I ain't had my bran muffins in quite some time, an' I'm plumb out o' Metamucil. You know, I told Jim all week, when he gits to town, go to the Rite Aid and git me the biggest bottle of Metamucil that's there. Does he? Does he remember? No siree, he don't. So see what happens? I got to set in the bathroom and here she comes. 'Dorothy. Dorothy. Dorothy!' It's enough to weary a person at this early mornin' hour."

Sadie felt the waves of humor, the beginning of a wonderful, deep-down, belly laugh, but she turned to start another pot of coffee before Dorothy could see her shoulders shaking and her mighty struggle to stay straight-faced.

The kitchen door swung open, and Jim strode purposefully up to Dorothy.

"I'm goin' to town. Ya want me to git ya anything? Boss needs some three-quarter-inch nails."

Sadie watched as Dorothy rose from her chair, all five feet of her. Her chest swelled to even greater proportions as she took a mighty breath. Sadie ducked her head at the coming tirade, watching as Dorothy's eyes narrowed and her lips pursed.

"Now, Mr. Sevarr, what would I possibly want from town? Isn't a thing. Nary a thing."

"But…I recollect there was somethin'. Wasn't there somethin' at the beginnin' of the week? Asprin or some-thin'?"

"If you'd give two hoots about yer woman, you'd remember."

Jim looked uncomfortable then, taking off his battered Stetson and twisting it in blackened, gnarled fingers. He searched his wife's face for any sign that would help him out.

"Toothpaste? Shampoo?"

Dorothy harrumphed her disgust, drank more coffee, and spilled it over the front of her dress. Then, she waved to Jim, telling him to go on, git to town, she'd get the item herself if he didn't know what it was.

Sadie knew, then, that all laughing was finished. Dorothy meant serious business, and she had better do her best in the kitchen. And if Jim knew what was good for him, he'd get out of Dorothy's kitchen soon.

Sadie worked efficiently during the following hour, side by side with Dorothy. The silence stretched between them comfortably and with the respect Sadie knew was required of her.

She finished the sausage gravy, and then mixed batter for the hotcakes, pouring perfect yellow orbs of it onto a steaming griddle and flipping the cakes expertly. She and Dorothy cooked mounds of scrambled eggs, shining pots of grits and baked oatmeal, and great square pans of bacon cooked to perfection. Then they carried the vast quantities of food to the beautiful dining room. The steam table sat along one wall, and they slid the pans onto the grids. The steaming water beneath the pans, heated by electricity, kept everything piping hot.

Sadie made sure everything was in order, setting out clean plates, napkins, silverware, mugs, and tumblers. Then she moved swiftly through the swinging doors as the clattering of boots and the rough voices of the jostling ranch hands were heard coming down the hallway from the main entrance.

She was never at ease being in the dining room with the men. Her mother would not let her work here at Aspen East Ranch if she thought Sadie would be among the ranch hands. It was unthinkable. It was bad enough the way she was always talking about horses with her boss, Richard Caldwell.

Mam was too strict, Sadie thought. Most of the men who worked at the ranch were married or had girlfriends. Richard Caldwell told her once that the white covering she wore reminded the men of a nun's habit. It scared them and made them think twice about misbehaving. It was good for them that she was there. It reminded them that there was more to life than running cows and racing trucks and chasing girls they didn't respect anyhow.

Sadie had assured Richard Caldwell that she wasn't any better than those men's wives. They were good women who treated their men well, and she didn't want to be viewed as someone who was better than they. She was certainly only human herself, regardless of her clothes.

Richard Caldwell had only looked at her, levelly, and said nothing. She didn't know whether he took what she said as truth or not.

When she returned to the kitchen, Dorothy had disappeared once again. With one look at the closed bathroom door, Sadie stifled a smile and bent to the task of cleaning up. She soaked pans in hot, soapy water, filled the large, commercial dishwasher, wiped counters, scoured the stove, and then felt dizzy and a bit weak.

She hadn't eaten her breakfast at home, that's what it was. Well, she'd drink some orange juice, then fill a plate after the men were finished eating.

What was that?

She straightened, turned off the hot water, then listened.

A knock, although a soft one. There. Another one.

Wiping her hands on her apron, Sadie went to the door and opened it slowly. She didn't see anyone, until she looked down. There was a very dirty, very brown, little boy, clutching the hand of a little girl who must be his sister. She was an exact replica of him, only grimier, if such a thing was possible.

Their hair was impossibly matted, snarled until it stood out from their little heads, stiff with dirt and dust.

There were brown streaks caked onto their faces. The little boy's T-shirt had been orange at one time, but now it was a color somewhere between brown and rust. The girl's skirt was torn, her T-shirt hanging from one shoulder, the neckline completely stretched out of shape. She was carrying a small, leather satchel, not a purse or a duffel bag, but a homemade bag bulging with items that were anyone's guess.

The children stared up at Sadie, their black eyes bright with fear.

Sadie opened the door wider.

"Hi!" she said, smiling brightly, hoping they felt welcome enough to share their names and what they needed.

They didn't answer.

"H...hello!" Sadie said, trying again.

"I'm Marcellus. This is my brother."

The voice was soft and musical, spoken in perfect English with only a hint of an accent.

"My name is Sadie Miller."

"My brother is named Louis."

"Hello, Louis," Sadie said quickly.

"Good morning."

Sadie was unprepared for the perfectly pronounced greeting, the voice as soft and cultivated as his sister's.

Looking around her, Sadie was undecided what to do. Invite them in? She did not want to get anyone into trouble, but she couldn't let these poor little souls out here by themselves.

Where was that Dorothy?

Taking a deep breath, Sadie asked them to come in. Immediately, the children stepped inside, dropping the satchel on the rug inside the door. Their black eyes opened wide as they took in the vastness of the kitchen area.

"Where ... where did you come from?"

"Our mother set us out of the car. She drove away. Our father went away first. There is a man who comes to our house. Our mother cries. We are not allowed to go with her. She will come back soon."

This was all spoken in perfect English, in the musical voice by the little girl named Marcellus.

There was an audible gasp, and Sadie turned to find Dorothy behind her.

"What in the world is going on here?"

Dorothy for once spoke calmly, in disbelief. Her usual bristling personality quieted at the sight of these little ones.

Sadie heard a sniff, then turned to see Dorothy lower her round, little frame to her knees, holding on to the kitchen chair as she did so. Tears pooled at the corners of her eyes, as she held out her short, heavy arms.

"Angels, that's what they are," she whispered. "Come here," she said, louder, in her usual commanding voice.

The children stepped over obediently, and Dorothy's arms enfolded them to her breast. She smoothed their filthy hair with no thought for the grime. She kissed the dirty little faces, murmuring to herself.

"It's God hisself came to our door. It's a test. These little angels," she kept murmuring.

Sadie bit down on her lower lip, trying to keep her composure.

When Dorothy asked them where they were from, Marcellus repeated what she told Sadie. Dorothy got up, still holding the grimy little hands close, then sank into a chair. Her hand went to her head as if it was almost more than she could bear.

"My little darlings!" she cried, suddenly. "Sadie, go

get Richard Caldwell. Hurry up! He's still eating in the dining room."

"But..."

"Go!" Dorothy thundered, and Sadie went.

A sea of faces looked up as she entered the vast dining room. She found the face of her boss quickly and went to him. He slid back his chair, knowing it was important if Sadie appeared in the dining room when he was eating breakfast with the men.

"Excuse me."

"Yes, Sadie?"

"Dorothy... I... You need to come to the kitchen for a minute."

Richard Caldwell followed her as she made her way through the swinging oak doors, then stopped at Dorothy's side. She watched Richard Caldwell's face as he looked at the children.

He gave a low whistle, then shook his head back and forth. "Likely some drunk threw his kids out," he muttered.

Dorothy's eyes flashed. "Now don't you go sayin' that, Richard Caldwell. These is angels sent from God to see what we're goin' to do with 'em. You ain't turnin' 'em out, so you're not. They ain't no drunk's kids neither. Listen to 'em. Tell the nice man where you come from, Mary. Marcy. Marcelona."

Marcellus looked seriously from Dorothy to Richard Caldwell, then told them the same story as before, with Louis nodding his head beside her.

"There now," Dorothy said triumphantly. "These kids has some upbringing. Can't cha tell?"

Richard Caldwell was speechless. He opened his mouth, then closed it again.

"I'm a goin' to give them a bath, then me and Sadie's gonna feed 'em. You go find your wife. Tell her to come to the kitchen in two hours. About 10 o'clock. You come with her. You an' me an' Sadie an' her gotta decide what to do about these kids. We ain't turnin' 'em out, neither, an' don't even think 'bout calling the police. When Jim gets back, tell 'im to git in here!"

And so Dorothy arranged her soldiers, ready to do battle for her God.

Chapter 3

DOROTHY BATHED AND SCRUBBED THE CHILDREN. She brushed their hair and dressed them in clean clothes she borrowed from a few of the ranch hands' kids. She fed them at the kitchen table, heaping their plates with scrambled eggs, toast, bacon, and hotcakes. The children drank thirstily before lifting their forks to eat the food. They had perfect manners, wiping their mouths with the napkins provided.

She huffed upstairs and back down, her face almost the same color as Barbara's purple kimono.

Barbara Caldwell came and watched Dorothy take care of the children. Her heavy, blonde hair was perfectly coiffed, her makeup applied expertly, the luxurious kimono she wore enhancing her elegance. She kept her emotions hidden, but there was no suspicion or judgment in her demeanor. She sat and observed, smiling, glancing at Richard Caldwell, occasionally commenting on the beauty of the children's hair or eyes.

Dorothy sent Sadie to clean the bathroom, dispose of the children's filthy garments, and clean the guest bedroom for them. She sprayed the tub with Tilex, cleaned the heavy mirrors and the ceramic above the sinks, then stopped when she spied an old leather satchel. It was not homemade at all. Rather, there was a tag, also made of leather, with foreign words inscribed on it.

Sadie knew enough about life to know what was affordable and what was not. This most definitely was not affordable, at least for anyone she knew, and it did not come from any store nearby.

But, these destitute little ones? Carrying a bag of finest...?

Glancing over her shoulder, Sadie lifted the flap and peered inside. Another bag. A cloth one. A drawstring. With fumbling fingers, she pulled it open and gasped. Quickly, she tightened the strings, closing the bag.

It couldn't be. Children didn't carry things like this. Who in their right mind would send two little ones, likely no more than five years old, out into the vast world with an expensive satchel containing what appeared to be jewels? Diamonds, maybe?

Sadie had no experience where jewelry was concerned, but she was pretty sure that when objects glittered and sparkled and were that heavy, they were probably real.

She considered opening the drawstring bag again, just to make sure she hadn't imagined what she saw, but decided against it. She shivered and looked at the satchel as if it was coiled and ready to strike.

Sadie cleaned the tile floor on her hands and knees, wringing the cloth well over a bucket of hot, soapy water. She hurried downstairs to dispose of the soiled water, told Dorothy the bathroom was finished, and asked if she needed anything else done in the kitchen before she tackled the bedroom.

"Nah, go on yer way. I'll keep an eye on Louise and Marcelona."

"Louis and Marcellus," Sadie said softly.

"I know. That's what I said."

Sadie didn't respond. She had to find Richard Caldwell. Or Barbara. Someone needed to know about that bag of jewels.

She put the bucket in the closet, then walked resolutely through the dining room and down the wide, oak-lined hallway to Richard Caldwell's study. Taking a deep breath to steady herself, she knocked softly and cringed when she heard that ear-splitting, "Come on in!"

She pushed the heavy, oak door timidly and was relieved to see her boss relaxed. He was tilting back in his great, leather chair. His feet, encased in heavy boots, were propped on his desk. His teeth flashed white in his tanned face as he smiled at her.

"Sadie!"

"Yes. Hello, again. I'm sorry to interrupt your..."

Her voice was drowned out by the shrill ringing of his desk phone. Richard Caldwell motioned for her to sit down, then picked up the receiver and yelled, "Richard Caldwell speaking!"

Sadie grimaced inwardly and imagined the person at the opposite end of the line holding the receiver away from his ear.

She tried not to listen, her eyes roaming the bookshelves and the expensive objects of art. She noticed dust on the wooden blinds and made a mental note to take time to wipe them tomorrow when she cleaned the study.

"Mike? No? Mark? Yeah, got it. What did you say? Paint? Pate? Can you spell that?"

His feet clattered to the oak floor. Tipping his chair forward, he grabbed a notebook and scribbled, yelling the letters as he wrote.

"P...ei... Huh?"

There was a pause before he finished with the "G...
H...T."

"Got it."

Then, "Yeah, come on down. I'll talk to you. Never
enough farriers to go around."

Another pause, then a chuckle.

"All right. See you this afternoon."

Sadie's eyes were two large pools of agitation when
Richard Caldwell turned to her.

"He sure doesn't have a lot to say. A new farmer.
Weird name. Hey, what's wrong with you, Sadie? You
look like you just swallowed your grandma."

"N...nothing. I mean...yes, there is. I... The children?"

Richard Caldwell nodded.

"They... After they had their bath and got cleaned up,
they...I found a bag of...of...I think diamonds or at least
jewels of some kind—in a leather...purse. It was upstairs
in the bathroom. I thought you needed to know about it."

"What? Now come on, Sadie. Kids that dirty and tat-
tered-looking don't carry around bags of jewels."

Sadie's eyes flashed.

"Would I make this stuff up?" she asked.

"No," Richard Caldwell shook his massive head,
laughing, "Not you, Sadie, not you."

He rose and asked her to take him to this leather
satchel.

Sadie walked down the hallway and up the wide stair-
case, acutely conscious of Richard Caldwell's heavy footsteps following her. She paused at the bathroom door
before walking to the well-lit counter and handing the
leather bag to her employer. She watched closely as his
thick fingers tried to undo the flap and then the drawstring. Muttering, he handed it to Sadie.

"You do it."

Her small fingers opened the drawstring efficiently. She held the opened bag out to him, her eyes searching his. Taking the bag, he spilled the contents onto the marble countertop, bent low, and whistled.

"What the...?"

He looked at Sadie, then bent to examine the small mound of glittering jewels, his heavy fingers raking through them.

"Earrings. Necklaces. Rings," he murmured, holding each one up to the light coming from the bathroom mirror.

There was a whisper of movement at the door, and they both turned to see the tall form of Richard Caldwell's wife, Barbara, enter the room.

There was a time when Barbara would have been suspicious, hateful even, of this Amish girl with the unusually beautiful face, her hair as dark as a raven's wing, her great blue eyes fringed with naturally dark lashes.

Sadie's presence had been a threat until Richard Caldwell helped her nurture the sick, broken horse, Nevaeh, back to health. During that time, Barbara's husband came to grips with his past and, as each day unfolded, he grew more loving and tender, especially toward his wife.

Now, seeing them both in the intimacy of the upstairs bathroom, Barbara's old suspicion and mistrust rose like sick bile in her throat.

"I don't suppose..." she began, despair clutching her throat.

"Barbara! Come here!"

Richard Caldwell's voice boomed out, and Barbara hurried to his side. All suspicion disappeared, and the despair fell away as her husband's arm encircled her ample waist, pulling her toward him.

"Look at this, honey."

This new term of endearment brought a thickening to the back of Barbara's throat, the place where tears begin, and she knew she would never be able to hear it enough.

Bending her head, Barbara peered at the jewels in disbelief. "Let me get my glasses."

The purple kimono swished expensively as she sailed from the bathroom, returning almost instantly with her reading glasses perched midway down her nose.

Then, "Wow! Oh wow! Richard! What is this?"

"They belong to the kids, I guess. According to Sadie."

"What?" Barbara was incredulous.

Sadie nodded. "When...when they had their baths, this was left on the countertop," she said, gesturing to the leather purse.

Barbara shook her head. "Are we sure we're not getting ourselves into something dangerous? This is unreal. Perhaps some...mobsters or gang members staged all this. They could be using those innocent children as a prop or something. We should absolutely report this to the police."

"I agree," Richard Caldwell said.

Sadie started to leave. But she turned. "Then I'll let it up to you. I just didn't feel right without at least showing you what I found. I'll return to my cleaning now, if you don't mind."

"Wait, Sadie," Barbara said, reaching out to her. "What do you think we should we do with these two little ones? I don't know... I mean..." she lifted her eyes to her husband.

Richard Caldwell acknowledged the questioning in

his wife's eyes with a very small shake of his head. Then he looked at Sadie, telling her that they didn't feel as if it was the right time for them to be caring for two small children. Did she have any suggestions? If the police were called in, the children would be placed in foster homes unless someone intervened.

"Would your family be able, or willing, to take them in?" he finished.

It was a hard question, one Sadie felt unable to answer. Her mother's mental health had been a real issue in the past. She had found help and resumed a healthy, balanced existence. Aided by her unwavering faith, she was peaceful and happy again. But to require this of her?

Sadie shook her head. "My mother hasn't been well, but there is a possibility. We'll discuss it and I'll let you know."

"Thank you, Sadie."

✿ ✿ ✿

That afternoon, Bertie, the gardener, asked Dorothy if she or Sadie would be available to help him plant the annuals in the garden down by the fishpond.

Dorothy was taking one of her many breaks, forking cheesy clumps of steaming macaroni and cheese into her mouth from the small microwavable dish in her hand. She washed it down with a resounding gulp of sweet tea, the ice clattering against the plastic tumbler as she set it on the kitchen table.

"Now, Bertie, I ain't goin' down there and breaking my back diggin' around in that there mud. It ain't no use. Come September, those plants will be froze stiffer'n my knees, so they will."

Bertie waved a hand in her direction, then snorted derisively.

"Aw, you old grouch. Then stay here in the kitchen and eat your macaroni and cheese. Where's Sadie?"

Sadie peeped out of the pantry door and smiled at Bertie, joy in her eyes. She loved Bertie, but she loved the banter between these two salty individuals even more.

"Sadie girl! You want to help me plant a few annuals down by the fishpond? My old back could sure use some help."

"Your old back? Well, why'd ya think my old back would be any different?" Dorothy spat out.

"I didn't ask for your two cents."

"Well, you got it."

Dorothy chuckled loudly before lifting another great forkful of macaroni to her open mouth.

Surprisingly, Bertie kept his peace and told Sadie he'd be ready in about half an hour.

"I guess, if it's all right with you, Dorothy?" Sadie asked.

"Yeah. May as well help him out if his back can't take it. We're havin' beef stew and rice for dinner this evening, so there's not so much to do. Go on and help him out, the poor, old man."

"You know, if you wouldn't be settin' there eating all that macaroni and cheese, you wouldn't be as…"

"Say it, Bertie! Go ahead and say it!"

Dorothy's eyes were snapping and twinkling at the same time. Bertie smiled, and Sadie suddenly became ravenous for the cheesy concoction Dorothy was enjoying.

"You want a dish of macaroni? Some sweet tea?" Sadie asked Bertie.

Sadie smiled to herself, thinking how English she could sound when imitating the lovely people that she worked with.

She heated more macaroni, punching the buttons of the microwave. At home, she would put her food in a saucepan, add extra milk, and set it on the gas burner of the stove. Then she would wait at least 15 minutes until it was heated through. She cringed at how Reuben burned food every time. He consistently plopped a saucepan on the gas stove, flipped the dial to high, and walked away. Sticking his nose in a magazine, he forgot about the stove until the house filled with the stench of burning food. Then he always blamed the girls for not making him something to eat. Using a microwave in an English person's kitchen was pretty handy.

Bertie settled into a kitchen chair, greatly enjoying his glass of tea and tucking into the dish of macaroni and cheese with as much enthusiasm as a much younger person.

Watching him, Dorothy started on a tirade of the different metabolism rates in people's bodies. Bertie said he didn't know, he never went to school for that. What he did know was this—if you ate too much, you got fat.

"Huh-uh. No. It ain't true. Look at you hoggin' that down. If I ate the way you do, I'd weigh 300 pounds!" Dorothy said testily.

"Is that all you weigh?" Bertie returned, then made a laughing retreat out the door and back to work, leaving Dorothy fussing and fuming and checking the refrigerator for some leftover coleslaw.

✿ ✡ ✿

Sadie found the flats of purple and pink petunias, the hose with the gardener's wand, and a trowel. Bertie wanted the flowers planted beside the brick walkways and on the side of the slope leading to the fishpond, but none in the shade by the trees.

"Petunias don't do well in the shade, you know," he explained. "If you need anything, give me a holler. I'll be mowing by the garage."

Sadie set to work, getting on her knees to dig, plant, and water. She loved the feel of the soil and reveled in the warm sunshine, the beauty of her surroundings, and the drone of bees as they flew busily from different sources of nectar.

Cows bawled, calves answered, horses roamed the paddocks and pastures, dogs barked, and pickup trucks came and went. But Sadie heard very little of these sounds that made up daily life on the ranch. Instead, her thoughts turned to Mark Peight.

Now why would he call Richard Caldwell? Yes, she knew he was looking for work, but... Did he know her parents forbid her to see him? No. How could he? She hadn't told anyone. Even her sisters didn't know. So, he wasn't coming to the ranch as a way to see her.

And now these children. A responsibility for someone. Had the police been here yet?

She was turning away from the dumpster after depositing the used plastic pots, when she spied Louis and Marcellus running toward her. What a difference the soap and shampoo had made! They were beautiful children. They almost seemed adjusted to the ranch, and they'd been here less than a day. Perhaps this was due to Dorothy's assurance that they would definitely be staying, that they had nothing to be afraid of, and that their mother was coming to get them as soon as she possibly could.

Sadie greeted them, and they answered with shy acknowledgement, perfectly worded in soft English.

"Would you like to help me?"

They declined, shaking their heads from side to side. Then Marcellus spoke up. "Gustav, our gardener, says we are too small to help."

Sadie nodded. Our gardener? Ach, my! The children must be from a well-to-do home.

Out of the corner of her eye, Sadie saw the tall form of Mark Peight enter the garden. He came down the brick walkway in his easy, cat-like stride. An electric jolt charged through her body, and, instantly, her hand went to her hair, leaving a dark smudge on her forehead. The children turned to face the tall stranger, keeping their eyes lowered respectfully.

"So there you are," Mark greeted her.

Flustered, Sadie got to her feet. "Hello, Mark."

"How are you, Sadie?"

"I'm doing well. How are you?"

"Good, good. Happy to be back in Montana."

He looped his thumbs in his suspenders and looked around appreciatively. "So this is where you work?"

Sadie laughed, "Not always."

"I didn't think so."

"Bertie, the gardener, asked me to help him out this afternoon."

"These Caldwell's kids?"

Sadie turned to Louis and Marcellus, and then introduced them. "We don't know their last names. They just came today. They..."

Sadie's voice was cut off by Dorothy's agitated yells, asking the children to come up here right now.

Sadie got down on her knees, eye-level with Louis, and told them to be very good. Some men were here to talk to them about coming to the ranch. She told the children that they should not be afraid. These were good men who wanted to help them.

Tears crowded her eyes as she watched Louis take Marcellus' hand protectively. Together they walked obediently up the brick walkway.

"What?" Mark began.

Sadie quietly explained the situation to him, omitting the jewels, then asked if he wanted to sit down. They seated themselves on the iron bench by the day lilies, and Sadie turned a bit sideways, tucking one foot under her leg.

"But…" Mark was curious.

"I know. It's the most unusual thing. You can tell by the way they talk that they aren't just some squatters' or sheepherders' children. Yet their black hair and eyes, their dark skin, all seem to…"

"They seem foreign."

"Mexican. Latino of some kind. The police are here now speaking to Richard and Barbara Caldwell. You know how it is, if no one wants them, they'll enter the foster system."

Mark looked unseeingly across the fishpond, the pasture in the background.

"Yeah, well, you're not going to let that happen, are you?"

Sadie shrugged her shoulders.

When she felt Mark's big hands grasp her shoulders much too tightly and give her a little shake, she snapped her head up in alarm, her eyes weak with fright.

"How can you sit there with that smug expression and shrug your shoulders?" he asked, his voice grating unevenly on the hard words.

His face was inches from hers, his eyes blazing with

raw fury. The force of his emotion drew the air from her lungs like a huge vacuum. She was too powerless to stop it, and her shoulders slid downward away from his grasp.

"Don't," she whispered weakly.

He released her, then abruptly turned to lower his face into his hands. She thought she heard the word "sorry" among the murmurings that followed, but she couldn't be sure.

He stayed in that position until a sick fear began in the pit of Sadie's stomach. What if he was mentally deranged, violent, or dangerous? Why would he become so agitated at the slight shrugging of her shoulders?

Just as suddenly, Mark sat up, brushed back his hair, cleared his throat, and turned to her.

"You have no idea, Sadie. None. If you did, you wouldn't sit there one second longer, knowing those sweet, polite children would be put in foster homes. Believe me, it's not a good place to be."

"How do you know? And how do you expect me to know, living the sheltered Amish life I have always lived?"

"How do I know? Because I was a foster kid," Mark said, emotion causing him to whisper.

Sadie was incredulous. "You were?"

"Yes."

"Why? I mean... How could you have been? Your parents were Amish. Why didn't your relatives keep you? Why in the world were you put in a foster home? Didn't you have any sisters or brothers? No aunts or uncles?"

The questions poured from Sadie, like water rushing and tumbling toward the ocean. Her desperate need to know more about Mark's life crowded out all reason.

"If I tell you why I was a foster kid, you will never look at me again."

The words were stiff, forced between clenched teeth, as if keeping his teeth in that position would keep Mark's past hidden and intact.

Sadie faced him, forced him to look at her. "Try me."

She had never seen eyes change the way his did, going from brown to deep black then back to brown. But it was a hooded, reserved brown. Suspicious even. Mistrusting. Finally, when Sadie's gaze did not waver, his eyes acknowledged her request, but without faith, barren and afraid. Then he took the plunge, baring his soul.

"I found my father. He was drowned. On purpose."

"No!" The word was wrenched from Sadie and she lowered her head, sobs completely controlling her.

"See. I told you. Now I did it. You will never speak to me again."

There were no words from Sadie, only the heaving of her shoulders as he got slowly to his feet.

She felt his presence leaving and was jolted to reality. She raised her tear-streaked face, and in a desperate need to keep him there, blurted out, "Oh Mark, you poor, poor thing! How old were you? I cannot imagine. Please don't say you'll never speak to me again. Don't even think it. I care about you, Mark. I do."

"No, you don't."

"Yes … I do. Please, Mark. You said…"

"Just forget what I said. Go back to work now. Go find yourself a good, normal guy who will make you a good, normal husband. Forget about me and the fact that I came back to Montana."

Suddenly Sadie grasped both of his arms, held on, and said clearly, "I am not going to do that. And neither are you. I'm only going to say this once, and then it's up to you. I love you."

Chapter 4

M<small>AM WAS ALARMED WHEN SHE SAW</small> S<small>ADIE AFTER</small> work that day. Her oldest daughter's face was so pale, she looked sick. Her typically sunny, blue eyes looked dark gray, as if thunder had hovered over them all day.

"Sadie? Are you all right?"

It was the tone of her mother's voice, the kindness in her face, that unraveled Sadie completely, a spool of yarn with one end tugged relentlessly.

She threw herself into her mother's arms, and like a six-year-old who felt she was punished unfairly, she hiccupped and warbled and cried and talked. Her sisters gathered around the kitchen table, clucking and oohing and aahing and sympathizing until the whole day had been laid bare for the entire family to examine. Even Dat caught the tail end of the story when he came home from work an hour later.

They laughed at Dorothy's view of Bertie, exclaimed at the jewels, and became doe-eyed when Sadie described how Mark Peight walked down the garden walkway. They all added their opinions, but grew completely embarrassed at Sadie's announcement of love to him.

Dat caught Mam's eye, and shook his head.

"So there you are. I know I'm not allowed to see Mark, but I also know I want to be with him until the end of my days. I love him. I know my life will not be as easy as some, but I need to be with him. I feel it's my destiny."

After a pause, Dat spoke softly, gravely.

"Well, Sadie, if you believe that it is God's will, would you give Mam and me a few weeks to pray about this? We're not going to forbid it, but we need to be very, very careful. Then we will see what unfolds."

"I can tell you what's unfolding right now, and that's my stomach. Whatever is up with having no supper?" Reuben announced, getting out of the recliner and clutching his empty abdomen.

"Let's get pizza!" Anna shouted.

"Pizza!" Reuben echoed.

"Who has money?"

"Not me."

"I would if we'd just get pizza, but till everyone has their cheesesteaks and ham subs and Pepsi, the bill will come to more than $50.00."

"I'll make a homemade pizza. We have leftover chicken corn soup…"

"No-o-o!" Reuben wailed.

"I'll pay 20," Dat volunteered.

"I'll pay 10!"

"Ten!"

"Who's going to order?"

"Who do you think?" Mam asked, pointing to Sadie.

Sadie laughed and got a scrap of paper and pen, wrote down the order, and went to the phone shanty to call the little rural pizza shop that delivered pizza to the homes spread around the lovely, Montana countryside.

On the way back to the house, Sadie's heart filled with love for her family. Her emotions had run a gauntlet that day, but how wonderfully firm was the foundation under her indecisive feet. The love and devotion of a family was a solid structure that held together through all of life's trials, above any storm that blew in. And how would life ever be manageable without her sisters and Reuben?

When the pizza arrived, the family was prepared with a stack of plates, tall glasses loaded with ice cubes, and Mam's bread knife to cut through the thick crust.

They remembered to bow their heads, their hands folded in their laps while they all prayed in silence. The girls had their own private joke about "putting patties down," the Pennsylvania Dutch version of saying a blessing, when pizza was ordered in. Dat never seemed to pray quite as long, and tonight was no different. Sadie was pretty sure Reuben didn't pray at all, the way he shrugged his shoulders and swung his feet. His head was only bowed halfway, and he watched the pepperoni on the pizza the way a cat watches a mouse nibbling on oats in the forebay of the barn.

When they raised their heads and Mam reached for the knife to cut the pizza, Sadie caught Rebekah's eye. They ducked their heads before Dat could catch their smiles.

It was delicious, as usual, the great slices of thick, crusty pizza dripping with tomato sauce, cheese, pepperoni, and mushrooms.

The subs were made with a special bread recipe, brown and firm, the ham and cheese melted to perfection, the lettuce and tomato still fresh and colorful.

No one said much, as they ate hungrily, then pushed back their plates and relaxed with their drinks.

Sadie watched Anna reaching across the table for one of the last slices, her third. Then she settled back happily on the bench beside Reuben, enthusiastically sinking her teeth into the thick pizza.

Reuben wiped his mouth with a napkin, surveying his hungry sister. "Boy, Anna, you ate a pile of pizza. Must be you were really hungry."

"I was!" Anna said, swallowing and nodding her head.

Reuben eyed her with concern. "You're getting chunky."

"So."

Her answer was about as indifferent as it could be, so Reuben shrugged his shoulders and said he was going to the barn.

"Are you riding?" Sadie asked.

"No. I have to clean my rabbit pens. Dat said."

Sadie figured she had better not persuade him to ride with her. Those rabbit pens were desperately in need of cleaning. Anna had told him that if he didn't clean the rabbit pens more regularly, she was going to call the Humane Society to come get the rabbits, and the animal rights people would put him in jail.

Horrified at the thought of being put in handcuffs, which Anna had explained in full detail, Reuben went crying to Mam. Anna was sent to her room after that. This had all occurred when Reuben was seven or eight, and things had not changed much at all. Reuben still loathed cleaning those pens.

Sadie slipped away from the house, telling Mam she was going for a ride on Paris. Mam nodded absent-mindedly while listening to Leah recount an episode from her day.

Paris and Cody were at the lower end of the pasture, as far away as possible. Usually when Sadie called, they came trotting to the gate, but not always. Depending on their mood, they stayed where they were, tails swishing, teeth crunching as they went on grazing.

Sadie climbed up and sat on the gate.

"Paris! Cody! Come on girls! Come on!"

The slanted evening sunlight brought out the rich gold of Paris' coat. She was the color of honey, the good, rich kind that came straight from the hives. Her mane and tail were a lighter shade of gold, almost off-white, the tone of some people's living room walls.

Paris whinnied, her nostrils making that funny rollicking noise that sounded like laughter. Sadie watched as she swung her head, then turned to make her way delicately across the pasture. Her head bobbed slightly as she walked up to the gate, prodded on by Sadie's gentle coaxing.

Nuzzling her skirt, Paris looked at Sadie as if to ask her how her day was.

"Hello, girl."

Sadie slid off the gate, her arms going around her horse's neck, and she squeezed tightly.

"Good, good girl. You're so beautiful in the springtime, Paris, you know that? You want to go for a ride? Hmm? Let's get some exercise, and I'll tell you about my day."

Paris' ears flicked forward, then back. She lowered her head to look for an apple, sniffed Sadie's palm, and followed her obediently into the barn and through the door of her pen. Her hooves clattered on the concrete as she went to the water trough.

Sadie lifted her saddle off the rack, then set it back down. She forgot the blanket. It was not on its usual rack, so she went to look for it in the harness cupboard.

Turning the wooden latch, she checked the interior. No saddle blanket. Hmm. That was weird.

Reuben came sliding across the gravel, making the sound of screeching brakes, almost colliding into his big sister.

"Reuben, where's my saddle blanket?"

"How would I know?"

"Nobody else uses it."

"I didn't use your saddle blanket. I'd never ride with a pink one, you know that."

"It's not pink."

Reuben turned his head to one side, then said loudly, "Phone!"

Sadie listened, heard the insistent ringing, and dashed to the phone shanty.

The sound of a phone ringing was a bit mysterious. If somebody was fortunate enough to hear the phone in the shanty at all, that person dropped everything and ran to answer it. That's because you never knew if the ring you heard was the first one or the tenth one, and you wanted to grab it before voicemail kicked on.

Breathlessly, Sadie lifted the receiver and said, "Hello!"

"Hey."

There was no mistaking that low, gravelly voice. She steadied herself for the usual plummeting of her heart, and the racing pulse that followed, before saying warily, "Mark."

"Hey, Sadie. I... should have stayed in the barn down at the ranch today instead of coming out to talk to you. I guess the sight of those children... I don't know. I over-reacted. Now you probably won't talk to me again."

Sadie smiled. "Why wouldn't I?"

"Well... I dunno. I guess..."

There was an awkward silence, then, "What are you doing?"

"Getting ready to ride. I was actually looking for my saddle blanket, which evidently sprouted legs and ran off."

"Can you... Come over to my place?"

"I can't." Sadie said the words automatically, without considering whether she could or not. It was late, but...

"Why not?"

"I shouldn't ride clear over there by myself. It'll get dark and it might not be safe for me to ride back."

"I'll meet you halfway."

Sadie bit down on her lower lip with indecision. She was dirty and unkempt from planting flowers in the sun and relentless wind, her stomach was much too full of pizza, and she had the start of a glaring red pimple on her chin.

"No."

There was a silence, dead and cold, before an exasperated sigh finally reached her ears. "Okay."

"Wait. Mark I don't want to be... Well, I don't want to hurt your feelings. Do you want me to be honest?"

She felt the humor rise in her chest and she stifled a giggle. Why not? She had already told him she loved him just this afternoon! "I ate way too much pizza with my family, and I have the start of one very large, very sore pimple on my chin."

There was the space of one heartbeat, then a loud, rolling laugh, pure and real and completely uninhibited.

Finally, "Oh Sadie. That is why I... came back to Montana. It is. I think once we know each other better, so many things are possible."

"I'm not coming over tonight, though," Sadie said firmly.

"Then I'm coming over there. Right now. Would your parents disapprove?"

"No. Yes. I don't know."

"Give me a half hour."

"All right."

Sadie slammed down the receiver and raced across the driveway and into the house while an exasperated Reuben closed the door to the phone shanty, shaking his head.

It was the quickest shower Sadie had ever had, and there was no time for making serious decisions about the color or fabric of her dress, either. At least she was more presentable, she thought, as she dabbed concealing lotion on the hateful protrusion on her chin. She hastily jabbed hairpins into her hair and plopped her covering on top, spraying cologne wildly across her wrists and collar as she heard a truck approaching.

A driver! He had asked someone to bring him over!

Her sisters plied her with questions, Mam looked worried, and Reuben was yelling something about Paris from the barn. But Dat just slept in the recliner, his glasses sliding down his nose, the newspaper spread across his stomach.

Sadie opened the door and was met by Mark coming up on the porch. His hair was disheveled, and he wore a blue denim work shirt.

"Sadie!" Reuben was screeching.

"Hi, Mark. Would you mind going with me to the barn? Reuben is seriously perturbed about something."

"Sure."

"You forgot your horse," Reuben said when they got to the barn.

Sadie had forgotten all about Paris. Her halter was still clipped to the chain by the water trough, and Sadie could tell she was not happy. She was throwing her head up, then back down, rattling the chain in the process.

"Sorry, Reuben."

"Hi, Reuben," Mark said affably. "How are you?"

Reuben was still scrubbing his rabbit pens, but he straightened his back, blew his bangs out of his eyes with an expertly protruding lower lip, and smiled. His eyes danced with mischief.

"I'm good. As soon as these rabbit pens are cleaned, I'll be better yet."

Mark bent to peer inside the hutches.

"Don't you like your rabbits?"

"Not really. I'm getting too old for these guys."

"Do you want to sell them at the livestock auction? I'll take you. Maybe Sadie could come, too. It's every Friday night in Critchfield. They have donkeys, horses, mules, geese, chickens. Everything."

Reuben's face was illuminated with excitement.

"Really?"

"Yep."

"I'll go! I'll sell all these rabbits and buy a donkey instead."

Reuben laughed at the very idea, and Sadie couldn't help but laugh with him, meeting Mark's eyes in the dim interior of the barn.

His eyes were laughing, too, but they contained so much more. It was as if her laughter opened the floodgates of his feelings for her.

That was the danger of being with Mark, Sadie thought later. He didn't say a word, but his eyes contained the depth of his... What was it? Did he love her at unguarded moments? Was he too shy or too proud to say what he felt? All she knew was that when the laughter had fizzled away, they were looking deeply into each other's eyes, a sort of assurance between them.

Reuben looked first at Sadie, then at Mark, shrugged his shoulders and returned to his rabbit cages. Sadie acted so odd when Mark was around, he thought.

They went for a walk, then, after releasing a miffed Paris back to the pasture.

Mark talked about everyday, pleasant subjects. He spoke easily and unhurriedly while Sadie bantered light-heartedly in return. He told her of his plans to remodel the old house and just how much work needed to be done. He worked on it every evening and all day on Saturdays.

Then he turned to her and asked her what sort of house she liked. It was so sudden that Sadie became scatterbrained and said something stupid about Richard and Barbara Caldwell's ranch house. She knew perfectly well that Mark could never afford a house half as big as their ranch. What was she thinking?

He steered her into the empty schoolyard, seated her on the cement porch, and sat very close beside her. He positioned his arm behind her and propped his shoulder on one hand, making her so nervous and confused that she didn't know what to say anymore, so she fell silent.

Then, easily, he began to talk. Really talk.

"Sadie, do you want to hear the beginning of my story? Do you know why I got so upset today? I'm sorry. I went a bit overboard. I'll try and do better from now on."

"It's okay," Sadie whispered.

"My first memory is being carried to a horse and buggy and sitting in the back seat with other children. They must have been my brothers and sisters. They say there were five of us.

"My father was a farmer, of sorts. I remember my parents milking cows by hand. I remember the sound of the milk hitting the steel pail, then watching the foam rise up as the pail filled. I remember cats drinking from a dish that my mother filled with the warm milk.

"The milk was stored in milk cans. You know, those big steel ones with handles? We stored them in cold water and then took them to the cheese house."

Sadie shook her head. "I wouldn't know. Dat was never a farmer. I think the farmers in Ohio, at least in our church, had milking machines and bulk tanks."

"Oh. Well, I told you I was raised in a very plain sect."

"Yes."

"Our house had no running water. We went to the wash house to pump our water, and then carried it to the iron kettle and heated it on a wood fire. My job was to carry the wood. We were poor, Sadie, painfully poor."

He stopped, shifted his position, and ran his hand through his black hair. Sadie watched the veins in his large, brown, perfect hands. She wanted to trace them with her fingers, just touch them to see if they were as secure and strong as they looked.

"My mother was a beautiful woman. They said she looked like an Indian from the southwest."

"She must have been," Sadie murmured.

"I remember her hair. When she washed it, it hung way down her back and was thick and sort of coarse. It was straight as a straw broom and swung back and forth when she walked.

"Her name was Amelia, but they called her Meely.

"I was the oldest, then Beulah."

"Beulah!" Sadie said, astounded. "That's not an Amish name."

"I know. I think my mother was a bit of... maybe rebellious toward the strict laws of the church. She named her children Beulah, Timothy, Diana, Rachel Mae, and Jackson."

"But that's six children counting you, Mark."

"But... I was told there were five. Well, whatever. Those were the names of my siblings."

"Why do you say 'were'? Where are they? Are they all... dead? What happened to them, Mark?"

"I don't know."

"You don't know?"

"Wait, Sadie. Let me go on. We must have been trouble for the church. I remember my mother asking my father many questions. She wanted out of the church. She wanted to move. She wasn't afraid of *bann and meidung*. I always thought she said "bone" or "bean," and I could never understand what a bean had to do with leaving the church and moving away somewhere.

"My father must have become despondent. Despairing, whatever. Our cupboards contained less and less. One time I was so hungry that I ate cornmeal from a white paper sack and drank water to wash it down. I shared it with Beulah and Timothy. Diana cried and cried. Her bottle was empty, so I put water in it to keep her quiet. She cried anyway, and I couldn't find my mother.

"I remember the smell of soiled diapers. I quickly learned how to open the large safety pins on the cloth diapers and change them. Sadie, this is one of the most painful things about my childhood. There weren't always clean diapers available, so my little brothers and sisters had to go without. I would watch, though, and clean up after them the best I could. I used a rag that I washed out over and over."

Sadie bowed her head, the knowledge of Mark's childhood pressing down on her very soul.

"I still don't know where my mother went. I just know she wasn't there for long periods of time, and neither was my father.

"I learned to keep the house fairly warm by adding wood to the range in the kitchen. I would get a piece of wood and lay it carefully on a chair. Then I would climb up on the chair, remove the heavy lid on the top of the range, and put the stick of wood into the firebox.

"Sometimes some women would come, and they'd be angry. Their black skirts swished all over the house while they cleaned with Clorox. I guess it was Clorox. It smelled very strong. The women used the wringer washer all day long and filled our cupboards with bread and cheese and cookies and apples. My mother usually cried when they did that. I don't know if it made her happy or angry or if she just felt ashamed of the way we lived."

"Well, where was your mother, Mark? Did she have to go to work, or was she out running around, doing things she shouldn't have been doing?"

"You know, I can't tell you, because I really don't know. She just sort of came and went. I was six or seven, so how much would I really know at that age?"

"But surely she could have explained and hired a babysitter?"

Mark shrugged his shoulders. "My father became increasingly quiet. Actually, he was sort of like a shadow in my life that came and went. I don't remember very much about my father. Only once ... no, it's too awful to say."

Sadie lifted her head, found his gaze. "Trust me."

"No. That can stay buried. I think my father was a man with no hope. Men of the church tried to help him, they must have. They would drive in with their horses and buggies and wide black hats, and stand in the barn for hours. They would talk and wave their hands to emphasize the force behind their words. My mother hated them."

Sadie drew in a quick breath. "Not hated."

"Yes. She hated them. She spat out the door once. It was a horrible sound, one I will always remember. I guess a little boy can absorb lots of things that seem evil, and it never really goes away. It's... I don't know."

Mark shook his head slowly, his eyes burning.

Sadie sighed, a quick intake of breath, then laid a hand on his arm as softly and gently as she could.

"There's healing, Mark. There is."

Chapter 5

THE WHOLE RANCH WAS BUZZING WHEN SADIE walked into the kitchen the following morning.

The television set in Richard Caldwell's study was turned up louder than normal as ranch hands huddled around the desk, sitting on the arms of the sofas and standing at the door. They shifted uncomfortably when Sadie walked into the dining room, casting furtive glances in her direction, shifting their snuff, tucking in shirttails, and clearing their throats nervously.

She wondered what was going on, but of course, she would never ask the men. The important thing at this point was to get the steam table ready for the large, square containers of hot breakfast food. She would drop the pans into the grids so the hot water underneath would keep the food warm, even for the latecomers.

Setting her plastic bucket of soapy water on the table, she added a dash of Clorox and went to work washing the sides and bottom of the table's long, shining enclosure. She wiped down the grids, the top, and the front, rinsing the rag every few swipes.

She stopped, her hearing strained, as she heard a yell of disbelief followed by exclamations of anger or dismay from a few of the most verbal ranch hands. Richard Caldwell was yelling too, his thundering voice bellowing above all the others.

"Aww! It ain't right! This is an outrage. Who in his right mind would do something like that?"

Sadie stood positively motionless.

"He's dead! A magnificent animal! I saw them load him in the truck. He was absolutely huge. Aw! It ain't right."

Sadie heard every word.

What? Which animal? It was all she could do to pick up the plastic bucket and return to the kitchen. She lingered reluctantly before opening the swinging oak doors.

Dorothy looked up from her post at the stove, viciously stirring a large pan of scrambled eggs. She was wearing an electric pink shirt over a brown, pleated skirt. The skirt rode up on her ample hips, leaving a few inches of her white, nylon slip exposed beneath the hem. Her hair was in a state of static profusion, held back by two very pink barrettes. Her eyes flashed blue amid all the pink surrounding her.

"It took you long enough!"

"I was listening. The men are all piled around the TV. Something about a dead animal on the news. Richard Caldwell was really yelling this time."

Without a word, Dorothy marched over to the small television set perched on a stand in the corner and turned it on, expertly pushing buttons on the remote control until she found the channel she wanted.

Sadie picked up the forgotten spatula and stirred the eggs, turning sideways to watch the flickering screen.

Dorothy positioned herself directly in front of the TV, obliterating any action from Sadie's view. Muttering to herself, Dorothy clicked the button, then turned around as the television screen went black.

"Nothin' much I can see. Some crazy person shot a horse. What's so strange about that? Horse likely had a bone broke. Those animal-rights people is plumb nuts. You ain't even allowed to dispose of a stray cat. You know what kills a cat so fast it ain't funny?"

Sadie lifted the heavy pan with both hands, and a golden yellow avalanche of scrambled eggs tumbled out of it and into the square container on the counter. She shook her head at Dorothy's question, biting down on her lower lip with the effort of lifting the heavy pan.

"I ain't gonna tell you."

"All right," Sadie said, shrugging her shoulders non-committally.

"You know why I ain't gonna tell you? 'Cause you'd tell everybody else, and next thing I know, I got those animal fanatics on my tail. I got enough to worry about now. Those kids. Those two precious souls, God love 'em. I can't imagine what's gonna happen to 'em. The cops has all the information they could get. They fingerprinted 'em, poor babies. Just like common animals, and what did they do wrong? Not one thing. Innocent as newborn babes."

Dorothy stopped for breath, her cheeks flaming. "I'm takin' 'em in! I am. I told my Jim, and this is what I said. I says, 'Now Jim, honeybun, you lookie here. We ain't never had no children of our own 'cause the Lord didn't see fit to give us any. I may be old and fat and half wore out, but as long as the Lord gives me the strength, I'm keepin' these young 'uns, sure as shootin'. They's sent straight from heaven.'"

She mopped her shining nose with the dishrag that lay beside the stove, then took a deep breath and launched into a vivid account of the room they were going to fix up for them.

Sadie buttered toast, nodded in agreement, smiling, nodding her head, whenever a question abbreviated the sentences.

"You know, pink for Marcelona. She should have pink walls, but that would never work for Louise. He needs blue or green. So what I'm going to do is paint one side of the room pink, about the color of my shirt, and the other side blue, probably about like your dress. Then... Oh Sadie!"

Dorothy clasped her hands tightly, gazing at the ceiling, pure joy stamped on her round features.

"At the Dollar Tree? In town? They have decals to paste on the ceiling that glow in the dark! They glow. I bought a package to test them before I knew about the children, mind you. Now that was straight from the Lord, too. He knew why I bought them stars. He knew! Two blessed children were coming into our lives. Me and Jim's."

She sighed ecstatically.

Sadie glanced uneasily at the clock.

"It's going past eight."

Dorothy looked, then fairly ran to the refrigerator, bouncing off the cabinets as she whirled toward the dining room.

"Lord have mercy, Sadie! Why'd you let me ramble on thataway? Git the bacon!"

Sadie never failed to marvel at Dorothy's speed. She was such a rotund little being, her feet clad in the questionable shoes from the Dollar General Store, moving with the grace and speed of an antelope, only rounder.

Barking orders, she swung the oak doors, her arms laden with heavy pans of steaming food, Sadie holding her breath more than once as she careened haphazardly between kitchen and dining room.

When everything was laid out to her satisfaction, she whizzed through the doors one last time, dumped steaming black coffee into her large mug, and flopped into a wide kitchen chair, reaching for a napkin to wipe her face.

"Whew! That was close!"

Sadie carried a plate stacked with hotcakes to the table, then went to the pantry for syrup, finally sitting across from Dorothy as she buttered the hotcakes liberally. Dorothy dumped cream into her coffee, stirred, then slurped the steaming hot liquid appreciatively.

"You better watch that butter, young lady."

Sadie laughed.

"I'm hungry. I love pancakes, melted butter all over them."

The door opened slowly.

Two small faces appeared, entering so timidly they seemed to slide against the wall, clearly uncomfortable in this vast kitchen so strange and unusual.

Dorothy's mug clattered to the tabletop as she leapt to her feet.

"There you are! Did Jim bring you in the truck?"

She was on her knees in front of them, brushing back their long, thick, black hair, adjusting T-shirts, tying shoelaces, clucking and fussing like a bantam hen with new chicks.

The children nodded, their eyes round with apprehension.

"My mother is coming to get us today," Marcellus announced, her eyes filling with unshed tears.

Louis nodded, speaking in his impeccable manner.

"She promised she would come soon. I think she will."

"Of course, she will. She'll be back as soon as she possibly can," Dorothy assured them, gathering them to her ample bosom, stroking their hair, murmuring endearments.

Straightening, Dorothy told Sadie to take them to the dining room and let them fill their plates. She did as she was told, a small brown hand in each of her own, swung through the doors, and looked straight into the brown eyes of Mark Peight.

"Good morning, Sadie," he said in his low gravely voice, the gladness in his eyes catching her unaware.

She felt the color rising in her face, lowered her eyes, and mumbled a good morning before checking the room for occupants who stared at them both. Clearly flustered, she bent to address Louis, handing the heavy white plates to the children.

Mark watched Sadie, the gladness leaving his eyes, brown turning to a very dark shade, and he turned brusquely on his heel and walked away.

"There you are!" Richard Caldwell boomed. "Come here!"

Sadie walked over to his table, after helping the children with their food and directing them to a small table along the kitchen wall.

"Good morning!"

"How are you, Sadie?"

"I'm doing okay."

"Hey, you need to hear this. On the news this morning, there's a story about the mysterious death of Black Thunder. Remember the horse?"

"What?" Sadie asked, incredulous.

"Yeah. Apparently, there's a guy, or a group of guys, I don't know, shooting horses just for the fun of it. He ain't the only one dead. It's the most disgusting thing. I mean, shooting a horse is just wrong. Especially a valuable one like that. His owner is heartsick. I called him this morning."

Sadie was aghast, the color draining from her face, as Richard Caldwell explained the situation in Lorado County. Ranchers keeping their horses inside, or the cowhands guarding the corrals, no horses allowed to be in pastures, and certainly not in the open range.

Sadie listened closely, thinking of Paris, grazing happily in the large, secluded pasture with Cody, Reuben's brown mare.

Surely the killers were not in this area. They couldn't be.

She launched into animated conversation with Richard Caldwell, spreading her hands for emphasis, the love for her beloved horse so apparent. Richard Caldwell watched her face, the expression changing from despair to panic then sadness as she remembered Nevaeh, the black and white paint that had broken his leg when she tried to clear a high fence.

Mark Peight had filled his plate, found a place to eat at the long table crowded with cowhands, and bent to his food, before looking up and seeing Sadie talk animatedly, with Richard Caldwell watching her face so closely.

The food-laden fork went slowly into his mouth, then out as he swallowed forcefully, never taking his eyes off the two at an adjoining table.

His eyes narrowed, his nostrils flared slightly as he slowly laid down his fork, color rising in his face. Putting both hands on the table's edge, he pushed back his chair, turned on his heel, and strode past Sadie and her boss, closing the door with a resounding "thwack" as he made his decided exit.

Her first instinct was to go after him, grab his sleeve, hang on, and ask him why he left so suddenly without acknowledging her presence.

Richard Caldwell watched Sadie, saw the distraction as Mark strode past, watched her turn sideways in her chair to watch him leave. Silently he took a sip of his coffee.

Sadie was clearly agitated now, but she sighed and met Richard Caldwell's eyes, resignation stamped all over her lovely features.

"You know him?"

"Yes."

"How well do you know him?"

Sadie shrugged her shoulders, pushed her dark hair back, bit down on her lower lip, and would not look at him.

"He's the best farrier I ever watched, and I've seen a bunch of 'em in my time. He shod Sage, that big gray brute, but ended up throwing him with the twitch to do it."

Sadie's eyes flamed.

"That's just cruel. You don't have to hurt a horse's mouth to restrain him."

With that, she got up, bid him a good day, and marched into the kitchen.

Richard Caldwell sipped his coffee, speculating, before a slow grin spread across his face, and he shook his head.

✿ ✡ ✿

Sadie and Reuben went riding that evening after the dishes were washed, Paris and Cody eager to run.

They held them in, with the horses chomping down on their bits, prancing to the side, even rearing in the air, balking a bit, as if they couldn't bear to be held back.

They went down the winding driveway and turned right, riding single file along the macadam road before coming to the field lane that turned to the high pasture along the ridge.

Sadie tightened her knees, leaned forward, and loosened the reins, grinning back at Reuben the instant Paris gathered her legs beneath her and catapulted up the lane.

There was no reason to hold them back. Just pasture grasses and wildflowers for at least a mile, so Sadie let Paris go.

The blond mane whipped across Paris' neck, her head pumped up and down, the dull, muffled sound of her hooves striking the earth sounding like pure music to Sadie's ears.

The wind tossed Sadie's dark hair, tore at her *dichly*, and still Paris pounded on. The grasses swayed, the trees blurred by, and she rode on, the enjoyment of allowing Paris to run free unfettering her own spirits, the worries about Mark Peight streaming behind her, lost on the wind, for now.

Out of the corner of her eye, a dark object crept into her vision. Turning her head, she yelled, goading Paris, who responded with a lowering of her head and an outstretched neck as her muscles renewed their strength, knowing Cody was gaining on her.

Reuben was bent low over Cody's neck, laughing. His hair was a shade lighter than his horse's mane, but they flowed together, rippling in the speed of the wind.

Sadie realized Cody might actually beat Paris, so she leaned forward, urging Paris on, talking, talking, and was rewarded by the sight of Cody and Reuben falling back, but only for a second.

As they leaned into the turn, Cody somehow got the inside, and Reuben yelled at Sadie as they inched closer.

On she came, Cody stretched out, running as Sadie had never seen the horse run. She was determined, all by herself, to beat Paris, Sadie could tell. There was a focus in her eyes, a determination in her bearing, and no matter how much Sadie urged Paris on, Cody and Reuben kept gaining.

"No!" Sadie screamed.

They were neck and neck now, coming down the stretch of pasture that led to the lane, so Sadie knew she had to pull Paris in, or they would run downhill at that speed. Sitting up, she pulled back slightly, turning Paris in a circle, back to the wildflowers.

Reuben was standing up in his stirrups, pumping his fist into the air, yelling at the top of his lungs, exultant, completely caught up in the moment.

"Cody did it, Sadie! She did! I don't care what you say! Cody beat Paris!"

Sadie was laughing, shaking her head, panting, as she pulled Paris to a stop. Cody came prancing up beside them, her nostrils moving rapidly, but clearly not finished running.

Paris was blowing hard.

"You did not beat me, Reuben!" Sadie gasped.

"I did! I'm sure I did. Cody's nose was ahead of Paris. I saw it!"

Reuben's tanned face was alight with victory, his hair disheveled, no Amish straw hat in sight. He decided long ago that there was no use wearing a hat to go riding. It wouldn't stay on his head longer than 10 seconds.

"All right! All right!" Sadie conceded, watching Reuben and glad he won, for his sake, although she didn't seriously think Cody had actually done it.

"Hey, I bet if I was English, I could race Cody at the rodeos!"

Sadie nodded, "I bet too you could! And you'd win!"

"Aw, I can't imagine! Think about it, Sadie. Riding like that in front of thousands of people, winning a bunch of money. Wouldn't it be unreal?"

"Yeah. But we aren't allowed to race like that. We don't go to rodeos and stuff either."

"Why ever not? That's so dumb. Who said?"

Reuben dismounted, threw the reins expertly over Cody's head, then stretched out in the grass. "Who said?" he repeated.

"Well, you know how it is, Reuben. We have rules. It's too worldly to be competitive with our horses. I mean, think about it. If you're born Amish, you grow up sort of knowing what's allowed and what isn't. It's no big deal."

Reuben grabbed the stem of a tall wildflower, peeled off the leaves and stuck it in his mouth. He pushed it to the side, as expertly as Jim Sevarr with his toothpick. "I'm going to go English, he said.

"Now, Reuben," Sadie said mildly.

"I mean it."

"You'd break Mam's and Dat's hearts."

Reuben nodded soberly, then spat out the stem.

"I know. I'm Dat's only boy."

"That's right. The least you can do for your parents is love and obey them. You know that."

Reuben nodded soberly, then sat up.

"I like Dat."

"Well, good for you, Reuben. Dat's not a hard person to get along with."

"I like you, too. Sadie, you're my best sister."

That was quite a stretch, Reuben saying that, Sadie knew. She reached out with genuine affection to touch her brother's hair.

"You're my best brother, too."

"I'm the only one you have," Reuben grinned.

"But my best one, anyway."

It happened so suddenly, the only thing Sadie heard was a high whining sound, sort of like a whistle, but more deadly. She didn't hear a crack. Not the way you're supposed to when you tell someone you heard a gunshot. It wasn't really the hard sound of a gun, the sort that makes you wince every time you hear it.

She knew only one thing: Cody was down. She hit the ground with a sort of grace, the way an accordion folds and produces a beautiful sound from the air pumped into its bellows. One moment she was grazing with Paris; the next, her legs folded beneath her as she made a short, groaning sound, sort of a whoosh. Her head bent back as her legs flailed, she made one pitiful attempt to right herself, then fell. She never took another breath.

Paris snorted, jerked the reins from Sadie's hands, then galloped off a short distance, her ears flicking, her head held high, watching the tree line.

Reuben cried out, a youth's cry of alarm, innocent in its raw terror. There was no anger in the sound, only the consternation of not being able to understand.

"Lie down! Reuben, lie flat in the tallest grass!" Sadie hissed.

He obeyed immediately, and they lay with their ears pressed to the ground.

Sadie was terrified.

Who would have done this? Surely not the same people Richard Caldwell talked about. That was in Laredo County at least a hundred miles away. It couldn't be. Likely a hunter, mistaking Cody's brown coat for a mule deer or an elk. But hunting season wasn't until the fall. It had to be someone shooting illegally. A poacher.

Her ear pressed to the ground, Sadie heard nothing except her own heart thumping wildly, seemingly tripping over itself, the blood rushing into her ears with each thump.

"Reuben?" she whispered.

"Hmm?"

"Do you hear anything? See anything?"

"No."

"We need to get out of here as fast as possible."

"I'm not leaving Cody."

Slowly they raised their heads, peering through the grasses.

When there was no movement anywhere, Sadie hoped they'd be able to make a run for it. She had never been so afraid. She was completely panicked now, her mouth so dry she could not swallow.

"Reuben, you have to go with me. We need to go, NOW! What if…that man with a gun was waiting in the trees or…"

"He probably left. I'm not leaving Cody."

Then he was up, walking to his beloved horse, dropping to his knees, stroking her neck, pushing the heavy mane aside with his hands.

Sadie crawled over on her stomach, much too frightened to stand.

Reuben didn't cry. He just hunkered beside his horse, his eyes flat with the truth of it. Someone had shot Cody.

Sadie couldn't bear his quietness. She put a hand on his shoulder.

Reuben shrugged it off.

"Don't."

"Reuben, listen. We'll get you another one. I will take this blame. We never should have gone riding. I knew there was trouble, but I just ... well, figured they were in Laredo County."

"You mean those men who shot Black Thunder?"

Sadie nodded.

Still Reuben stayed, stroking Cody's neck, her face. When he turned to look at Sadie, the disbelief, the inability to comprehend such evil, turned his eyes a darker color, the corners drooping with the weight of his sadness. His mouth trembled, but no words followed.

"We have to go. Please."

"Not yet."

There was a dark pool of blood seeping out beneath Cody's chest. Sadie watched Reuben carefully, willing him away from the sight of it.

Suddenly, he drew a sharp breath.

"C ... Cody is bleeding."

Sadie nodded.

"She's really dead."

He bent his head then, put both hands over his face to hide it, as great sobs shook his thin frame. Sadie gathered him in her arms and cried with him, wetting his shoulder with her tears.

She cried for Cody, for Reuben's pain, for life when it turned cruel, and for the fact that she didn't understand everything.

Did she understand anything?

Why was Mark angry? Surely he would not have become so upset that he would shoot a horse? But Reuben said his home was filled with guns.

He wouldn't.

Sadie stroked Reuben's back, the only way she knew to comfort him, and when he stepped back, dug out a rumpled red handkerchief and blew his nose, he looked at her and took a deep breath.

"I'll be okay," was all he said.

Chapter 6

IN THE DAYS THAT FOLLOWED, THE WHOLE FAMILY rallied around Reuben.

Anna bought him his favorite candy bars, baseball cards, and red licorice from the store in town.

Rebekah let him drive Charlie when she went to visit Aunt Elma who lived about eight miles away. Mam baked pumpkin whoopie pies and chocolate ones, filled with thick, creamy frosting and wrapped in Saran Wrap individually.

Dat called the hide and tanning company. He traveled with the truck up the field lane to the field of wildflowers, where they loaded the carcass. He never said a word about any of it to Reuben, which had to be the best, leaving him to remember his horse as he loved her, alive and well, running fast.

There was a huge controversy going on down at the ranch. Sadie busily pieced together snatches here and there, unable to come to a conclusion of her own. It was difficult pondering why any person or group of people would aim a rifle and shoot an innocent, unassuming horse in its own pasture.

There were no tracks, no leads for the police. A few days of discussion on the news, then nothing.

The Miller family did not report Cody's death; it was their way of staying out of the public eye. They looked on the incident as something God allowed to happen. Whether it was evil or not, it had occurred. The family accepted it, mourned the horse, then everyone moved on, including Reuben.

Only Sadie understood his pain. Really understood it.

When he flopped on the recliner and stared into space, then picked up a hunting magazine to hide his face, Sadie knew he was biting down on his lower lip, blinking madly as he vowed not to cry.

One evening, when dusk was settling over the back porch like a soft, gray blanket of comfort, promising rest to the tired occupants of the porch swing, Dat broke the silence. He was building a screened-in deck for a man who had an old buckboard he'd give to someone who would restore it.

Instantly Anna sprang up, clapping Reuben's shoulder.

"There you go, Reuben!"

Reuben snorted.

"What would I want with a buckboard? I don't know how to fix it up, and besides, I have no horse."

"Paris," Anna countered quickly.

"She's not broke to drive."

"Charlie!"

That was met with an unenthused snort.

"Would you restore it, Dat?" Sadie asked.

"I don't know. It's not really my thing."

"Who does that?"

"I have no idea. Plenty of people in Ohio, but here... I don't know of anyone Amish, anyway."

"Would you do it, Dat?" Sadie asked.

"I don't really want to."

"If Reuben and I help? If we get a horse that matches Paris, we could really have something neat. Maybe even drive them at horse sales."

"Or shows! Or rodeos!" Reuben shouted.

"Now!" Mam said.

That long drawn out "now" was always Mam's way of reprimanding gently but firmly, sort of like pulling back the reins on a horse. You knew you had to stop and consider, not go so fast; there might be an obstacle along the way, and you needed to be aware of it.

Still it was an idea.

For one thing, it might help Anna. She desperately wanted to feel needed and to rebuild a kinship with Reuben, the way it was when they were younger. Sadie often felt guilty for taking Reuben from Anna the way she did. But unlike Reuben, Anna was not a rider. She was becoming quite chubby, her cheeks round and rosy with good health and lots of good food, and absolutely not a care in the world about it.

Her face was very pretty and tanned, with greenish-gray eyes that looked blue when she wore a blue dress and gray when she wore anything else. She was going on 15 now and looking forward to being finished with school. Anna was as happy and easy to get along with as any of her sisters.

Sadie sat up, adrenaline filling her body with energy.

"Dat! If you bring the buckboard home, we'll fix it up, and we'll keep watching for a horse for Reuben, and we'll teach that horse and Paris to be hitched double. Anna can help."

Anna was chewing on a hard pretzel, sounding very

much like a horse crunching an ear of corn. Reuben watched her out of the corner of his eye.

"Do you have to crunch that pretzel so hard?" he asked, his eyes narrowing.

"What's it to you? Maybe my pretzel's good!"

Mam got up, yawning, gathering her housecoat about her, saying it was time all decent, hardworking people went to bed.

Sadie caught a whiff of Mam's talcum powder as she neared her chair, the same warm, silky scent she always wore, sort of like fresh baked bread mixed with a flowery odor of roses. She had just washed her graying hair; it hung down her back, held fast by a black, elastic ponytail holder. The long, thin ponytail made her seem as vulnerable as a child.

Mam always had her hair up in a bun, a white covering obscuring most of it. She appeared neat, clean, and in charge of her life and her family. Somehow, at moments like this, Sadie knew Mam was a tender sort of person, though still dependent on medication. Her mental condition had greatly improved but was still delicate.

Mam despised the fact that she was on "nerve pills," but she never wanted to return to the abyss of breakdowns she had earlier slid into.

Thankful now, Sadie said goodnight. She took a cool shower and tumbled into bed. She was too sleepy to read. It was too warm to be very comfortable, so she lay on her back, her hands propped behind her head, and stared wide-eyed at the ceiling, thinking.

The giggles from Rebekah's room irked her. It irked her more when the giggles rose to shrieks of glee and Leah dashed across the hall to the bathroom, slamming the door.

Sadie harrumphed inwardly. They acted so childish these days. Both of them were very interested in their guys and acted as if it was the only subject worth thinking about. Likely they'd soon be dating.

Sadie felt old and a bit useless, except for Paris and the ranch. If that Mark Peight insisted on acting so *bupplich,* then she'd just ignore him, and he could go fly a kite for all she cared. She was getting thoroughly sick of his strange ways. Besides, anyone with a childhood like that was bound to have some dysfunctional issues, and she wasn't going to marry anyone like that.

She had felt so sure that God was leading them together, that this was her destiny. Well, no more. She was done. She rolled on her side, punched her pillow, and sighed.

So that was how it was going to be. Mark Peight would just have to live in Montana if he wanted to; it didn't mean she had to be his wife anytime soon. Or... anytime at all.

Suddenly, a train of nostalgia rolled over her heart, its mournful whistle causing her to wince with remembering Ezra.

He was so good. So kind, uncomplicated, and easy to figure out. Life with Ezra would have been like calm waters, serene, her days floating by with no turbulence.

It was unreal, at times. He was no longer here on earth. If anyone deserved a home in heaven, it was surely Ezra. Maybe she was meant to be alone, then reunited with him once she got to heaven. Who knew?

Pi-i-ng!

The sound was only heard in her subconscious mind. The second time she heard it, she figured the temperature must have been higher than usual this afternoon, the way the house was creaking and snapping.

She heard another pinging noise, this time against glass.

What?

She sat straight up, kicked the sheet off, and headed to the window.

Crack!

Sadie recoiled, taking a few steps backward.

Someone was throwing a small, hard object against her window, above the screen.

Clutching her throat in horror, she stood in the middle of the room in total darkness, wondering what to do. Grab her robe and make a dash for the stairs? Get Leah and Rebekah? Wake Reuben?

She heard her name, a hissing sound.

Someone was out there. Someone who knew her and knew which room was hers.

"Sadie! It's me!"

A hoarse whisper. "It's me! Mark!"

Mark Peight! Throwing pebbles at her window like some lovelorn hero of the past. What a loser!

Anger gripped her, its claws tightening her senses, until she realized it would never work to go to the window and tell him exactly what she thought of him. Storming out of the ranch house because of who knew why, then showing up at her window in the middle of the night almost.

She had a notion to stay exactly where she was until he went away.

"Sadie! It's me. Mark!"

Again, she heard the urging in his voice.

"Sadie!"

Pushing her face against the screen, she looked down at his tall dark form, his face lifted as he eagerly awaited her answer.

"What do you want?"

She didn't mean to sound as grouchy as she did. She wished the words, or rather, her tone of voice, would stick in the screen and stay there, or dust the night breeze without harming anyone.

"What do you think I want?" he hissed in return. There was so much anger in his tone, Sadie took a step back, her eyes opening wide.

"I have no idea."

"I need to ask you something."

"Ask away."

What possessed her? Why did she answer with barbs emphasizing every word? She wanted to hurt him, like he'd hurt her by storming out of the Caldwell dining room, then ignoring her, and leaving her to wander a desert of insecurity.

How could she ever have felt he was her destiny? He was too hard to understand.

"Come downstairs."

The words were a curt order.

She pursed her lips, considering her answer. She no longer felt that panicky heartbeat in his presence, which uncomplicated things a lot. Folding her arms, she took her time in giving him an answer.

"Well, I need to get dressed."

"No, you don't. Just grab a robe."

"Hush! You'll wake Mam!"

Sadie knew Mam was a very light sleeper, as alert as the mouser in the barn. There was no way she could creep down the stairs without Mam knowing. Dat would go right on sleeping, the proverbial log. If Mam caught her sneaking outside in her night clothes, she would be in some very serious trouble.

"Hang on!"

She dressed quickly and crept down the stairs, her heart pounding now, which puzzled her. She thought she had surely moved on from that childish emotion. But by the time she reached the kitchen door, it was hammering against her ribs, drying her mouth until her tongue felt like cotton. She was still trying to be angry, but she couldn't keep the anger if the excitement of seeing Mark again drove it away.

Rounding the side of the house, she found him sitting on the lawn, his back to a tree, looking as if he had been there all evening. It was dark, but not so dark that she couldn't see his features or the shape of his head, the slope of his shoulders.

Dropping to her knees, breathless now, she said, "This is a weird time for you to come talk to me."

"Yeah, well..."

There was a silence, swelling with question marks.

Then, "Sadie, I have to know. What does Richard Caldwell mean to you?"

"Mean to me? What are you talking about?"

"I...was eating breakfast, and... You have never talked to me like that. Never. Your whole face lit up. You moved your hands. You pushed back your dark hair. It was like...suddenly you had a great reason to care about life. Almost like... I don't know."

He leaned forward, his elbows propped on his knees, the picture of misery. The great shoulders slumped in dejection.

Sadie sat down, pulled her skirt over her knees, and said nothing.

How could he? Surmise, presume, suspect, whatever. It was all the same. She could not believe him.

"Mark, he's my boss. I work for him. That's all."

"It didn't look that way."

"He's old enough to be my father!"

"So? That doesn't mean anything in the English world."

"It does, too."

"Look, Sadie, I know a lot more about that world than you do. A man like him, with his wealth, his status..."

"What about me? You think I would actually encourage him to... to...? So that's what you think I am?"

There was no answer.

Sadie's chin lifted. She felt the anger literally course through her veins. Scrambling to her feet, she stalked across the lawn, through the darkness, glad for its cover as the heat rose in her face.

She felt no tears, she was far too angry.

"Wait!"

Sadie did not wait. She walked as fast as she could, past the shrubs, up onto the porch. She had just reached for the door handle when she was caught, a hand on her waist. She was forcibly whirled around to face a very tall, ominous Mark.

"I didn't say that."

"You meant that!"

The screen door opened, and they were both caught in the blue glare of a blinding LED flashlight.

The deep, sleepy voice of Jacob Miller boomed, "*Vass geht au?*"

Dat!

Mark smiled sheepishly, then stuck out his hand.

"Hello, Jacob Miller. I'm just... here to talk to Sadie about something."

"You that Peight guy?"

"Yes, I am."

"Well, if you have something to talk about, I suppose the porch swing would be a proper place to sit, and since I doubt if you want me to hear what you're saying, I'll go back to bed again."

With that, the flashlight clicked off, the darkness covered them, soft and merciful, the screen door closed softly, and he was gone.

Mark cleared his throat, shuffled his feet.

"Can we sit down?"

The last thing Sadie wanted to do was share the intimacy of the porch swing with him, but she said stiffly, "We can."

Like robots they were now, turning and sitting down as if on cue. Sadie sort of hit the edge of the swing, miscalculating its position in the dark. Then she sat back too far and almost slid off, causing the swing to lurch like a boat hitting waves. She had to brake with her feet. Then the whole ridiculous situation hit her, and she burst out laughing, a sort of unladylike snort that caught her totally unaware.

They were both laughing now. With great swells of relief, the tension between them evaporated, welcome as summer showers on a parched earth.

Laughter was like that. A smile worked the same magic. It eased tension, opened the way for friendly conversation; it lowered a drawbridge for large ships that had to arrive at their destinations on time.

"You just about sat on the porch floor," Mark said finally.

"Hard, too!" Sadie laughed.

"What was I going to say?"

"You were talking about my boss. Mr. Richard Caldwell, himself."

"Yes, I was. And I plan on finishing my questions. What were you talking about?"

"Didn't you hear the men's conversation? It's all over the ranch. Someone is going around killing horses. Like a sniper. It started in Laredo County, sort of... well, I think the area where the horse thieves were. You know those thieves were never caught and brought to justice. Black Thunder, the leader of the wild horses—he's dead. His owner is devastated. It's awful, Mark. You surely heard about Reuben's horse?"

"What?"

"Reuben's horse. He was shot. Up on the field of wild-flowers where we caught Paris and Cody."

"You can't be serious!"

"Yes. It was horrible. Reuben is being brave, but he'll never forget it. He's so young. I mean, I was what, 18 when Nevaeh died? I'll always remember that day."

"I will, too. Certainly. That was the day I finally held you in my arms. I could have died there. On that wagon. My life was fulfilled then. I knew what heaven feels like."

Sadie did not know what to say, so she said nothing. The chain attached to the heavy steel hook creaked with each moment of the swing, and Sadie could sense Mark's agitation.

"That's why I get so... I don't know."

Suddenly he burst out, "I am so jealous of you, it's scary. When I saw you talking to your boss, I felt like a great black beast that wanted to... punch him, drag him away from you. It's shameful and awful, but I don't know what to do about it."

"What hurts me most, is that you would even think I would be... having an affair with him or something? How could you?"

His answer, a lowered head, moving back and forth, was his denial. "I'm like a colt that's been mistreated. I don't trust anyone. Not one single person. I want to, but…"

"I would never do anything as out of…just plain unheard of…" She was cut short.

"It's not unheard of!" he shouted.

Instinctively she put a hand over his mouth, like she would to try and shush a small boy.

"Shhh!"

"Sorry," he said quietly. "My mother, my lovely, beautiful mother, had a horrible affair with a real estate man. They slunk around the house like deceiving liars. Snakes. That's what they reminded me of. You know the kinds of snakes that are the exact same color as the grass and twigs and leaves?"

Sadie nodded.

"That's how it was. His car would drive in, my father would be in the fields, dragging that rusty, ancient, screeching harrow across his rocky soil with two skinny brown mules that looked as if they'd fall over any minute. He'd knock at the front door…and, well, I was only a kid, but I wasn't dumb. I knew. I think finally, that was the end of everything. The farm was sort of put up for sale, I guess, and that's when my father…wanted to stop living."

"But…did your mother run away with the real estate man?"

"Yes. There was an awful fight."

"But…I don't understand. If your parents were of the Amish faith, why did they act like that? Wouldn't they… I mean, surely they knew they did wrong?"

"My father did nothing wrong! Not one thing. He was a good man. He tried his best. I think he married way out of his league, if you know what I mean. Dat was sort of ordinary looking, a bit thin, and didn't have the... I don't know. Mam was beautiful, probably could've had any guy she wanted."

He paused, then turned and looked Sadie in the eye, and said, "Like you."

"Not me," Sadie whispered.

Mark bent over and caught both of her hands in his. He held them, securely, warmly, and kept them. The swing creaked, the night sounds shrilled and warbled and hooted, a symphony of nature resplendent in its variety.

"Yes, yes. Sadie, listen to me. It's why I ran off to Pennsylvania after I held you in my arms. I figured if I let myself love you, if I went falling headlong over a cliff without any thought to my past, of who I am, look what could happen. And when I saw you at that table with Mr. Caldwell... I... well, I went a little crazy. Can you blame me? You're so beautiful, Sadie, and how do I know that inside you there's not a promiscuous heart, like my mother's?"

"But, Mark, your mother was one in a million! That doesn't happen among our people. We are raised and kept to a commitment to God. The church, our marriage vows, all are taken very seriously. I have never heard of anyone... I mean, your mother was... Whew!"

Sadie had no words to describe her disbelief.

"I think she joined the church and wanted to do what was right in the beginning. She bore five children in five years, the way the church wanted it, doing nothing to prevent it. And perhaps, she simply couldn't handle the drudgery, the sleepless nights, the endless work, I don't know."

Sadie nodded, quiet now. She pulled her hands free,

hesitated one second, then brought her hands to his forearms, slid them up to his shoulders, and pulled him close, laying her head on his hard, muscled chest.

"Mark?" she whispered.

He groaned softly before crushing her to himself, his head lowering.

"I want you to know you can trust me. I can only say that, and the rest is up to you. I'll try and be someone you can place... I mean, for you to tell me these things, is just amazing. Where have you learned to confide in someone? So often, troubled children aren't able to do that."

"You are the only person who knows. Well, the counselor, but..."

She nodded, and stayed quiet.

"Sadie, do you believe in distant courtship? Are your parents very strict about these things?"

"I think that's pretty much up to us. I can't imagine... I don't know."

Clearly, she was becoming quite flustered, floundering with her words.

He chuckled softly. "I think I know what you mean, Sadie."

He kissed her softly, then soundly, and Sadie knew she had never felt closer to anyone in all her life. The will of God was so clear she could almost hold it in her hands, like a bouquet of wildflowers on the ridge, their fragrance enveloping them both, promising a future that was not smooth and untroubled. Rocky and steep at times, stormy at other times, their love was a vessel of strength that would bind them together, like two souls in a fortress of might.

And she'd be very careful how she talked to Richard Caldwell.

Chapter 7

IN CHURCH A FEW WEEKS LATER, THE *KESSLE-HAUS*, where the single girls stood, waiting to be called in and seated on the benches assigned for them, was abuzz with the shootings.

Erma Keim, a garrulous, big-boned girl of 28, who had never bothered about boyfriends or marriage, her white organdy cape and apron wrinkled and limp, her hands pumping the air for emphasis, expounded loud and long about this latest atrocity.

"I don't believe it," she was saying in a voice not meant for the quiet of a pre-service *kessle-haus*.

"I mean, this is ridiculous. Finally, we got those wild horses out of here, and now they claim someone is shooting horses on purpose. I refuse to believe it."

She tucked a strand of wavy, red hair beneath her covering, which sprang back out in defiance, looking wavier and redder than before. Her covering was limp and out of line, like her hair. She socked herself back against the counter, her green eyes bulging as she folded her arms across her skinny waist.

"It's true. Reuben's Cody is dead," Sadie said bluntly.

"What? Your brother? Is Cody his horse? What do you mean?"

Erma was fairly shouting now, her eyes looking as if they could leave the sockets of her face, were they not attached by strong muscles.

"Yes, yes, and yes," Sadie said, nodding soberly.

"But shot? I mean, just plain out of the clear, blue sky?" Erma shouted.

Sadie nodded, then told the attentive listeners the story of the race, the shot, the fear that followed.

"*Upp*!" Erma said, nodding in the direction of the kitchen door, where Maria Bontrager, the lady of the house, stood, motioning them to come to the service.

Erma always went first, being the oldest by more than a few years. Today was no exception, with Sadie following on her heels, and then Leah and Rebekah. The group of girls fell in line as they wound their way to the living room to be seated with the remainder of the congregation.

The open windows promised a breath of air in the already stuffy room. Sadie knew all too well how warm it would become before the three-hour service ended.

Her heart jangled a bit when Mark Peight led the row of single boys. He was so tall! So dark. How could she ever remain the same when she saw him? She was so glad no one could tell how her heart jumped and skipped a beat at the sight of him.

She sighed, a small expulsion of air, when she saw the boys being seated in the kitchen, out of their sight. She couldn't see him at all during the service, but maybe it was just as well; she'd keep her mind on the sermon.

When the strains of the first song began, she opened the small black *Ausbund*, the old German hymnbook written by the forefathers in prison. She turned to share it with Leah, who shook her head slightly as she busily unwrapped a red and white striped candy, which she popped into her mouth. She rolled the cellophane wrapper into a small bundle and tossed it below the bench ahead of her.

Sadie stuck her elbow out, punching Leah's arm. She turned to look at her sister with bewilderment in her innocent blue eyes.

Sadie drew down her eyebrows, pointed with her chin at the cellophane wrapper below the bench and mouthed, "Pick up your paper."

Leah shrugged, enjoyed her peppermint, and opened her mouth to help with the singing, its volume building by the minute.

Sadie leaned over. "Give me one, please," she whispered.

"Don't have another one," Leah answered.

Sadie answered by tapping on the pocket of Leah's dress below the apron, where the presence of a few candy-sized lumps resulted in a meaningful stare from Sadie and an upturned hand.

"Give me."

Leah frowned but lifted her apron, producing a candy obediently before settling back to help with the singing.

Sadie unwrapped the peppermint discreetly, bent her head to pop it into her mouth, folded the wrapper, and put it in her pocket along with the ironed handkerchief.

Leah watched from the corner of her eye and mouthed, "Goody."

Sadie grinned, then ducked her head when she felt the grin spreading.

The girls knew they were to behave with circumspection in the church at all times. But on a warm summer morning, a bit of sisterly fun helped ease the boredom of sitting on the hard benches for three hours, less alluring today than it ever was.

The slow rhythm of the singing swirled around her. The wave of tradition and comfortable Sunday-morning sounds were as much a foundation for every Amish young person as the regularity of the services.

It was a form of worship they could adhere to, be content with, and grow in grace and spirituality without asking hows and whys. Lots of people chose to question, though. They became contentious, berating the ministers and their sermons, and sometimes taking their families to "go higher," which meant they joined another church that allowed them more worldly things, like cars and electricity.

Parents shushed their crying babies. Fathers with crying two-year-olds looked to give the children to their mothers, who may have been upstairs with other tiny siblings. So an aunt or grandmother scrambled to relieve the father of his unhappy offspring. After questioning the child closely, she'd offer a drink of cold water or a small container of pretzels or fruit snacks.

When the minister rose to begin the sermon, the congregation grew quiet, eagerly awaiting his words. He did not disappoint. The graying patriarch expounded on the word of God in a dynamic, undulating voice that gripped his listeners.

Sadie noticed a disturbance on the bench where the younger girls sat, a few rows ahead. Anna was extremely restless, her head turning first one way, then another, fixing her cape, then her covering.

Sadie became uncomfortable. What was wrong with Anna? It seemed as if she could not sit still for a minute.

Her face was pale, and she kept grimacing in the most unattractive manner.

Just when Sadie could stand it no longer, Anna rose and made her way carefully between the rows of girls, making a hasty exit up the stairs.

Sadie thought no more about it, guessing that Anna went to the bathroom, and resumed singing. When they stood to hear the Scripture, after kneeling in prayer, Sadie went to the *kessle-haus* for a drink of cold water and noticed that Anna was not among the girls her age. As she turned to go upstairs through the kitchen, she lowered her eyes demurely. She did not want to meet Mark's eyes, already feeling flushed as she walked past him.

She closed the door firmly, went softly up the stairs, and turned the knob of the bathroom door. It was locked. She stood back, her arms crossed, waiting until the bathroom was unoccupied.

She heard the water running, a pause, then Anna, very pale, opened the door. Sadie looked at her closely, noticing the swelling of her eyes. Was it just the warm summer weather?

"You okay?" she asked.

"Course, why wouldn't I be all right?" Anna said, her voice strained. Hoarse? Had she been crying?

Erma Keim thumped her way upstairs, and Anna pushed past Sadie, quickly disappearing down the stairway.

Sadie and Erma entered the bathroom together, Erma saying quite loudly, "Something smells bad! Eww! Someone threw up or something!"

Sadie winced, never knowing Erma to be tactful. She sniffed, then pushed aside the lace curtains to open the window wider.

"How can you tell?" she asked.

"I just can. Hey, my job at the produce market is coming to an end in September. Do they need someone down at Aspen East, where you work? I need to get serious about a job."

Sadie smiled to herself, knowing they were not supposed to discuss business or monetary concerns on a Sunday. But typical Erma, speaking loudly what was on her mind, no matter the day or the circumstances.

"I can check for you."

At the thought of Erma Keim and Dorothy Sevarr together in one kitchen, Sadie resigned herself to culinary war, with Dorothy defending her kingdom as queen of the domain, and the invading Erma trying to steal the crown in the first week.

The room was becoming quite warm. Women groped in their pockets for a square of folded, white handkerchief, lowering their faces to wipe discreetly at the perspiration beading their foreheads.

Little boys sat patiently beside their fathers, their bare feet swinging, their bangs dark with sweat, as the fathers swiped at their collars, loosening them slightly. The tired and restless babies grew too uncomfortable to sleep, while mothers patiently held them, their eyes a picture of submission.

The second speaker, a shy young minister who had only been ordained a few years ago, droned on. His monotone voice led the older men down a ramp slick with sleepiness, lassitude, then sleep, until they jerked back to consciousness—and embarrassment.

The minister did the best he could, Dat said. The Lord had chosen him, and someday, he'd overcome his quietness and shyness. Dat always had a soft spot for Phares Schlabach, who Dat said was truly humble, a good servant in the Lord's vineyard. And don't you kid yourself; if you paid attention, he said some profoundly interesting things, pointing out bits of Scripture no one else thought about.

Dat was like that. He respected and admired the quiet ones. The simple men of the community who struggled to make a living were often overlooked. They stayed in the background, smiling, and thoroughly enjoying the more talented storytellers who drew all the attention.

Dat said his girls would do well to marry a man like Phares.

After services, Sadie helped set the long tables with the Sunday dinner they always ate at church. The women spread long, snowy white tablecloths on benches elevated by wooden racks to form tables. For each place setting, they supplied a small plate for pie, a cup, knife and fork, and a water glass. Along with plates of sliced, homemade bread, the women served butter, jam, cheese, peanut-butter spread, pies, pickles, sweetened little red beets, and plates of ham.

It was the traditional meal at every church service, and so delicious each time. It was more like a snack or a hurried lunch. There were no elaborate dishes. They did no cooking, except to make a large pot of coffee. But it was a church dinner, a taste of home and community, a meal shared after services, as talk and laughter moved among the good food. Everyone ate hungrily and revived their spirits.

Sadie and her sisters washed dishes, filled water glasses, served coffee, whatever was necessary. They talked with their friends as they held fussy babies so mothers could sit down to eat in peace.

Erma Keim dashed among the tables, every movement

well calculated, the picture of efficiency. Sadie couldn't help but wonder what that presence would accomplish down at the ranch. But she dismissed the notion quickly at the thought of Dorothy's snapping eyes and her unladylike snort.

"They need pie on the men's table," Erma said, whisking past with an empty water pitcher held aloft.

Sadie turned to the pie rack to extricate one, then slid out another before turning to head for the men's table, where she found Reuben enthusiastically spreading a huge glob of the peanut-butter spread on a thick slice of whole wheat bread. She held her breath as he lifted it to his mouth, then grinned when he gave her a thumbs-up sign, peanut butter spread all over his fingers, the knife, and his face.

Sadie chose to walk home in spite of the heat. It would be worse, packed in the surrey with her sisters, Reuben yelling and complaining as always. Rebekah said she would accompany her and invited her friend Clara and, of all people, Erma Keim.

"Why Erma?" Sadie hissed behind a horizontal palm.

"She gets lonely on Sunday afternoon," Rebekah said quietly. "Besides, you're almost the same age. Both entering spinsterhood."

There was no time for an answer. Erma caught up from the rear in long, purposeful strides, her face alight with the prospect of spending an afternoon at the Miller home.

"Boy, that pie was nasty!" she bellowed into Sadie's ear. "Must be Ketty was baking again!"

Sadie shrank from the grating sound of Erma's raucous laugh, but smiled politely.

"Poor Fred Ketty."

The whole afternoon was spent in the kitchen, making popcorn loaded with melted butter. They tried all different kinds of seasoning, laughing uproariously when Reuben sprinkled hot pepper sauce on top of his dish, then raced for the water faucet, his tongue on fire.

Mam even joined in the fun, and Dat read *The Budget*, grinning behind it, sometimes lowering the paper to peer over his glasses when Erma said something exceptionally peculiar.

There was no doubt that she eyed the world in a different light and with strangely colored lenses. Men were a huge bother, not worth the ground they walked on, except for Moses in the Bible, Abraham Lincoln, and maybe John F. Kennedy, although he was a Democrat and they were a bit liberal for her taste. She thought the locals all looked alike in their cowboy hats, though the hats vastly improved their faces, which, the way they spent all their time outdoors, resembled the surface of the moon.

Not one boy had ever asked her out. Not one. She was as uncaring about that fact as she was about her looks, though Sadie wondered if this was really true.

She made a homemade pizza from scratch that tasted better than anyone's, she assured them airily. She ate four square slices of it, belched, wiped her mouth, excused herself, and decided it was time to go home.

"I know we're not supposed to call a driver, but I don't have a horse and buggy, so how else am I supposed to get home?"

With that, she marched to the phone shanty and called her neighbor lady, then sat on the porch swing to wait for her.

"Why don't you go along to the supper and singing at Melvin Troyer's?" Leah asked.

"Me? You want me to? Nah. People would say I'm setting my hat for Yoni's Crist. He's 40 now, did you know that? Everybody thinks he should ask me for a date, then, you know, marry me. I wouldn't take him. He has no ambition. You can tell by the way he walks that he doesn't like to get up in the morning. Not for me, no sir."

Sadie laughed. "Come on, Erma. I'm going to set up a blind date for you."

Erma leaped out of the porch swing, coming down squarely on both feet, her hands in the air, her mouth open wide.

"No!"

"Why not?"

"Because."

"Come on, Erma. Please? We'll get a driver and go to Critchfield. You pick your favorite restaurant, okay?"

"No. Absolutely not. I do not want a man. Certainly not Crist."

"Why not?"

"I told you why not."

"If I ask Mark Peight to go?"

Erma's eyes narrowed. She plopped back on the swing.

"Sadie Miller, you are crazy for hanging out with that guy. If anyone is shooting horses around here, it's him. He's not really right, is he? Good-looking, yes, but he scares me.

"*Upp*, here's my driver coming. Hey, thanks for the popcorn. I had fun. Come see me sometime. I live behind my Dad's house now. In a trailer."

"Do you really? We'll come see it," Leah assured her as Erma was off in a cloud of dust.

The supper and singing proved uneventful. Mark Peight was absent again. He never came to the suppers and singings anymore, which irked Sadie more than she cared to admit.

What did he do on Sunday? Why didn't he ask for an ordinary date like normal people? He probably had some deep, dark secret of his own, like Erma Keim thought.

Sadie played volleyball. At supper with her friends, she sat at the singing table and sang with everyone else, her thoughts far away.

Was she crazy, the way Erma Keim said?

She watched Yoni's Crist Weaver. He was tall, wide in his shoulders, dressed nice enough, with a receding hairline. Actually, his hair, what there was of it, was thin and brown. His eyes were pleasant, not too close to his nose, which was large and took up a lot of room on his face. He seemed shy, quiet, not very comfortable in the girls' presence. Sadie thought he'd make a wonderful companion for the boisterous, colorful Erma. She would fill his days with her never ending viewpoints, and her unique take on life would completely change him. Wasn't there an old saying about opposites attracting?

Later that evening, Sadie sat at the kitchen table with Rebekah, drinking a Diet Pepsi, munching on "old maids," the leftover unpopped kernels of popcorn that remained in the bottom of the bowl.

"You should somehow get her fixed up a little. How would you go about telling her those limp coverings are simply a disaster?" Leah giggled, covering her mouth with her hand.

"Her hair is worse. Hasn't she ever heard of hair spray?"

"She has a nice figure, she's thin, at least, but her feet are so scarily big. I bet she wears a size 11 or 12."

"That's okay. Crist is bald almost, and 40."

"They'd be so cute together."

"I don't believe her one bit about men."

"I don't either."

Sadie looked at the clock.

"Shoot. Midnight," she said, yawning.

"Where's Leah?"

"I have no idea. She was talking to a group when we left."

They drained their Pepsis, wiped the table, and were just ready to go upstairs to bed when headlights came slowly up the drive.

"Hmm, Leah," Rebekah said, watching as the buggy approached.

Then, "Oh, my goodness! The... They're going to the barn. I bet you anything Kevin... Oh, my!"

Catching Sadie's sleeve, she tugged, and said, "Come on, Sadie! He's coming in! Quick!"

Together they dashed up the stairs, flung open the door of Sadie's room, and collapsed on the bed, giggling like school girls. They heard Kevin's deep voice and Leah's nervous laughter.

The girls whispered about the lack of cookies or bars in the house, anything Leah could serve to him on that first, much-anticipated date.

"There are chocolate whoopie pies in the freezer," Sadie said.

"He doesn't want a frozen whoopie pie."

"They're best that way."

"Well, go down and set one on the table for him."

They dissolved into giggles imagining Leah's anger if they did something so completely senseless on her very first date.

They were both sound asleep when Leah finally came upstairs. She had managed well on her own, asking him politely if he wanted a snack, which he declined, saying he ate a big helping of cheese and pretzels at the singing. Really, he was far too nervous to eat anything after working up the nerve to ask Leah if he could take her home.

✡ ✡ ✡

Sadie arrived at work the following morning in a state of melancholy. Not only had her younger sister been on a date, but she seemed to be back to square one with Mark.

When Dorothy fussed and fumed, Sadie became more irritated than usual and told Dorothy she needed to get more kitchen help or retire. One or the other, take your pick. She meant every word she said, and when Dorothy sat down on a kitchen chair and ignored her the whole forenoon, Sadie didn't care.

Marcellus and Louis came to the kitchen with Jim. The kids were sweet and clean, with only a hint of the usual anxiety in their eyes. Sadie turned on her heel and started savagely stacking dishes in the commercial dishwasher. She resented the way Dorothy turned into another person the minute the children made an appearance.

She felt old and dissatisfied with her life. She was bitter about Mark and his strange ways. She was tired of it now. She wanted a home of her own, a husband to love and cherish. She wanted to quit slaving away at this ranch. She wanted, well…Mark.

When Jim came in, she barely acknowledged his jovial smile.

"We're a bit sour this morning?" he asked her, chuckling.

"A bit."

"Want to ride with me to town?"

"Yeah, take her with you. Dry cleaning needs picked up," Dorothy said flatly.

So that was how Sadie found herself in Jim's pickup with a list of groceries in her hand. Her foul mood lifted as the truck wound its way along country roads, dust flying from under the tires.

She rolled her window down, flung an elbow out the side of the door, watched the scenery roll away, and listened to Jim's good-natured conversation.

They picked up the dry cleaning, zipped it carefully in a navy-blue garment bag, and laid it on the truck bed. They bought groceries and picked up salt blocks at the feed store. Then they stopped for a cup of coffee.

It was pleasant sitting in the truck, watching the hustle and bustle of the people. Everyone seemed intent on their own personal business. They were all a variety of achievers but working together to make the town a place that was busy and industrious.

A shining, 15-passenger van came slowly down the street, the driver and the occupant of the front seat straining to read the street signs. The women's coverings were heart-shaped and their hair combed back severely, shining and sleek. Another group of Amish from Lancaster County, Pennsylvania, visiting the west.

Sadie turned her head, hoping they wouldn't see her. She simply was not in the mood to talk to strangers. When the van stopped, she willed herself to be invisible to them.

Just when she thought they had moved on, she heard a rich masculine voice say, "Excuse me."

She turned her head, and her gaze found the bluest eyes she had ever seen. He had a mop of streaked blondish-brown hair, a square jaw, and a very nice smile.

She was going to say "Hello" or "Hi," but nothing came out of her mouth. Nothing.

When she finally got her bearings, she stuttered a bit, became flustered, yanked open the door of the pickup, and stood on the street. Later she wondered why in the world she did that when she could have given him directions from her seat in the pickup just as easily.

"I'm looking for Bozeman Avenue."

She gave him halting directions as he watched her face intently. She wished he'd ask her name, but he didn't. The group was from Lancaster County, as Sadie had suspected. They were staying for a month or so. He said his mother was in ill health, and Sadie said she was sorry to hear it.

Then they simply stood there for several moments and looked at each other. He turned to go, then stopped and asked her name. When she told him, he smiled and said, "See you around."

Sadie felt as if a smile like that made anything possible. He left her standing in the street beside the old pickup, but twice he looked back.

Chapter 8

Eventually, Sadie persuaded Dat to hire a driver and get the buckboard she wanted. She said she would pay for it and do all the painting herself if he would build new seats and replace the floor. They had an extra pair of fiberglass shafts, although Reuben airily informed his father they weren't worth much if they were going to hitch Paris double.

Dat lifted his eyebrows, then lowered them, took off his straw hat and scratched his head. His graying hair was in disarray, but it didn't matter because his hat would cover it anyway.

"Thought you weren't going to get another horse," he said slowly.

"If we find one that looks like Paris, I will."

"Good."

Sadie made a phone call and told Dat that John Arnold would be here at two to pick him up. Then she swept the buggy shed, picked up baler twine, swept the forebay, washed her saddle and bridle with saddle soap and wax, then, to pass the time, she swiped at cobwebs hanging around the barn.

She called Paris. The horse was grazing at the lower end of the pasture with Charlie. Paris answered with a lazy lift of the head. She pricked her ears forward and lowered her head, her tail swishing steadily.

Charlie, however, decided it might be worth a try for some feed. He came obediently, his brown head bobbing in easy rhythm with every step, his shoes clicking against the small stones on the path.

"Come, Paris! Come on!"

Sadie coaxed the horse with her hands cupped around her mouth, but Paris refused to budge, staying under the shade of the large oak tree, her head lowered sleepily.

Sadie shook her head and turned to go when she heard the truck returning in a spray of gravel and a cloud of dust. Dat and the driver leapt from the truck, losing no time in unhitching the trailer, before John Arnold sped off down the driveway in a great swirl of rolling dust.

"What is up with him?" Sadie asked.

"There's been another shooting. Poor sheep farmer over in Oaken Valley. Name of Ben Ching. He had two champion quarter horses. The only thing he owned worth anything. Both shot this morning, early."

Sadie stared at her father, her eyes filling with tears.

"But who...?"

Dat shrugged. "His wife works at the dry cleaners in town. They're Chinese, or Japanese, or foreign something. Their daughter is a barrel racer."

Sadie crossed her arms and shivered, then looked off across the valley. Dat turned to loosen the straps that held the buckboard, which looked more like a decrepit old wreck with each passing moment.

"It's like a bad omen, Dat. Those horse thieves on the loose, the wild horses scaring us, and now this. It's almost as if someone is determined to... I don't know, make us all afraid of something unknown."

Dat unhooked another strap, straightened, and said wisely, "Well, I wouldn't say that. I think it's unsuccessful horse thieves who are still mad and taking revenge on their failure. They won't get away with it."

Sadie nodded. "How did they know the spot on the ridge where Cody was shot? You know, sometimes I wonder if it's not someone closer than we think. Who else but us knows of that field of wildflowers?"

"The people you work with down at the ranch?"

Sadie shook her head. "I doubt it. I mean, there is not one single person down there who seems even vaguely suspicious. Well, these two children..."

"What two children?"

"You know, Marcellus and Louis."

"Who?"

Dat stopped working, straightened, and looked at Sadie, switching the piece of hay in his mouth to the other side.

"Those...dark-skinned Latinos, Mexicans...whatever they are. Beautiful children. I told you."

"No, you didn't. I heard nothing of this."

"Well, you must not have been home when I told the rest of the family."

She told her father the whole story down to their impeccable manners, Dorothy's total devotion to them, and the jewels in the drawstring bag.

"Hmmm."

That was all Dat said before Reuben came out of the house holding one cheek and with a sour expression on his face.

"Reuben!" Sadie called, "Look what arrived!"

Reuben looked, snorted, then said, "Piece of junk."

Dat smiled and Sadie stifled a laugh.

"What's wrong with you?"

"Toothache."

"A serious one?"

Reuben nodded. "Hurts plenty. Mam's taking me to the dentist at 4:30."

✡ ✡ ✡

Sadie cooked supper that evening with Anna's help. Rebekah and Leah were working late at the produce market, so it was an ideal time for Sadie to spend time with her youngest sister.

As Sadie peeled potatoes, Anna shredded cabbage on a hand-held grater, her head bent to the task. She answered the questions Sadie asked, but the usual youthful chatter was completely absent.

"Now, for coleslaw. Fix the dressing. A few tablespoons of mayonnaise, some sugar…"

"Not mayonnaise," Anna said sharply.

"Why not mayonnaise?"

"Miracle Whip. Half the calories and fat."

"Anna! Seriously? When did you start worrying about calories?"

Immediately Anna became flustered, nervously tugging at a covering string, refusing to look at Sadie.

"I'm not. I…just…like the taste of Miracle Whip so much better. That's all."

"Just so you know, you aren't fat, Anna."

"Yes, I am. I'm grossly overweight. I'm obese."

Sadie leaned against the counter, pursed her lips, and watched a red-faced Anna mixing sugar into the shredded cabbage.

"Whatever gave you that idea?"

"The scales."

"You don't weigh more than me, Anna."

"I weigh a lot more."

"How much do you weigh?"

"I'm not saying."

No amount of coaxing would persuade Anna to reveal the troubling number. Sadie detected a note of genuine sadness in her sister's voice, so she let it go. No use prompting and upsetting her younger sister more than she was.

They ate at 6:00. Leah and Rebekah did dishes together while Sadie tidied the kitchen. She put magazines and newspapers in the basket beside Dat's recliner, then wandered aimlessly from the porch swing to the living room and back. Finally, when she realized the hour was quite late, she became concerned.

Where were Mam and Reuben? His appointment had been at 4:30, and it was getting close to eight. Oh, well, likely they had gone to buy groceries.

She wandered out to the barn, having heard hammering noises coming from that direction. Dat was tearing up the floor of the buckboard. Sadie was clearly delighted, unable to believe he was already starting on a project he didn't want to do in the first place.

She watched from a distance, then decided not to approach him or praise him for his work. Sometimes when you did that, Dat turned gruff, downplaying his emotions, even walking away.

Sadie went into the phone shanty and sat on the cracked plastic chair at the counter. Flies buzzed at the screen, half dead or still trying in vain to escape. If they would only turn around and look in another direction, they'd be able to fly straight out the door to the great, wide, freedom outside.

Flies were like that. Idiotic, annoying little insects that drove you crazy in the summertime, hibernating in the cracks of the windows in winter, making a brand new appearance in spring. So far, Sadie could find no purpose for flies, other than making life miserable for humans and beasts alike. Horses swished their tails endlessly all summer long, cows swatted, stamped their feet, swung their heads, and still the flies tormented them. Housewives swatted flies, hung fly paper, yelled at children to close the screen doors, and still the flies found a way in.

She picked up the phone and heard the familiar "beep, beep, beep" that indicated someone had left a message. But there was none, so she replaced the receiver and swatted aimlessly at a pesky fly. As she turned to leave, the shrill vibration of the phone pierced her consciousness and made her jump.

Instantly, her thoughts, as always, turned to Mark Peight. As sure as the sun came up every morning, whenever the phone rang, her heart leaped within her, and Mark came to mind.

She picked up the receiver. "Hello?"

No answer.

Sadie waited a few seconds and decided to try once more. "Hello?"

She heard raspy breathing. But only that. No words.

The silence now turned ominous.

Quickly she replaced the receiver, then stood watching the phone as if it might turn into some dangerous object if she wasn't careful. It rang again, that shrill sound, and shivers went up her spine.

Should she pick it up? What if someone was playing a

joke? Mark Peight? Would he do something like that? What about Mam and Reuben? Maybe there was an accident? That thought goaded her as she immediately picked it up.

"Hello?"

Only the same raspy breathing, almost the way a snake sounded as it slithered across a rock.

Once, when she was walking with her friends on the way home from school, a snake had made its way up the side of a rocky cliff. It seemingly made no sound at all, and yet, it was there, just like this breathing.

She hung up firmly, resolved not to pick up the receiver again, and walked out of the phone shanty. She was determined to put it from her mind. It was nothing. Just a wrong number.

She was grateful to see headlights winding their way up the hill in the deepening twilight. Mam and Reuben! Fear and uncertainty faded away at the thought of Mam coming up the hill with a grouchy Reuben in the backseat. Mam was her anchor at times like this.

The car stopped and the interior light came on. Mam paid the driver, then emerged from the vehicle and opened the back door for Reuben.

Sadie and Anna helped unload groceries, scattering the bags across the kitchen table and countertops.

Mam threw her bonnet on the counter, her face colored slightly, her blue eyes snapping.

"Now that's the last time I'm doing something like that!" she announced firmly.

Oh, here we go again, Sadie thought wryly.

"I absolutely hate it when a driver does that to me!" Mam fairly shouted.

"I called him first. Yes, he can go. Fine. He comes to pick up me and Reuben, and once we're in the van he says he hopes we don't mind taking Dave Detweiler, Sally, and guess who else? That Fred Ketty, of all people! Oh, I was about nuts. Here I had an appointment, and he still had to pick up these other two women. And you know Fred Ketty? She's as slow as molasses in January, never ready when the driver comes. When she finally came lumbering out the sidewalk so slow, I had a notion to tell her to go back and change her apron. She had food all over it. Talked the whole way to town in Dutch, of course, picking her teeth with a toothpick. Oh...!!"

There were no other words to describe her trip to town except for that final exasperated "Oh!" Mam wiped her face with a paper towel, then rummaged through the plastic grocery bags muttering about her ice cream being nothing but milk.

"Now, Mam," Sadie said soberly. But her heart was full of joy and thanksgiving. The old Mam was truly back. Her spirit. Her passion. It was all there, a banner of well-being.

Mam liked going to town by herself. She would rather pay twice the amount than split the cost with other riders. It was more convenient to go her own way to the stores where she wanted to shop, and then have the space to load everything in the small van, rather than crowding in more people who, in Mam's words, "stopped at every fencepost."

"Then Reuben's tooth was infected and the dentist pulled it, saying he thinks he has him numbed up, but here was Reuben in all this pain and misery, and Dan Detweiler's wife had an appointment at that quack chiropractor, what's his name? Bissle or something. I wouldn't take my cat to him, but Sally goes every week. Says he helps her sciatica, or however you say that. Well, there we sat, Fred Ketty talking my ear off, still shoving that toothpick around."

Suddenly she stopped, turned to Sadie, and said, "Did you know about those quarter horses being shot?"

"I heard," Sadie said, opening a box of Raisin Bran Crunch, pouring a liberal amount into a bowl.

"It's a bad omen. Fred Ketty said there's no way anyone would find her sitting in a buggy. It's downright dangerous. I had a notion to tell Ketty she don't have to worry, as tight as Fred is with his horse feed. That poor, hairy creature they drive is too pitiful to shoot."

Sadie laughed, then put her arms around her mother, laid her head on her shoulder, and held her close.

"Mam, I love you so much. You are back to being my Mam again."

"Ach, Sadie. Ach, my."

Mam's voice sounded choked with emotion. When Sadie stepped back, Mam held her at arm's length, her eyes soft and watery.

"Let's give God the credit."

"I will."

It was more than the gas light that cast the kitchen in a warm yellow glow that evening. The love of God was so near, Sadie could touch it.

Mam hummed softly, then laughed.

"You know, I'll probably never be able to share my town trips well. Isn't that awful? I should be ashamed of myself."

"No. You are so my Mam," Sadie answered, as she poured cold milk on her dish of cereal and headed for the porch swing.

The view from the porch was magnificent. The navy blue night competed with the disappearing blaze of the sun, casting the clouds in burgundy, magenta, and powder blue. The pines were black and pointed, like a silhouette of soldiers standing at perfect attention, the glory of the sunset their leader.

A mockingbird sang his plaintive evening cry, its warble a drumroll for the pine trees to begin their march. After that he imitated a robin, chirping shrilly, on and on, stopping only when the car bearing Leah and Rebekah wound its way up the drive.

The sisters tumbled out, saying goodnight, then plopped on the porch swing.

"Slide over, fatty. Whatcha eating? Mm! Give me a bite."

Leah grabbed the bowl, while Rebekah lifted a spoonful to her mouth.

"Mmm. Did Mam get a fresh box of Raisin Bran Crunch?"

"Yep!" Sadie said happily.

Home was like this. A place where everything came together. All the anxieties of jobs, insecurities, the whole wide perplexing world and its difficulties were put to rest the minute you opened the kitchen door and met your sisters or Mam.

Not one person on earth understood you the way a mother or a sister did. They could see straight through you. So there was no use trying to be cheerful when you really weren't, or pleased when you were horribly disappointed, or anything that made you out to be something you weren't.

"Hey, don't eat all that cereal. It's mine, remember?" Sadie said.

"I'll get you some more. Hey, did you hear about that poor family whose quarter horses were shot? Everyone is talking about it down at the market. It's just pathetic. The parents were hoping their daughter would take first place in the barrel race at the end of August."

Reuben came out and flopped down on the concrete steps, one hand held delicately to his swollen cheek. He sighed loudly. Then he rolled his eyes in the most pitiful way, sighing deeply again. When that didn't get much of a response, he said loudly, "My tooth was infected."

Leah had just launched into a vivid account of the tragedy and the beauty of the reddish quarter horses. Sadie and Rebekah listened wide-eyed.

"My tooth was infected," he repeated, much louder.

Leah stopped, turned to Reuben, and asked if it hurt.

"Oh, yes. I think the dentist used a digging iron and a crowbar to loosen it."

"Reuben!"

"It felt like my whole jaw was coming apart. I'm never going back to that dentist ever again."

The girls clucked sufficiently, pitying him until he was satisfied that he had impressed them with his bravery. He sat back against the porch post, listening as the girls talked of the sheep farmer and his daughter.

Reuben sat up, listened intently, then began waving his hands.

"This is odd. This is really odd. Listen to this."

He had his sister's full attention now, so he leaped up from the steps, his aching mouth forgotten, took a deep breath, and proceeded to tell them about the character at the dentist's office.

"He was skinny, greasy, his hair in a ponytail, tattoos all over his forearms, and I guess I was staring 'cause Mam told me I'm not allowed to. He was... Well, I'd hate to meet him in the dark."

"What's so odd about him?"

"I'm not done yet. His cell phone rang. You know, people with manners usually go outside to talk, or else they talk quietly. Boy, not him. He stayed right there and talked in the oddest way."

He hesitated, then asked, "What's a chink?"

Sadie looked at Leah. "Isn't that a slang word for a Chinese person?"

"I don't know. You're the reader, not me," Leah answered.

Reuben continued, "He said a lot of swear words. Mam's mouth got tighter and tighter. He said something about those chinks. And talked about a target, then got really angry about some messed up operation."

"It couldn't be."

"Who knows?"

"Was it someone who knows something about the quarter horses?"

"Oh, dear, Reuben, you should have gone out to the parking lot and got his license number."

That brought a solid snort from Reuben.

"How could I? I didn't know which vehicle he was driving. And besides, I don't know if he's connected with that quarter-horse deal."

As darkness fell, the girls made plans for a chicken barbecue dinner. Dat joined them on the porch and offered some advice. Mam contentedly sipped a tall glass of sweet tea on the wooden rocker.

Sadie noticed Mam's covering was crooked and that she had a pinched look around the corners of her mouth. Sadie could only imagine the restraint it required to accept the long wait at the chiropractor's office and then endure her distaste for Fred Ketty's toothpick.

They decided to organize a bake sale and give all the

proceeds to Ben Ching and his family, the quarter horses being such a terrible loss. They'd make chicken corn soup, barbecued chicken, and whatever else the Amish folks could think of. All the food would be donated. Mam suggested a consignment auction, which the girls thought was a great idea, but Dat said they'd need some of the settlement's active leaders to give the "go-ahead."

In the days that followed, the girls wrote letters and made phone calls while Dat organized a meeting the following Thursday evening. The men who attended solemnly planned the event and voted unanimously to hold it at the Orvie Bontrager farm on the second Saturday in September. As they drank coffee and ate chocolate whoopie pies, they chose Dat to speak to Ben. They asked the women to plan the bake sale.

Sadie offered to give spring wagon rides with Paris—for the English people who turned up for the benefit. Reuben snorted so loudly at the suggestion that Old Emery Weaver turned the whole way around to see where the noise came from. Reuben slid way down on the recliner behind his book so no one could see his face. Anna giggled out loud, and her face turned bright red as she ran out on the porch to finish laughing.

Sadie rose straight to the challenge. Let them laugh. She knew she could do anything she wanted with Paris, so she'd show them.

She coaxed Dat into putting temporary seats on the old buckboard. She painted it a glossy black and put an old piece of carpet on the floor, and it was just fine. Rebekah pronounced it a mighty chariot of goodwill. Sadie couldn't have agreed more.

Reuben refused to participate. No amount of wheedling or promised sums of money made a difference. He sat on the fence like an obstinate little owl, blinking his eyes wisely, chewing on a long piece of hay. He mostly snorted or made cutting remarks. When Sadie told Dat, Reuben was taken down a notch by having to stack firewood on the north side of the barn.

Anna loitered on the outskirts of the pasture, but when Sadie gestured for her to help, Anna disappeared into the house. Finally, in exasperation, as Paris sidestepped and tossed her head trying to get rid of the blinders, Sadie tied the horse to the fence and went to find someone to help.

Reuben was slowly stacking firewood, so angry that he threw a sizable stick at her. Sadie marched up and pulled his ear as hard as she could, and he began yowling in earnest until Dat appeared around the corner of the barn.

Sadie found Anna at the kitchen table, her head in her hands, blinking back tears. She swatted savagely when Sadie asked her what was wrong.

"Sadie... I would love to help you, but..."

She stopped, her plump shoulders slumping dejectedly as she whispered, "I'm too fat to help you give buggy rides."

Instantly, Sadie slid into a chair opposite her sister, reached across the table, and took one of Anna's soft, brown hands.

"Anna, look at me. You are the perfect one to help. We'll wear the same color dress the day of the sale, and you can drive. Help me, Anna. I can't do this by myself."

"Reuben would be better."

"Not for this. He's a wonderful rider, but driving is better for you. You genuinely like people, and you'll be friendlier. Reuben would be so...so...snorty all the time."

Anna wiped her eyes, a flash of self-confidence in her shaky smile.

Chapter 9

THE COMMUNITY WAS ABUZZ WITH PLANS FOR the consignment sale. There were always new messages on the phone and people donating things they thought would sell well: sofas, kitchen chairs, lawn mowers, bedding, old quilts, anything they didn't need and would help to form a lively auction.

The old buckboard was sort of a do-it-yourself job, Sadie knew, but it looked clean and glossy. The wheels were solid, and the new pair of fiberglass shafts fit perfectly. Paris was a picture of regal beauty once she was fitted between them.

Sadie and Anna had two weeks to work with Paris. It wasn't as long as Sadie would have liked, but it would have to do. The first time Sadie put a harness on Paris, she pranced and snorted at the unaccustomed attachment on her back. Anna held her steady, walking behind her with the reins while Sadie spoke gently to the horse as they walked and then trotted around the pasture. Paris pranced and tossed her head, but Anna was consistent, holding the reins steady as Sadie led her around the pasture.

"Stop throwing your head," she admonished her horse. "You know you're not acting like a good horse should."

They stopped, and Sadie stroked her neck, adjusted the collar, then stepped back. She had an idea.

"Anna, take her by yourself. I don't think she likes me hanging onto her bit. You try."

Anna bit her lip and shook her head.

"I can't."

"Try. Just lift the reins a bit and cluck, the way Dat does with Charlie."

"I can't. I'm not you. She won't listen."

"Anna, please. Just try."

Sadie could see the resolve in her sister's face as Anna straightened her back, lifted her chin, and nervously said, "*Komm*, Paris."

For one split second, Sadie was afraid Paris would not obey, then, her head lowered only slightly, she leaned into the collar and pulled, the buckboard rolling smoothly after her.

"Turn her in a big circle," Sadie called, and when Paris lifted her head and stepped out with a fancy gait, Sadie got goose bumps. She felt like crying, then laughing, clasping her hands together so hard her knuckles hurt.

Look at her! A genuine show-off, she thought. A real one. Oh, Paris, you gorgeous creature. You look like a horse in a show ring. Her light mane and tail streamed in the stiff, evening breeze. She made a perfect circle, trotting slowly, then stopped obediently when Anna pulled in on the reins.

"Whoa."

"Oh, Anna! That was perfect! Absolutely! You are simply a natural driving Paris. I wouldn't even have to be there!"

Anna drew in a deep breath, sat up very straight, her eyes shining, and said, "Do you really mean it, Sadie, or are you just saying that for *goot-manich*?"

"No, no, I'm not just being kind. You did a wonderful job."

From that day on, Anna flourished. Her confidence in her ability to drive Paris steadied both horse and driver. And when Anna finally took Paris down the drive, the horse flicked her ears only when Anna slammed the lever forward and the old brakes screeched.

They trotted Paris down the road, passersby waving and turning to watch. Anna sat straight, waved, and smiled. Sadie knew the buggy rides would be a hit with the sale patrons. And they'd do wonders for Anna's confidence.

✡ ✡ ✡

The day of the consignment sale turned out to be cloudy in the morning. Sadie ran to the window countless times to see if the gray clouds were churning with darker ones that promised rain. Finally, she walked outside, licked her forefinger, and held it up to the breeze, which was very slight. But she could still feel the difference, the side to the west drying quicker.

Yes! It would not rain today. A few sprinkles or scattered showers, perhaps, but not a pelting rain with no let up.

She dressed quickly. The new pale-blue dress shimmered over her shoulders as she put it on. It was a beautiful color, a happy one, if there was such a thing, she thought. She pinned her apron quickly and gave her appearance a final check in the mirror. She grabbed her purse off the oak clothes tree in her room and hurried down the stairs.

She was alarmed to meet Anna, who averted her tear-stained face as she busily tied her shoes, sniffing quietly. Mam was wrapping chocolate shoofly pies in Saran Wrap, thoroughly flustered. Dat hitched Charlie to the sparkling clean surrey outside.

Ach, my, Anna, Sadie thought.

"What's wrong with Anna?" she whispered to Mam.

Mam turned to look, saw Anna's face and asked, "Anna, why are you crying?"

"I'm not."

Mam shrugged her shoulders, wrapped another pie, and quickly slid it into the pie rack, a homemade tower with 12 shells surrounded by screen, with a door and a handle on top. It was the easiest way to transport 12 pies in a buggy, or any vehicle for that matter.

After they left, Sadie caught Anna's eye and raised her eyebrows in a silent invitation to spill her sadness. Immediately, Anna's chin quivered.

"My dress is too tight, Sadie. I look so awful. It's… I look like a pale blue elephant!"

The last word was drawn out on a wail of despair, the self-hatred so evident you could taste it, a horrible metallic taste of untruth wrapped around Anna's conscience until it eliminated all rational thinking.

How? How did a person go about correcting this?

Sadie put one arm around Anna's soft shoulders and slid two fingers inside the belt of her apron. She assured Anna that there was room to spare, and whatever made her think the dress was too tight?

"Everything I wear is too tight," Anna said, shrugging Sadie's hand off her shoulder.

Standing before the bathroom mirror, Anna burst out in another long, drawn-out exclamation of disgust.

"My hair! I hate my hair."

"Anna, stop."

Sadie was firm, standing behind her, finding her gaze in the mirror.

"No! Look at me! I'm a fat ugly ... toad. My hair isn't right."

"Anna, come. Sit down."

Sadie told her God made her unique, according to His will, and it was wrong to think of yourself in such a harmful way. These thoughts were of the devil, and eventually, she would believe them, which could cause harmful behavior, like anorexia or bulimia.

"What's that?" Anna asked, wide-eyed.

"I'll explain it sometime. Driver's here!"

The Orvie Bontrager farm was a kaleidoscope of color and movement. Vehicles crept along the driveway and parked in fields and ditches. Children ran about in bright colors, constantly changing the scenery—a red dress here, a green shirt there, yellow straw hats bobbing along on little heads, sticky little fingers clutching colorful candy.

The auctioneer's cry rose and fell as he sold horses and surreys, ponies, sheep, goats, pigeons in cages, a litter of kittens. The crowd pressed close, eager to hear the bidding.

Sadie and Anna went to find Paris. They had decided to bring the horse down the evening before to familiarize her with the throng of people, vehicles, and other animals. When she saw Anna and Sadie, she nickered a good morning, shoving her nose into Anna's palm for her usual treat of an apple, a carrot, or a few sugar cubes.

"How was your night? You didn't like it down here, did you?" Sadie whispered.

Anna nudged Sadie's elbow. "Look who's here!"

Mark Peight was striding purposefully in her direction, a broad grin on his handsome face.

"Hello! What are you doing with Paris here?" he asked.

Sadie struggled to keep the anger from taking control of her tongue. *If you'd date me the way normal guys do instead of storming out of a dining room and then coming to throw those silly pebbles at my window, you'd know what I'm doing here.*

"Buggy rides," she said, and none too friendly.

The broad grin folded in on itself, the white teeth obliterated by fine lips that gave no hint of a smile.

"I see."

Sadie busied herself with the currycomb, brushing much faster and harder than normal, until Anna cleared her throat nervously.

Mark shoved his one foot against a bale of hay to reposition it, then sat down, loosely, easily, with that cat-like grace he possessed. He pulled out a piece of hay and chewed it. Patting the bale beside him, he smiled at Anna and asked if she wanted to sit there. Anna, gazing at him with adoring eyes, obliged him immediately.

"I'm sure Paris is brushed well enough," he said slowly.

She didn't give him the satisfaction of a reply, just yanked the black harness off the hook and threw it savagely onto Paris' back.

"Whoa!" she said, when Paris sidestepped.

"We're a bit testy today," Mark said, his deep brown eyes teasing her.

Sadie faced him, her hands on her hips.

"No, we aren't. I mean, no, I'm not testy. I just have work to do, unlike you, who does only what he pleases all the time."

"You look awful pretty when you're mad."

With that, he got up and strode purposefully out of the barn. Sadie watched in disbelief, then remorse, as he strode up to the doughnut stand. Lillian Yoder, in a beautiful lime-green dress, hurried over to take his order, bowing and dipping, her blond hair shining with every toss of her head.

As Mark became drawn into a serious conversation with her, it was all Sadie could do to turn away from watching the scene at the doughnut stand as she picked up Paris' bridle.

Anna giggled, "He bought six doughnuts."

"Hmmph."

Anna shrugged her shoulders, convinced Sadie would be an old maid forever, the way she acted about Mark Peight.

Sadie led Paris to the fence near a big handmade sign: "Buggy Rides, $2.00."

Sadie backed Paris between the shafts, as Anna held them aloft.

Sadie loosened the britchment straps, making sure the collar was not pinching her neck, and polished the bridle with a clean rag. A crowd was already forming, holding out the dollar bills required.

Sadie smiled, accepted the money, and helped the first six people into the spring wagon. Then she drove off with Paris acting like a perfect lady. She let Anna take the next six people, secretly gloating at the thought of having already accumulated $24. All the angry thoughts of Mark Peight slipped away.

The barbecued chicken smelled wonderful, the thick gray smoke rising from the pits as it rolled over the crowd. Sausage sandwiches, doughnuts, funnel cakes, and burritos—there was so much food Sadie wondered how to decide what she wanted most.

As she pulled Paris to a stop, she saw a middle-aged Asian couple climb up on the auctioneer's platform, followed by a boy about Reuben's age and a petite young girl dressed in traditional western garb.

The barrel racer and her family! The auctioneer introduced them as the Ching family. He told of the shooting, of the loss of their beloved animals, to a crowd hushed with sympathy. When he announced that the proceeds of the sale would go to help them buy more horses, hats went sailing into the air, and the crowd erupted in a cheer of goodwill and charity.

The Amish men kept their hats on their heads, stoic and quiet, as was their way. More than one straw hat was bent, white coverings alongside, as they wiped furtive tears.

Mr. Ching took the microphone and spoke in halting English of his deep gratitude. The crowd was completely quiet, listening reverently. He spoke from the heart with the good manners of the old Chinese, his arm at his waist as he bowed deeply, his wife nodding her assent at his side.

"For all the world like two beautiful little birds," Dorothy would say later, shaking her head in wonder.

Mr. Ching introduced his daughter, Callie, who would be the real recipient of this day of unselfishness. She stepped up to the microphone and spoke in a low, musical voice about her loss, the heartbreak of finding the two quarter horses dead in the pasture, the bullet holes, and the investigation that followed.

"Last, I wish to thank all my friends of the Amish for this day."

She bowed, waved, and stepped down, her black hair swinging down her back, her boots clicking on the wooden platform.

The auctioneer announced that no one would want to miss the making of egg rolls, wontons, and Chinese chicken and vegetables under the blue and white tent, all made by the relatives of the Ching family who had come from Indiana for the benefit.

Sadie stepped down from the spring wagon, and Anna took over. Sadie went to find a cold drink of lemonade, her throat parched by the sun and the dust.

Mark Peight stood by the lemonade stand in lively conversation with Callie Ching and appeared to be quite taken with her.

Had he no shame? The nerve of him! What a flirt! And she being English and all.

Sadie took two deep breaths to steady herself. Common sense finally settled in. He was a grown single man and could hold a conversation with whomever he wished. It was none of her concern. They were not dating, and she had no right to these ugly little monsters of jealousy that cropped up every time she saw him with another female. It was ridiculous.

But when Callie put a hand on his arm, and he bent his head toward hers, Sadie's emotions skyrocketed into the wild blue sky.

Why did she care so much? He made her stomping mad with his...his ease and his grace and his smile and his pitiful past. Why wouldn't he ask her for a decent date and stop being so secretive? She was just going to forget about him, and the next time he wanted to confide in her, she'd suggest he tell Lillian Yoder or Callie Ching. But she knew she couldn't say that, because what if he did?

She felt all mixed up and evil inside, so she prayed hard for help right then and there. I need you, I am not being who I should be, she prayed.

Was love supposed to be like this—a standoff between feelings of wonderful heights and valleys so low they were unbearable, with the unexpected avalanche of emotions she could not understand thrown in randomly?

Well, she definitely was not thirsty for lemonade anymore.

She bought an ice-cold Pepsi from Reuben and his rambunctious friends at the drink counter. He threw a handful of ice at her, and she told him he'd better behave or she'd tell Dat. But Dat wasn't there, Reuben reminded her, because he went to town for more ice.

Sipping her Pepsi, Sadie made her way through the crowd, smiling to herself at the sight of Fred Ketty leaning intently over a counter watching an aging Chinese woman making egg rolls.

"Oh, for sure, for sure," she heard Ketty say, and hoped she didn't have that ever-present toothpick dangling from her teeth.

"Oh! Oh, I'm sorry!" Sadie said.

She had bumped solidly into a broad chest and spilled her Pepsi all over a striped blue shirt. She stepped back and looked directly into the same blue eyes she had met in town.

"Sadie Miller, right?" he said.

She could feel the heat in her face and knew the blush quickly spreading across it was a telltale sign of...of what? Remembering him?

"How are you?" he asked, seeming confident in his ability to win her.

"I...I'm okay. I...I was on my way..." She jerked her thumb toward Anna on the spring wagon.

"Don't let me keep you," he said smiling.

"I'm...That's my horse, Paris. I'm giving buggy rides for $2."

"Will you take me for a buggy ride?"

"But you're Amish. You've been on a buggy plenty of times."

"Will you take me anyway?"

"I will."

"Just me?"

Sadie lifted her chin.

"Yes."

She persuaded Anna to let her take her turn driving. She climbed up on the driver's side and took the reins. He hit the seat beside her with a solid thump, his shoulder landing squarely against hers.

"This your horse? Named Paris? That's awesome."

He turned to look at her, and their eyes met. They both grinned a happy smile of recognition and shared admiration.

"I don't even know your name," Sadie said.

"Guess."

"Hmm. You're from Lancaster. Isn't everyone named Stoltzfus or...um...Zook? Strictly guessing!" she said, laughing.

"I love how you say Lancaster. LAN-caster. We say LANK-ister, sort of the...well, whatever."

"You still didn't tell me your name."

"Guess. Hey, how come you're circling around? We don't want to go back yet. My name is Daniel."

"Just Daniel?"

"Daniel King."

"Oh. Hi, Daniel."

He stuck out his hand and she grasped it warmly, a good solid hand, smooth and strong. She did not want to let go but did so reluctantly, the current between them so strong that they fell silent immediately.

Paris was tiring, her steps becoming slower as they made their way out Orvie's driveway and past parked vehicles, the sound of the auctioneer's sing-song voice fading rapidly.

"It's so unreal out here in Montana. I've never seen anything like it. I don't want to go home ever again."

"We like it here, although we've definitely had our trials."

Paris was walking uphill now, her head nodding with each step. Sadie told Daniel about the wild horses, Mam's illness, the ranch, everything. Words came so easily, they were nearly unstoppable, a brook bubbling in a rich stream of memories and feelings.

Daniel spoke of his home, the hustle and bustle of Lancaster County, the tourism, the pace, while Sadie nodded her head in understanding. Holmes County, Ohio, was no different. They both agreed that bit by bit, in small devious ways, the world slowly encroached on the old traditions, threatening Amish culture.

Suddenly, Sadie took notice of their whereabouts, spying a sign that said,

Atkins Ridge, 3 miles.

"Oh, my goodness, we've come too far. We have to get back. Anna will wonder what has become of us."

"Let her wonder. She'll be okay. Your parents are there."

But Sadie felt uneasy now. Anna wanted to give more buggy rides, she felt sure, and she did not want to disappoint her sister this way.

A pickup truck came over a rise, and Sadie pulled slightly on the right rein, making sure she was on her side of the road. When she glanced at the truck, Mark Peight's bewildered brown eyes looked directly into hers. She lifted her chin, set her shoulders, and did not answer his wave as the pickup moved past.

We're not dating. You are not my boyfriend. You sneak around enough to keep me on a string, and I'm resisting you now. If I choose to live this way and be with someone else, I have the right. It's up to you to honor my companionship, and you have not been doing that. I'm moving on.

She became stronger with each thought.

"Someone you know?"

"Yes."

"Boyfriend?"

"No."

No, just someone who has the ability to tie my heart in knots. Someone who loves me, then hurts me. Someone I don't think I'll ever understand fully.

"We're leaving next week."

He cleared his throat, then turned sideways on the seat. "Sadie, I can't remember when I felt so... I don't know. I feel as if I've known you all my life. If you don't... If you aren't seeing anyone, could I take you out to dinner on Saturday evening? I know that's not our typical way, but I'm not from around here, and I don't have much choice. I would like to spend some time with you before I go."

Only the space of a second passed, a butterfly movement of hesitation, before she turned to meet his gaze.

"I would like that, yes."

He had said, "Go out to dinner." Just like classy English people do. They had dinner in the evening and lunch for lunch.

His hand reached up to touch her hair.

"I can hardly believe your hair is real. It's so black, it shines blue. I love the way you comb it. I'd love to see you without your covering."

Sadie did not know how to respond, so she said nothing, just shook the reins across Paris' back to urge her toward the auction where her safety lay.

"I didn't count on … you. I mean, I hadn't planned on meeting someone like you. Now I don't want to leave."

Her conscience jabbed her. She had told Mark she loved him, she wanted him to ask her for a real date, the way normal guys did. But he refused. Was it wrong to go on a date with this Lancaster-County Daniel? Surely she was not doing anything wrong. She could not wait on Mark Peight forever. She wasn't getting any younger. Besides, someone with a past like his was risky.

So, no, she was not doing anything wrong. Yes, she would go out with Daniel. It was just dinner.

Suddenly, without warning, Paris lowered her haunches, then lunged into her collar. She took off running, her ears flicking back and staying that way.

Grimly, Sadie gripped the reins with all her strength as a pickup truck passed at a dangerous speed, the diesel engine revving, black smoke pouring from two silver pipes, gravel spitting from the broad tires.

The same color! It looked like the same pickup containing Mark Peight!

Sadie fought to control Paris, calling out to her in a strong voice, trying to still the panic rising in her own chest.

Daniel leaned forward, gripping the seat, watching quietly, letting Sadie take control of her own horse.

When Paris slowed, he grinned and put a hand on her shoulder. "Good job. I can tell you're one with this horse. It's awesome."

Then, a high, whining, deadly sound.

The reins snaked out of Sadie's grasp as Paris went up, up, and came down, hitting the macadam at a dead run.

Someone was screaming and screaming, a volume of sound that made her throat hurt. Who was it? Daniel? Herself?

Paris was galloping in a complete frenzy. She had no one to guide her, no rein to hold her back, all her instincts goading her away from the sound of that gunshot. She ran at full speed.

Sadie remembered. The dark night. Captain. Ezra. The ridge. The black beast running, running, gaining on them. Was this how it would all end? She had been spared before. This time, instead of snow, the sun was shining and the cornflowers were blooming. Yet once again, the specter of death loomed before her.

Chapter 10

GRIPPING THE SEAT WITH ONE HAND, SADIE CLUNG to Daniel with the other. The spring wagon swayed and bounced, and the dusty air made breathing difficult. The black reins slapped the surface of the road, then flew away, as out of control as everything else.

"Should we jump?" she screamed, falling onto her knees as the spring wagon lurched.

Daniel shook his head. "Call Paris! Keep talking to her!"

When he saw Sadie's whitening face, he screamed, "Sadie! Stay with me! Talk to your horse!"

She was so frightfully dizzy. How could she get up and call Paris if the whole world was out of control? Bile rose in her throat.

"Sadie!"

Daniel reached out and slapped her, hard. Her head flew back, then up, and back to reality. Sadie called and called.

"Paris! Come on. Whoa, whoa, good, good girl. Stop, Paris. The bullets are gone. It was only one. Slow down, babe. Slow down, Paris. Stop running now. You're going to upset us."

Was Paris tiring? Was she responding?

Without warning, Daniel got up and stood on the shafts, steadying himself on the dash of the spring wagon. His face was white, his mouth set in concentration as he calculated the distance.

Oh, those flailing hooves. Sure death if he fell! The steel wheels! If they rolled over him, he would never survive.

"Don't scream, Sadie! Keep talking."

She had never been called on to muster all the reserves of courage she had. With extraordinary effort, she continued talking, pleading with Paris.

Daniel crouched, then sprang, a released tension, propelling himself forward by sheer force of will, until his legs grasped Paris' haunches. Searching and finding the reins, hauling them back, he eased Paris into a controlled run.

They came to a stop beneath an overhang of pine branches. Paris was a deep brown color, soaked with her own sweat, her sides heaving, her nostrils moving in and out by the force of her panting.

Daniel slid off her back, went to her head, put his hand on her mane, and slowly lowered his forehead against hers.

Sadie fainted, evidently, and awoke lying by the roadside under the pine boughs, heaving and gagging, as she threw up like a little child who had become thoroughly carsick. Daniel held her head, rubbed her back, and offered her a clean, white handkerchief. She thought she would surely never look at him again, gripped in a fit of nausea.

"I'm so sorry. Please forgive me."

"It's all right. You did an awesome job."

Sadie wiped her mouth, blew her nose. There was that word *awesome* again. It must be his favorite word.

"I have to go to Paris," she said.

He quietly helped her up, supporting her as she clung to Paris' neck, weeping softly, whispering heartbroken endearments.

"I couldn't live without you, Paris. You are the best horse ever. Thank God we're alive," she murmured, over and over.

A car passed, the driver watching them, presuming their horse got a bit overheated and they'd be fine, waved, and moved on down the road.

Daniel remained quiet as Sadie wiped her face, kissed Paris' nose, and laughed shakily.

"Sorry. I love my horse. Oh, Daniel, who is shooting these bullets? Who is endangering these lives? I'm so afraid."

He looked into her eyes. "We need to report this when we get back."

"No! Not to the whole crowd. I'll do it later from our phone shanty at home. Please? I don't want the…fuss, the publicity."

"Whatever you want."

His quiet strength was hers now. Calmly, he helped her into the spring wagon, a hand on her back to support her.

They decided it would be best to drop Daniel off at the sale. He would tell Anna and her family what happened while Sadie took Paris on home.

"Aren't you afraid to drive home alone?" he asked.

"No. They won't be back. It's only a mile or so."

She desperately needed time alone to clear her head. The staggering thought that Mark Peight could be the sniper completely did her in. It had to be the same truck.

It was, wasn't it? How could she even begin to understand this complex person, this result of two terribly dysfunctional parents? Or was even this a fabrication, a lie, told in the most convincing manner?

She prayed, "Dear Lord, you're going to have to show me the way. I'm in a maze, lost, can't make any sense out of this. I felt your leading, I did. Now I don't know anymore."

She needed space, she needed her family. She needed, above all, the calming presence of her Lord and Savior. Hadn't he said his yoke was easy, his burden light?

As Paris plodded up the driveway, her neck stretched out in weariness, Sadie sang softly,

> *His yoke is easy. His burden is light.*
> *I've found it so. I've found it so.*
> *His service is my sweetest delight*
> *His blessings overflow.*

Peace wrapped her in its loving arms. She cried with joy and thanksgiving as she bathed her beloved Paris, wiped the harness and put it away, then fed the horse a double portion of oats and corn and a block of the best hay. Sadie kissed Paris' nose and told her goodnight, walked into the house, and collapsed on the sofa, where her family found her a few hours later.

❉ ☼ ❉

"I don't care what you say," Dorothy said forcefully, steam enveloping her face and shoulders as she unloaded the commercial dishwasher. "You're going to keep on messing around with them horses until you get yerself kilt, and I mean it."

It was Monday morning after the lavish breakfast had been served. Sadie cleaned the floor, swishing the foam mop across the ceramic tile, cleaning corners longer than necessary just to hide her smile.

"But..." Sadie began.

Dorothy turned, a stack of clear plates in her hands, and shook her head from side to side, her eyes snapping.

"Hm-mm. Don't 'but' me. I ain't listening. If'n yer parents had a lick of common sense, they'd take that crazy gold horse and sell her for ... for dog food. She ain't safe! Now a well-trained horse would not have bolted like that. What n' na world was you thinking in the first place, hitchin' 'er up like that?"

Sadie kept mopping back and forth, scrubbing at a stubborn spot on the tile. Then she straightened, pushed back a stray lock of hair, and faced Dorothy with her hands on her hips.

"Paris *is* well trained. Any horse would bolt with that sound of a rifle, gun, whatever it was, being fired. It was an ... an accident, a weird thing that happened."

Dorothy's eyes flashed.

"An act of God, you mean. That's what you get for prancing around with a stranger from ... oh, wherever. Did you ever think for one moment about what Mark thought when he saw you?"

Rebellion rose in Sadie's throat, a sort of thickening, causing her voice to become harsh.

"I don't care what he thought. I'm not seeing Mark Peight. I don't ever want to date him either. He's a coward and a ... a ... Oh, he makes me so mad! Why can't he come to the house and ask me out for an official Saturday night date? Huh? Answer that, Dorothy!"

Dorothy didn't answer, her lips set in a firm line.

She put a large stockpot on the shelf, yanked her apron down, smoothed it across her stomach, and reached for her large, purple mug.

"Sit down!" she barked.

"No! I'm not finished mopping."

So Dorothy sat and slid off her shoes, putting her feet up on a low bench, revealing the nylons she cut off at the knee, rolled, and twisted to a firm knot. She never bought knee-high nylons, never, saying they slid down your legs, and then what did you have? A sloppy-looking ring around your shoes, which did no honor to them pretty shoes from the Dollar General in town.

Dorothy dashed an extravagant amount of cream in her empty mug.

"Fill this for me, Sadie. Please."

Sadie propped the handle of her mop against the refrigerator. She turned and filled Dorothy's mug at the coffee maker, resisting the urge to set the mug down on the table with a severity that was unnecessary.

"You know if you put your cream in the cup first, then pour the coffee on top of it, you don't need a spoon?" Dorothy asked.

Sadie took her revenge by remaining silent. It was a sweet sort of gratification. Dorothy had no right talking about Paris that way.

"So now you're mad. Well, you got reason to be. Shouldn't'a said that, I guess. But you, young lady, need a talkin' to."

"About what?"

"Your horse, for one. And your guy."

Sadie leaned forward, her hands propped on her knees, her eyes bright with the force of her words as she looked straight at Dorothy. "He's not my guy."

"If you did the right thing, he would be."

"What's that supposed to mean?"

"Just what you think."

Sadie shook her head back and forth, a pendulum of denial. Dorothy got up heavily, her face the picture of frustration. She went to the pantry and returned with two cold, leftover biscuits. She slammed them into the microwave, punched the buttons solidly, then turned to face Sadie.

Yanking open the door of the microwave, Dorothy slapped the biscuits on a plate and spread an alarming amount of butter on top of each, then sank her teeth into one.

Sadie wished she'd stop eating biscuits or slurping that disgusting coffee in between each gigantic bite.

"I don't know where your parents are. You should not have been allowed to take that... What's his name?"

"Daniel."

"Whatever. You shouldn't have taken him on that horse and buggy ride alone. Where was your mom and dad? Now you have all these fancy-dancy notions in your head about a stranger from... wherever, Canada, Iraq, Iran. Who knows?"

"He's from Lancaster, Pennsylvania," Sadie said dryly.

"Lancaster? That great Amish place everyone talks about?"

Sadie nodded.

"Hmm. Well, maybe he could turn out all right, but you are committed to someone else, you know you are. You love him."

When Sadie began her denial, Dorothy lifted her chin and held up one finger. "App! *Upp*! Stop that! Anyone that gets mad when someone doesn't ask them for a date wants to be with that person. Look at me and Jim. My James. He waited. Took his good old time. I persuaded myself that he made me angry and I didn't want him, but in truth, I did. I sure did. I got me a good man. The salt of the earth, he is."

Sadie took half of a biscuit, spread it with a thin layer of butter, then turned the plastic honey bear upside down and squeezed. Holding the bread carefully above the plate, she answered, "But Jim likely had a normal childhood, not like Mark's."

She bit into the sweet, buttery biscuit, watching Dorothy's face.

"I don't know what you call normal, unless gettin' up at four a.m. to milk 30 cows when you're nine years old is normal. His parents divorced when he was in third grade, too. Had a paper route to help keep his family going until his mom remarried, but his stepdad kicked him out when he was 15. Made his own way, so he did."

"But that's still not quite as bad as Mark's childhood, and I have a feeling I only know the tip of the iceberg. Aren't people like Mark seriously damaged their whole life long?"

"Some of 'em."

"I don't know him that well. What if Mark is seriously disturbed?"

"That's where you come in at."

"What do you mean?"

"You need to be there for your man. He…"

"He's not my man."

"As I was saying, you need to be there for your man. He needs a good woman behind him, one that comes from a firm family structure. If ever anyone had a good family life, you do. You need to…"

Before Dorothy could finish, Bertie Orthman, the aging gardener, made a grand entrance, holding a gigantic bouquet of orange, yellow, and peach-colored daylilies. He got down on one knee and closed his eyes, one arm sweeping the air in time to his humming.

> *"Flowers for my lady fa-a-ir.*
> *My beautiful lady fa-air!"*

Dorothy drew herself up to her full height, lowered her eyebrows, and let out the biggest snort Sadie had ever heard.

"Bert! For Pete's sake, don't you think you're layin' it on a bit thick?"

Bertie dipped and bowed, then swept his arm in an arc, presenting Dorothy with the beautiful bouquet. "There you go, Dot. Beauty presented to the beauty of my life!"

Another snort. "You know I ain't beautiful. Give 'em to Sadie."

Sadie laughed and accepted the gorgeous display. Bertie laughed with Sadie, then told her it was all in fun, to brighten their day.

These two, dear, old souls. What a joy to be with them! English people were just more open, more at ease to create a scene like this. They lifted her bogged-down spirits on this humorless morning, when the whole world seemed serious and dangerous and dreadful.

"You jes' can't take a joke, can ya, Dot?"

Dorothy threw him a nasty look. "You know, Bertie, if you ever let that cat of yours over into my yard again, I'm gonna shoot the flea-infested thing. She gits on my bird feeder, and then she sits, lickin' her lips, just waitin' to latch onto one of my birds."

Bertie's mouth closed in on itself. The sparkle left his

eyes, his eyebrows lowered, and he glared at Dorothy.

Shoving his face up to hers, he said, "If you … ever, ever shoot my cat, I'll have the law on you."

"Then keep her over there."

Sadie burst out laughing.

"It ain't funny."

"Sure, it's funny," Bertie said. "You know, Sadie, she sits on her front porch, rockin' and rockin', watchin' her birds, and I'm right across the road, lookin' out the same direction on my back porch, rockin' and rockin', holdin' my cat. We're like two people on a bus, facing the same direction, never communicatin' 'cept here at work. Never give each other the time of day at home."

"You know why? 'Cause I'm afraid if'n I get too friendly, you'll think I don't mind about that cat of yours, and I do."

"Aw, Caesar Augustus ain't gittin' yer birds."

Dorothy's mouth fell open in disbelief. "That yer cat's name?"

Suddenly the door ripped open with such force that the conversation came to a halt. They all turned to see who would fly into the kitchen in such a hurry, surprised to find Richard Caldwell himself, looking weary and shaken, but with a light in his eyes that no one had ever seen before.

"Her name is Sadie Elizabeth Rose."

Dorothy was the first one to find her voice. "Who?"

"Our daughter was born at 5:15 this morning!"

Sadie sputtered but could form no words at all. She just stared at Richard Caldwell, eyes wide, mouth agape.

"She ain't yours," Dorothy said brusquely.

"She's ours. Barbara's and mine!"

"But why? How come no one said anything about it?"

"We kept it a secret."

Dorothy's eyes became cunning, and she nodded her head, pursing her lips.

"I knew there was somethin' in the works, so I did," she said matter-of-factly.

Richard Caldwell walked over to Sadie, who was still speechless, and put both of his big hands on her shoulders, looking into her face with the most tender expression she thought he was capable of.

"Your namesake. We want our daughter to be just like you, Sadie."

Sadie opened her mouth to say thank you, to be polite and gracious and classy and grown up, but her mouth wobbled and her nose burned and she burst into the most embarrassing tears of her life.

Instantly, Richard's huge arms went around her. He was sniffing and wiping his eyes and laughing. Dorothy joined in hugging them both, and Bertie clapped his old, worn hand on Richard Caldwell's shoulder, congratulating him in very colorful language.

The tiny, six-pound, 14-ounce Sadie Elizabeth Rose caused quite a stir at Aspen East Ranch. Everyone said they knew something suspicious was going on, especially when the boss started eating breakfast upstairs with his wife. Sadie didn't think anyone guessed the Caldwells were anticipating a baby. Barbara was a big woman, so her clothes easily concealed the pregnancy. Even so, it was a remarkable feat for both of them to keep it secret.

No baby showers, no nursery, no nothing, Sadie thought. But the minute the birth was announced, the house became a beehive of activity. The painter, the interior decorator, the carpet cleaner, had all been on standby.

Within a few days, the bedroom adjacent to the master suite had been turned into a nursery a mother could only dream of: pink and green rocking horses on the curtains, the crib set, the rugs. Even the new swivel rocker had a shawl with the same horses across the back. Little horse shoes adorned the walls, and luxurious pillows were strewn everywhere.

Sadie dusted and vacuumed, scoured the bathrooms, cleaned the mirrors, and scrubbed the floors. Bertie brought in great armfuls of lilies for every room, while Dorothy ran in circles and cackled and fussed and wore herself out completely.

When Richard Caldwell brought Barbara home from the hospital, everyone at the ranch saw the change in her. She was wan but absolutely elated, and she looked 20 years younger, as if this was the crowning moment of her privileged life—a precious daughter of her own.

Sadie was in awe of Barbara. Being Amish, she had seen lots of babies, even helped out as a *maud*, but never had she seen such devotion and unabashed joy as this. The Caldwells considered their beloved child a miracle, pure and simple.

Even Richard Caldwell's booming voice had quieted. He talked softly, walked lightly, even closed doors gently. He carried his tiny daughter in the crook of one arm, showing her to all the ranch hands as if he, alone, had thought up the whole idea of the human race.

When the days turned shorter, the evenings cooler, the Caldwells decided to throw a huge cookout for all the help at the ranch to celebrate their daughter's birth.

At first, Dat frowned on it, saying it would be no place for Sadie. She explained how Dorothy needed her. He sighed and said he guessed she could go if she wanted to.

Sadie wanted to go, more out of curiosity than anything else. She would help with the preparation of the food, then find a quiet corner to watch everyone else.

Maybe with Mark? Where was he? It had been almost a month since the shooting on the day of the consignment sale. She had been convinced it was Mark shooting from that truck. Killing. All those guns were evidence, weren't they? She could tell Reuben thought about it, too.

She tried to distance her heart. She tried thinking only of Daniel, but she couldn't forget about Mark. Not entirely.

The evening before Daniel had left to return to Pennsylvania, he came to say goodbye. He had been so kind and so sweet, just as he'd been on their dinner date. They had gone to an expensive steakhouse with dim lighting and delicious food she never knew existed. Daniel was handsome, talkative, always laughing. He told her about his family, which sounded very much like her own, only with 10 children. They had their everyday spats and ordinary disagreements, but no argument stayed serious for long. He loved his mam and got along great with his dat, except during the time when he wanted to get a car and join the wilder group of youth. His dat put his foot down, and Daniel didn't have the heart to hurt his father, which touched Sadie deeply.

Here was a normal, happy, well-adjusted young man, who was so good-natured it bordered on disbelief. Was he really so kind to everyone?

He had not kissed her. Sadie wanted him to, then felt guilty for thinking about it.

She had been swept completely off her feet and began a long-distance romance that would be kept alive through letters and phone calls.

Had Mark caused her to be this way? Was it wrong? She knew attitudes about distant courtship varied greatly from one Amish community to the next. She agreed that it was not good to touch each other before marriage.

Or was it? Mam didn't think so. In fact, she was quite serious about this subject and adamant about her views on dating. She was strict about flirting shamelessly, staying pure and chaste, but didn't everyone need to know who their partner really was before marrying?

Sadie knew what Mam meant, without her saying much at all. She did not like the new trend of thinking that you could be above reproach, better than your peers, free of all temptation.

Still, Sadie wished Daniel had kissed her, to see if she liked him. He hadn't hugged her; he only shook her hand and looked deeply into her eyes when he said goodbye.

She had his address and phone number. They promised to write and call each other every week.

As always, she tried not to think of Mark. Who could she trust, ever?

Daniel likely had every girl in Lancaster "setting her hat" for him, as Mam used to say. Could she depend on a husband from Lancaster County? The distance was so great. Oh, he said he loved it out here, but did he really? As close as he was to his family, especially his brothers?

This business of finding a husband was just not her thing. She was no good at it. And yet, when she held little Sadie Elizabeth, she knew with complete certainty that she wanted a darling baby girl of her own someday. She wanted a house and a kind husband, someone who was easier to understand, easier to love, than that Mark Peight and his strange and strong silences.

Chapter 11

THE CALDWELLS HIRED EXTRA HELP THE WEEK
before the cookout, or "shindig," as Dorothy put it.
She was taking extra vitamin B-12s all week. Her nerves
would plain get the best of her if she wasn't careful.

Barbara Caldwell had spent entirely too much time
in the kitchen, and Sadie knew it made Dorothy uncomfortable. But Barbara had planned the menu and stuck
around to make sure everything was done to perfection.

The Caldwells asked Reuben to come to work with
Sadie and help with the vast amount of yard work that
needed to be done around the large house. Bertie always
kept the plants and shrubs looking their best, but this
was a special evening, and he had more work than usual
to do. Besides the ranch hands, all the wealthy ranchers
and their wives, the Caldwell's business associates, and
even the physicians from the hospital were to be together
as friends for one special evening.

When she saw the large, red riding mower whizzing
along at an alarming rate, Sadie wondered what in the
world had come over Bertie. Taking a closer look, she was
horrified to find Reuben hunched low over the steering

wheel, his elbows lifted, clearly pretending he was driving something other than a lawn mower.

Now he was coming into the homestretch, zipping around a low lying willow tree. He straightened his back as he jammed on the brakes, slammed to a stop, and took a long drink from the red-and-white Igloo thermos Mam had filled with his favorite fruit punch.

Back on the mower, Reuben lurched off at high speed, and to Sadie's chagrin, loud singing ensued.

> *Shall we gather at the river?*
> *The beautiful, the beautiful river!*

Sadie held her breath as he sped around a tall blue spruce, leaning way over to steady himself. She dropped the dish towel she was holding and ran outside to talk to her brother about his lack of driving skills.

Her pink dress rode up as she ran, an annoyance to every Amish girl who wore a dress with a pleated skirt. She slowed to a walk and pushed down the unruly skirt, waving her hand. She gasped as he spun around the pillars at the entrance, narrowly missing the famed roses climbing the trellis beside it.

"Reuben! Hey!"

She hoped he'd hear her before he overturned the mower and pinned himself beneath it. Her shoulders slumped as he took off in the opposite direction, leaving her standing at the edge of the lawn with nothing to do but watch him go.

A tall form emerged from the barn, closing the distance between them in long strides. Now who was being nosy enough to come and help her out? She didn't need help. This wasn't exactly a dilemma; Reuben just needed to be warned a bit.

"Need some help?" a familiar voice called.

Sadie turned, a cool answer on her lips, to find a hat-less Mark Peight, his hair disheveled, his short-sleeved white shirt stuck to his body with perspiration, and a streak of dirt across his tanned face.

The cool answer fizzled away into despair, the feeling when you know you were wrong and there's not one thing you can do about it. She despaired of seeing him and not being able to catch her breath, leaving her thoughts completely scrambled, nerveless fingers fumbling at an apron that had been straight in the first place. She marveled at his deep brown eyes that crinkled at the corners, and his mouth so perfect she could only stare at it, wondering why she had ever thought another person existed.

She lifted her hands in a helpless gesture. "Looks like it."

Reuben was in his own world of imagination. The mower buzzed up an incline. At the top Reuben leaned over, twisting mightily on the steering wheel, then racing back down, practically airborne.

"He's going to throw that thing over," Sadie said between clenched teeth.

She began walking quickly toward him. Mark laughed as he watched Reuben's antics. Just as Reuben went whirling around a yellow bush, his song caught Mark's ears, and he bent over double, laughing even harder.

"He will be gathered at the river!" he gasped.

Sadie glanced at Mark before spasms of her own laughter overtook her. The longer they watched, the funnier and more absurd the whole situation became, until they were caught in a helpless tide of laughter.

Finally, Sadie caught her breath. "Richard Caldwell would not be happy. We have to stop him."

They both walked quickly toward Reuben. When he finally saw them, he shut the mower off, sat back, and beamed, clearly pleased with himself and happy to show off his expertise as a lawn-mower driver.

"Hi, Mark! How are you?"

"Good. I'm good. Looks like you're enjoying yourself."

"I sure am. This is totally cool."

Sadie cringed at Reuben's *rumspringa* language. She glanced sideways at Mark, who was clearly enjoying Reuben's company.

"Reuben, you have to slow down. You're going to flip that lawn mower."

Reuben leaned way back in his seat, turned his face to the side and yelled, "No way! These things don't flip over."

"Reuben, they do. All you know is pushing our reel mower. You have never driven one of these, ever. You have to slow down, please."

Sadie was serious. She was afraid for Reuben's safety, although she assured him he was doing a good job and that Bertie would be pleased about how soon the mowing was done. Reuben grinned, waved, and was off without reducing his speed one bit. He zipped around the corner of the corral and lurched across the cement walkway with a clatter.

Mark began laughing again.

"It's not funny."

They walked together across the lawn, and Mark asked Sadie if she wanted to see the horse he was shoeing at the stable.

Sadie stopped, looked wistfully in the direction of the barn, but said she should help Dorothy, since she was all in a stew about the coming cookout.

"You going?" he asked nonchalantly.

"Dat doesn't really want me to go. He says it's no place for me."

"It probably isn't."

She looked up at him, surprised. That sounded rather strict, coming from Mark. However, when their eyes met, everything else vanished. His dark brown eyes were warm, caring, wanting, a conveyor of his longing, an insecurity bigger than the ability to speak of his love. She could not look away.

A thousand questions crowded her mind until she felt caught up in a whirlwind of emotions that shook her entire being. This was her Mark Peight, the one she met on that snowy road with Nevaeh so long ago. Before the questions. Before the partial telling of his life's story. Was he just shy? Or was he hiding something?

"Don't go," he murmured, his voice catching.

"I have to help Dorothy with the food."

"Is there no one else?"

"No."

He nodded and looked off across the corral.

"Well, come in and see this horse. It won't take long."

He was a magnificent animal, no question. Gray, with dapples across his rump, he stood tall and regal, heavy in the shoulders, his mane and tail a shimmer of light, grayish-white hair.

"Wow."

"One of the best horses I've ever seen." Then, "How's Paris?"

"She's doing well."

"Even after the runaway?"

"What do you know of the...that day?" she asked with accusation dripping from every word.

"I passed you. Remember?"

She whirled, her eyes flashing with anger and disbelief. He caught her arm and held onto her with a vise-like grip.

"It wasn't me. I didn't shoot."

"How can I know that for sure? You disappear for months at a time. You...you..."

There was a scraping of boots as a small, swarthy figure burst into the shoeing area. He held a whip aloft, ready to bring it down on Mark's head, or rather, up, as it would seem to be the case with this short person.

He stood behind Mark, his feet planted squarely, his heavy shoulders stretching the fabric of his shirt. He was a picture of righteous indignation and chivalry, rescuing the damsel in distress.

"You!" he yelled in thunderous tones. "Let her go. Release the lady!"

Mark stepped back, his face registering surprise.

"Sorry. I didn't mean anything. We were..."

"You let the lady go. I am Lothario. My name is Lothario Bean. You do not treat ladies this way. You Americans are such...such baboons. You must learn to take care of your women. They need protection. They need your devotion and aid at all times. My Lita. I do not grasp her arm or talk harshly to her. Now you go back to shoeing your horse, and *I* will assist the beautiful lady back to her kitchen."

He drew himself up to his full height, emphasizing *I* with great pride and dignity. Then stepping up to Sadie with his head held high, he offered his arm and bowed his head.

"Come," he said, in a heavy Latino accent.

Sadie smiled with a quick glance at Mark. Lothario escorted her out of the barn, across the drive, and to the kitchen door.

"Now, if you ever have any problem with that man who shoes horses, you just call on me, Lothario. I do not stand by and let any lady become a victim of bad treatment. No. No."

"Thank you, Lothario. I appreciate your help. Give my regards to Lita and the girls."

His dark face shone with love for his family.

"God has blessed me. God has been good. I thank him all the time. I sing to Jesus in praise. Someday, I play my guitar for you. Not him. Not him." He jerked his short dark thumb in the direction of the barn.

❀ ✡ ❀

Sadie was ill at ease the remainder of the day. She constantly ran to the windows to check on Reuben's lawn-mowing progress. Dorothy was impossible to deal with, so Sadie stayed out of her way as much as possible. When Barbara came into the kitchen yet again, Sadie was afraid for her, knowing Dorothy's temperament was a pressure cooker of suppressed frustration.

"Why them fancy kabobs? Why not hot dogs and hamburgers and homemade beans? Fiddle falutin' people!"

Sadie thought as she read over the menu. Shortcakes. Peaches. Real whipped cream. Tamales. Shish kabobs. No wonder everyone was in a tizzy.

Sadie and Dorothy worked together quite well preparing for the cookout. Dorothy miraculously calmed down, becoming efficient and making every step count until the evening of the cookout. The mound of food that was prepared was remarkable. Richard Caldwell—jovial, wearing a tall white chef's hat, talking in his usual stentorian tones, waving his spatula wildly—handled the grill by himself, producing perfect strip steaks.

Dorothy and Sadie carried out tray after tray of delicious sides. The cabbage slaw was crisp and chilled, the thick rolls warm and crusty. There were mounds of twice-baked potatoes that had almost been Dorothy's undoing, mixing the cheese, bacon, and chives to the right consistency.

Dat had asked Sadie to come home after the food was served, which she planned on doing. Lita Bean would help Dorothy finish up. As Sadie untied her apron in the kitchen, Mark Peight appeared at the door.

"Do you have a way home?"

Oh, Mark! She shook her head, unable to speak one word.

"Could we walk? I know it's... four miles?"

"More like five."

"Then I'll get someone to take us."

"No. No. We can walk. We have all night."

They thanked their hosts and wished everyone goodnight. The warm feeling of belonging to a large family of workers and friends followed them.

Their footsteps were the only sound, except for a dog barking somewhere in the night. The stars hung low over Montana, like a black dish of night with holes punched in it, the stars a beautiful wonder.

"You tired?"

"I'm okay. The stress was almost worse than the actual work. Cooking for ranch hands and dumping the food onto a steam table is entirely different from cooking for the... well, wealthy people who are used to chefs and unusual food."

"It was delicious, Sadie. I've never had better cabbage slaw."

"Thank you."

Their steps were the only sound for a length of time until Mark cleared his throat.

"So, did Mr. Bean escort you to the house okay?"

Sadie laughed. "Isn't he something? You know, many Latinos are staunch Catholics. A very strong, dedicated faith. He's a good man."

"Isn't that the church we supposedly came from?"

"I guess. Hundreds of years ago."

"You think we're better than they are now?"

Mark's words were heavy with bitterness, hatred almost. Sadie stopped involuntarily and turned to face him. She wanted to question him, but thinking better of it, she turned to walk on.

"What?" Mark asked.

"Nothing."

"Yes. What did I say that upset you?"

"It's just the way you said it. You don't like plain people, do you? Why did you join the Amish faith if that's how you feel? You don't even like us much, let alone have faith in a group of people to help you travel through life."

Mark sighed, a long, deep sound expelling from his chest.

"I guess I'll always carry the burden of my past on my back, waiting to explode at the slightest opportunity."

Sadie did not speak. What he said was true. He was a walking tinderbox of buried hatred. Why did she keep trying?

Her thoughts whirled. Suddenly, she became weary, her head heavy, her feet dragging. It was no use. This man was scarred for life. She felt trapped in a situation she had very little control over. The only way out was to stay completely away from him.

Before she could follow her weary thoughts, he caught her hand in his.

"Come, let's sit down. I want to talk."

And he did. He talked for hours, as Sadie listened, crying at times, amazed at others.

His mother was excommunicated for her sins, the promiscuous *ungehorsam* life she led. His last memory of his mother was her waving out the window of a red car, her hair streaming behind her, wearing heavy black sunglasses, leaving with that real estate man. His father cried and cried and cried.

"You know, Sadie, his crying seemed so...final. The depth of his loss is stamped on my heart forever. He was so...so pitiful. I held the baby. I remember the smell of her filthy dress that hadn't been washed for who knows how long? Dat never recovered. To this day, it haunts me. Why didn't I do more? Maybe I could have prevented his death."

"No, Mark..." Sadie began.

She was silenced by his harsh words, torn from his tortured mind. "Yes! I could have. I was so busy with the children. If I would have kept closer watch, he wouldn't have died."

He sighed, and a torrent of words followed. "The men, the elders of the church, they came often. They blamed Dat. They said he was going to hell. Anyone who couldn't keep his family in line was not worthy. What did they mean? Worthy of what? Heaven? God? So is my father suffering in eternal flames for the wrong my mother did to him?

"I hate my mother. I hate her so much I can't tell you. If I would see her again, so help me, I don't know what I'd do.

"Why didn't any of the church members take us children? They could have tried. Nobody did anything. We were basically cast out.

"Dat must have gone to look for my mother. I remember him dressing in English clothes, cutting his hair, shaving his beard. He would go English for her. He left me alone at night with the little ones.

"The baby would cry and I'd get up to fill her bottle with water. There was no milk. She screamed and cried. I flavored the water with strawberry Jell-o. That hushed her for awhile. Good thing we had strawberry Jell-o.

"Dat gave up then. He stopped searching for Mam. His hair and beard grew back. He got a job at a welding shop. We had milk. I learned to make soup with beans and tomato juice and hamburger. The only thing I couldn't do was sew. Our clothes were torn and much too tight.

"I thought my father was doing better. He read his Bible a lot. He sang to us. One time his parents came. They cried. Mommy Peight brought us food, clothes. She hugged us. I think they weren't allowed to be there and came in secret because I didn't see them until last year when I went back.

"That day..." he began, then hung his head.

A shudder passed through him. His head stayed bent. Sadie put a hand on his shoulder and kept it there.

"Dat didn't come home. I made soup for the little ones. We slept alone. The next morning, I searched the barn, the woods."

There was a long pause. Sadie stroked his shoulder as if comforting a small child. Or Paris.

"He was half sunk in the water, half out of it. He was covered with algae. That's why I didn't see him right away. There were dragonflies on his back. Flies."

"But, Mark, if he was half out of the water, maybe he was trying to get out. Maybe it wasn't a suicide at all. Maybe he had an accident."

"No. He didn't want to live. He couldn't handle all of us children. We were the ones that should have never been born. The counselor tried to tell me differently, but I know how it was. We were a mistake, born to two people who would have been so much better off without us.

"I imagine my mother was a free spirit, liberal, always rebellious. She gave birth one year after another, the way the church required. Dat was too simple to see it, or too much in love, whatever it was. I spent my whole life wishing they hadn't had any of us."

"Mark, you can't think that way. There is a purpose for every soul brought into this world. I truly believe that. God wants you here on earth or you wouldn't be here. He loves you as much as he loves anybody else. Likely more, even."

"No, he doesn't."

"Mark!"

"He can't. Not after what I did. After Dat drowned himself, the church had nothing to do with us. We were tainted children then. So the authorities put us into the foster system. We were all separated. I was eight.

"We became English. I went to a public school. The kids were nice enough; so were my foster parents. They drank a lot of beer. Keith became drunk a lot, but not angry drunk, just...stupid drunk. Sharon gave me good things to eat. I found out what pizza was. And cookies.

"I don't understand what happened then, but I was suddenly placed in another home. I lived in fear of their 17-year-old son. He...well, I won't go into detail, but when I was 12, I ran away, alone, at night. I found my way to an Amish home in another community. Betsy, the family's mother, took pity on me and allowed me to stay. I worked in their produce fields all my teenage years. The Amish man, I think, was bipolar, schizophrenic, whatever. He had vile temper fits. Blamed Betsy for everything, but he never touched her. Never. It was always me. He beat me regularly. Either with a whip or a hammer. The hammer was the worst.

"The whip would hiss through the air, catch my legs, then my back. It burned like fire. After awhile, though, I got used to it, if such a thing is possible. I can still hear the tomato plants being whacked off by the force of his whip. I picked the tomatoes too green. Too rotten. Filled the hampers too full or not full enough. Everything wrong was my fault.

"But what he did to me was better than what the 17-year-old did to me. Sadie, I'm a ruined person, basically. I've seen just about everything there is to see.

"Betsy was a saint. She even baked like an angel. She lived with that man to the best of her ability, and I bet to this day their community has no idea who he is or what he did.

"The night he broke my ribs with the hammer, that was the night I left. I just walked away, no extra clothes, no nothing. The dog barked, but I didn't care. I'd be better off dead, I thought, so I just walked. My ribs burned in my body. I couldn't lie down, it hurt too bad, so I kept walking. Some guys picked me up. Told them I fell off a wagon. The took me to the hospital. I stayed there for two days.

"My life after the hospital was basically English. I worked odd jobs in construction, at McDonalds, anywhere I could make a bit of money to save for an apartment. I started drinking, and I can't tell you what alcohol meant to me at that point. It was the wonderful substance that eased all my pain. It bolstered my self-confidence, it made me happy, it made me laugh, it made me forget, at least for a time. It was like a god that finally had mercy on my torment.

"You see, Sadie, I hated myself. I still blamed myself for my Dat. And that Wyle, that 17-year-old, I guess I felt that was my fault, too. I was a mess, and I don't know why I even try to persuade you that I'll be okay.

"Do you understand, now? Why I went back home to get away from you? I spent a whole year in rehab, a facility to help people get away from drugs and alcohol."

Sadie gasped, "Drugs?"

Mark nodded. "I tried it all. Anything to make it all go away.

"The counselors at the rehab were wonderful. Trained professionals who are used to dealing with people who are … well, like me. Or, like I was. I came out clean, sober, and healed, to an extent, I guess.

"I always leaned toward the Amish, though. I guess they were my roots. When I left rehab, I found out that my parents' church had sort of fizzled out. It was a bunch of radicals who had lost the *frieda* with the real Amish of that area. I visited my Grandfather Peight. My Daddy. He is the single source of my greatest healing."

"Besides God," Sadie said softly.

Chapter 12

Mark continued, "No, God was in my grandfather in the form of forgiveness, love, tears, and a kindness so huge I couldn't wrap my warped mind around it. He even looked like God. His hair and beard were white, his face unmarked, his eyes…"

Mark's voice dropped to a whisper. "Sadie, if I ever get to heaven, I imagine God's eyes will look exactly like my grandfather's. Pools of kindness without end.

"He told me how their church fell apart, fueled by evil hatred and harsh unbiblical practices. They had no communion for years. They were being led by a group of… Well, I won't say it. But thankfully they moved away. The rest of the church saw the error of their ways and became better people.

"My grandfather told me, if there was anyone to blame, it was him. He should not have believed these ministers. He was so glad to see me. He taught me my love of horses, how to shoe them. I stayed with him after rehab until I heard of Montana. I had some money. I just wanted to see what it was like here, you know? A young man's yearning for adventure and all that. So I came out here by Amtrak. I was here two weeks and was taking a horse to Richard Caldwell's ranch. It was snowing, there was a dark form on the road, a young girl waving her arms, clearly scared out of her wits, which she must not have had too many of, being out on a slippery road with a dead horse..."

"He wasn't dead!"

Mark's laugh rang out, his arms went around her, and he held her so close she could feel the fabric of his shirt stamped against her cheek.

"That was when my real problems began. I almost returned to alcohol. Sadie, I loved you the first minute I saw you. I did. I don't care what people say about love. For me, it was love at first sight, and God was in that snow, too. He was pure and white and... Well, he was there.

"But since... I dunno, Sadie. It seems as if my enemy is my past and the way it makes me feel about myself. When I think of you and your family, your perfect little life, I hardly have the audacity, the daring to be with you. Or your family."

He stopped, shook his head, his hair falling darkly over his eyes.

"Mark, don't be sarcastic when you say, 'your perfect little life.'"

She was hurt beyond words. As if he was mocking her for being who she was, which was grossly unfair. Her first attempt at dealing with the belittling comment was sort of soothing, assuring him they were far from perfect, to make him feel better about himself. But then she caught herself. He could not shift the blame on her.

"I wasn't."

"Yes, you were."

"Oh, okay. I was. You know better."

"Mark, perhaps I do. You carry the blame for the sordid things in your life, but you are much too eager to shift it onto someone else's shoulders, or you would not have spoken to me that way. You drag yourself down constantly and want to drag others down with you."

Now the sarcasm came thick and fast.

"So where did you go to college?" he asked. "You sound exactly like some trained counselor. You think you're smarter than me?"

It was a whiplash of words, ruthless and stinging. It goaded Sadie into action. She sprang up and started running toward home. She ran blindly, uncaring, just to put great distance between them. She ran until her breath came in hard puffs, her chest hurt, and her legs felt as if the bones and tendons had liquefied.

She saw the silhouette of her home on the hillside, the driveway a winding ribbon of silver. It all swam together in the film of her tears.

She had never seen him look as handsome as he did tonight. He wore a brown, short-sleeved shirt of some rough-looking fabric, almost like homespun. His dark brown eyes matched his shirt, his black broadfall trousers were neat and clean. When he took off his straw hat and tousled his dark hair, Sadie could not tear her eyes away. There was simply no use.

Was it all because he was so handsome? Was she so shallow?

He was impossible. She replayed his words, the story tumbling through her senses. What agonies! So young!

She cried the whole way up to the driveway—for him, for the father of those children, for life's unfairness. But mostly she cried because he did not bother to run after her. Where was he now?

When she heard a car coming, she quickened her steps. If she hurried, she'd reach the safety of the driveway before the lights approached. Reaching the mailbox and paper holder, she relaxed, slowing her pace. She turned to the right, more out of habit than anything else, to see if she recognized the car.

The headlights went out. Only the glistening of the silver on the mirrors and the bumper were visible. The steady brrm, brrm, brrm of the engine was plainly audible, and the sound indicated it was a diesel. A pickup. It was barely moving, as if it was in slow motion.

Wait!

Two smokestacks! It was the same truck! The one that had passed her with Daniel.

Fear washed over Sadie's body in powerful chills. It sent her up the embankment where she pressed flat against a pine tree. The needles scratched her face and arms, the sticky resin stuck to the palms of her outstretched fingers.

The truck beat a loud staccato, her ears pulsed with the beating of it. Then it stopped. The motor was off.

Sadie turned, grabbed a low branch, and scrambled up the pine. The branches of a pine tree were just like a ladder, only pricklier. The branches were close together and straight so that you could climb easily.

She climbed up about 10 or 12 feet and settled herself on some thick branches. She remained as still as possible and listened. There was no sound at all.

She craned her neck, peering around the trunk of the pine tree, but there was only an incomprehensible blackness. She could see nothing, not even the silver of the mirrors.

Had she imagined it all?

Wait. Voices.

A truck door opened. As Sadie watched, the tall form of a man emerged, then turned back to help two small ... what was it? She squinted her eyes and peered into the darkness. If she moved anymore, she was sure to slide sideways out of the pine tree. Shifting her weight, she leaned back, holding onto a branch above her. There. Two children.

The tall man helped them out. One of them disappeared in the thicket beside the road. He stooped to speak to the other one.

Suddenly the lights were back on, a brilliant bluish-white. They startled Sadie so much that her fingers convulsed and she lost her grip. The last thought she had before she fell was the realization that the wicked inhabitants of that pickup truck would kidnap her as soon as she hit the ground.

The thing was, she never hit the ground. Instead, she became sandwiched between two branches like a hot dog in a roll, her body doubled-up quite painfully, her breath constricted.

The truck's engine started, revved, pulled out onto the road, and moved slowly past. Someone laughed, a voice spoke.

Now the shot, Sadie thought. I'll be shot just like the horses.

The truck moved on around the bend in the road, disappearing into the warm night.

She had to get out of this tree. Every muscle of her body was cramped. She twisted first one way and then the other, the rough pine bark digging red brushburns into her arms and legs.

Redoubling her efforts, she twisted, turned, and wriggled, but with no luck. Her arms were becoming quite painful, her hips wedged tightly.

She needed to stop panicking, think clearly.

Okay. If no amount of twisting would get her out of here, her best bet would be to find a firm handle somewhere, anywhere. Then using her hands as a lever, perhaps she could pull herself up and out.

Flailing her arms on both sides, her fingers found a branch to the left, but was it too far away? She twisted her upper body again as hard as she could and was rewarded by the feeling of a good, solid, pine bough. She grasped it firmly and heaved with every ounce of strength she possessed.

There was a ripping sound as her skirt caught on a broken knob, but slowly she pulled herself upright.

Glory, Hallelujah! She was out.

Still shaking, she climbed down from the tree, branch by branch, until her feet hit the soft, spongy, pine-needle-laden soil beneath the tree. She felt like kissing the ground, like weary sea voyagers of old had done.

She assessed her situation. Her muscles groaned and her back hurt, but she could move both legs without too much pain. She scrambled down the embankment and began the walk up the seemingly endless driveway.

What if the truck returned? What if it was filled with those horse-killers?

Her feet pummeled the earth now, as she raced up the driveway. Clattering onto the porch, she flung herself on the swing, her breath coming in hard, short whooshes of air. She imagined that this was how Paris felt after a race with Cody through the field of wildflowers.

No wonder she was so grouchy at work the following day. Her back hurt, her head hurt, her arms had bruises on them, stinging horribly when she lowered them into the dishwater.

She was sure she had torn a ligament in the calf of one leg. She hobbled all day about the kitchen, her eyebrows lowered, speaking to no one unless absolutely necessary.

Dorothy hid her smiles of enjoyment as she ate one leftover dish after another. That was the thing that really irked Sadie to start with: the sight of Dorothy at the kitchen table with a dish of cabbage slaw, a slice of carrot cake, and a large mug of coffee at six o'clock in the morning. Watching Dorothy nauseated Sadie. No wonder Dorothy had trouble with her constitution.

Finally, when the tension in the kitchen became so thick it was unbearable, Dorothy clapped a hand on Sadie's aching shoulder, lifted her chin, closed her eyes for emphasis, and said, "Sit down!"

"Ouch!" Sadie said, rubbing her sore shoulder.

"Sit down, I said, Sadie darlin'."

"Why would I sit down? Can't you see this place is a horrible mess? And all you do is eat all morning."

Dorothy's answer was a tilted head and a great guffaw of sound.

"Sit down, Sadie. Either a bear got ahold of you, or you fell out of a tree, or I'd say you got heart problems. And them heart problems ain't the physical kind, now is they?"

Sadie lowered her head into her arms and groaned. Dorothy went to the coffeepot, filled a mug, and set it firmly on the tabletop in front of Sadie.

"Drink this. And here."

She went to the cupboard, came back with a bottle of Advil, and shook out two pills.

"Not with coffee," Sadie said, peering out of her arms with one eye.

"Oh, take 'em. Go on. Won't hurtcha.

"Now, tell me what happened. For one thing, if'n you'd wear better shoes, 'stead of traipsin' around in them there sneakers of yours, if you'd go to the Dollar General and get a pair like mine, you wouldn't be hobblin' the way you are. You go for looks instead of good, solid quality. I have a hunch you're doin' the same thing with that heart o' yours. Ain't nothin' gonna match good, solid, down-to-earth men. Same as shoes."

Dorothy paused. "Ain't you gonna tell me what happened?"

Sadie lifted her head, swallowed the pills with coffee, and grimaced.

"No."

"An' why ever not?"

"It's none of your business."

"Has nothin' to do with that Mark guy, now does it?"

"No. Yes. I don't know."

Sadie stared miserably into the distance.

"He's quite a looker," Dorothy continued. "Even Barbara commented on it. Caught that doctor's wife checkin' him out, so I did. Jes' shook my head to myself and thought, he can't be easy. He's got that brooding look about him. Too quiet. Never smiles right. Just one of them there plastic smiles he hides behind. You love him, don't you?"

"I did."

"You don't now? You want some more of that carrot cake? I'm havin' me another slice. I run my feet off last night. Not that I minded it, not that I minded it. Not with my Dollar General shoes, mind you."

She cut herself a generous slice of cake, scraping the cream-cheese frosting from the wide knife with her tongue as Sadie watched, swallowing her nausea.

"So, what happened?"

"Nothing."

"Now don't give me that. You come to work looking like you got run over by a truck, and you say nothing happened."

Sadie eyed her warily, sighed, then told her everything, ending with her stay in the pine tree.

"I mean, suppose Mark is the shooter, going around killing horses? And what about Louis and Marcellus? It could have been them, all these mysterious goings-on. We don't have any idea where they come from either. For all we know, they're little spies or something, planted here to find out where the horses are."

Dorothy snorted so loudly, Sadie jumped.

"You ain't got a grain of common sense, girl. Now don't you go belittling my Marcelona or Louise. Them kids is definitely victims of domestic abuse. Rich kids. Their parents likely involved in some illegal mess. We know their names now. Police contacted 'em, or tried to. Couldn't come up with nothin'. They evidently skipped the country. No, that pickup you saw. Likely some dad cartin' his kids around and one of 'em had to go potty. Your mind blows everything way outta line."

"Huh-uh, Dorothy."

"Oh, yes it does. Even with Mark, it does."

"What do you know about Mark Peight?"

"Probably more than you think."

Sadie blinked and looked away. Now she was curious. But she was too proud to ask Dorothy what she meant by that remark, so she dropped the subject.

They served leftover steak and fried eggs for breakfast. They made toast with store-bought bread and pancakes from the big commercial box of mix. Since everyone had overeaten the night before, they figured breakfast could be scant. Besides, they had the whole flagstone patio to hose down and chairs and tables to wash and put away. The work loomed before them.

Jim brought Marcellus and Louis, who were each set to work with a plastic bucket of hot soapy water and a rag, and promises of a swim in the pool as soon as the job was completed.

The children were blossoming under Dorothy's care. They loved to help around the ranch when they could. Jim hovered over them, seeing to it that the job was done properly. Bertie came to the patio, engaging Jim in a long, heated conversation about politics, which made Dorothy hiss beneath her breath until she was fairly steaming. She told Sadie if that old coot would get off the porch and let Jim go, he'd get more work done.

An hour later, the men were still standing at the exact same spot, and Dorothy'd had her fill. Marching up to the grizzled old gardener, she placed her fists on her hips and told him if he'd shut his trap, her James could get something accomplished, but she guessed people who worked for the government didn't need to worry about working to earn their money.

Bertie waved his arms and yelled. Then he stomped off the porch and went to find garbage bags, while Dorothy turned on her heel and marched self-righteously back to her domain, the kitchen.

Sadie turned the garden-hose pressure nozzle on high and washed down the flagstones from the previous night's party. She was sleepy, the flies were pesky, and her leg hurt worse as the forenoon wore on. She had never felt quite so depressed in her whole life.

What was the point of hanging on to Mark Peight? He obviously was not an easy person to understand.

What made him say those unkind things one minute, then become one of the nicest people anyone could ever hope to meet in the next?

Her mind was a million miles away until she saw Richard and Barbara Caldwell come out of the house, walking purposefully toward her. Sadie let go of the lever that powered the water spray and turned to greet them with the respect a boss required.

"Good morning," she said evenly.

"Yes, it is a good one. How are you?" Richard Caldwell boomed, his wife smiling at Sadie.

"You have dark circles under your eyes," Barbara observed.

"Do I?"

"We're being too hard on you, right? You're overworked."

"No, no," Sadie demurred.

They told Sadie what was on their minds. More horses had been killed the evening before. There was a serious threat in the area, and the local police needed telephone numbers to leave messages and warn the Amish.

This time, a full-blooded Tennessee Walker, the pride of the Lewis Ranch, the LWR, had been gunned down in broad daylight, along with a prize mare. And as an afterthought, three miniature ponies had been killed also, all in a drive-by shooting. They had, however, one vague clue. There was a truck, a blue diesel, seen in the vicinity, driving by slowly about the time of the shooting.

Sadie's shoulders slumped as color drained from her face. She plucked at a dead geranium without thinking, trying to bide her time before lifting her face to meet the piercing gaze of Richard Caldwell.

"Sadie? Do you know anything at all?"

Sadie sank weakly into a lawn chair, then met their questioning gazes. She told them honestly everything she knew, including the shot ringing out when she was with Daniel King and the truck the evening before.

Richard Caldwell fairly shouted at her, the veins protruding in his thick neck. What she was doing, traipsing along the road in the dark like that? Barbara placed a well-manicured hand on his arm and patted it a few times to calm him.

"The police have to know this," Richard Caldwell bellowed.

"They do," Barbara agreed.

"Everything? Even last night's incident?"

"No. There's more than one diesel truck in this area. Likely a kid needed to go to the bathroom, as Dorothy said."

☆ ✡ ☆

As the Amish people listened to the phone messages from the police, fear settled over the community like a cloak of heaviness. Parents feared for their children's safety. They kept their horses in barns, and children no longer rode on carts hitched to ponies. Local drivers took them to school in vans.

Families walked whenever possible. When distances were too great, they drove their teams cautiously, glancing furtively to the left and right, never relaxed, goading their horses to a fast trot.

Dat shook his head and said Fred Ketty may be on to something when she said the end of the world was nigh with so much evil in rural Montana.

Then two of Dave Detweiler's Belgians were found below their pasture. The fence had been cut with wire cutters, and the great horses had been chased out, then gunned down. There were no footprints or any trace of the killers left behind.

The Amish people were shaken but took the news stoically, as is their way. No use crying over spilled milk, they could have been struck by lightning, and God would not be mocked. These men would be brought to justice.

Sadie was afraid for Paris, so she kept her inside the barn. Dat said he wasn't keeping Charlie off that good pasture. He guessed if they got the horse, they would. That comment made Sadie so angry she felt like telling Dat a thing or two, but she knew she shouldn't.

Paris hung her head over the door and whinnied all day, while Charlie stood in the pasture and whinnied back. Reuben got so tired of it he brought Charlie into the barn and closed the gate. The whinnying stopped, and Dat never did anything to change it.

Reuben claimed aliens were hovering over the pastures in green flying ships and shooting horses for revenge. Mam scolded him thoroughly. She said there's no such thing as aliens, and he better watch it or he'd have to go work in John Troyer's truck patch, helping to clean it up as fall approached.

That shut Reuben up.

Sadie was afraid to ride. Still, when summer breezes turned into the biting winds of autumn, when the frost lay heavy in the hollows and the brown leaves swirled among the golden ones from the aspens, she could no longer hold back.

She asked Reuben to accompany her on Charlie. He looked up from his word-search booklet, his eyes round with fear.

"If you think for one minute that I'm going riding with you, you're nuts. Charlie isn't a riding horse. It's like riding a camel. He trots, and you bounce up and down, rattling all your teeth loose. I'm not going."

"Reuben!" Sadie wailed.

"Nope. Go by yourself."

"Okay. I will."

"You're crazy."

With that, Reuben went back to his word search, shaking his head wisely.

Mam was down in the basement, rearranging jars of canned goods. Sadie contemplated asking for permission, but she knew the answer would be a dead no. So she just left, though she felt a bit guilty.

Dat was at a school meeting and wouldn't be home until later. But she met Anna coming down the stairs from the haymow, holding a black cat who was struggling mightily, clearly displeased at being removed from the warm, sweet-smelling hay.

"Whatcha doing?" she asked innocently.

"Riding."

Anna shrugged her shoulders, hanging on grimly to the cat struggling to be free.

Sadie laughed, then whistled happily as she caught Paris' chin, kissed her nose, and began brushing the sleek, golden coat.

"We're going riding, Sweetheart, for better or for worse. Here we go!"

Chapter 13

THE FEELING OF BEING ON HORSEBACK AGAIN WAS one of jubilation. Sadie loved seeing Paris throw her head high, her ears swiveling forward then back, tuned in to Sadie's commands. Of course, there were no commands, and there wouldn't be. All Sadie had to do was give Paris a slight squeeze on the ribs or lay the reins easily on her neck. The communication between the two was so complete as to be almost imperceptible. But Paris knew, and so did Sadie.

Paris wanted to run. Should Sadie take her to the field of wildflowers? Sadie shivered. Taming Paris and Cody among the wildflowers had been so beautiful, but now a dark sort of foreboding hung over the field, turning it gray with her own apprehension. Could she ever ride there again?

She would never forget Reuben's sobs and the despair that shook his young body. He still had no horse. He wanted nothing to do with another one.

She held Paris in until the road wound uphill, then she let the horse run. She would let her stretch out, let her gather her feet beneath her, lunge with those powerful haunches, her heavy shoulders, feel the wind in her face just up this ridge. Then she'd turn around and go back.

Paris lowered her head. Power surged through her body as she raced up the winding road of Atkin's Ridge. Sadie leaned forward, sitting low in the saddle, savoring the wind that rushed in her ears.

They were almost at the top of the ridge. The light was darker here, the trees dense. There was a high embankment to her right, a heavy growth of trees and another steep incline to her left. It would be best to turn around and let Paris go slowly back down the way they had come.

A mockingbird dipped in the air ahead of her, his silly calls following him. First a cardinal's call, then a thrush, and finally a seagull. Had this saucy bird no shame, mocking these beautiful birds of the air? She turned her head, following his whereabouts until she located him high up in a scraggly pine.

She guessed that was why she didn't see the pickup truck until it was directly in front of her.

The throbbing, pulsating diesel sound pierced her awareness. A shot of raw fear surged through her with the power of a streak of lightning.

No! Not now! Remorse followed on fear's heels. Why had she been so foolish?

The truck was coming steadily, slowly. The blue color gleamed in the twilight.

There was only one way out. Up the embankment. Paris could do it.

Turning the horse, Sadie laid the reins on the left side of Paris' neck.

"Up, Paris! Up, girl." Sadie leaned forward, preparing herself for the powerful gathering of her hooves, the leaping.

Paris obeyed to perfection. Oh, wonderful horse! Her feet were sure, her hooves ringing on the rocks as she scrambled up, up, sideways up the incline. Sadie leaned over her neck, speaking softly, goading her on.

The occupants of the pickup yelled something. Sadie heard their harsh anger. But what did they say? Would they follow her?

The forest was green and brown, yellow and red with autumn, decked out in its final show before winter winds would howl through it, turning everything stark and white.

"Dear God, keep me safe. Stay with me, protect me, and keep me from harm," she prayed like a little child.

Paris took one last leap up the incline before pushing her way through the thicket, brushing nervously past two trees. Sadie pulled in the reins, sat up, listened, her heart racing.

There. She could still hear that truck idling. They had not moved on!

What was their motive? Who were they looking for? How could they terrorize a peace-loving, sleepy, little Montana community this way? Sadie was convinced the blue diesel truck held the shooter—or shooters.

Suddenly, anger overtook her common sense, and she turned Paris to the left. If she could get close enough, she might be able to see the license plate through the trees.

Should she tie Paris or stay on her back?

The truck was still idling, and Sadie was afraid to look and see if its occupants were inside or out. Better stay on the horse.

"Shhh, Paris," Sadie whispered.

They moved quietly through the trees until the rear of the pickup was in sight. But it was too far away now. She leaned to the right, her eyes straining to see the figures on the metal rectangle. All she needed was that license plate number.

Was that a six? Or an eight?

She screamed then, a sound of pure terror, as two heads appeared coming up over the embankment. Paris lifted her head. Sadie loosened the reins and screamed again.

"Go, Paris! Go!"

She bent low and let Paris take control. Horses could always find their way home, and Sadie trusted Paris more than anything. They raced through the forest, zig-zagging first uphill, then sideways downhill, over rocks, between trees. Sadie looked back, her eyes wide with fear.

What would happen once Paris broke out of the woods? She couldn't go back on the road. Did those men know where she lived?

A feeling of despair enveloped her, threatened to choke her. She couldn't go home. Besides, Paris wasn't going home. She was running downhill in the opposite direction, away from home. She slowed, her ears pricked forward, before wheeling, veering sharply to the right and running diagonally down the side of the forested hill.

The sun was getting very low in the west, dust-laden streaks of light slanting between the trees. The browns and reds turned into stripes of flaming color.

A fence!

Instinctively, Sadie pulled back, but Paris had seen it and was slowing of her own accord.

"Whoop. Watch it, Paris. There's a fence."

Horses! This was someone's pasture.

Well, they'd have to find their way around it.

Paris picked her way carefully now. The horses in the pasture lifted their heads, whinnied. Paris answered with a high cry of her own.

The biggest horse lifted his head farther, then trotted over.

Hadn't she seen him somewhere before? He was so massive in the shoulders. And that color. So distinct. The grayish-oatmeal color of an Appaloosa mixture.

Sadie rode carefully as the horse trotted up to the fence, tossing his head, his mane whipping in the brisk wind.

The fence dipped into a culvert, then went almost straight up a steep hill. Sadie rode easily, but she was tense, her fear a support that kept her vigilant.

She remained alert for any unusual sound, the sight of a human being, the rumbling of traffic, anything that could mean she was being followed. As she crested the hill, she saw the rooftops of a barn, shed, then more outbuildings.

This, too, seemed vaguely familiar. But, no. She wasn't far enough out to be on Mark Peight's property, was she?

The fence stopped at a corner, then turned straight across the hayfield to the barn. She stopped Paris, indecision making her falter.

As if on cue, she heard the low rumbling of traffic. Was it the diesel truck? Well, if it was, they could just drive straight on past Mark Peight's place and be gone. She was safe for now.

Suddenly she became rigid with anger. Who in the world did they think they were? Riding around like cowards, wreaking havoc on people's lives, wrecking livelihoods, creating heartache.

The police were doing what they could, but there was no evidence, so they weren't making much progress. That made her mad, too.

Something had to be done. Someone had to take charge. If Mark was any sort of man, he'd stand by her and help out.

Besides, if he truly was innocent of ever having anything to do with these twisted individuals, who seemed to receive some sort of nameless thrill by killing innocent animals, this would be his chance to prove it.

Over and over he had assured her that this thing was way over his head. He couldn't fathom it, this senseless killing. In typical Mark-fashion, he had pouted and ignored her, his way of letting her know she had hurt his feelings by refusing to place her trust in him.

Hadn't he pledged his word the night of the cookout? That long magical evening when their words flowed, an artesian well of entwined emotions, a night she would never forget.

Kicking the stirrups and yanking on the reins, she startled Paris into a gallop across the hayfield and into the barnyard. She hauled back on the reins, then waited.

When she heard no one, she called his name.

Mark rounded the corner of a building wearing a nail pouch, his sleeves rolled up, hatless, surprise written all over his face from his wide-open eyes to his open mouth.

"Sadie Miller! What on earth...?"

She dismounted, led Paris into the forebay, and said, "Shut the door."

He obeyed immediately, latching it securely.

"Mark, I want you to listen to me. I need your help. These men are shooting horses again. I went for a ride, and they..." She caught her breath. "They saw me."

"Who are they?"

"How would I know? It's that blue diesel pickup. They have the gall...the...the...indecency to ride around wrecking people's lives as if a horse, a beautiful creature, was a...a *stump* used for target practice. And listen, I think they're after Paris. For a long time I didn't want to believe that, but now I'm sure Paris has something to do with it.

"Remember the black?"

Mark nodded.

"Well, he was shot. So was Cody. I still think there's a connection between the horse thieves and these shootings. Now they must be after Paris. I think she's a valuable horse in some way I don't even know.

"Mark, let's get close to the road, maybe put a road-block across it. They're in the area. We need to get that license-plate number. I'm tired of everything. The fear. The not knowing. If no one else does anything, I will."

In the dim interior of the barn, Mark could see this was no lady in distress. He watched her face intently and saw her honest resolve. She meant business, and she meant it now.

He smiled at her. "You really mean it?"

"Yes, I do. Now hurry. Can Paris have a drink? Some hay? She's been ridden hard."

Snapping a neck rope around Paris, Mark loosened her bridle, then took it off, hanging it on a nail nearby. Paris dipped her head as if to acknowledge the kind gesture, then drank deeply, her nostrils quivering.

Sadie laughed. "That's funny. She never drinks out of water troughs she's not used to."

Mark lifted his eyebrows suggestively. "A good omen for us," he teased.

Sadie blushed and kicked at some loose straw, as if her concentration could push his teasing away.

They tied Paris in a stall, gave her a block of fragrant hay, and turned to go. The sun was setting behind a distant ridge, and Sadie's heart sank along with it.

Sadie had to let Dat and Mam know where she was.

Bewildered, she asked Mark what she should do. He steered her into the implement shed where a black phone hung on the wall.

She picked up the receiver, dialed the number, and, of course, no one answered. She left a quick message, saying she was at Mark Peight's house with Paris, and they were not to worry. She couldn't tell them how she'd get home because she didn't know. Darkness was fast approaching.

When she hung up, she looked at Mark.

"Can we put a roadblock across the road?"

"I don't think that's legal."

"Can we stop them somehow? Can you flag them down? What reason could we give for trying to stop them?"

"Don't worry. I'll think of something."

He strode off toward the barn, returning with a heavy Stihl weed whacker.

"I'll work at the weeds around these buildings. You sit behind that row of pine trees."

Sadie assessed the trees, and then nodded her head.

"I'll climb up. They're easy."

They parted ways, Mark going to his designated area, Sadie to hers.

There was plenty of light. Good.

Mark pulled at the weed-wacker rope again and again until it sputtered to life, then moved it back and forth in long, sweeping motions.

Sadie listened, wondering if they would hear the sound of the diesel truck above the whining of the weed wacker.

Sadie watched Mark, the play of his shoulders, the ease with which he handled the heavy equipment.

Why did he have to be so complicated?

A little while later, Mark laid down the weed wacker and looked in the direction of the pine tree.

"You still up there, Sadie?"

"Yep!" she answered.

"I think your buddies went home the other way."

"I guess so."

When had their friendship turned into this? They were both more relaxed this evening than ever. It was an easy, natural feeling. It seemed as if she had known Mark all her life, and this was an evening where everything would go right. He had come to the end of his driveway with her. Not once had he laughed at her or made sarcastic remarks about the Amish. And that was something. Perhaps it was the circumstances, the danger, or maybe it was Paris, or something other than themselves to worry about.

Uh-oh. There they came.

At first she thought it might be a tractor; they were moving so slowly. Then she saw the gleaming silver smokestacks and heard the rumbling of that diesel engine. Her heart beat faster with the realization that they might be stopping.

Were they dangerous, armed men? Or was this all a figment of her imagination? Maybe this truck had absolutely nothing to do with the drive-by shootings.

The truck came slowly—slowly—over a low rise. She could see three men in the vehicle, all wearing hats pulled low. The driver was a big man; the other two were smaller. They were watching the road and the fields intently for any movement.

Oh! There was Mark. He just stood there with the weed wacker. Sadie shifted so she would be able to see the rear of the pickup. The truck slowed even more when the driver spied Mark.

Sadie could see the license plate. The numbers! She could see them!

Just as Mark stepped forward and Sadie thought the truck would stop, the driver accelerated. The tires screeched as the truck seemed to lift in the front. It fish-tailed as the driver gunned the motor, and they were off down the road at a dangerous speed.

Mark stood by the side of the road, scratching his head in bewilderment, while Sadie scrambled out of the tree and ran to his side. She was breathless when she reached him.

"I could see the license plate as plain as day!"

"Definitely something odd with that bunch."

"They're smart. Oh, Mark, I know they're the ones doing this. I just have this feeling. An intuition or something."

"I bet you anything this is the end of the diesel truck," Mark said shaking his head.

"Why?"

"They'll use another vehicle now. They didn't trust me at all, or they wouldn't have taken off like that."

"Oh."

"Well, there's not much we can do now," he said. "So? You want to come in? See where I'm staying? I don't have a house yet, you know."

Sadie looked around at the fast-approaching night.

"How am I going to get home? I can't ride Paris."

"What were you doing on the road riding that horse to begin with? Don't you know it simply is not safe right now?"

"I do now."

"I'll take you home. Paris can stay here."

He laughed in a low, gravelly sound. "You could stay here all night as well."

"Mark!"

"Just teasing."

As it was, she stayed far too long anyway. He showed her the room he had done up for his living quarters. It was surprisingly tidy and neat. His bed was made with a brightly-colored Indian blanket. A huge gun cabinet contained many guns of all sorts, and there were racks of guns on the wall. A glass-fronted cabinet held almost as many hunting knives.

His dog, Wolf, rose from the floor in front of the brown leather sofa. He was a magnificent animal, but fearful-looking. The wolf in him was so apparent he didn't really seem like a dog at all.

"The color of his eyes!" Sadie exclaimed.

"Isn't he beautiful?"

"He is. But, oh my, Mark, I'd hate to meet him in the dark."

"That's why I have him. I met too many ghosts in the dark as a child."

"You mean you had him when you were little?"

"Fifteen."

"Seriously?"

"About the age I learned to protect myself, yes."

Sadie sat down as Mark continued to speak. She sat quietly, her hands in her lap, watching his face. He never looked at her when he talked this way, which was all right if that made it easier to bare his soul.

She hung onto every word, knowing that understanding his aching past is what would play the most powerful part in understanding this man.

"See, before I started with … the substance abuse, oh… Did I tell you about my uncle? He was Amish. A member of my parents' church. I don't know how old I was, but we … my brother and I were there for a time to help in his produce fields. That's when my whole world flipped upside down and I felt as if I had nothing … no gravity, even, to keep me upright, centered. I was basically floating around in a misery of having nothing to hold onto.

"You couldn't trust English people, but neither could you trust Amish. My uncle, anyway. I often wonder how much he had to do with my mother's leaving."

"Is this uncle the same man you told me about before? What was his wife's name? Betsy?"

Mark nodded.

"Why didn't you tell me he was your uncle?"

He shrugged his shoulders. "Embarrassment. Afraid you'd never look at me again. Never date me…or marry me."

Sadie remained quiet.

What had he just said? Marry me? She bit her lip, hard.

"When I worked for my uncle, I realized that Amish people, men of faith, were lower in nature than even the foster system. That's really when the pins were knocked out from under me. Every person needs something they can believe in, and often, for children especially, God is not that real. So children depend on good people to give them food and clean clothes and love. But when you live without the love of your parents, you're like a stray dog. You have to scrounge through trash cans to get whatever you can. A smile here, some food there. You look for any tiny bit of kindness and grasp it with greedy, hungry fingers, and you never forget it.

"So my parents were gone, but the hardest part of my life was when even my uncle betrayed me. At first, I looked up to him. I wanted so desperately to believe he was good, that he was someone I could finally trust. Even the first beating, Sadie, I thought I deserved. My self-blame made him seem like a better person.

"So I tried even harder. I checked every tomato, every cucumber, and placed it carefully in the basket. When he tied me in the silo chute overnight for accidentally knocking over a stack of plastic tomato hampers, I gave up. There was no goodness, no mercy in this vile man. Recognizing that was a sort of freedom, but that's when I could no longer keep my feet on the ground. I free-floated in a world of hatred.

"The hate bit into my wrists that night I was tied to the steps of the silo. Those ropes became the hate in me, and that hate gave me strength to pull free. I almost lost my one hand to infection."

"Not hate, Mark. God helped you become free."

Mark shook his head. "No, Sadie. There was no room for God in that silo chute. It was filled with rage, my silent screams, my determination to kill that man."

"No, Mark! Please don't say those things."

"So now you see. Now you know why I'm not good enough for you."

"It's in the past."

"Never totally. I guess finding God is harder for a person who has hated the way I have. The alcohol was a sort of haven for awhile. So were the drugs. But I couldn't go on. Once I was so messed up, I almost died one night. I guess... that was probably the first time I could recognize God in my life. It must have been him, or else I'd be dead.

"But God acts like a missing parent sometimes. He's often hard to find. At first, you have to survive on bits and pieces. A sunset, for instance. Or a sunrise. Little things sort of pierce your armor of hardness, but it's elusive. God is terribly hard to understand. Why does he allow a life like mine? Why?"

"Your life is good, now, Mark," Sadie said quietly.

"By all outward appearances, yes. But I struggle. It's tough. I want to be free of my past, completely, but...I can't."

"Is that … is that …?"

"What?"

"I can't say it."

"Come on, Sadie. Out with it."

"Is that why we don't date like normal young people in an Amish community do?"

"Yes."

She was silent at that. Mark paused.

"You see, Sadie, I'll hurt you. My jealousy, my anger, it's not fair to you. I hurt you now, and we're not dating."

Like a star falling across the night sky, the knowledge awakened her. She almost gasped audibly. She clasped her hands firmly around her knee to keep them from going around Mark's shoulders.

She knew then. She knew that she was the link, the gravity, the conduit of God's love to Mark. He needed her. Her love was from God. She was only a vessel he had prepared, and would continue to prepare, as long as Mark needed her.

What did it matter? Her life would not always be safe or secure. She would, no doubt, suffer at times. But only at times. They would have their good days, and many of them. If the bad times came, God would be there for her. Yes, he would. Oh, how he would!

She drew in a soft breath. Turning to him, she laid a hand on his arm.

"Mark, can we have a date on Saturday evening?" she asked.

Her arms slid around his shoulders when he bent his head toward hers, not knowing if the tears of joy between them were his or hers.

Chapter 14

SADIE LAID IN HER BED FULLY AWAKE. WHAT WAS that sound? Was it the creaking of the siding, the snapping of wooden floorboards? She heard it again. A hoarse sort of sound.

Retching. Someone was being sick.

She swung her legs over the side of the bed, tiptoed quietly across the hall to the bathroom door, and turned the knob. It was locked securely.

"Reuben?"

Her answer was another tearing sound. Someone was really sick.

Knocking, she called again, "Reuben?"

There was no answer, only the sound of the bathroom tissue being unrolled.

"Anna?"

"Go away." The words were garbled, almost indistinct.

"Anna, let me in. Are you sick?"

"I'm all right. Go back to bed."

"No."

Sadie leaned against the wall outside the bathroom, crossed her arms, and waited.

Finally, the door opened a tiny crack, a thin sliver of yellow light from the kerosene lamp showing through. Anna appeared, carrying the lamp. At first, Sadie shrank back against the wall, then gave up and stepped forward.

She was shocked to see Anna's face. It was so pale, with red splotches on her cheeks. Her lips were ballooned to twice their normal size, tear streaks in jagged, glistening paths down her swollen cheeks.

"Anna!"

"Go away!" Anna hissed, pushing past her.

The lamp chimney rocked unsteadily as Anna turned to enter her room. Her hands outstretched, Sadie followed her.

"Anna, stop! I'm going to wake Rebekah and Leah if you don't act normal. Why are you so angry? Do you have the flu?"

"Course I have the flu! What does it look like? You think I *want* to throw up, or what?"

Sadie stepped up and took the kerosene lamp from Anna's nervous hands, guided her back into the bedroom, and closed the door noiselessly.

"Yes. I think you want to throw up," Sadie ground out, pushing her face very close to Anna's, watching as her pupils dilated with fear.

Sadie set the lamp on the small dresser. Turning, she said, "Sit down."

Anna obeyed, hanging her head in shame. It touched Sadie's heart. So young and still obeying her elders in her innocent way as she was trained to do. At 16 years old, when she started her years of *rumspringa*, she would be given more freedom to make her own choices. But for now, she still obeyed the voice of her parents or older sisters.

"Anna, listen to me. You don't have a stomach virus, do you? You want to throw up to get rid of food you ate because you feel fat. Am I right?"

Anna shook her head from side to side, her eyes downcast, picking at her white T-shirt with fingers that never stopped moving. Sadie said nothing until the back-and-forth movement stopped.

"Have you been making yourself vomit for a long time?"

"I don't...do that. I feel sick."

"Then we have to take you to a doctor. You may have a serious disease that causes the nausea."

"No!"

"Why not?"

"I hate doctors. They...they weigh you."

"You've been losing weight, Anna."

"I am?"

Anna lifted her head, hope shining from her swollen eyes. Sadie watched quietly as Anna pulled her T-shirt tightly across her stomach, then released it abruptly.

"Anna, it's okay if you want to lose weight, but you can't do it like this."

"Like what?"

"Purging. Making yourself throw up."

"I don't."

"Yes, you do."

Confronted with the truth, Anna began to cry. It was a pitiful mewling sound at first, then deeper, hoarse sobs. She twisted her body and threw herself face-first into her pillows.

Sadie sat down on the twin-size bed, her hands in her lap. Instinctively, she knew it would be better to let Anna's misery boil over for awhile.

Her eyes roamed the small room. She noticed the poster of dogs, the cheap Wal-Mart candle that didn't match any color in the room, the clothes in a heap by the closet door, a cellophane wrapper by her bed.

The furniture was mismatched hand-me-downs of dressers that had been used by her sisters as they grew through their early teens. When Anna reached 16, she'd have a larger room filled with new furniture, beautiful things, art on the walls, a room that stated her own tastes.

A wave of pity washed over her Sadie. Poor Anna was stuck back here at the end of the hall, in a room that was almost an afterthought, unimportant, forgotten—too much like Anna herself. As the youngest daughter, she sat in on her older sisters' conversations, listening in awe to their vivid accounts of weekends with girlfriends and interesting boys, all of it a faraway, scary place for Anna to imagine.

The *youngie*. As she approached *rumspringa*, her own inadequacies quadrupled in size, her apprehension mounting into inconsolable proportions. She filled that worried place with food, the source of her comfort and happiness.

Anna was quiet now, only an occasional hiccup reminding Sadie of the sobs, the onslaught of her despair. Slowly, she placed a hand on Anna's shoulder.

"Anna, you aren't fat."

There was no answer, only a long, drawn-out shudder.

"Do you know how much I weighed when I was 15?"

Silence.

"140."

Anna sat straight up, staring at Sadie.

"You did not!"

"Yes, I did."

"I only weigh a little more than that," Anna whispered, the corner of her lips lifting.

"Of course, you do."

Anna pulled up her pajama-clad knees, wrapped her arms around her legs, and talked. She told Sadie she had been perfectly content to be who she was until some friends had a sleepover at Sarah Ann's house. There they compared skin problems, hair color, sizes and weight. Jeanie told Anna that she was the heaviest by 10 whole pounds, and why was she so much bigger than her sisters? Why was her hair lighter?

After that, Anna had sat in the sun all summer spraying vinegar-water in her hair, then lemon-juice water, then baking-soda water, anything to change the color. She had even tried spraying it with mosquito repellent, but all she got was an itching, flaky scalp.

She was always hungry, that was the thing. She could eat all day long, every day. Doughnuts, peanut butter crackers, chicken corn soup with saltine crackers, applesauce, hot dogs with sauerkraut, and potato chips. She loved Mam's snickerdoodle cookies and Subway's sandwiches. Everything in the whole world was delicious, except brussels sprouts. They tasted like spoiled cabbage.

At the dentist's office, she watched a lady on the television eat spaghetti. It made her so hungry for spaghetti that she asked Mam to make it for supper, and she ate it for days and days with dried Parmesan cheese sprinkled all over it, and homemade bread with butter and garlic powder, oregano, and more cheese. She put it in the broiler of the oven, and it was the best thing ever.

At the produce stand where she worked with Leah, she loved to eat a garden-fresh tomato, sliced thick and sprinkled with salt and pepper. She ate great sections of cantaloupes and oranges and blueberries, as well.

"Then I gained over 25 pounds," she said sadly.

Sadie laughed, a sound of genuine understanding.

"It's all right to eat. You're hungry, you're growing, and you're healthy."

Anna shook her head. "I'm fat!"

Sadie looked at her steadily, unflinchingly. "You are not fat."

"According to Sarah Ann and Jeanie, I am."

Sadie nodded. "Girls can be so cruel. So terribly, unthinkingly, crushingly cruel. So mean. But you know what, Anna? The reason they say those things is because of their own insecurities. They don't feel good about themselves, or they wouldn't put other girls down.

"Every 14- or 15-year-old girl has her own struggles with feeling adequate, secure, able to move among her peers with ease and confidence. It's tough out there. We have a close circle of people being raised in the Amish way, but we're only human beings, and we suffer in the early teen years same as everyone else."

"I can't believe that you did."

"I sure did. Sometimes I wished the end of the world would come so I wouldn't have to be 16. I was terribly hurt by the loss of Paris and by moving to Montana. I hated it."

Anna told Sadie about how she felt left out by her and Reuben, with their tremendous riding skills and their way with horses. She felt as if she had no talent at all. She couldn't even sew a decent dress on the sewing machine.

Sadie listened quietly and felt some remorse. A plan formed in her mind.

"I'll tell you what, Anna. If you cross your heart and promise that you will never, ever, as long as you live, make yourself *cuts* again, then I will get a horse for you. Reuben won't ride with me anymore, so you can. I'll teach you."

"No."

"Why not?"

"I'm too *blottchich*."

It was then that Sadie realized that the brick wall Anna had built around herself was impossible to breach in one heartfelt talk. How deep was her problem?

Oh, dear God, Sadie prayed silently. Bless Anna, look upon her with grace. She's so young and so mixed up about what's important in life.

She yawned and stretched.

"Well, if you think you're so *blottchich*, then we'll drop it."

She stood up, gathered her robe around her, shivering.

"Winter's coming," she said sleepily.

Anna watched her wearily.

"I…I can't ride a horse. I'm scared of them. I'm not like you. You just look at a horse and it likes you. They don't like me. They bite me."

Sadie laughed. "You know that's not true."

"It is."

"Goodnight, Anna. Sleep well. No *cutsing*, okay?"

"Okay."

The wind was moaning among the eaves, a sad sort of harmony with the night, as if they had put their heads together and written this symphony for the approaching winter.

Sadie heard very little of it, falling asleep the minute her head touched the soft pillow.

✿ ✪ ✿

In the morning, Dat sat at the table poring over the newspaper as Mam expertly flipped the sizzling golden rectangles of cornmeal mush in the cast-iron frying pan. Each year when the leaves turned color and the air carried a frosty nip, Dat wanted fried mush for breakfast. It was an item of food that had been passed down for many generations. He liked it cut in thick slices, then fried in oil for at least half an hour. He ate it with two eggs sunny-side up and a glass of orange juice. Then he had oatmeal as a sort of breakfast dessert, often accompanied by shoofly pie.

Sadie wondered whether to tell them about Anna's problems.

Mam put the mush on a platter, then cracked the eggs into the same pan. Sadie poured the juice, looking up as Leah walked into the kitchen.

"Morning."

"Mm-hm."

"Cleaning today?"

Leah nodded.

"Can someone make toast?" Mam asked.

Sadie sliced thick slices of homemade white bread, raising her eyebrows at the lack of whole wheat flour.

"Out of it," Mam said, observant as always.

"That's unusual."

"Well, I called Johnny Sollenberger yesterday to take me to town. He's my least favorite driver, but no one else could go, and guess who he had going to town with him?"

Sadie pushed the broiler closed with a squeaky bang and looked at Mam.

"Fred Ketty."

"Ach, my."

"So I just didn't go. Figured we could eat white bread."

Dat chuckled. "Ach, Fred Ketty. She means well."

"I'd go into hiding if I was called Fred Ketty," Leah observed sourly, pulling up her chair.

Reuben slumped in his chair, rubbing his eyes with his fists.

"Where's Anna?"

"Let her sleep. She was up late."

They bowed their heads, asking a silent blessing on the morning meal. When they raised their heads, Sadie decided to bring up the subject of Anna's purging.

Mam listened wide-eyed while Dat shook his head in disbelief. Reuben promptly stated that nobody noticed Anna, same as him, and she was just doing it for attention. A generous portion of egg and fried mush churned in his mouth as he spoke, until Dat told him to swallow his food first, then finish speaking. This sent Reuben into a dark silence, and he shoveled food into his mouth at twice the speed.

Mam said it was more than just ordinary teenage angst, which Sadie agreed was true. Leah nodded her head in acknowledgment as well.

"She needs a horse," Sadie said.

"You think that would help her snap out of it?" Dat asked.

"Anything to build some confidence."

Reuben snorted. "Well, what about me? I still don't have a horse. If it would help, I can start throwing up."

Dat explained patiently to Reuben that he had shown absolutely no interest in another horse, so they figured he'd have to be ready for one first.

"I hate horses," Reuben said quite abruptly.

He left the table, hurried into the living room, and threw himself on the couch, burying his face in his arms. Mam opened her mouth to call him back, but Dat waved his hand to quiet her.

"He'll be okay. This thing with Cody will take time."

It was Saturday, so there was no hurry, except for Leah going to her housecleaning job. Sadie lingered with her parents, discussing the issues of the day, then told them that Mark would be coming to the house that evening.

Dat drank his coffee to hide his smile, but Mam lifted her eyebrows in concern.

"He's sure given you the runaround already," she observed dryly.

Sadie nodded in agreement, deciding not to try and prove a point. She'd have one date and see what occurred. She giggled to herself, wondering what her very proper mother would say if she knew that Sadie had asked for the date, instead of the other way around. But Sadie knew it was all right. At this point, they were closer than many couples who had been dating for some time.

She cleaned the refrigerator and defrosted the freezer while Mam baked shoofly pies, discussing Anna and Reuben all the while.

Mam poured water on the mixture for the pie crust, felt it with her fingertips, then poured on a bit more. She pushed the mound to the middle of the stainless steel bowl and molded it into a perfect pile of moist pie dough.

She went to the flour canister and scooped some into a bowl. She scattered a generous amount of the snowy white flour onto the countertop. Pinching off the right amount of dough, she sprinkled more flour on top. Then she grabbed the rolling pin and began an expert circular motion until she had a perfect orb of evenly rolled dough.

Folding it in half, she pressed it into the tin pie plate, then took a table knife and cut off the extra, overhanging dough.

She made six pie crusts, ladling the brown sugar, egg, water, molasses, and soda mixture into it, measuring the amounts carefully. Mam said if there was too much liquid, the pies ran over in the oven; too little and you had a dry shoofly pie.

Next she took up a handful of crumbs made from flour, brown sugar, and shortening, sprinkling large handfuls of them on top. It never failed to amaze Sadie how the liquid and crumbs merged to create the three perfect parts that made a shoofly pie: the "goo," the cake, and the crumbs on top.

Mam was an expert, her shooflies always turning out with the deepest amount of goo, the softest cake, and just a sprinkling of crumbs. She said it was from doing it over and over for years.

"Well, if you have a date, perhaps I had better make a ho-ho cake," Mam said, her smile wide and warm as she watched Sadie clean the shelves of the refrigerator.

"A what?" "A ho-ho cake. A chocolate cake with creamy white filling topped with fudge sauce. You eat it with ice cream. Or without."

"Oh, yes. They're a lot of trouble, aren't they?"

"Well...yes."

"Then don't."

"Of course, I will. You have a date!"

Sadie grinned, then her nose stung as she tried to hold back the tears. She would never forget the anxiety of passing through the dark valley of her mother's mental illness. She hoped she'd also never forgot to thank God for her mother's ordinary, everyday awareness and love for life.

There were still times when she would catch her mother gazing out the window with tears gathering in her eyes. On those days Sadie's heart would plummet to her stomach as she wondered if the depression would return. But it never did as long as she faithfully followed her doctor's orders, with Dat's full support.

Sadie sincerely hoped Anna was not following in her mother's footsteps. Sadie knew depression could be hereditary sometimes, and she wondered if Anna was showing signs of it.

As Sadie cleaned the rest of the house with Rebekah's help, she noticed it was close to dinnertime. What time might Mark show up? Had he made plans with anyone else?

"Isn't Kevin coming over this evening?"

"No. He has church tomorrow."

Reuben brought the mail, thumping it down on the kitchen table as loudly as he possibly could. Letters rained down on the freshly scrubbed linoleum, squeezed out from between the magazines and catalogs.

"Letter for you! Looks like a guy's handwriting!" Reuben said, chortling.

"No, it's not," Sadie said automatically, before examining the handwriting.

She held very still as she gripped the blue envelope with both hands. She felt a slight tremor as the handwriting leaped at her.

Reuben was right!

Oh, had Mark done the same thing again?

Her breath came in quick gasps that she struggled to hide from Mam and Reuben. Rebekah peered over her shoulders.

Oh, please God, no. Not now.

With shaking hands, she tore open the envelope, unfolded the single white sheet of writing paper, flipped it over, and read the signature.

Daniel King.

She sagged in the recliner in pure relief, her limbs folding as if the joints were liquid.

Dear Sadie,

> *I am miserable. I cannot forget you. I'm almost 2,000 miles away, and all I want to do is go back to Montana. I think I love you. Why don't you write to me?*

Sadie's fist went to her forehead, and she thumped it without thinking.

I didn't write because Mark became a very important part of my life, that's why, she thought wryly.

His letter was full of his praise for Sadie and reproach for the terrible distance between them and his aching heart. Sadie folded the letter slowly, then shoved it back into the envelope, her eyes unseeing.

He was one of the nicest people she had ever met. She knew he would be an easy person to love, to marry. He was so normal, with such a good heart, a grounded attitude, a wonderful appetite for life and love.

Suddenly, she was unsure about seeing Mark that night. She felt waves of doubt lift and bear her away, floating up and out, dipping low as a wave dropped her, and then rising up when the next one came. She drifted in an ocean of restlessness that never ceased movement.

Daniel. His hair streaked blond. His laughing eyes. Always smiling. So easy to understand and...well, get along with. Her life would be so easy.

Reuben peered at her. His intense gaze brought her back to earth.

"Well, who was it? Mark skipping out on you again?"

As if in a trance, Sadie shook her head.

"No, not this time."

Perhaps he should. Perhaps he should go back to Pennsylvania and find his English mother and all his siblings and leave her entirely out of his complicated life. He'd never be normal.

"Mam, I think I'll go to my room. I need to sort through some of my clothes and organize them."

Mam looked up from her dishwashing.

"You sure it's your closet you need to organize?"

"Now you sound like Dorothy."

Mam laughed.

"May I read his letter? It's from that Lancaster boy, right?"

Sadie smiled at her mother. "Someday," she whispered.

Mam shook her head as she sprinkled detergent on a kettle and resumed her scrubbing.

Chapter 15

Sadie pulled the heavy, purple hairbrush through the wet, thick strands of her hair. She winced as she thought how nice it would be if her hair were not quite as thick and heavy.

Mam said in the older days, it was strictly forbidden to cut women's hair, no matter how long it became. She remembered seeing her aunt with hair hanging to the back of her knees. She would wind it around the palm of her hand over and over, securing it with nearly two dozen hair pins.

Now, Sadie and her sisters kept their hair trimmed to below the shoulders, making it easier to wash and dry. Even the coverings fit better, although she knew it was still a controversial subject. Some of the more conservative mothers absolutely forbid their girls to cut their hair.

With a fine-tooth comb Sadie drew her hair up and back, securing it with barrettes.

That didn't look right. The whole top of her head looked horribly lopsided. She unclipped the barrettes and started over, leaning as close to the mirror as she could, drawing the comb slowly and carefully through her thick tresses.

Still not right, she thought grimly.

She ground her teeth in frustration at the sound of loud, thumping footsteps. It could only be Reuben. Now what did he want, the nosy little beggar?

"What?" she said to the mirror, as his beanie-encased head appeared in the doorway.

"Mark's here!"

"No, he's not."

"I know he's not!"

Yelps of glee accompanied his retreat as Sadie shook her head and snorted. Now her nerves were on edge for sure.

She sat on the bed, one side of her hair combed and held with clips, the other side hanging heavily down the side of her face. As she looked in the mirror, it struck her that her appearance matched the state of her heart. Unfinished. Two-sided. One side so different from the other.

She wished Daniel King lived in Montana. Perhaps if she saw him again, she would know if he was the one God meant for her.

How could you tell?

She had no time to feel alone after Daniel left. Mark had reappeared immediately. He was at the ranch, in church on Sunday, involved with the incident with the blue diesel truck and Paris. They had talked of his past again, which was very meaningful to their relationship.

But surely if she loved Daniel, she wouldn't be so content to stay here in Montana and love Mark. Hadn't she felt so clearly once more that he was the one?

Getting up, she fixed her hair again and decided it looked all right this time. She had already planned what to wear, so there was no hesitation at the closet. She slipped the paprika-colored dress over her head. It was a dark burnt, but muted orange color.

Orange and yellow were considered much too flamboyant for plain girls. Pink was frowned upon but tolerated for some occasions. This color, Sadie was sure, would cause a stir if worn in church. But this was a Saturday evening date, so she could push the envelope a bit.

She loved the fabric, the way the pleats hung in luxurious folds from her waist. The sleeves were just below the elbow and fit perfectly. Yes, she liked this dress.

She put on her covering with confidence, pinned it, then sprayed cologne from her collection in the drawer.

Mmm. That certainly was the most wonderful smell.

She straightened the comforter on her bed, adjusted the shams, picked up a pair of hose that had a run in them. Mam said she would go to the poorhouse buying stockings for her girls if they didn't try to be more careful, so Sadie felt a bit guilty as she stuffed them in her brown wicker wastebasket.

There. She was ready for her first genuine date with Mark Peight.

He arrived on time, his horse and buggy spotless. He looked so good, Sadie felt weak just walking toward him. His hair was black, so thick and dark, combed just right. Was it carelessly or carefully? Whatever it was, he took her breath away, as usual.

His eyes never left hers as she walked toward him, one elbow leaning on the shoulder of his horse. He was wearing a white, short-sleeved shirt, which only made his complexion appear darker, his perfect mouth widening into a smile of welcome.

"You look like a leaf still hanging on a birch tree in that color!"

Sadie laughed. "It's not yellow!"

"It's pretty, whatever color it is."

His elbow dropped, and he glanced toward the house. "No hugging, right?"

"Better not."

He nodded. "You want to drive to town for ice cream?"

"I'll get my coat."

The ice cream was wonderful. They ate it while seated at a small table on the porch of the little shop, the wind just nippy enough to add color to their cheeks. They talked easily about everyday, uncomplicated subjects, careful to keep the serious things hidden. Sadie learned he liked coffee ice cream, also her favorite. She took that as a good omen rather than a coincidence.

Daniel King wasn't in her thoughts at all. She studied Mark as she ate her ice cream, admiring his hands once more. She felt as if she would never doubt her love for him ever again.

That is, until she saw a man leaning against his white pickup truck. He looked so much like Daniel, for a second Sadie thought it was him. That smile! Her hand went to her chest as her breath left her body, making a soft whooshing sound.

"What's wrong with you?" Mark asked watching the color leave her face.

Sadie waved a hand reassuringly. "Oh, it's nothing. I just thought..."

She stopped, knowing she had gone too far, like trying to park a car and hitting the curb. She should just stop, not telling him what she thought.

"What?"

"Oh, it's nothing Mark. Just someone I thought I knew."

"That guy leaning against his truck?"

Sadie said nothing.

"Okay. Be that way. Don't talk. You thought it was that guy from Lancaster. That Daniel King. Your knight in shining armor who rescued you from the evildoers who shot at Paris."

His words dripped with sarcasm. Like acid they ate away at her sense of well-being, destroying her confidence by the second.

"No, no, it wasn't him."

"'Course not, but you thought it was. Your face turned white as a ghost."

"No, no, it didn't. I mean, he's... It's nothing."

Their ice cream finished, they walked toward the horse and buggy. It was tied to a sturdy hitching rail provided by the store owners for the Amish to use, but it was behind the store, and they had to walk through an alley between two brick buildings.

Suddenly, Mark stopped and lowered his dark head. Sadie instinctively backed away. She felt the porous texture of the brick with her hands as she shrank farther from him. He had suddenly turned ominous, his features slated with gray, his shoulders hulking.

"That is precisely why I don't date," he said in a tone Sadie had never heard before.

He stalked off as a man possessed. She followed him slowly, shocked and afraid. She never once thought he would leave. Not once. The rasp of the wheels against the concrete of the hitching rack proved her wrong.

She ran, her hand outstretched. "Wait! Mark! Please wait!"

The horse lunged against its collar. The buggy swung at a dangerous level as it careened around a bend, spraying gravel. Then, around the next set of buildings, it disappeared.

Darkness had fallen. The only light was from the yellow street lamps and the bluish-white lights from the storefronts. She stood in the middle of the alley, biting down on her lower lip. No matter how hard she tried not to cry, she cried anyway. She cried for the hopelessness of their love and their relationship, which was as delicate as dominoes standing in a line, ready to topple at the slightest touch. Like the dominoes, their relationship had no foundation at all. It was all because he was handsome, and she was a hopeless flirt.

Self-hatred infused her being until she sagged down on the concrete around the hitching rail and let the blame overtake her. It was all her fault.

She should have shut Daniel firmly out of her life, and she hadn't. His attention had soothed her and puffed up her vanity. Now she had lost Mark because of it.

Sadie lifted her head and assessed her situation. She was alone in town. She needed to call someone to come get her, but who? If she called an Amish driver, the whole community would know what happened. There was no such thing as asking them to keep a secret; they spread gossip to every Amish person they drove.

Did Mark really leave her? Surely he'd be back. This was simply unreal.

She considered walking home, but decided against that as soon as she heard booming rock music in a low-riding car that crept past, the occupants yelling at her as they drove by.

No way.

She was still crying, so that had to be taken care of first. She dug into her purse, grabbed a wad of tissues, and honked her nose into them. Then she dabbed at her eyes and cheeks and drew a long, steadying breath.

What about James Sevarr. Dorothy's Jim. She had his phone number in her purse. All she needed was a phone.

Summoning all her courage, Sadie re-entered the brightly lit shop and stood in line. When she got to the counter, she timidly asked if she could use the phone to make a local call. The proprietor was very kind, simply falling over himself in his eagerness to help her, which almost made Sadie cry again.

Jim answered the phone, said he was laid up with gout, but Dorothy would come get her.

She had never felt quite as alone as she did waiting for Dorothy. She sat at the very same table she had shared with Mark earlier, trying to keep from crying again.

When Dorothy appeared in her rusted orange Honda, her head not nearly as far above the steering wheel as it should have been, Sadie didn't know whether to laugh or cry. As it was, she did a lot of both, first blubbering and sniffing and blowing her nose, then shaking and laughing hysterically when Dorothy said she would go after that Mark Peight in his horse and buggy and run him off the road.

Dorothy turned the wheel abruptly when they came to the first stoplight, saying she was hungry for Wendy's chili.

So they sat in a blue booth beneath an orange light, ate chili and french fries, sipped Cokes, and talked.

Sadie was belittled. She took the blame for the whole incident and told Dorothy so, which immediately set her off like a rocket.

"Now see here, Sadie, you're gettin' yerself into a dangerous position you are. It's like them abusers. They slam their wife or whatever and git 'em so befuddled, they actually think it's their own fault. It happens over and over, and you're too thick in the head to see it.

"He ain't to be trusted. You mark my words, Sadie Miller."

Dorothy was angry to the point where she seriously wanted to go to Mark's house, confront him, and make him apologize. Sadie shook her head adamantly, of course.

The thing was, Sadie knew that Mark's past drove him to act the way he did. Dorothy didn't know much about Mark's difficult childhood. For all she knew, Mark was perfectly normal. But Sadie could not, in good conscience, betray Mark's trust and tell Dorothy the secrets of his past. No, she was the only one to blame.

Between gigantic spoonfuls of chili, Dorothy said more than once, "You deserve better, my love. You deserve better."

"You want a vanilla frosty?"

Sadie shook her head.

Dorothy heaved herself out of the booth, her green polyester slacks catching on the table. She tucked her red plaid shirt securely into the elastic waistband, pulling the pants up as high as they would go. The bottom of the pant legs barely reached her beige-colored ladies shoes from the Dollar General, but she strode purposefully up to the counter, returning in short order with a large vanilla frosty.

"Mmm, these are the best thing ever! Don't know how they git 'em so creamy."

Dorothy shoveled great mouthfuls of the creamy milkshake into her mouth, then she suddenly leaned back and clapped a palm to her forehead.

"Oh, shoot! Brain freeze. Ate too fast."

She leaned over the table, moaning in agony, saying, "Whew!" over and over, until a kindly old gentleman came to their table and asked if there was anything he could do to help. His only answer was a glare of pain from Dorothy and a tart reply about hadn't he ever seen anyone with a brain freeze? So he shuffled off bewildered.

Sadie slumped over the table, her shoulders rounded with dejection.

"So now you know, Sadie. He ain't for you," Dorothy concluded, carefully tilting the paper frosty container as she scraped out the last of the ice cream. "No, sir, he ain't."

Then she put down the empty cup and reached over and held both of Sadie's hands as gently and softly as the touch of an angel.

"I know this ain't your way, Sadie, but I'm prayin' for you right here this minute. You need it, honeybun."

And she prayed in a beautiful singsong voice, the most compassionate prayer Sadie had ever heard.

"Heavenly Father, I know you're watching over my Sadie girl. You really need to get serious and show her the way. Right now her future is in the balance. Thank you for providing everything she needs to get through this difficult time. Continue to bless her with your strength and your wisdom. Amen."

"Thank you," Sadie whispered, her voice choked with emotion.

"Now don't you go thinkin' I prayed that to be seen and heard of men. I didn't. God just needs to hear some serious prayin' going on right now. That Mark don't trust you right, and you so in love with him. You're like a love-sick little puppy, so you are."

The ride home was quiet, except for Dorothy's occasional "rifting," as she called it. She rubbed her ample stomach and complained of indigestion, saying she hadn't taken her usual dose of Gas-X yet today, and here it was almost bedtime.

Sadie was numb to any kind of emotion. She answered when she was expected to do so, laughed when it was required of her.

When the orange Honda wheezed to a stop at the back porch of the Miller house, Sadie pushed a 20-dollar bill in Dorothy's direction, which she declined furiously, saying that's what was the matter with this world—no one did anything for anyone anymore unless they expected to be paid.

Sadie went inside to find her parents in their usual recliners. They looked up with concern when she came in.

"You're home early? With a vehicle?" Mam asked, her eyes round with concern.

"Something came up. Mark had to leave early," Sadie said, averting her eyes as she made her way up the stairs.

"Goodnight," Mam said, quietly, then raised her eyebrows and rolled her eyes in Dat's direction.

Dat shook his head and resumed his reading.

✿ ✡ ✿

Sadie woke with a groan, punching her pillow in frustration when she thought of the events of the night before.

Reuben worked on a jigsaw puzzle, humming the same tune under his breath the whole entire morning until Sadie thought she might lose her good sense and sound mind.

She wandered out to the barn, but Paris was at the far end of the pasture. Sadie didn't feel like calling her, so she let her go. Besides, there was no use calling the horse if she couldn't go riding.

Uncle Samuel's came for supper, but Sadie was in no mood to visit with his loud and jovial family.

So she sat in her room instead. She wanted to answer Daniel King's letter, but was too numb to think of anything to say. Picking up a book, she read halfheartedly, wishing the whole time that she had never met Mark Peight.

She was getting terribly hungry when Anna opened the door very quietly, slipped inside, and sat down on the beige-colored loveseat. Her eyes were large and round with concern. Sadie noticed a definite jutting of her collarbones and a thinness around her neck.

"What happened, Sadie?"

"I'd rather not talk about it."

"Seriously?"

"Yes."

"I need to talk about the vomiting."

Sadie looked at Anna, really looked.

"Have you done it again?"

"No."

Anna's eyes were downcast, averted, and she was completely unable to raise them to meet Sadie's gaze.

"You're telling a *schnitza*."

"I didn't feel good."

"Did you force yourself to throw up?"

"No."

"I don't believe you."

"I don't have to force myself anymore. My stuff comes up real easy."

"Anna!"

Sadie was horrified. All the thoughts of Mark and his sordid behavior flew from her mind, replaced by a concern much more immediate and serious.

Things like this only happened to English people with serious body issues. Not her own little sister! Where had it started? Were they all so concerned about their appearances, their weight, their figures, who was cute and who was not? Was it God punishing them for being too worldly?

All these thoughts crowded into Sadie's mind like a rampage of fear and anxiety, until she remembered Dorothy's prayer. It rose in its power and light, pushing back the onslaught of fear and panic.

Yes, God, please help us, bless us with wisdom and understanding for each other. For Mark, for Anna, for us all.

To get at the reason she hated her body, Anna would need compassion and understanding, but she would also need a firm hand. Should Mam be the one to deal with Anna?

So many problems, so many decisions.

✿ ✡ ✿

It was only at work the following week that Sadie found a measure of peace. It came by way of Bertie Orthman, of all people, the aging gardener and veteran of a troubled life.

She was emptying a large dishpan of potato peelings into the compost bin beside the lily bed, when Bertie's balding head protruded from the window, followed by his arm holding a steaming mug of tea. He was chortling with glee.

"Come here, Sadie girl. Lookee what I got. My old bones is starting to ache about this time of the year, and nothing helps like a hot cup of tea with milk and sugar. Join me?"

Sadie looked over her shoulder, wondering if Dorothy was expecting her.

Bertie saw and hissed, "Come on. That old bat don't need to watch every move you make. She ain't the boss. Richard Caldwell is, and a right good one he is, too. Can't really put my finger on it, but he's made the biggest change in his life I ever seen. His heart's in the right place. It is. I ain't much for talkin' about the Lord, but he's not the way he used to be. One of life's mysteries. You don't always understand the way things work, so you just take the good with the bad, sorta sift through it."

He paused, waving his hand toward the door. "Come on."

Sadie entered the garden shed, her eyes adjusting to the dim interior. It was as clean as Dorothy's kitchen, every tool on its own hook, every insecticide and fertilizer in its own container labeled with blue tape. An electric hot plate took up one side of a small counter where a red teakettle bubbled merrily.

"This is so cute, Bertie!"

He beamed with Sadie's praise as they each sipped a mug of thick, fragrant tea. When the subject turned to Dorothy, Bertie smiled and declared confidently that if Dorothy ever became a widow, he would marry her in no time flat.

"A heart of gold, that's what she has. You know, people aren't always the way they seem. She's had a rough life. Her past is likely one of the most pitiful stories ever. She came through with flying colors, that girl did. Her dad was the town drunk, and she was beaten nearly every night. But she's smart enough to know that you can't blame other people for your past. You gotta make the best of it. She's feisty, and so she came through, so she did."

Is that how it was? Could people turn out all right, no

matter how mistreated they were?

She wanted to tell Bertie everything about Mark, then decided against it. It wasn't fair to Mark. He had confided solely in her, and she would not betray his trust.

But why did she care? Why? Especially after that abominable display of immaturity? It was all his foolish jealousy, his... his... She didn't know what.

Her miserable train of thought was derailed by Bertie's soothing voice.

"Yes, life ain't all roses. But them blessings, the good stuff, is all you need to take with you. You can get all tangled up in the thorns if you want to. Wallow in 'em for a little while, and all you do is hurt yourself. Jes' look at them two kids Dorothy took in. They don't understand what happened with their mama. They don't try and figger it out neither. They cried awhile, but they know that right now, Dorothy's their mama. Ain't it amazing, Sadie?"

Sadie nodded, smiling a smile that was less than genuine.

Bertie saw and nodded his head.

"You got troubles of your own, Sadie girl. That smile is playin' with shadows, as Mum used to say. It'll work out, it'll work out. The Man Above works it out. All you gotta do is wait. It'll be okay in the end."

Sadie thanked him for the tea. Her spirits definitely lifted as she made her way up the flagstone path to the kitchen. Patience. She would wait on the Lord, who would renew her strength, as the Bible said.

Chapter 16

THE FIRST SNOW OF THE SEASON DROVE IN HARD, icy little pellets that made pinging noises against the windows to the north. The lowered sky was gray-white, the air filled with the whirling iciness.

Inside the Miller house, the wood stove in the living room cracked and popped, the good, dry oak logs burning cheerily, the flames dancing against the glass front. The braided rug in front of the stove was charred in places where a hot coal had fallen out as Dat was loading up the stove with logs. He always muttered under his breath and stomped on the burning coal when it fell. Mam said it was better to ruin a rug than her hardwood floor. Mam kept the wide floorboards polished and varnished to perfection. She mopped that floor with a dry mop and furniture polish and got down on her hands and knees to wash it gently with vinegar water. Mam even had rules about moving furniture across it: the furniture had to be put on a thick rug that slid smoothly across the floorboards, so there'd be no scratch marks left behind. That hardwood floor was the one thing in which she admitted having pride.

Sadie sat in the big, brown recliner, a cotton throw across her knees, a box of tissues on the propane light stand with a few crumpled ones strewn across it. She had just come home from work at the ranch, putting in a whole day of overtime by working on Saturday. Her head cold made the day drag on and on. Dorothy was nursing a sore hip, so there had been very little love lost between them: Sadie coughing, sneezing, and blowing her nose, Dorothy limping and complaining the whole day long.

The only bright spot of the day had been listening to Marcellus and Louis conversing in Spanish as they sat on the kitchen floor sorting through yard after yard of white Christmas lights. The children coiled them carefully in separate containers so that Bertie could hang them from the eaves, doors, and windows, and even drape them across shrubs and pines.

The children's voices were always low with a wonderful lilt, a sort of singsong to their sentences that flowed and rippled in a sweet cadence. Sadie never tired of the sound.

Dorothy believed the children had lived in a mansion rather than an ordinary home. They had talked of gold faucets, sunken bathtubs, and servants. Cooking, cleaning, ironing, and laundry was all done by someone who was not their mother.

Richard Caldwell had spoken wisely, saying the jewels had to be shown to the police. Meanwhile, he had taken them to his personal safe-deposit box at the bank. First of all, he said, there was the danger of receiving stolen goods, and secondly, if the children did come from a wealthy home, there was a chance they may have been kidnapped for ransom.

All of these uncertainties had made Dat and Mam cautious and skeptical, stoic in their reluctance to becoming involved. It was not their way. The wealthy children were of the English, and what future could they possibly have among the Amish? What if they did agree to give them a home, and then the children grew to adulthood, found their biological parents, and became torn between two cultures?

Dat and Mam assured Sadie they would never leave them out in the cold. If no one else offered to take them, they would, but only temporarily. Sadie was distraught, her face pale, showing the strain of events on the ranch.

"But Dat, think about it. We're supposed to be the Christians, full of charity, love, and all that good stuff. And here we are refusing them.

"You have a point, Sadie. You really do. We won't leave them abandoned."

Sadie lifted her tear-filled eyes. "I don't think they were abandoned. I think... I still wonder if someone didn't just... I don't know. It's just a big mystery, and it drives me crazy. They talk of a huge lawn, golf, servants, pools. Why would they appear at the ranch in dirty, pitiful clothes, with a small drawstring bag of jewels?"

Mam put a hand on Sadie's shoulder. "Sadie, it's good you're concerned. But you must be careful. Listen to your father. He's right. I still think the perfect arrangement is to let Dorothy have them. Dat said that's all Jim talked about when he took him to the horse sale last week."

Sadie nodded. As usual, she could place her trust in her parents' decision. When they were side by side like that, when God had a hand in Dat's and Mam stood beside him, you just had to reach out your own hand and place it in Mam's. They were so rock-solid.

So the mystery of the children remained a large question mark. Dorothy said "them jewels in the pouch" would stay in the vault at the bank, and if she died, it all went back to Marcelona and Louise, as she called the children. The jewels sure weren't hers, and she wanted no part of them. All she needed was that piece of paper that made her and Jim legal foster parents of those precious angels sent straight from God.

Sadie often marveled at the perfect way God had taken care of those adorable children, who, without a doubt, came from a very troubled background.

Sadie laid back in the recliner and closed her eyes. Her head was throbbing. As soon as the Tylenol began working effectively she would have to write to Daniel King. She had not replied to his letter, struggling with indecision, and she could not put it off any longer.

The thought of that whole situation increased the pain in her temple, and she groaned silently.

She had just drifted into that blissful state between waking and sleeping, when you are only half-aware of your surroundings, when everything is soft and warm and safe.

Suddenly, the door opened with a bang, followed by a much louder one as it was flung shut. Then an agitated, "Mam!"

Sadie grimaced, rolled her head to the side, and said hoarsely, "Mam's not here, Reuben."

"Where's Dat?"

"They went to an auction at the fire hall. Why didn't you go along?"

Reuben did not bother answering.

"It's just that... Oh, Sadie!"

That was all he could say before his white face crumpled and he began to cry little-boy tears. He rubbed his eyes, gulping and making a desperate attempt to stop the tears.

Sadie pulled on the lever at the side of the recliner and sat up with a thump. Concern for Reuben made her forget her headache for the moment.

"Reuben! What is it?"

He twisted his body to hide his face in a throw pillow on the couch, then sat up abruptly, tears streaking his cheeks with a brown smudges where his fists had rubbed them.

"Sadie! It's so awful! I...I had my BB gun. I was shooting sparrows. You know Mam doesn't want those sparrows at the feeder?"

Sadie nodded, "Go on."

"Well, a flock of starlings flew behind the barn, and I guess I lost track of where I was, and before I realized it, I was in the horse pasture.

"I let Charlie out this afternoon because he kept carrying on so bad in his stall, and I thought he might settle down if he got some exercise. I got down to the lower pasture, and... Sadie! He's dead! Just exactly like Cody."

The last words were a sort of despairing scream, hoarse with fear and disbelief.

"I heard the shot. I saw them. They saw me. As soon as they saw me, they took off, but their car got stuck in a ravine. A little ditch.

"Sadie, I was never so scared in all my life. I had to take that chance. It was too late for poor Charlie, but I had to try to catch that license-plate number."

"Reuben, you didn't!"

"I did. I ran without thinking, taking the chance that they wouldn't shoot people. Boys.

"I was running so fast, the snow hurt my face. It's all a blur. They sat there, spinning their tires, revving the motor, but nothing happened. I kept running. One of the men jumped out, swearing and yelling, waving his arms. Then he leaned all his weight against the car. He was big and fat. Really heavy."

"The car? Wasn't it a blue pickup?"

Reuben shook his head.

"It was a low black car. One of those crazy ones. The fat man saw me then, got back in the car. The wheels spun and spun and spun. Blue smoke came out, and that's when I thought I wouldn't be able to get the license number. Because of the smoke. Then I saw it. As plain as day."

He paused, his face a mixture of painful fear and accomplishment.

"You're not going to believe this. It was one of those license plates that has words, whatever you call them. Special ones, where people spell names or nicknames."

Sadie nodded, leaned forward, her eyes intently on Reuben's face.

"What is it?"

"If I have it right, it's T-R-A-D-R, then a space, and J-O."

"Trader Joe?" Sadie asked.

"That's what it said."

"Oh, my goodness. Oh, my, Reuben. We have to get Dat. We have to contact the authorities. The police have to find these men. I'll call a driver, okay?"

She got out of the recliner in spite of a pounding headache and another fit of coughing. Catching her breath, she asked Reuben to go out to the pasture and make sure Charlie really was dead and not suffering alone in the snow.

Reuben shook his head, but obeyed without another word.

✻ ☼ ✻

The driver came quickly and took Sadie and Reuben to the fire hall where a lively quilt auction was being held. They found Dat without any trouble, and the news spread like wildfire.

The police arrived and questioned Reuben, who stood with his beanie pulled low on his forehead and his blue denim coat hanging open, the collar of his green shirt frayed and crooked.

Even so, his face was clean, his blue eyes direct and honest, and for a young Amish boy, he was very well-spoken. He stood by Dat and Sadie, explaining exactly what had happened in great detail. He politely addressed the uniformed police officers with a quiet, "No, sir" or "Yes, sir."

Sadie was impressed by her brother's fortitude and composure in the face of such a shocking event. Reuben was clear, articulate, and highly believable in his forth-right manner. He did not hide anything; neither was there any grandiose embellishment. It was a simple, truthful story explained clearly by a young boy. The police had no reason to doubt his honesty.

The police drove Dat, Sadie, and Reuben to the scene of the crime in the back of the police car. Reuben's eyes darted constantly from the leather holsters containing gleaming pistols, to the computer and the electronic gadgets on the dashboard, to the hats and gold wrist-watches they wore. He missed nothing at all.

True to Reuben's words, they found Charlie lying on his side, stretched out in the cold snow, his faithful life as a buggy horse over.

A huge lump welled in Sadie's throat as she remembered another time, another place, with Jim and Nevaeh—and seeing Mark Peight for the first time.

She swallowed her tears and felt sorry for Dat, who was struggling with his emotions as well. A driving horse was a close companion, that was the thing. There was a bond between horse and driver that didn't break easily. When the horse died, it was like losing a dear and close pet.

Charlie had been especially faithful with his plodding, steady gait. He started running and stopped readily when commanded. He never balked and seldom shied away from 18-wheelers or trucks with flapping canvas tarps or obnoxious motorcycles. He just took it all in stride and trotted right along.

Even in winter, Charlie was as sure-footed as a mule or a donkey. You could close both buggy windows, fasten them securely, and hold loosely to the reins through the small rectangular openings.

With Charlie, a buggy ride was relaxing. You could put your feet up on the dashboard, let the reins hang loose, and sing along to the steady clapping of his hooves. You could eat an ice cream cone with one hand and drive with the other, or if the ice cream dripped, you could hold the reins between your knees while you cleaned up the mess with a napkin.

If ever there was a horse you could describe as good, Charlie was it.

Sadie got down on her knees and stroked Charlie's neck, arranging the coarse black hair of his mane just so. The icy pellets of snow were already accumulating in the heavy brown hairs of his side, their staying a stark reminder of the lack of warmth, of life, within his body.

"Goodbye, Charlie. Thanks for all the good times," she whispered brokenly.

She looked up to see Reuben and Dat shaking hands with the policemen. She got up, and all three stood together, the silence a comfort that needed no words.

They turned to go in unison, their heads bent, shuffling softly through the snow. Their heads were bent with acceptance of another act of God in their lives. It didn't make sense, but they accepted it and bore it stoically.

A high whinny brought them back to reality.

Paris! Sadie had almost forgotten about her. Now Paris would be terribly lonely. She would whinny and whinny all day long, a relentless cry for Charlie to come back to her.

"Hear that, Dat? She's going nuts!" Sadie said, anxiety in her voice.

Dat nodded. "We have to get another horse immediately. Can't go to church on Sunday if we don't."

"Where will you get one?"

"They have that sale in Bath every month. Don't trust them, though. Too many drugged horses there."

That was how they found themselves at the livestock auction in Critchfield the following Friday evening. Jesse Troyer told Dat there were going to be a few of Owen Weaver's drivers there.

Clapping his shoulder the way he always did, laughing along with his words, Jesse had told Dat the local hearsay was that Owen was as honest as the day was long, only his days were just a bit shorter than most.

Dat had shaken his head at Jesse's generosity of spirit.

"You know, Jake, at the end of the day, we all have to make a living, and if Owen wants to tweak a few ends here or there, that's his choice. He's a horse-dealer, Amish or not."

There were as many Amish folks as English at the auction, Sadie decided. Or almost.

The acrid smell of the sawdust mingled with horse smells, dust, and burning charcoal-broiled burgers from the cheaply paneled kitchen, along with the sounds of squawking chickens and bleating sheep. It was all the part of the quintessential country auction.

Sadie loved a lively animal auction. Being seated high up on the elevated rows of built-in chairs was the closest she would ever come to sitting in the bleachers of a ball game, an event strictly forbidden by their *ordnung*. Amish usually did not attend organized sports, whether as viewers or as participants. The auction, however, was permitted as necessary to buy a good driving horse.

Many of the older men came to the auction barn in Critchfield almost every week. It was their source of entertainment, something to look forward to after a week on the job. They ate their cheeseburgers and french fries, drank strong coffee, and visited with the grizzled old farmers and ranchers. They watched the sales of various animals, listened to the local gossip, then returned home to their wives who clucked in consternation over their quilts or embroidery as their husbands related all the good stories to them.

Small children hid shyly behind their fathers' trouser legs, but older ones ran loose, clinging to gates like little squirrels in their agility, running across corridors,

laughing and shouting, their faces sticky with the lolli-
pops, Nerds, and packets of Skittles they consumed.

Sadie knew their mothers, who prided themselves on
their housekeeping and child-rearing abilities, would be
shocked to see their faces sticky with the sugary treats
they bought at the counter, their hands dirty from holding
yet another baby lamb or goat. The indulging fathers, on
the other hand, took no notice, often busily engaged in
conversations with friends.

The auctioneer's voice rose and fell, amplified to crashing proportions by the loudspeakers on the wall. He sold
baby rabbits, roosters, hens, geese, and ducks, followed
by hordes of frightened, bleating sheep and goats.

That was the part Sadie did not like. The men who
herded them into the sales ring cracked their heavy whips
above the terrified animals' heads, creating a sort of panic
in them. Their eyes became wide with fright as they tried
to scale the wooden walls.

Why did they have to crack a whip at all? Simply to
show their inhumane authority, that was all. She often
felt like going down there and yanking that beastly whip
out of their hands and flinging it on them to see how they
liked it. The whip should not be allowed. A good border
collie or a simple herding stick would do the job just as
well, she felt sure. She sighed with relief when the last
baby lamb disappeared through the steel gate.

The auctioneer took a hefty swig of his warm Mountain Dew and began to talk about horses. The horse auction began with a team of magnificent Belgians, led by
Owen Weaver himself. His portly frame looked shorter
than ever, dwarfed by the huge beasts on either side of
him.

He took the microphone and expounded expertly on the unequaled merits of these fine horses. His flowery descriptions of the animals showed he was obviously a veteran horse-seller. As his words flowed, Sadie grinned to herself, remembering Jesse Troyer's comment to her father. Surely Owen's day wasn't very long at this auction.

The team was sold for $6,000, but no one could tell if Owen was pleased or not. No emotion showed on his blank face. A true professional, that one.

A black Percheron was sold after that, followed by a string of driving horses. Sadie caught Dat's eye, and he gave her a thumbs-up signal accompanied by a hearty wink. She raised her eyes with a questioning look. Dat answered by jutting his chin toward the gate. Sadie turned in time to see Mark Peight riding Chester.

The whole auction barn seemed to tilt at an angle, and everything went black, but only for a moment. She was unaware of Dat's bidding, of the auctioneer's voice, of Anna and Reuben bouncing up and down with glee when Dat bought the black gelding they wanted him to buy.

Why was Mark selling Chester?

When the gate opened, Chester pranced out. Mark held him back. He looked relaxed, leaning back on the horse, one hand on his thigh. He eased him into a perfect canter, then a trot, moving as one with his horse.

The bidding escalated. The auctioneer's helpers stepped out, stretched their arms, and yelled piercing cries of "Ye-ep!" each time a bidder nodded his head. When the sum reached $5,000 the crowd erupted into whistles and applause. Sadie felt goose bumps on her arms and tears pricking her eyes.

Oh, Mark!

She knew then that she had to talk to him. At the very least, she had to let him see her and watch the reaction on his face. It would be easier to know if he hated her than to not know how he felt at all. If he rejected her, it would be her final answer. Then she could reply to Daniel King's letter.

On shaking, unsteady legs, she got up and excused herself as she wedged past the crowd of bidders. Biting down hard on her lower lip, she ran down the remaining stairs, hurried to the right and up the steep wooden steps lending to the horse pens.

She didn't notice the smell of hay or the rancid odor of fresh manure. She only knew she had to see Mark.

He was leading Chester, a girl in jeans with blond hair hanging to her waist following him. He listened to what she was saying, a smile on his face, as he tied Chester in a pen with two other horses.

Sadie hung back, afraid. She twisted her burgundy-colored apron in her hand. She smoothed her hair, lifted her chin, and stepped out.

"Mark!" Her voice cracked, and she hastily cleared her throat. She called him again.

"Mark!"

He stopped and looked in her direction. As if in a dream, his eyes found hers. What was the expression in them? Yes. It was anger. He hated her, wanted nothing to do with her.

Then...oh...then...his brown eyes lightened, and he came toward her. His mouth widened into a soft grin of welcome. The light in his eyes was not hatred; it wasn't even annoyance or disappointment. But, oh, wonder of wonders, he was overjoyed to see her!

He didn't stop until he had wrapped her firmly in his arms, bent over her, murmuring words of endearment into her ear. Her ribs hurt with the pressure of his hugs, and she suddenly became aware of her surroundings.

"Mark. Mark! Someone will see."

"Let them."

"Mark, please, let me go."

He did, then stepped back, looked deeply into her eyes and said, "I'm sorry."

That was all, but it was enough. It was more than enough. It was a treasure chest filled to overflowing with precious gold coins worth much more than anything Sadie had ever owned. She was rich, wealthy beyond measure. God had provided the answer she so desperately sought.

He was only human. His apology was his way of taking responsibility for his own actions. He did not blame his mother or his father, his past, anyone, or anything. He had done wrong, he knew it, and he repented. The coins in the treasure chest of this love glittered and sparkled.

The blond-haired girl stood awkwardly at the gate, annoyance written all over her face. She cleared her throat, a nasty twang to her voice as she said, "Excuse me?"

Mark apologized, politely showed her out, then returned to Sadie's side.

"We need to talk."

"You want a greasy, sloppy, burned cheeseburger?" she asked.

He laughed. Oh, that beautiful sound! Then he caught her hand in his and took her to a stained table at the top of the stairs, in the smoky, plastic-paneled dining room of the food stand.

They took huge bites from the cheeseburgers, that were slathered with heavy mayonnaise, thick slices of tomato, dill pickle, onion, and lettuce, and served on cheap white rolls. They shared an order of greasy steak fries loaded with salt, pepper, and ketchup, wiping the excess off their faces with lots of thin paper napkins from the smudged holder against the wall.

He talked a lot. More than she had ever heard him. It seemed as if that one, solitary "I'm sorry" had opened a floodgate of goodness. But he confessed he still had a difficult time with trust.

"I just go a bit crazy when I think you are attracted to someone else, even if you say you love me. I'm sure my mother told my father that she loved him many times, and he believed her. That's what terrifies me. I'm afraid that I will give my heart to you, and that you'll hurt me, just like I've always been hurt. I trust no one, least of all, you. It's awful having to tell you these things, but I hope you understand why I overreacted to situations that normal guys can just shrug off."

Sadie nodded.

Later he would tell her that he had never loved her more than at that moment when she nodded, quietly understanding and accepting his insecurities, his *bupplich* attitude. Her love was the strongest chain he had ever had to hang onto, especially when the quicksand of his past threatened to submerge him yet again.

People of every kind came up to their table to talk to them. They smiled politely, endured the needless chatter, but were eager for everyone to let them alone.

It was Owen Weaver himself who told them that Fred Ketty had spread the rumor that they had broken up. She was in town and saw them eating ice cream together.

On her way home again, Sadie was sitting by herself at the same table. She figured they had an argument and stopped the friendship. So Owen had to look twice to see if it was Jake's Sadie sitting there with Mark.

Mark was at a loss for words, but Sadie rescued him smoothly, saying Mark had to move his horse from the hitching rack, which was the truth.

Owen shifted the toothpick in his mouth, scratched his rotund stomach, and laughed good-naturedly.

"Ah, that Fred Ketty. She's a sharp one. You have to give her that. Between yard sales and the Laundromat in town, she sees a'plenty, now, don't she?"

He clapped a thick hand on Mark's shoulder, rattling the ice in his glass of Coke. Mark grabbed his glass, held on to it firmly, not daring to take another sip with the affable Owen ready to pound his shoulder at any moment.

"So why are you selling that horse of yours, Mark? He's a beauty."

Mark grimaced, then slid over in the booth, turning his upper body to see Owen better. Also, Sadie guessed, to get out from under the descending, good-natured hand clapping on his shoulder at regular intervals.

"I have too many. It's turning into a habit. I come to the horse sale and think I have to buy one."

Owen's toothpick fell out when he grinned widely, nodding his head until his hat slid sideways. "I can see it. I can see it! Young man like you, a paycheck and no wife to spend it. Ah, enjoy your horses. Soon enough you won't be able to afford it with a good wife and a buggy-load of youngsters to take care of that paycheck."

He gave Sadie a meaningful wink. She would gladly have slid under the table and stayed there.

Mark and Sadie continued to talk into the evening. It was only when a seriously worried Anna came through the door, her face pale and her eyes burning with unshed tears, that Sadie remembered the rest of her family. She clapped a hand to her mouth and gasped.

"Anna! Over here!"

Anna was so relieved, she sagged into the booth beside Sadie and laid her head on her shoulder.

"Where in the world did you go? Dat is frantic!"

"She's with me," Mark said, smiling. "She's with her boyfriend."

Anna sat straight up, clearly flustered.

"You guys are just different. One day you're happy, and the next day you're...whatever."

Mark laughed, and Sadie put her arm warmly around Anna's shoulders, hugging her close.

Chapter 17

Sadie wrote to Daniel King on a plain white sheet of notebook paper, telling him in the kindest way she could about her relationship with Mark. She felt quite sure Lancaster County was full of girls he could date. He was close to his family, so it was likely best for him to stay and move on with his life.

That winter proved to be the turning point in her relationship with Mark. They went to hymn singings and supper crowds where the youth would assemble and visit. They spent Saturday evenings with other couples, most often Kevin and Leah. And when they went on dates alone, they stayed up and talked for hours.

Sadie slowly adjusted to Mark's personality. There were times when he withdrew into a dark place inside himself, and he didn't speak unless she spoke first. Even then, his answers were curt, accusing, as if she had done something to make him feel so down. No amount of questioning or pleading made any difference. These times were when he felt lowest about himself, and if she tried to talk him out of it, he only pulled her down with him. So she learned to leave him alone at such moments.

He had never promised her the relationship would be easy, but was it always going to be this way?

Anna lost weight all winter long, a strange flush in her cheeks every evening. She was taller than Rebekah now and nearly as tall as Sadie. None of her dresses fit anymore, so the girls helped Mam to sew new ones for her.

Sadie spent hours discussing Anna's problem with Mam and her sisters, but everyone had a different opinion, so nothing was ever resolved.

Mam maintained her stance that as long as Anna kept a reasonable weight, ate good, healthy food, what was the harm? Everyone ate the occasional doughnut and wished they hadn't.

Leah tended to side with Mam. Rebekah thought she should be taken to the same doctor that had made such a wonderful difference in Mam's life.

Too much money. No insurance.

What about the money they received for finding the stolen horses?

Mam's hospital bill.

What about the rest of it?

It was Sadie's.

And on and on, with no real conclusion.

Sadie still felt the same. Anna needed a horse. So did Reuben. If Dat didn't do anything by springtime, then she would take matters into her own hands.

Sadie noticed the change in Anna just as spring arrived. The reason she remembered was because it was the same day that she first heard the Chinook.

Dat called it that. It was the first warm air of spring, blowing from the south so softly it was barely noticeable. The light sighing sound was nature's way of breaking down the long icicles that hung from the eaves. It would still take weeks and weeks for the Chinook to wear down the snowdrifts.

Sadie did not sleep well the night she heard the Chinook. Mark had gone home early from their date, but that wasn't what kept her awake. It was the steady dripping of the melting icicles that kept her up all night.

She would have loved to burrow into her pillows, pull the comforter up over her head, and sleep until dinnertime. She was tired, cold, and in no mood to sit on a hard bench for three hours or be stuffed in the surrey with all her sisters and Reuben.

She burned her fingers on the broiler pan when she retrieved the toast and snarled at Anna because of it. Mam scolded her in clipped tones, telling her to stop taking out her foul mood on Anna.

Her dippy egg was undercooked, and Sadie swallowed her nausea as she pushed the plate away. Mam never finished a dippy egg properly. More nausea pushed at her throat as she watched Mam dip a corner of her toast into a glob of swimming egg white. Maybe she should make her own eggs from now on.

Dat slurped his coffee in the most annoying way, and Reuben dumped almost the whole plastic container of strawberry jam on his toast. He laid the sticky knife on the tablecloth and promptly set his elbow on top of it. He devoured almost half the toast in one bite. That was the last straw.

"This family has the most indecent table manners," Sadie said tartly, wincing at the sour taste of orange juice in her mouth.

Dat and Mam looked at her with surprise, Anna ducked her head in embarrassment, but Reuben shoved the remainder of his toast in his mouth and blurted, "Sour old maid!"

"I am not an old maid," she fired back.

"Why doesn't Mark marry you then?" Reuben asked, victory shining from his eyes.

Sadie swallowed her anger, gathered all her common sense and Christian virtue—it was Sunday morning, after all—and told Reuben that he'd better get ready for church.

✿ ✡ ✿

Her mood lifted when she entered the *kessle-haus* and her friends greeted her with warm hugs and girl talk. This was a part of her world that she so often forgot to appreciate, she knew.

The girls walked to their seats, and a few minutes later, the boys came in and sat on the opposite side of the shop, facing the girls.

The singing began, the voices ebbing and flowing as they always did. Out of the corner of her eye, Sadie noticed Emery Hershberger's Leon leaning a bit to the left, looking at something, then correcting his posture again.

At 15, he was turning into quite an attractive young man, with a tall, easy gait, wide shoulders, and auburn hair. He used to be a heavy-set red-haired boy with a spattering of freckles and a loud, obnoxious voice. Now, his hair had turned darker and his complexion settled into a smooth, healthy color. He certainly was not the boy he used to be. Why hadn't she noticed that before?

Leon leaned over again, and this time Sadie leaned forward ever so slightly to see the object of his attention. Her eyes traveled Leon's line of vision, and she nearly gasped aloud.

Anna!

Her head was bowed demurely, the way it should have been, but there was a decided blush coloring her wan cheeks. Her thick lashes swept them as she kept her eyes downcast, her brown hair swept up in a thick, shining mass below her white covering. Her dress was the color of the ferns that grew beneath the pines on the ridge, a woodland color that complemented Anna's complexion.

Oh, my Anna! My dear little insecure sister. You are growing up, blossoming into a maiden of the forest, right beneath our eyes. A beautiful young girl, unnoticed for so long, with all the attention going to your older sisters.

Sadie could barely look at Leon. She was an intruder, an outsider who had no business looking for any sign between them, and yet, she couldn't help but see what was so painfully evident.

Ah, Anna. You're not yet 16. So innocent and unspoiled, so pitifully sure you're overweight and ugly.

What was best?

Sadie felt old and a bit careworn at that moment. It seemed as if she and Mark were an outdated grocery item to be taken off the shelf and replaced with a fresh one.

She grinned, then bent her head. Boy, wouldn't that get Mark all fired up when she told him?

✿ ✡ ✿

That afternoon, when Mark stopped at the porch to pick up Sadie, his horse and buggy as immaculate as always, she greeted him lightheartedly. It was a wondrous thing to be so happy and confident in their relationship. She marveled at the natural way they could be together, even at the simple act of climbing into the buggy and sitting beside him. That intimacy was a privilege. They talked easily now, with no self-consciousness—words, expressions, smiles, a familiar part of their lives.

The first thing she told him was about Leon Hershberger and Anna. Mark raised his eyebrows, smiling. Sadie never tired of his smile. When they were 80 years old, that smile would still amaze her. However, it didn't stay. The horse plodded on gaily, but a sort of coldness crept over the buggy's interior.

Sadie talked on, then watched him a bit uncomfortably before blurting out, "Is there...something wrong?"

He said nothing.

Then after wiping the wooden dashboard of the buggy with his handkerchief, he cleared his throat.

"My mother wrote me a letter."

His words had the impact of a sledgehammer. Sadie went cold all over. She became numb, then senseless, blinded by blackness for a second, before her heart began to beat again, but harder.

Oh, no. Now what?

They'd come so far. Would it all be stripped away now?

She knew there would be no easy way out of this. Dread in all its forms hovered over her. His whole past would be flung in his face yet again, this time in physical form.

Oh, dear God, look upon us with mercy. *Barmherzikeit.*

Her voice was very small when she said, "And? What did she write?"

Mark's hand reached over and pulled at the handle of the small wooden door built into the dashboard. It was a place in the buggy to put lighters, small flashlights, clean handkerchiefs, or tissues. It was the catchall for necessities, like a vehicle's glove compartment. Sadie thought it could rightfully be called a glove compartment, as there was almost always a pair of gloves in the back of it. You had to wear gloves to drive a horse in cold weather, especially if it was an unruly one, opening the window for better control.

He handed her a plain white envelope, saying nothing, his jaw set in that firm line.

She looked at him, questioning.

"Go ahead. Read it."

With shaking hands, she removed the letter from the envelope and unfolded it. Just an ordinary sheet of writing paper. There was no date or return address. The handwriting was cursive, neat, the type many Amish teachers teach their pupils.

Mark,

I got wind of where you live through the Internet, an object of the devil for you, but a necessity for me. HA.

Sadie's eyebrows turned down. She looked at Mark. "Wow."

Mark remained still, a statue of control.

I'm still out in the world and I plan on staying here. My kids are scattered all over. They know who I am, but they don't care about me. I guess I deserve that, I don't know. You're the only one I can't find. You are the oldest of the pack.

What a bunch of kids I had! Have had almost as many husbands. I'm on number four. Married this guy for his money. Can't stand him. I can't sleep at night, have to take all kinds of junk to put me to sleep.

I want to see you. Sure hope you're not Amish. Are you

married? If you are, bring your wife.

This is my home phone number. Please call soon.

I still do love you, you know. At least I wrote now, to let you know I care.

Your mother,
Amelia Van Syoc

Sadie folded the letter slowly and put it neatly into the envelope. She smoothed the dust blanket over her knees before daring to look at Mark. His expression remained unreadable.

Carefully, she laid a hand on his arm, then slid it underneath his arm and laid her head on his shoulder, tears forming beneath her eyelids.

She just could not imagine. How could his own mother, his flesh and blood, be so callous?

Slowly, Mark put down the reins, turned, and crushed her to him. He held her as if she was his only hope of rescue, the single life preserver in a swollen sea, where dark troughs of rolling water threatened to take him down into the awful abyss of his past.

Sadie slid her arms around his wide shoulders, willing him to know that she would remain by his side where she belonged. She would help him to keep his head above water during the rough times.

He groaned, a broken cry, then kissed her with a new intensity.

"I love you so much, Sadie," he said hoarsely as tears fell on the shoulder of her black woolen coat.

"I love you, too, Mark. I love you more with each passing day."

He gathered up the reins, then laughed quietly as he

wiped his face.

"Good thing Eclipse keeps trotting right along, isn't it?"

"He's a good horse," Sadie replied, slipping her hand into his. She loved holding Mark's hand. He had perfect hands, she thought.

"So now, what will you do?" she asked quietly.

"Nothing for now. I want to pray about it, think about it. I have no clue where she is. If I go see her and she sees I'm Amish, she might shut the door in my face."

"I'll go with you," Sadie said instantly.

"You will?"

"Yes."

Yes, she would go. He needed her beside him every step of the way to support and encourage him. She would follow him to the ends of the earth.

He kissed her passionately again, and Sadie realized their love had reached a new level that brought another whole set of concerns. She must talk to Mark about their physical interactions, but she hardly knew how to open the subject without causing serious damage to his feelings—and his ego.

Dat and Mam had talked to her about their concerns, knowing Sadie and Mark did not hold to the strict code of distant courtship. Sadie was the oldest daughter, and they trusted her conscience, but dating is dating. They, too, had been through those years and knew the intimacy of late nights together. Like many couples, they struggled to remain pure until the day they married.

"Things are changing, Sadie," Mam began on the day she and Dat sat down with their oldest daughter. "Over a hundred years ago, we held with the practice of 'bundling,' or sharing a bed fully clothed, under a comforter or quilt, to stay warm on cold winter evenings. This practice stayed in one form or another in some communities, even in some families. Some groups of concerned parents worked hard to eliminate it altogether; others adhered strictly to the old ways.

"There's a lot of pressure in our community to practice complete distant courtship, the way the higher churches do. Some of the New Orders have a much stricter dating code than we do. And it's worrisome to me. Even though we drive horses and buggies, our moral standards are more like the English than some of the people who leave our community and choose to drive cars. Some who leave for the New Orders have higher morality than we do, yet we're the so-called conservatives."

Dat nodded in agreement as Sadie listened carefully to Mam's words.

Sadie could only be perfectly honest about her feelings. "Do you both agree that absolutely no touching, not even holding hands, is what God intends?" she asked.

Her parents were clearly uncomfortable with that question.

Finally, Dat spoke up. "I can't imagine it."

Mam quickly broke in, "It's what everyone says they want now. It's the new, better way of dating."

Sadie bent her head. She was embarrassed to speak the truth to her parents, but she told them that she and Mark kissed and held each other but did nothing further. Her face flamed with the confession.

Her parents were full of understanding. And in Dat's eyes, was that a twinkle of knowing?

"Then let your conscience be your guide," Mam said. "You know when it's time to stop. Probably the perfect way would be to remain distant."

"I disagree," Sadie said firmly.

Mam was taken aback and watched Sadie's face intently.

"I do. I don't feel guilty for the things we've done, but I know I will soon if it goes any further."

Dat threw his shoulders back and laughed, releasing the tension. Now they were just Mam and Dat and Sadie. Honest. Completely comfortable. Not false or competing to see who could be the best Christian.

"We are who we are, and each man must answer for what he allows himself to do," Dat said. "It's between you and Mark and God."

Sadie knew she had to approach Mark about this subject, but she also knew that now was not the time, not after the letter from his mother he had just shown her. He was so delicate with things pertaining to his ego, his sense of well-being.

She held his hand and entwined her fingers in his. Their love was a wonderful gift from God and the single best thing that had ever happened to her.

✿ ✿ ✿

The police department's search for the snipers had come to a dead end. The license plate led to a stolen car. There were no fingerprints, no leads to pursue, only the same brick wall they always came up against.

For the rest of the winter, there had been no shootings. Most of the Amish argued that it was too cold to be out and too dangerous to make a getaway on the slippery roads. At any rate, a sense of safety pervaded the community, and people relaxed as they got out their horses and buggies to go to town, visit, or travel to church. Would that change now that spring was on the way?

Richard Caldwell shook his gray head, his neatly

trimmed mustache bobbing as he warned everyone it was a lull in the storm, that the worst was yet to come.

"They're mad. They're out for revenge, and they're not giving up any time soon, you mark my words," he told anyone who would listen.

The kitchen work at the ranch had been almost more than Dorothy and Sadie could handle, especially last Christmas. There had been parties, showers, and dinners all winter long, with little Sadie Elizabeth the center of her doting parents' extravagances.

Dorothy was not happy with all the plans Barbara Caldwell was making but knew that if she wanted to keep her job, she better keep her mouth shut.

Richard Caldwell expanded the ranch. He hired an additional five men to build bigger pole barns for hay and equipment. He increased the size of the cattle herd, and he added sheep to his financial ventures, which brought in every relative Lothario Bean could find to work at the ranch.

They cooked large meals for all the ranch hands and work crews, until one day Dorothy threw her hands in the air, marched into Richard Caldwell's office, and told him that they needed another person in the kitchen, and if he didn't get one, she was going to up and quit right there.

While Dorothy argued with the boss, Sadie remained in the kitchen, peeling potatoes and keeping a low profile. She smiled to herself and wondered how it was going in the office. Dorothy really lost her temper this time.

Sadie looked up as they came through the swinging doors of the kitchen. Dorothy's face was the color of salami, her eyes spitting blue sparks. Richard Caldwell looked somber, every inch the gentleman. He was holding

Sadie Elizabeth, who was wearing a little pair of Levi's with a plaid shirt, already dressing for a life on the ranch.

The look in Richard Caldwell's eyes gave Sadie goose bumps. What a father this oversized, noisy, uncouth man had become. Little Sadie had molded him into a gentle, devoted daddy.

She had her own puppy already, a little brown dust mop that shed hair over everything, which made more housework for Sadie. It was the sad story of the stray dog that Richard Caldwell had buried when he was a boy that brought the little brown puppy. He was striving to be a good father in every respect, not wanting to make the same mistakes his father had made in the past.

Barbara Caldwell wasn't fond of Isabel, as the dog was named, but she didn't complain as long as Sadie kept the rooms vacuumed. That was part of the reason Dorothy had marched into his office.

"Dorothy says she's quitting."

"Is she?" Sadie asked, laughing as she put down a wet potato and paring knife. After drying her hands on her apron, she reached for little Sadie Elizabeth.

"She says so. Unless I get more help. You know of any Amish girls looking for a job? One of your sisters?"

"Anna. But she works at the farmer's market."

"No friends either?"

"Uh…I think…there's Erma Keim. She's almost 30, never married, a real workhorse. She was looking for more a little while ago."

So that was how Erma Keim began working at the ranch, opening a whole new chapter in the kitchen for Sadie and Dorothy.

Erma was a diesel engine of hard work. Her large,

freckled hands flew, her long, sturdy limbs simply catapulted her from kitchen to dining room and back again. Even so, Erma had a rough start, not fitting in with the kitchen responsibilities—or with Dorothy—as Sadie had hoped. It might have been smoother for Erma if she had started off quietly, perhaps with a smidgen of humility. But no, Erma knew how to do everything and do it better than Dorothy, which was like setting fire to a long fuse that sizzled and crackled slowly. Sadie came to work everyday eyeing the burning fuse with caution, completely uncomfortable with Erma's loud voice.

On her second day, Erma said Dorothy's sausage gravy could be much improved, although she'd never eaten a better biscuit. On the third day, she asked why they never served breakfast pizza. It was a huge favorite at Erma's house.

Dorothy had been making frequent trips to the restroom all morning. Sadie knew her constitution was way off, which spelled serious trouble for Erma if she kept on talking about Dorothy's food.

Suddenly, Dorothy had enough. She threw her balled fists on her hips and said loudly, "I've been here for 30-some years, and you've barely been here that many hours. I know what the men like and what they don't, and I highly doubt that your newfangled pizza would be appreciated."

That shut Erma up. She started scrubbing the wall behind the stove, muttering to herself and casting poisonous looks in Dorothy's direction. But now she knew where she stood in the pecking order, though she contested it every chance she got.

"Why don't you ever serve dinner rolls?"

"Men don't want them little bitty rolls. They want a thick slice of bread they can latch onto."

When she suggested changing the pancake recipe, Sadie put a warning finger to her lips and sighed with relief when Erma let it go.

When Erma wasn't around, Dorothy complained to Sadie. "She ain't normal, that girl. Ain't no wonder she ain't got a husband. I wouldn't marry her either if I was an Amish man."

However, Erma made a friend for life when she struck up a conversation with swarthy little Lothario Bean and began discussing the merits of keeping eggs and the best way to build a good henhouse.

Sadie decided the human race was full of surprises and unlikely friendships at every turn.

Chapter 18

A<small>ND THEN, JUST LIKE THAT,</small> R<small>EUBEN BONDED WITH</small> another horse.

Reuben began suggesting he call a driver to go to Critchfield on Friday nights. Dat would grin behind his paper and ask Reuben what he wanted there. Reuben would say an ice cream cone at the food stand or a chicken at the animal sale. His answer never failed to bring a genuine laugh from Dat and a smile out of Reuben.

The horse was brown with a black mane and tail, just like Cody. The ears were small with a curve, giving him an intelligent look.

Reuben named this horse Moon. There was no particular reason for the name. He just liked to say "Giddup, Moon" or "Whoa, Moon." Reuben said it sounded professional.

The girls had a conversation about the merits of naming a horse Moon, but they agreed to keep quiet and never once mention anything to Reuben.

Reuben spent hours in the barn brushing, cutting and trimming the mane, and washing his saddle with the pungent saddle soap, humming under his breath all the while.

He spent a whole day cleaning the pens, getting fresh shavings from the feed man, throwing down hay, and sweeping every bit of it carefully into Moon's stall.

Sadie had never seen a horse as spoiled as Moon. He quickly became overfed and used to having his own way. When Moon had a mind to stay inside, Reuben could not get him out of the barn no matter how hard he tried.

He sidestepped and crow-hopped, snorted and lunged, until Sadie felt like using a riding whip on him, something she thoroughly disliked. Sadie clasped her hands until her knuckles were white.

Reuben usually handled a horse easily, but he had to be cautious when Moon was putting on a show like this. Reuben was clearly frustrated. His navy blue beanie slid around on his head, completely covering one eye. His nose was red from the stiff March breeze, and the snow wasn't helping matters at all.

"Just stop him," Sadie called out. Her commands were like throwing kerosene on a small fire.

Reuben hopped off the horse, grabbed the reins, and stalked over to Sadie, his eyes spitting his anger. "There you go, Miss Professional, you do it if you think you're better than me."

Sadie raised one hand, as if to take back her advice.

"Go! Get up on him and see what you can do!" he yelled, swiping angrily at a dripping icicle.

Sadie caught her breath as the icicle clattered to the concrete, shattering into a thousand fragments. Moon jerked his head, wheeled around, and tore the reins from Reuben's hand. He took off down the driveway at a gallop, his haunches gathering beneath him as he gained momentum.

Oh, no, Sadie thought.

"Now, look what you did!" Reuben shouted, clearly too upset to talk sense.

How would they catch this horse? He hadn't been here long enough to call this home. Where would he go?

"Reuben, come," Sadie called, already heading for the barn. "You can ride double with me. Come quickly. Hurry."

Sadie slipped the bridle over Paris' ears and swung herself up. Reuben followed without further urging, his arms sliding around her middle.

"You dressed warm enough?" Sadie asked over her shoulder.

"Yeah."

Paris was eager, needing little urging to run. There was no sight of Moon on the road. Sadie pulled back on the reins, then decided to go right. She urged Paris into an easy gallop, keeping her eyes on the road ahead for any sign of Moon tearing along.

As Paris' head bobbed, her mane flowed back in a cream-colored mass. Sadie always loved the sound of her pounding hooves on the macadam, that strong, rhythmic sound of power.

They searched open fields, woods, and ravines. Cars passed, curious drivers peered out at them, but they could find no sign of Moon.

As twilight deepened, Sadie realized they had traveled much farther than they should have. She reined Paris in.

"Reuben, I don't know if Moon turned in this direction. Should we turn around and try the other direction? Toward Atkin's Ridge?"

Reuben swiped at his running nose with the back of a gloved hand and shrugged his shoulders miserably.

"We'll try," Sadie said, hoping her voice sounded more

encouraging than she felt.

"If we don't find him, someone will. Likely he'll run into someone's barnyard," Sadie said, squeezing Reuben's knee reassuringly.

She laid the rein expertly across the right side of Paris' neck, which turned her around. She was eager to run again.

"Why are you holding her back?" Reuben yelled.

"Hang on!" Sadie called, loosening the reins as she did so.

Paris gathered her hooves beneath her, stretched out, and ran. She ran joyously, with that deep, easy stride that was so characteristic of her. Sadie relaxed, not particularly watching for Moon in the joy of the ride.

She and Reuben were both laughing when the car passed them on the left, then stopped in front of them. Their laughter stopped immediately, the sound corked in their throats as two men emerged at the same moment. They stepped forward, holding their arms out as if to form a human fence, a barrier to halt the horse and riders.

Sadie realized the danger of the situation. The men may be armed. If she stopped, they could force her off Paris, and if she didn't, they might shoot.

Indecision crowded out her fear, but only for a moment. She compressed her lips, leveled her eyes, and focused on the road behind the two men.

"Stay low, Reuben. Here we go."

She loosened the reins, kicked Paris' sides, startling her into an instant full gallop. The men's faces were covered with ski masks of black stretch fabric, with only the horrible whites of their rolling eyes showing.

Bent low, she goaded Paris toward the middle, where there was only a small opening she could break through without hurting anyone.

Would Paris do it?

She called out with all the power she could gather from her unsteady heart. "Go, Paris!"

She heard the men yelling obscenities. With a powerful leap, Parish crushed through the obstacle they had made.

"Go, go, go," Sadie whispered.

Out of the corner of her eye, she saw that low black car creeping up beside them, slowly crowding them farther off the road. They rode desperately now, bent low, their breath coming in gasps. Around the next corner, up this last grade, and their house would be in view. But never had the distance seemed so long.

The car was coming closer, the windows down, the men leaning out. Would this be the end of her life then? Had God spared her when he took Ezra, only to have it end this way?

"Stop! Stop!" one of them yelled.

Her answer was another kick in Paris' stomach. She could almost make out the schoolhouse fence in the snow.

The motor revved, the car crowding them off the side of the road and toward the ditch. Now there was no alternative. She had to stop Paris very suddenly.

"Reuben, I'm stopping."

She could feel him bracing as she hauled in on the reins with every ounce of her strength. Paris responded immediately, almost sitting down in her desire to perform for Sadie.

The car flew past, then braked. The men in the car looked back in bewilderment. That was when Sadie leaned forward and begged Paris to take them past the car yet again.

"Go, go. Oh, Paris, you can do this!"

The hulking black vehicle was a blur as they hurled past.

The driveway!

If they could just make it to the end of the driveway, they would have outwitted these men. Sadie was convinced they were not armed, but why?

Paris ran low and fast, her feet pounding the macadam. They were on the wrong side of the road, the car closing in fast. But they were still ahead.

Oh, no! A truck was coming!

"Reuben! Stay with me!" she screamed, breathless now.

Sadie whipped the reins so that Paris veered to the left, never slowing her pace. The truck driver turned the wheel desperately to the right, narrowly missing Paris, almost scraping the black car, the driver shaking his fist and pumping the horn with the palm of his hand.

Sadie saw the mailbox and the paper holder. Oh, thank you, God.

They raced around the boxes, gravel and soil flying from beneath Paris' hooves as they hit the driveway. The ringing of hooves on macadam is very different from the sound of them on dirt and stone. It was a sound so sweet, it was almost Sadie's undoing. She knew they had made it. She became limp, without strength, like a rag thrown about. She rode numbly, looking over her shoulder for the shape of that dark vehicle.

Sadie's eyesight was blurred by her tears, but she saw the slowly moving hulk of a car. Its hoarse cries assailed her senses, a foreboding so thick it was impenetrable. A sound so violent, the only suitable word to cover it was evil. What did these men want from her?

Paris kept up her desperate pace, lunging up the driveway, running low past the house. Leah was just stepping out of the phone shanty, Mam's old sweater wrapped tightly around her shivering body. She jumped back as the horse went sailing past, then shook her head and walked after them as Paris slid to a halt.

"Sadie, what is going on? You scared us so badly. What were we supposed to think when Co...I mean, Moon, came running fast up the drive without a rider! One of these days you guys are seriously going to get hurt with your *ga-mach*."

Leah's face was white, her words cutting, her anger barely controlled. Mam and Rebekah entered the forebay, breathless, old sweaters wrapped around their shoulders as if they had grabbed them off the hooks and raced out the door.

"Sadie!" Mam's word was sharp, her relief evident.

"You're just crazy!" Rebekah said, loudly, accusingly.

Reuben slid off Paris and opened his mouth to answer when he saw Moon's face hanging over the gate of his stall. Charging along the forebay, he grabbed his horse's face with both hands and planted a loud kiss on his nose.

"Aw, Moon, my Moon," he crooned. Then he turned, his face alight, and said, "Hey, he ran home. He knows where he belongs!"

Sadie smiled, her dimples deep with genuine warmth and admiration. That Reuben could ride!

As Paris drank deeply from the trough, Sadie told them what happened. She tried not to elaborate, knowing Mam would become too upset. As it was, Mam crossed her arms and said there was no way they were allowed to ride until the law got to the bottom of this.

Dat and Anna entered the barn, wiping slivers of wood from their work coats. They had been piling wood in the basement all evening. They listened as Sadie related the incident yet again. Dat glared with disapproval, admonishing their behavior with sharp words. Anna stood at his side, her eyes large with fear.

"It's Paris!" she said finally. "They want her. She's the only one left from those wild horses. She's a beautiful horse. She likely has an expensive bloodline in her or something."

Leah and Rebekah nodded solemnly.

"If you know what's good for you, you'll stay off the road with her."

"Better yet, don't ride her at all."

Sadie stared at her family in disbelief. The incident wasn't her fault.

Dat looked at her.

"The encounters you've had recently tell me that they must be watching this place quite regularly. You better listen, Sadie."

"They don't want me and Moon, do they?" Reuben asked innocently.

"Probably not. But you better not take any chances," Dat replied.

As the family walked back to the house, Sadie stayed to rub down Paris, then gave her a small amount of oats. She brushed her mane and tail, stroked her neck, crooning her words of admiration, before closing the gate. Sadie could still see Dat's head bowed soberly, his hat a silhouette in the disappearing light.

✿ ✪ ✿

The incident caused quite a stir down at the ranch. Richard Caldwell called the police, giving Sadie no chance to back out. He put a hand on her back and escorted her into his office.

The officers intimidated her, and she felt as if, some-how, she had broken the law and that they would haul her off to jail and make her pay a stiff fine.

The younger of the two was obese, stuffed into his clothes, the belt under his ample stomach tucked away from view, which caused the black holster at his side to jut out awkwardly. He had a sandy crew cut, drooping moustache, and red freckles dotting his nose.

The older officer was more mature in his ways. Some-how Sadie couldn't take her eyes off of his large, bobbing teeth. They were long and yellow, just like Paris'. She couldn't help wondering if his toothbrush was still in the plastic packet it had come in.

She greeted them politely, with a bowed head, and answered their questions as precisely as she could.

No, no facial features were visible.

Black ski masks, yes.

No, she didn't know the make of the car. She wasn't familiar with vehicle types.

The men were silent as they wrote on yellow legal pads. Their radios crackled. Richard Caldwell looked stern, and Sadie pleated her apron over and over, trying to remain calm and composed.

When they looked up, they told Richard Caldwell that they would do what they could, but so far, they had not been able to accomplish much. All they had were leads leading to a dead end. This, however, had been the most serious incident, and they warned Sadie to stay off the road.

Sadie nodded, said, "Yes, sir," then returned to the kitchen, a cloud of humility over her head.

Erma Keim accosted Sadie before she even reached the large granite-topped worktable. Erma's red hair was static with curiosity, but Sadie was in no mood to explain or let her in on one single secret.

"Well?" Erma asked, her knife stopping midair.

Sadie shook her head, offering nothing, her mouth a serious, straight line. Erma laid the knife down carefully, took up a stalk of celery and bit down on it as if her life depended on how large a chomp she would take. Glancing sideways at Sadie, she tried again, "Well?"

"They were talking to Richard Caldwell."

Another gargantuan bite, followed by a snort of epic proportions.

"I'm not dumb, Sadie. There was a reason why he so politely escorted you into his office with those policemen. Look, I won't tell, but I can't stand the suspense. You have to tell me what happened. Did you steal something from the ranch, or were you caught with something illegal, or..."

Sadie raised her eyebrows. "You think I'd do that?"

"No, of course not, but if you don't tell me, I'll make up my own reasons why you were in with those police."

Sadie laughed, and then related the incident as minimally as possible. Even so, she had to endure Erma's popping eyes, her clucks, her shrieks of alarm, and her dramatic warnings and finger-shakings.

Dorothy entered the kitchen carrying a huge piece of beef in paper wrapping, her breath coming in fits and gasps. Flinging it on the worktable, she grabbed her side, leaned forward, and grimaced.

"Ow! Pulled a muscle!"

"You should have let me help you," Erma offered kindly.

"I can carry a beef roast up them steps as good as anybody else. Thank you," Dorothy said formally.

Sadie turned her head to hide her grin. This was the merry-go-round the ranch kitchen had become: Dorothy desperately seeking control over every aspect of the cooking, Erma muttering under her breath or complaining about the way things were done, and Sadie caught in the middle, forever attempting to find common ground between the two.

The menu for the meal that evening was beef stew with dumplings, baked beans, a lettuce salad, pickled beets, and homemade bread with apple butter.

The lettuce salad had been Erma's idea. It wasn't an ordinary salad with a mixture of vegetables, but rather a salad of lettuce, thin slices of onion, and sliced, hard-boiled eggs. Dorothy grudgingly allowing it, and Sadie wondering what the men would say.

To go with the salad, Erma cooked a wonderful hot bacon dressing with plenty of bacon chips in the creamy mayonnaise-based concoction. Sadie filled a small dish with the salad and ate it while they cooked. It was delicious. Dorothy hovered in the background, not saying a word no matter how hard Sadie tried to pull her into the conversation.

The lettuce salad was a huge hit, and many of the men complimented the cook, as Dorothy was called. She bowed her head, batted her eyelashes, and put on a show of humility as she accepted the praise, never mentioning Erma or her recipes.

Richard Caldwell noticed the change in recipes as well and came into the kitchen with a broad smile softening his granite features.

Erma was still in the same stage Sadie had been in a few years ago, when the sound of Richard Caldwell's voice made her drop the Pledge furniture polish. Erma tried to pass it off as nothing, but Sadie could tell he unnerved her by the way her speed increased when he entered the room.

Richard Caldwell clapped a hand on Dorothy's rounded shoulder and congratulated her on another outstanding meal.

"That dressing was the greatest thing I ever poured on lettuce!" he boomed, causing Erma to scrub the pans with a new intensity.

Dorothy nodded, the deep pink color in her apple cheeks turning to crimson. She said nothing, turning to look apprehensively in the direction of Erma, who was slathering a roaster with dish detergent, squeezing the soap bottle so hard Sadie was afraid they'd never get rid of all the leftover suds.

"So who gets the credit for the recipe?" he yelled.

There was more furious scrubbing in Erma's corner while Dorothy drew herself up to her full height. She pursed her lips and narrowed her eyes in concentration.

"My grandmother had a recipe like that," she said.

It wasn't a lie. It was the truth.

And it was all Richard Caldwell needed to know. Assuming the recipe came from Dorothy, he smiled and thanked her again. Then he left the kitchen, picking up a biscuit on his way out and winking at Sadie, who smiled back.

Oh, boy, Sadie thought.

Erma kept scrubbing for a full minute before turning and wiping her forehead with the back of her hand, leaving a white shelf of suds across her eyebrows.

Slowly, much too sweetly, she said, "I didn't know we used your grandmother's recipe."

"We didn't."

"I guess that's a useless bit of information Richard Caldwell doesn't need to know."

"'Course not."

The kitchen was a beehive of tension after that. Erma scurried back and forth, her eyes popping, her hair standing on end with resentment. Dorothy's expression indicated no good either, in that haughty state where she became unapproachable.

Sadie's own mood hovered between irritation and resentment. Work just wasn't the same with Erma in the kitchen. The mounting tension had steadily increased all week. She was exhausted.

For the first time she could remember, she did not want to come back to work in the morning, Oh, she had her sleepy Monday-morning blues like everyone else, but nothing that blackened her entire day the way these two did with their silly squabbles.

Sadie finished boiling the potatoes for the morning's home fries, washed her hands, then said she was going to find Jim. It was time to go home. She tiredly stuck her arms into her coat sleeves, shrugging the coat over her shoulders.

"The floor ain't done," Dorothy said evenly.

"I'll get it," Erma said, stepping forward. "You can go."

Dorothy's eyebrows shot straight up, and she watched without comment as Erma filled a bucket, added soap, and bent to begin her task.

"You sure you can handle it?" Dorothy asked.

"What?"

"The floor?"

"It's not a big floor," Erma answered, swiping furiously.

Dorothy shook her head, smiled, and winked at Sadie. Then she bent to find Erma's gaze.

"You piling coals of fire on my head, or what?"

"No, I'm washing the floor with soapy water. I have no plans to pile coals on your head."

Dorothy burst out laughing, and after a pause, Erma sat back and laughed with her.

"No stupid ol' lettuce salad gonna ruin us, now, is it?" she chortled, wiping her eyes.

Erma nodded, a hint of tears glistening in her own eyes.

Chapter 19

Perhaps the unbalanced relationship between Erma and Dorothy was a good thing. Mark told Sadie that his mother had sent another letter stating her desperation to see him. He would go this time. Sadie didn't hesitate to tell him that she would accompany him on the trip to visit her.

The ranch could be run smoothly without her, even if Dorothy and Erma were like a team of horses that jerked on the singletree, one lunging forward while the other held back.

They planned a trip by train on Amtrak. Their destination was almost 600 miles to a town in North Dakota. As they made arrangements, Mark became reserved, offering only a minimal amount of information, his eyes dark pools of restraint. Sadie wondered if he wanted her to go along at all. So a few days before they left, she voiced her concerns, haltingly.

"Mark, I'm not sure how you feel about taking me with you."

"Why do you say that?"

"You're... It's tough... I guess I'm scared. She doesn't

want you to be … Amish. What will happen when she sees me? You could go alone and dress English, and she'd never know the difference."

Mark looked at her coldly, his expression unreadable. Then he bent his head, hiding his eyes in his hands.

"I wasn't going to tell you, Sadie. My mother is very, very ill. She's dying, I think. I wasn't going to tell you," he repeated.

"Oh, Mark!"

"We actually spoke on the phone a few times, and, Sadie, she's so bitter. I'm still reeling from those calls. Her voice so weak…" He paused, then, "What can I do? I don't feel as if I'll be able to help her. I have so much baggage of my own to carry. It'll be like the blind leading the blind, two mixed-up, bitter people."

"Your baggage is lighter than it was."

"You think so?" His tone was mocking. Then, "You have no idea."

✡ ✡ ✡

Sadie prayed as she packed her things that night. She prayed as she showered, dressed, and said goodbye to her family the next morning. She begged God to stay with them, impart his wisdom, and erase all the old hatred that lingered in both Mark and his mother. Somehow, she knew that hatred was the only thing keeping Mark and his mother from true happiness and peace.

Reuben took Sadie aside and told her not to worry about Paris. He'd take good care of her. Besides, he was planning to teach Anna to ride, now that she had lost so much weight. Sadie told him she would depend on him, but to be very careful with the snipers still on the loose.

Reuben was almost as tall as Sadie now, their eyes almost level. The sudden knowledge of this surprised her. Dear Reuben.

When Mark pulled up to the porch with a driver, Sadie was ready to go. She turned to say goodbye to her family, but the lump in her throat made it difficult.

Mam smelled of frying corn mush and laundry detergent. Sadie breathed in deeply as she hugged her tightly.

Dat's expression was gruff, but his eyes were liquid with love. Sadie's sisters handed her a packet of tissues and a pack of Juicy Fruit chewing gum. Reuben smiled, then dipped his head to hide his tears.

In the van, Mark tried to keep the conversation light. He bantered with Adam Glassman, the driver, telling him they were eloping, which caused heat to infuse Sadie's cheeks. But when the train pulled in and they were settled in their seats, a cloud settled over Mark. His features darkened until he turned away from her and pretended to be asleep.

Sadie sat still and watched the other passengers. She smiled at a baby no older than six months. The harried mother acknowledged her smile gratefully, glad to have a friendly person sitting so close.

"Are you used to babies?" she asked timidly.

"Not in my immediate family, but yes, there are lots of babies in our community," Sadie answered.

"I'm so nervous about taking Braxton on a trip this way. What if he cries and I can't make him stop?"

"You'll be fine. He looks perfectly happy," Sadie answered.

She picked up her magazine, flipped through it, and began to read an article about training a horse to drive. It absorbed her interest completely until her stomach began to rumble.

She was surprised to find it was almost lunchtime. When her glances at Mark's back did nothing to rouse him, she picked up another magazine and read one boring article after another.

The baby fell asleep, the mother noticeably relaxed now. The train's wheels hummed beneath them, taking them farther and farther from home.

The Juicy Fruit gum took the edge off her rumbling stomach, but she was still hungry and then grew irritable. She had not eaten breakfast but only drank two cups of coffee, which she definitely should not have done. Why hadn't she packed a few sandwiches? When would Mark wake up?

Finally, he sat up and turned to talk to her. Sadie could tell by his eyes that he hadn't slept at all. He just shut her out of that deep, dark place he went to at certain times. No amount of prodding ever uncovered the reason why.

He said nothing about food. In fact, he didn't talk at all for the next hour. Sadie attempted short spurts of conversation, but she felt as ineffective as a housefly bothering a horse, getting only grunts for answers.

The lack of food and support from Mark drew her spirits down until she was in one of the worst moods possible. First, she wished she hadn't come; then she wished she had never met Mark Peight at all.

She was blinking back tears when an announcement came over the speaker saying they'd be stopping in the next town for approximately an hour and a half.

She glanced at Mark and was rewarded by his gaze.

"Hungry?"

She nodded happily.

He returned to her then, attentive, polite, and kind as always. He told her to order whatever she wanted and not to worry about the cost. This was sort of a vacation for them both.

She decided to try something new from the menu, a pasta dish consisting of a flat spaghetti. It was a word she could not pronounce: linguini. It was covered with sauce called marinara, another word she had never heard of, and topped with little shrimp and the most heavenly tasting cheese. There were slivers of thin garlic toast, and a salad made of fresh lettuce, dark spinach, croutons, cheese, and a spicy dressing. It was wonderful.

"Definitely not Amish food!" she laughed.

"Nope. No mashed potatoes and chicken gravy here," Mark replied.

For the remainder of the journey, he remained attentive, talkative, almost lighthearted. He emerged from his swamp of hopelessness as if it had never occurred.

There was no one to meet them in the town of Ashton, of course. The station was small, the old building consisting of crumbling bricks, an aging wooden cornice, and battered window frames. A remnant of white paint clung stubbornly to the graying wood of the exterior, weathered by hot winds and freezing blizzards.

Even in the light of early spring, a gray despondency hovered over the flat little town. There was nothing except scrubby emptiness that went on and on and on in all directions. Dirty tumbleweeds, covered with the dust that rusty pickup trucks agitated, clung to buildings as if hoping to escape their journey into oblivion.

Sadie shivered, glancing at the hovering water tower in the sky, a sort of peeling, steel sentry, crumbling along with the brick buildings and the windowpanes.

The wind blew constantly, just like at home, pulling at her skirt and ruffling Mark's hair.

Sadie crossed her arms and looked around a dusty waiting room with a filthy carpet, a cow skull on the wall, and dusty chairs. She decided right then and there that Mark was the only safe thing in this town.

He talked to the girl behind the desk, asking if there was any taxi service available, handing her the address from his pocket.

She chewed a huge wad of gum, snapping and popping it at regular intervals. She nodded her head in recognition.

"Ya see there," the girl said, pointing out the window with an index finger, the nail polished to a crimson hue.

"Cross the street. Jeff don't have a sign over his store, but go in through that open door, and he'll give ya a ride. If yer folks are on Killdeer Road, Jeff can find 'em."

She fixed Sadie with a frank, curious stare.

"Ya Mennonite? No, lemme guess, yer Mormons, right?"

She batted her lashes, those thick heavy spiders of mascara, and grinned up at Mark. He laughed, clearly enjoying her open approach to their different way of dressing.

"None of those. We're Amish."

"What kind of animal is that?" she asked, her penciled eyebrows drawn down.

She burst into laughter so loud, she almost lost the enormous wad of gum.

"It's sort of Mennonite," Sadie offered, seeing this girl was clearly baffled. No use trying to explain.

"Well, you're awful good-looking, whatever you are. You said yer mother lives out on Killdeer Road? Ain't never seen anybody wearin' those kinda clothes, so she must have left the fold."

Mark nodded. "She did."

"Nice yer goin' to see 'er. She'll be glad. That's good."

Sadie felt the goose bumps begin on her arms, and quick tears sprang to her eyes. Those words from this person with no guile somehow seemed prophetic, a good omen.

This worldly girl helped them cheerfully and sincerely wished them well. She was the sort of person who would have helped the poor man in the Bible who was assaulted and beaten, lying in the culvert by the side of the road.

The Spirit of the Lord was like the wind. You saw what it did, but you couldn't tell where it came from.

"Hey, tell you what. If'n it don't suit Jeff, jes' come back. I'll call my mom to fill in for me, an' I'll take ya."

Mark thanked her, and as they turned to go the girl waved her hand and told them to leave their luggage. It wasn't in anyone's road, no how.

Jeff was a portly individual, his overalls grimy with grease and mud. The clasps at his shoulders the only clean thing about him, except for his teeth, which were long and surprisingly white.

He greeted them with a curious grin, quiet eyes, and a hearty, "Ya lost?"

Mark smiled back and told him that perhaps they were. He told Jeff about his mother's residence on Killdeer Road, and Jeff pondered the length of it in his mind.

"The only place I know out there is that... Naw, that ain't yer ma. She's crazier 'n a coyote with fleas. Tain't her."

Mark froze, a statue of indecision. The panic and foreboding in his face was almost Sadie's undoing.

Why had they come? They knew nothing of this strange woman. She meant nothing to Mark. Would they regret this wild-goose chase? Would it hurt rather than help Mark?

"If'n this woman's yer ma, you gotta be prepared. Talk has it, she ain't right in the head. Haven't seen her in a while, huh?"

Mark shook his head.

"Sorry, I don't mean to be a' gossipin'. Lord knows there's way too mucha that goin' on. An, besides, she's yer ma."

Jeff called over the half-door to his wife, telling her that he was leaving for a little while. Then he went to get his keys.

Sadie slid her hand into Mark's. He tightened his hand and gave her a grateful look. But the pallor of his face gave away the fact that he was in turmoil, finding Jeff's words to be fiercely disturbing.

They made their way to the aging, white pickup, the running board rusted so badly, Sadie stepped over it entirely.

Apologizing, Jeff pushed aside the trash: empty tea bottles, sticky orange-juice cartons, screwdrivers, duct tape, dirty little receipts, crumbling newspaper, an assortment of junk that must not have been disturbed for months.

"Don't nobody ride in my truck hardly ever," Jeff said laughing good-naturedly. "Shoulda taken Lila's car. She keeps it a sight cleaner."

They eased out of town, Jeff waving at each person on the sidewalk, pressing down hard on the horn when three dogs crossed the street in front of them. A mangy-looking sheep dog, a German shepherd that looked less than friendly, followed by a large dog of various descents, ambled across.

"Ol' Bertha's got her dogs loose again. What this town needs is a dog warden. Mayor, such as he is, says we can't afford one. Well, we can't afford the accidents these big bruisers cause, trotting all over town as if they own it."

Jeff shook his head, pushed back his cap, glanced in the rearview mirror, and made a hard left.

"Trouble is, ain't enough of us. Work's not so good anymore. Most of us worked for the wheat farmers or the big gas company, only the gas ain't producin' the way it used ta."

Jeff rambled in his friendly manner. The truck swerved around potholes and bounced across skips in the macadam. Jeff turned the steering wheel first one way, then another, grimacing as the right front wheel hit an especially large pothole.

He pointed to tall grain bins, their sides coated with rust, sienna-colored messengers of time and neglect.

"See them?"

Mark craned his neck.

"Part of the ranch we're headed to. Nothin' left hardly. It's yer typical sad story. Good man, that Scout. Scout's his nickname. His real name is Bill Van Syoc. Hard-working. Owned half the county in acreage. Wheat farmer. Cattle. Married that... Well, I can't say in front of you people what I normally would. Excuse me, but she ran everything into the ground. The town people saw him go from a proud, ambitious person to a wreck in no time flat. Took to alcohol. It's a shame."

Mark sat beside Sadie tight-lipped, so she said nothing and just looked out the window at the landscape.

North Dakota was literally as flat as a pancake. There were no rolling hills, no dips, just long stretches of prairie. The roads were as straight and flat as the land.

Weather-beaten grain bins seemed to cling to the earth. Occasionally one appeared slanted, almost as if the wind had pushed at it steadily until, inch by inch, the building had leaned in the direction the wind wanted it to go. Rusted sign posts stood like rail-thin, starving people. There were no fences, which made everything seem loose and free.

An occasional meadowlark warbled from the top of a wooden mailbox post while smaller birds dipped and whirled across the sky. The grasses were showing hints of green, although the entire landscape still showed its brown winter hue. This land seemed foreign, somehow. The vastness of it made Sadie feel like she was in another country.

Jeff looked to the right, squinting beneath the visor, then pointed with a gnarled finger.

"See them buildings?"

They nodded their acknowledgment.

"That's where we're headed."

As they drew closer, Mark's eyes folded into slits. The mailbox sagged on a post hanging on by a thread. The post stood haphazardly in an opening much too large to hold it upright.

The house was unconventional for the area, built by someone with oversized dreams, as if the builder attempted a sort of mini-castle, then found his funds depleted and stopped all the work, finishing it as cheaply as possible.

The roofline had no sense of balance due to the gable ends, turrets, and balconies. Parts of the house had beautiful gingerbread cornices, but the rest was plain and finished with ordinary vinyl siding. Some of the windows had black shutters, but most of them had nothing at all, making them appear unprotected and unfinished. There was a large front porch with expensive urns that were filled with weeds. Weeds climbed the house too, their sadness spilling over the windows and door frames in brown destitution.

Poison ivy covered the chimney, the massive sandstone apparatus that consumed almost the entire south side of the house.

Jeff drove slowly, trying to avoid the deep washes in the unkempt driveway. Beneath a towering tree were the remains of a water fountain, a hammock, roses growing wild.

When Sadie saw an elaborate statue of a little girl holding a basket of flowers, her skirt blowing in the wind, almost buried beneath wild ivy, she thought her heart would break. Once, there had been a beautiful garden, but time and neglect had turned it into a forlorn picture of sorrow.

Oh, the complete desolation!

Jeff stopped the truck, then looked at them levelly.

"Now are you sure you don't want me to wait? Let's just say I'll set right here until you go knock on that door, all right?"

"I'd be obliged, but we'll try and make it short. I'm sure you have work to do at home," Mark said.

"I'll be fine."

Sadie smiled at Jeff and was rewarded with a look of sincere warmth. Then she looked up at Mark. He would not meet her gaze, his face having lost most of its color, his mouth set in a grim line.

The sidewalk had been beautiful sandstone laid to precision, but it was covered over now by an assortment of weeds and vines.

Surely no one lived here. Certainly no one visited anymore.

She followed Mark up the steps of the front porch, her heart hammering against her ribs. When he knocked on the large oak door, still wondrous in spite of the neglect, she bit her lip and clenched her fingers.

There was a chorus of barks, howls, and yips, and then the door swung slowly inward.

At first Sadie thought the woman could not possibly be a real person, only a caricature someone rigged to the door to frighten intruders. She was so thin! Way too tall, too white, the cheeks sunken, the black hair hanging in dirty tendrils around her shoulders.

The woman threw them an angry glance, a black look of suspicion. The look was so that Sadie clutched desperately at Mark's sleeve, but he shook off her trembling hands.

"Whadda ya want?"

The voice was only a thin rasp, barely audible above the chorus from the dogs. She slapped halfheartedly at the largest, a white Siberian husky, with blue eyes and the dark brows so often seen in that breed.

"I am... I am Mark Peight. This is my girlfriend, Sadie Miller."

He could not say more or less. It was straightforward, mincing nothing. His family of origin, his marital status, and the Amish religion was all there for her to comprehend and absorb.

The dogs quieted when one thin, white hand went to the husky's head. The other hand went to her throat, clutched at the black satin robe, then fell to her side. A long, thin breath whistled through her dry, white lips.

Suddenly, she lowered her head and the lank hair fell over her face. Sadie thought she was going to fall and moved forward to catch her, when the woman put one hand on the door frame, swayed slightly, then steadied herself.

"Aaah." It was a hoarse, broken cry.

Then her head came up, the eyes large and black with defiance. She took a step back.

"You're... A-Amish!" she whispered hoarsely.

"Yes. I am also your oldest son."

"Just... just go. Leave me alone. You'll condemn me to hell. It's where I'm going soon enough anyway."

"Don't, Mam."

"What did you call me?"

Her voice was painfully raw. If a voice could bleed, it would sound like this.

"I called you Mam. You are my mother. You asked to see me, so I came."

"But... you can't come into my house."

"Why not?"

"You... you have to shun me. I am *im bann*."

"I know."

"Just go." The words were tired, broken, so weary they left a trail of complete exhaustion across Sadie's heart. But she ignored it, stepping forward bravely.

"No, we're going to stay here with you for a little while," she said.

She met Sadie's eyes, saw the innocence, the guile-lessness, and wavered. Her indecision was so apparent, flickering in her large dark eyes.

"Why would you?"

"We traveled all this way to be with you, and we'd love to stay, talk, and..."

"I'm ill. I won't live long. You don't want to be here."

"We'll just bring in our luggage, if that's all right," Sadie answered.

They bade Jeff goodbye. He gave them his cell phone number, shaking his head in worried disbelief that they were actually staying there.

When Mark and Sadie walked through the front door, the dogs rose to greet them. They were quiet now, and Mark bent to stroke them all, fondling their ears like a true dog-lover.

His mother stood by the wall, supporting herself on the back of a red wing-chair, watching with an expression that had no name.

Chapter 20

SADIE NEVER THOUGHT THE WORD "DESPAIR" would be suitable to describe a home, but it was the only word that fit the place where Amelia Van Syoc lived. It wasn't the dust and grime as much as the atmosphere of a person living without hope.

The house had been full of beauty at one time but now held only decay. The carpet, the hardwood floors, and the ceramic tiles were covered in years of dust and dog hair. Every window was covered with insulated drapes, dark blinds, or simply with fabric. Even the sunshine and fresh air were trapped outside.

There were boxes piled everywhere, as if she had tried to fill the emptiness by purchasing things. Over time she accumulated huge containers filled with all kinds of useless items. There was a path between the boxes through the living room, kitchen, and dining room. Otherwise, they had to set things aside to be able to reach the bedrooms where Amelia had told them to put their suitcases.

They had each sleepless nights on lumpy mattresses. In the morning they sat across from each other at the kitchen table with nothing to say. There was no food in the cupboards, and they found the refrigerator almost empty, so Sadie made coffee and drank it black.

Mark was in that dark place, answering Sadie's questions through averted eyes. He glanced at the bedroom door his mother had entered the evening before, gasping for breath as she did so, telling them she was tired and going to bed.

Was she still alive? Would she allow them to stay?

Sadie longed to get started on cleaning the house, but Mark had not yet given her permission. So she sat, drank the awful coffee, and gave up trying to engage Mark in any further conversation.

Sunlight filtered through the lone uncovered window, creating a bright patch of light on the ceramic floor. Sadie placed her foot on it, as if it would beat back the darkness creeping into her body and mind as she contemplated this lonely woman's life.

The heavy oak door creaked on its hinges as Mark's mother slowly pulled it open from the inside. Sadie looked away from the white face and piercing dark eyes that were creating a sort of panic in her chest.

She never said a word, only shuffled to the bathroom, her black satin robe clutched to her skeletal frame.

The dogs had been sleeping at Mark's feet calmly, as if they knew help had arrived and were glad of it. Obediently, the dogs rose as if she had called them. They followed her down the hallway and laid outside the bathroom door.

Sadie tried desperately to met Mark's eyes, but he had shut her out. His face was like cut granite, his eyes flat and black.

There was a hoarse cry, a shattering of glass, and a thump from behind the closed door. Instantly, Mark was on his feet with Sadie at his heels.

"Are you all right?" he called.

When there was no answer, he turned the knob, then went in. Sadie gasped when she saw the pathetic figure huddled by the commode, a glass shattered beside her and a bottle of pills scattered around her, absorbing the puddles of water on the floor.

Mark knelt beside his mother and called her name.

"Meely! Mam!"

The face was even more colorless now, the eyes closed.

Mark felt for a pulse, put his ear to the thin chest, then scooped her up in his arms like a child. He carried her from the bathroom to the living room, folding her long, thin body on the cluttered, brown sofa.

Out of habit, Sadie quickly returned to the bathroom to pick up the shards of glass and mop up the water. When she returned to the living room, Mark was calling his mother's name yet again.

When she finally responded, he was so visibly relieved it was heartbreaking. Meely cried in low moaning sounds, her thin lips drawn back in agony. She turned her face away, a gesture to save her withering pride.

"I'm…," she whispered.

Mark bent, then went on his knees beside the sofa, his hands hanging awkwardly by his side as if afraid to touch her.

"I'm…," Meely tried again.

A long, broken breath.

"I'm…going to die."

"Not yet, Mam. We're here. Sadie and I."

She nodded, struggled to sit up, then fell back on the sofa, closing her eyes. Her hands fluttered restlessly over the satin robe.

Sadie reached out, pulled up the heavy fabric of the robe, and laid it gently across her stomach.

"Meely." The word was new, but she said it quietly, bravely. "We're here to stay. We're going to take good care of you. Is it okay for me to clean and buy some food?"

Another weary nod, then she twisted her body as she strained and heaved, completely sick to her stomach.

Sadie glided noiselessly to the kitchen, found a container, and returned to the living room, stroking Meely's back as she strained.

"It's okay. We're here. You'll be all right," she crooned.

Mark watched her and remembered. The snow, the cold, the horse so thin, so evidently dying. Sadie kneeling by the horse, holding its head, stroking the mane, whispering words of endearment in Pennsylvania Dutch. It was then he had fallen in love with her, and that love had only grown stronger with time.

He was suddenly overwhelmed with emotion and put a hand reassuringly on Sadie's shoulder. He did not look away when she turned to meet his gaze, burning now with intensity.

Meely wiped her mouth with a crumpled tissue, then moaned softly, waving her hand in dismissal. Slowly she turned to face the wall.

Sadie watched as Meely's eyes closed, then turned and headed for the kitchen. Mark was suddenly behind her. He slid his arms around her and held her as if she was the anchor that grounded him to his very life.

"I love you so much," he whispered in her ear.

"And I love you, Mark. Always," she returned.

Anything was possible with Mark's love. Her spirit lifted to new heights.

They cleaned all morning. They carried boxes to one designated room, swept, pushed aside the drapes, cleaned windows, scoured bathrooms, emptied waste cans, and moved furniture. By mid-afternoon they were absolutely ravenous.

They called Jeff, who whisked them off to the local grocery. They bought fresh meat and cheese, salt, flour, oatmeal, cereal, and all the staples they would need to cook nutritious meals that they hoped would tempt Meely's appetite. They returned and filled the freshly cleaned cupboards and refrigerator.

They toasted bagels in the toaster, cooked thick sausage patties, and melted Swiss cheese all over them. They scrambled eggs and built huge breakfast sandwiches with ketchup slathered liberally in the middle.

They drank cold orange juice, talked with their mouths full, licked their fingers, and then Sadie jumped up for a roll of paper towels.

"No napkins. Mark, we forgot."

"Sit down, Sadie."

His voice was low and very serious, so she slid carefully into the heavy oak kitchen chair and watched his face as she wiped her hands on the paper towels.

The air was heavy with unspoken words and feelings too deep to be brought to the surface easily. The only sound was water dripping from the newly polished faucet at the kitchen sink.

"Do you...?"

His voice was drowned out by a piercing scream from the living room, propelling Mark out of his chair so swiftly, it fell over backward. He hurried through the arched doorway and into the living room to find Meely with her head pressed into the pillow, her body arched as she strained to escape the pain assaulting her back.

Her lips drew back and released another cry of agony.

Instantly, Sadie slipped an arm beneath her and held her thin shoulders.

"Meely! Don't. It'll be all right. Don't cry. It's okay."

No amount of coaxing or massaging would soothe the poor woman. Finally, Mark suggested calling an ambulance, anything to still her cries and ease her pitiful suffering.

"No! No! No!" she cried.

The dogs rose, whimpering, until Mark let them outside.

After the initial wave of pain wore out, Meely calmed down and obediently swallowed the Tylenol they offered. Then she asked for hot tea.

"You should eat," Mark said.

"No."

"If Sadie makes chicken soup, would you eat that?"

"No."

She drank the tea, then asked for more pillows.

Sadie went to the kitchen and put some chicken breasts in water to make homemade chicken corn noodle soup. Then she asked Meely if she would like a warm bath and a shampoo.

"No."

"Meely, I think it would help you feel better."

"Nobody's going to bathe me. No."

"Would you do it yourself?"

"No."

Sadie sighed and looked at Mark. The sour odor from her unwashed hair and body was loathsome, but she was afraid to mention it, not wanting to offend Meely, or Mark for that matter.

The tea seemed to give her a measure of strength, and she patted the pillows with nerveless fingers, a sort of repercussion from the caffeine in the tea.

"I have to talk." She spoke loudly, the words coming in quick succession, as if she might never be able to say the necessary words if she didn't say them now.

Sadie quickly walked to the kitchen to turn down the burner on the stove. When she returned, Mark was sitting on the red-wing chair. Sadie stood beside it, a hand on the arm.

"Sit down," Meely barked, angrily.

Obediently Sadie brought a chair from the dining room and sat beside Mark.

"I have cancer. It's in my bones. It started in my breasts. Had that taken care of, or so they thought. You know..."

Her hands fluttered like white birds swept by a gale, seemingly propelled by forces beyond their control.

"The doctors don't know what happened. Told me to quit smoking. Couldn't do that. I always smoked. Well, not always, but..." A terrified glance at Mark.

"After I left, I smoked a lot. Helped my nerves. Evan smoked. The... you know, the man I left with."

Mark nodded.

Her black gaze adhered to Mark's eyes with a certain wildness.

"Say you don't remember," she ground out hoarsely.

Mark sat motionless, made of stone. Then he nodded again.

As if her soul were in Mark's hands, Meely searched his face, earnestly hoping he did not remember the past.

"No. You don't. You can't. You were too young."

Why didn't he speak? Was it pride that kept Mark so still?

The dripping faucet in the kitchen violated the dead silence as effectively as a hissing scream, until Sadie thought the very atmosphere would fly apart.

"I remember everything, Mother."

Sadie's heart slowed, then dropped, when she heard Mark's words, spoken in Pennsylvania Dutch.

"*Ich mind allus.*"

"Oh, God!" The sick woman understood. The words, spoken in the language of her past, sealed her fate, and it was a thousand times worse than she feared.

Out of the depths of her ravaged soul came the words, "*Nay! Nay!*"

Her response in Dutch made Sadie shudder. If ever there was a time when she felt helpless in the face of these horribly buried pasts, this was surely it. She breathed a prayer to God to stay here, in this room, with his power and strength.

Meely became defensive then.

"It wasn't my fault. Atlee should have done something. He was so set in his ways. The farm was going downhill all the time. He...was so unconcerned. All he wanted to do was...lay around the house.

"He loved me too much. It drove me insane. I couldn't deal with it. When you were born, it was okay, but they just kept coming. The babies. Crying, wanting food, there weren't enough diapers. The washer was broken. Atlee... None of it was my fault. A person can only take so much. Not my fault."

She turned her face away, the subject closed. The past was smoothed over by adjusting the blame to someone else.

Mark's eyes blared with black fire, disgust, and fury leaping out of them. His mouth opened and then closed. He gulped like a dying fish receiving no oxygen but still floundering.

When he finally spoke, the words were cased in searing heat from anger pushed deep inside for much too long.

"No, Meely. Huh-uh. You're not going to get out of this so easily. I don't care if you are sick, you're going to hear what I have to say. I was only eight years old, but I knew. I knew what you and that... that Evan were doing. I can still see him, that cringing lizard at the front door, coming to mislead my Mam. I can still see you leaving in his red car, the babies crying. No, Meely, it was not my Dat's fault.

"He's dead, you know. Dat. Atlee."

She turned her head to face Mark, checking his face for any untruth.

"No!"

"Yes. Atlee killed himself after you left. He drowned. I found him."

There was a snort of derision from the sofa.

"Guess you had a shock, huh?"

Mark stood up, towered over her. She shrank into the cushions of the couch, afraid he might strike her.

With a hoarse, nameless cry, he turned on his heel and stalked out through the front door, slamming it so hard the windows rattled.

Sadie looked at Meely, who looked back with a blank, cold stare. The dark glare withered any sense of goodwill Sadie may have had.

✿ ✪ ✿

The smell of chicken soup floated through the house, creating a homey warmth. Mark had disappeared, and Sadie hoped she could get his mother fed and bathed by the time he returned. They might resume talking then, opening old Pandora's boxes, battling the spirits that spewed forth.

Sadie wheedled, coaxed, even joked, to get Meely to eat the soup. No amount of coaxing could persuade her. Finally, Sadie told her she needed some sort of sustenance to withstand another attack of pain. Nothing could persuade her to try a single spoonful.

"I hate that Amish stuff."

The words were shoved violently at Sadie and made her flinch. She stood her ground.

"English people make chicken noodle soup. Not just Amish."

"Don't want it. You're Amish."

"Okay. Then starve. We're going home."

"No. No. Don't." she cried pathetically. "I'll taste it."

"It's made with ingredients from your grocery store, so it's English soup," Sadie teased.

That brought a weak semblance of a smile, and she reached for the soup bowl. She tried some, then raised the black eyebrows.

"It's good."

She ate every drop, then asked for water with ice in it, which Sadie brought quickly. Meely drank half of it.

"You don't mean it," Meely said, her shoulders drooping. Then, "Why do you want me to live?"

"I want you to live long enough to reconcile your feelings with Mark. I care for Mark. I love him very much, and you're his mother, so I care about you, of course. You're his mother."

"You don't love me."

"I would if you'd let me bathe you," Sadie said smiling. A small twinkle flickered in her deep brown eyes.

"I'm a disgusting person, aren't I? Sick and dirty and weak. I wasn't always like this, you know."

Sadie nodded.

"I'll bathe myself. You can help me shampoo."

Sadie could hardly believe her good fortune. While Meely bathed, Sadie vacuumed the sofa and tucked clean sheets along the cushions. When that was finished, she glided noiselessly across the carpet and pressed her ear to the bathroom door. Meely was not yet ready for her shampoo, so Sadie hurried away to put the soiled sheets and quilt in the washer.

She was thankful for her experience of working at the ranch. She was accustomed to toasters, microwaves, washers, and dryers even though the appliances were not a part of her life at home.

Meely called from the bathroom, and Sadie braced herself, knowing it would take courage to enter.

When she quietly opened the door, Meely was submerged in water up to her shoulders. Her face was turned away, and she refused to meet Sadie's eye.

"Don't hurt me now." The voice was soft, like a child's, and it enveloped Sadie's heart.

Poor, frightened woman. Was she any different than Nevaeh, that sick beautiful horse, so pitiful in her weakness?

As Sadie gently massaged Meely's grimy scalp, working the shampoo into it, Meely closed her eyes. Sadie could see the beauty that had been ravaged by disease and malnutrition. Her eyebrows were like dark wings, once plucked to perfection, now beautiful in their fullness. Her eyes were wide half-moons fringed with black lashes. Her cheeks were sallow and mottled, but the bone structure was perfect, just like Mark's.

As Sadie washed the matted mass of hair loosening under her hands, the water turned gray and then brown. She rinsed, shampooed again, then worked the conditioner in before the final rinse.

"There, Meely. Do you need help to finish?"

The "no" was quick and emphatic. But she had to call Sadie to help her dress in clean pajamas, warm socks, and another robe, a white one this time, which improved the stark outline of her figure.

Sadie led her to the red wing-chair and gently brushed her hair until all the tangles were smoothed. Sadie was amazed at the amount of black hair Meely still had, despite her illness. She was only graying a bit at the temples.

"I lost all of it before, you know. Chemo kills you," Meely said wryly.

"I've heard people talk of chemotherapy."

"It's as horrible as they say."

That was all she said. Her body was limp with exhaustion, so Sadie helped her to the sofa, pulling the quilt around her thin shoulders. Meely tried to speak, but her eyes, those beautiful half moons of light, fell. Her breathing deepened, and she was asleep.

Sadie stood, then reached out and tentatively smoothed the hair away from her pearly brow.

Dear God. *Unser Himmlischer Vater.*

As she prayed in Dutch, a wave of homesickness rushed over her. She missed her family. Reuben especially. She missed Paris and hoped Anna was riding her with Reuben and Moon. She missed Dorothy, too. She would call tomorrow.

She washed dishes, fed the dogs, ate some of the chicken soup. She was still hungry and decided to make *toast brot, milch und an oy*. It was an old satisfying dish when the stomach was not quite right or the body needed a bit of comfort within the next 15 minutes.

She put a small amount of milk in a little saucepan and broke an egg into it. Then she put a slice of bread in the toaster. When the egg and toast were ready, she dumped the egg and milk on the toast, salting and peppering it liberally.

She took a bite and closed her eyes, savoring this dish straight from Mam's kitchen.

Where was Mark?

She couldn't blame him for leaving. She couldn't imagine how difficult it would be to face those memories again, especially from his own Mam. It was almost beyond her comprehension.

When Mark returned a short time later, they sat in the neglected garden and talked. At first Mark was curt, defiant even, but as the late afternoon turned to evening, the dusty sunlight filtering through the trees, he spoke of his pain. He desperately longed to forgive his mother, but he didn't have the strength to do it.

Sadie could only slip her hand in his, lay her head on his shoulder, and listen. His pain was as raw as the day his mother had left so many years ago. Sadie knew then that he would always be bound by the fetters of his past, even if he reached a measure of forgiveness.

Perhaps forgiveness was like love. It came in small portions, but it was the exact amount you needed, poured out by a loving Father above.

Life is imperfect. To believe that painful things could be completely washed away, never to return, was wishful thinking.

The painful things of the past remained, but with forgiveness and love, you could lock them away if the key to that lock could be maintained by love. It was God who supplied the key of love yet again. He was always there.

So was love.

Chapter 21

THE FOLLOWING MORNING THERE WAS A RESOUNDING knock from the rusted knocker on the front door, followed closely by two insistent peals from the doorbell. Instinctively Meely clutched her robe with one hand and grasped at her quilts with the other, her eyes wide with terror as the dogs began their ear-splitting cacophony.

"They're coming to get me, aren't they?" she hissed, her dark hair flying about her head as she searched for a way of escape.

Before Sadie could stop her, Meely lifted the quilt, flung her legs over the side of the sofa, raised herself up, and with a frightened cry, fell headlong onto the carpet.

As the doorbell repeated its insistent peals, Mark and Sadie rushed to Meely's side, hoarse sobs escaping the pitifully thin body. Choking and crying, clawing the air with her thin, white fingers, she was clearly horrified now.

"Get the door," Mark said curtly.

Sadie went to the door, hushing the dogs as best she could before pulling it open tentatively, peeping out to see a large African-American man. Instinctively, she was reluctant to ask him in.

She stepped outside and kept her hand on the door handle in case she needed a quick escape back inside.

"How ya doin', honey? I'm Tom!" He extended his large hand and crushed Sadie's in an all-encompassing grip.

Then, rushing on, giving Sadie no space to introduce herself, he filled the air around him with a steady stream of words spoken loudly but in a rich, lovely baritone that sent shivers down Sadie's spine.

"I'm Tom, the preacher man. I've been tellin' the Lord that he needs to let me know if there's anything I can do for this lady. She never comes out of the house, but I'm trusting him to let me know if she needs help. Last night I saw someone walking around here as I was comin' home, an' sure enough, I knew right then that the Lord needed me here. How's she doin'?"

Sadie shook her head.

"I figgered. I figgered. Honey, she in a bad way?"

"She doesn't have long."

"Aw, honey!"

With that, Sadie was enveloped in what she could only describe as a bear hug, from which he released her just as quickly.

"You relation?"

"My ... boyfriend's mother."

"Aw, honey!"

There was a sweet lilt to his words, a butterfly perched on a question, a dove of peace on every endearment.

His words always came with a smile. His eyes were a constant glow of good humor, his white teeth a flash of goodwill. All this was apparent in these first few moments.

"She needs saved, right?"

Sadie nodded, hesitantly. The English used the word *saved*, but Sadie, like most Amish, was wary of the term.

Amish teaching instilled the fear of God as a strict master who demands that the faithful stay within the rules of the church and adhere to the keeping of good works. It was the Amish way, and it made them stumble at using the word saved to describe a believer.

"You think I'd be eaten alive if I walked through that door?" Tom asked.

Sadie smiled. "Oh, no," she said. "Follow me."

Sadie led Tom through the foyer. She did her best to keep the dogs at bay. Meely was lying on the sofa, still crying, her head moving constantly from side to side.

"Mark, this is Tom, a minister."

Mark looked up as Sadie caught her breath. How would he react?

Mark straightened, standing as tall as Tom. Then he extended his hand, a curious welcome in his brown eyes. Sadie breathed out, grateful now.

"Tom Dockers," he said, grasping Mark's hand with a firm grip. His white, white teeth and his eyes with their never-ceasing good humor won him immediately.

"Mark Peight. How do you do?"

"Fine. Your mother?"

"Yes."

Tom nodded. His eyes softened, then filled with warm tears of mercy. Slowly the massive form moved toward the frail woman. He stood over her, his head bent, his lips moving. He was clearly a powerhouse of prayer, faith, and love so great that Sadie felt sure she had never met anyone quite like this man.

Slowly, Tom placed his hand on Meely's restless shoulder. He closed his eyes. Tears squeezed between the lids.

Meely ceased her restless movement and breathed peacefully. Slowly she opened her eyes, then drew in a sharp breath. Her eyes popped as she screamed, high and desperate now.

"No! No! No!" she wailed. "Don't! Oh, don't. Don't torment me before my time!"

Her torment was visible and audible. The dogs whined in response, the large white shepherd beginning a howl of sorts.

Sadie moved quickly to let the dogs out before a situation arose that would have dire consequences.

Tom did not remove his hand. Instead he gently moved it back and forth, as if to calm the flailing woman on the sofa.

"Now listen, honey child. Nobody's gonna hurt you. I'm just here to talk awhile. Nobody's gettin' you."

His voice was drowned out by a piercing scream of agony. Still he kept talking. Half-reassurances, half-prayers. He talked on and on while Meely railed against him, cursing, crying, begging Mark to take this awful man away from her.

They felt the time had come for professional help, when they could no longer control the pain. Meely's lucid thoughts and words were fewer. The strain of trying to keep her comfortable was showing in Mark's eyes.

The local hospital had been extremely helpful, giving them telephone numbers, explaining various services, until they found an organization they were comfortable with.

At first Mark had resisted, until Sadie reasoned with him. His memories of foster care made him suspicious of anyone coming to help professionally. They were all part of "the system" in his words. Only the moans of intense discomfort from his mother's bed finally convinced him. He nodded, a sort of pitiful caving in of his resolve, when Sadie said she would make the call.

When a heavy-set nurse from Hospice showed up at the front door, Meely's screaming only increased. Undaunted, the blond-haired woman waved them all aside, telling them to "git," which they obeyed. Mark led Sadie and Tom to the kitchen, leaving the nurse to administer professional care.

They sat around the kitchen table with mugs of coffee and a blue packet of Oreo cookies. Tom took the time to introduce himself fully, explaining his life's mission as a small town "preacher man," counselor, mentor, cook, husband, and father of three: Levi, Jeptha, and Samuel.

"They my men, they my men," he chortled, swallowing yet another Oreo.

Sadie sipped coffee, quietly absorbing this man and his larger-than-life personality. She had never talked to a black man before. So she listened and became increasingly amazed by this man and his speech. He was completely and totally devoted to his Lord, his God. "My Man," as Tom called him.

Just how close could a person actually get to God? Was it possible to have a personal connection? It was a bit scary. Completely unnerving, really.

"We gotta pray us through this," Tom said. "Prayer is what my Man wants from us, y' know? He got the power. We don't, even though sometimes we think we do, y' know?"

That lilting "y' know?" served to include you fully into his outlook in a way that was not forceful or intimidating. Certainly, this man was not *fer-fearish*, the Pennsylvania Dutch term for being misled. The Amish were always alert for anyone with beliefs strange to them. They exhorted on this subject quite regularly.

Somehow, Tom was not to be feared, Sadie could tell. He just lived his faith in complete fullness. Nothing stood in his way. The way people dressed, their skin color, their way of life, their beliefs, their doctrine, it was all the same to him. He was amazed at the Amish way and glad of it.

"We all people. We all lose sight of the Glory. We sin, slip away. We come back when the Man chastens. He's the God of Glory, y' know?"

Is that how God worked? That would settle a lot of things, Sadie thought.

Tom nodded toward Mark. "Tell me about you and your mother."

So Mark told him his story. His voice was gruff, his eyes hooded sometimes, his manner brusque. But he spoke simply, leaving nothing out.

While they talked, Sadie refilled their coffee cups. She glanced at the clock, then set about grilling sandwiches and heating the chicken corn soup.

All the dishes and utensils in the kitchen were of the highest quality, bought in stores Sadie was sure she never heard of. She loved the feel of the heavy silverware, the weight of the pots and pans, and the china that was so smooth when she ran her hands across it.

"Noritake," it said on the back. Never heard of it, she thought.

Tom's hand was on Mark's now as tears dropped on the leg of his trousers. His head was bent so far, his dark bangs hiding his eyes safely from Tom's gaze.

Tom was praying, his lips moving to the words. Mark looked up and wiped his face.

With tears now in his eyes, Tom said, "We'll pray us through this, my man. You my man, Mark. You my man."

What absolute beauty in those words. Tom spoke as if every prayer went directly to God, who was so glad to have his power acknowledged that he, in turn, made all things possible. What a new and unbelievable thought.

No, unbelievable was not the right word. It was believable. It was just different. Tom had a large, hopeful perspective on God's promises.

After inhaling his lunch, Tom left with a promise to return the following day.

The Hospice nurse also left, but not before giving Mark and Sadie clear instructions. She was professional and precise, giving only the necessary information. She was friendly but firm. Hospice would send over a hospital bed. The morphine would have to be administered in regular doses with no let-up. Once the pain threshold got out of control, there was no bringing it back down easily. They were to give her any food she could keep down, but no caffeine.

The nurse said she'd return each day on a regular basis, and with that she was gone.

✶ ✡ ✶

Tom and the Hospice nurses from Lutheran Home Care became a grounding regularity, especially as Meely's condition deteriorated.

There were also phone calls now. Long, emotional calls from Sadie's Mam and sisters begging her to come home. Reuben told her that Paris wasn't eating her oats. He said it jubilantly, as if that fact alone would bring Sadie flying back as fast as Amtrak could carry her. He also informed her that Anna could finally ride now that she was as thin as a rail. Sadie stiffened with fear and insisted he put Anna on the line right now and get out of the phone shanty while they talked.

He turned the phone over to Anna, but not before he told Sadie about the latest horse shooting. They shot a palomino, but it survived. The police traced the caliber of the rifle. Many detectives were now on the case, according to the local paper.

"It's Paris they're after," Reuben concluded sagely.

Anna said she was not as thin as a rail. No, she was not throwing up. Neither was she forcing herself to purge the food she ate. Yes, she was eating healthily.

The rasping note in her voice set off an alarm in Sadie's mind, but she said nothing. She would deal with troubles back home when she returned. She had more than enough concerns here with Mark and Meely.

Mam was wonderfully supportive and sympathetic. She even cried tears of joy when Sadie told her about Tom. Mam told Sadie that, as she went through life, she would meet people from all walks of faith. Her view of God would widen and deepen. But no matter where her life led her, Mam told her to never lose sight of her wonderful heritage. She was privileged to be born and raised in an Amish home.

"We're people same as everyone else, Sadie, but hang on to your background. It is worth something."

✿ ✡ ✿

When possible, Meely would have a bowl of soup or some oatmeal. Sometimes she asked for a soft-boiled egg or a piece of dry toast. Most of the time, she didn't eat at all, just drifted in and out of sleep.

Once, when the sun was unusually hot and the dry prairie winds began to blow, she asked to have her bed raised. She asked Sadie to come sit with her and Mark, and she began to talk.

She asked about Tom first in her hoarse, weak voice.

"Who is that big, black guy that's in here? He walks through my dreams. He's always calling me, and I'm tied to the bed by my ankles. So I can't go. I can't reach him."

"He's a preacher," Sadie said.

"I figured," she whispered.

Then her tone changed, and she spoke forthrightly. "Yeah, well... I'm not stupid. My time is almost here, and I want to talk. I'm done, now. What I mean is, I'm done blaming everyone else for my life. You know I've always done that?"

Mark nodded in response to Meely's question.

"You don't know if I did or not, Mark, so why are you nodding?"

She was sharp, Sadie thought. She was surprised to see Meely let go of the pitiful thrust of defiance. There was a new expression in her eyes.

Mark said nothing, kept his eyes hidden.

"It's okay. I blamed Atlee. Then I blamed my father. Even my mother. God rest her soul."

She said the last few word in the softest whisper possible, but Sadie heard.

"To blame other people is how you do it, you know. You justify leaving a devoted husband and six beautiful children only by the power of blaming others. It's the easiest way. As long as you can do that, you can convince yourself that you're okay; you're a good person. It's the others, the bad people, who made you this way."

She stopped to cough. She was so weak that it raked

against Sadie's heart and brought tears to her eyes.

"So you do what you want," Meely continued. "You don't do what you know is right. You…you…*recht fertich*—justify yourself—by your own way of thinking. It starts to grow like a parasitic vine that eventually kills the tree that hosts it. The vine is your attitude—killing the truth. Soon you don't know what's right or wrong anymore. And you don't care."

Meely bowed her head, her black hair hiding her tortured eyes.

"I'm so afraid of the truth," she whispered.

Neither Mark nor Sadie knew how to respond. They remained quiet. The clock in the corner supplied the only sound for several minutes.

"What if I say it was all my own fault? Then what? My sins are so…monstrous, there's absolutely no way I can even hope of getting to… Ach, you know. I can't even say the word. I'm too dirty and wretched and lost."

The dogs whined at the door. The clock kept up its rhythmic sound. The refrigerator hummed in the kitchen.

"Mam, at least you admit that what you did was wrong," Mark said quietly. "That's a start, isn't it? I'm no saint either, Mam. But it seems to me, you'd be on the right track."

Mark was suddenly embarrassed by his halting speech in front of Sadie, not sure how she felt about his mother to begin with.

"Well, no doubt about it, if I die, I will go to hell. The devil made me believe I was this pitiful person all my life. Well…not all of it. I have six beautiful children. I see their faces every night before I go to sleep."

A sob tore at the ravaged throat, but she lifted her head and pressed on.

"Beulah. How happy I was to have a daughter! Oh, she was so cute. Even the midwives fussed about her when she was born. Eyes like half moons, a little button for a nose. I kissed her little face constantly. We named Beulah out of great joy. *Beulah* sounds almost like 'bugle.'"

The happy glow that spread across her face was replaced by a look of despair as she described Timothy's birth the following year.

"I wasn't ready. I resisted this little boy growing in my stomach. Oh, where is Timothy now? I pity him so *veesht*.

"He was so thin when he was born. I didn't eat right, I... Oh! Do I have to confess everything? Tell the whole truth?" she groaned. "Well, I have nothing to lose.

"I didn't want Timothy or any of the others after that. I tried to starve myself... I was selfish and mean and thought of no one but myself.

"Diana was as cute as Beulah, but so colicky. Atlee rocked her at night or carried her around on a pillow while I slept. He was always good with the babies. He wanted to name her Elizabeth. Lissie!"

Meely spit the word out with all the force she could muster.

"Lissie! His fat, vile mother. How I hated her! She accused me of so many things. How was I possibly supposed to keep all the laundry clean and white and have the meals ready on time with a colicky baby? That's when I..."

She lowered her head yet again, then asked for a drink of tea. She took a tiny swallow of the icy liquid before she resumed her story.

"When Rachel Mae was born, I knew there was no way I was going to make it. I had no interest in my children anymore. I just wanted out. I planned my exit secretly. Atlee felt it. He became steadily more despairing.

"Because I clung to tradition, I continued my wifely duties, at least for a while. Atlee was very conservative, too. He said the wife is subject to her husband in all things, and I believed him, although I rebelled inside. So horribly.

"I had already started seeing Evan when Jackson was born."

Suddenly Mark burst out, "Mother! Why? Why did you have all these children? It wasn't our fault that you couldn't stand your own life, but you blamed us all the time? That's all you did! Why did you bring innocent souls into this world only to raise them like some stinking...*vermin*!"

He spat the last word into her face, and she cringed beneath his hot wrath. He clenched his fists to his side.

Sadie rose partially, her hand outstretched as if to stop the flow of seething lava from the volcanic crater that was Mark's past.

"Don't, Mark," Meely whispered, weaker now.

"I will if I want to!" he seethed. "In your wildest imagination, Mam, you will never fully realize what you did."

Mark was panting now, his eyes terrible in their anger.

Sadie then broke in calmly in what she hoped was a quieting tone. She talked about Dorothy and Jim and how they couldn't have children and how they felt that God had finally answered their prayers by sending Marcellus and Louis into their lives.

"Perhaps," Sadie concluded, "God is answering your prayers. Perhaps things are not as bad as they looked."

Meely raised her eyes to Mark's. His fell first.

"Mark, I know that I've done a lot of wrong. But will you promise me one thing? I won't live long enough to find my children. Will you find them for me? I can die easier if I know that somehow, you will know where they are and…what they're doing. It might help for you to forgive me, too. Can you promise me that?"

"I'm not made of money."

Sadie could not believe her ears. How could he deny his mother's dying wish? How could he be so cold, so…uncaring?

She opened her mouth to tell him, then decided against it. She could never know what he'd been through or what it was like when he struggled to keep his little siblings from starving.

Who was to be pitied most? It was unanswerable. The past hung over them like a black shroud of misery.

Was Meely the only one at fault, or did Mark do wrong, too? Perhaps he hadn't as a child, but how long would it be until he came to grips with his past? Did those wrongs condone his festering grudges? How long was long enough?

Forgive us our debts as we forgive our debtors. How often do we say that? Sadie wondered. How often do we do it?

Was Mark's unforgiving spirit as bad as his mother's sins in God's eyes? Sadie shrank before the truth. Then she thought of Tom. We'll pray our way through this, she thought.

"Mark, listen. I want to contact my lawyer. You will get all this: the house, the farm, such as it is. I have no one else. Before you showed up, I considered leaving it to the dogs, but that's just nasty. And it is my wish that somewhere, somehow, you can find my…little ones, especially Timothy. Oh, he was so skinny. Please find Timothy someday."

Mark said nothing.

Meely sighed, a long, shaking sound. Then she let her head fall back onto the pillows. Her long dark lashes, so peculiarly thick in spite of the cancer treatments, brushed her cheeks as she closed them.

"I need to rest now."

There was nothing for Mark and Sadie to do but go to the kitchen. When they sat down at the table, Mark wouldn't even look at Sadie. His face stony, the features closed as tightly as a prison door.

Sadie was more than grateful when the phone rang. She grabbed the receiver like a drowning person grabs a life preserver. She smiled when she heard Dorothy's nasally voice say much too loudly, "Whatcha doin', Sadie?" followed by a lengthy list of all the wrongs Erma Keim performed every day, turning that whole ranch upside down.

She glanced out the window and saw Mark whacking furiously at weeds in the garden with an old sickle. She laughed out loud and let Dorothy think it was because of her.

Chapter 22

SHE CALLED LATE AT NIGHT. HER VOICE WAS STRONG, laced with the force of her terror. Her hands fluttered furiously as she kept repeating, "I'm lost. I'm so lost. I have no idea where I am."

Sadie panicked. Her forgotten robe fell open as she grasped Mark by the sleeves and pulled him away, whispering, "Mark! What if she's going? What if her mind is going before she's saved? We have to call Tom!"

Mark turned away from her as she grabbed the strings of her robe and tied them about her waist.

He snapped on the bedside lamp before sitting on the side of Meely's bed. His hair was tousled, his clothes thrown on hurriedly, his shirttail hanging over his trousers, his feet bare.

"Mam," he called softly. Then again, "Mam."

He reached for her moving hands, held them firmly, then released them when Meely thrashed her head about.

"Mam."

Suddenly she sat straight up and glared at him. "Don't 'Mam' me. You're as lost as I am." That was all.

Mark watched her face. Sadie slipped out of the room and went to the kitchen. She found the slip of paper with Tom's number on it beneath a magnet on the refrigerator. She dialed the number.

Tom arrived quickly, just as Sadie knew he would. He hugged her at the door and Sadie clung to him unashamedly. She led him inside. He clapped his hand on Mark's shoulder, called him "My man," then bent to look into Meely's face.

"What's up, honey?" he asked softly.

At the sound of his voice, Meely cried, softly at first, then with increasing force, until Sadie was afraid Meely's thin body would not hold up beneath the powerful sobs that ravaged her.

Tom placed his huge hand on her shoulder to soothe her and began to pray.

Mark and Sadie, unaccustomed to anyone praying verbally except for the prayers read from the German prayer book during church, felt a bit uncomfortable. Sadie was glad for the shadows in the room as she lowered her head and Tom prayed on.

Tom put a hand on Meely's head and prayed for the Lord to visit this woman now, to make known his presence. But she gave no notice that she heard Tom at all, or was beyond caring. Finally she turned her face away.

"Go away," she told Tom.

"I ain't goin' anywhere, honey."

And he didn't. He stayed right there by her side and read to her from the Bible. He read verses of encouragement and hope until Meely slowly quieted.

When she looked up a short time later, they noticed a change in her. The storm had passed and left behind it a woman who was completely void of anything. Her eyes were quiet pools of emptiness in the light of the bedside lamp: no defiance, no despair, but no hope either. There was simply nothing.

Then she lowered her head and spoke to Tom.

"Tom, what would you do in my shoes?"

She asked the question so softly, so pitifully, that it broke Sadie's heart.

"I'd ask Jesus to save my soul," Tom answered quietly in his magical voice.

"He can't anymore."

"And why not?"

"You know why. I'm too wicked. I've been too bad. I've had three other men. I killed Atlee."

"Now wait a minute. You what?"

"My first husband. The father of my children."

"You killed him?"

"Yes."

"How'd you do that?"

"Well, he drowned himself. But it was because I left him."

"I see."

Tom sat quietly for a long time until Meely began weeping violently again.

Then Tom said quietly, "Why don't you look the other way?"

Meely stopped crying. "Which way?"

"Look to Jesus."

"I can't find him. Besides, he won't forgive me."

"You'd be surprised, Meely."

Tom talked about salvation in minute detail. Every word was a caress, the love of God so evident with his "y' knows?" and "my Mans." He assured her that she had already taken the most important step: admitting her sinful past. Now she had to move on and ask for mercy.

"Just accept it."

"I can't. They excommunicated me. I'm given over to the devil."

Tom raised his eyebrows, then looked to Mark, seeking his help.

Mark explained the Amish way of excommunication that occurs when a member is disobedient or breaks their vows to the church.

"It is actually a form of love, Mam," Mark said, speaking softly. "It's a reminder of your wrongdoing so that your spirit may be redeemed."

Suddenly, Meely understood.

"Aah!" The cry was long and drawn out.

"Yes! Oh, how I do understand that, Mark! My guilt went with me everywhere I went. Especially when I lay in bed at night. My children's faces. Atlee's face. The fact that I had been disobedient. The shunning. The ban. It bothered me every day of my life. But..."

Here her eyes opened wide as she seemed to grasp a solid fact.

"Do you suppose... Could it be...? Now I'm sorry. Can I still be saved?"

"No doubt about it, honey. You messed up badly. But Jesus is still your only hope of salvation. He's the light that will get you safely to the other side."

Still she wavered. Still she doubted.

Tom prayed again, then began humming the first bars of "Amazing Grace." He asked Mark and Sadie to join him, which they did gladly, though sometimes they stumbled over the words.

Meely fell asleep, then, and Tom stood up, shaking his head.

"We're gonna have to pray our way through this," he said. "Stay with me."

✡ ✡ ✡

The cancer soon began invading Meely's nerve endings and tissue, causing excruciating pain. The morphine did little against the constant waves of torment, so the Hospice nurses adjusted the dosage.

The medication caused Meely to slide in and out of consciousness. Sometimes she spoke lucidly; other times she was completely bewildered.

During one particularly good afternoon, she asked Mark to sing the *Lob Song*, an old song in the German hymnbook that was sung at every Amish service. It was a song from her childhood, her past, even the years of overwhelming responsibility as a mother.

Sadie joined him, self-consciously at first, but their voices gathered strength as they sang. It proved to be a healing balm, a salve of love, that opened the way for Tom to minister to Meely.

When Tom spoke this time, she couldn't speak. She just nodded. Soon warm tears ran down her cheeks as she kept nodding, understanding, taking it all in.

Tom's words were like a warm summer rain that fell from kind skies, nurturing tiny, hard seeds in a cold, dry earth. The seeds cracked, broke, and new life crept upward. Finally, in the spring, the plant burst through the soil into the marvelous sunlight.

Tom's words finally produced light in her eyes.

"I do accept Jesus Christ."

She spoke quietly, the words illuminated by a first light of grace, and the angels sang.

Mark's face reflected the light in his mother's. Sadie had never seen such soft, broken, mellow light emanating from his eyes. It was almost holy. None of the old brashness was there.

Meely was quiet after that, and Tom respected her silence. He simply sat by her bedside, his hand on hers.

Sadie couldn't help but think how Amish it was. So quiet, with little fanfare. It was still Meely's way after all these years. Tom recognized this, and later called it right.

They left her then, and went to the kitchen, talking in low tones.

✿ ✡ ✿

They often sang for her now. Sometimes in German, other times in English, they sang any hymn they could remember.

One day when Sadie thought Meely was asleep, she chuckled quietly. Sadie thought nothing of it, thinking Meely may have been laughing in her sleep.

"Remember '*Schlofc, buppli, Schlofc*' ('Sleep baby sleep')"? Meely asked Sadie.

"Yes."

"I sang that little song at least a thousand times."

She opened her eyes, and in a pathetic, reedy whisper, she began:

> *Schlofc, buppli, Schlofc,*
> *Da doddy hüt die schofe,*
> *Die mommy melked die rote kie*
> *Kommt net hame bis mya frie*
> *Schlofc, buppli, Schlofc.*

Meely sighed. A tear trembled on her eyelid.

"Poor little Timothy. I sang that to him all the time." She turned to Sadie with an earnest look in her eyes. "If you ever see Timothy, promise me you'll tell him how I wish I'd been nicer to him. Please?"

Sadie nodded solemnly.

✧ ✪ ✧

Meely lingered longer than anyone anticipated. The shroud of approaching death cast a dark pall over each day. Sadie's sense of homesickness grew.

One day Tom unexpectedly offered to stay with Meely and sent Mark and Sadie out for the afternoon.

"Pack a lunch. Go somewhere and have a picnic."

So they did. They packed ham sandwiches, fruit, and some of the chocolate cake Tom's wife, Malinda, had sent along over. They put ice in an old, plastic, two-quart jug and filled it with iced tea. Then they started out as the sun was climbing to noontime.

It was a warm spring day. Butterflies flapped and fluttered, hovering over wildflowers in the overgrown garden. Birds dipped and trilled their endless songs.

Mark was attentive, helping her over the broken board fence, holding her hand, teasing her, slipping a lean, brown arm around her waist. For a few hours they would forget. For a few hours they would remember they were young and in love with a bright future.

Mark did not mention his mother's account of her will, and neither did Sadie. It seemed too unreal, like a mirage. The delusional words of a dying woman. Better not approach the subject with any real amount of hope.

The lawyer had come and done all the necessary work

to fulfill Meely's dying wishes. Mark was the sole heir. If any of his siblings were found, they would be given their share.

It was quite a large sum of money, making the 20,000-dollar reward for rescuing the wild horses seem paltry. The sale of the farm would make the sum even larger.

They came to a creek of sorts. It was really only a trickle winding through a ditch and snaking along the prairie grasses and sagebrush. A few old willow trees grew along its banks, their roots reaching down into the water as if to sustain life by the small trickle the creek offered. The grass was thick and lush, however, especially beneath the dancing willow leaves, the long green fronds whispering as they moved gently in the breeze.

Mark threw himself on his back, his hands behind his head, his knees bent in a V-shape. He sighed contentedly and closed his eyes.

Sadie sat beside him, her arms wrapped around her knees. She watched the rise and fall of his broad chest beneath the blue denim of his shirt. He was so unbelievably handsome, the way his dark hair fell over his eyes. And that perfect mouth. Was it enough to base her love on that face?

She knew it wasn't, but she knew just as clearly that this was where God wanted her, beside this man and all his baggage. Yes, his past would return again and again to torment him. He would always battle between darkness and light. Even so, she knew she was right where she was supposed to be, directly in the center of God's will.

So she sat quietly as Mark feigned sleep. She pulled a few grasses, fingered that tender yellow part that rises from the earth, and thought of home.

She smiled to herself as she thought of Dorothy's last phone call. She had ranted on in the most erratic manner about Erma Keim, claiming she was in love with Lothario Bean, poor man. He was a good Catholic husband to his beautiful wife, and here was that red-haired giraffe after him with no shame.

Sadie had laughed out loud and told Dorothy it was just Erma's way. She was extremely outgoing, exuberant, and a bit overboard, but she was certainly not a man-chaser.

Dorothy huffed indignantly.

"Sadie, you can try and be the peacemaker all you want. But I know when I see a girl settin' her hat for someone. She's out of line. And you should see how Lothario acts about her fruit pies. It's unreal! He goes on and on about that Dutch apple she makes. You know, the one with the crumb topping? With streusel? Now if that ain't out-and-out flirting, I don't know what is. She even straightens her apron when my Jim walks through that kitchen door, so she does."

"It's just her way," Sadie repeated.

"Well, them fruit pies? She's gonna make 'em for all the men now. To take home. They're not *that* good. If you ask me, she's a bit stingy on the sugar. Now my blueberry pies, on the other hand, can't be beat."

Sadie assured Dorothy that her pies were the best, but she liked the idea of Erma pleasing those ranch hands with her apple pies. Erma needed a little praise and affirmation.

"Dorothy, you know as well as I do that an old maid like her needs love and attention, too. We all do."

"That's exactly right, Sadie. I ain't dumb. That's why she's after all them men, even Richard Caldwell. Why, when those two get together, I have to take my hearing aids out, so I do. The other day they was havin' a slice o' pie in my kitchen, mind you, both of 'em roaring like hyenas. That old Erma was a-slappin' her knee when she laughed. The boss, he eats it all up, same as her apple pie. Now that pie, Sadie, could do with at least another cup of sugar."

Suddenly Mark turned his head to look at her, his intense gaze interrupting her thoughts.

"Sadie."

She couldn't answer. There was a tone of endearment in the way he said her name that drove away her power to speak at all. Her limbs turned to water when he sat up, his gaze never wavering.

"Sadie."

He said her name again, a caress this time. She could not answer.

"Will you marry me?"

The words were spoken softly, then hung in the air between them, veiled in cascades of white roses and lilies of the valley. She heard lovely music from somewhere deep within, the sound of love starting in her mind and seeping into her heart and soul.

"Oh, Mark!"

The wonder of his question flowed through her being, through her hands. They fluttered to his as he sought them, laced her fingers together with his. She breathed the scent of the flowers into her answer.

"Oh, Mark! Yes! Yes, I will marry you!"

He crushed her to him, his lips finding her willing ones. Breathless now, they broke apart. Tears came to Mark's eyes.

"I wanted to find a perfect time and place, but... I'm not real good with words and romantic stuff... you know? Like getting down on my knees with a ring the way English people do."

Sadie laughed and kissed him again, never wanting to let him go.

"Mark, you don't need to. But I do want a clock," she teased.

A clock was the traditional Amish engagement gift. Once a young girl received her clock, whether a grandfather or a pendulum clock for the wall, the union was sealed for coming nuptials.

"I will let you have my mother's."

Suddenly, after that, he became shy, sensitive to the fact that this may be bad timing with his mother dying. Was it all too dark and foreboding for her? How could she say yes? There was no way her life would ever be easy. Perhaps she had no idea how hard.

"I probably have a pretty good idea what I'm in for. I mean, our dating has been a bit complex at times. To put it politely."

"All my fault. Every time."

"No, of course not. I just have to remember that you are … well, not like other people."

They laughed together, Mark held her and murmured his love. The fact that she would marry him put him in a state of disbelief.

"But why? Why would you marry me?"

"It's so simple, Mark. I love you. I know we'll have many dark valleys to go through, but this love will sustain us. I want to be with you. I want to make your breakfast, pack your lunch, wash your clothes, fold them and put them away…"

"Hopefully sleep in the same bed with me."

Sadie felt the color warm her face.

"That, too, of course."

"Sadie."

Suddenly, there was a different tone in his voice. Again she became quiet.

"I have been with other women. I'm not..." He couldn't go on.

Sadie nodded.

"Mark, it's okay. I figured as much. But..."

She needed to know, even if it was a question that would be old-fashioned and maybe even offensive.

"That was before you gave your heart to Jesus? Before you were baptized into the Amish faith?"

"Of course, Sadie."

"I'm so glad," she whispered.

And she was. His sins were forgiven, washed away by the blood of the Lamb. Thanksgiving welled up in her heart as that realization settled in, brighter and more real than ever before. For without the love of God, what would their union become?

Sadie's nature was not perfect either. She was full of selfishness, jealousy, and other weaknesses that would not serve his insecurities well.

Search my heart, O God, and show me my weaknesses. That was all she could think until it became a sort of benediction.

They sat together for a long time, talking of their future and making plans for the wedding. At last Mark spoke of his longing to find Timothy.

"It breaks my heart, to think of Mam's sadness for Timothy. I remember him well. He was so thin, whining and crying. I honestly think he drove her nuts. I'll do anything to honor her wish to find him."

"But Mark, why were you so cold when she asked you to find him?"

"Sadie, listen. There's one thing you will need to understand. Every single time I'm confronted with my past, I want to lash out, hurt someone, blame someone, make it all go away by the power of my own anger. Do you have any idea how horrible it is to remember the things I am forced to remember? Did you ever hear a child crying steadily all night long because of an empty stomach? The Jell-o... I can still smell it, feel the sticky, sugary powder against my hand as I shook a portion into the stinking, plastic, milk-stained bottle. I can't eat strawberry Jell-o to this day. I did what I had to do, but the gigantic despair I lived with is like a coiled snake, ready to strike. I can't really explain it... fully, I guess."

Sadie closed her eyes as tears leaked between her lashes and made wet trails down both her cheeks. Mark held her closer and kissed her forehead.

"Timothy wasn't very healthy to begin with. And Mam... Well, she wasn't really abusive, but she took out a lot of her frustrations on Timothy. That... in a way, is why I'm almost afraid to find him. How could he possibly have turned out to be a normal human being? He sure didn't have much to go on those first few years. His little bottom got so sore from his constant diarrhea. I feel so bad about that. I did the best I could, but there weren't always clean diapers. I..."

Sadie cut him off.

"All while I was in Ohio, eating my mother's good cooking, wearing her well-washed laundry, playing on the manicured lawn, living with the love of two good parents. I had no clue I had something special going on in my life."

Suddenly she sat up and turned to meet his brown eyes.

"And, Mark, I guarantee, if I would have been able to, I would have brought you a whole bunch of groceries. Better yet, I would have packed all of you in a car and brought you home."

"But..." Here Mark threw back his head and laughed, a free and beautiful sound.

"You probably weren't even born yet!"

Chapter 23

M EELY'S PAIN WAS THE DEMON THEY ALL BATTLED, but Tom's dark face and wondrous smile had a way of brightening even the most trying hour.

Hospice provided more pain-killers. They also brought the best mattress available, with a large gel-filled overlay. The gel moved through the well-built tubes of the mattress to relieve the pressure on her thin body.

Even so, no one could touch her. The softest, most gentle touch evoked shrill cries of alarm, pain, and horror.

She cried, begged, then finally, when her newfound faith found its footing, she prayed.

The hardness in her eyes was gone. They were now clear pools of love. She spoke of it, she whispered of it, and she sang songs of God's love. She sang "Shall We Gather at the River?," "How Great is Our God," and "Beulah Land," then lapsed into a soft conversation about her darling baby Beulah.

"You know, I must not have been all bad. I loved her. If I could only tell her that. You will someday, right, Mark? Tell her how cute she was, how I kissed her. I did love her.

"But you know, the love I have for her is such a tiny drop compared to the love we receive from heaven. The angels love me now, Well, I guess they did before, but I just didn't accept it. They're waiting for me. Not me. My soul. It'll fly away when I stop breathing.

"You know, I loved Atlee at one time. I love him now. I can't wait to see him. And I don't have to tell him I'm sorry. He already knows. Isn't that wonderful?

"Praise his name! Praise his goodness!"

And she was singing softly, humming under her breath. Then she slept, her thin chest heaving, then rising and falling slowly.

Her lips were so dry, so painfully cracked and brittle. Ever so gently, Sadie wet a sponge and moistened the once-beautiful mouth. Meely moaned with pain in her sleep.

Tom sat with his head bent. He held Meely's hand, whispering his prayers, still praying her through this.

Sadie sat wrapped in her robe, her dark hair pulled back in a ponytail, her head resting on the back of the red wing-chair, her legs drawn up and curled beside her.

Mark sat on the carpet, his head resting against the arm of the chair. They could barely stay apart from each other now. Their engagement opened a whole new world of love, dispelling any insecurities or doubts about each other's feelings that they may have felt before. They often discussed their plans to spend the rest of their lives together.

Tom had cried openly when they told him about their engagement. He cried, laughed, rejoiced, even danced around the kitchen, singing an English wedding song. Mark recognized it, but Sadie was completely perplexed.

He brought a cake, served it with ice cream. Malinda and his three "men" came, too.

Malinda was at least 250 pounds and had the most beautiful face Sadie had ever seen. She wore a multi-colored silk head wrap. Her beautiful eyes were pools of liquid amber, and perfect black eyebrows accentuated her golden brown complexion. Her full, soft lips were always drawn into a half-smile. Her clothes made her look like an African queen in swaying, brilliant skirts. A smartly-cut top made her silhouette appear well formed. A person of unquestionable presence, her movements sort of sailed through the rooms.

Their three boys, whom Tom called his "men," were polite, well-spoken, and seemed completely happy and well adjusted. Teasing their parents, — "Jus' jivin' wid ya," they'd say—their handsome faces were wreathed in smiles almost all the time, their laughter quick and easy.

Sadie wondered what kept those loose jeans from falling down, the only saving grace being the looser T-shirts that nearly reached their knees. Their odd shoes were either orange, green, or purple. Jeptha wore what looked like black pantyhose on his head, while Levi wore his hair in long coiled cornrows.

The family was full of an endless stream of laughter, love, and a generous helping of goodwill toward everyone in the room and outside of it.

Sadie asked Malinda if the family always got along in this manner and was astounded to hear an adamant, "No! Oh, no. Huh-uh, man. Who you think we are, huh? We people."

After they all left, Sadie and Mark looked at each other and laughed.

"What a great family!" Mark said, shaking his head.

The Hospice nurse left a short while later, so they went to the bedroom to sit with Meely while she slept. They didn't try to touch her at all, knowing it would only bring pain rather than comfort.

They took their seats and made themselves comfortable, ready to keep the vigil once more. They noticed something different. There was a quiet aura about Meely —too quiet.

Mark looked at Sadie, a question in her eyes. She responded with raised eyebrows.

Had she passed away so suddenly? When she was all alone? But, no. She was still breathing, though it was shallow and erratic, almost imperceptible. Then she stirred.

Mark reached her first. He put out his hands to guide her as she slowly sat up, but surprisingly, she needed no assistance.

Sadie was at Mark's side, astounded.

"We can't..." she began.

But Mark held a finger to his lips. They watched in disbelief as she turned her body and moved to put her feet on the floor. Their hands were outstretched, ready to catch her, but there was no need.

Was the setting sun casting this golden glow throughout the room? Or was it the glow of hovering angels?

Slowly, Meely's thin white feet touched the carpet. As if in a dream, she lifted her thin arms and walked to Mark. She smiled, and her dark eyes filled with a light beyond earthly comprehension.

With a soft cry, Mark enfolded her in his strong brown arms. Then they swayed, back and forth, in soft, undulating movements.

"Goodbye," she whispered, her dance of love complete.

Mark bent his head and kissed his mother's cheek, then led her back to the bed. He laid her down quietly and gently. He held Sadie in one arm, his dying mother in the other, while cleansing tears of healing rained down his cheeks.

"Goodbye, Mam," he choked.

And then Sadie knew she was gone. Her soul had taken its flight.

It seemed she had been partly in heaven and partly here on earth when she danced with Mark. She only needed to give away this great love before she left to be with Jesus.

Mark knelt by his mother's bed, sobs coming hoarsely at first, until the power of them sent him to the floor, where his grief turned to tormented keening that could not be stopped.

Wisely, Sadie stayed back. This was not ordinary grief.

This, she supposed, is what happens when a person takes her own way. She is like a barge propelled by a huge diesel engine of self-will, leaving disappointment and all-consuming sadness in its wake. When the end comes, when the barge runs aground and spills toxic oil into the pristine sea, it is those left behind who deal with the slick, poisonous hatred of unforgiveness for the rest of their lives.

But there was Jesus' forgiveness, yes. And there was closure for those damaged in the wake, oh, yes!

Sadie would never forget this moment. Sadie would never forget the sweetness of that whispered, "Goodbye." But to see Mark in the throes of this disappointment was almost more than she could bear. The disappointment of a wasted life. The anger of every hardship he had ever endured. The desperate, endless, life-draining swimming to get out of the toxic oil.

Now he had partially saved himself. He had to try and save his siblings. At least find them.

The future looked daunting and dangerous. All Sadie could see was a black dragon breathing fire, and she had no sword to slay it.

But she suddenly remembered, neither did David when he went up against the giant and slew him. How often had she heard that story? As a child she always sat up and paid attention when the preacher spoke of David and Goliath. Perhaps Mark's past and the deep grief of his mother's death, perhaps all that was their Goliath, a giant they must face together.

Then slowly the storm ceased, leaving Mark in a fetal position, his hands tucked between his knees. He shuddered, relaxed, then slowly rose to his feet. He stood silently with his back toward Sadie, looking at the still form of his mother.

Suddenly he turned on his heel. "Call Tom. I'm going out," he said brusquely, refusing to meet her eyes.

"But..." Sadie began to protest, then closed her mouth, wincing as Mark slammed the door on his way out.

Feeling more alone than she ever had, she walked over to the bed and gently pulled the sheet up over Meely's still body.

Mark's mother. May God rest her soul.

Sadie had loved her sincerely. She had.

✿ ✪ ✿

The following days were a blur of activity. Tom knew what to do and helped with the funeral arrangements. Samuel and Levi worked the computer, desperately trying to find Mark's missing siblings, coming up with nothing. Malinda cooked up a storm, delivering great casserole dishes of southern cooking, huge coconut cakes with slivers of pecans all over the top.

Neighboring farm wives came. These well-meaning women dressed in clean cotton frocks brought Pyrex dishes of homemade scalloped potatoes, lasagna, burritos, fried chicken, and green-bean casserole. The quantity of food was endless.

The kindness of ordinary people is a wondrous thing, Sadie thought. She wished Meely could see how these simple country folk turned out in droves to deliver their condolences in the form of warm food.

Tom's great laugh rang out while he and Mark sampled all the food. He spent a great deal of time with Mark, beginning that first evening after Meely's death. They spent hours outside under the trees, Mark sitting in the hammock, Tom on a rusted bench.

Sadie wondered if Mark would ever tell her what they talked about.

The viewing at the local funeral home was pitifully small. There was no long line of friends and acquaintances waiting to sign their names at the entrance. There were only a few people from the Hospice service, the man who brought salt for the water softener, and the fuel-truck driver. Mark was the only family.

Meely was still lovely, laid in a bed of white satin. Great banks of flowers surrounded the coffin, as she had wanted.

A soft, early, summer rain fell on the heads of the small group of mourners at the burial. A few well-wishers from Tom's congregation shook their heads at the sadness of it all. Their faces were a haven of kindness for Mark and Sadie now.

Tom spoke a eulogy of love. He read the Twenty-Third Psalm, called Meely "sister," and led the group in a hopeful hymn. Mark and Sadie bowed their heads and cried tears of cleansing. The past was partially settled, or at least as much as it could be in a matter of a few days.

They went back to the house, where Malinda served up a banquet of delicious food, urging everyone to take heaping servings of everything.

"Y'all tried this here chicken? Y' need more Coke?"

Mark ate hungrily. He smiled at Sadie, who sat across from him at the dining room table.

"You look amazing in your black dress," he whispered, sending her pulse racing.

✧ ✡ ✧

They finally made arrangements to return home. They said many tearful farewells to Tom and his family, who promised to visit. Then they climbed into the Amtrak train, that speeding wonder that would deliver Sadie once again to her family. Her heart pumped with excitement.

Going home!

Mark watched Sadie's face before commenting on it.

"Your eyes are just shining, Sadie."

"Yes, Mark, I am so happy to return home. It seems like a long time since I've seen everyone."

"Yeah, well, you're lucky."

That was all he said before turning his face away.

Oh, boy, she thought. Here we go again.

Anger bubbled out of a seething cauldron of hurt. A part of her wanted to sit up and actually hit him, yelling, "*Bupp! Grosse Bupp!*"

Would he always hold up that daunting shield of his past? Would he always make excuses and ask for pity? Or when he was jealous, would he take the role of a martyr?

Then Sadie sighed and fluctuated between self-blame and anger.

I know I'm lucky. I have a wonderful family. Maybe I shouldn't show how happy I am. It's my fault.

The steady rhythm of the train put her to sleep. It must have been a deep sleep, because she didn't remember letting her head fall on Mark's chest. She awoke completely confused, with Mark's arm around her securely.

He was in a jovial mood. He teased her and bantered incessantly about their wedding. He acted as if he had never been unkind, never left her out of his thoughts.

Complicated person, for sure, was her only rational thought.

☆ ☆ ☆

Arriving home was everything Sadie knew it would be. There were hugs and tears of welcome. Reuben hovered self-consciously in the background, wearing a brand-new shirt for the occasion. Sadie squealed and ran after him, giving him a very warm hug. He shrugged it off, but his wide grin gave away his true feelings.

Anna was alarmingly thin, just as Sadie suspected she would be. Her thin face made her eyes look abnormally large. All the loose fabric of her pretty teal-colored dress was tucked into her apron.

Sadie had to work hard to hide her fear, mentally shelving the talk she would have to have with Mam and Dat later.

It was Saturday, so no one had to go to work. Everyone piled into the kitchen and chatted over each other. There was so much to say.

Mam had prepared a wonderful brunch. There was

a breakfast pizza, made with a homemade crust, fried potatoes, sausage, eggs, tomatoes, and cheese. There were golden biscuits and sausage gravy, fresh fruit, orange juice, homemade yogurt, and granola. The coffeepot was never empty for long, but no one had room for any of the doughnuts available in great variety.

Not even Reuben's eyes were dry when Sadie spoke of Meely's death. Dat marveled over the whole thing and said he never heard anything like it. What would the ministers say about something like that?

What about the Bible story of the woman at the well? Mam asked. Wasn't that woman a sinner? Five husbands she had, and the man she was with that day was not her husband. Yet she recognized Jesus when those self-righteous scribes and Pharisees had no clue.

"Jesus offered much forgiveness and great love," she concluded. Her nostrils flared a bit. She got up to refill her coffee. It wasn't really necessary, but she was worked up by Dat questioning whether Meely was saved.

Mark listened closely. He had never heard Sadie's mam talk like that.

Dat quickly agreed, patting his wife's shoulder with a soft touch of contrition. Mam lifted her face to his, a soft smile spreading across her features. Dat returned it with one of his own.

That beautiful exchange was what came after 30 years of marriage, Sadie thought. Their own Goliath definitely had dwindled in size in the face of this long-practiced trust between them.

What a foundation! Surely it was worth more than gold. Surely she and Mark could make it, too.

After the long, drawn-out brunch, Mark followed Dat outside. Sadie knew he would tell Dat about their engagement. She decided to wait to tell Mam, anticipating the surprised expressions of her sisters and Reuben.

Her room was a welcoming haven. She had forgotten the tasteful simplicity of it, the calming white curtains and sand-colored comforter, the off-white walls, the candles and greenery blending so perfectly. She loved her room all over again.

She went to the bathroom to straighten her covering and check on the condition of her hair. She paused to sniff the familiar scent of Dove soap in the holder and to take in the border of seashells on the wall.

She raised her eyebrows when she saw the black plastic bottle of men's body wash. Was it Reuben's? Oh, my goodness.

Before long, Reuben would be going with the youth. *Rumspringa.* That was the time of "running around," when youth first experience the world and are forced to make some of their own choices. Some would be good, others bad. And yet, he would still be within the Amish arc of friends and under the scrutiny of a close community where things of a disobedient nature traveled through the grapevine at the speed of lightning. He would still have to pay the consequences once his poor behavior reached Dat's ears.

Anna was a far greater concern. Dat's frightened smile told her everything.

Sadie pushed the problems aside. She would wait to talk to Dat after Mark announced their happy news.

Mam's face actually turned a different shade and her eyes darkened, when Mark said they wanted to get married in September. She mentally calculated the months.

"June, July, August," she breathed shakily.

"Congratulations!" all her sisters yelled, in their "Happy Birthday" voices.

"Who's going to *huck nâva*?

"I will."

"I want to!"

"I'm the oldest!"

Reuben said nothing at all but just kept eating doughnuts and washing them down with milk. Sadie watched
him, then noticed him blinking his eyes and twitching the
corners of his mouth into a downward tilt. It was the way
he looked when he was not going to cry, no matter what.

For a moment, it erased Sadie's joy as clearly as a wet
rag erased words on the schoolhouse blackboard.

Would that special bond with Reuben disappear when
she married?

"I want Reuben to *huck nâva*," she said clearly.

He looked up, mid-chew, a slow smile starting in his
eyes.

Nâva hucking was a high honor. He was young, but
easily tall enough to escort one of Mark's family, whomever he chose, to the bridal table. He would even hold
her hand.

"You want to?" Sadie asked.

"Of course," Reuben answered, his chin tucked in to
make his voice sound much more masculine then it actually was.

They decided on Leah, Sadie's next oldest sister, to
be the second attendant, along with Kevin, her steady
boyfriend.

Mam was in a state of happy panic; it was honestly the
only way to describe her. Dat was gruff and businesslike,
but he snapped his suspenders too often and drank way
too much coffee.

Mark offered to pay for the wedding, telling them
about the inheritance from his mother.

There was so much to say, so much to plan, that they quickly grew tired. Dat flopped on the recliner and reached for the *Botschaft*. Mam frantically washed dishes, no doubt mentally counting all the relations on both sides of the family and calculating how much food it would take to feed them all two meals.

Sadie stole away, then, to greet Paris. She entered the barn eagerly, slipping into Paris' stall, and flinging her arms around the horse's neck, noticing the condition of her honey-colored coat, the well-rounded stomach, the muscles well developed in her deep chest.

"Oh, Paris, I missed you so much! How I wish I could take you for a ride. But I can't yet. Dat said I can't even leave you out in the pasture because of those evil men. Well, they're not going to get you."

She kept caressing the silky coat, murmuring her words of love, when she looked up to find Reuben hanging on the gate.

"Why do you have to go and get married?" he asked, his voice cracking in mid-sentence.

"Reuben, I know..." she broke off, her emotions catching her off-guard.

She gave Paris one last pat, letting the horse nuzzle the palm of her hand with that wiggling, velvety nose. Then she turned to Reuben, desperately willing herself to stay happy and lighthearted.

Why did this bother him so much?

Before she could speak, he wailed, "You'll never ride with me again! You'll have a whole bunch of babies the way everyone does, and you won't ride at all."

Sadie opened the gate and put her hands on his arms, looking squarely into his innocent eyes.

"Reuben. I will always ride Paris, married or not.

And if I have babies, I guess Mark is just going to have to stay home and watch them so we can go riding together."

Before he could respond, she pulled him into her arms and squeezed him tightly.

Chapter 24

THERE WAS NO USE TRYING TO KEEP ORDER THE remainder of the summer. Dorothy and Erma were every bit as bad as Mam. Between the three of them planning the menu for the wedding, Sadie's mind was full of at least 30 different dishes, none of them even close to what she really wanted.

Erma, of course, insisted on Dutch apple pie. When Sadie told her that Mark's favorite was coconut cream, Erma wouldn't speak to her for two weeks. This bit of news escalated Dorothy to a state of glee, saying she was an expert at cooking homemade, cream-pie filling. Then Mam said there was no way anyone was going to cook coconut pie filling except herself. Dorothy pouted for a week after that, saying no Amish cook could outdo the pies she always made for the fire hall.

Sadie ended up having a serious heart-to-heart talk with Mam about the importance of give-and-take. Why couldn't Dorothy have the honor of making the pies? Especially if they decided to bread the chicken with Mam's recipe rather than Dorothy's?

The weather grew stifling hot. The heat rolled off the sun and pressed down on them with its force, like a steamroller made of hot air.

Sadie worked only three days a week at the ranch now because of all the work to do at home. She looked forward to the times she spent in the air-conditioning, though it did little to cool Dorothy's and Erma's hot tempers. Dorothy was always in a dither these days, with Erma wielding her red-haired power. Sadie flung back and forth between them like a tennis ball, until one day when she had less patience than usual.

She had just fought with Mam about the sleeves for her wedding dress. So when Dorothy and Erma started their bickering, Sadie stood in the middle of the kitchen, balled her fists, squeezed her eyes shut, and demanded some peace and quiet. Couldn't they both stop bellowing as if they were two-year-olds? She told Erma she did not want the seven-layer salad for her wedding. She didn't like all that mayonnaise spread on top of the lettuce. Dorothy could forget about making biscuits. Amish people ate dinner rolls. She wanted all whole wheat, and she was going to order them at a bakery.

That outburst brought an end to the competition, at least temporarily. Dorothy muttered under her breath for a long time afterward, and Erma took to helping Lothario Bean in the office at the stables whenever possible. Dorothy lifted a hand to her mouth and whispered in Sadie's ear that she didn't trust that Erma, and if she didn't stay away from that "little Mexican," she was going to contact his wife, sure as shootin'.

Sadie told Dorothy she was being overly suspicious. With Lothario being the staunch Catholic he was and Erma the Amish member she was, there was absolutely nothing to worry about. They just enjoyed each other's company.

Dorothy swiped viciously at a roaster, then held the sponge aloft like a judge's gavel, water dripping off her round elbows. She told Sadie to get off her high horse right this minute. She didn't care how religious they were, those two were human beings and were spending entirely too much time alone.

So Sadie approached Erma in church the following Sunday, telling her about Dorothy's concern. Erma's eyes opened wide, then wider, before a horrified shriek broke forth from between her open lips. Then she quickly clapped two hands across her mouth as three overweight matriarchs gave her a disapproving glare.

"Oh, my word!" she hissed with a disgruntled look on her face.

Sadie burst out laughing, then clapped her own hand to her mouth.

"He's ... half my size! He's married! He's ... he's Catholic! I'm just his friend! Oh, Sadie! To think Dorothy... Even bringing up that subject is enough to ... to ..."

"It's okay, Erma. Dorothy means well. She's just being careful. I think sometimes we Amish girls are a bit naïve. In our culture, married men are so off-limits, it's like they don't exist. But it's different in the English world."

Erma chewed on a thumbnail, then shook her head in frustration.

"That is just the plight of old maids. We're always being watched, talked about, matched up with someone ... Ach, Sadie, it goes on and on."

Erma gazed unseeingly out the window, her eyes darkening with emotion, a cloud of sorrow passing over her usual animated glow. She continued, "It would be entirely different if we could...do something about our... Oh, whatever."

Sadie watched her, saying nothing. What could she say? Erma shrugged her slouching shoulders and went back to biting the thumbnail. She slumped down farther against the wash-house cupboard.

"It would be different if we...well."

She stopped. Suddenly she straightened, took a deep breath, and self-consciously tugged at her waistband. "See, you're one of the lucky ones. Mark loves you. You're getting married. Mine married someone pretty. He was mine, Sadie. We dated for a year. In the end, I wasn't enough."

She put up a hand to her coarse red hair. "My skin looks like...the Sahara. Nose like a crow's beak. I'm nothing to look at. But, Sadie, he loved me once."

"Who?"

Erma shook her head, closing the conversation.

"But.." Sadie began.

Erma closed her eyes and held up a hand to stop Sadie. She didn't want to discuss it anymore.

✿ ✡ ✿

That was how Sadie got the idea of asking Erma to *nâva huck* with Reuben. Mark had been unable to come up with any distant cousin as Reuben's partner in the wedding party. They had been racking their brains over whom to ask ever since.

When Sadie approached Reuben, he all but stood on his head in refusal. He shook his head back and forth so violently, his hair swung in his eyes, and he said no so many times, it became a sort of chant.

No amount of coaxing would help. Sadie even offered to buy him a new saddle, a brown one, brand new, from the tack shop in Critchfield.

"Nope. I'm not *nâva hucking* with her. She's twice my age. She's taller than me. She's too loud. No."

As time went on, the thought of a new saddle weighed heavily on his mind, slowly tipping the scales away from the avowed no. The turning point came about a week later. Surely he could do that for his best sister. For Mark.

Mark was not nearly as hard to deal with as Reuben. He smiled constantly, shrugged his shoulders, and said anything they planned was fine with him. All he wanted was Sadie. She was so happy, so completely in love with him, and so glad she had made this choice to marry him in spite of their rocky courtship.

He worked tirelessly on his house. He gutted the interior and replaced the old plaster with pine boards. He replaced the flooring and built all kinds of furniture. He hoped to have most of it finished by the day of the wedding for his new bride.

Sadie spent many evenings with him, sanding and varnishing. He laid the stones of the fireplace himself, working so late that Sadie fell asleep on the dusty old chair in the corner. Wolf laid at her feet, his head resting on his paws, his blue eyes watching Mark's every move.

He was as loyal to Sadie as he was to Mark, never barking or showing any hostility. He faithfully followed both of them around the property, keeping an eye out for any intruders.

Sadie was glad to have Wolf. Mark's place was so secluded. The road was about a quarter of a mile below the house, without much traffic. There were certainly no neighbors to run to if she needed help.

The house was surrounded by woods, although there was enough space for a nice lawn in the front. Mark had cut down quite a few trees to make the lawn larger. Then he chopped the trees into firewood and stacked it neatly in a shed for many winters to come.

Originally Mark had made plans to raze the house. Then he decided to preserve it by keeping the structure, the western character, the odd corners, and the dormers built into the front of the roof.

The house was brown, covered with stained oak boards. The new windows were a dark brown color as well. The door was made from heavy oak boards with narrow windows on each side. A deep porch ran along the front and left side of the house. There were no steps or sidewalks yet, only a few boards that led up to the porch.

Sadie didn't mind. She knew everything would take time. She often wondered if it was right to love a house so much. She adored the looks of it. She loved the way the house blended with the surrounding trees and how the large, old barn complemented the whole area.

She couldn't wait to put her brand-new furniture in the house, decorate the interior, keep it clean, do laundry, make meals, and do all the other everyday things married women did in their homes. It was a joy to think about and imagine.

Then one Sunday in church, the deacon announced Mark's and Sadie's upcoming nuptials. Mark had gone to speak to the deacon previously, who came to visit Sadie and confirm her desire for marriage. It was an age-old tradition and one that Sadie fully appreciated.

After the services, members of the church approached the Miller family wearing wide smiles of anticipation. Women offered to make food for Mam. Men shook Dat's hand, clapping his shoulder with work-gnarled hands. It was their way of saying, "We're here, we're happy for you, we're looking forward to a wedding. What can we do to help?"

Dat grinned and grinned, then he batted away his tears when Sadie's uncle came to tell him he had raised a remarkable daughter. The way she had placed her love and trust in this Mark Peight was commendable.

"They'll be blessed," he said wisely, shaking his head.

"I think that boy's come a long way, from what I've heard about his family."

Dat nodded, unable to speak.

On the other side of the room, poor Mam threw up her hands with laughter. So many people offered to make food that Mam asked Leroy Betty for a notepad to write everything down.

Betty would bring bars the day before the wedding for the relatives to eat while they gathered to prepare the food, the shop, the tables, or whatever else was to be done.

Leroy Betty – Banana Nut Bars.

Leroy Betty was the traditional way of identifying Betty. She was not referred to as Leroy Troyer's wife, Betty, but just Leroy Betty.

Simon Mary – Oatmeal Cookies.

Dave Lavina – Molasses Cremes.

Lod-veig Andy Sarah – Macaroni Salad.

The name *Lod-veig* is Dutch for apple butter. Who knew how Apple-Butter Andy got his nickname? He likely came from a long line of men who cooked apple butter and sold it, or made it exceptionally well. At any rate, once a nickname like that was applied, it stuck for generations.

Sometimes, there were simply too many Andy's within a 20-mile radius, and that was a sure way of knowing which Andy was being mentioned. There were also Pepper Bens and Cheese Haus Sams, and on and on.

Later that day, Mark went to the Miller home for supper. Mam had made fried chicken with the breading recipe they would use for the wedding. She wanted everyone's opinion of it so she could perfect it before the wedding. She also cooked potatoes mixed with an onion sauce and cheddar cheese. There was a roaster of homemade baked beans that had bubbled all afternoon, the bacon and tomato sauce sending up a heady fragrance.

Right before they ate, Rebekah tossed a salad, Leah made the dressing, and they all sat down to a table of happy laughter and endless chatter about the coming wedding. It was less than three weeks away.

Dat said the shop was ready, but everyone protested loud and long, contesting his statement that it was "ready."

The shop was a sort of large garage. It served as Dat's workshop and was where he kept the carriage and spring wagon. Bikes, extra picnic tables, folding chairs, express wagons, and pony carts were also stored there. So was anything else Dat bought or found or thought he needed.

Amish weddings are mostly held in the shop instead of the house because it is a huge areas of unfettered space and 200 or 300 people can be seated there. Tables are set up the day before with white tablecloths and dishes. A neighbor usually offers to host the service, where the actual ceremony is performed during a church service of three to four hours.

David Detweilers agreed to hold the service for Mark's and Sadie's wedding in their shop. Then the wedding guests would walk or drive the half mile or so to the Millers' home for the remainder of the day.

"You've only power-washed the shop," Mam gasped.

"The windows! All those windows!" Leah shrieked.

"The fly-dirt on them!" Anna joined in.

"What did you do with that old picnic table? Surely you're not going to leave it in there?" Mam asked.

"What picnic table?" Dat asked defensively.

Mam laughed and waved a hand, assuring everyone that they had plenty of time. Then she promptly sat down, took off her glasses, and began rubbing them so vigorously that a lens popped out. She quickly got to her knees, scrambling furiously for the missing necessity.

The pandemonium continued when Dat couldn't find the kit to fix Mam's glasses. Sadie upset her glass of water, soaking the clean tablecloth. Leah shrieked and jumped to get a clean tea towel, spilling another glass of ice water with her elbow. Reuben threw up his hands, declared everybody nuts, and went to the refrigerator for more ice.

Mark laughed more than Sadie had ever seen him laugh before. He seemed relaxed, his eyes calm, his smile quick and broad as he reveled in the joy of "his" family.

"Everybody needs to keep calm," he observed, laughing yet again.

"I agree!" Dat called from the living room, followed by a frantic question as to the whereabouts of the eyeglass kit in a tight voice about two octaves higher than normal.

It was a happy time of joy and anticipation, but also of quick, loud responses fueled by worn and edgy nerves. That was what an upcoming wedding did to a family, and you simply couldn't help it. At least that was Sadie's conclusion.

The girls pressed their dresses and hung them neatly

in the closet. They had made a dress for Erma, too, planning and scheming how best to help her with her hair without hurting her feelings. Between sewing projects, they cleaned the house.

Dorothy smirked all week long, batting her eyelashes coquettishly, baiting Sadie with little remarks.

"I went to the Dollar General store, Sadie. Gittin' close to wedding time, now ain't it?"

Sadie nodded happily, her eyes sparkling as she carefully extracted an English muffin from the toaster. She spread a liberal amount of butter all over both halves, took a big bite, and closed her eyes in contentment, her lips glossy with butter.

Dorothy watched her, then sniffed. "Y'know, that's an awful lot of butter on there, young lady. You gonna turn into one of those women that double their weight after they git married?"

"Dorothy!"

"Well, I'm jus' sayin' is all."

"Yep. I went to the Dollar General."

When that bought no response, she cleared her throat loudly.

"Yeah, just thought I should go. Don't really need new shoes but had other stuff on my mind that I needed to get."

Sadie munched her English muffin, saying nothing. Dorothy cleared her throat loudly.

"They got some awful nice wedding wrap."

Sadie's thoughts were far away, thinking of Leroy Betty helping Mark with his wedding suit. She had generously offered to order the suit and all.

"Didn't know if I should get the bag shaped like a gold bell, or the pink with gold polka dots. I told myself that a purple bow would look awful nice on a package like that."

Leroy Betty had even hemmed the sleeves and trouser legs for him and pressed the whole suit afterward. She certainly was the salt of the earth.

"You listenin' ta me?" Dorothy stood over Sadie, hands on hips, her head tilted like a little robin waiting for the earthworm to emerge from the dirt below.

Sadie stuffed the last of the buttered muffin into her mouth. Then she looked up wide-eyed and startled.

"What? What?" she stammered, thoroughly confused.

"Well, I ain't repeatin' myself."

Sadie shrugged her shoulders, gathered up the cleaning supplies she needed for the morning, and headed to the bedrooms.

While dusting the dresser in the master bedroom, a movement in the yard below caught her eye, so she laid down the dust cloth and went to the window.

There was little Sadie Elizabeth, toddling toward the bent form of Bertie, shrieking with glee when he scooped her up in his arms. The regal form of Barbara Caldwell moved across the lawn toward them. She was dressed in the latest fall fashion, her hair coiffed to perfection. Sadie watched the sweet-mannered way she patted Bernie's arm.

It hadn't always been like that. The darling baby girl had done wonders, completely changing Richard and Barbara Caldwell. These two wealthy landowners had it all, but their one real source of happiness was their cherished daughter.

Sadie sighed, then turned back to her dusting, polishing the top of the dresser to a rich sheen as she contemplated the people and her work at the ranch.

Did she really, for sure, want to give up this to become Mark Peight's wife? She knew she'd no longer be able to keep her job at the ranch when the first baby arrived.

It was the Amish way. Women stayed home and took care of the children and their husbands. For generations, mothers prepared their daughters for this important role by teaching them the art of running a home smoothly.

Yes, she was eager. She was prepared to be Mark's wife. She looked forward to her new life with him. But she would miss these people so much. She would come back, yes, but it would never be the same. She wouldn't know the same camaraderie she had known from working among these people day in and day out.

She set the heavy brass candleholders back on the dresser, then frowned as the taper candle wobbled in its socket. Grabbing a tissue, she tore it in half, folded it a few times again, wrapped it around the bottom of the candle, then put it firmly back in the brass holder. It stood straight and strong.

Sadie smiled to herself. What they don't know won't hurt them.

She would miss this house. She loved just being in it, even if it meant cleaning. She enjoyed the work, lifting and replacing and touching objects so far above anything she would ever own.

A muffled screech broke through her absentminded reverie, and she turned to look out the window once again.

She put her hand to her mouth when a shrieking Erma Keim came barreling out of the tack room, her legs churning, her skirt flying above her white knees. A grinning Lothario Bean followed quickly on her heals, both hands holding the pressure nozzle at the end of a long green hose and the water following Erma's yelling form.

Oh, dear.

Sadie laughed as some of the water connected with the retreating back and laughed again at Lothario's obvious glee.

But still. She had pooh-poohed Dorothy's idea of Erma overstepping her bounds with Lothario. She still felt that way. But the scene in the yard was a bit unsettling, nevertheless.

Sadie knew Erma's behavior would be looked at disapprovingly among their people. The scene playing out in the yard below was why some Amish mothers frowned on their girls working "out."

Sadie winced as Barbara Caldwell turned to watch, then relaxed as she saw her laugh with Bertie. As long as Erma knew her place, it would be all right, although Lord knew she had sorely overstepped her designated "place" in Dorothy's kitchen.

As she ran the vacuum cleaner, she thought again about her decision to have her in the bridal party with Reuben. What if she became noisy and, well, like she was today? She was just so overboard.

Back in the kitchen, she spoke to Dorothy about it, which was a big mistake. Sadie wound up defending Erma's reputation and desperately trying to hush up Dorothy before poor Erma returned.

Dorothy said she would have thought better of Sadie. How could she even think Erma would keep that mouth shut long enough to be in a bridal party? And how did she think that red hair would ever lie flat long enough to be in a wedding?

Sadie spent the rest of the day in a sour mood. When she got home that evening, everything got worse. Anna was throwing up again out behind Paris' stall, just one easy retch and she emptied her stomach of the food from supper. She was wiping her mouth when an angry Sadie appeared. All Anna could do was sink to the floor of the barn and deny everything.

Sadie confided in Mark, who said she couldn't expect to fix everyone's problems. Anna was just passing through a phase. This, too, would pass.

As far as Erma Keim was concerned, he wouldn't worry about that either. She was a delight. He was glad she was going to be *nâva hucking*, and he planned on finding a husband for her as soon as Sadie helped her tame that red hair.

Chapter 25

THE DAY OF THE WEDDING DAWNED.

Actually, the day began in the pitch-black hour of four o'clock in the morning when the battery-operated digital alarm went off and woke Jacob Miller from a sound sleep. He found his wife getting dressed in the bathroom. Unlike her husband, she had been wide awake since two-thirty, her mind tossing at the thought of all the disasters that could occur.

He bent to kiss her good morning but was brushed aside like an overgrown housefly.

Aah…well. Mam had a lot on her mind.

Mam woke the whole household, sparing no one, not even relatives in the basement, or Eva and Sadie, who had rejuvenated an old, old bond, by talking until midnight.

Mam popped breakfast casseroles into the oven and got out cups for water and coffee. There was no juice or toast this morning. Cranky little cousins yelled as mothers wet their hair, pulling fine-toothed combs through the long tresses. Mam helped pin capes and adjust coverings.

Erma arrived at five-thirty with a driver and was whisked upstairs with the speed of lightning, though she looked back at the breakfast casserole with genuine longing.

Leah produced all her best hair products and explained the need for neat hair. Rebekah nodded in agreement, exclaiming the wonder of the gels and sprays. They sprayed and pulled and pinned until they finally stepped back and smiled.

"Look at you!" Rebekah cried. "You're gorgeous!"

Erma bent her head to look in the mirror, then put her hands to her cheeks in dramatic fashion.

"Well, you may as well have ironed my hair and been done with it."

They put a new covering on Erma's glossy, now-subdued, red hair and were astounded at the results. What a difference it made!

Sadie combed her hair at least five times before it suited her. She needed both Leah's and Rebekah's help in pinning the white organdy cape and apron.

Mark appeared in his new black suit, his shirt as white as white could possibly be. His hair cut to perfection. Sadie took one look and knew she had never seen him look better.

Was it really true? Was this striking man about to become her husband?

Sadie glanced toward Reuben and winced when Erma linked her arm through his. She smiled gamely at him, bolstering his courage with a quick whisper of, "Remember the saddle."

Poor Reuben.

Sadie hung on to Mark's arm in sheer alarm when a whole army of buggies, vans, buses, and vehicles of every description wound their way up the rural road toward the Detweiler home. When their own ride was at the door,

Sadie gulped down a few swallows of black coffee before following Mark to the waiting carriage that would take them to the Detweilers for the service.

The glossy pine benches in the Detweilers' spotlessly clean shop were set in neat rows. The wedding guests took their seats. Mark and Sadie sat beside each other with Reuben and Erma on one side, Kevin and Leah on the other. They greeted the wedding guests: family, friends, and members of the community.

There was only a handful of Mark's relatives from Pennsylvania, but Sadie was grateful for every single one that came, for Mark's sake.

The family belonged to a sect of the Old Order Amish who dressed a bit different from Sadie's community. They greeted Mark with a sort of curious fascination, as if he was an ancient relic that had survived a remarkable amount of excavation.

He had been given up as a bad sort, a black sheep. Was it any wonder, coming from that sort of family? And here he was, looking normal. It was a miracle. Atlee and Meely's oldest. My, my.

The single boys filed in and were seated on the men's side of the shop, the girls on the women's side. The service began when the first song was announced, a wave of slow, undulating tunes from the German hymnbook enveloping them in the familiar way.

The ministers rose to go to an adjacent room for a conference with Mark and Sadie. This was when the ministers explained the rules and value of Christian marriage and asked if they wished to become man and wife. The ministers wished them many blessings, as was the custom.

When they were dismissed, Mark and Sadie were joined by their *nâva huckers*. Blond-haired Kevin was so striking alongside Leah; Reuben's face was white and tense, while Erma averted her eyes in the greatest show of humility she had ever managed.

Slowly, they walked among the congregation and sat in six special chairs in the ministers' row. The three women sat facing their men, their heads bent, their eyes downcast in the proper way.

The singing ended when the ministers came back from their conference. Then the first speaker stood up and spoke. When he finished, they prayed. Then the second minister stood up and told the story of Tobias, a touching tale of a youth and his bride.

When he came to a certain part in the story, he announced to the wedding guests that Mark and Sadie wished to be united as well.

Very solemnly, their eyes downcast, Mark and Sadie rose. The minister asked them if this was their wish, and they promised it was with a subdued "*Ya.*" The minister joined their hands, pronounced a blessing, the congregation stood in prayer, and they returned to their seats.

Never once did they raise their eyes while the remaining ministers gave testimony. Only when they rose from the last prayer, and the final, rousing, German hymn had begun, did Sadie dare raise her eyes to Mark's own.

He met her eyes. One fleeting look.

How could a lifetime of love be poured forth from those dark eyes in a few seconds? It took her breath away.

She loved him so. With all her heart and soul. Even the fear of the tough times ahead diminished in the face of this love. She was so secure now. His love to her was real. She could never doubt that.

When the song ended, he looked at her again and smiled, a slow easy smile that warmed her the whole way through.

"My wife," he whispered for her ears alone. Her eyes shone into his.

The remainder of the day was a movement of color, warmth, smells, hands shaken, hugs accepted, senses awed by light and sounds.

Their wedding table was a corner. Mark sat on one side, Sadie on the other, their attendants on either side.

There were candles, chinaware, stem glasses, and silverware on white tablecloths of Sadie's choice. The cloth napkins were an off-white color, as were the placemats and accessories.

The mashed potatoes and fried chicken were cooked to perfection, although Sadie hardly remembered what she ate or how it tasted. The women slaved over ovens and stove-tops, getting everything just right.

Sadie loved how the butter was molded in a perfect butterfly-shape on the butter plate. She exclaimed over the perfection of the whole wheat dinner rolls, sadly disturbing the butterfly to spread a small amount of butter on her roll.

Would she ever forget Dorothy's remark about doubling her weight?

Jim and Dorothy dressed in their wedding finery. Dorothy wore a blazing-pink polyester suit with a large corsage from the Dollar General firmly imbedded in the lapel. Her hair looked really good, for Dorothy. Jim smiled and beamed beside his portly, brightly-colored wife.

Richard and Barbara Caldwell were seated at the English table, the one that had special servers for important guests. They were as resplendent as Sadie had imagined, and little Sadie Elizabeth was a vision in yellow.

Beside them, Bertie Orthman and Lothario Bean and his lovely little wife, followed by their beautiful daughters, were all laughing and seemed to be enjoying their first Amish wedding.

Then Marcellus and Louis came back from wherever they had gone and Sadie leaned over. "Mark!"

He looked to where Sadie pointed, and his eyes became soft with emotion as he looked at the two lovely children, their dark faces alight with interest. He watched as Jim bent to tie a shoe and brush off a bit of dust. Dorothy hovered and filled their plates like a pink mother hen.

"They're definitely two of the lucky ones," Mark said meaningfully.

Sadie nodded, found his hand, and squeezed it reassuringly.

After dinner, they opened a towering mound of gifts. Richard and Barbara Caldwell came to talk to them, and Sadie found herself choking up, unable to speak. Richard Caldwell quickly gathered Sadie into a bear hug while Barbara patted her white organdy cape.

The Caldwells' present was a painting of horses, the kind Sadie never thought she would own. It took her breath away. A band of horses running against the wind, with a thunderstorm in a background of gray, beige, blue, and green clouds.

Dorothy's gift was encased in the gold, bell-shaped gift bag. Inside were the two ceramic crosses with pink flowers that she had promised Sadie a long time ago.

"One for each side o' yer hutch cupboard," Dorothy beamed.

There were so many gifts. A gas grill. A pair of Adirondack chairs. Dishes, cookware, towels, blankets, shovels, brushes, utensils, wooden racks, clothespins, tea towels, bakeware, lanterns, batteries. Would they need to buy anything at all?

Rebekah wrote it all down in a notebook, listing the gift and the giver.

The rest of the afternoon was filled with hymn-singing.

They served a supper of scalloped potatoes, home-cured ham, lima beans and corn, and a tossed salad. There was also more wedding cake and Dorothy's coconut cream pies, which even Erma pronounced the best she had ever tasted.

Sadie was feeling a bit wilted now, ready for the day to come to a close and be alone with her new husband.

Evidently Erma still had energy to spare. She was having an animated conversation with Reuben. When she flicked a spoonful of meringue at Reuben, hitting him squarely on the nose, they both fell into a fit of convulsive giggles that they were powerless to stop.

"Whooo!" Erma said in the most unladylike voice Sadie had ever heard.

Reuben, however, was thoroughly impressed. He eyed Erma with a newfound respect. Anyone who could flick a spoon and hit the target directly was pretty awesome. So she showed him how to do it.

Mark grinned, then laughed outright when a glob of meringue landed squarely in Kevin's lap, barely missing Sadie.

Mam frowned in the direction of the wedding tables, her eyes looking completely exhausted. Somehow Dat was still going strong, although he had a look about him like a hot-air balloon getting ready for its descent.

Sadie caught sight of Rebekah seated beside Benjamin Nissley, their heads bent as they sang in unison. It was only a matter of time for those two.

Sadie sat back and let her eyes roam the room. She thought of weddings she had been to in the past, sitting beside boys she barely knew, eating food that tasted like sawdust, gamely making attempts at conversation, relieved beyond words to be finished with the singing.

Her eyes landed on Anna, who was seated much, much too close to Leon Hershberger. Leon seemed to be leaning in close to her, his auburn hair cut in the English style, the disobedience glaring from his bold eyes. Anna had a spot of color on each cheek, her smile wide, her eyes never leaving his face.

Sadie's heart sank. Would Anna ever understand the fullness of her self-worth and the beauty of her character?

Sadie silently grieved for Anna, if only for a moment. She could not solve the problem today, not on her wedding day.

After the last guest finally bade them a goodnight, Mam and Dat kicked off their shoes and sat down with fresh mugs of coffee. Rebekah and Leah wearily sagged in kitchen chairs, Anna seated on the bench.

Reuben went straight to bed, but only after eating another slice of wedding cake and calling Mark "brother" with a toothy grin.

Mark asked Sadie if they should ride Paris and Bruno, Mark's new horse, over to their house for their first night together.

It was a wonderful idea!

Sadie raced up the stairs to change clothes and pack a bag. Then she hugged her parents, telling them they'd ride back in the morning to help clean up.

"But..." Mam started protesting.

"She'll be okay," Dat broke in, looking at her meaningfully.

Mam closed her mouth, then smiled as Sadie dashed out the door, her duffel bag swinging.

When Sadie reached the barn, Mark had Paris ready, the saddle securely in place. Bruno pranced beside her.

"Oh, Paris!" Sadie burst out, then swung up while Mark secured her duffel bag behind his saddle.

The moon was not completely full, but almost. Sadie couldn't really tell, except that one side seemed a little lopsided. It outlined the ridges, the trees, even the winding road in front of them.

Bruno pranced, wanting to run. He hopped sideways, then bucked lightly.

Paris walked slowly down the drive, her head up, her ears pricked forward, alive to every movement around her. Her mane rippled and flowed, the moonlight catching the white highlights. She picked her way carefully, as if she thought she was carrying royalty.

Was it only Sadie's childish imagination, or did it seem like Paris knew this was a special evening?

No, Paris would know.

After Bruno settled down, Mark rode very close to Sadie. He extended his hand, his white shirt sleeve silver in the moonlight. Sadie met his hand halfway and grasped it.

The saddles creaked, the horses hooves made a dull thunking sound. Far away, a coyote barked, then wailed eerily. The pine trees stood tall and straight on either side of them while the stars twinkled above.

"This whole day has been unbelievable," Mark said. "I feel like I'm in a dream."

His voice was gruff, the emotion he felt making it sound ragged.

Sadie smiled at him. "Why?"

"I simply do not deserve you. How did you ever agree to become my wife?"

"It's so easy, Mark. I love you. This is all I ever wanted."

Then they galloped their horses up the side of Atkin's Ridge. The cool breeze fanned their faces; the stars disappeared when they rode beneath the trees. Rounding the corner of the ridge, they slowed the horses for the downhill ride to their home, their start to a life lived as one, for better or for worse, in sickness and in health, until death parted them.

The End

LINDA BYLER

THE
DISAPPEARANCES

SADIE'S MONTANA
Book 3

Chapter 1

Now that the snows had come, Sadie missed Reuben the most. Oh, it wasn't that she was lonely or discontented. After all, she could go home whenever she wanted, as long as the snow was not too heavy.

It was just Reuben, his guileless blue eyes, the way he tossed his blond-streaked hair away from his face, that often brought a lump to her throat.

She was a married woman now. Somehow, she felt no different than she ever had, except for the love that had come to fulfillment with Mark Peight, her husband of exactly two months and five days.

Sadie Peight. Or Sadie Anne Peight. Sadie Miller no more.

In the Amish world in which she lived, that close-knit community of plain people in Montana, she was "Mark Sadie" now — not "Mark's wife, Sadie," in the proper way. Just plain "Mark Sadie." No last names were needed. Everyone knew who "Mark Sadie" was.

Her family, the Jacob Millers, had moved to Montana when she was 15 years old. She had had to give up her beloved palomino riding horse, Paris, as well as her best friend and cousin, Eva, moving thousands of miles away from her home community in Ohio.

In time, she came to love Montana, working at Aspen East, the huge ranch that employed dozens of men, cattle drivers, farmers, horsemen, the list went on and on. She cooked large meals in the kitchen with Dorothy Sevarr, whose husband, Jim, transported her to and from the ranch. The Sevarrs came to be beloved friends, as well as Richard and Barbara Caldwell, the wealthy owners of Aspen East Ranch.

Sadie had met Mark when a horse appeared from seemingly nowhere in a snowstorm, falling sick and disabled in front of Jim Sevarr's pickup truck. Sadie opted to stay with the horse, a beautiful but dying paint, while Jim went for help. Mark Peight and his driver found Sadie in the snow with the dying horse. There was an instant mutual attraction between Mark and Sadie. A long, imperfect courtship followed, imperfect due largely to Mark's troubled, unusual past.

Wild horses had been a danger, running uncontrolled through the isolated areas, terrifying the Amish community. The large, black leader of the herd threatened unassuming horses and buggies traveling the countryside.

Sadie and her brother, Reuben, had spent many weeks on a grassy hill taming the few remaining horses. Among them was the outstanding palomino mare Sadie now owned, which she named Paris, in memory of her beloved horse from Ohio. The palomino had been given to Sadie as a gift of appreciation from the owner of the wild horses, which turned out to have been stolen by clever horse thieves in Laredo County. After the thefts, someone started going around the county randomly shooting horses, Reuben's among them. Paris and Sadie managed more than one harrowing narrow escape. But the sniper—or snipers—remained at large and the motive for the shootings a mystery.

She felt safe now, snug and cozy in the house Mark was renovating. There had been no sniper activity for almost four months. The Amish community breathed a sigh of relief. People went on with their lives, shaking their heads at the seeming incompetence of the local police, but, in the Amish way, taking it all in stride.

The home Mark had bought before the wedding had been a forsaken homestead nestled at the foot of Atkin's Ridge. The buildings were covered in old, wooden, German siding, the framework amazingly sturdy, but almost everything else was crumbling with age.

When you came in the driveway, the unique shape of the barn, with its series of gable ends and various roof slopes, was so completely charming that you forget to look for a house, which was farther up the slope in a grove of pine trees. Despite its lamentable state of disrepair, the property was as cozy and attractive as a nursery-rhyme house.

There was an L-shaped porch along the front, dormers on the roof, and a low addition on the right side. Besides the broken windows, sagging porch posts, and torn floor boards, sparrow nests were built into every available crack of the decaying lumber, the floors littered with their feces. Bats flew in and out of the upstairs dormer windows at will, and mice scurried in terror at their approach.

Mark had put in long hours repairing the barn first. His hard labor resulted in a remarkable building with a beautiful forebay, horse stalls on either side, wide enough to drive a team of horses attached to a manure spreader through it, for easy mucking out. There was a workshop in another section and room for the carriage, spring wagon, and various lawn tools in another, all on top of a solid, new, concrete floor.

The barn was their pride and joy, especially when Paris adapted so well, becoming quite sleek and flirtatious with Mark's horses.

Sadie would stand at the wooden fence, her arms propped on the top board, one foot on the bottom, watching Paris nip at Truman, the new horse, then squeal and bound nimbly away.

She still loved Paris and rode her as much as ever. But whenever she went to visit her parents, she drove Mark's steady, brown standardbred driving horse hitched to the shining, black carriage. Since the sniper incidents had quieted down, she felt safer and often returned home with the back seat of the buggy full of items that had been left behind after the wedding.

The house was not finished; only the lower floor was livable. Mark's original plans changed after his mother passed away from bone cancer, leaving them a substantial amount of money to be shared with his five siblings when they had been located.

Mark hired a cabinetmaker and a crew of carpenters to finish the main floor, resulting in a well-crafted home.

The kitchen was all done in oak cabinets, with wide plank floors also made of oak. The countertops were a speckled black and gray, so Sadie had chosen to paint the walls a gray so light it was almost white. Three windows side by side provided a full view of the driveway, the sighing pine trees, and the barn.

Sadie placed her furniture where she wanted it in the house, then told Mark she was unworthy to be the housekeeper of such a beautiful home. Mark ran a hand through his black hair. He said nothing, just grabbed her and swung her around. His glad brown eyes and perfect smiling mouth told her everything he thought she should know. Their love was an all-consuming flame, their marriage a union of God—a blessing that, after all they had been through together, they would never take for granted.

Oh, they had their times, like Mark's sliding into his silences, becoming absorbed in a sort of blackness when she least expected it. She would always revert to self-blame, her shoulders tightening, a headache developing, watching his morose face with a sort of hopeless intensity. What have I done? What have I said to bring this on?

She would be completely miserable, afraid to approach him, until she remembered his past and the awful times after his mother left with a real estate agent, leaving eight-year-old Mark to care for his five younger siblings.

The slightest put-down, often going unnoticed by Sadie herself, could bring on those quiet times. A dark fog, as impenetrable as the proverbial pea soup and about as messy to clean up, surrounded him.

Sadie had been raised in a secure, loving home, imperfect perhaps, as most homes tend to be, but completely normal. Her three sisters, Leah, Rebekah, Anna, and one brother, Reuben, all younger than herself, had been loved, disciplined, and nurtured.

Their mother, Annie, endured mental illness that resulted in hospitalization. In the end, it only bound them closer, enveloping the family in a shroud of thanksgiving for Mam's well-being.

Sadie was often quick to speak her mind, the words tumbling out happily before she thought of their consequences. Mark would be hurt, returning to that place where only he knew, leaving her floundering, reeling from the rejection in his eyes.

The latest bout had been brought on by her happy evaluation of the oak kitchen cabinets. Sitting back in her chair, wrapping her soft, white robe securely around her waist, she crossed her legs, kicking her slipper-clad foot, shaking back her long, dark ponytail, saying simply how no one could build cabinets the way a cabinetmaker could.

"They just know exactly what they're doing, don't they? Such perfect raised panels on their doors!" Forgetting, like a dummy, that he had built the ones in the office and had been terribly proud of his accomplishment and the money he had saved by doing it himself.

He had nodded his head, agreed, using words to that extent, finished his coffee, and abruptly left the table, returning to the recliner. He stayed there without offering his usual Sunday-morning dish-drying assistance.

Amish people hold church services in a home every other Sunday. This is an old tradition, allowing the ministers and deacon to visit other communities if they feel so inclined. Church members have an in-between Sunday, allowing long sleep-ins, leisurely breakfasts, a day for resting, visiting, Bible-reading, studying German, or, as is often the case, simply relaxing and doing nothing.

Which is exactly how that Sunday turned out. Doing nothing. Not one thing. Finally her insides were in knots. The book she was reading gave her the creeps. Her legs became so restless she thought they might run away by themselves. She wished she had never married Mark Peight. She wanted to slam doors and spill a whole container of water over his head or pound her fists into his chest.

What she did do, finally, was kneel by his recliner and

beg him to tell her what was wrong. But he feigned sleep, grunted, stuck up an elbow as if to shake her off, rolled on his side, smacked his lips in the most disgusting way, and resumed breathing deeply.

Sadie got up and walked blindly to the kitchen, then stood in the middle of it. She wanted to go home. She wanted to lay her head on Mam's shoulder and, smelling the talcum powder that always wafted from her, cry great big alligator tears and ask Mam why she hadn't warned and better prepared her little girl?

She felt like a buoy anchored to the sea floor, tossed about by the waves. But she stayed right there in the middle of her kitchen, anchored to the beautiful floorboards by her marriage to him. Oh, he made her so mad!

It wasn't right, this anger. All her life, she had been groomed to be a submissive Amish housewife. The husband is the head of the house, and his wishes are to be respected. Your life is now no longer your own.

No doubt.

Your life is doled out in portions by his moods. If he falls into a black one, your life could be measured by the tiniest measuring spoon. Approximately one-eighth of a teaspoon. Barely enough to keep a person going. No cup runneth over here.

Ah, well. She knew their life together would not be perfect, the way he had always been so hard to understand. But this? This standing in the middle of the kitchen, completely afloat, by that tall dark stranger sunk into a vile mood for which you were unprepared.

Then he would get over it, usually by going off to work the following morning, his lunchbox swinging in one hand, the red and white Coleman jug of ice water in the other, his faithful driver and coworker, Lester Brenner, waiting at the end of the yard, idling the diesel engine of his pickup truck.

Mark was a farrier and a good one. He shod all of Richard Caldwell's horses, as well as those of the Amish who owned more than one horse, and still the telephone messages kept coming.

After he spent a day doing hard physical labor, getting out among people, talking, forgetting himself, he would return home a changed person. Smiling, his arms enfolding her, her head fitting so perfectly into that hollow of his shoulder, she would smell the rich odor of horses and his own musky, salty essence. She would close her eyes and thank God for her husband, forgiving him another time of blackness.

That was when the eighth of a teaspoon turned into immeasurable quantities, and Sadie's life made great, big, happy sense, like a tree filled with great rosy-cheeked apples, its roots by a blue lake, watered constantly by the love of God.

So when it was Tuesday morning, and the snow was coming down thick and fast, too fast to attempt a drive to her mother's house, she decided to unpack some of her extra things and wash the dishes, fold the towels, and store them in the bottom drawer of the bureau in the living room. It was a job she had meant to do at least a month ago and still had not accomplished.

She was unwrapping a set of salt and pepper shakers, the newspaper around them aged and crumbling from being stored in her parent's attic for many years. Mommy Hershberger had given them to her on her tenth birthday. Purple grapes with green leaves swinging from a sort of tree, all made in shining ceramic. Oh, my. And she had thought they were so cool back then.

Smiling, she put them on the countertop to be washed in soapy water, then she retrieved a small white basket filled with yellow plastic roses, the greenish faces having changed color from the heat of the attic, waxy, smelling like old plastic. Grimacing, she pulled out the artificial flowers and threw them into the trash can with the old newspapers, then set the white basket by the purple salt and pepper shakers.

She had just found a small cedar chest with a glossy top, a gray and white kitten smiling from the lid, surrounded by pink flowers and a red handkerchief. Ugh. A gift from a names exchange in seventh grade. Oh, dear. She should keep it.

Barking from Wolf, Mark's large gray and silver dog, brought her head up, her gaze automatically going to the driveway. His bark was deep, full-throated, but not threatening. She watched as a black Jeep, (four-wheel drive, she hoped) made its way slowly up to the end of the yard before stopping. The driver shut off the engine.

Sadie stood up, smoothed her white apron over her stomach, adjusted the sleeves of her lime green dress, then checked her appearance in the mirror above the sink in the laundry.

Covering straight.

Wonder who would come visiting in the snow?

Three men slowly opened the doors of the vehicle as if hesitant to subject themselves to the cold wetness of the snow. They all wore some semblance of the usual Stetson hats so common in Montana—brown, black, slouched, but seemingly clean. Their clothes were presentable, clean blue jeans, tan Carhart coats. Adjusting their jacket zippers, they looked to the boards leading up to the porch.

No sidewalks or strips had been built yet, so the

boards leading from the porch floor to the ground would have to do. Covered with snow, though.

Why were all three of them coming in? Usually, only one person could state their business.

Well, no use getting all flustered, she'd be okay. Once fear invaded your life, it could easily take control and make you subject to it. She'd be okay.

The leader was evidently heavyset, his large form rocking from side to side with each purposeful stride. His gray mustache hid all of his mouth, his hair tied in the back, a long gray ponytail hanging down the back of his coat.

He stopped, evaluating the slope of the boards, the accumulation of snow, before turning to his friends, saying something.

Sadie started to go to the door to advise them, then decided against it. They'd find their way.

The other two men were smaller in stature, with clean-shaven faces, not unpleasant. One wore glasses low on his nose, which he pushed up every time he squinted toward the house.

Wolf kept barking but followed them, his tail wagging. Sadie knew he was friendly, but one command from Mark could change the situation entirely, and he would attack a person or animal if Mark wanted him to.

None of the men seemed to be bothered by Wolf, completely unafraid, barely acknowledging his existence. That was odd.

They were all up on the porch now, huddled, talking in hushed tones. Should she simply disappear, glide noiselessly away, up the stairs or into the bedroom, and hide? No, that was cowardly. She was here by herself except the days she still worked at the ranch with Dorothy and

Erma Keim, the garrulous spinster who had been hired to make the work load easier.

A resounding knock. Nothing timid about them, that was sure.

She wasn't afraid when she opened the door, and when they greeted her with friendly smiles, she invited them inside, the man with the glasses still pushing them up, squinting at her as he did so.

The heavyset man introduced himself as Dave Sims, the other two shaking hands with her politely, saying their names, which she promptly forgot.

Sadie gestured toward the kitchen table.

"Would you like to sit down?"

"Actually, we will."

Silently, they all pulled out chairs, Dave grunting a bit as he folded his large form into the chair that had appeared quite sturdy before but looked very small and feeble now.

"What we're here for..." he began. Then, "How much do you know about the two children who came to the Caldwell place?"

Whoa. How did they know she worked there? Why come here? Why not talk to Richard Caldwell? Or Jim and Dorothy?

Taking a deep breath, Sadie said carefully, "Not very much."

"You work there?"

"Yes."

"Were you working when they arrived?"

"Yes,"

"What did they look like?"

"Just...well, two very dirty, poor children. Their

clothes were in tatters. Too big. They just hung on their thin shoulders."

No answer, just a nodding of three heads in unison.

"Where are they now?"

"Why don't you talk to Richard Caldwell, the owner of the ranch?" Sadie asked, a bit hesitantly, yet braving the adversity she felt would come.

"We did."

Instantly, Sadie felt more at ease. She visibly relaxed, let go of the hem of her white apron, which she had been twisting between her thumb and index finger. If they talked to Richard Caldwell first, and he sent them here....

Yet, there was a lingering doubt.

"They are adopted, the way we heard."

"Yes, I think legally."

They nodded.

Then, they all showed their identification. They worked for the government, some kind of detectives who handled special kinds of cases. (Sadie didn't completely understand it.) Apparently, the children had disappeared with their mother. The father was a fugitive, a person of interest who was running from the law. The mother was also under suspicion, although her complete disappearance was the only reason. They needed information. Everything would be recorded. How much did she know?

Sadie told them everything from the moment the children appeared at the kitchen door, about the bag of costly jewelry, the safe where it was held, their impeccable manners, their names.

When she mentioned their names, two of them shook their heads.

"No, no. Not their real names."

Sadie's eyes opened wide.

"Really?"

"No. Their mother, or whoever took them away, did a good job of masquerading the real kids. Their names are Sebastian and Angelica Hartford, of the Dallas Hartfords?"

Sadie shrugged her shoulders.

"Ever watched the TV show, *Dallas*?"

"No."

"Well, there's more money than you can ever imagine involved."

"These kids are victims of a serious ring of horse thieves. The only thing they ever did wrong was to have eyes and ears. They know too much, and, we're surmising, so does their mother. There is an old, old bloodline running in the veins of some of these horses, an Arabian strain, that makes them worth thousands and thousands of dollars. There was one stable here in Montana that unknowingly housed a stallion carrying the bloodline. The horse thieves knew this. Stole a lot of horses. I think what happened, it was a mistake gone completely haywire."

Sadie swallowed hard. The room spun, then righted itself, her breathing came raggedly now, as she acknowledged the fact that she knew a whole lot that could help these men tremendously.

But...should she?

With all her heart, she longed for Mark. He would know what to do. She had seen the identification. But why the ponytail? The mustache? Their clothes did not fit her mind's description of a detective. Was that only the Amish way instilled in her?

You expected people to dress a certain way, to look the

way you think they should. Men wore hats and suspenders buttoned to broadfall trousers. Older women combed their hair flat, wore larger coverings, wore darker, plainer fabric and colors. Young girls arranged their hair in nicer waves, wore smaller coverings, brightly colored dresses. Little boys wore straw hats, denim trousers. Everything was in order and expected to appear a certain way.

People who worked for the government wore uniforms and cut their hair close to their heads, didn't they? She would have to know. So she asked them. Hesitantly at first, but gaining strength as she talked.

"What do you think 'undercover agent' means?" the heavyset man asked, a broad smile on his face, widening to a likeable grin.

The man with the glasses, (what was his name?) pushed them up again, squinted more than ever, but smiled genuinely.

So she told them everything. The black stallion's return, Cody, Paris, the shootings, the close calls, the Amish people's frustration with the local police.

At the mention of Paris, Dave Sims' eyes bore into hers. He shook his head from side to side as she mentioned the narrow escapes.

"Do you have any idea of the danger you are living with?" he finally ground out, his face turning a dark shade of red.

"Are you here alone, every day?" the thinner man asked, keeping himself professionally in check.

"No. I work at the Caldwell…Aspen East. Aspendale," she stammered.

"Your husband?"

"A farrier. Works for Richard Caldwell."

"Where is this horse named Paris?"

"In the barn."

They all looked at one another, compressed their lips.

"Do you have the registration papers?"

"Yes. In fact, I do. They were one of the last things I brought from my parents' house. I'm...it's been a bit over two months since we've been married."

"That's wonderful. Congratulations."

"Thank you."

"Can we see the papers?"

"Yes, of course."

She found them in the pocket of the notebook, where she had filed more important documents until she could arrange them properly in Mark's bottom file drawer. When she produced the papers they needed, Dave Sims extracted an envelope from an inside pocket of his coat. They all bent their heads, clucked their tongues, read portions out loud, then sat back. Dave Sims told Sadie she was the owner of an extremely valuable horse who was in grave danger and would have to be taken away if she wanted the horse to stay alive, or wanted both herself and Mark to remain safe.

"But you can't take Paris!" she burst out, unashamed now, her only thought how much Paris would miss her, how unhappy she'd be away from Truman and Sadie and Mark and Wolf. In the end, she gave in. There was no other way.

Chapter 2

When Mark arrived home she threw herself into his arms and cried and sniffed and mumbled and blew her nose, her eyes red, her nose swollen, her hair disheveled, until he led her to the new beige-colored sofa with the gray cushions. He told her to stop crying, calm down, and start all over.

He held her hands and stroked her back reassuringly as she repeated her story much slower this time, hugging him and begging him to try and do something about Paris. They simply could not take her away.

"And the thing that worries me just as much—what in the world will happen to Dorothy if she finds this out? She'll be beside herself without those children."

Mark said she wouldn't have to know, and Sadie said that wasn't one bit fair, that it was better to tell her, which is what she did when she went to work the next day.

She went straight to Richard Caldwell's office, glad to hear his voice welcoming her in, glad to hear every word he had to say about her and Paris.

Yes, he believed it was as serious as the men had said. Paris would have to go to an undisclosed location, despite

Sadie's vehement protests that Paris would be perfectly all right in the barn.

"Who knows I got married and live with Mark now?" she finished, a note of rebellion hanging on the question.

"You want my personal opinion, Sadie? You better do what you're told. Until this whole thing is cleared up, anyway."

Sadie said nothing, still hoping for a chance to keep Paris in the barn where she would be perfectly all right, thank you very much.

However, they agreed to tell Dorothy about the children together. When she was called into the office, she waited a good 10 minutes before making her appearance, then blew through the door, prickly with irritation, sat solidly on a leather wing chair, then almost slid off, her short legs putting a halt to it by digging into the carpet, definitely not helping her dignity.

"Now what do you want, Mr. Caldwell?" she said, putting all the impatience she could into the "Now."

"This is very important, Dorothy," Richard Caldwell said soberly.

"Hardly more important than my roast of beef. That Erma don't know how to trim it, so she don't."

Sadie squelched a giggle. Erma Keim had only one name here at the ranch, and it was "That Erma."

Continued combat, she thought.

Richard Caldwell assured her it was much more important than roast beef and proceeded to tell her in a level, quiet voice everything that had occurred, which left poor Dorothy rocking from side to side in agitation.

"Oh, come on now, they can't take my babies. They're in school! You can't take kids out of school. They're mine. I don't care if those men say they're the government, you can't take kids out of school."

With that, she pulled a bobby pin out of her gray hair and dug so viciously in one ear that Sadie was afraid she'd never find it again. Dorothy remembered what she was doing and put it back in her hair, clearing her throat self-consciously.

A wave of pity rolled over Sadie's heart. Dorothy was so small and plump, her polyester slacks too short around the ankles, her beige shoes from the Dollar General splattered with bacon grease, her multicolored shirt exposing too much of her wrinkled neck, a cloud of bluster and sense of self riding solidly on her gray head.

Richard Caldwell went on explaining patiently. If they found the mother of their children and she was proved innocent, Dorothy would have to give them up.

Shaking a plump finger in Richard Caldwell's direction, Dorothy told him the Lord had sent Marcelona and Louise; they were her beloved angels sent straight from heaven, and he'd not allow them to be taken away. And don't you kid yourself, she was going to go back to her roast beef, and if he wasn't going to do anything about Erma Keim trimming off too much fat, then she'd have to do it herself, or he'd be eating a roast beef that had the taste and texture of good shoe leather, and she meant it.

She slid off the leather chair after that display of territorial words and bustled straight back to the kitchen, leaving a vapor of martyrdom behind her. Richard Caldwell shook his head, then exploded in a volcanic bellow of laughter that brought one just like it from Sadie.

They wiped their eyes, smiled, then agreed to let it go. They had told her the truth, and now it was up to Dorothy to accept it.

Sadie vacuumed and dusted, scoured bathrooms, and

as always, thoroughly enjoyed cleaning this grand house. There was just something about being in a home as beautiful as this that fulfilled a sense of longing for the finer things in life.

In her circles, Sadie knew this lust of the world, this lust of the eyes, was accompanied by a firm denouncing of it. She was admonished to take up the cross, deny herself, and follow the narrow path of Jesus, which she felt was good and right. Sadie wanted no life other than the one she led, the goal of which was to live in a way that would lead to heaven.

That was how she was born. Amish. To parents who wanted this way of life, this security for their children. The heritage passed on from generation to generation.

It was hard to explain when English people asked questions, implying the senselessness of driving a horse and buggy or having no electricity. And if it was so wrong, why ride in a car at all?

It wasn't wrong for Richard and Barbara Caldwell to have their beautiful home. They were living their lives the way their parents lived theirs, doing what, to them, was right. That was fine.

Sadie loved her employer and his wife, defending their lifestyle if anyone dared say anything negative. They were kind, caring people, who did what was right for their employees, even if they lived lavishly, according to Amish standards. She would never judge them.

She stopped in the upstairs bathroom to lift the slatted wooden blind and gaze out across the snowy ranch land. It spread as far as the eye could see, the scenery so beautiful it could take your breath away, especially in winter.

She would have to ride Paris this evening. One more time before they took her away. Paris loved the snow, taking great plunging strides, spraying clouds of it when she ran, the cold air slamming into Sadie's face, Reuben at her side, yelling and laughing.

She'd have to leave a message for him on her parents' phone. Maybe he could ride over tomorrow after work.

As it turned out, Reuben had to work late. Dat started a new log cabin that needed the concrete poured for the footer before the next snow arrived.

A week later, the government men came and took Paris away. Sadie refused to watch, throwing herself on their bed, shutting out any sound with the pillow clamped over her head as tightly as possible. She lifted it cautiously to listen for any sounds before emerging from the bedroom, her ears red, her eyes swollen from crying.

Catching sight of herself in the mirror, she was shocked to see how old and careworn she appeared. So she took a shower, changed to a dress the color of cranberries, brushed her teeth, and decided to grow up and stop being so immature about Paris. She was just a horse.

Then Sadie thought of Paris stepping down from that trailer after a long cold journey, her large brown eyes with the thick, bristly lashes looking at everyone and everything with so much trust in them. Sadie's lips trembled, her nose burned, and she started sobbing all over again.

Mark told her to go home and spend the day with her mother and sisters. She needed it.

And that's exactly what she did, being greeted with cheers and hugs and coffee and French toast, maple syrup and chipped beef gravy, fried cornmeal mush, and Mam's perfect dippy eggs.

Leah was working at her cleaning job, but Rebekah and Anna were at home. They caught up on the latest news, the life of dating, being with the youth, their work,

Reuben turning 16 before too long, and Mam's concern about Reuben's time of *rumspringa*, literally translated as "running around," which is exactly what the youth did after they turned 16.

Mam was in high spirits, making them all laugh with stories about the last quilting she had attended. She had to get started piecing Leah's Mariner's Star quilt, with the feeling goading her that Kevin had marriage on his mind.

"But, can you imagine, a Mariner's Star in black and beige? It's enough to give me the blues. All that black!"

"Get Fred Ketty to piece it," Rebekah suggested.

"Fred Ketty?"

"They said she did one with black and ... I forget what else, but she got over 900 dollars for it."

"Where?"

Mam was so incredulous her mouth formed a perfect O, then closed tightly after she pronounced the "where."

"She sold it at the fire hall, remember? That auction in August."

"See, that shouldn't be allowed. That's too much display ... of ... Well, it's just too worldly, parading a quilt like that at a fire hall. Likely it was raffled off or whatever, and that's too much like gambling, and that's strictly *verboten*, you know that."

Mam became so agitated she started scraping leftover crusts of French toast into the garbage, her face with heightened color, her nostrils flaring.

Rebekah winked broadly at Sadie, with the sort of look that said, "Mam's just jealous," but in a loving way. You could never hate your mother. You could get irritated, even angry for a short time, but if she had a whole list of failures, you sort of loved even the shortcomings. Mam so obviously prided herself in her own ability to piece outstanding quilts that this sort of news was a bit much.

After the conversation lagged, Anna got up, saying she had a dress to sew, so Rebekah and Sadie could do the dishes.

"What color are you making?" Sadie asked.

Anna brought out a three-yard piece of fabric, the color a hue of brilliant magenta with a decided stripe in it.

"Mam!" Sadie gasped. She was clearly shocked.

Why would Mam allow a color that bold, a stripe that pronounced? She obviously hadn't. Calmly, Mam laid down her plate, then came over to peer at the offending color and texture.

"Where did you get this, Anna?"

"Walmart."

Anna's eyes were very large in her too-thin face, the angle of her beautiful cheekbone so pronounced, her chin so tiny, the cleft in it showing so plainly. Her dress, as usual, hung on her thin frame, gathered about her tiny waist by the broad belt of her apron.

Anna was the youngest and battled eating disorders. With little sense of self-worth, always appearing over-weight and ugly in her own eyes, she had taken to purging. Sadly loathing herself and her pitiful ability to be a friend, she felt she had nothing to contribute to a conversation or any circumstance in which she found herself. Anna was one of the reasons it had been difficult for Sadie, often acting as a mentor to her troubled sister, to leave home.

Mam pursed her lips now and said evenly, "I hope you know I can't let you make a dress with that fabric, Anna."

It was all Anna needed to release the spring of tension, the bottled up volcano of rebellion against Mam, or

Sadie, or anyone who tried to take this dress away from her. It was completely essential that she wear this dress, the object that would surely grab and keep Neil Hershberger's faithful devotion.

"Oh, no! You're not taking this dress away from me!" she shouted, her beautiful eyes already forming tears. "I paid for it with my own money! No. You're not. I'm going to wear it!"

She turned, sobbing, running up the steps, the priceless magenta-colored fabric clutched tightly to her thin chest.

Mam started to follow, a hand out, calling her name, but Sadie stopped her. "I'll go after awhile."

"I don't know what to do. She is so different from all you other girls. I plum don't know how to handle it."

With that, Mam sat down wearily, suddenly overcome with her daughter's rebellion coupled with Fred Ketty's 900 dollar quilt.

"Mam, you know her whole problem is that she has to be on top of the pile," Rebekah said harshly.

"Ach, Rebekah," Mam said sadly.

"I'm serious. She can't give up. If that would have been me, you would not have been overwhelmed very long. Bingo! In the trash! Subject closed!"

Mam laughed, her plump stomach shaking with mirth. "Now stop it," she said, still laughing.

✿ ✡ ✿

When Sadie got to Anna's room, she found it hard to see her sister that way, lying on her stomach, as close to the wall as she could get, her fingers in her ears the minute Sadie opened the door. Human nature made Sadie feel like smacking her, calling her a big baby, and telling her to get off that bed this minute, go eat something, and stop obsessing about yourself and Neil Hershberger. Maybe that's what Sadie should have done.

There were too many big girls in the family while Anna was growing up. Somehow, she had been shorted, whether it came from Mam's mental illness, or whether she was born with this decayed sense of her own worth. Whatever the cause, she needed help.

"All right, Anna. Stop it. Get your fingers out of your ears. Look at me."

"Go away."

"All right, I will."

She walked away, closed the door firmly behind her, then heard it open and Anna calling, "Come back, Sadie."

"Not unless you're *chide*." (nice, normal)

"I'll try."

Sadie picked up the fabric, took it over to the window, parted the curtains and looked at it, peering closely, as if it were a foreign object.

"You weren't really going to make this, were you?" she asked, kindly and unaccusing.

"'Course I was."

Her words were hard stones pinging against Sadie's flinching face. Somehow that answer was a solidified thing, an assurance that Anna was no longer the harmless little girl who ate great dishes of Lucky Charms cereal. She was actually a concern, a problem to be addressed, like a broken porch step or a refrigerator that stopped working. You had to acknowledge that it needed fixing and then apply yourself, even if it put you in a state of despair. This thought swam into her consciousness, like a shark in a peaceful barrier reef.

Softly, but firmly, Sadie addressed her sister. "Wouldn't you be afraid? Ashamed to wear it to the hymn singing?"

"Huh-uh!"

"I bet you would."

"Hah-ah." So pronounced, her words were almost guttural.

"Come on, Anna. It's way too bright. The parents would have a fit."

"Hah-ah."

"Tell you what. I'll buy you another one if you'll go shopping with me."

Anna rolled over on her back, then sat up, pulling her knees to her chin, wrapping her arms around them. Her dark hair was disheveled, a lock hanging into her large, dark eyes and the dark shadows of ... what? Tiredness? Lack of good nutrition? Her eyes made her appear older, much older in fact, than her years.

Anna said nothing and just looked at her steadily, unflinching, with a cold look Sadie could not fully perceive.

"I want the dress I chose." The voice was flat, the words hard as nails.

Sadie said nothing, sighed, turned toward the dresser, picked up a small bottle of cologne, winced, gasped in shock at the words written diagonally across it. Still saying nothing, she plucked off the cap, spritzed a small amount on her wrist, rubbed it with the palm of her hand, and sniffed. "Mmm."

Anna's face brightened.

"You like it?"

"Yes, it smells ... different. Where did you buy it?"

"Neil gave it to me."

The defiant note in her voice is what gave away the lie. There was an angry retort on Sadie's tongue, but she caught herself just in time, knowing that a thick, suffocating confrontation would follow, driving a wedge of cast iron into the fragile relationship between them.

"He did? No birthday, no nothing?" Sadie turned, her eyebrows raised, surprise in her voice. "And you're not dating?"

Anna came up off the bed in one movement, her face darkening as anger propelled her. Standing boldly, one thin hand on her hip, her pelvis jutted out in defiance, she clipped her words short.

"No, we're not dating. Which I hope you know is none of your business. If I remember correctly, you weren't dating Mark for a very long time. Just sort of creeping around."

It was the sarcasm that did it. Turning, she felt the heat rise in her face, did nothing to stop it. She stepped within a foot of her sister, thrust her face close to hers, and let her words fall where they would.

"Anna, you know Neil did not give you that cologne. You also know that you are on a dangerous road, completely obsessed with a person of … of questionable intent. You can't do this, Anna. He doesn't seem like someone you should be spending time with."

"You don't know him."

"Yes, I think I do. When I saw you two at my wedding, I could tell. You have no idea how you two appeared. The…"

She was cut short. "Shut up!"

Sadie's mouth fell open in disbelief. "Anna!"

"Get out! Get out of my room and stop talking. Go!"

Sadie opened her mouth, closed it, turned, and walked

through the door, closing it firmly behind her.

The remainder of the day passed in a blur. Mam prattled away happily about Kevin and Leah, how absolutely wonderfully he treated her, how much money he made, being the same as foreman on that logging operation, but then his father always was a good manager. Everything he touched turned into money.

Mam said this innocently, but Sadie caught the underlying pride. She wanted to tell Mam to be careful, but she was suddenly too tired, too beaten down by Anna's outburst to try and remedy anything at all. She just wanted to go home. Home to Mark, to her clean, uncluttered life, where the unpleasantness came only from Paris's absence, which would turn out all right in the end, she felt sure.

She hitched up Truman with Rebekah's help. She waved good-bye as he pulled the carriage down the drive, and a deep sense of anticipation settled over her.

There was no need to question whether it had been God's will for her to become Mark Peight's wife. With a deep, abiding knowledge, she knew the rightness of it, of returning to him with this joy after spending a day with her family.

She would worry about Anna, the magenta-colored dress, Neil, the questionable cologne, but she would be able to put all of it out of her thoughts, for a time, anyway. Perhaps it was just a phase.

The cream-colored SUV passed her from behind, traveling so slowly she almost had to hold Truman back to keep from catching up to it. Annoying driver... Why didn't he accelerate? Just get going? She did pull back on the black leather reins then, or she would have driven too close. Probably an elderly couple afraid of the snow-covered back roads. Truman wanted to run, so Sadie held back firmly now, glad to see the car ahead of her pick up speed.

Driving horses were all the same, she thought. When you got them out of the barn and hitched them to the buggy, they trotted along willingly, took you where you wanted to go, settling down to a level trot, even if they felt a bit spunky at first, dancing around, balking a bit, or crow-hopping sometimes. But if you let them stand at a barn, or along a fence, or tied to a hitching rack for any length of time, then hitched them up to return home, they pricked their ears forward and clipped along at a much better pace, knowing a good cold drink out of their own trough, a nice pile of oats, and a block of good hay awaited them at home.

Home was where all horses wanted to be. Me, too, Truman, Sadie thought, smiling to herself. She had some cold chicken breast in the refrigerator. She would make the chicken and rice casserole for Mark this evening. No broccoli, so she'd substitute peas. She had a whole pumpkin pie in a round Tupperware container under the seat, a gift from Mam, bless her heart. Pumpkin pies were complicated to make. She smiled to herself, thinking of Mam's distaste for any uncovered, or loosely covered, food items put under the seat of a buggy. No matter how hard you tried to avoid it, there was always a certain amount of horse hair floating inside a buggy, always finding its way to the top of a container. But not one hair would be on the pumpkin pie. Mam double-checked the famously secure Tupperware seal.

The beige-colored SUV approached her again from the opposite direction, driving as slow as before. The windows were tinted, so there was no use checking for the occupants. That was some expensive vehicle, Sadie guessed.

She wondered vaguely what she would drive if she was English. She smiled at the thought of turning the ignition key, stepping on a pedal, and moving off. Wouldn't that be different?

She wished she had sunglasses to wear. The late afternoon sun was blinding. That would be different, too. A pair of black sunglasses on a face framed by an Amish bonnet. Likely she'd get her picture on the front page of the local newspaper.

Truman was gathering speed for his dash up the side of Atkin's Ridge, so Sadie relaxed the reins, letting him have his head, knowing he had to make it up the hill on his own terms, rounding the curve on top like a racer, leaning to the right.

She pulled back in alarm when the same SUV roared past from behind, disappearing up the side of the ridge in a whirl of snow and grit. Boy, for all the time they wasted going back and forth, probably looking for a certain road sign, they must have suddenly decided they knew where they were going.

And when she came upon this vehicle parked across the road, she hauled back on the leather reins as hard as she could, thinking they should have been more careful, having suddenly hit an icy spot. She hoped no one was hurt, and she was glad to see the vehicle had not turned over. There was no way around it, with the high bank on one side and the steep incline on the other, so she opened the window, calling "Whoa."

Chapter 3

Truman obeyed, although he raised and lowered his head, pulling at his bit, impatient at the obstacle in his path.

Sadie was surprised when the doors flung open and two men wearing black ski masks quickly ran to the buggy. Her first thought was about their lack of common sense, wearing ski masks this time of the day when the temperatures weren't that low. Later, during the night, the temperature would hover below zero. It was only when she saw the small black pistol in the fat man's gloved hand that she felt the first stab of fear.

"Don't give us any trouble and you won't get hurt."

The words were muffled, as if the opening in his mask was at the wrong place. His breath was coming fast and hard, like he had been running. The barrel of the pistol was so tiny. It looked like a toy, actually. Maybe it was. That thought was fleeting, instantly replaced by the knowledge of danger and the alarming position in which she now found herself.

Truman's ears flicked back, he lowered his head and tested the reins.

"You're coming with us."

She knew she couldn't do that. Who would care for Truman and the buggy? What about Mark? His chicken-and-rice casserole? Her eyes sought an opening, a way through. Not enough room. Could she jump out, make it on foot? Not in this snow. Panic spread its oily fingers across her chest, squeezing her lungs till her breathing was only coming in shallow puffs.

"Get down." The words were garbled, surprisingly mild, and, in a way, mannerly.

"I can't." Her voice was hoarse, her dry throat now aching with a sort of despair, an acceptance that this time she could not go dashing away on Paris. She didn't even know where Paris was.

"You will get down." The words were forceful now, spoken much louder. The gun was positioned again, shoved up against the frame of the buggy where the door had been slid back.

Wildly now, her eyes darted, searching for an escape route, realizing there was none. Slowly, methodically, she lifted the lap robe that kept her legs warm.

"I can't just let ... Truman ... the horse, loose."

"Get down now."

There was nothing to do but obey. Not with that pistol stuck in her face and the two men waiting for her. It was when she laid the reins across the glove compartment, slid the lap robe away from her legs, and grasped the frame of the buggy to lower herself that a total loss of hope clenched her heart. Here, on Atkin's Ridge, again. This time, would it be her last? She was too afraid to pray.

Like a robot, she moved. Her foot hit the step, then the ground. She was immediately seized on either side, her elbows encased in gloved hands like vices clamping down and propelling her forward. Stumbling, sliding, looking back at Truman, she begged them to let her take care of the horse and buggy. Yanking on her, they stuffed her into the back seat. She saw a roll of duct tape appear.

"No!" She screamed, then kicked, flung her arms, and hit the fat man with every ounce of her strength.

"Get in and drive!" The fat man's accomplice instantly slid behind the wheel and locked the doors. Still she fought until the fat man shoved the sinister little pistol to her face.

Sadie became more terrified. She was being taken to an unknown destination, to an unknown end. And for what reason? She shuddered and slid back against the leather seat as the fat man encircled her wrists and ankles, the sticky tape digging into her flesh. The car was moving now, going down the side of the ridge.

Oh, Mark. It was then that she cried. If this was the way her life would end, then she was deeply aware of having had these short months with Mark and so very grateful of his love. That he had chosen her to be his wife still seemed like a miracle. The days they spent together were idyllic, except for the bad times, which, so far, had proved to be temporary.

What would he do? If there is such a thing as telepathy, a sort of mental communication, just let him know I'm safe, so far.

Then she remembered God. Of course, God was here. He knew where she was. Her fate was in his hands, not the hands of these men. He had the power to rescue her, keep her safe, or end her life. It was all in God's hands.

How often had she heard that phrase? *In Gottes Hent.* Over and over, the Amish people used that phrase. It was the way they lived. The way they believed. Everything happened for a reason. To God on his throne, it all made perfect sense, so they lived simply, peacefully, not having to understand everything, their faith a substance of things not seen.

Like one of Mam's homemade, pieced comforters, his presence wrapped itself around her shoulders, loosening the clutches of fear. As if God wanted to comfort her, she clearly remembered the story of a girl who had been kidnapped and knew to remain friendly, talkative, complying with her abductor until they became friends of a sort. They finally agreed on a compromise. The man who abducted her acknowledged that he needed help and became a much better person in the end.

Well, there were two kidnappers, and as far as she could tell, they were still hurtling along on an interstate. The joyous thought entered her mind of the driver going far over the speed limit, a police car overtaking them, being rescued, and these men being caught. Hopefully, the driver was pushing about a hundred.

She couldn't swallow without straining, the duct tape biting into her cheeks and jaw every time she did. She desperately needed a drink and wondered how long a person could go without using a restroom. She thought of a tall glass of sparkling lemonade with chunks of ice, which made her swallow, bringing much more discomfort.

"Better watch it. Cops'll be after you." The driver slowed down.

Sadie was lulled to a stupor, a sort of gray area, neither asleep nor awake, but always aware of the moving vehicle and the men beside her. The emotions of fear and panic were blanketed with a fuzzy warmth, a dissociation from reality.

She didn't know how long she stayed in this position; she only knew they were slowing, then came to a stop. The men exchanged a few whispered comments.

The driver got out. She smelled gasoline, so she knew they were filling up at a service station. Was it dark outside? What time was it?

Please, please, let me have a drink of water. Her throat was beyond dry; it was ravaged with thirst. Any saliva she could summon was instantly absorbed by the rags, sponge, cotton, or whatever it was that they stuffed in her mouth.

The driver returned; they moved on. She heard tractor trailers moving slowly through the parking lot. Cars moved, honked their horns. The men were drinking something. She heard the crack and hiss as the fat man opened a bottle of soda pop, the liquid gurgling from the bottle down his throat.

She was so thirsty that she cried. Tears squeezed from between her lashes, wetting the blindfold. She was glad of the blindfold, absorbing the tears, her sign of weakness. She would have to be stronger. She would be. She would will away her thirst.

Her feet were going numb. The duct tape dug into her ankles and cut into her black stockings. Her hands throbbed. She imagined them growing twice as big and turning purple, then falling off. That's what happened if you banded a little piggy's tail. After the circulation was shut off for a length of time, it simply shriveled away to nothing and dropped off. She hoped it took hands a long, long time.

Her ears were pressed so hard against the side of her bonnet, she could barely feel them. If she moved her cheekbones, or imagined moving her ears, it helped. So she knew she could actually change the position of her ears, even if it was only for a short time before the numbness and tingling returned.

All night, they drove. Sadie alternated between sleep and a half-awake stupor. Her thirst raged in her throat now, a constant thing she could not escape. As a child, she had often imagined being kidnapped, the pain of fetters, but never could anyone imagine the cruelty of her thirst. No wonder people died of thirst way before they succumbed to hunger.

The vehicle stopped. The back door opened. She lurched awake, strained against her blindfold, screamed a silent scream of alarm when rough hands seized her.

"Get out."

Sadie tried to wiggle the duct tape loose, leaned forward, swung her legs over the side of the seat. The air was cold and wet, sharp as a knife against her senses.

"Loosen her feet."

Sadie brought her teeth together, clenched her jaw, willing herself not to cry out. If she moved as much as a tongue muscle, the pain was excruciating. The tape made a tearing, sticky sound. She felt it being unwound, the blood rushing into her feet, a thousand needles pricking like a swarm of yellow jackets from the swamp in Ohio.

"Get out. Walk."

She slid down, her feet hit the ground, and she crumbled into a heap, crying in her throat, raw from the thirst and pain and hopelessness.

"Get up." The fat man was angry.

"She can't with the tape," the driver said.

"Get her."

Two hands went under her arms, lifted her, but she crumbled into a heap the same as before. The fat man snorted with impatience. Grabbing her, he threw her across his shoulder, the same way any man would pack a hundred-pound sack of feed or bag of potatoes. The blood rushed into her head as she bobbed along, being carried up one flight of stairs, then another. Doors opened and closed. It was warm. Something smelled good, very good, in fact. Like pine woods or the first of the wild flowers.

The fat man dumped her on a soft sofa or bed. She lay completely still. Somehow playing dead like a possum seemed safe.

"Unwind her hands. The duct tape."

Again she heard the grinding sticky sound. Her hands fell into the bed, containing no strength of their own.

"We need to talk. We're going to unwind the tape around your mouth. We will loosen the blindfold if you promise to stay. Any attempt at leaving will mean death. We are serious. You are of no consequence to us."

Her head turned from side to side by the force of the tape being removed. It was all irrelevant. No matter. The pain was bearable. She'd be able to see, to swallow. Would they allow her a drink? She gagged when they removed the object in her mouth. But she recovered quickly, summoning her courage and resolving to remain strong.

When they removed the blindfold, she untied her heavy black bonnet with groping, numb fingers that felt as big as bananas and about as clumsy. She kept her eyes closed, afraid to open them. Where was she? Slowly, through shaking eyelids, her eyes focused, bringing the room into view.

At first she saw only beige walls, then the ornate molding in a darker shade. Slowly, as her eyes cleared, she saw that she was in a bedroom, sort of a guest bedroom. The carpeting was beige, as well as the bedspread, the curtains, and pillows. There was a red sofa, a glass coffee table, and red objects of art. Black lamps cast a yellowish light into the corners, and huge, navy blue, plaid pillows were strewn across the sofa in the glow of the lamps. Very pretty, she thought wryly.

"May I please be allowed a visit to the restroom?"

She tried to say this, but her voice was only a whisper, her vocal chords refusing to accommodate her. The fat man pointed to a door behind the bed. Slowly, carefully, Sadie set one foot on the carpeting, then the other. Clutching the side of the bed, she moved around it, bent over, wincing with the pain of the returning circulation.

She never knew a person could drink so much water. She cupped her hands beneath the gold faucet and drank and drank and drank. Water seeped between her fingers. She sucked at it greedily, hating to wait until her cupped hands were filled again so she could slurp at it like an animal dying of thirst.

It was only after her thirst was sated that she knew how hungry she was. She looked at the pink guest soaps in the white seashell dish and considered eating them. She had to have something to eat. They'd have to feed her. Allow her some kind of food. Did kidnappers starve their victims to death? Who knew?

Tentatively, she opened the door of the bathroom, hobbled out, still clinging to the side of the bed.

Immediately the fat man began. "You cooperate, you're fine. If you act stubborn, you're not. Got it?"

Sadie nodded, her eyes on the carpet.

"Where's the palomino mare?"

"I don't know."

With the speed of lightning, his hammy fist smacked her mouth, snapping her head back. Sadie didn't cry out. Tears came to her eyes, and blood spurted from a torn lip. She lifted the hem of her blue apron to sop up the flow.

"I told you. You work with us, you're fine."

The driver shifted uncomfortably, his gaze wavering, clearing his throat as if he wanted to say something, then thought better of it. From behind the apron, Sadie shook her head.

"They took her away."

"Who?"

The fat man's eyes bored into hers, a sick light of greediness shining.

"Four men came to my house. Was it a week ago? Something like that. They said I was in danger. So was Paris."

"Who's Paris?"

"The horse."

"The palomino?"

Sadie nodded. "They said they were taking her to an undisclosed location."

The two men looked at each other and nodded. "Are you telling the truth?"

"Yes. Why would I lie? I just want to go home. You can have the horse if you spare my life. I don't want to die."

"We ain't killin' anybody," the driver burst out before the fat man held up a hand, giving him a scathing look.

"Looks as if you're gonna be here awhile, young lady. We want the horse. At any cost. We figure we'll get her if we use you to acquire her."

At this, the fat man's eyes glittered again. "There's more ways than one to acquire our needs," he chortled.

"All right," Sadie said, not unpleasantly. "If you have to keep me here, am I allowed to know where I am? How long I have to stay? Will I be able to have some food? You're not going to tie me again with that duct tape?"

The driver shook his head wildly behind the fat man's back.

"You're a long way from home. You'll be staying until we can persuade them, whoever it is, to give us the palomino. We'll feed you, and if you stay cooperative, we'll keep you locked up in here, but no duct tape."

Sadie nodded. "Thank you. I am appreciative of this freedom. I won't attempt an escape as long as I'm treated decently."

"If the people hand over the palomino, you're good to go."

Sadie nodded again. She lifted her head then, "Am I alone in this house?"

"This is a big place. No, you're not alone. This place is full of housekeepers, gardeners, cooks. It's a big place," he repeated.

So her imprisonment began. The digital clock read 11:09. The big red numbers against the black face were her only companion. There was no telephone, radio, or television. She went to the window, parted the heavy curtains, pulled on the cord that raised and lowered the blinds. Yes, as she thought, she was housed in a palatial home. Looking down from her third-story room, she saw there was no doubt about the immensity of the gardens, pastures, and the vast corrals and barns. It made Aspendale East seem quite ordinary.

The snow was thinner here, with brown tufts of grass showing like eyebrows on an old man's face. As far as the eye could see, there was only flat earth, a level landscape with rows of fences and trees creating a crisscross pattern that looked like one of Mam's homemade comforters.

Sadie had no communication with the outside world, only the fat man or the driver appearing with trays of food at whatever hour they chose. Her first meal had consisted of cold cereal, milk, and an apple, blistering in its sourness on her raw tongue and throat. The cereal tasted heavenly, savoring each sweet, milky bite the way she did. Sometimes she fared well, eating good, hot, Mexican dishes. Other time she went to bed hungry, dreaming of Mam's breakfasts.

She tried to keep her thoughts away from Mark. She always ended up sobbing into the pillow if she let her mind wander to him. She missed her family. She hoped Mam and Dat would be okay. She figured Reuben would waver between anger and indignation, between bluster and little-boy tears.

She paced the room, did sit-ups, stood at the window for hours on end. She was always thankful for good, hot baths, the ability to wash her clothes in the bathtub, to have clean towels, soap, and a good bed to sleep on. Her situation could have been so much worse.

She prayed for her rescue. She prayed the government agents would deliver Paris. She cried about Paris, too. But if it meant her life...

Had she been too *gros-feelich* (proud)? Didn't the Bible say we reap what we sow? Had she sown pride and arrogance with her beautiful Paris? Why had God allowed this to happen? How long until this ordeal ended?

Then one day, when she felt as if she would surely lose her mind if she had nothing to do, she decided to houseclean the room. It would give her exercise, keep her occupied, simply save her wandering sanity. She shaved some of the pink soap into the vanity bowl, grabbed a heavy, white washcloth, dunked and swirled it in the soapy water, then wrung it out well.

She started with the bathroom cupboards. She carefully took out towels, soap, a hair dryer, and what she guessed was a hair-curling apparatus, an assortment of combs and brushes, a box of guest soap. She washed each shelf thoroughly, replacing the objects, before tackling the bathroom closet. She stood on the vanity stool to clean the top shelf, pushing aside a stack of perfectly folded blankets.

Ouch! Her fast moving hand struck the corner of a hard object. Pulling out the stack of blankets, she let them fall to the floor before procuring the cause of her pain. She held it in her hands, incredulous. A radio! It must be. She didn't know much about electronic devices, living all her life without them, but she did know what a radio looked like. Eagerly, the blood pounding in her ears, she unwrapped the long, brown cord, plugged it in, then turned the dial with shaking fingers.

Nothing. Her disappointment was palpable—big and heavy, black, as dark as a night without moon or stars. The depth of her disappointment fueled her anger, her desperation. She jiggled wires, shook the radio, twisted and turned dials with a sort of viciousness, yet there was nothing.

Then she thought of Jim Sevarr's old rusted pickup truck and the wire coat-hanger stuck on the end of his broken antennae. Oh, dear God, let it be. Dashing to the closet, she flipped frantically through a long line of plastic or wooden hangers. Just one. I just need one wire hanger. Over and over, she went through them, finally acknowledging that there were none.

When a knock sounded, she had time to close the bathroom door. The fat man called her name; she told him she was in the bathroom and would he please wait until she came out. Her evening meal consisted of a great, steaming pile of roast pork and corn tortillas with tomato sauce, which absorbed her tears as she ate.

Chapter 4

Richard Caldwell and his wife, Barbara, were at their wit's end. They had already run the gauntlet of emotions in the weeks that Sadie had been missing. They had badgered every police department in the state of Montana. The computer was never idle, searching relentlessly for new avenues of discovery.

Dorothy's way of dealing with Sadie's disappearance was blaming the country, the president, Wall Street, the love of money, the devil, and most of all, the local police for not being able to track down the horse thieves, the snipers, the whole crazy lot of them in the first place. Erma Keim nodded her head, pursed her lips, and worked like a maniac, saying her nerves couldn't take this if she didn't use her muscles. She agreed with Dorothy on most subjects but stopped at Wall Street and the president.

The news media had posted regular news about the disappearance that first week, leaving the Amish community reeling. They had to be very careful, as being on TV was strictly *verboten*. So was speaking on radio or other forms of "worldly" news.

They were most comfortable "doing" for Jacob Miller's family and Mark. People came in great, caring buggy loads. They cleaned the stables, washed Mam's walls and windows, cooked so many casseroles and baked so many pies, half of them were thrown out.

Dat's face aged week by week. They all feared for Mam the most. Hadn't she been emotionally weak? Hadn't she been mentally ill? Yes, she had. But her strength now was amazing. She was a matriarch, a fortress of long-suffering and patience. She assured her family it was that palomino; the money or the horse would eventually show up. She prayed for Sadie's well-being. The only thing that set her face to crumbling now was the thought of Sadie having to suffer.

Anna became steadily more fragile. She blamed herself. She was afraid of God. He was up there on his throne, raining fire and brimstone down on her family because of her magenta dress and the secrets about her and Neil Hershberger. She roamed the house, a sad ghost of her former self, disappearing when company arrived. Leah and Rebekah hung posters on the local store windows. They prayed together, cried together, tried to include Anna, and were always supportive of Dat and Mam.

Mark moved in. He couldn't live in their house without Sadie. He lost weight, and deep lines appeared beneath his eyes. He had come home that evening, found Truman hitched to the buggy by the fence, shivering with cold. He became irritated. Why hadn't she unhitched him? He took care of Truman, noticed his leg bleeding, found the pumpkin pie, and Sadie's purse. Alarmed, Mark ran to the house, called for Sadie, and tried to stay calm.

Wolf had whined, and Mark even asked Wolf where she had gone. Men and dogs searched for days that turned into weeks. Helicopters throbbed in the sky. It was all a bad dream. He would surely wake up soon. But things like her nightgown hanging on a hook in the bathroom are what made him move in with her family. He simply couldn't take it—the sight of the boots she wore to help him do chores, the smell of the soap on their vanity, the essence of his darling Sadie.

They talked a lot, Mark and the Millers. They said things they probably never would have said if this had not occurred, leaving an impenetrable bond that would always hold.

Reuben got mad. He said Sadie was foolish, driving her horse and buggy around the way she did when she knew her life was at risk. The whole thing was—she had no fear. She never did. She should have taken a warning way back when she had that near-accident with Paris and the spring wagon and that guy from Lancaster County. It probably had something to do with that fat guy in the dentist's office. He reasoned with a lot of common sense for a youth of 15 years old.

He almost had it down pat; the only thing missing was more information. Which, with the hand of God moving in mysterious ways as it always does, was partially supplied when Richard Caldwell asked Reuben to come help Louis and Marcellus get the tack ready for the horse fair in February. There were piles of silver buckles and rings to be taken off the saddles and bridles, polished with silver polish, and reattached. It was a perfect job for Reuben, and one for which he'd be paid the astonishing amount of $12 an hour. In his eyes, he was amassing a fortune.

Dorothy fussed about that, too. She said the tack room was too cold. The children were too little to work, but Erma Keim told her they were not either. Little Amish children did lots of chores at that age, and Dorothy got her dander up and told her they were no better than English kids, and who did she think she was? Erma went home in a huff, slid down the washhouse stairs, and scraped her backside on the concrete steps, which Dorothy never learned of.

As it was, Dorothy supplied the young workers with cranberry juice and ginger ale, warm chocolate chip cookies, and ham salad to eat on warm rolls, all packed in a tin basket, telling them to come into the kitchen to warm up if their feet got cold.

Louis warmed right up to Reuben. They talked nonstop. Reuben asked Louis where they really came from, and Louis dropped his voice and told him the whole story in his little-boy wisdom.

"We're from far away. The town of Santa Fe, New Mexico. It's a big town. My parents owned a ranch. We had too many horses to count. My dad got greedy, and I think he stole other rancher's horses. My mother became very sad. After that she became angry. They were always fighting. Bad men came to eat at our table."

Louis paused, wiping absentmindedly on a buckle.

"There is a big fat man with a mustache and very long ponytail. His name is Oliver Martinez. He steals the horses. Him and a whole bunch of other men. They appeared at our door and continued to do that for many months. Mother would cry.

"My dad would not listen. Then she had to go away and said she would be back for us, but she never came. That's why Jim and Dorothy—they're our parents now. We love them okay, only they don't look as nice as our real parents. Our house isn't as nice. Our dad's name is Lee Hartford!"

Marcellus chimed in, laughing. "Grace Hartford!"

Reuben laughed, then shook his head. "Whoever they are, you probably have a wise mother."

When Richard Caldwell paid Reuben, he asked if there was any news of Sadie. Reuben shook his head, but related Louis's story, giving him the name of the man named Oliver Martinez. When Richard Caldwell's eyes became quite big and round, and he swiveled his chair immediately to his computer, Reuben figured he was onto something.

He rode home, fast and hard, the bitter cold searing the skin visible between his coat sleeve and his glove, Moon throwing the snow in chunks. He found Mark slumped over the kitchen table, his head in his hands, waiting for supper to be ready.

"Hey, guys! I think we're onto something!"

Mam turned sharply. Mark lifted his head, his two big eyes piercing into Reuben's, his face devoid of color.

Reuben related the story, finishing with, "I bet you anything that Oliver guy is connected here somehow. Richard Caldwell is already on it. He wants to search all the old police files. I mean, that little Louis and Marcellus are likely victims of this whole horse thieving thing, don't you think?"

Far into the night, Richard Caldwell sat hunched over his computer. Mark lay sleepless. Reuben knelt by his bed in his T-shirt and flannel pajama pants, put his head on his hands, and prayed like never before. He had to see Sadie again.

✫ ✫ ✫

Erma Keim walked out to the tack room to take some hot chocolate to Reuben, (still her favorite buddy, she told him) and met up with Lothario Bean, who promptly began bowing and scraping his feet in his total delight at seeing her again. Reuben watched them both in bewilderment, Erma giving off those loud guffaws of pure delight at Lothario's antics.

Wasn't he married? Reuben shrugged his shoulders, went back to polishing saddles, but held very still when he thought he heard the name Oliver.

"Very big. Very big!"Lothario Bean stretched his arm up high above his head to show Erma how big Oliver was, then extended his arms out in front of his stomach to show the size of his girth.

"He a good friend of ours. My wife cook up wonderful Mexican food for him. He won lottery. Lucky fellow. Bought brand new SUV. Cream color. Look like Dallas people on TV. Bought it at Gregory Cadillac in town. Nice man. Like to eat. Oh, yeah, love hot chocolate just like this. He marry a person like you. Make him hot chocolate this way."

Reuben froze, then began slowly polishing buckles, his mind whirring like Mam's egg beater when she made lemon meringue pie. He got up, stretched, and casually walked to the house, straight to Richard Caldwell's office.

"Gregory's Cadillac. In town! Oliver Martinez bought a new car there. He's a friend of Lothario Bean!"

Reuben leaned over his desk, his hands reeking of silver polish, his eyes very big and blue, desperate with longing.

"I'll call the police immediately, Reuben."

The police came to interview the family and found Lothario Bean, who gave them all the information they needed. Then they went to Jim and Dorothy's house, where they found Louis and Marcellus in their pajamas, having their evening bedtime ritual of graham crackers and milk.

Still as mannerly and well-spoken as ever, they answered questions forthrightly with childish sincerity. They proudly produced their address label on the inside of their drawstring duffel bag, having discovered it only the week before and told Dorothy, who refused to look at it, saying no one knew whose address that was.

The police were onto something, and they knew it immediately. They went back to the Miller home, found Mark still awake, pacing the kitchen floor, and delivered the good news. Mark bent his head, nodding, his mouth working as he fought to control his emotions. At last, a thread of genuine hope. With promises of keeping him posted, they left, but there was very little sleep for him the entire night.

❊ ✪ ❊

Sadie was finished cleaning. She felt as if her mind was slipping, slowly leaving her without the good foundation of genuine reality. Had this all happened? Was it a bad dream? This couldn't have happened in real life. Amish girls driving around in horses and buggies were not accosted on rural roads. Another car or truck would have passed them, been aware of a suspicious-looking situation, stopped, and helped her out.

She checked her appearance in the mirror. She still looked the same, only thinner, circles casting shadows beneath her dark eyes, and definitely like someone who was, yes, slowly losing her mind.

If she only had something to write on or something to read. She had asked but was refused. Why? Why couldn't they let her have something to read? She wrote poems in her mind. She thought of words, put them together in a sequence, sort of, until she memorized verse after verse.

She considered kicking her way out of the door. Not the door. The drywall would break easier. Just kick and pound, bludgeon the wall with whatever she could find, and sneak out. Or, like a rat, chew slowly away at an opening, slip out during the night, and run. Run wildly, crazily, screaming for help.

Another scenario that held more logic was knotting the bed sheets, the bedspread, the towels, and whatever else she could use, hanging them down the side of the great house, and slipping away during the night. But who could measure how many sheets it would take to reach the ground? What if she stayed dangling halfway, unable to climb back up, and the distance too great to drop down? The alarm system in a home this grand was another thing to be reckoned with. Probably not even a cat could roam these grounds without someone being aware of it.

She stood at the window, watched the wind blow the brown tufts of grass, prayed to be allowed to feel the wonderful breezes caress her face. Sometime she felt as if she was riding Paris, Reuben beside her, laughing, the wind tearing at her *dichly*. She would smile, remember, and then tears would rain down her cheeks, missing Reuben.

The fat man was becoming increasingly forgetful, leaving her without breakfast, and sometimes without anything to eat until evening. Once, she received only a stack of stale saltines and a warm bottle of Dr. Pepper without apology. He seemed to become more agitated as time went on, peering over his shoulder before he entered, his fingers drumming on the window pane as he stood, parted the wooden slats of the blinds, then turned sharply.

"They're not responding yet."

Sadie looked up sharply. "Who?"

"The people we think have the palomino."

"Maybe they don't even have her."

"Do you know more than you're telling us?"

"Absolutely not. I told you the truth."

"I don't believe you."

"Please. I don't know where they took her or who the men were."

"Why wouldn't they respond?"

Suddenly Sadie became physically ill, her stomach churning with fear, the knowledge hitting her, slamming into her with the force of a hurricane: the kidnappers must not have alerted the police or government agents, or they would have responded a long time ago. It was becoming clear to Sadie that these men weren't really interested in the horse. Paris had little, if anything, to do with her abduction.

Sadie felt a cold sweat break out on her back and shoulders. Her hands shook of their own accord as she clenched them in her lap, desperately trying to still them before the fat man saw her fear. Play dumb. She would need to be an opossum, playing dead. It was the only way.

"Perhaps they don't have her."

"That's what I'm thinking."

The fat man was pacing now, extremely agitated. "So, if we can't get the horse, and we take you back, I'll spend time in jail for having taken you in the first place. It's not looking good."

Sadie nodded.

"And ... if you were to disappear ... Just weighing my options here."

Another lurch of Sadie's stomach was followed by her mouth drying up, her breath coming in shallow puffs, the color draining from her face. Play dumb. She heard the words this time. She forced herself to meet his eyes, found his sliding away, furtive, sensitive, unstable.

"You mean you'll let me go, right?" she asked, as normally as she could possibly manage.

"No."

"Why not?"

"You'd turn me in."

"What does that mean?"

He gave her a look of disbelief.

"You mean you don't know?"

"No."

Sadie squared her shoulders, sat up, took a deep breath, summoned her courage. "Don't you have a wife, children, anyone you care about?"

"Used to."

"Did you love her? Or your children?"

"Yeah, at one time I did. But I got to messing with this ... uh ... operation, and they left."

"Who left?"

"They did."

"You mean your wife and children?"

"Yeah."

"Do you own this house?"

"No! Who do you think I am?"

"I have no idea who you are."

"No. I don't own this place. I just work for the guy who does. Things are just so out of control right now. I mean, he always dealt in horses. Done real good for himself. Beautiful wife and kids, found out about the...I can't say...and plumb lost his mind. Started thievin' and doin' illegal stuff just to get his hands on these horses. Offered me...I can't say."

"So, if you just work for this man, why can't you let me go? Does he know I'm here? Does anyone know why?"

"Yeah. Well, in the beginning he did. But I'm not sure he didn't...I can't say."

"Well, if you don't know how I can go home, why don't you just put a stop to this whole deal and let me go?"

He looked at her, and she saw the wavering in his eyes, the doubt, a certain dipping of his eyelids.

"Because I'm getting a bunch of money if we get that horse. I mean, a lot. And...I thought if I have so much money, maybe Adele will come back to me. See, she needs money to keep her happy, and I just couldn't make enough for her. I mean, to keep her with me, happy— you know?"

He looked up. "Adele's a terrific cook. She cooks the best sausage and eggs with salsa, fried tomatoes with chilies, it's unreal. I loved her. Did anything I could to keep her. The kids though, that's what really broke my heart."

Sadie nodded. "Must be hard, losing your wife."

"You could live with me. Just disappear. Can you cook? We could go across the border. I don't want to go to jail."

Suddenly, he appeared to Sadie as his true self, undisguised. A fat, lonely man, afraid, who had only been trying to make enough money to keep his spoiled wife at his side. Perhaps he was as afraid as she was, only in a different way. Was he capable of harming her? She doubted it.

Quickly, she weighed her options, measured them on the scale of pros and cons. To go with him, out of this room. To refuse, stay here, with no promise of escape. It was the confinement that was hardest. She would go. She would risk it. What did she have to lose?

"You take me, I'll go."

He looked at her, then shook his head. "Can't do it. I have to wait. Surely I'll get the money."

Sadie felt the desperation assail her, became fueled by it, burst out, "But if you don't even know if your ... your boss is trying to contact the men who have Paris ... the horse, then how is this thing ever going to come to an end?"

She was crying, then sniveling, pleading, groveling at his feet.

"Just please take me home. Get me out of here. I've done nothing wrong except own a palomino horse. Supposing I was your daughter? Your son?"

In the end, the fat man hardened his heart, became harsh, adamant, refusing to budge or listen to her cries. She knew without looking at him when she heard him heave himself from the chair, open the door, turn the key in the lock, and leave.

It was the large sum of money. Her despair felt like a heavy backpack that wore down her resolve, her hope, her courage. There was truly nothing left. They would let her die in this room.

Well, she wasn't going to die. She had too much to live for. Mark. She pictured him. Tall, dark hair tumbling over his forehead, a new line of dark hair appearing along his jawbone, growing the beard in the Amish style of the married man, so handsome, so gentle. How she loved him! And she had Mam, Dat, Reuben, her sisters, Dorothy. No, she would not give up.

Eyeing the bedspread, the towels, estimating a sheet's length, she sat on the beige sofa and planned. As her thoughts were fueled by a shot of adrenaline, she formed a plan. It was absolutely doable. Yes, it was. The hardest part was determining how to secure the end of the rope of sheets firmly enough to hold her weight. The door? The bed? The doorknob? Would it hold? Oh, dear God, help me.

As night fell, she knew it was this night or never. To pass time, she took a long hot bath, shampooed her hair, hung up the towels, rinsed the tub and bowl of the vanity. She straightened the cushions on the beige sofa, then found extra sheets, towels, whatever she could knot together to form a rope of sorts.

With her teeth, she gnawed at the sheet's end, beginning a small tear. Sometimes with fabric you could pull with all your strength and you'd be unable to tear it apart. But if you put just a tiny cut in it, you could rip it easily. Even if her teeth hurt, she kept chewing, until she had a delicate beginning.

Would he be back? He never came to check on her after her evening meal was delivered, but you never know. To stay safe, she worked on the floor on the opposite side of the bed, so if anyone did appear, she could quickly stuff it all beneath the opulent bed skirt. What a wonderful sound! That ripping, tearing sound of a sheet being torn—the sound of freedom!

She worked steadily, her ears tuned to the slightest sound from the hallway. When there was none, she continued tearing, then knotting. She knotted the sheets with the same knot she used to tie Paris or Truman to a hitching rail. The *gaul's gnipp*. The horse's knot. Over and under and around. If the knot was done properly, the harder it was pulled, the tighter it became. Sometimes, a horse could pull until it became dangerously tight, and still there was no way it would loosen.

She planned her escape route, considered the distance to the road, the crisscross of fencing, and where the fence rows and the trees were. She wondered whether she might trigger alarms and lights as she scurried across the property. There was a row of square bales and a place she hoped was a ravine.

She had never seen her coat or her bonnet after they had brought her to this room. Her only hope to keep from freezing was the white terrycloth robe that hung on the ornate hook on the oak bathroom door. It would work as a coat of sorts.

The red numbers on the clock were 10:22.

Chapter 5

Sᴀᴅɪᴇ ʟᴀʏ ɪɴ ʙᴇᴅ, ʜᴇʀ ᴇʏᴇꜱ ᴡɪᴅᴇ ᴏᴘᴇɴ, ᴘʟᴀɴɴɪɴɢ her getaway. How strong was she? Powerful enough to cling to a rope of sheets and lower herself to the ground? Reuben would be. So would Mark.

She tied the end of the sheet around the leg of the bed, having determined that it was made of heavy steel. She secured it to the hinge on the door as well, just to be sure, sliding a length of sheet carefully into the crack of the door when it stood ajar. Surely, secured in two places, it would hold.

Better to wait till close to the morning hours. Hadn't she heard, somewhere, that people slept most securely at four o'clock in the morning? Four o'clock, then; that was her goal.

She didn't sleep a wink. Every shadow of the room imprinted on her mind. She pictured every knot, every length of sheet. At midnight, she got up, sat on the sofa shivering. She shivered with a case of nervous energy coupled with fear. She shook out the heavy bathrobe, put it on, secured it around her waist with the belt on top of her blue dress.

She wore no covering since they had taken it with her black bonnet. She had been taught to pray with her head covered, so she laid a washcloth as a makeshift covering. She caught sight of herself in the mirror, and looking so silly, she decided surely God would hear her prayer since these men had taken her covering away and she was in such dire need of help.

What about that Magdalene, or whatever her name was, in the Bible? Hadn't she wiped Jesus' feet with her long hair? She didn't wear a covering, and Jesus said she had done him a far greater service than anyone else. Or maybe she did wear a covering, one of those long biblical cloths they wore thousands of years ago. Who could tell?

Sadie prayed reverently, tearfully, begging God to keep her safe. I'll take pain, fear, whatever, but just give me strength to do this, she prayed.

Her mind raced, her nerves jangled. She wished she had something to put in the deep pockets of her bathrobe. A package of crackers. Some pretzels. A bottle of water. It couldn't be too far to a house. A car would pass.

What about dogs? The great rangy creatures flew like agile wolves at the heels of the cattle scattered all over cattle country to protect the livestock from predators. She'd just have to deal with them. She surely did not want to die like Jezebel in the Old Testament either. That was such a tale of warning, the way Jezebel had held her own spiritual meaning far above her husband's, and he was likely closer to God than she was. Women could be such misled creatures, being the weaker vessels the way they were.

Boy, she got herself in trouble saying that to Dorothy. Sadie had finally conceded, saying all right, Dorothy, we Amish are sort of old-fashioned in our views about women knowing their place, being submissive to their husbands. Dorothy did not go along with that. Where would her Jim be if she didn't keep him on his toes? Huh? Answer me that.

One thirty-six. Soon now. Soon she would know. The wind moaned around the corner of the house. Hmm. It hadn't been windy. She hoped there wasn't a storm coming. There was no snow, only cold.

Would a car come along before the dogs, or the fat man, or the hired hands, or whoever else was in the wealthy man's employ? She must have dozed off. Not really slept, just entered the gray zone, the way she had done while they traveled to this house.

Three forty. She jerked, her whole body froze. Twenty more minutes. Oh, dear God. What difference will these 20 minutes make? I must go. She felt a numbness, a maddening listlessness steal over her legs, her arms. You can't do this. You are weak. Tears rose from the hard lump in her throat. Yes, she was weak. No, she couldn't do this. She couldn't.

The Apostle Paul had said the same thing. He was weak, but in Christ Jesus he could do anything with his power. A warmth stole over her body, an assurance of strength. Adrenaline followed it.

She sat up, swung her legs over, secured the belt of the white bathrobe, checked the security of the knots one last time, then slowly loosened the crack of the window. In one turn, she was rewarded by a loosening scrape. She turned steadily, until the long, narrow window was propelled out, allowing enough room for the rope of sheets to be thrown over. Leaning out, she peered desperately into the semi-darkness.

Oh, no. It did not reach the ground. Well, it had to

be close. The sheets passed both windows of the second and third stories, went to the first story. She had to go.

With a deep breath, she climbed up on the windowsill, grasping the sheet. It was so thin. The actual taking hold of the sheet was much harder than she had imagined. How to do this? She finally realized she'd have to sit on the windowsill, with her legs dangling down the side while keeping her hold on the sheets. She'd have to sit forward, then take the plunge, twisting her body to keep her feet against the wall.

She looked back. Three fifty-eight. A good omen. A little before the set time. Grasping the rope of sheets in both hands, she pushed herself off the windowsill, her teeth clenched in the desperate effort to keep a firm grip.

She swung out too far. There was a tearing at her shoulders. Her hands slipped. Oh, no. She couldn't do it. She would fall. Such thoughts tumbled through her mind, but only for a moment. Then her arms rippled with strength. She propelled her body sideways, then in a turn, her feet slid against the stone wall.

Slowly, hand over hand, she lowered herself. The air was so cold. Should have thrown this bathrobe down, the way it billowed out. The first knot. On down. Ouch.

She was going too fast. The sheets burned the palm of her hand. Grasping them more firmly, she slowed her descent. Better to take her time. She didn't want bleeding palms on her hands. The last knot.

She looked down but could not determine the distance to the ground. Was that a shrub? A low tree? She had to stop or let herself fall to the ground. It couldn't be too far.

She dropped. A gasp tore from her throat as she felt nothing at all, only the air rushing past her face as she fell.

She suddenly landed on her feet, one twisting sideways with the impact of her weight.

A red hot, searing pain shot up her leg from her ankle. She lay on the ground, her hands propping her upper body, her eyes squeezed shut, her lower lip caught firmly in her teeth, as she struggled to keep from screaming out a high cry of pain and weakness.

She spun her head. A light went on. No! Oh, please, God, no. She never knew how she got up and started running, but she did. She ran with pain her constant companion. She lowered her back, pumped her arms, her knees raised and lowered, propelling her toward the ravine she projected as her destination. She didn't look back, afraid of what she might see.

Her breath was coming quickly now. She imagined herself in school, running with that effortless, little-girl gait. The time when you could run and run and run, and still you could breathe all right and keep running. She had always been good at it. She would've won every fast race if it hadn't been for that long-legged Henry Mast. They should have let the girls and boys race separately.

Still she ran. Why stop at the ravine? She ran along fences, across water-filled ditches. They would be ice at home. Headlights? A car! A blessed car. A real vehicle. She ran toward it, waving her arms. The vehicle slowed, but then accelerated.

Sadie would never know how the employee at the Quick-Mart, heading to work on the early morning shift, his face now drained of color, said he had seen a real ghost, white, flapping its arms. It didn't take him a second to step on the gas and get out of there. When his co-worker eyed him coolly and said that's how those stupid Bigfoot rumors get started, he got hopping mad and told her off, pouted the rest of the day, and wouldn't speak to her till she brought him a homemade Boston cream pie.

When the second vehicle zoomed by in all its disregarding splendor, Sadie thought of the bathrobe. She took it off and rolled it up, carrying it under her arm.

Dogs! Barking in the distance. Who knew though, if they came from the house she had just escaped from? She walked now, backward, holding out her thumb, a hitch-hiker. In desperation she kept her arm out. Her breath was coming in quick succession, her fear a palpable thing. The dogs. Coming closer? Yes. They most definitely were. Were the dogs merely herding cattle? Bringing home milk cows?

What was the best thing? Revert to fleeing across the fields? No, better to stay with the safety of the highway. Another vehicle. Her teeth were chattering, the shaking spreading to her limbs as the pain in her ankle worsened. She could not keep walking backward like this.

When the truck rolled on past, not even bothering to slow down, an idea entered Sadie's mind. She would appear to be carrying an infant, a helpless baby, clothed in white. She stepped aside, rolled the white bathrobe into the form of a blanketed baby, then held it in her arms, walking backward, slowly, limping now. Would anyone have mercy? No. A tractor and trailer roared past, spraying her with an odorous sulphur, tiny bits of hard gravel, and a wave of hopelessness.

Then the dogs were on her. Clutching the bathrobe, she stepped back, which was completely insufficient. There were four. They touched her, milled about, snapping playfully at each other. They were so big. Collars. Tails wagging? Yes! Oh, yes!

"All right," Sadie squeaked from a throat gone dry. The leader, a large brown and white dog with short, heavy hair grinned up at her, his tongue lolling. The heavy black one reached up to sniff the bathrobe.

Headlights made her wince, close her eyes momentarily. She tried hard to pay attention to the dogs, any sign of aggressive behavior, so she did not really comprehend the slowly rolling vehicle coming to a stop on the shoulder of the road.

It was only when the door opened, and the form of a heavy man emerged, that she lost her courage, her resolve, everything that brought her this far.

Had the fat man caught up to her? Her legs became traitors, turning to Jell-o at the knees, her arms lost their strength until she could barely hold onto the bathrobe. Then the lumbering giant came closer, the round, ruddy face surrounded by stiff bristles of white hair, his eyes intent, assessing her predicament.

"Git! Git! Git goin' there! Ho! Git!" Waving his arms, taking control. Did God not look exactly like this?

She wasn't aware that she was crying. She talked, laughed, showed him the bathrobe, became hysterical, and wept in earnest. The dogs bounded off across the level fields, the man helped her into his car, handed her Kleenexes, offered her his cup of coffee, listened, then told her he was on his way to work, had to be there by six, but he was taking her to the police barracks and would call in late. The brilliant white lights of the police building made her shield her eyes, feeling like a castaway, a stray cat brought in until the local humane society rescued it.

Sadie related her story, saying she didn't know where she had been, only that she ran for close to an hour. The house had three stories; they had horses; she wasn't sure how long she had been held there. The officers made her feel as if she was the one who had done something wrong with their stern expressions, gun belts slung across their hips, all creased and crisp and professional. But the morning light brought a bit of understanding, like a jigsaw puzzle when you finally found the missing border section. Things began to make more sense after she was shown to a waiting area with comfortable chairs, pillows, and warmth.

Gratefully, she accepted a steaming cup of coffee but waved away the sugary croissant, her stomach rolling now. When she winced from the pain of her ankle, the policeman insisted on having it checked at the city hospital.

While the cruiser moved through the city, the sun brought everything into reality, along with a glorious knowledge that she was safe. She was here in this wonderful vehicle, protected by a man who worked for the good of humanity, in a big city filled with people who walked all sorts of different paths. The wonder of those tall buildings!

The feeling of appreciation swept through her when white-coated professionals poked and prodded at her ankle, pronounced it a torn ligament, no broken bones, wrapped it in some heavenly, soft brace, and then wheeled her out to the police cruiser. Later, she laughed softly with the officer.

To Sadie's surprise, the heavy, white-haired gentleman was waiting at the barracks till they returned, introducing himself as Harry Magill.

When she laid her head on the back of the sofa and closed her eyes, he immediately brought her a pillow and blanket, then stayed with her the remainder of the day until it was time to return home to his wife, receiving Sadie's profound thanks as a sort of benediction.

✿ ✡ ✿

When the call came, no one answered the phone, as usual. The black telephone in the phone shanty shrilled its eight rings. But the wind was blowing the snow around in cold, painful little spurts, and Mam stayed in the house.

Dat and Reuben were at work, putting in a fireplace for a friend of Jim Sevarr's who lived in town.

Anna was down with the flu, having retreated to her room in a huff after Mam told her it was her own fault, the way she stayed out on Sunday night until who knew when.

When the second phone call came, Rebekah had just closed the door of the white minivan that took her to and from her housecleaning job, having finished early because of new carpeting going in. She thought she heard the phone, but in this wind she couldn't be sure. Better check the messages. Too cold for Mam to be out in this.

There were three. Three messages relating the same thing. The same unbelievable news that made Rebekah sit down on the cold plastic chair and cry big sobs of gratefulness, then forget to replace the receiver and close the door of the phone shanty so that it slapped back and forth in the wind, blowing snow into every crevice and chasing the calendar pages up and down all afternoon. She was hysterical by the time she reached the kitchen, frightening her mother so badly, she had to sit on the recliner, seeing spots in front of her eyes.

When the police car pulled up to the door, Mam waved

a hand in Rebekah's direction, who answered the door with tears streaming down her face and dropping on her dress front. Dat and Reuben were brought to the Miller homestead, Mark came with Richard Caldwell, clearly beside himself with joy, Richard's voice booming as if he really was holding a megaphone. The police had offered a phone to Sadie so she could call her family.

Leah, after she learned of the joyous news, told a most amazing story. Her sleep had been restless all night. But a few minutes before four o'clock, she awoke with a great and intense urge to pray for Sadie.

"All the while, I had this sensation of falling. But after I prayed, I fell asleep, deeply, better than I'd slept all night."

No one at this point knew how or when Sadie had escaped, or even if she had escaped, but they all agreed—wasn't Leah's dream something? Wasn't it awesome how God heard and answered prayer?

Next they discussed whether they should let Sadie fly home. Riding in an airplane was *verboten.* Should they confer with the ministry to see if it was allowed in a case of emergency? Dat said just fly her home. Mark said the same thing. And everyone also agreed that Mark should be the one to make a return phone call to Sadie. He was, after all, her husband.

✡ ✡ ✡

She was asleep on the sofa at the police barracks, wrapped in her cocoon of safety, when Mark's phone call came through. Gently, Cindy, the tall, thin receptionist, woke her.

"Sadie Miller? There is a phone call."

Immediately Sadie sat up, throwing back the blanket in one clear sweep, stumbling a bit, but following her eagerly to the cordless phone, taking it with her to a corner of the room where she could squeeze her eyes shut and blow her nose and sob and talk and laugh, and no one would see her.

His voice! She had forgotten that deep, gravelly baritone. She couldn't talk at all, just cry, until Mark thought there was no one there and said, "Sadie? Are you there?"

She had to answer, and all that came out was a hoarse squeak. Finally she croaked a pitiful, "Oh. Oh, Mark!"

Then he began crying, and no one said anything for quite some time, until finally Sadie took a long, shuddering breath and said she was fine and asked how soon were they coming to get her.

"No, I do not want to fly home, Mark. I had enough of being too high up in the air to suit me for the rest of my life."

✿ ✪ ✿

When they hired a driver, he figured his GPS system would get them to Brent, Colorado, in about 12, maybe 13 hours. He could leave after two o'clock. Everyone went along, the 12-passenger van holding them all quite comfortably. No one wanted to stop to eat or sleep, rolling into gas stations, grabbing sandwiches, and back on the road they went.

They encountered a snowstorm after about six or seven hours of travel, slowing them to a mind-numbing crawl across a corner of Wyoming. The driver peered through a whirl of white until he proclaimed the roads unfit for travel.

They were forced to stop and stay at a motel, the rooms reeking of stale air and cigarette smoke, the beds hard as nails, in Reuben's words, and nothing to eat except stale crackers and bitter coffee. The fact that he found the Discovery Channel on TV soon smoothed over the sadness of stale crackers and coffee, and when he discovered Animal Planet on another channel, he was quite beside himself with amazement.

Twenty-four hours later, they rolled into the Brent police barracks with the voice from the GPS as their guide. "What an absolute miracle," Dat proclaimed the small device.

Sadie had been taken to the Hilton Inn a block away. She was pacing the second-floor lobby, dressed in the much-washed blue dress, still without a covering, but showered, her hair combed neatly, running to and from the windows on the second floor.

When she saw the black van, she knew it was George Gilbert's. She went down a short flight of stairs as fast as the brace on her foot would allow, then stood rooted to the carpeting, gripping the back of the sofa, until her knuckles turned white. Mark walked up to the glass door. With a cry, she flung herself into his arms, oblivious of anyone or anything around her. They clung to each other, the amazing, unbelievable joy of being alive, safe, and having come through this together, restoring their emptiness, their hopelessness.

Dat stood back, his hands in his pockets, shy, ill at ease, as everyone held Sadie in their arms, crying, laughing, then crying again. Sadie saw him then. "Dat!"

There was no self-consciousness. It was not customary, but she needed to feel her father's arms around her to make her homecoming complete. She put her arms around him. He clutched her tightly to his denim-clad chest, his gray beard caressing her forehead, his tears anointing her head.

Her parents had aged and had both lost weight. Reuben looked terrible, but he said it was because he had been up all night watching TV and drinking that sick coffee and eating disgusting cheese crackers. He shook his hair into his eyes so no one would see the tears. He was too old and cool to be caught crying over a crazy sister.

They sat in the lobby, listening quietly as Sadie related her story from start to finish. Mark got them all rooms, and the driver, too, so he would get a solid day of sleep before the long drive home. Mam and Dat welcomed a long-awaited rest, along with the joy of having seen their beloved daughter again.

For Mark and Sadie, it was very nearly heaven on earth.

Chapter 6

IT WAS ALL OVER THE NEWS, ON EVERY TELEVISION station and in every newspaper. Richard Caldwell informed them: the horse thieves were caught. The whole ring of them would finally be brought to justice.

They had been extremely intelligent at first, but as the band of thieves grew, so did their lack of security and loopholes of leaking facts. When they abducted Sadie, it was the beginning of the end.

Reporters requested interviews with Sadie, but they were all turned down, as was the way of the Amish. No one could appear on TV, so there were no on-camera interviews, although she spoke to many other people about her experience.

The government agents returned Paris to her golden glory. Sadie laughed to Mark about how they could tell Paris was pouting, standing in her stall batting her eyelashes, a haughty princess who believed a great wrong had been brought on her head.

Sadie bathed her and brushed her. Then Sadie bundled up in numerous layers of warm winter clothing and rode the horse across the snowy fields. The wind froze Sadie's face as tears welled in her eyes. Paris ran, kicked her heels joyfully, lifted her head and whinnied high and clear, the sound borne away on the freezing wind. Sadie leaned into her neck, reveled in the motion beneath her, that quivering mass of muscle and speed, understanding the gift of freedom as never before.

Mark rode with her sometimes on Duke, the new gray gelding he purchased from Sam Troyer. Duke was a magnificent animal, a bit raw around the edges, perhaps, but with careful training, he would improve. Sadie winced, however, when Mark began using the quirt. How she hated that evil-looking little whip! It only served to increase Duke's nervousness, being a bundle of alarm waiting to implode as it was. Mark was short on patience. He was too quick to use that hateful quirt, as Sadie explained to him, gently trying to keep from deflating his always fragile ego.

The thing was, life was so good, and, like a delicate egg, she carried their relationship with care. The specter of his dark moods served to put a hand over her mouth, an ear attuned to his derisive snorts of annoyance. It was one of his quirks, this tumble into darkness where he would stay, entombed in a silence of his own making, brought on by who knew what.

"Mark, that Duke is absolutely fearless. After the snow melts, we're going to race. Reuben could bring Moon."

They were in the forebay of the barn, watering the horses. Sadie pushed the barn broom in a short, quick motion, sweeping loose hay and straw into the open stall door.

"Duke would win."

"Not if you don't quit using that hateful quirt on him."

The words tumbled out even as she realized their harm, but it was too late to save herself. Deliberately, Mark turned Truman, slid the steel pin into place and ground out, the words serving to box Sadie's ears. "You think you know more than I do about horses, Sadie. You don't. Paris is spoiled rotten."

Uh-oh. When he spoke in that tone of voice, the harm was done, so she may as well have her say. Besides, she couldn't avoid it, her anger serving as the propeller that lent wings to her hot words.

"Paris is not spoiled. She listens to anything I want her to do. Without using a *quirt*."

She turned, flounced her skirt, steamed her way through the snowdrifts, thumped up on the porch, her cheeks blazing with the lust of her indignation.

They ate supper in silence, dipping spoons into the home-canned tomato soup, then lifting them to their mouths. They dipped grilled cheese sandwiches cut in half into the steaming tomato-y goodness, but they spoke no words. Sadie swallowed water from her glass noisily. The only sound beside Sadie's clumsy gulping was the ticking of the clock. It wasn't that she didn't try. She did.

"Do you have plenty of horses to shoe this week?"

When there was no response, she tried another tactic, wrapping her arms about his waist. But they were firmly loosened and set aside as he made his way to his recliner. With a heavy heart burdening the slightest task, she slowly washed the soup bowls, each seeming to weigh 10 pounds now.

Everything had been so perfect, their love elevated to new levels after her escape. The homecoming, and now here she was, sunk to the bottom again, her life draining away because of what she had said. It was all her fault. That realization, like light entering a darkened room through a slowly opening door, was more and more apparent. She needed to be careful. No words of correction, no unkindness, no rebuke. She would be perfect soon.

When Mark spent the night on the couch, his dirty work clothes covered with their beige throw with their wedding date, names, and "Love Is Forever" monogrammed on it, his stocking feet sticking out like two questioning gray puppets, a fear arose in her throat. Would it always be like this now?

She slept well enough, but at 5:30 her heart raced, wondering why he wasn't up, the propane lamp lit, going to do chores. Was he dead? People passed away in their sleep. Was he so angry that he would leave or just stay lying on the couch all day? Perhaps, like Mam, he was depressed, and it was all her fault.

Nervously, she cleared her throat, waiting for Mark to come into the bed, lifting the covers the way he always did, taking her into his arms, apologizing, clearing the air. This would never happen again. Never.

But he didn't. He showered and shaved, banged doors, slammed drawers, and said absolutely nothing. Sadie's heart wavered within her. She tried meeting his eyes, but they were flat, black, unseeing. Breakfast was as silent as the evening meal had been.

✤ ✤ ✤

"But Dorothy!" Sadie wailed at work, sitting at the table, her untouched coffee turning cold in its ironstone mug.

"You need to stand up to your man. He's controlling

you with his temper. Huh-uh. You ain't allowin' it. It ain't gonna happen."

"How can I love him so much, and yet last night when he lay on our clean, new couch with his dirty work clothes ignoring me, I...I almost hated him. He makes me so mad I don't know what to do. Just because I told him about that stupid quirt."

Dorothy buttered a warm biscuit, her arms beneath the too-short sleeves of her white T-shirt flapping with each stroke.

"Sounds a lot like marriage to me," she chortled.

"But what causes it? Why can't he take any correction or...Oh, whatever."

Sadie's voice ended in a wail.

"What'd I tell you? He's a tough one. Most men don't like for their women to tell 'em what to do. The normal ones. Your man ain't normal. So keep yer mouth shut."

Sadie winced. "What if I don't like the way he uses that quirt?"

"Shut up about it, or learn to live with his moods, then, if yer not going to stand up to him and tell him to grow up."

"What do you mean, grow up? Reuben is 15 years old, and he never ever acted like Mark."

"Reuben had a normal childhood."

"But how can Mark go through life like this, always blaming his childhood?"

Sadie lifted her hands on each side of her head, bringing down two fingers of each hand, mocking the word *childhood*.

"I mean, it's a crutch. Suppose I would go lay on the couch and pout because he did something I disapproved of? There wouldn't be a whole lot going on at our house."

Dorothy's arms wobbled along with the rest of her as she shook with glee, infused in her own delight of finding out how human Amish people were, obviously. She buttered another biscuit, popped half into her mouth, then flipped the bacon on the hot griddle.

"I ain't no shrink. I don't have all the answers."

She looked at the clock.

"Five more minutes and it's Erma Time."

Dorothy shoveled bacon into the steel pan, and Sadie lifted herself off the chair, placing her mug of coffee into the microwave and punching the minute button.

She was busily flipping pancakes when Erma Keim breezed in, her red hair frozen and her covering smashed beyond help by a brilliant purple head scarf. The freckles on her nose were unforgiving, doing absolutely nothing for her very white skin.

As usual, her mood was ebullient, which was about the only word to describe Erma. Gregarious was another, Sadie thought wryly, watching her with tired, creased eyes.

"Good morning, my ladies! Top of the morning to ya! Did you hear the Chinook, Sadie? Waters going to be running shortly. Snow melting! Whoo-ee!"

Dorothy shook her head, then turned to watch Erma as she fairly danced to the coat hooks and shimmied her way out of her black wool coat.

"Ya musta slept good," she observed dryly.

"Oh, I did! Pillows from Fred Ketty's store. Did you know she has super-good quality foam pillows? She's really getting that little dry goods store up and running."

Suddenly a wave of longing wrapped itself around Sadie, bringing with it a sort of wanting, an unnamed but nonetheless real feeling of wishing. Yes, to be straightforward, she wished she was Erma Keim. No one else to worry about. No relationship as tricky as a cracked egg to juggle continuously.

She shouldn't have married. The thought squashed her whole day. The vacuum cleaner clogged, she broke the leaf off a rabbit statue, her back hurt, her head swam with a million negative thoughts. Black crows of unsettling resolve about her future and her past added to the mountain of unscalable heights growing out of this one incident.

She told Erma Keim her apple pies needed more brown sugar and hurt Dorothy's feelings when she criticized her ability to keep the refrigerator organized.

"You don't need butter in three places, Dorothy. The butter goes in the door. The one to the left."

She swiped furiously with a cloth wrung from a bucket of Mr. Clean and piping hot water. Her hands were red, chapped, and she had a nasty hangnail, that annoying little piece of skin that got so painfully in the way of every task.

"Well, ain't we Miss Hoity-toity, now? That butter to the right is old. Outdated. I'll use it for bakin'. So don't tell me where to put my butter. I know what I'm doin'."

Sadie knew she should have apologized, but she was too upset to do it. Why was one's whole life upside down and strewn about when you fought with your man?

She didn't want to go home. She wanted Mam. She wanted to be in her old room, giggling with Leah and Rebekah and Anna, not a care in the world, except who was cute, who they would like to date, while eating sour cream and onion powder on a big bowl of freshly popped corn.

Why did she ever think Mark was handsome? How disturbing was that? Those huge feet sticking out from

the much too short afghan, unwashed socks, smelling—
no, reeking—of his work as a farrier.

Bouncing home in Jim Sevarr's rusted old pickup
truck, she slunk against the door, her face pale, her mouth
an upside-down "U" of disenchantment. Jim shifted his
toothpick, watched her sideways, turned the steering
wheel with gnarled fingers, then sighed.

"Wal, Missy, ya look under the weather, now, don't
cha?"

"Oh, I don't know."

"Honeymoon over, eh?"

"I guess."

"We is all alike, honey. Black, white, suntanned, or
Amish, Chinese, or Tippecanoe. Two people git hitched,
problems follow 99 percent o' the time. Ya gotta work
through 'em. See what works. See what don't. Learn by
it. Appreciate what you got. My Dorothy's a salty one,
now ain't she? Tells me off, but no more harm than a fly."

Slowly Sadie turned her head, watching the lined features, the creases opening and closing like an accordion
as the words slowly came from his mouth, the toothpick
disappearing as he shifted it to the other side. That was
quite a speech for Jim. The equivalent of an hour, actually.

"Well, Mark is more harmful than a fly," she burst
out.

"I doubt it."

"He is!"

"What happened?"

In brief detail Sadie told him, finishing with Mark's
black silences.

"It's a tough one. I used to do that. Hang in there. It'll
get better as time goes on."

The truck ground to a halt, and Sadie hopped down.

"See you in the morning," she called.

Jim touched his hat brim, ground the gears of the truck, and was off down the drive. Wolf bounded up, his nose snuffling the creases of her coat. She ruffled his ears, stroked the broad face, and walked slowly up the melting, snowy path to the door of the washhouse. Mark wasn't home yet.

Laundry hung on the great, wooden rack, waiting to be folded. In winter, clothes were dried on lines in the basement, if there was a woodstove, or on racks in the washhouse or kitchen.

There were many different kinds of clothes-drying racks. Some were round and made of PVC pipe, with wooden clothespins attached to the ring by a small chain to hang small articles like socks, washcloths, or under-wear. Wooden racks mounted to the wall had arms you could spread out. These held all the laundry you could fit on them. Clothes dried quickly by the wall behind a good stove. The large adjustable wooden folding racks that sat on the floor were used for hanging larger items like T-shirts and denim trousers. Dresses on hangers were all drip-dried in the washhouse beside the gleaming new wringer washer.

Whenever possible, Sadie hung clothes outside in spite of the cold, even though she'd bring in half-dry, half-frozen laundry. It still retained that outdoor scent. The clean, sun-washed fragrance never ceased to make her heart glad.

Today, however, the laundry didn't stir any gladness at all. It just hung there, stiff, still damp in the armpits and hems, smelling vaguely of old Snuggle and residue of Tide and bleach. She noticed the gray stains on the heels of

Mark's socks, which increased her feeling of inadequacy.

The kitchen was dark. What was that smell? Going to the waste can, she flipped back the lid, bent, and sniffed. Eww! She remembered then, the plastic wrap of the tray of chicken legs and thighs, the yellow Styrofoam tray containing the heavy padding of chicken juices and blood. When did they have fried chicken? Saturday evening. Her stomach churning, she grabbed the top of the waste can, fairly hurled it onto the countertop, hauled the garbage bag out, and swung it through the door and out to the garbage can, replacing the lid with a bang.

Now what to make for supper? If Dorothy wouldn't have been quite so testy, she would have asked her for a small portion of the chicken and dumplings she made in the gigantic cauldron, as Sadie called it, for the ranch hands' evening meal. After Sadie had complained about the unorganized refrigerator, Dorothy sizzled with displeasure. Her mouth a thin line, her eyes snapping, she did not stop to have her afternoon tea and leftovers, but moved grimly, methodically, until Sadie felt like screaming at the top of her voice, especially when Erma Keim began singing, "When the Roll is Called up Yonder" in a reedy, high voice that sounded like tree frogs in the early spring.

Opening the refrigerator, Sadie found a square Tupperware container of leftover spaghetti and meatballs. She'd warm that in a saucepan with a bit of water, open a can of green beans, and use Mam's leftover homemade bread for garlic toast, all possible in 10 or 15 minutes.

She set the table, pleased with her supper, her thriftiness, the cheese and garlic wafting from the oven making her hungry at last. When Mark did come home, her heart skipped, then plodded on, giving her a headache in her right temple. Eagerly she searched his face, ready to welcome him home, put the ugliness behind them.

He put his lunch bucket on the counter, followed by his Coleman water jug, then disappeared through the laundry-room door. She heard him wash up, wanted to follow him, plead with him, but stayed where she was. Quickly, she dished up the steaming spaghetti, added a pat of butter to the green beans, and arranged the garlic toast on a pretty platter. Mark came in and sat at the table, averting his eyes. Nervously, Sadie poured the water from the blue pitcher in the refrigerator, spilling some beside Mark's glass. With a gesture of annoyance he got up, yanked a paper towel from the roll, and wiped at the spill before throwing the towel in the trash can.

They bowed their heads in silence. Mark cleared his throat. He surveyed the food, then said gruffly, "What is this?"

"What?"

"This?" He pointed to the garlic toast that minutes before had been so inviting.

"It's garlic toast. With cheese."

"It smells like feet."

"It's the Parmesan."

"You know I don't like string beans."

Sadie literally counted to 10. In her mind, she said the numbers, a first-grader in the class called "Marriage." What had Jim said? See what works. See what don't. She knew what "don't." Criticism of any kind. Ever. Was it because of the quirt? This senseless criticism of her cooking? Is this the way it works?

She watched as he helped himself to a large portion of the spaghetti and meatballs, ignoring the string beans and garlic toast. Going to the refrigerator, he bent to find the applesauce, then dumped half the container onto his plate, spooning it up as fast as he could. Like a hog.

Sadie couldn't help her thoughts. She had a notion to say it, but instantly knew she wouldn't. Well, okay. If this was how he was going to be, she'd learn from it. See what works. See what don't. Learn from it.

She spent another night alone in bed, but she did not cry. She read part of a book called *Love and Respect* she had received as a wedding gift, her feelings numb, the words jangling through her nerves that only felt dead.

In the morning, when she sprayed the couch with Febreeze and threw the beige-colored afghan into the rinse tubs to be washed, she cried great big tears of disappointment and hurt.

✧ ✡ ✧

When she arrived at the ranch, there was an ambulance parked at the barn. She forgot all her personal struggles. A hand went to her mouth as she lifted questioning eyes to Jim Sevarr's concerned face. He hopped down quickly, disappeared behind the entry door, and reappeared after a heart-stopping few minutes.

"It's Lothario Bean. The Mexican. Got kicked by the new mustang. Better git off to the house."

Sadie did as she was told, finding Dorothy and Erma by the window, their eyes wide with concern.

"It's Lothario Bean. He was kicked."

Erma's hand went to her mouth, her eyes opened wide, popped out the way they did when she was concerned or surprised. There was an air of solemnity about the three of them all morning after the ambulance careened out the drive, lights flashing, sirens screaming, sending chills of dread up Sadie's spine. When Jim Sevarr came slowly into the kitchen, his eyes soft, Sadie knew before Jim said a word that Lothario Bean had died.

"Smashed his skull. Bled internally. Didn't last long."

Erma cried quietly. Dorothy shook her head, brought a box of tissues to her, said it was a pity. That dear man was the salt of the earth, and what would that poor widow do? And those beautiful daughters? Sadie cried for the little Mexican. She was glad he was a Christian. She imagined his great enjoyment in this wonderful place called heaven. He had been such a loving man.

✡ ✡ ✡

When Mark came home from work, he found Sadie curled on the recliner, still numb, her eyes red from crying. There was no supper on the table, the house was dark and cold, the laundry still hung on the rack stiff and dry. Sadie was beyond caring. If he wanted to go ahead and muddle around in his black fog of silence and self-pity, he could. She was not going to apologize if she didn't do anything wrong. So she turned her face away and did not say one word. If he wanted to know something, he could ask.

She heard him go outside. Wearily, stiff with cold, she got up, made her way to the bathroom, then soaked in a long, hot bath, shampooing her hair over and over. Wrapped in a heavy robe, she took two Tylenol for her pounding headache and laid back on the recliner.

It was 8:00 before Mark came in. He stood awkwardly by the table, his arms at his side, watching her. He turned to go to the refrigerator, then changed his mind, going to the pantry, and emerging with a box of cereal.

His shoulders were as wide as ever, bent over the dish, as he hungrily shoveled the food into his mouth. His dark hair was disheveled, in need of a good wash.

She would have to tell him about Lothario Bean. If she waited for him to speak first, they'd grow old like this. It was ridiculous. She would have to be the one to make amends, innocent or not. She knew better now. See what works. See what don't. Learn by it.

Slowly, she let down the footrest of the recliner. Mark turned, a question in his eyes.

"Lothario Bean was kicked by a horse at the ranch. He's dead."

"No!" Mark's voice was incredulous, filled with raw disbelief. Then, "Aw, the poor man."

He came over, scooped her out of the chair as if she was a child, then held her on his lap as he kissed her, gently, tenderly, murmuring words of endearment. Sadie told him she was sorry about the quirt, and he said it was okay, he was acting childish as well. All of Sadie's happiness came back multiplied by 10.

Chapter 7

They all attended Lothario Bean's Catholic funeral service, Richard Caldwell and his wife, Barbara, seated with the many Latino relatives. Mark and Sadie were amazed at the similarities to the Amish, the close sense of community, the caring love shown for each other by these dark-skinned people from Mexico. Lothario Bean's daughters surrounded their mother, who was dressed in traditional black, a veil over her face. Bravely his wife received condolences from the many people he had encountered in his life.

Afterward at the ranch, they had a memorial service of sorts, seated informally in the dining room, eating pulled pork sandwiches and scalding hot bean soup, coffee, and Erma's banana cream pies, filled with sliced bananas and piled high with genuine whipped cream. They reminisced about past events, Lothario Bean's eagerness to please, the humility he possessed, his outstanding love and support for his wife and daughters. A new sense of closeness enveloped them. This mixture of cultures, all human beings now, wrapped in a sense of loss felt so strongly that it was touchable, a thing to be cherished.

Sadie never wanted to quit her job at the ranch, knowing she had an extended family in all of them. Mark told her she could work as long as she wanted. They didn't need the money now, but if that's what she wanted to do, she should.

Richard Caldwell hired an Amish man to replace Lothario Bean. He had just moved into the area from Indiana. Richard Caldwell asked Sadie if she knew him at all. She didn't.

"He says he's worked with horses since he's three years old, which I think is a bit unlikely, but you never know. Check him out for me tomorrow morning, okay?"

So when breakfast was served, she lingered, wrapping silverware, filling the ice bin, observing from the background as the ranch hands filed in. She heard him before she actually saw him. He had a deep, hearty laugh, which seemed to never stop. It rolled out of him after every sentence, each of which was punctuated by what could only be described as enthusiastic listening. He had to be a great personality.

His hair was longish in the back, which was good, helping to balance the long neck, the beaked nose, and the dark rimmed glasses he pushed up or down on his nose, depending who or what he wanted to examine. Clearly this man was a great lover of life. No beard. Single.

The cogs in Cupid's wheel were matching perfectly. Sadie wrapped her arms around her waist and held very still, listening, observing, and then fairly skipped through the swinging oak doors to the kitchen.

"Where's Erma?"

"Upstairs," Dorothy said, from her sink full of dishes.

Grabbing her apron strings, Sadie pulled her in the direction of the dining room.

"You have to see this. The perfect man for Erma Keim!" Pushing her through the doors, Sadie stepped back, giggling, waiting for Dorothy's return.

"I ain't never endorsing no man for that giraffe. I told you!" Dorothy exploded the minute she was back in the kitchen.

"Dorothy!" Sadie wailed, her disappointment keen.

"I mean it. He's much too nice lookin' for her. She'd completely make his life miserable. The poor man. I ain't sayin' a word, and you better not, either. I'm serious."

When Erma came back to the kitchen for a Diet Pepsi, she popped the top, took a long swig, and spilled a rivulet of the freezing soda down the front of her dress. She snorted with impatience before lifting the can to repeat the process again, running to the sink for a clean, wet cloth to dab at her dress front, her hair and covering a hopeless mess. Sadie decided to obey Dorothy. Perhaps it was for the best.

Goodness, that Erma Keim was a sight. They had helped her with her covering and showed her how to use hairspray at the time of Sadie's wedding, which evidently was all lost. Dorothy shook her head, wiping her hands on a clean dish towel.

"See, she can't even drink a soda properly. Now I ain't Amish, but there's a big difference in your hair and that white thing on your head. Hers looks as if she was in a hurricane."

Sadie laughed, agreeing, and decided to drop the subject.

✿ ✤ ✿

Spring breezes did their best to lift everyone's winter blahs. New green weeds poked their way through brown, dead growth, but the patches of snow and the cold rains were persistent into April.

Mark and Sadie were on their way to church, the cold spring rain splattering the windows of the buggy, leaking through the small rectangles cut into the window frame to allow the reins to pass through. The top of the glove compartment got wet. Mark wiped it off with a clean rag whenever he thought about it. Truman's hooves splashed through the puddled water, the wheels slicing through it, but everything was dry and cozy inside the buggy, with a light, plaid blanket across their legs just to keep the chill off.

Sadie pinned a black wool shawl securely around her shoulders, and she wore a black bonnet on her head. The shawl was usually only worn to church. At council meeting they were encouraged to wear the garment wherever they went, but very few of the young women did. It was cumbersome, knocking things off shelves, and not very suitable for shopping. But it was warm and perfectly suited to a chilly Sunday morning buggy ride.

Mark looked so handsome, his new beard in perfect symmetry, his jaw line in sharp relief against the whiteness of his shirt collar. He was in a quiet mood, which was normal and comfortable when not accompanied by the blackness and anger that devastated Sadie.

They had forgiven, forgotten. Life was smooth and so good.

"A penny for your thoughts."

Mark smiled. "You don't want to know."

"Mm-hm. Yes, I do."

"I'm thinking of my mother's dying wish. She wants me to find my siblings. Do I want to honor that? Or wouldn't you do it?"

"You won't have any closure, rest, whatever you want to call it, if you don't."

"I know. But... I'm scared."

"You have reason to be."

✿ ✡ ✿

The best part of attending church services was seeing her family. Her excitement at seeing all of them lent wings to her feet. She walked swiftly to the washhouse door.

All the joy of her morning evaporated when she saw Anna, a wan reed, her complexion blue-white, her eyes enormous in a face almost skeletal, sagging weakly against the wall, her feet propped against the cement floor as if to keep her standing erect.

Summoning all her strength, Sadie desperately tried to appear normal. Anna's smile was mocking, a pulling away of her mouth setting her teeth free. Her eyes were hard, boring into Sadie's, a challenge.

"How are you, Anna?"

"Good."

A thousand questions screamed in her mind. Where was Mam? Dat? Her sisters? Why was no one trying to help? Surely this was evident to the entire community. It was so different and yet so similar to Mam's illness. These things could be hereditary.

When Neal Hershberger walked in, his hair cut in the English style, chewing and popping his gum, his eyes brazenly searching the girl's bench, a hot anger welled up in Sadie's throat, a bile threatening to choke her.

Oh, my. Dear God, I have forgotten to pray. Wrapped in my own problems, I am not being watchful. Am I my sister's keeper? Please answer me. She bent her head to hide her tears from the men and boys facing them.

When she saw Neil Hershberger openly flirting with Suzanne Stutzman, saw Anna cringe backward in desperation, Dat sitting sound asleep in the front row as the young preacher droned on, she felt as if she had to do something.

Dat and Mam were so dear. Sadie's love for her parents had only increased with her absence, but they were by all means sticking their heads in the proverbial sand, either unwilling to face the disaster that was Anna, or just tired and optimistic, hoping it would all get better soon. She had to do something. Anything. She bet Anna weighed a hundred pounds, if that.

Asking Mark's permission after services, she invited her parents, sisters, and Reuben for Sunday supper, especially including Anna.

"I can't. I'm going away," she countered.

"Where?"

"The supper crowd."

"Can't you skip? This once?"

"No."

Anna wouldn't budge. Sadie gave in, glad to have her parents and Reuben even though her sisters were with the other young people. Mark was jovial, talkative, keeping Dat entertained, while Sadie prepared meat loaf, scalloped potatoes, and a salad of lettuce, bacon, sliced hard-boiled eggs, thinly sliced onion, and shredded carrots, with a homemade mayonnaise dressing.

After the meal as they sat around the table, full and content, Sadie braved the subject of Anna, a forbidden one, she knew. Her desperation, her only strength, grabbed at straws of reassurance.

"Dat?"

"Hmm?"

She had his attention; his eyes were kindly upon her.

"Does Anna even weigh a hundred pounds anymore?" she asked, her eyes giving away her fear.

Mam looked startled.

"Oh, of course. She isn't that thin."

"Do you realize she is sick, Mam? She needs help. Someone should at least talk to her about her... Mam, now come on, you can't tell me otherwise. She is definitely going through an eating disorder."

Dat burst out, quite uncharacteristically.

"That eating disorder you're talking about is named Neil Hershberger!"

Reuben was eating his second slice of chocolate layer cake, soaked with milk and shoveled with a small tablespoon into his mouth, which was opened wide to accommodate the entire mountain of cake. He chewed, swallowed, and shook his head up and down.

"That's for sure."

"Anna is completely obsessed with him," Dat continued. "I hardly know how to handle it. I'm afraid if we get too strict, she'll do something... completely crazy."

Mark nodded.

Sadie shook her head. "She's way, way too thin. Do you think she'd come live with us for awhile? I think I could at least get her to talk to me. She's pathetic."

"I'll come live with you," Reuben shouted, waving his empty spoon before digging into the soaked cake for another round.

"Nothing wrong with you!" Mark said, laughing.

"Nothing cake can't fix," Reuben grinned.

✿ ✡ ✿

After much coaxing, begging, pleading, and numerous phone calls, plus the promise of going to the mall in Chesterfield, Anna relented a few weeks later and agreed to stay with Sadie for awhile. Sadie welcomed her with open arms, fighting tears as she gathered the skeletal frame against her body. Leah and Rebekah accompanied her, turning the day into a sisters' day, helping Sadie houseclean the kitchen cupboards. Leah was dating Kevin, with plans of becoming his wife in the future, and Rebekah had just begun dating Jonathan Mast, a shy personable young man of 22.

As Sadie knew she would, Anna stayed in the background, listening, very rarely taking part in the conversation. She ate almost nothing all day, maybe a half of an apple, a few bites of cracker, a few sips of water. When Leah and Rebekah hitched up Charlie, waving their way out the driveway, Anna turned to Sadie.

"So start right away. Start lecturing me. That's all you want me here for, anyway. You want me to tell you something, Sadie? I'm just here because Neil can pick me up in his car. Mam and Dat won't let me go away with him. I sneak out. So get used to it, sister dear. I'm going away with Neil."

If Sadie would have acted on impulse, she would have smacked her sister's sneering face. Sadie's anger boiled, but not to the point she couldn't control it. So to bide her time, she kicked at a pile of dirt, absentmindedly extracting small rocks.

"What makes you think I'm going to lecture you, other than your guilt?" she ground out evenly.

"I'm not guilty," Anna said, pushing one hip out impatiently.

"Okay."

Sadie pretended to lose interest, changed the subject, and walked back to the house. Chattering about mundane subjects now, she put clean sheets on the guest bed upstairs, helping Anna hang her brilliant array of dresses in the closet. They did chores together and fed Wolf, who Anna seemed to bond with immediately, throwing a small stick for him to retrieve over and over, a thin color showing in her wan cheek from the exertion.

"He is so cool!" she cried, her eyes alight.

Quite clearly Anna adored Mark, his dog, his horses, his barn, everything. That was a good thing, Sadie decided, keeping her happy to be here. She even got Anna to try on the trousers she always wore to ride Paris. When Anna couldn't walk in them without losing them to a puddle around her ankles, Sadie looked genuinely surprised.

"But..."

She looked up, floundering now.

"You're not fat," she said, completely bewildered.

"No, I'm not."

Sadie decided to leave it at that.

Anna had her dress tucked under her chin, bent over, unable to grasp the fact that she would not be able to keep the trousers from sliding down over her hips.

"But I'm not...I'm not this skinny."

"Yes, you are, Anna."

"Well, good! Neil loves skinny girls. He doesn't like fat."

"Who is Neil?"

"Neil Hershberger."

"Oh. Him." Then, "Are you dating?"

"No, not really. Well, we go out."

"You go out. Where do you go?"

"I'd rather not say."

Sadie walked out the door, down to the barn, with Anna following in silence. It was one of those spring evenings in Montana that was achingly beautiful, every slope and plane of the land in contrast with the majestic sky, the colors so vivid, it made you want to fling your arms out and take off running, the way six-year-olds did quite regularly. Anna helped Sadie saddle up, brushing Paris's long mane and tail, her thin, white face pensive.

"Do you have any idea how much I wanted to be you already?" she asked suddenly, angrily.

Sadie stopped, eyeing her sister closely before returning her answer.

"Why does it make you angry to want to be me?"

"It doesn't. I'm not angry. Just forget I said that."

Sadie bit off the words of rebuke, knowing there was no sense pushing her point of view. Shrugging her shoulders, she turned to throw the saddle blanket across Paris's back, followed by the well-polished saddle. There was just something about throwing a saddle on a horse's back that made the horse lower herself ever so slightly, without actually seeming to do it. A certain readiness, a locking of her knees, perhaps. As if she knew the weight of it would settle solidly on her back and was prepared.

Nothing was said as Sadie tightened the girth, then tightened it again after Paris let out the air she had used to stretch her stomach, the way she always did. As she slipped the bit into her mouth, with that satisfying chunk that meant it had slipped between Paris's teeth, adjusted the leather strap over her ears, buckled the chin strap and threw the reins across her neck, Sadie ground her teeth to keep from spewing unwelcome words at her sister.

She was as delicate as a spiderweb and as strong as one. If you took a hose with the nozzle turned to jet and squirted a fragile-looking spiderweb, you still could not loosen it from the object to which it was attached. You just couldn't.

How to help her? That was the thing. Force was certainly not going to do it. Or was there a time coming when force would be the only way?

Love would be the answer. Build up her character, bolster her self-esteem, slowly allowing her to see herself as she really was. Who knew?

"Okay, Anna! Up you go!" The words were spoken brightly, with too much enthusiasm, her thoughts cloudy with distraction.

"I'm not riding." With that, Anna stalked off, her shoulders squared.

"And just why not, after all the trouble I went to, saddling her up?" Sadie yelled after her.

"I can't ride," Anna called back, breaking into a run.

Her mouth pressed into a straight line boding no good, Sadie threw the reins over the hitching rail, jerked them into a knot, and raced after her sister, her feet sliding in the watery slush in the driveway. She soon caught up, jerking Anna backwards by her shoulders, bringing her to a stop. She was appalled to see how fast Anna was breathing after that short sprint.

"Oh, no, you don't, Anna. You're not going to manipulate me with your moods. You are going riding."

"I don't want to. You can't make me."

"Yes, you are. You wanted to go riding, now we're going."

"No!"

"Yes!"

"Why?"

"Because."

Anna sighed, dropped her shoulders, relented, handed over her resistance.

"Good. C'mon."

She saddled Duke, swallowing her misgivings about him. He lifted his head obnoxiously, making Sadie stand on her tiptoes to attempt an entry with the shining steel bit. Instead of losing her temper, she went to the cupboard where the harness was kept, extracting a box of sugar cubes and a carrot, offering them on an open palm, stroking his neck, crooning to him, rubbing his face. Anna watched, her arms crossed tightly around her middle.

"Boy. I'd never go through that to get him to put the bit in his mouth," she observed dryly.

"Only thing that works."

After letting Duke savor the carrot, allowing him to nuzzle her hand, Sadie made another attempt at inserting the bit. After a moment's hesitation, he willingly took it.

With Anna on Paris and Duke beneath her, hopping, sidestepping, doing anything he could to make it hard for Sadie, she had to concentrate on keeping her seat, trying to control him as best she could. He lifted himself off the ground, his front feet flailing the air, then came down crow-hopping, bouncing sideways as Sadie tried desperately to perceive her next move. He was a handful.

"He's gonna buck you right off of there," Anna shouted.

"I hope not!" Sadie yelled back.

After he settled down, they rode together, Paris walking sedately as if to remind Duke what a loser he was and to show him how it really was done. The pasture was green and brown, with the only patches of snow on the north side of dips and hollows or beneath low spreading pine trees. The ground was wet, the earth still absorbing the piles of winter snows, so they rode slowly, carefully. The smell of the earth and sky, the woods, the wet rotting leaves, the calls of the jays, the mockingbirds' warbles of mimicry all lifted Sadie's mood. Anything was possible on an evening like this.

Sadie looked over at Anna. Her face was set in stone, her mouth grim, her eyes darting from Paris's ears to the ground below, alternating between pulling back on the reins and holding the saddle horn. She was afraid! So very afraid! Oh, my goodness! Is that why she never rode? She was terrified.

The trail across the pasture took a steep downturn, wound around a grove of trees, the shadows looming long and black. Anna's eyes opened wide as she grabbed the saddle horn, bracing herself for the descent, her face whiter.

"I'm not going down there," she said softly.

"Come on, Anna. Paris is used to it."

Sadie led the way, Duke prancing and sidestepping, unwilling to be completely controlled.

Paris followed daintily, Anna's expression inscrutable. When the trail evened out, Anna breathed a notable sigh of relief. Sadie grinned at her.

"That wasn't so bad, was it? You're doing great. Straighten your back now. Relax. You're doing great."

"I am?"

"Of course."

They rode on, the horses' hooves making a dull, sucking sound in the mud. Then, suddenly, Anna spoke.

"Sadie?"

"Hmm?"

"Does...does it mean a...a...boy, a guy, loves you if he wants to take you out in his car?"

"His car? A vehicle?"

"Yes."

"You're surely not seeing an English boy? Guy?" Sadie mimicked, smiling genuinely.

"No. But...Neil...you know. Neil Hershberger bought a car. He doesn't want to be Amish. He...sort of hates his dad. He says I don't love him if I don't ride with him in his car."

Oh, boy. Problem number 162, Sadie thought wryly. How to answer?

"You really like Neil, don't you?"

Anna nodded, her expression containing so much pain, it was like a contortion of her features, a clouding over.

"Why?"

She shrugged. "He's cute."

"He definitely is that," Sadie agreed.

Chapter 8

"He's wild, but ... I think he'll change. Once we start dating, he'll ... change. He just says ... I think if I agree to go places with him in his car, he'll ask me for a date, because that will show him that I love him, right?"

Oh, boy. Literally walking on eggshells now. How to correct her without tearing down the frail stepping-stone they had placed so inefficiently a few minutes before?

"Well...," Sadie breathed. She was at a loss for the correct words now.

"I think he loves me," Anna blurted out, her voice abrasive in its desperation.

Paris whooshed air through her nostrils, lowering her head. Duke responded with a snort of his own. They came to a knoll, a sort of elevation, between two lines of trees. The rolling Montana landscape unfolded before them, dressed in the dull greens and browns of the time between winter and spring. Sadie knew a few weeks of sunshine would make all the difference, coloring the earth in those wonderful shades of green, like an artist who decides his palette is depressing sets about correcting the dullness with broad, bold, tumultuous strokes.

"Look, Anna!" Sadie said, pointing.

"What?"

"How beautiful it is!"

"Oh, yeah. But, Sadie, if I refuse to go with him, he'll tell me off. Our friendship would be over before it even got started."

Her words ended on a wail of wretchedness, a sound so deep and primal, Sadie knew she had to respond the only way she knew, telling her the hard truth, letting her deal with it.

"It's the best thing that could happen."

The words were blunt, clear, flung into the cold, Montana air. Anna's head came up, her eyebrows lowered, her face twisted into a mask of anger.

"You sound just like Mam. See? You're all against me! Every last one of you. Even that goody two-shoes Reuben! I hate you!"

With that, she jerked on Paris's rein, surprising the horse. Sadie saw the confusion in her eyes, her bearing before Anna dug in her heels, leaning forward, goading Paris with the power of her terrible rebellion. Paris ran then. At a speed much too fast for an inexperienced rider.

Wheeling Duke, Sadie screamed, "Stop! Paris, whoa! Stop! Anna!"

Paris was confused, frightened as she had been that day hitched to the spring wagon with Daniel beside her. The only instinct she knew was to get home as fast as she could. But with Anna sliding and flopping around on the saddle, they'd never make it.

Leaning forward, Sadie urged Duke, who was just waiting for the order to run. His feet gathered beneath him, his haunches lowered, as power surged through his magnificent legs. His neck stretched out, his head moved up and down, for a moment Sadie thrilled to his power and speed in spite of the dread that wrapped itself around her senses, a claustrophobic tentacle squeezing the breath from her body.

Oh, dear God! Keep Anna on her horse! she begged. That turn around the alders! At this rate, they'd never make it.

"Whoa, Paris!" Sadie screamed again, screamed over and over till her voice was hoarse and inconsistent.

Still they pushed on. Then it was over so fast. It only takes a second for a very thin person like Anna to be flung from a fast-moving horse's back. She looked like a limp rag doll with barely any stuffing inside the fabric of her arms and legs. She flew through the air and hit the muddy ground, folding in on herself, the arms, legs, the black of her coat, the brilliance of the dress. A sickening, mud-filled clunk. A little pile of muddy clothes.

Was Sadie screaming? Or was it Anna? She had to haul back on the reins with every ounce of strength. Duke wanted to follow Paris, who had already disappeared around the corner of the alders, heading home, with or without her rider.

Sadie didn't remember dismounting. She just knew her knees were shaking so badly she had to concentrate on every step to reach her sister, whose face was turned away. She was lying on her side, her legs flung out, her arms drawn in. How badly was she injured?

A low moan was the first thing she heard. She was alive. That was all that mattered. Praise God! Another moan.

"Anna!"

There was no coherent answer, only another moan. Never move an injured person. Sadie called Anna's name over and over, moaning sounds the only response. Wildly,

Sadie looked about her, then hurled herself into the saddle, urging Duke without meaning it, an unnecessary thing done out of habit.

When they slid into the barnyard, Mark came racing down the path from the house, waving his arms.

"Sadie! What is wrong with you? Riding like that? Duke? Why Duke?" he yelled, his agitation an engine of words tumbling over each other.

"It's Anna! Is Paris here? Did you see her run home?"

As she spoke, she dismounted, running through the forebay opening, then slumped visibly, relieved to see Paris outlined against the water partitions.

"Oh, Mark! She's here!"

"What happened?"

Mark shook his head in disbelief as she quickly related her story. Then he ordered her back on Duke, quickly leaping up behind her. As long as she lived, she would never cease to be amazed at Mark's ability to leap onto the back of a horse, cat-like, springing up as if it required no effort on his part. She remembered the first time she had seen him springing, no, bouncing off the truck that day on the snowy road.

Duke took off, Mark's weight holding him back, his gait a fraction slower. They found Anna, still moaning, her breath coming in painful jerks. Mark bent over her, calling her name.

"Anna! Anna!"

She began crying then. Whispering how much it hurt. She couldn't breathe. It hurt. Was she going to die? In the end, Sadie stayed with her while Mark rode to the phone. Anna was so cold. Why did it hurt so badly?

"I think you have a few broken ribs, Anna. Or worse."

"It hu...urts." She could only gasp in broken whispers.

Birds twittered their good-evening calls. The cold settled like a harsh blanket as the sun slid behind the mountain, a warm kindness that bade them farewell. Why did
it take them so long? Then she heard it. The wail of an
ambulance. Shivers chased themselves up her back as
quick tears sprang to her eyes. Help was on the way.

With Mark's direction, the ambulance drove as far as
they were able to across the muddy pasture, driving slowly, a red and yellow beacon of hope as Anna continued
gasping for breath, crying out in pain. Two men carried
a stretcher. Her shrieks of agony began when they poked
and prodded, then carefully slid the stretcher beneath her
battered body.

Sadie let the telephone ring and ring and ring, repeatedly pressing the redial button. Reality suddenly hit. How
much would her poor Mam and Dat be able to take?
Now Anna. And Sadie just home from her own ordeal.
God chasteneth whom he loveth. Yes, this was true. But,
like children, there was no chastening if they behaved
themselves. Must be God saw plenty wrong with them,
or he wouldn't try to fix them the way he did.

Please answer! If they didn't, she'd have to send a
driver to tell them to come to the hospital. Then, sure
enough, Reuben.

"Hello?"

"Reuben? Oh, I'm so glad you answered."

"I just got home from work."

That gruff voice! Reuben was growing into a young
adult right before everyone's unseeing eyes.

"Listen. Anna was thrown from Paris. She was taken to
the hospital. Get yourselves over there as fast as you can."

"Is she...is she, okay?"

"Well, yes. As okay as she can be. See you, Reuben."

✿ ✡ ✿

Anna had three broken ribs, her right lung was punctured, she was battered and bruised, but there were no life-threatening injuries other than her emaciated state. That awful thinness from years of depriving herself of good, wholesome food.

Dat and Mam, of course, were visibly distressed, but so glad to find their daughter alive and responding to the doctor's care. It was an attribute to their Amish upbringing, this receiving of bad news with grace and dignity borne with calm acceptance. Stoic was the best description, Anna thought, as she watched Mam clasp Anna's forearm, her eyes wet with unshed tears, her face a harbor of love, a safe, sound place for her battered Anna.

"*Siss kenn fa-shtandt.*" Mam's usual exclamation.

They asked many questions. Nodded their heads. Leah and Rebekah came in, their eyes wide with questions. Reuben had his say, then, his love for Anna fueling the jet stream of his words.

"Sadie, I think it's time you took a lesson from this. You are always in some sort of trouble with this crazy horse business with Paris. It's okay, but one of these days, someone's going to get killed. You had to have your own special horse, and look at all the troubles she brought us. It's about time you retire from.... Well, just slow down and take it easy for once."

After that, he became self-conscious, kicking the toe of his sneaker against the footboard of Anna's bed until Dat made him stop.

Mam nodded. "My mother's favorite saying was, 'What most we long and sigh for, might only bring us sorrow.'"

"But, Mam!" Sadie burst out.

Mark put his arm protectively around her shoulders, his presence letting her know he was on her side, as she told her mother Paris had brought so much more than sorrow. Mam remained adamant, Dat backing her. Reuben glared at Mam. Leah and Rebekah's faces were inscrutable.

"But...but..." she floundered.

"You need to be more careful, Sadie. Horses can be a source of danger, as you should be aware of by now, surely," Dat said firmly. "It's a wonder you're not dead."

Reuben's words were blunt, but sort of like one of those squishy things you throw against a wall and they slowly slide off, although they leave a sticky residue. Sadie considered them, but only a small part. Paris was a part of her life, like Mark, her beloved house beneath the trees, the ranch, Dorothy. She couldn't imagine life without any of them.

✾ ✡ ✾

Anna moved home and was kept like a queen in a hospital bed as she healed. The doctors diagnosed her anorexia and prescribed medication. The family set up an appointment for counseling.

Sadie visited often. Mam firmly took matters into her own hands, deciding Sadie was part of Anna's problem, and asserted herself. Late one Saturday morning she made a pot of coffee, then opened the oven door to reveal a large pan of homemade sweet rolls, the spirals of brown sugar and cinnamon tantalizingly curled among the puffs of sweet dough baked to a golden brown. She poured a soft caramel frosting over the warm rolls before serving them on pretty plates, accompanied by a breakfast pizza, which consisted of potatoes, eggs, cheese, and sausage.

Sadie sighed happily. "Dear Mam. I can't imagine being happier than I am at this moment. Your food!"

That voice of appreciation made it harder for Mam, but she remained strong, a matriarch of wisdom, knowing her oldest daughter needed to be lovingly rearranged, put in place. The conversation drifted to a quiet lull, allowing Mam to open the subject of Anna's disease, the dreaded anorexia.

"You know, Sadie, you are the oldest daughter, and you do have a way with Anna. I'm grateful for everything you've done so far. She needs building up now. I think…"

Here Mam hesitated, searched Rebekah's face, then Leah's, as if seeking approval.

"You can't help being you, Sadie. You are beautiful, you have a gift of riding, a way with horses, and now you have Mark, your kind and handsome husband. But to view yourself through Anna's eyes…"

Here Mam stopped again, then reached out to put a hand on Sadie's arm.

"Believe me when I say you are blessed, and being you is not what makes Anna what she is. But I don't think you realize the depth of Anna's self-loathing. She has always looked to you as a sort of idol. An *opp-Gott* almost. To attain your height was the despair of her life. And Sadie, this is not your fault. But… we need to understand how frail she is. She's like the Bible verse where the house is built on sand, not the rock of Jesus."

Sadie gasped.

"You mean… you actually mean Anna doesn't have Jesus in her heart?"

"Does she?"

Mam searched Sadie's eyes, and Sadie's lowered first.

"She needs the Lord. But we can't do that for her. She needs to let him into her heart, so we'll just be here for her. And Sadie…just back off a little. Don't lecture, or…how can I say this in the right way?"

At first Sadie reeled from Mam's judgment of her. Slowly, though, as time went on, the truth became apparent. She was always the fixer in the family, the one who always got it right, the queen, the oldest. Yes, Mam was right. The experience brought a new humility over the coming weeks.

She visited Anna, telling her of Mark's dark moods, her own insecurities, the socks she ruined by soaking them in pure Clorox, the sausage gravy she burnt to a crisp at the ranch. And all the time Anna was recovering, with all the friends she received, the bouquets of flowers, the cards, the gifts, not once did Neil Hershberger as much as try and contact her in any way. There were no messages on the telephone's voice mail, no cards, no flowers. She searched feverishly through each envelope, but each day there was nothing.

One evening, when the light of a spring day lingered into that softness that is so beautiful you can hardly stand it, Sadie sat on her parents' porch swing, rocking gently with Reuben beside her. Anna lowered herself painfully into the wooden porch rocker by their side.

"Ouch. Everything hurts!" she exploded impatiently.

Sadie laughed. "It will for awhile yet, my dear."

Dat and Mark had gone to the end-of-the-year school meeting, so Sadie stayed with Mam and the girls, an event that never failed to bring her joy.

When the distant, shrill ring of the phone began, Reuben leaped off the swing and raced to the shanty. It was a dash of desperation to catch the caller before the voice mail came on and before they left their phone shanty, because no matter how many times you called back, they were gone and you never found out what they wanted. It was one of those minor annoyances of Amish life, like searching for a lighter that was always to be kept in a small basket at the base of the propane lamp, yet someone always took off with it. Some folks tied a lighter to the propane lamp. But it looked so ridiculous, that brightly colored plastic lighter hanging in midair by the black carpet string, that Sadie never bothered. She just kept a large box of long matches in a drawer that no one, not even Mark, knew about. It worked.

Reuben raced back, threw himself on the swing and announced there was a group of Amish friends coming with pizza.

"Who?" Anna asked, her face leaking its color like a deflating balloon.

She was visibly afraid. Sadie could see her chest heaving, her heart beating thick and loud. It was Neil, she knew. Would he be with them? It was too painful, this complete obsession.

Sadie helped her shower and comb her hair, laughing and joking, trying to keep the atmosphere lively, upbeat. She remembered Mam's words, remembered to let Anna choose her own dress, nodding approval. She was so pretty. But in her own eyes, so ugly. A pitiable caricature of her true self.

Neil Hershberger, of course, was not among them. Lydia, Suzanna, Ruth Ann, and Esther. Her best friends, bearing a stack of steaming pizzas from the best pizzeria in town. Followed by Melvin, Michael, Jerry, her cousin Danny, and Merv Bontrager.

Merv Bontrager! Oh, my goodness. He was at least three years older than Anna. It was as if he stepped out of the surrounding shadows and into the illuminating light of Sadie's knowledge. Why not? Goose bumps roused the fine hairs on her arms as she thrilled to this new prospect. Why not? He was perfect for Anna. He had enough confidence to keep them both afloat, that was sure. She would not say a word to anyone.

She watched Merv from the background, watched him like a hawk. He ate lots of pizza, laughed and talked, but his eyes rarely left Anna. When she spoke to him, it was like a queen extending her royal scepter, he was so honored. But—how to get Neil out of her head?

The group of youth around the table was quite boisterous, enjoying themselves, the bantering, the youthful zest for life. They were at an age Sadie had almost forgotten. It seemed so long ago that she was one of them. But, oh, the sweetness of this! She had forgotten the simplicity, the innocence.

When the school meeting was over and Mark returned, Sadie did not want to leave, glad to see Mark sit down and help himself to a large slice of cold pizza, turning his attention to Merv, who responded to Mark's questions politely. Yes, he was busy. Yeah, it was a bit hard to start his own roofing business, but that was only in the beginning. Yeah, there was a real need for roofers. Tear-offs, for sure.

His brown hair was cut neatly, his blue eyes alive with pleasure when Anna spoke to him. His white short-sleeved shirt was open at the collar. He was relaxed, at ease, able to maneuver his way in a conversation so well. Oh, the possibilities!

Anna said she was thirsty, so Merv was instantly on his feet, getting ice from the freezer, filling a tall glass with cold water, then bringing it to her, totally devoid of self-consciousness. Handing the glass to Anna, their hands touched, his eyes a caress on hers. Was that a blush spreading across her too-pale cheek? Their eyes held, stayed.

✿ ✡ ✿

Sadie was fairly bouncing up and down on the buggy seat the whole way home, grabbing Mark's arm, squeezing it with both hands to get her point across. He laughed easily, held her close, and told her to calm down.

Mark said the school meeting dragged on longer than necessary in his opinion, shaking his head at the audacity of Fred Troyer. They needed another schoolhouse built, and David Detweiler offered a piece of ground, a nice, central location, but Fred had to throw a monkey wrench into the works and put in his two cents, saying the school should be built a few miles to the north. His grandchildren wouldn't have to pay transportation then; that was the only reason, everyone knew.

"He's as bad as his wife," Mark finished.

Sadie instantly changed the subject. "But, Mark, you know what? If Neil would just stay away now, I think Merv would have a chance. But I'm afraid when Anna is better, she'll return to the youth's events, the singings and suppers, and then what? Huh?"

"Oh, don't worry yourself about it. As I said, that Fred and Ketty are something else. But, you know how *goot-manich* that David Detweiler is? Of course, he said it's all right with him, they voted on it, and old Fred got his way. Sure would have liked to see it go the other way, but who am I to say? We don't have any children yet, so, of course, it's all right. Whatever the older men decide."

"And, Mark, you know what? If someone could put a bug in Merv's ear, he could just ask her for a date. Anna, you know, she might say yes. She just might. Neil isn't going to ask her. Do you think Neil will ask her out? I mean, for a real date?"

"I don't know, Sadie. But the thing that gets me, look how many families will have to pay transportation now. Even at five or six dollars a day for each family, at 130 days, that's over a thousand dollars. Fred should have thought of that. I wouldn't be a bit surprised if we have another meeting."

"Probably. Why do you think Neil doesn't come visit Anna?"

"Likely because he drives that old clunker around."

When they turned into the driveway, the deep barking of Wolf welcomed them, a sound Sadie had grown to cherish. He was such a good, faithful dog, so devoted to Mark, easily adopting Sadie as his second master.

Sadie hopped off the buggy and went to say good night to Paris, after helping Mark unhitch Truman. He had a nasty habit of running out of the shafts before the britchment snap was released, which could result in a bucking horse and broken shafts, among other things.

Where was Paris?

"Hey, Paris. Are you lying down already?"

Sadie walked to her stall, peering through the vertical, steel railing, certain of seeing Paris standing in the darkened area. Only the headlights gleaming through the door illuminated the forebay, but it was enough light for Mark to unharness his horse and put him in his stall.

"Paris?" The fear began in the pit of her stomach, taking her breath away. No. It couldn't be. The horse thieves were caught. It was all over. This could not be.

Chapter 9

Bᴜᴛ ɪᴛ ᴡᴀꜱ. Pᴀʀɪꜱ ʜᴀᴅ ʙᴇᴇɴ ᴛᴀᴋᴇɴ ᴏᴜᴛ ᴏꜰ ʜᴇʀ stall, the door closed and latched behind her. But what really broke Sadie's heart was imagining how obedient Paris would have been, her large eyes questioning, unsure but obedient. She was gone. No amount of consolation did any good. Absolutely none.

The next day Mark went to work weary from a restless night, the endless searching, Sadie's questioning, his inability to make this right for his beloved wife. They called the police, of course, but were received with a sort of tired disbelief, as if this surely had to be a joke, which made Mark angry. Banging the receiver down into its cradle and stalking about the phone shanty muttering to himself brought a fresh onslaught of tears from his stricken wife.

✸ ✡ ✸

In time Sadie accepted it, gave herself up to it, in the Amish way. Paris was gone. The neighboring community kept an eye out, watched their own horses, but knew she was an extremely valuable horse, and perhaps it wasn't the will of God that Sadie had her at all.

Hadn't Sam Detweiler preached last Sunday about where our treasures are, there will our hearts be also? Sadie better watch out; that palomino horse was taking the place of God. This the grandmothers discussed at the quiltings without malice, certainly not wishing any evil on Mark Sadie, just stating a fact. She surely had a streak of bad luck, that girl and her horse. They felt so sorry for poor Mark Sadie. But you know, she'll be in the family way before long, and then what good will the horse do her? All these discussions of wisdom, wise in the ways of life, were spoken out of love and concern for Sadie's safety.

Sadie persuaded Mark to till the soil so she could start a garden. He thought the ground was too wet, but Sadie remained adamant, remarking that Mam already had planted her peas and onions. So Truman pulled the plow, and they evened the ground with a harrow and an old bedspring, which worked just great. Sadie was ecstatic. Mark put in stakes attached to a heavy string, and she planted a pound of peas in perfectly aligned rows.

They bent side by side, poking the papery, yellow onion sets into the damp soil, covering them loosely with the hoes they had been given as wedding gifts. When Sadie insisted on planting the red beets as well, Mark gave in, shaking his head in disagreement, saying it was too early. They would need them pickled, preserved in quart jars for church services at their house.

"Oh, imagine, Mark! We're an old married couple. We'll have church services at our house. The deacon will announce in services that church will be at Mark Peight's, and all the women will offer to bring something!"

Mark grinned. "We'll have to have church in the basement."

"I figured."

✿ ✡ ✿

She told Dorothy that sometimes she heard Paris whinny from the barn and ran down to see if she was back, but she never was. Dorothy shook her head.

"I'm tellin' you, though, yer better off. That Paris is a peck o' trouble. Ya don't need her."

Not even Erma Keim understood. "Why a horse? Why trouble yourself? She's gone. Good riddance. You're still alive, and, you know, you could be dead."

Dorothy said Erma didn't have a very nice way with words after she went out to rake the lawn of its winter debris.

"I mean, she has about as much tact as a steam engine. It's why she don't have no husband. Imagine the poor guy's life?"

"I know."

Sadie was snapping green beans to cook with new potatoes and ham. She sat by the window, watching Erma's long, powerful strokes of the rake, her red hair a veritable flame in the strong sunlight, her covering blowing off repeatedly, which she dashed after and pinned back on her head.

Sadie was almost finished when a dark figure approaching Erma Keim from the barn caught her attention. He wasn't wearing a hat, which wasn't unusual in the Montana wind, which caught hats in its grasp and whirled them away without warning, tore off coverings, and made a complete mockery of hairspray.

Steven Weaver! The man from Indiana!

"Oh, my word! Come here, Dorothy!" Sadie hissed excitedly.

"Can't!" Dorothy called, stirring her famous white sauce for baked macaroni and cheese.

"Turn the burner off!"

Dorothy complied, walking heavily to stand by Sadie's chair. Slowly she breathed in, then out. Steven walked up to Erma, stuck out his hand, a broad grin on his friendly face. Erma looked at him, then brought her arm back, her elbow protruding under the sleeve of her red dress and met his hand with a solid smack.

Sadie winced, and Dorothy shook with a deep belly laugh.

"What a giraffe! She don't even know how to shake hands! Especially with a man."

When Steven dropped his hand, it didn't look as if he minded how firm her handshake had been. He looked delighted, if anything. Their tall forms stood in the middle of the lawn, talking, the wind whipping his hair and the legs of his trousers, her skirt twisting and flapping and her red hair a complete disaster, the pins sliding out yet again.

She was laughing when her covering went flying off. She grabbed desperately for it but could not catch the elusive object. Just then Reuben came dashing by at his usual unsafe speed on the riding mower, caught sight of the rolling white object and slammed on the brakes, leaned back, his arms stiff as a board to the steering wheel, as he brought the mower to a halt, inches from the white covering. Reuben swung his legs over, hopped off, grabbed the covering, and brought it to Erma.

Steven was bent at the waist, slapping his knee with pure merriment, watching intently as Erma tried to pin it back on, taking extra pins from her belt. She had to turn her back to Steven, the wind coming in that direction, as she struggled to pin it in place.

"Come here!" Sadie hissed.

Dorothy had been on her way back to her cream sauce, but she turned immediately, peering eagerly through the window just as Steven reached up to hold her covering in place so Erma could pin it.

"Oh, my lands!" Dorothy breathed.

Sadie watched, spellbound, when she saw how flustered Erma became, picking up her rake, catching her covering strings, looking down to her shoes, then to Reuben, who stood observing them both with innocent curiosity. He said something, and Erma slapped his back so hard he took a few steps forward, then laughed.

"Oh my, she must be really worked up," Sadie said. "She almost knocked Reuben on his face!"

"What'd I tell you? If that Indiana chap knows his good, he'll hightail it right back to his home state. She'll make his life miserable. Mark my words! Miserable!"

But she had a light in her eyes and was humming a silly little love song when she returned to her cream sauce, dipping and waving her spoon in time to her song.

✿ ✡ ✿

Sadie's life remained completely peaceful, except for the ache in her heart about Paris, who had disappeared that night leaving no trace, much the same as so many horses before her. The sun gently drew the seeds into sprouts that pushed their way up through the hard, wet soil in late spring. The nights were still crisp and cold, the air brisk and snappy when Sadie hung laundry on the line in the early morning, that unceasing Montana wind tugging at the heavy towels and dresses as she pinned them securely, sometimes needing more than one clothespin on each corner to ensure her peace of mind while she was at work down at the ranch.

Erma Keim remained a constant source of entertainment, spicing her days with a dash of peppery comments, clashing with Dorothy's bristling wit like a bad summer thunderstorm.

In the evening Mark would lean back and howl with laughter when Sadie related an especially bizarre incident, but of late he had become increasingly withdrawn yet again. It was always the same. First she would blame herself. Scouring the past days, even weeks, for a certain thing she had said or done, enabling the black cloud to hover over his head, raining down the sadness, the dissociation, that extracting of himself to another, darker place. She dreaded it.

She prattled senselessly, as incapable of changing the descending cloud as changing the horizon or the order of nature. Still she tried to bring him back, knowing it wouldn't work, then went about her work with a lump in her throat, knowing she had let him down yet again.

It was especially bad this time. He slept on the couch, his face to the back, his knees drawn up almost to his chin. His dirty work clothes reeked of barns, horse manure, and other scents that Sadie could only describe as dirty.

No amount of wheedling would make one stitch of difference. First, after her shower, she sat on the space where his knees left an indentation and put an arm across his wide back. Slowly she began a relaxing massage, asking him softly if he felt ill, or if his head hurt, willing him to break the silence and tell her what had happened to bring this on. A rude shrugging of the shoulders, a grunt, a burrowing into the couch cushions, followed by a long drawn-out sigh was her only answer.

So she got up, went to the bedroom, groped around till she felt her box of long matches, struck one along the side of the box harder than was necessary, took off the glass lamp chimney, turned up the wick, and lit it. Tears dropped onto the surface of the nightstand. Replacing the chimney, she pulled back the quilt and top sheet and slid into bed with her book of the week. Swiping viciously at her eyes, she opened the book, but all the words swam together, a black-and-white blurb of unreadable nonsense that only made her cry harder.

Was it the lack of a good, hot supper on Thursday? Had she become too snippy about leaving his soiled boots beside the stove on Wednesday? That was likely what it was. She would have to remember next time. Place a rug along the back of the stove for his boots, then shake out the accumulation that hardened on the soles afterward. She'd have to be more careful.

Having reached a reasonable conclusion for herself made all the difference, so she laid her book down, blew out the lamp, and soon fell asleep. You just had to know how to work at these things. Didn't even the experts say marriage wasn't easy?

When Mark disappeared on Saturday morning, she presumed he went to town, or forgot to tell her he had a few horses to shoe, or went out back to chop more firewood. She cleaned her house all morning, starting in the back, throwing open every bedroom window, allowing the spring breezes to enter, filling the room with the sweet smell of new growth, rain-washed earth, and spring flowers. She swept the wide-plank oak floors with the soft broom she had just purchased at Fred Ketty's new dry goods store. All Amish women had to have a Soft Sweep broom. Inexpensive, the bristles so soft and pliable, it allowed a much cleaner sweep than those stiff bristled ones at Walmart.

The thing was, English women used vacuum cleaners, which whirred across the floor and sucked up the dirt and dust and household accumulation of questionable things, like pet hair and dander and bugs and spiders. When she cleaned at the ranch, she dusted first, then ran the powerful vacuum cleaner across the carpeting or hardwood floors.

At home she swept first, raising little puffs of dust and woolies from under the bed, making a pile outside the bedroom door before collecting it in a dustpan, then liberally spraying her cloth with Pledge furniture polish. She removed the candles, lamp, tray of lotions and colognes and worked the cloth energetically across the surface. When everything was replaced, she used the Swiffer, picking up any dirt and dust the broom had missed.

There. Now for the bathroom.

At the ranch, she had to dry the huge garden tub, then spray it with Tilex. Never anything else. Barbara Caldwell considered it the best product, so Sadie used it and never said a word. It was Barbara's bathroom, and if she was happy with the result of her cleaner, it was good.

But at home Sadie used cheap old Comet. The dry stuff you shook out of a tall green container, wet a cloth, and scrubbed away. It never scratched anything she knew of and had a cleaner, smoother finish. No water spots.

She was on her hands and knees, scrubbing happily away at her new white bathtub, the water running, when she thought she heard someone calling her name. Quickly, she yanked down on the lever, stopping the flow of water. She stepped outside the door, looked left and right, but couldn't see anyone. Wolf hadn't barked, had he?

"Sadie!" There. Someone was calling.

Wiping her hands on her apron, she hurried to the front door and was gratified to see Mark standing by the barn door, waving a piece of paper.

"What?" she called, so glad he was talking to her.

"I'm going to the ranch."

"Okay."

She stepped back, eager to finish cleaning the bathtub. Why did he let her know now? He had been gone all morning without letting her know of his whereabouts. Pushing back the resentment, she tried to think of more pleasant subjects. She wished he'd finish the porch steps so she could wrap up her landscaping project. She could hardly wait to plant shrubs and flowers, especially since Dorothy had offered to take her to Rhinesville to a huge nursery and greenhouse combination. She promised the use of Jim's truck so she could buy anything she wanted, even trees.

The thought of Dorothy weaving that rusted pickup truck in and out of traffic, her short legs and arms barely able to reach the pedals or the steering wheel, driving the same way she did everything else—as fast as possible—talking all the while, definitely caused Sadie a few misgivings. If only she wouldn't maneuver the turns like that—seemingly on two wheels, sometimes spinning gravel from under the tires when her foot hit the gas pedal too firmly. But still, it was a free trip.

That was an awful bunch of dust and woolies on her broom. Stepping outside, she whacked it down on the porch railing to loosen them, and after a distinct crack, was left holding half a handle, the remainder of her broom lying in the mud below. Oh, no. That was the only broom she had except a porch broom, and she certainly did not want to use that. So she decided she needed a few dresses for summer, and she'd hitch up Truman and drive to Fred Ketty's store. The cleaning would have to wait till she returned.

Smoothing back her hair, she pinned on a clean, white covering, grabbed her purse, and was out the door.

The loss of Paris was always worse at the barn. She hated going there and struggled to keep her eyes from wandering to the empty stall. The currycomb still contained honey-colored hair from Paris's coat. She raked it out with her fingers, savored the softness as she sifted it between her thumb and forefinger, slowly letting it fall to the concrete floor of the forebay. Setting her mouth determinedly, she brushed Truman hard, willing the dark brown horsehair to drive away the endless longing for Paris.

She knew, now, that Paris was a very valuable horse, so perhaps it was for the best. She'd be in good hands, likely making some rancher wealthy with that bloodline of her past. She'd have to give up. Wasn't that the way of it? What you couldn't change, you had to accept.

Throwing the harness across Truman's back, she adjusted it, fastened all the snaps and buckles, the collar riding well on his thick neck. Leading him to the buggy, she told him to stay, then hurried back to lift the shafts. There was always that small space of time when you were never sure if the horse you were hitching up would stand obediently until the shafts were lifted. Even then, if he had a mind to, he could have gone running and kicking, free of doing his duty of pulling the buggy. Truman was well trained and, with a slight tug of the britchment strap and a command of "Back," he responded, stepping back lightly, fitting between the shafts neatly.

Truman was in high spirits, and Sadie's arms felt as if they had quite a workout by the time Fred Ketty's store came into view.

That Fred. Sadie smiled to herself as she noticed the gray siding on one side of the building, white on another, and beige-colored siding on the front. Likely he'd been scavenging the local lumberyard to build his wife her dry goods store. The dubious-looking stainless steel chimney poked its way out of the black shingled room, a thin, white column of smoke whirling away on the breeze. Why a fire in the stove? Sadie barely needed her sweater. The door stuck, so Sadie shoved harder, entering the store with a bang and two quick steps.

"Sadie!" Ketty boomed.

"H...hello, Ketty," Sadie said, floundering a bit, grabbing for composure.

"Welcome to my store!"

"It's nice!"

"Really nice, isn't it? My Fred is something. Never saw anyone that can put up a nicer building for less than 2000 dollars."

"Really?"

Ketty nodded proudly, then lowered herself around the cash register to whisper confidentially that Fred is good buddies with Jack from the lumberyard. Gave him stuff he can't sell anymore.

"That's good," Sadie said, smiling.

It had to be close to a hundred degrees in the place. Sadie took off her sweater, asking if she could put it by the cash register.

"You too warm? Well, I got a bunch of cheap apples from the fruit man, and we don't eat so many apples, me and Fred. I hate to see them go to waste, so I told Fred if he starts me a wood fire, I'd cook down the apples for *loddveig*. Nothing better than *loddveig* on a warm dinner roll, *gel*, Sadie?"

Sadie nodded, smiled, said all the appropriate things, her eyes looking for the right shade of blue, her fingers searching for a good, lightweight, sturdy fabric. She scratched her head, then wiped her forehead with a clean handkerchief. This was absolutely miserable. What was wrong with this woman? Why didn't she open a window? Perspiration beading her forehead, she quickly made her purchase, steering clear of the red-hot, potbellied stove snapping and crackling in one corner, a heavy pot of apples bubbling and steaming on the top.

"Three yards of this, please."

"Sure."

Fred Ketty made a sweeping motion with her arms, a grandiose gesture of the experienced store owner, one who would become quite well-to-do the minute she had sold Sadie her fabric.

Sadie looked behind Ketty to the plush recliner, the cup of coffee, the heavy book. What had she been reading? On a Saturday? This early in the morning? A half-eaten cinnamon roll lay haphazardly across the Saran-wrap-covered plate that contained five more.

War and Peace? Fred Ketty was reading *War and Peace*? Sadie looked sharply at Fred Ketty as if seeing her for the first time. Was she a genuine intellectual? People said she was way smarter than she looked, which was a blunt statement, but honest.

She imagined Fred Ketty with her hair down, dressed in English clothes. She was tall, statuesque, actually, her eyebrows quite regal-looking. If she wasn't wearing the rumpled dress, the too-small glasses, the lopsided covering, she could probably look quite distinguished. A lawyer?

Sadie imagined Fred Ketty walking the streets of New York City, wearing a black belted trench coat and large, dark glasses, carrying a designer briefcase, four-inch heels coming down on the paved sidewalk. She bet she could do it if she hadn't been born Amish. But here was Fred Ketty, her keen eyes looking at the world through her plain glasses, perfectly happy, avidly curious about the world's goings on, about history, especially World War II. It was an innocent outlet for a mind that could have been taught so much more. It was the way of it. No sadness in this birdlike happiness.

"How's marriage treating you?" Fred Ketty asked, folding a three-yard length, her bright eyes looking straight through her.

Sadie opened her mouth to say, "Fine," but instead, ended up with a catch in her throat, her mouth wobbling. She sat behind the counter with Fred Ketty for an hour, eating the softest, most wonderful cinnamon rolls with cream cheese frosting and drinking chai tea, which Fred Ketty said was good for the sinuses, among other things.

She told her about Mark, and Fred Ketty clapped a warm hand on her shoulder and said that boy had a rough start. How in the world could she ever figure it wouldn't show up sometimes? The human spirit could only take so much and not more, and he was likely doing the best he could, and she'd always said that Mark had married exactly the right girl, as strong as Sadie was. She was the perfect helpmate for a guy like him, and if he went into a depression like that, she'd have to detach herself and go on with her life and know she couldn't change him. And if it got too bad, she could come over and sit in her store and eat sticky buns and drink chai tea.

She laughed so deeply and genuinely when Sadie told her about Mark sleeping on the couch, that it rolled between them and caught Sadie infectiously until her whole world looked better and better.

"It's called marriage, Sadie dear!" she gasped, lifting her too small glasses to wipe her eyes, and Sadie was so glad Fred Ketty was here in her cheap little store and not a lawyer in New York City.

Chapter 10

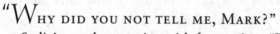

"Why did you not tell me, Mark?"

Sadie's words were ripe with frustration. "Why? Why put me through all these days of silence, the months of not knowing what in the world is eating you, and suddenly, bingo, you let me in on your wonderful secret, which you had absolutely no right to hide from me at all?"

Mark leaped up, pushed back his kitchen chair, and slammed the door behind him as he left the house, giving Sadie no answer. She was so angry.

It was sweltering. Dry, hot wind tugged at the curtains, stirring the thick, tepid air but giving no real relief. In Montana the summer was not as unendurable as in Ohio, but there were always a few uncomfortable weeks, and this year had been no different.

Absentmindedly, she stirred the cold soup, that sweet concoction the Amish still considered a good, refreshing alternative to cookies on days when no one was comfortable. A large amount of fresh blueberries in the bottom of a generous pottery serving bowl, a liberal amount of sugar, a few slices of heavy homemade bread broken on top, and ice-cold milk poured over everything. *Kalte sup*.

It was so good. Sweet and creamy and fruity. Dorothy shivered to think about it, which made Sadie smile.

Wearily she began gathering knives, spoons, and forks, heading for the sink. Why had he done this on his own? Searching, going to the library, asking Duane Ashland, of all people, to use the computer. *Genealogy*. The word was hostile somehow. Against her. So now, out of the clear blue sky, he announced he had contacted his brother Timothy, and they planned to meet. He lived in Oregon. He was going, and did she want to go?

What about the months of wondering if she'd actually made a mistake? Marrying him the way she had, thinking her whole life would be one long day of love and adoration. She felt angry, bitter, and betrayed by his secrecy. So angry, in fact, that he was going to know it. She was absolutely not letting him get away with blithely skipping over these past months of hurt and disappointment.

She rattled the dishes as loudly as she could, somehow taking delight in banging them. She jerked the dish towel off its rack, snapped it into the air, and began drying dishes as if her life depended on exactly how dry they would become. To punish him, she wouldn't go. He could go by himself. He could pack his own suitcase, too.

Being all alone in one's kitchen, letting anger and bitterness eat away at your soul like battery acid, was not the thing to do. It was plain to her after a miserable evening. Something would have to give.

Dear Father in heaven, I am so mad. I am such a complete mess. I can't forgive Mark. I can't stand him, even. You know my heart. All my horrible hatred and bitterness. Cleanse me now. Let my sins be washed away. Give me a new start.

So she prayed, swinging back and forth on the porch

swing, the new porch steps beside her a tribute to Mark's hard work. She turned her head to listen. A buggy? Yes, a horse and buggy was traveling down Atkin's Ridge, coming in their direction. Oh, she hoped it was someone from her family. She missed them all so much. It had been too long since she had been back home with Mam and her sisters.

Listening eagerly now, she stopped the swing. The crunch of gravel on steel wheels was gratifying. It was Reuben and Anna! Leaping up, she began waving long before they reached the house, then ran down the steps and across the yard to greet them.

"Check out my new buggy!"

Reuben was 16 years old now and was still eager to tell Sadie everything he knew, blurting out the good news without as much as a hello.

"Wow! Sharp!" Sadie burst out.

Anna was grinning widely, and Reuben tried hard to maintain his air of grave manliness, but he couldn't hide his little-boy delight.

"Look at this! Gray and red! The carpeting is black and gray!"

"The glove compartment is very nice, too! Wow! Dat paid a lot for this rig!" Sadie said.

Mark came up from the barn and duly exclaimed about the new buggy, the harness, and where did he get the horse?

"It's Charlie!" Reuben crowed.

It was Charlie, a bathed and currycombed one. Even his mane and tail were clipped.

"Go tie Charlie and come in," Mark ordered.

They needed no second invitation, quickly gathering on the porch in the hot, still evening. Reuben seemed almost shy about the fact that he had turned 16. There was always a big fuss when one of the girls reached that age, which he never understood, displaying plenty of disbelief in the entire ritual. But when it was his own turn, he soaked up the attention like a dry sponge.

"So now Anna has a ride to the suppers and singings, right?" Sadie asked, smiling appreciatively at Reuben.

"I guess so," he said gruffly.

Anna winked broadly.

"How's life treating you, Anna?"

"Okay, I guess."

The usual noncommittal answer from Anna.

"No Neil Hershberger yet?"

A look of pain crossed Anna's face, and she bent her head.

"I guess not. He's dating Sheryl."

"He's what?"

Sadie was clearly disturbed.

"Sheryl?"

Anna nodded.

"Why?"

Anna shrugged her shoulders, her eyes downcast, biting her lip. Reuben shushed her with his eyes, drawing his eyebrows down with a slight shake of his head, rolling his eyes in Anna's direction. Sadie nodded slightly, then changed the subject.

Mark suggested they go fishing. He was hungry for some fresh trout, and with Danner's Creek this low, they'd have a good chance at a few fat ones. Reuben jumped up, clearly beside himself at the opportunity to show Mark his fly-fishing skills, which left Sadie with Anna for another hour or so before darkness folded itself across the land.

Sadie went to the kitchen, bringing back tall glasses of lemonade, the fresh-squeezed kind that Mark loved so much. Anna sipped daintily at hers, making a face afterward.

"Sour," she commented.

"It's the way Mark likes it."

"I'm never getting married," Anna said bluntly.

"I wouldn't."

Anna's head came up, and a smile crinkled her eyes at the corners. Her face was still gaunt, but not as angular, not quite as skeletal as it had been in the spring. The belt on her apron was tied loosely, so she still had the appearance of being painfully thin.

"Why do you say that?"

Sadie shrugged. "We just aren't … It's been a difficult summer. He finally came out and told me today, today, mind you, what has been so heavy on his mind."

Sadie told Anna the story, coming to a close with a frustrated, palms-up, arms-outspread jerk of her arms.

"Go figure! Go around leaving me in the dark."

Anna nodded. "I know how he feels."

"You do not."

"I do. I know exactly."

"Tell me."

Anna was quiet, sipping her drink, alternately making horrible faces till Sadie laughed, asking why she put herself through all that misery drinking that lemonade.

"I don't know how to explain it, but I know how he feels."

"Please, Anna."

"Well, you don't talk as if you're afraid people will think you're dumb if you say what you think."

"Can you say that differently?"

"I'm not a good talker. Like now, I can't…. Often the words don't come out right. Then if I do say … say how

I feel, I imagine you … all my sisters think I'm dumb. So I don't talk."

"Why would we think that?"

"You do. Often I am dumb."

"Anna!"

"Well, all my older sisters are beautiful and smart … and … and someone. If you love others a lot, look up to them, it's pretty scary. Because if you do give an opinion, they'll think it's stupid. I am not smart like the rest of you. So I stay quiet."

"And then you don't eat because it's something you can control?"

Anna shrugged, sipped her lemonade, and pursed her lips, which Sadie saw but was thinking too deeply to notice. What were the right words?

"So you think Mark feels the same way?"

"Probably."

"He was afraid I'd laugh at him for looking for his brother? But we had talked about it before!" Sadie burst out.

Anna nodded. "Still, think about it. He's afraid of you, in a way."

Anna looked off across the lawn, her eyes softer than Sadie had seen them in a long time. "He's afraid you'll laugh at him. Think he's *bupp-lich*."

Sadie shook her head in disbelief.

"Ask him," Anna finished.

She told Sadie, then, about her return to the youth's events, how Neil acted as if nothing ever happened and that their friendship would continue, begging her to go out with him in his car. She had gone, of course, she would always go with him, so glad he wanted her back, telling herself he was too shy to meet her parents or ask her for a real date. How she loved him! Sadie nodded, understanding.

Then one night about a month ago, she realized he had no good intentions toward her and, selfishly, wanted her to leave her family and the Amish community for good. How he had pleaded. He said if she loved him she'd prove herself and go away with him. She almost went. She hadn't told anyone, knowing they would think she was foolish.

One night she dreamed Neil was leading her with a rope, the rope tightening around her neck, and she woke up screaming and screaming, choking and crying.

Mam had mentioned Anna's nightmares to Sadie. They had both agreed it was only normal after her accident. But this?

After she told Neil she would not leave the community, he had retaliated by dating Sheryl, a good five years his senior, and certainly a pitiful choice, leaving only a trail of heartache.

Anna finished miserably, "Now, he's trying to prove to me that he's staying Amish, obeying his parents, only not doing it for me."

"You don't care, do you?"

Anna shrugged her thin shoulders.

"Are you eating?"

"Better."

"Good girl, Anna. I'm so glad to hear you say that."

Anna smiled, a small timid lifting of her lips, but a smile nevertheless.

✢ ✪ ✢

The following Saturday, Dorothy insisted they were going to the nursery. The summer was almost gone, and early fall was a good time to plant evergreens. She wanted a white pine of her own.

Sadie had hoped she would forget about it, especially when she remembered the steering wheel of the old pickup being stubborn at certain times. With Dorothy, though, there was no forgetting. Erma Keim could cook by herself, she said, since she knew how to make everything better than Dorothy did, anyway.

So Sadie dressed in her lightweight blue dress, combed her dark hair carefully, spraying it liberally with hair spray and pinning her covering with extra pins. She knew that with the lack of air conditioning and Dorothy's love of a strong breeze, the windows would be lowered the whole way down, as they hit speeds nearing 75 miles an hour if there was a good highway.

Mark watched her pin her covering and laughed.

"I can only guess what you'll look like coming back."

"If I come back!" Sadie laughed.

Mark sobered, then walked over and put his hands on her shoulders, bending his head to kiss her deeply before holding her tenderly against his body.

"Please be careful. I couldn't live without you. You are my life, the reason for my existence. Nothing else makes any sense."

Sadie clung to her husband, turned her face away, and felt the bitterness, the sadness, the impending sense of failure, leave a trail of debris as it was ushered out the door of her heart. When she cleared her throat, the debris followed, leaving a clean, white trail, sparkling with stardust, accompanied by the strains of angel harps.

Forgiveness, then, was incredibly important when two people became one, united in holy matrimony, as the minister had said. Sometimes their union had certainly not been holy. Or sacred. Why didn't someone write a manual about *after* your wedding day? A complete list of how-to's in every situation.

Well, for now, on this wonderful, glad morning, hope sprang up, completely new, stronger than ever.

"I love you, Mark," she whispered.

"I love you, too," he answered, taking a deep breath.

It's one of life's greatest mysteries. No matter what, you simply were not happy if you were angry with your husband. Even if you had more than enough reason to be. Even if you believed yourself to be a victim of his selfishness, his manners, you still did not have the all-consuming happiness that came with forgiveness. She felt like skipping out to the truck when it ground to a halt at the end of the new walkway Mark had finished.

"Good morning, Dorothy!"

"Don't you look nice, Honey?" Dorothy said, her way of greeting.

"Thank you!"

She slid the truck perfectly into drive, shifting gears much better than her husband ever did, her short arms and round fingers finding the gears as expertly as any truck driver. They wound their way along the rural roads, the morning air cool enough to keep the windows closed except for an inch or so at the top and still be comfortable.

"Where are we going, Dorothy?"

"To Rhinesville."

"How far away is it?"

"'Bout an hour."

"So, we get on 26?"

"Yeah."

Sadie glanced over at Dorothy, quite suddenly looking shorter and older, her arms outstretched, her small feet barely reaching the gas pedal or the brake. Sadie thought of the big rigs passing them from behind, with their furious speeds, and swallowed.

"Are you used to driving this truck?" she asked, quietly.

"Who? Me? 'Course I can drive this truck. I drove it for years. 'Fore I worked at the ranch."

"Oh."

"Don't you worry, yer in good hands. You wanna stop at the Dollar General? They have a big one in Rhinesville. Clorox is a dollar a gallon. It's up to a dollar and 29 cents at Walmart. See what I mean? You can't beat the Dollar General. You know their off-brand a' Ritz Crackers? They're a dollar sixty-nine. Mind you, real Ritz at Walmart's up to two ninety-eight. It's a sin. How 'n the world do they expect a person to pay their bills? Now nobody needs three bucks for them crackers. I ain't buyin' 'em."

Sadie nodded in agreement.

"I told Louise the other day, there ain't no way I'm packin' their school lunches no more. I give 'em three dollars, and they get a hot lunch at school. Bless their hearts, those kids is so good. So sweet. Sadie, the Lord smiled on me the day those kids came into my life. I'd give 'em everything I got. So would Jim. Love 'em to death, so we do."

She leaned over to check her mirror.

"Somepin' comin'?"

"No," Sadie said.

"Well, here we go, then."

With that, Sadie was introduced to the wildest ride she had ever encountered, with Dorothy pressing her foot on the gas, clutching the steering wheel with both hands, passing anything in her path. They shot past tractor trailers, wove in and out of all the traffic, hardly ever going below 75 or 80 miles an hour. Sadie chewed on her lower lip, watching the mirror on her side and then the smaller cars ahead. The scenery was beautiful, with yellow beech trees, dark green pines, large horse farms, and cattle ranches dotting the countryside. Sadie sincerely hoped she'd reach Rhinesville safely and be able to return home without too much anxiety.

The nursery and greenhouses were worth every tense mile. Acres of land were covered with healthy looking shrubs, perennials, trees, and evergreens, as well as greenhouses containing the last of the season's flowers. Dorothy walked tirelessly in and out of rows of flowering shrubs and bushes before purchasing a small white pine for $9.99.

"It's not so dear," she commented. "And when I'm dead and gone, this tree will remind Louise and Marcelona of their foster mother, now won't it?"

Sadie nodded agreement, settling for two arborvitae, two blue junipers, some ivy, day lilies, and hardy sage. She enjoyed her time at the nursery so much, she was reluctant to leave, buying a birdhouse for her porch at the last minute, Dorothy scolding and shaking her head.

"Now what's that gonna do you good? Ain't no bird gonna build a nest in that teensy hole."

"They might. You never know."

She couldn't tell Dorothy the birdhouse was simply "for nice"—for display. She would never get over that, bringing it up every day for a month. That was just how Dorothy was, and Sadie had learned a long time ago not to tell her things she wouldn't approve of.

"You know Mark coulda made you that birdhouse fer nothin'?"

"He doesn't have time."

"Why not? He has to run around shoeing horses as fast as he can so's you kin spend it all on birdhouses?"

"I guess so."

Dorothy shook her head. Sadie was almost splitting her face to keep from laughing. If anyone else would have said that, Sadie likely would have been offended, but not Dorothy. She didn't have a mean bone in her body; she just felt it was her Christian duty to warn Sadie.

They traveled slowly through the town, looking for the Dollar General. It was beside a McDonald's, which left Dorothy fairly hopping up and down with glee. She parked the truck with a lurch, reached down and got her imitation brown leather purse, and dug, pulling out two coupons.

"Which one do you want? McDonald's or Burger King?"

"It's your call, Dorothy."

"I like McDonald's. I like their sundaes. Hot fudge. Maybe we better go to the Dollar Store first, make sure our money lasts. Nothin' else, we don't have to splurge. Eating out is so dear, you know. We can get a bag o' chips at the Dollar Store."

She almost ran across the parking lot, her green polyester shorts slapping about her knees, her white blouse embroidered in a rich teal thread around the neckline.

"Here, Sadie. Here's the carts. You better get one out here. This is a popular store. Never any carts. Never. We're lucky we got one this time, so we are. Mark my words, the Dollar Store's gonna put a hurtin' on Walmart. One o' these days, we'll read it in the paper."

Dorothy's hair was sticking straight up, completely electric with excitement, when she discovered the shoes were only $17.99, on sale from $24. She bought two pairs, saying she'd really have to explain it to Jim, but likely they'd last till she was about ready to retire.

She bought and bought and bought. She exclaimed loudly about every price, stocking up on Clorox, Ritz Crackers, chocolate sandwich cookies, saltines, handker-chiefs for Jim, socks for the children, until her cart was full to overflowing with various useful items.

At lunch, Dorothy ate a Big Mac with the dressing squeezing out from beneath the sandwich, spreading it across her face and completely unaware of it, talking between bites, saying this was the funnest day she had since she was 50.

And when she backed into a utility pole, giving Sadie's head quite a lurch, she got out to check the back bumper and said Jim could whack it out. She'd tell him someone hit her. They had. "They" was the utility pole. Why'd they put a pole at such a busy place? People didn't think, that's what. That's why the world was the way it was. Nobody thought.

They roared down the highway, the yellow Dollar General bags flapping and waving, the shrubs and bushes tilting this way and then the other, depending which way Dorothy turned in or out of traffic. Sadie prayed they wouldn't blow a tire. When they wheezed up the drive-way and came to a skidding stop, Sadie leaned back and sighed, only not loud enough for Dorothy to hear.

Dorothy waved away the proffered gas money, saying Jim would fill it up, he had nothin' else to do with his money except go to the fire hall an' play Bingo, and she'd a' liked if he didn't do that. He was better off at home. Her Jim was a good-looking man. You never knew.

Chapter 11

WHEN THE BREEZES TURNED COOLER, THEN COLD, Mark said it was time to go. His work had slowed enough to allow him to plan the much-thought-about trip to Oregon. He became withdrawn, pensive, but not sullen or angry. He talked again of his past, the times he remembered Timothy. They discussed the reason his dying mother carried so much grief for him, if she barely mentioned the others.

Sadie could tell Mark was in an agony of indecision, even after the tickets had been procured, all the necessary arrangements made, and he had talked to Timothy on the phone. Still he wavered. Would it be for the best?

Timothy would try and contact his siblings, but hadn't elaborated if he had accomplished this. They were simply stepping out into the unknown, having no reason to believe any good would come from it.

Sadie could ask questions, but more often than not, she would receive a shrug of the shoulders, or a denial, an "I don't know," or words to that effect.

Sadie had decided to go along. Reuben and Anna would take care of Wolf and the horses. Leah would fill in for Sadie at the ranch. She was Erma Keim's good friend, so Sadie figured if things got too rocky, Leah could always tell Erma to back off. Mam made a new coat for Mark and a nice one made of wool for Sadie. They bought new shoes, a few shirts for Mark, packed their suitcase, and waited nervously for the driver to take them to the Amtrak station.

"At least no one is terminally ill this time," Sadie quipped, trying to bolster Mark's mood.

"Yeah."

"It'll be okay. You might be surprised how normal everyone is. If you feel no bonding, no connection, then just come back home and continue living your life without them. Nothing will change."

"But what will they think of me? My being Amish. I'm sure they think I'm just one big joke. A loser, who isn't even nearly as good as he thinks he is."

"We'll see, Mark. Don't be so hard on yourself."

He went to the refrigerator, helping himself to a slice of deer bologna, followed by the jar of bread and butter pickles. He folded a slice of Swiss cheese into the bologna, piled on a generous amount of pickles, and crunched all of it between his teeth.

"Mm, that's good! Those pickles are the best thing ever."

"Give me a bite."

Sadie jumped up, eagerly reaching for the bologna combination, only to be slapped away playfully.

"Come on, Mark!"

Elaborately, he dropped the last bite into his open mouth, then hunched his back as Sadie rained blows on his arm.

"Ow! Ow!"

"You need to learn how to share!"

Just as he had made another roll, the driver stopped at the end of the walks, with Sadie chewing a great mouthful on her way out. Her garden had yielded well for a brand new one. But then came the tedious job of peeling those gigantic cucumbers, cutting them in halves, scooping out the seeds, cutting them in long spears, and making banana pickles out of them. They were called that because of their resemblance to bananas: long, yellow, and curved, till they were all packed in the jar properly, standing upright, with the turmeric, that orange spice that turned everything yellow (including fingertips and countertops and wooden spoons), making them a beautiful color. Banana pickles were often served in church, fitting perfectly inside a roll of ham or eaten with cheese. Or like now, wrapped inside a roll of Swiss cheese and bologna, creating a burst of sweet and sour in Sadie's mouth.

The driver, Tom Nelson, the oldest, most dependable driver, with an impeccable driving record, having driven a huge 18-wheeler for "40-some" years, was in a sour mood, grunting a surly hello, throwing his cigarette reluctantly out the window when they got into the 15-passenger van.

"Whyn't ya tell me there was only the two of you? Woulda brought the truck."

"I thought I did," Sadie offered.

That was greeted by another grunt. "Gonna cost ya more."

Mark said nothing, so Sadie kept her peace. Observing Tom from the seat behind the driver, she decided he'd likely be in a better mood if he shaved and got a haircut. That gray hair looked itchy and uncomfortable, growing in stubbles all over his face that way. His glasses could have done with a good cleaning as well.

Sadie grimaced as he reached for his ever-present bottle of warm Coke, twisting the red cap off and draining it in a few gulps before returning it to the cup holder, wiping his mouth and belching softly, as he scratched the plaid flannel fabric of the shirt stretched across his stomach.

"So where we goin'?" he rasped.

"Oregon," Mark answered.

"What?"

The beady brown eyes peered at Mark, the head elevated slightly to see him better, his eyes adjusted to the bifocals in his glasses. Mark laughed.

Tom bent over his steering wheel, pulling himself into a more comfortable sitting position before saying, "You better be pulling my leg!"

Mark was still laughing when he told him about the train tickets, which seemed to put him in a better mood, caught up in Mark's good humor.

He drove well, the way these retired truckers did, watching for wildlife, his head constantly swiveling from side to side. "Eagle," he pointed out. Or, "Mule deer." Sadie would never quite figure out how he kept the van on the road while spotting all the wildlife. Mark wasn't driving, and he didn't find all the interesting things Tom did. Sadie guessed if you logged as many miles as this driver did over the span of 40 years, with uncountable hours spent behind the steering wheel, it all came automatically and you didn't even think about it. Sort of like frying an egg or hanging out laundry for an Amish housewife, repetitive things you never thought about on most days as you did these mundane tasks.

"I told Thelma, some of these cats is gonna hafta go.

I can't take it. I'm allergic to 'em. Hackin' and coughin,' you'd think she'd listen to me. I'm the one has the hairball in my throat, not them cats, she says. Says, I quit smokin' these cigarettes, I quit coughin'. She says it ain't the cats. Sure it's them cats. Hair floatin' all over th' trailer, so it does. Cats on my table, cats in my bathroom, on my recliner, all over the house. Shouldn't a' got married that second time, that's what. She told me she had a few cats, she didn't tell me they'd have little 'uns. Wouldn't a married her, I'da known."

Sadie smiled to herself, wondering how often she had heard this very same story. Who had put in the new pet doors? Or bought the electric water cooler type cat dish that kept their water fresh?

"How many cats do you have?" Sadie asked, same as she always did just because she enjoyed hearing these cat stories so much.

"I dunno. Big gray bruiser named Rex. A dog's name, ya ask me. Rex is big. That cat weights 30 pounds, I bet. We got Lulu, she's a smart one. Won't drink out a' the cat dish. Opens the spigot in the bathroom. Jes' sits there batting at the handle until she gets it open."

One by one, he ticked off the cats' names, their attributes, as proud as any father with his family. When Sadie told him this, he denied it so vehemently she was actually afraid she had offended him. She was relieved when he changed the subject to something more interesting, in his opinion.

Trains are funny things. You sit quietly and don't really know you're moving until you feel a faint shudder and the buildings beside you start moving of their own accord, or so it seems. Sadie had been looking forward to the ride, remembering well the long, quiet, time they had spent prior to their marriage going to stay with his dying mother in North Dakota. There was just something soothing about sitting close to Mark, relaxed, knowing she was doing something for him, something he cared about deeply, a service she did gladly. Enjoying the sights, the sounds, and rhythm of a train, the atmosphere of togetherness where people of all ages, names, backgrounds, sat together in a common bond of traveling, all depending on the power of the wheels beneath them to take them to their destinations. There were always talkative folks, friendly, inquisitive, and those who ignored you, pretending you didn't exist, which was okay with Sadie either way.

Mark was quiet, falling asleep an hour after the train began moving. Sadie traced the soft line of the black hair growing along his jaw line with the tip of her finger, watched the way the thick eyelashes fluttered as she did so, and smiled to herself. So big and so strong, shoeing horses, building houses and barns, wielding a chain saw, swinging an ax, and yet so vulnerable when it came down to it. Victim of a puzzling past, he was now hurtling through the state of Montana, across Idaho, and into an unknown city in Oregon to find a brother he had never known, perhaps to uncover another painful, long-buried incident and face down yet more demons of his complex nature. Well, if it was too difficult, they'd leave. Sadie would not allow it to become a situation that would only make his life harder.

She smoothed his blue shirt collar, flicked off a piece of thread from the sleeve of his new gray coat, then adjusted her own seat to a more comfortable position before closing her eyes. But she was too excited to sleep, so she sat up and looked around her.

A portly gentleman was unwrapping a cupcake. Sadie's mouth watered as she watched him unwrap the entire cake and fold the creased paper carefully before holding it up to the light for closer inspection. It had to be carrot cake, according to its orange color. The tiny white flecks were undoubtedly coconut, the heavy frosting applied so liberally it had to be cream cheese. When he inserted it into his mouth, easily biting off half of it, she had to restrain herself from reaching forward and extracting a tantalizing morsel for herself.

When the complete cupcake disappeared entirely with one more wide-open chomp, and he leaned down to rummage in a small box, his face growing quite florid with his efforts, he produced another one as big as the first. He proceeded to unwrap as precisely as before, licking his fingers carefully before folding the paper perfectly. Sadie swallowed. She was really hungry.

She wondered what a person had to do to acquire some food. She blushed when the portly gentleman caught her eye and smiled. Surely he couldn't read her thoughts? Had she appeared as beggarly as she felt?

The ring of white hair around his red face reminded Sadie of a white bottle brush bent in a V-shape and Super-glued to his bald head. She wondered if his hair was like Mam's, each new white hair having a will of its own, in her words. He was just as round as a bowling pin, his shirt front gleaming with buttons, his little round knees protruding not too far away from his rotund stomach. To her embarrassment, he caught her eye again, chuckling out loud now. Quickly, she turned her head, desperately hoping he hadn't seen her close observation.

"You know, if looks alone could get one of these cupcakes, they'd be flying across the aisle," he chortled, reaching below the seat with a grimace and a grunt, producing a plastic container.

"Will you do me the honor of sharing my dessert? Compliments of Sir Walter Bartlett."

His little blue eyes were diamonds of merriment, topped by a shelf of bristling white eyebrows, small bottle brushes to match the one around his head. His nose was so small and red it almost eluded the observer, his mouth wide, hid by his sagging bulbous cheeks, filled to capacity with his dessert.

"If you want, I'll allow you one!"

"Oh, no! I couldn't. They're yours." Sadie said demurely.

"Of course not. I bring these on the train to share. Last time it was cherry croissants, which, I believe, are the lesser dessert, according to my way of judgment. But you know, never take a treat for granted, and the bakery on Second Street has a vast array. A vast array of yet untried possibilities."

He laughed so happily at the thought, a gurgle of laughter welled up in Sadie's own throat. Leaning across the aisle, he offered the box of cupcakes with a flourish and a sweeping motion that reminded Sadie of an orchestra conductor.

"Please accept my humble gift," he chortled.

Sadie chose one, then thanked him politely. "You shouldn't have offered them," she concluded.

"And why not? It only increases my pleasure of a fabulous dessert to be able to share it with such beauty as yours. Are you Hutterite? Or perhaps Mennonite?" he asked as quickly.

Sadie shook her head. "Neither. We're Amish."

Completely flummoxed, he shook his head in confusion. "Never heard of 'em."

Sadie barely heard his reply as she bit into the sweetness of the richly textured cupcake. She had never tasted better. She closed her eyes in appreciation to find Mr. Walter Bartlett leaning eagerly across the aisle in anticipation of her evaluation of his gift.

"Simply the best carrot cake I've ever tasted," she told him honestly.

Waving a short, puffy finger delightedly, he bent forward at the waist, then sat back, still waving his finger. "Aren't they? Aren't they, though? If I compare them to the pumpkin, however, I do remain a bit indecisive for the reason of the frosting. I believe the maple-flavored icing on the pumpkin cupcakes complements the pumpkin better than the cream cheese does justice to the carrot, pineapple, and coconut. Then there's always the question of the lack of raisins. I have yet to find a single raisin that I feel would elevate the essence of the carrot and pineapple so splendidly."

Suddenly a genuine sadness, almost grief, pulled down his happy features until he appeared unusually morose. "But, oh, the day they pulled the German chocolate! That was a hard day, indeed. I walked home that day, opened my umbrella to the pouring rain, so fitting to my loss, and I thought, Where? Where in all the world will they bake those little Dutch chocolate cakes topped with the brown sugar, coconut, and pecan topping? Since, however, I have come to grips with the lack of my favorite cake, substituting the coconut-covered devil's-food ones. In a way, they are a sad replacement, but it's all right. I'm no longer grieving."

He took a deep breath and sat up straight, squaring his shoulders in a brave and manly fashion, then turned to her with martyred eyes. "So hard, sometimes," he said quietly then.

Sadie nodded her sympathy, which brought a sniff of resignation. Mark stirred beside her, and Sadie turned instinctively, but he resumed breathing deeply, lost in his slumber.

"Husband?" Walter asked politely.

"Yes," Sadie nodded.

"May I ask your destination?"

"Barre, Oregon?"

"So far?"

Sadie nodded. "We're going to find my husband's brother, or siblings, we don't know how many will be there. His family was broken when the children were small, so he's trying to reunite."

Walter nodded happily. "Very good. Very good. Genealogy is such a wonderful thing. With computers now, you just Google everything. So easy." He nodded companionably.

Sadie could have told him about her lack of computer knowledge, but decided not to, the Amish and their ways being such a complete mystery. Besides, he had plenty of hardship in life with the baker pulling the German chocolate cakes from the shelves, therefore exposing poor Walter to such deprivation. Dear little round man. Sadie wanted to go home and find a good recipe and bake him two dozen cupcakes and present them to him warm from the oven.

God made such a wonderful variety of people, all so different and all so special. God must love people like Walter very much, their friendliness, their guilelessness. Likely that's what one of the disciples looked like when Jesus saw him beneath the olive tree, "and there was no guile in him." There was no deceit. No cunning. No sly behavior. That was the sort of person Jesus needed to follow him. The honest, the loving, the ones you could just hug and hug, like Dorothy. She was so full of fussing, spitting, complaining, but she was as guileless as this man. This rotund little Walter whose worst vice in life was the sweet desserts on a baker's shelf, who handed out compliments, wished everyone well minutes after he met them, and seemed unaware of life's darker side. He was much too busy being Walter Bartlett. Sir Walter Bartlett.

Sadie was sorry to see him weave his way down the aisle, clutching his plastic box of cupcakes, waving his fat little hand in her direction. She'd never see him again. But that was okay. He had touched her life with one wonderful carrot cupcake, a fat little fairy that touched her with his magical wand, filling her train ride with happiness.

Leaning over, she kissed Mark's cheek, waking him in the process.

"You smell like ... ?" he said softly. "What were you eating?"

Sadie giggled and kissed her husband. She loved him when he woke up with that sleepy "little boy" crease on his forehead.

"Oh, a fairy gave me a carrot cupcake with cream cheese icing."

They reached their destination with surprising swiftness, the hours on the train clicking by as quickly as the clicking of the rails. When they emerged with the flow of passengers, standing inside the station, awed at the city lights, the height of the skyscrapers, the smallness of two people alone in a foreign (or so it seemed) place, Sadie clutched Mark's hand as he called a taxi, then relaxed when the taxi arrived only a moment later.

Mark had a conversation with the driver, and they were whisked through rain-slick, light-filled streets, a kaleidoscope of brilliance and energy, honking horns, strains of music, shouting pedestrians, and people just moving, moving, moving. Into a hotel lobby, their steps muted on deep, plush carpeting. A few words to the man at the desk, while Sadie looked around at the gigantic green plants growing up toward the windowed ceiling. Was it just a glass ceiling?

The lights were low and people spoke softly. The women wore high heels, and she felt like the country mouse in the city, which she knew she was, though she sort of enjoyed the privilege, smiling back at inquisitive faces, holding Mark's hand, glad she was the wife of this tall, dark man who received his share of appreciative glances.

Sadie felt the hotel room was too costly. Was it really right to spend so much money on one night's sleep? This seriously bothered her conscience until Mark put it to rest, saying they could sleep in a motel for half the price, but, for safety's sake, he was not about to go looking for the seedy section of town with the cheap motels.

"We are Amish and look just different enough to attract attention, so I feel safer right here where folks don't need my wallet."

After that, Sadie relaxed and enjoyed her stay at the beautiful opulent hotel. The fixtures in the bathroom were gold, so she touched them tentatively, carefully, and wiped them clean after her shower just because she felt guilty leaving them water-stained. They weren't real gold, were they? She asked Mark, and he laughed for a long time, saying no, they didn't live in King Pharaoh's time. Sadie felt like a country mouse all over again and told him so. He laughed again and said that was a part of his attraction to her: her childish honesty, the way she spoke her mind.

"Even when I tell you cabinetmakers are good at their trade?" she asked eyeing him sharply.

A dark cloud passed over his face, covering his features, then left again when he took a deep breath. "Just forget it, Sadie," he said gruffly.

So she did and went to the window, pulling the braided, gold cord to draw the heavy brown drapes aside. She stood, her hands on the wide windowsill, and leaned her forehead on the cold glass, peering down on the streets below, all glossy and golden with light. How did men build a skyscraper? Who ever had enough audacity to attempt it, even? It was amazing. But she guessed as long as there were human beings on the earth, God would impart the wisdom to enable civilization to do whatever was good and necessary.

"Look at the Egyptians," she muttered softly without realizing she had said anything at all.

"What?" Mark asked from his pillows on the bed.

"Oh, I was just thinking about building skyscrapers. They always did. The Egyptians built those pyramids. A bunch of other things. How could they without equipment? It all seems so brave and...well, who thinks this stuff will even work? Who knows if the concrete and rods and bolts and stuff will hold? It's the same way with bridges. How can they go ahead and do this awesome amount of work and know it will work?"

Mark smiled. "It's called courage and faith. It's what I need in great quantities for tomorrow. Think about it, Sadie. Our tomorrow is not so different. We planned this, we're going through with it. We're hoping what we're doing will work. No going back now. With a bit of faith and well ... let's not be afraid. It'll be a spiritual bridge or skyscraper or whatever we want it to be. Imagine, Sadie the possibilities are so ... promising. And yet ... I'm so terribly afraid. Come to bed. You're my number one support in this bridge-building project."

Chapter 12

In the morning, Mark was quiet, his face taut with apprehension. He did not want a hearty breakfast so they had bagels and coffee brought to their room. Sadie noticed Mark's untouched bagel and the tremor in his hand when he reached for his coffee mug.

She held her peace, however, knowing he did not like any display of weakness, especially for her to notice and bring it to his attention. This she had learned the hard way, having her feelings hurt repetitively by blurting out a few unmasked words. The silence was broken only by the soft sound of lifted coffee mugs, swallowing, or a clearing of the throat, a napkin dabbed.

Finally Sadie asked, "You have the address?"

Mark nodded.

"So all we need is a taxi, right?"

"Right. Ready?"

There was no smile, no affirmation of his love, only a rapid thrust of his arms into his coat sleeves, a shrugging of his shoulders, and a quick pull on the gold door handle, stepping back, his eyebrows raised with impatience as she shrugged into her own wool coat.

The taxi driver was skilled, talkative, and knew the streets well. Before they had a chance to wonder how far it was, the taxi pulled to a fluid halt, the driver assuring them this was the proper address.

They peered out the right window, taking in the old brownstone, the Georgian façade, the enormous front door, the huge windows flanked by heavy wooden shutters. The stone on the exterior was aged to perfection, three stories in perfect symmetry, an old, sturdily built home kept well with loving care, standing the test of time.

The boxwoods surrounding the low windows were trimmed to precision, the inlaid stone walkway and steps leading to the front door a tribute to skilled masons.

A copper-plated sign by the post beside the stone walkway read "Jackson Peight, MD."

"He's...he's a doctor?" Sadie whispered.

Mark said nothing. Then, "Let's just leave."

Sadie shook her head. "Does he know you're coming?"

"Of course."

"Then we're going."

Sadie opened the door, stepped out of the cab, and breathed deeply. The smell of cold winter air mixed with city odors of traffic and asphalt, that indistinguishable no-name aroma that cloaked all cities. It was not offensive; it was a smell of energetic people and vehicles and food and grass and trees.

Mark followed and the taxi moved off, leaving them standing on the sidewalk looking up at the house as if it might swallow them alive. Sadie shivered, shaking off the foreboding that threatened to envelop her with its tentacles.

Mark's face was ashen. "I can't do this Sadie. Please. I'm nothing. He's an English man. A doctor. He's so much more than me. He'll laugh in my face."

Sadie turned, her hands going to his coat front, giving him a small tug the way she would to a child as a way of slight rebuke.

"Stop it. Those feelings are of the devil, in Mam's words. Don't listen to them. Come."

It was Sadie who led the way, who pressed her finger decisively to the ornate doorbell, who rocked back on her heels, lifted her chin, and smiled a much wider, braver smile than she felt.

A few seconds and the door opened, swung wide. A replica of Mark stood aside. An English replica, his black hair cut short, but the same eyes, the perfect mouth, a plaid button-down shirt tucked into relaxed jeans.

"Come in. You must be Mark."

Mark nodded, his eyes flat, expressionless. He offered his hand and received a firm grip of welcome.

"Jackson."

"Mark." Then, "Do you remember anything about me?"

"Oh, yes."

Mark introduced Sadie. Their coats and luggage were quickly whisked away by an older person Sadie could only guess was the housekeeper. They were led to a room with a fireplace crackling on the far side, facing beige and white chairs and sofas. Tables and various antique dressers holding tastefully displayed vintage items sat atop expensive rugs strewn across the worn oak flooring. Candles flickered on the mantle, lamps gave off a yellow pool of light, illuminating the room in small circles, as if they were a helpmeet to the stripes of sunlight stealing through the heavy wooden slats of the venetian blinds.

It was a lovely room. The touch of old decor mixed with new required an expert's eye. Jackson was a year younger than Mark, or was it two? How had he acquired so much at this young age?

Sadie smiled at appropriate times, answered questions, but was so involved in her assessment of the room, she feared she'd be impolite.

Jackson was effusive in his welcome, and Sadie could tell Mark was responding, the hooded, evasive light in his eye replaced by a spark of interest, a small smile that wouldn't be reined in too much longer.

They were joined by a heavy-set woman who floated into the room on waves of cologne, her dress swirling about her buxom figure in swirls of red. Her hair was dark, cut to just below her chin, her face wide with curiosity, taking an interest in everything surrounding her.

"Hi! I'm Jane. Just plain Jane," she laughed.

Introductions followed, Jackson pulling her large form against him closely. He introduced her as his wife of exactly six months and a few days, Jane dipping and beaming, exclaiming at the likeness of the two brothers.

They were all seated and served coffee and tea before Jackson settled in for a serious talk.

"Yes, Mark, I do remember. Not everything, likely, the way you do, but I remember the bad times probably just as distinctly as you. The thing, the one single thing, that's hardest for me is—how could she? How could our mother leave us hungry, uncared for, and simply drive away with that man? You know, it's funny, but I don't remember him at all. Can't imagine his face, his features. That act of a mother abandoning her children is one of the biggest hurdles of my life."

Mark nodded. "You feel as if there was something you did wrong. Like, perhaps if we had been better children, or we had done more, or looked better, she wouldn't have done it. Like *we* failed *her*."

Jackson watched Mark's face, incredulous. Finally he shook his head. "I find it unbelievable to hear you say that. I thought I was the only one who wrestled with that demon of my past."

Jane clucked her tongue, then laid her head reassuringly on her husband's shoulder and was instantly gathered into the safety of his arm.

Jackson continued. "It was tough. Still is. I allow, though, it's as tough as we let our past control us. The reason I studied medicine...it was a sort of block. The more I buried myself in my studies, the better I was. I was ravenous to learn, to move up the ladder, to excel, to prove myself worthy. I was far ahead in my classes, always. But it really was my saving grace. To stay busy, challenged, immerse myself—it just worked well. My foster parents had the money to put me through college, so I was very fortunate, I realize that. My dad is a surgeon. My mom is the greatest person on the face of the earth. I'm serious. I don't know why the Lord smiled on me the way he did the day I was put in the foster system, but he did. They are my parents, my stronghold. It's amazing to this day."

Jane nodded, her eyes wide with emotion.

Sadie shrank inwardly when Mark cleared his throat and said gruffly, "Yeah, well."

There was a space of silence where Sadie watched nervously, knowing Mark was fighting that internal battle of feeling worthless. He drank coffee, ran a hand across the knee of his trousers, fought to rise up against the tide of black nothingness his mother had pitched him into the day she left.

Then Mark lifted his ravaged eyes. "Yeah, well, you're lucky."

"I know that," Jackson responded sincerely.

Then Mark launched into his own tale of the foster care system. The abuse, the existence of a loveless world, the hunger for stability, the batting around from home to home, unwanted, used, the drugs, the alcohol, and finally, his grandfather, the reason he became a member of the Old Order Amish church.

Jane got up and extracted a box of Kleenex from a heavy holder, dabbed her eyes daintily, clucked, and gasped, shaking her pretty head from side to side as Mark related his story.

"Wow," Jackson breathed, finally. "What kept you sane?"

"I know what it's like to walk on the edge, let me tell you," Mark said, with a harsh laugh.

"Have you gone for counseling?"

"Oh, yes. A lot of good, positive feelings about myself and my past have come to light through counseling. It's a good thing. God imparts wisdom to those people, I don't doubt. I probably would not have made it through my early twenties if it wouldn't have been for counseling."

Sadie nodded.

"And Sadie."

Sadie turned to Mark, a glad light in her eyes, met his own, ignited, but as was the Amish custom, they remained seated apart, awkward and ill at ease with any public display of affection.

"I'll have to tell you how we met," Sadie offered. She began a colorful account of the wintery day with Nevaeh lying in the snow, desperately flagging down the cattle truck that had been moving too fast to begin with. Mark laughingly explaining when you drive a rural Montana roadway, you do not expect to meet a half-dead horse and a very pretty girl in the middle of a snowstorm.

Jackson and Jane were delighted, and the conversation took a lighter turn for awhile, until Mark related the demise of their mother, the dark valley of guilt that finally brought her to her knees, the peace she had before meeting her Savior.

Jackson kept shaking his head, repeating, "Unbelievable. Absolutely." The brothers struggled to restrain their emotions, then got up and left the room together, Jackson turning to Jane, saying thickly, "We'll be back. Why don't you show Sadie the rest of the house?"

Jane was just the most lovely personality, Sadie soon decided. She was bubbly without being overbearing, humble in showing Sadie her home, and genuinely interested in Sadie's upbringing, her family, and the Amish culture.

They ended up in the surprisingly small kitchen, lined with tall dark cupboards and a bar with comfortable bar stools. Sadie perched while Jane served her another cup of ginger tea and made grilled roast beef and goat cheese sandwiches with spicy mustard and olives.

"I love these sandwiches," she announced happily.

"I probably should have waited till dinner, but, oh, well. You knew Timothy was coming, didn't you? We're all going out to dinner later today."

When the doorbell rang late that afternoon, the talking still had not ceased. Like the floodgates of a dam built into a levee, the river of words burst through and continued to flow, surrounding the two brothers with a sense of stability, closure, and certainly memories, both unpleasant and downright absurd, coming to light. Each was examined with a blood brother's viewpoint and discarded or put away, leaving in its wake a new kind of peace, threaded with uncertainty, perhaps, but a peace, nevertheless.

As the afternoon wore on, shoes came off, feet were elevated on stools, pillows put behind backs, accompanied by a sense of brotherhood swirling about both of them, infusing their laughter, discovering how much alike they really were. They both loved fresh-squeezed lemonade without too much sugar, slept on their stomachs, had huge appetites, and had a cowlick on the left side of their foreheads.

Finally Jackson looked at the clock. "He said he'd be … be here around 4:00."

"How much do you know about him?" Mark asked.

"Not much. He's the only one who responded. You know Beaulah was killed in a car accident, in November of '08?"

"Really?"

"Yes. She was hit by a fuel truck when she pulled out of a street in town. She lived in Ohio somewhere. She was 24 years old. Not married. I know very little about any of the others. I don't know, maybe it's just as well."

"I agree. So, you never feel as if you're being sucked into a giant whirlpool?" Mark asked suddenly with urgency, as if he needed to clear this with Jackson before Timothy arrived.

Jackson looked up sharply. "Why would I?"

"I mean, don't you have days when you feel everyone is against you, and it's just a matter of time until you can't take another day of battling these feelings of inadequacy? Of not being enough?"

For a long while, Jackson said nothing, leaning forward, his elbows on his knees, staring at the floor between his feet. Then, "I guess I do."

"Jackson!" Jane exclaimed.

"No, nothing serious, my darling," Jackson said, sitting up and rubbing her soft shoulder with affection.

"It's just that, yes, I know what you're talking about. When that empty feeling does threaten, which is less and less, now, I put on my shoes and go running. I run for as many as seven or eight miles. It's wonderful therapy."

Mark nodded in perfect agreement. "I ran a lot."

There was a distinct bell-like tone, and they all looked at each other.

"Timothy."

Jackson nodded, went to the door.

Involuntarily, Jane touched up her hair, sat straight, while Sadie tucked a few stray hairs behind her white covering. What would Timothy say?

Jackson returned, followed by a strapping youth, his long, unkempt, dirty-blond hair hanging over his eyes, his ears, and well down into the hood of his gray sweatshirt. Loose jeans hung sloppily below the waistline of his boxers, the hem torn and scuffed, the threads gray from contact with the ground.

His eyes weren't visible at first glance, until he picked up a hand and pushed his hair back, then everyone could see that they were as dark brown as his two brothers'. He had the same perfect mouth, but his teeth were brown and crooked, decay spreading across the neglected grayish-white objects in his mouth.

His cheeks were packed with deep scars where acne had taken its toll, the worst of it gone now that the teen years were behind him. He smiled an unsteady smile, an unsure separating of his lips that had nothing to do with his eyes.

"Hey."

He shook hands limply, a mere sliding of a sweated palm against his two brothers', a nodding in Jane's and Sadie's direction, his eyes glancing nervously at his feet, a small cough, a sniffling sound before tossing his hair to the side again.

"How y' doin?" he muttered in the general direction of the women.

"Good. Good. It's nice to meet you!" Jane said effusively.

Sadie murmured something, she wasn't sure what, her throat swelling with the same emotion she felt that day when Nevaeh stumbled out of the woods, down the embankment, and crumpled her pitiful body onto the road, surrounded by that cold unrelenting snow.

Here was a youth surround by a cold, unforgiving, joyless existence. Sadie sensed in him the same hopelessness, the same victim of circumstances that had shaped his life so much beyond his control. She bit down on her lower lip, averted her eyes as goose bumps raced up her arms and across her back.

"Sit down, Timothy," Jackson offered.

"It's Tim."

The words were spoken defensively, that self-conscious sniff following the words, as if the sniff sent the words out and supported them.

"Okay, Tim. So…you came. That's good."

"Yeah, well. I ain't staying."

"But you will have dinner with us?"

"Yeah."

The first awkward silence of the day followed.

"So, you...want to tell us about yourself?"

"No."

Mark said that was all right, he'd go first, and proceeded to tell Tim his life's story. He got as far as the Amish uncle, when Tim lifted his head, the anger creating dark, brown fury, turning his eyes into blazing outlets of raw anger.

"I hate him."

Mark's eyes opened wide. "You know who I'm talking about?"

"Yeah."

"Were you raised Amish?"

"Yeah."

"Surely not by him."

"No, but I know what he did to you."

"How?"

"Word gets around."

"Who raised you?"

"Aunt Hannah. The old maid. Till I turned 16. Then I left. Went to New York City. Big mistake. Came back. Hannah was dead. Heart attack. I stayed in the area among the Amish but never really went back. Guess I'm half-Amish. Remember all of it. It's good, in a way."

He shrugged his shoulders, picked at the hole in his jeans, pulled at a thread, then rolled it between his thumb and forefinger, unsure of what to do with it before straightening his back to put it in his pocket, blinking with a terrible embarrassment. As he lowered his head, the curtain of long hair obliterated him into the safety of his shell.

Sadie had to restrain herself from going to him, peering under that hair and telling him he was just fine exactly the way he was.

"So, what do you do?" Mark asked.

"I'm a roofer."

With that he actually straightened up, flipped his hair back, and looked directly at Mark, a tiny spark of pride passing quickly through his brown eyes.

"In Illinois?"

Tim nodded. "I'm a good one. Boss said."

Again he lowered his face, picked at a scab on his arm.

"I'm sure you are, you've got some shoulders on you for a...What are you? Twenty? Twenty-one?" Jackson asked.

"Twenty-two, I guess. You know they never found my birth certificate. Had a...mess when I applied for my driver's license."

In the course of the evening, they found out Timothy had a steady job, but that was the only stability in his life. He lived from one paycheck to the next and ran with a questionable group of friends who led him from one bad habit to another. But they were the only real form of love and friendship he knew.

Sadie listened, watched, and observed his total lack of support, his free-floating existence, before sitting beside him on the sofa, reaching out a hand, placing it tentatively on his gray sweatshirt.

"Tim, did you ever consider returning to your roots? You know when your mother passed away, you were the only one of her children she really worried about. She mentioned you so many times, asking us to find you. It was her dying wish. I think of all the deep regrets she carried with her, you were the worst. In her own way, she loved you the most."

Tim shrugged, sniffed. "Yeah. Well, Hannah loved me. Sort of. She died. My mother's dead. So that's as far as that goes. Poof!"

He illustrated with a rapid opening of his fingers, a short, derisive laugh, followed by a backward movement of his shoulders, and then he slumped against the back of the sofa, his long legs splayed in front of him, tapping his feet in time to remembered music.

Well, he was up and on his feet, Sadie thought. Sick and thin and maybe dying, yes, but on his feet! He had, in his own way, admitted that his real love was Aunt Hannah, his substitute mother, and not in the sort of life he led.

"Would you allow Mark and me to try?" Sadie asked, turning to look at Mark as she spoke.

Mark's mouth literally fell open. He stared at Sadie in a way she knew was without total comprehension.

"You're not my mom."

"I'm your sister-in-law."

There. She had reached out and stroked Nevaeh under the unkempt mane, where her poor neck was so thin and scrawny, the hairs so matted and pitiful. Now she had reached out to Tim, offering her love.

Was it too much? Too soon? Would she drive him away?

The foot kept tapping. The hands were jammed deep into the pocket of his sweatshirt. His shoulders hunched. He sniffed, then coughed. He scratched his stomach, smoothed the sweatshirt, then looked at Sadie. Really looked at her.

Then he smiled, a small one, but a smile, no matter what he would choose to call it. Sadie could feel the leaning of Nevaeh, a sort of turning her neck in her direction, as if to let her know she appreciated the gesture of affection.

"I guess you are."

His voice was small, stripped of its coolness, the mask of bravado he wore every day, leaving his words as vulnerable as a newborn baby, completely dependent on someone else's care. Babies did best on their mother's breast, but if that wasn't possible, they could thrive easily on a substitute of another human being feeding them a good formula.

"Mark is your real brother. You were raised Amish. We are your family. Your real family," Sadie went on.

Jackson and Jane exchanged a knowing look, a smart doctor who could see the miracle unfolding before his eyes. He also knew Sadie had gone far enough; this would take time.

As if on cue, Sadie backed off. "Well, Tim, you know where we live. If you decide to change your life, you know where we are."

Tim nodded, a strange melancholy landing on his features, clarifying the desperate sadness in his brown eyes.

"Yeah, well I'm . . . guess you'd say caught in a spider web of my own making. I'll go back home. I'll let you know. Give you my cell phone number."

He sniffed again, self-consciously, and Sadie lifted triumphant eyes to Mark.

Chapter 13

When they left the brownstone on River Drive, Sadie could tell Mark had left a sizable chunk of his worst childhood baggage behind, hopefully buried beneath the city streets, never to be picked up again. His step was light, he was ravenously hungry, he teased Sadie with a new lighthearted attitude she had never seen before. They ate sandwiches at the train station, they ate on the train, and they ate when the train arrived at the station in Montana. As Sadie watched her husband, she could only guess at the price he had paid to make that visit into the unknown, reminding herself yet again that he didn't have that strong system of support from a normal home life the way she did.

When their life resumed its usual rhythm, Sadie thanked God they had gone, returned, and met Timothy and Jackson. Doing so had instilled a sense of worth in Mark. Was it because Mark had filled Timothy's bottle with Jell-o water? Had helped Jackson eat his oatmeal? Had found a new sense of having done something right? In that time of darkness and pain, had he somehow found that in all situations some good can come of it? Surely he had.

This spring in his step, this light in his eye was a miracle. Sadie had been afraid that Jackson being a doctor would intimidate Mark, lowering his fragile self-esteem, but it had worked the opposite way. Mark was so proud of Jackson and so concerned about Timothy, a new sense of purpose surrounded him.

The winter came early, its harshness arriving along with it. The cold was mind-numbing, the thermometer hovering below zero every night in spite of the sun's feeble rays during the day. Snow enveloped everything. It clung to pines and firs, placing a huge burden on the sturdy limbs with its weight. It was not unusual to be awakened during the night by the sound of a gunshot, jolting Sadie out of a deep sleep, before realizing it was only the sound of branches snapping beneath the snow's weight. Mark said ice and snow were nature's pruner, something Sadie had never thought about. She guessed they were.

Dorothy was not doing well at work, which caused Sadie a few moments of anxiety. Her hip was bothering her quite a bit, and her usual quick movements turned into painful hobbles, her mouth a tight line of determination. Erma Keim accosted her at every turn, telling Dorothy to go to the chiropractor, which, of course, was like igniting dry tinders.

"That quack ain't touchin' this hip. Let him crack backs and collect his 30 dollars. He ain't gittin' a red cent off'n me."

And that was that. Erma told Sadie if that thick-headed old lady wanted to be that way, then she'd just have to live in her pain. She guaranteed that Dorothy's hip and pelvis were out of line, and if Doctor Tresore was allowed to take an X-ray and adjust her a few times, she'd be so much better. Sadie nodded agreement, but added that maybe Dorothy's hip joint was actually deteriorating and she needed a replacement, which gave Erma so much hope of running the ranch kitchen all by herself that she immediately stopped harassing Dorothy about the chiropractor, leaving an aura of peace in the ranch kitchen.

Richard Caldwell was getting ready to host the annual Christmas banquet, as usual, spending more time in the kitchen, Barbara joining him as they pored over recipe books. He watched Dorothy limping between the refrigerator and the pantry before putting an elbow to his wife's side. When she looked up at him, he shoved his jaw in Dorothy's direction, shaking his head in concern.

"Your hip bothering you, Dorothy?" he boomed.

The sound of his voice alarmed Dorothy to the extent that she dropped a five-pound block of Colby Jack cheese on the linoleum, then snorted impatiently.

"Now look what you made me do, Richard Caldwell! No, my hip ain't bothering me at all."

Erma pursed her lips and raised her eyebrows, a hand going to her unruly red hair, leaving a trail of flour and bits of pie crust in its wake as she returned to crimping her apples pies. Sadie stirred brown sugar into the baby carrots and said nothing.

Later that evening when she was getting her coat and scarf from the hook on the wall, Dorothy approached her after Erma had gone to talk to Barbara about a Jell-o dessert. Dorothy's eyes were mirrors of humility, tears brimming on her lower lashes.

"Sadie, if'n I tell you what's bothering me, you ain't gonna tell anyone, right? Least-ways not Erma."

"Of course not, Dorothy. I'm just afraid you're going to have to go to the hospital and have surgery."

"No, no, no. It's not my hip."

Dorothy raised herself on her tiptoes and held a short hand to her mouth. Sadie bent her head slightly to receive the long-awaited secret.

"It's corns. I got them corns all over my toes. I bin using them little adhesive tapes, you know. Those Dr. Scholl's. They don't help a bit. I got 'em so bad, I can hardly walk. The Dollar General is letting me down so bad. You know, if them shoes were worth what I say they are, I wouldn't get corns, would I?"

"Oh, my, Dorothy. Corns are extremely painful. I know just what to do. You can have them removed at the doctor's office, or you can use tea tree oil. Just dab it on with a Q-tip for a few weeks."

Dorothy nodded, her eyes downcast.

"It's heartbreaking. The Dollar General is letting me down so bad. I can't buy any more shoes there. In fact, I'm not sure them Ritz crackers is fit to make my chocolate-coated crackers anymore."

Her withdrawal from Dollar General was obviously quite painful, so Sadie assured her it was okay to change stores. Suddenly she had a great idea, assessing Dorothy's round stature and small feet. Those Crocs everyone wore! The perfect footwear for Dorothy. Sturdy, wide, slip-proof.

"Dorothy! I have the perfect idea for you. Crocs! I'll go to town with you, and we'll fit you into a completely trouble-free pair of shoes. Your corns won't be touching anything and will heal in no time at all."

It was love at first sight. Dorothy slid her poor, corn-addled feet into a pair of sturdy Crocs, stood up, and began walking down the aisle of the local shoe store, her head bent, concentrating on the placement of each foot, so much like a small child. Slowly a beatific grin spread across her face as she stopped, turned, and walked back to Sadie.

"It's like walkin' on air. An' I don't have to bend down and tie 'em. Oh, it's a miracle, Sadie. The Lord heard my prayers and took mercy on me and…" She lowered her voice and hissed behind a palm, "…my corns!"

Sadie nodded happily. There were no brown or black ones for Dorothy. She was undecided between bright pink or lime green, then settled for a furious shade of purple.

"Next time I'll get the lime green."

When she opened her wallet to hand over a crisp 20 and a 10, she pursed her lips, but told Sadie quietly that wasn't so dear if you counted the comfort. And when they drove steadily past the Dollar General without stopping, Dorothy shook her head with great sadness and wisdom.

"See, that's what the world's coming to. You pay for a cheap product, that's what you get. And you know what else I thought about? They sell them Dr. Scholl's corn adhesives *right beside* them shoes. They know whoever buys them shoes will return for corn thingys."

She arrived at the ranch the following morning, no limp in sight, her purple Crocs flashing with each step. Erma asked what happened to her limp. Dorothy said she went to the chiropractor, winking broadly at Sadie behind Erma's back. Dorothy's gait was new and refreshing, rocking slightly from side to side, the shape of her Crocs making her appear so much more like a lovable little duck.

✻ ✡ ✻

There was no phone call, no warning, not even a letter. Just the sound of an aging motor driving an old Jeep up the driveway, making its way steadily through the deep snow. And then, nothing. The rusting Jeep just sat at the end of the walkway. No doors opened, no lights blinked or horn blared.

Mark went to the washhouse, slipped into his boots, and shrugged his coat on quickly before making his way down the walks. Sadie watched behind the half-drawn curtains as he bent his tall form to peer through the window. The interior light was too dim for Sadie to see who the person was, so when the washhouse door slammed shut and she heard Mark speaking to someone, she immediately put down the book she was reading and watched the door to the kitchen. It was Timothy.

"Here's Tim!" Mark announced.

Tim stood just inside the door beside the refrigerator, a timid smile playing across his features. Sadie closed the space between them, hoping he would extend a hand, but there was no move to do anything at all. Definitely no hug. Not a handshake.

"Hey."

That was all. That noncommittal "Hey."

"Hello, Tim."

She bit off the last part of his name just in time and sighed with relief, watching his face, the way he sagged at the hips, a certain lowering of himself as if to convey his feelings of inadequacy. Well, here he was. All six feet of complexity. The challenge was staggering.

Too cheerily, Mark asked, "So? What's up? You here for a visit? Are you here to stay? Did you drive that Jeep the whole way?"

Tim actually smiled, revealing all the crowded decaying teeth, then quickly put up a hand, painfully aware of his teeth.

He said, "I'm just here. Work's slow. Thought I'd come check out where you guys live."

Sadie nodded, smiled. *"Kannsht doo Amish schwetsa?"* (Can you speak Dutch?)

Tim smiled only with his eyes, his hand going up to cover his mouth. *"Ya, ich kann."* (Yes I can.)

"Alles?" (Everything?)

Again, a smile with his eyes, a nod.

So the conversation switched easily to the Dutch language. Sadie put on the coffeepot, then brought out the square Tupperware container of molasses cookies.

"Did you have supper?" she asked.

He shook his head, swallowed as he eyed the molasses cookies. He was obviously very hungry.

Quickly Sadie moved from the stove to the refrigerator and back again, heating the leftover chili from their evening meal. She placed a few squares of cornbread on the stoneware plate, put aluminum foil over it, and turned the oven on. She brought out some saltines, applesauce, and slices of dill pickles, arranging them on the table with a glass of cold water. Conversation lagged as he lowered his head and ate ravenously, refilling his bowl, crumbling more saltines, spreading the cornbread liberally with soft butter.

"Didn't have time to stop to get something to eat," he murmured.

Sadie knew he had more than likely been penniless, unable to pay for even a single meal. She said nothing, just shook her head with understanding. All they really got out of him that first evening was that he'd be there for awhile, check out the land, see if he liked the people.

"You mean, the Amish or the English?" Mark asked.

The question caught him by surprise, so he gave no real answer. After eating almost everything on the table, he could not stay awake after driving so many hours. Mark showed him to the guest room, the upstairs bathroom that was almost finished except for the trim work, and helped him adjust the wick on the kerosene lamp, providing a lighter for him.

"Don't need a lighter. I have one."

"If you smoke, Tim, we expect you to quit if you want to stay with us, okay?"

Mark said it quietly but firmly. Tim nodded but said nothing.

Sadie was cleaning up the few dishes when Mark came back down, a light in his eyes.

"Well, Sadie, my love, he's here! Are you sure you're going to be okay with this?"

Sadie stopped rinsing the chili bowl and said quietly, "I am, Mark. I may not always be, but, yes, I'm willing to give it a try."

"We may be in for the roughest ride of our life."

"You think so?"

"I know so. This young man is…well, this will take a lot of effort, a lot of wisdom, and whatever else we can scratch together to help him straighten out his life."

Sadie nodded soberly.

Since they both had to leave for work the following morning, Sadie left a note and hoped they could trust him with Wolf and the horses.

When Jim's pickup bounced up the drive in the evening, the Jeep was gone, and Sadie raced into the house, becoming breathless in the process, looking for Tim, calling his name, but he was nowhere to be found.

They were deeply disappointed, eating their evening

meal in near silence, wondering why he had stayed, only to leave again. There was not a trace, no clothes, no duffel bag, the bed made neatly, the quilt tucked beneath the pillows as if Sadie had made the bed herself.

Mark sighed, then told Sadie what he had said about his smoking. "Do you suppose that was the reason? Like I just said too much too soon. I didn't want to appear like some holier-than-thou, but still...I don't want him here with any of his old habits."

Sadie nodded. "It's tough. And we're so young. We certainly don't have any experience raising teenagers. We're barely out of that stage ourselves."

"I am!"

"Well, yes, you're ancient. Going on 30, which is alarming."

That was as close to lighthearted banter as they could manage, wondering all evening where Tim had gone and why. They discussed his teeth, and Mark said there was no doubt in his mind that poor boy did not have the proper nutrition he so badly needed as a small child.

"I can't imagine how he ever became as tall and well built as he is," he concluded.

"Aunt Hannah."

Mark nodded.

That night they both lay sleepless and restless, wondering what had happened. The next morning Sadie stayed home from the ranch to make candy and cookies for Christmas, it being only a few weeks away.

Mark loved chocolate-coated "anything," which had become a private joke between them. She had acquired plenty of coating chocolate, and with a song of Christmas in her heart, set about melting it in a large stainless steel bowl on top of a pot of boiling water, noting carefully Mam's handwritten warning on the directions: *Don't leave on burner after water has been boiling for a few minutes. Overheated chocolate will become clumpy.*

"A few minutes"? Typical Mam. Not two minutes or five minutes. Who knew what "a few" meant?

Should she wait until Mam arrived? She had promised to spend the forenoon with Sadie, bringing Anna, the only sister who had off work. She sighed her disappointment when she saw the horse and buggy pull into the driveway and only Anna hopped off, pulling the reins through the silver ring and knotting them expertly.

Sadie ran to the door, yelling to her sister. "Need help, Anna?"

"No, I'm fine."

Sadie shivered, closed the door, heated the coffee, and waited eagerly for Anna to arrive at the house. When the washhouse door banged closed, she greeted her eagerly, inquiring about Mam.

"She never comes over here when she says she will," Sadie moaned.

"She said to tell you she's sorry, but Fred Ketty's having a quilting for the teacher's quilt, and it has to be done by Christmas. She said Abe Marian started the whole project back in October, but with those five little ones, she can't accomplish much in a week. Don't know why she took it on. Why doesn't she let the older women tackle it?"

Sadie shook her head, a wry grin spreading across her features. "That's Abe Marian."

That was the way of it, the Amish community woven together with its intricate ways, personalities, individualities carefully held together by the Master's hand. Each one was known by the others, accepted, loved, sometimes talked about or clucked over, but forgiven in spite of small blunders and, often, large ones.

Anna was looking so pale, her skin was translucent, narrow blue veins threading their way up past the delicate skin around her beautiful eyes, the dark shadows beneath them a grayish-white. When she turned to go into the kitchen after hanging up her coat, her waist was alarmingly narrow, her dress folds hanging limply over her nonexistent hips. She folded her angular form into a kitchen chair, a mere whisper of her former self.

"Anna."

"What?"

Her dark eyes looked to Sadie, bearing defiance, guilt, fear, and what else? Desperation? Acknowledgment of starving herself?

"You … you're not looking well."

A shrugging of the shoulders. A waving of the hand. A dismissal.

"Are you eating okay? Throwing up?"

No use hiding anything. Sadie had nothing to lose this morning, this ghost of Anna's former self seated at her kitchen table.

"Oh, be quiet, Sadie. I'm here for two seconds and you're already starting in on me."

"Somebody has to. Mam and Dat won't say a word about anything. Neither will Leah and Rebekah. Everyone at home just lets you go right ahead killing yourself."

Sadie's words were pointed, harsh, spoken loudly, the words coming slowly and thickly like a predator stalking prey already caught in a steel-jawed trap.

"Shut up!" Anna screamed suddenly, lunging at Sadie, pummeling her with weak, white fists, propelled only by her anxious fury. It took Sadie completely by surprise.

The blows rained on her shoulders, her arms, her back, Anna's face a twisted caricature of her normal features.

"Anna! Please don't."

She closed her eyes, cringed, turned her back. Somewhere she heard a door opening, as if in the distance. The blows stopped.

"Hey, hey, what's goin' on here?"

Timothy! He had an arm around Anna's waist, pinning the stick-thin arms to her wasted body as she tried weakly to escape.

"Sadie, help me! Let me go! Get away from me!" Even her cries were weak and pitiful, the meowing sounds of a starved kitten begging for its mother.

Sadie adjusted her apron, smoothed back her hair, and told Timothy to release her. Anna slumped onto a chair, bent over, and sobbed, her head in her trembling white hands. Timothy stood, his hands in his pockets, his shoulders squared, and looked at Anna with an expression as raw and vulnerable as Sadie had ever seen. It was pity, pure and simple. He understood. He met Sadie's eyes, raised his eyebrows in question. She shook her head, raised her own. Suddenly Timothy was on his knees, holding Anna's fluttering, blue-veined hands in his own, murmuring, stilling them.

"It can't be that bad. Nothing could happen that makes you want to beat up..."

He lifted questioning eyes to Sadie. "Your sister?"

Sadie nodded, grimacing.

Timothy gave Anna's hands a small tug. "Give her a break. It can't be that bad."

Shuddering sobs were the only answer. Tim stood, stepped back, and shrugged his shoulders.

"*Voss iss letts mitt ess?*" (What is wrong with her?)

"She's … anorexic. Bulimic." Sadie mouthed the words.

Tim understood. His eyes opened wide, his eyebrows lifted, he puckered his mouth into a low whistle, shaking his head as if he realized the sad significance of it. Slowly he rolled his eyes to the melting chocolate, the shadow of a grin reaching his features. Sadie looked, caught his meaning, held a hand to her mouth to stifle the smile beginning there, her eyes betraying her merriment. Their eyes caught, the humor a piece of shared chocolate, a bond acknowledged, accepted, a trust crackling to life.

Tim became self-conscious, then, shuffled to the recliner and sat in it, staring out the window. Sadie went to the light stand, pulled at two tissues and handed them to Anna, who grabbed them and blew her nose without lifting her head. Finally she raised herself, her eyes brimming, averting them from Sadie before looking in Timothy's direction, the anger consuming her again.

"Who is he?" she croaked.

"Mark's brother, Tim. Timothy Peight."

Tim cleared his throat.

"Tim, this is my sister Anna."

Tim stood up as Anna lifted her eyes to his face. "Hello, Anna, I'm pleased to meet you."

Anna said nothing, her glare the only response. Sadie bit back words of rebuke, but they rushed to the surface again when Anna blurted out, "Oh, go brush your teeth."

Chapter 14

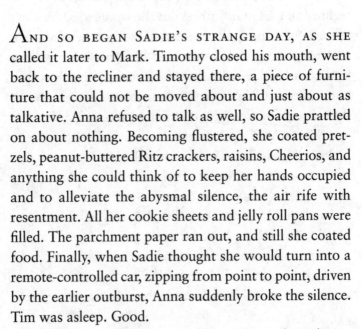

AND SO BEGAN SADIE'S STRANGE DAY, AS SHE called it later to Mark. Timothy closed his mouth, went back to the recliner and stayed there, a piece of furniture that could not be moved about and just about as talkative. Anna refused to talk as well, so Sadie prattled on about nothing. Becoming flustered, she coated pretzels, peanut-buttered Ritz crackers, raisins, Cheerios, and anything she could think of to keep her hands occupied and to alleviate the abysmal silence, the air rife with resentment. All her cookie sheets and jelly roll pans were filled. The parchment paper ran out, and still she coated food. Finally, when Sadie thought she would turn into a remote-controlled car, zipping from point to point, driven by the earlier outburst, Anna suddenly broke the silence. Tim was asleep. Good.

"Sadie, I...didn't mean to hurt you. I don't know what got into me. My life is so plain down weird, I can't handle it. I was doing much better, felt like eating, and didn't hate myself quite as much. Then Sheryl broke up with Neil. Now I'm back to where I started. Square one."

Sadie said nothing. Waited.

"See, Merv ... You know Merv?"

Sadie nodded.

"He's really a nice guy. I prayed and prayed for God's will. I know he will ask me, eventually, and I would do well to become his wife. But ... "

"It's Neil." It wasn't a question; Sadie only filled in the obvious.

Miserably, Anna nodded. "I can't control Neil, I can't control my future. The only thing I can control is my figure. And, I am finally thin enough now. I no longer feel fat."

Sadie shook her head. Slowly, Anna's hand crept out, one finger unfolded, the tip coming down on a speck of chocolate. Lifting it, she held it to her tongue, then closed her mouth, tucking her hands below her armpits as if to keep them from straying for more chocolate.

Sadie watched her, lifted a chocolate-covered pretzel, still warm and a bit sticky, to her mouth.

"Mmm," she said, closing her eyes.

Anna swallowed.

"Go ahead, Anna. Eat one. Eat the whole cookie-sheet full."

Anna laughed, a small, hard, sound.

"So is Neil paying attention to you?"

Miserable eyes, then a miserable voice, talking, talking. It was all a matter of time. He would, eventually, come around. He would settle down. She could help him by dating him, just being with him. But he....

Her voice trailed off into a state so abjectly pitiful, Sadie stopped all movement and strained to hear the whispered words.

She thought he.... In whispered words, the root of her trouble was spilled over the table, the horror curdling Sadie's stomach with its wrongness.

"No!" The plastic spatula she was holding sliced through the air and smacked the table with a resounding splat.

"Oh, no, you don't, Anna. Believe me when I say this. It's not what he wants. It's not what you want. He means you nothing good. You have *got* to get rid of this guy, this Neil."

Tim stirred, sat up, the recliner rocking as he released the handle. Quietly, with Mark's cat-like grace, he came to the kitchen, went to the sink, and helped himself to a large tumbler of water. Anna's eyes went to Timothy, assessing the long, dirty-blond hair, the tall, lean figure, the loose jeans. Did she notice his scarred cheeks? His decaying teeth? The teeth, definitely, she thought. Her face was unreadable.

Tim came to the table, folded himself into a chair, raised his eyes to Sadie's, and asked if he could help himself. She nodded, still watching Anna's face. Tim threw a whole chocolate-covered Ritz cracker into his mouth, chewed twice, and swallowed, reached for another, then another. Anna swallowed, watching him. He ate six, then asked if they had plenty of milk. Sadie nodded, and he moved to the refrigerator to fill his large glass with milk, guzzling all of it in five or six large gulps, promptly reaching for more crackers coated with chocolate.

"I hope you're going to pay rent," Anna remarked sourly.

"Think I should?" Tim asked, meeting her gaze squarely, challenging her. Infuriating her, Sadie observed.

"Yes, I think you should," Anna said.

"You know, it's absolutely none of your business."

Sadie winced. Touché. Immediately she changed the subject to something trivial, her words tumbling over each other in her need to smooth things over, but was rewarded by the lack of even a single comment. Tim ate a chocolate-covered pretzel, then tried the raisins, Anna watching him with an increasingly nauseated expression.

"You know," Tim said, slowly putting Anna on the edge of her seat, bristling with defense at the mere sound of his voice. "Couldn't help overhearing your little conversation there. Looks like you got some guy trouble."

He paused. "Is it true, Anna?"

Anna's face flamed, and she ignored the use of her name.

"Like I said, Anna. I couldn't help overhearing. Sounds as if you have some problems. Bill. His name Bill?"

Anna could not have been more contemptuous, her eyes flashing as she faced him squarely. "I wouldn't say anything if I couldn't hear."

Tim laughed easily, then, his hand going to his mouth to cover the offending teeth. "Oh, I can hear all right. You just weren't speaking very plainly."

"I was, too!"

Tim shook his head.

Where did he come up with this sort of audacity? Sadie wondered. This poor self-conscious individual who could barely lift his head when they first met. With Anna he was at ease, completely in control with a sort of teasing banality. Was it Anna's vulnerability? She was a scarred, troubled creature like himself. Whatever it was, Sadie realized he enjoyed Anna's company or he would have left. Or perhaps he suspected he knew how to help her.

"As I was saying, you can't have this Bill guy..."

"Not Bill. Neil," she broke in, quickly.

"Believe me, this guy does not want you. Not in the right way. I know. I've been there. You don't want him.

He's no good."

"What do you know about him? Nothing. Why don't you just stay out of it?"

"Okay, I will."

And he took down his coat and went outside, leaving Anna peering out the window, turning her head to watch as he slipped and slid down the sidewalks to the barn, his arms waving wildly to keep his balance.

"Now where's he going?"

"I have no clue."

Sadie smiled to herself, watching Anna. She was clearly frustrated but curious now. They ate a lunch of turkey, tomato, onion, and lettuce sandwiches on Kaiser rolls, with mustard, of course. Sadie knew Anna would not touch the sandwiches if there was as much as a speck of mayonnaise on them, the fat-laden condiment containing the ability to put 10 pounds on her.

After she had actually eaten half of a sandwich, Anna's mood shifted. She became lighthearted, talkative. She related incidents of her weekends, who was dating whom, the pitiful creature that Sheryl had become after breaking up with Neil, hardly ever coming to the Sunday evening singings, how cute Reuben was, so certain the whole world was his, driving Charlie and that brand new buggy. When Sadie wondered at the ability of Charlie to keep up with the youth's horses, Anna laughed, telling her old Charlie could still kick up his heels with the best of them. They were laughing when Tim came back into the house, but stopped when they saw his expression.

"Hey, Sadie, I hate to trouble you, but I had the barn door open, decided to clean out the stable, and this...this yellow...sort of yellow...horse came stumbling into the barn. Do you have a horse loose somewhere? He acted as if he's been around the barn."

Sadie dropped her spoon, heard it clatter to the floor as her mouth opened in disbelief.

"Y...Yellow?"

"Sort of."

With a cry, Sadie ran to get her coat, pulled her boots on, tied her head scarf as she ran, slipping and falling the whole way to the barn, propelled by one single thought— Paris.

At first, she thought it was Paris. Then she thought it wasn't. But when the dirty, unkempt, horse turned its head and nickered, she knew without a doubt it was her horse who had found its way back. She was thin, her coat was coarse and long, but it was Paris. Sadie was unaware of anyone or anything other than throwing her arms around the thin neck and staying there. She cried and whispered to Paris, told her of the times she missed her most, then stepped back to assess the damage that had been done to her beloved horse.

She appeared to have lost weight but was in better health than Nevaeh had been. She didn't stand on the right hind foot. No matter, she'd heal everything up. Crying sometimes, then laughing to herself and talking, she was unaware of Tim's and Anna's presence until Tim cleared his throat self-consciously, the way he sniffed when he was ill at ease.

"I guess you know the horse" he said, finally.

"Yes, Tim, I do."

Anna, completely forgetting her former animosity toward this stranger, filled him in with the details about Paris, the enduring relationship through all the trials. And now, after Sadie had given her up completely, she had come back. Tim's face was an open book as Anna spoke.

He watched her large eyes, the shadows of deprived nutrition beneath them, the thin, white hands gesticulating. They watched as Sadie continued stroking Paris before going to the wooden cupboard and taking down a currycomb.

Slowly, lovingly, she worked, cleaning the mane, the burrs and dirt falling on the cement floor of the forebay. Anna offered to help, but Sadie waved her away, so Tim told her she could help him clean the stable for Paris.

Anna looked at Tim, the pitchfork he held toward her, back at the stable, and then at Tim again. She wrinkled her nose and wrapped her coat tightly around herself, rocking back on her heels.

"I don't know if I'm strong enough."

"You would be if you'd eat normally."

"Define normal!"

Tim laughed uproariously and admitted he was on the other end of what was considered normal. But she sure was on the extreme opposite. So which one was the healthiest? Sadie could tell that Anna knew the answer, but the younger sister went right ahead cleaning Paris's coat as if she hadn't heard.

Supper was not ready when Mark came home. The house was dark, chocolate-covered food all over everything. The fire burned low, but surprisingly, a bright light shone from the barn window. When he stepped inside, he couldn't fathom the horse Sadie was still grooming, applying antiseptic to scratches and open wounds, while Tim swept the loose hay in a pile and fed it to Truman and Duke.

With a cry, Sadie dropped the antiseptic and ran to his waiting arms, hysterical with the joy of Paris's return. Mark held her, soothed her, and held back his own emotion. He shook his head in disbelief, the only way he could convey his feelings.

When Tim joined them, Mark smiled at him and said he was genuinely glad Tim was back. Mark asked where he'd been. Tim looked down, scuffed the cement floor with the toe of his shoe.

"I had some business to take care of."

"Okay," was all Mark said, asking no questions.

Anna had taken her leave, declining Tim's offer of assistance, obviously very uncomfortable under his watch. He said something, Anna replied, and she was off down the drive, turning to the left at an unsafe speed.

Paris had been sufficiently groomed, cleaned, and her wounds treated. Sadie returned Paris to her stall, which had been strewn with clean shavings as well as a large portion of oats, corn, molasses, and two blocks of good hay. Sadie finally turned to leave the barn, joining Mark who was patiently waiting by the door, the lantern in his hand creating a circle of yellow light around him. They walked to the house together, followed by Tim with a hand on Wolf's collar, throwing a snowball for him before entering the house with them.

Sadie was starved, her stomach rumbling as she scooped up the chocolate candies and stacked them neatly in Tupperware containers, popping the seal to assure the airtight quality. Turning to Mark, she asked if it was all right to make "*toste brode, millich und oya*" (toast, milk and eggs).

"Sure, you know how much I like that," Mark said grinning.

Timothy nodded. "Aunt Hannah made it."

Heating a large saucepan, Sadie poured a generous amount of milk into it, then cracked open and deposited the insides of a dozen eggs, leaving them to poach. Opening the broiler of the gas stove, she carefully laid six slices of thick, homemade bread on the broiler rack, then stood up, closing it with her foot. Hurriedly, she set the table with a clean tablecloth, three soup plates, utensils, a bowl of applesauce, some leftover red beets, and half a chocolate cake. When the eggs were soft-poached, the milk almost to the boiling point, the toast dark and crispy, Sadie put two slices of the toast in each bowl, set the eggs and milk on a hot pad in the middle of the table, then poured the cold water in each glass.

It seemed as if Tim's self-consciousness became more noticeable when he was expected to bow his head for a silent prayer before mealtime. He never made eye contact, his sniffing became more frequent, and he shuffled his feet uncomfortably when Mark said it was time for "Patties down," the Amish term, in child's language, for silent prayer.

Tim helped himself to six of the eggs, as Sadie had expected, politely asking if she and Mark had all they wanted. He ladled enough milk over everything to fill the soup bowl to brimming, then added a liberal amount of salt and pepper before digging in. He ate all the red beets and half the applesauce, accompanied by a chunk of chocolate cake so large Sadie could not believe he ate it all in less than six bites.

They talked of Tim getting a job, of his offer to pay rent, and whether he was thinking of returning to the Amish. Mark did not set any rules, but by that first warning about not smoking, Tim knew about what was expected of him.

After Sadie washed dishes, Tim asked her what really was wrong with Anna. He spoke in a quiet, nervous manner that completely won Sadie over. As accurately as she could, she related Anna's sad story about her obsession with Neil. But Tim said nothing at all when she finished. He made his way to the stairs with an abrupt "good night" before closing the door quite firmly.

☆ ✡ ☆

Richard Caldwell had a fit, as did Jim Sevarr and the ranch hands who knew Sadie and Paris's story. Richard Caldwell slapped his knees, gleeful in his exclamations, chortling about the rotten luck of the horse thieves or the tattered remains of the ones that had slipped between the cracks of the law.

"Good for 'em!" he yelled, his *Schadenfreude* completely consuming him. "For all they put you through," he shouted, "good for 'em!"

Dorothy shook her head and said no good could come of it. She thought they were done with that cursed palomino once and for all. Sadie became so insulted she had to blink back tears.

"She ain't a blessing, that's sure, unless you figure every time Sadie got out of her scrapes alive was one. Ain't no blessing to me, so she ain't."

Erma became completely defensive and said that palomino was not cursed and that was an awful term to use. Her face got red and she opened her mouth for her usual fiery retort. Sadie held a hand over her own mouth and shook her head, her eyes begging her to keep her peace. She knew Dorothy meant well; it was just her way of protecting Sadie.

They were into the Christmas season at the ranch, baking extra pies, dozens of cookies, and huge fruit cakes, besides the everyday cooking. The ranch was prospering; the price of beef spurred Richard Caldwell into acquiring more land, more cattle, as well as more horses and equipment. The usual 20 cowhands that ate in the huge dining room often doubled, especially for the evening meal.

Dorothy, who was in her element, barking orders, wearing the brilliant purple Crocs, would have to admit defeat around three or four o'clock every afternoon, succumbing to the pain in her lower back or a cramp in her leg. That was usually when the pressure was on to have the huge evening meal ready and waiting on the steam table, with napkins and utensils, everything clean and in perfect order.

So in the middle of everyone scurrying around in the usual manner, Dorothy sat, her one leg elevated on the seat of a kitchen chair, holding a bowl of macaroni and cheese and one of chocolate pudding. Erma's baked beans had turned out a bit dry, so she was adding some warm water, leaning over the hot oven door, her brilliant red hair only a shade brighter than her face. Dorothy chewed with great enjoyment, savoring a too-large mouthful of macaroni and cheese, watching the heat rise in Erma's face.

"Told you to do them in the electric roaster."

Too slowly, Erma replaced the lid, shoved back the oven rack, and closed the door, adjusting the knob in front. She watched Dorothy slurp her coffee before spooning up more of the cheesy concoction, Erma's eyes mere slits in her red face.

"I'm not used to electric roasters at home, Dorothy. And besides, they're slow."

"No, they ain't."

"Yes, they are."

"No, they ain't. I know that for a fact."

"You better not eat all that chocolate pudding," Erma said with concern, changing the subject as abruptly as she could.

"An' jes' why ever not?"

"I'd get terrible heartburn. Coffee, chocolate pudding, and macaroni and cheese." Erma visibly shivered.

"Don't know what heartburn is."

"That's good," Erma said, rolling her eyes in Sadie's direction. Sadie was slicing a roast of beef, the meat falling away under the direction of her knife.

"Is the gravy made?" Sadie asked curtly. Sometimes these stupid little spats just irked her, and today, patience was in short supply.

"Ain't no hurry," Dorothy said around her macaroni before slurping yet more coffee.

The kitchen door opened slowly. Steven Weaver poked his head through the opening and asked if they wanted a few bushels of Rome apples, leftover from the market in town.

"The guy said I can have 'em, but I have no use for 'em."

Erma almost cried in her haste to fix her hair and covering, desperately spitting on her hands and smoothing the wayward tendrils, making her look like a skinny, wet cat. Oh, dear. Sadie cringed when Erma wiped her hands after washing them, then charged through the bathroom door, her elbow already pulled back like a bowstring, ready to fire. She literally slapped her hand into Steven's, accompanied by her loud, jovial yell.

"Where you been, stranger? Haven't seen hide nor hair of you in a coon's age!"

Dorothy stopped chewing, her mouth a straight line,

her cheeks bulging, as she opened her eyes wide, her eyebrows shooting straight up. And when Steven Weaver met Erma's hand halfway and they laughed great guffaws of pure merriment together, it was obvious they were so happy to see each other. Sadie realized God had surely sent the perfect match for Erma Keim. Who else but Steven would enjoy a cymbal-crashing greeting like that? It was enough to send a half-dozen other men running for cover.

When Erma accompanied Steven to the door, offering to bring the apples in, Steven waved her away. But she charged straight through the door anyway, following him like a devoted puppy. When 10 minutes passed and no Erma or apples followed, Sadie smiled to herself. You go, Erma.

Sadie found Dorothy rattling bottles and mumbling to herself in the bathroom, the door of the medicine cabinet ajar. She just closed the door quietly and continued whipping potatoes.

That Sunday in church, Erma looked a bit crestfallen, for her. Her hair was slicked back tighter than usual with less *shtrubles*, her covering pulled forward well over her ears. Her usual effusiveness was dampened to a gentle, "How are you, Sadie? Nice dress."

Sadie walked into the kitchen to stand with the women and noticed Erma following her, a wistful expression on her face. Sadie shook hands with her usual friends and family, noticing Mam's new covering, then accepted everyone's sincere congratulations on the return of her beloved horse. She acknowledged it humbly, her eyes shining nevertheless, the days of missing her horse gone now, reveling in the pleasure of seeing her, touching her.

When she watched the boys file in and Steven Weaver was not at the head of the line, she swallowed her disappointment. Surely he had not returned to Indiana, leaving Erma without hope! During the service Sadie prayed for her friend, for the strength she would need to rise above this, if, in fact, he had decided to return. Erma was such a dear person. So genuine, so human. Seemingly imperfect, but so unselfish, and above all, sincerely caring about everyone in the community, English people as well as her Amish. Surely God would not be so cruel.

So often, though, this happened. Young men were lured to the west by the breathtaking scenery, the hunting, the adventure, but then yearned for their home folks, their busy way of life, and sooner or later, returned to their home state. The minister expounded the wisdom of Solomon, but Sadie was only half-listening, watching Erma Keim's display of emotions across her face. Poor dear.

Chapter 15

THEY WENT HOME TO DAT AND MAM'S FOR SUPPER, a time of renewal, the scents of Mam's kitchen bringing a lump of emotion to her throat. Mam was frying chicken, Mark's favorite, and had a casserole of scalloped potatoes in the oven. Leah was tossing a salad and Rebekah was setting the table, both of them dressed in their Sunday best, waiting until Kevin and Junior came to pick them up. They talked as fast as they could about Tim, and about Anna's meltdown, Mam staring in disbelief as Sadie related the whole incident.

"It's that Neil," she whispered. "I had no idea." Helplessly, she looked at Rebekah. "I thought you said she liked Merv."

"I thought she did!"

"Somebody is not communicating," Sadie said firmly.

Mam turned the chicken, hissing and snapping in the pan, before turning to Sadie.

"And just how do you communicate with a rock? How? If I ask her questions, I get no answer. Only a shrug of her shoulders. It's just as if she's another girl. I know how skinny she is. I know, too, that the more I say, the worse it gets. It's just a vicious circle, and as long as that Neil is in the picture, it's not going to change."

Mam choked back tears bravely, a matriarch over petty emotions, a strong pillar of the family, having overcome so much adversity herself. Mothers were like that. When the storms of life blew in, creating chaos, uprooting younger people as they struggled to understand situations in life that were beyond their control, talking, talking, restlessly trying to figure out situations, mothers wisely knew there was no use. God was up in his heaven and knew everything, including the reasons, something mortals did not have to know. That's what faith was for, no doubt about it. Same as Dat. Except Dat was perhaps more of a disciplinarian. So parents were a wonderful thing, when it all came down to it.

Dat teased Sadie about changing Paris's name to Lassie, that it was just like the old classic story of a dog finding its way home. Sadie smiled and smiled, she was so glad to be at home with her family, thinking of Paris in the barn, safe, warm, and secure.

Timothy would not accompany them to Sadie's parents, so they left him at home.

Sadie asked Dat about Tim, what would be the best way to approach him to make the decision to come back to the Amish.

Dat shook his head. "It's going to be tough."

Mark disagreed, saying he had his share of wild days and was thoroughly sick of the whole scene. He had been sick of it even before he came to meet Jackson.

"I think he's just too shy to tell anyone how he feels. To change back into Amish clothes, to make all new friends, feel at home in the community. It's a big mountain to scale for a person as bashful as Tim."

"Bring him sometime," Dat said. "Christmas would be as good a time as any."

Sadie looked at Mark, raised her eyebrows in question. Yes, they would bring him. Or try to.

Mam's fried chicken, as usual, was outstanding. And as usual, Sadie could not resist that second piece, followed by a large slice of homemade butterscotch pie. The coffee was perfect. Reuben came dashing in at the last minute just to say Hi, being otherwise occupied, in his words. Two of his friends were waiting in the buggy, so he grabbed a piece of chicken on the run, Mam calling after him about taking one for his friends, and he yelled back they didn't need any, which made Mark laugh and Dat smile and drink his coffee.

The atmosphere was so cozy, so homey with Mark beside her, his wide shoulders leaning back in his chair, at ease, happy to be here, confident in Sadie's love, a place to call his own, a reason for living after the overwhelming ordeal that had been his childhood.

"Only forward." Sadie seemed to hear the words, and yet there was no voice. I bet God just put those words in my head, she thought, looking around to see if anyone else had heard them. Just keep our eyes on the finish line, run the Christian race with Jesus Christ our Savior by our sides, and we won't go wrong. Thankfulness washed over her, along with a deep sense of purpose where Tim was concerned. There was so much good in Tim.

At work on Monday morning, Erma Keim walked quietly, even sedately through the door, unbuttoning her coat as she went, hanging her scarf neatly on the hook. Turning, she smiled, wished them a good morning, then turned to look at herself in the mirror. Sadie looked at Dorothy, and they both raised their eyebrows. What was going on? Sadie's heart sank, her sadness for Erma slowly churning in her stomach.

Dear God, she prayed, please give her the strength. Tears were close to the surface as she begged God to help Erma Keim through this time of trial.

Erma's hair was again combed back severely, her covering forward, well over her ears. She walked softly, rocking her feet from toe to heel, then asked Dorothy if she needed help with the bacon.

"I...guess," Dorothy stammered in disbelief.

Serenely, quietly, Erma placed bacon on the hot griddle, averting her eyes. Sadie put water on for the grits, sliced oranges, arranged the apple and pineapple for the fruit compartment, her heart heavy. Should she approach Erma? Offer condolence? Ask her outright whether Steven had returned to Indiana? After they served breakfast and filled their mugs of coffee, Sadie slid an arm around Erma's narrow waist, laying her cheek on her upper arm.

"Erma, tell me what's troubling you. Please feel free to confide in me. I pitied you so much when you looked so sad in church yesterday. You're just not yourself at all this morning, either. Is it Steven? Did you two...sort of have something going? It..."

She raced on, feeling as if she was sinking, unable to bring any happiness to Erma this way.

"Did he...he return to Indiana?" she blurted out, ready to accept Erma's sad fate.

Erma slid a long, thin arm around Sadie's waist, then released her, stepped back, and laid her large hands on her shoulders.

"Oh, Sadie, you are a dear. It's nothing like that." Bending her head, looking over her shoulder, then at Dorothy, she whispered, "I have a date."

The breath seemed to leave Sadie's body, she had no voice or air to start her words after that. She remembered Dorothy's look of disbelief, then her peal of laughter ringing through the kitchen, slapping her knees, her elbow catching the handle of her cup, dangerously rocking it, spilling a small amount of the steaming liquid on her sleeve.

"Who with? That long-nosed Mr. Weaver that comes in here?" she screeched.

Erma smiled, an angelic version of her usual rich-throated guffaws.

"Yes, him."

That was all she said, smiling sweetly at Sadie before turning to her coffee. Sadie squealed, congratulated her, then begged her to be herself.

"You don't have to change, Erma. Seriously. We love you just the way you are. Evidently, so does Steven!"

Erma looked confused, a bit sad, even. Looking around, making sure no one would hear her, she whispered, "I don't want to wreck my blessing!"

Christmas was a time of heightened activity in the Amish community. Hymn singings, school programs, Christmas dinners, caroling, shopping, gift exchanges, baking and cooking among the most important events. So Mark and Sadie had very little time to spend with Tim or fret about Anna's problems.

Paris remained lame in the hind right foot in spite of Mark's expertise, removing the shoe, cleaning the hoof, telling Sadie it may be the start of laminitis, which was like an arrow to Sadie's heart. They soaked the foot in warm water, applied the secret home remedy, that strong black salve that was a miracle cure for most horse hoof ailments. Still the reddened, infected tissue remained.

On Christmas morning, a storm blew in. The sun appeared for only a short time, cloaking the valley in shades of lavender and orange, only to disappear behind a heavy gray bank of clouds swollen with churning winds. Icy snow fragments began pelting the earth just as Mark and Sadie tucked themselves into the buggy, the presents and chocolate treats placed under the back seat.

Truman was a handful, crow-hopping, shaking his head to dislodge the bit in his mouth, pulling on the reins, wanting to break free and run too fast, putting the light shafts connecting him to the buggy in decided jeopardy, the way he was carrying on.

This was a serious storm, Sadie decided, when Mark opened the window and clicked it fast to the holder on the ceiling. "Can't see," he murmured, as he squinted into the steadily increasing snow.

Sadie wrapped her black, woolen shawl tightly around her shoulders, her gloved hands holding the fringes to keep it in place. Shivers chased each other up her back, and she let go of the shawl to pull the heavy lap robe up over her shoulder on the right side.

"Cold?"

Sadie nodded, relieved to see him reach up and unhook the window, letting it slam into place, then adjust the reins through the small rectangular holes in the frame.

The buggy swayed, slid, then righted itself as Mark slowed Truman, hanging on to the reins with both arms stretched out. Sadie could feel the weight of the buggy being pulled partly by Truman's mouth and his determination to run at breakneck speed, propelling them along, winding uphill over Atkin's Ridge.

The house on the side of the hill was the most welcome sight, the yellow glow of the gas lantern a friendly beacon through the whirling, biting, whiteness. Home was always an anticipated pleasure, but at Christmas, a horse just couldn't go fast enough. Sadie hopped eagerly off the buggy before Mark had time to pull the reins through the window.

Even with the long uphill run, Truman wasn't winded. Steam rose from his body, some hairs on his flanks were frosted from the moisture, his breathing accelerated only slightly as he tossed his head up and down, his way of asking Mark to hurry up and loosen the neck rein so he could lower his head.

Mam greeted Sadie at the door with a quick hug, taking the presents, then Dat shook hands warmly as he shrugged his coat on, going to help Mark with his horse. Leah and Rebekah were helping in the kitchen, rosy-cheeked, smiling, so happy to see her. Reuben was sprawled across the recliner, dressed in his "good" trousers and red Christmas shirt. He was definitely turning into a nice-looking young man, an air of confidence in his manner, and a wide, teasing grin. He slapped the footrest of the recliner down before bouncing to his feet to greet Sadie.

"Hey, Sis! Where's Tim?"

Sadie shook her head. "Couldn't persuade him to come."

"Why not?"

"Claimed he had nothing to wear."

"I'll hitch up Charlie and go pick him up."

Sadie shrugged her shoulders. "Good luck!" she said soundly, meaning there was hardly a chance he could be persuaded.

When Anna came down the stairs, Sadie had to fight the rising panic in her throat. Dear God in heaven. The prayer began before she was even aware of it, automatically switching to a plea for higher help.

Huge dark circles lay like harbingers of death below each eye. Her cheekbones were prominent, the white skin taut over them. Even her teeth seemed to protrude from the pale lips, the square jaw containing only a hint of flesh. Her eyes were enormous, filled with fear. Did she know she was being controlled by something she could no longer handle?

"Hello, Anna! Merry Christmas!"

Her voice came out cracked, high, breathless. When Anna smiled, it was only a parting of those pale lips. The eyes remained flat, afraid. She gripped the back of a chair, then slid into it, folding her skeletal frame weakly against it.

Reuben scurried through the kitchen, pulling on his beanie, his coat buttoned against the cold on his way to collect Tim, as he put it, grinning assuredly at Sadie. Numbly, she went about the kitchen, grating cabbage, washing dishes, putting whipped cream on the coconut cream pie, watching Anna from the corner of her eye. She sat in her chair, her breathing coming in short gasps, then actually reached down for support, her long, thin fingers gripping the sides for a prop, her shoulders sagging weakly when she let go.

Instantly, Sadie was by her side. "Anna."

There was no answer.

"Anna, do you hear me?"

Anna stared ahead, her eyes seemingly locked.

Suddenly, very afraid, Sadie shook her by the shoulders. "Anna! Talk to me!"

As soon as Sadie's hands left her shoulders, Anna began to slide in slow motion, her head outweighing her neck and shoulders with no strength to hold it, like a sack half-full of feed sliding along the back of the chair before crumpling to the floor. They were all around her then, Dat lifting her to take her outside to revive her from her faint, Mam hovering over them, her face ashen, Leah and Rebekah angry, then crying, Reuben running from the barn, his eyes wide.

Grimly, Sadie heated milk in a saucepan, added sugar, then chocolate syrup. Likely her blood sugar was so slow it wasn't even readable, or else she hadn't eaten in days. Or—she had eaten too much and then purged the food from her body. How had things gotten so out of control? Catching Mark's eye, Sadie shook her head.

When Anna came out of her unconscious state, she lay weakly on the sofa, her eyes dry, still terrified. There were no tears, just this dry-eyed lethargy, coupled with the wide eyes of fear. Sadie brought the hot chocolate and asked her to drink it, which of course, Anna refused.

"I'll be fine. I have the flu," she croaked, her voice edged with panic.

"Drink it!" Sadie hissed.

Anna remained adamant, her lips compressed into a straight, thin line of determination. Sighing, Sadie got up from her crouched position, sighed, dumped the hot chocolate down the sink drain. The light of Christmas was only a flicker, tossed by a harsh wind of fear and doubt, for the remainder of the forenoon. The ham was carved, the pineapple sauce falling away with each slice, the mashed potatoes were piled high, browned butter dripping from each cavity. No one wanted to eat, but, like robots, they went through the motions, their eyes sliding to Anna, a mere bump under the quilt she had pulled over herself.

As Sadie helped wash dishes, she formed a plan: There would be no presents until the family held a conference, a no-holds-barred meeting about Anna. Reuben still had not returned, and if Tim showed up with him, he'd just have to sit in. Something had to be done, Christmas Day or not.

How to approach Mam was the next problem, but when she came to dry dishes while Sadie washed, she plunged right in, grateful for Mam's understanding. With tear-filled eyes, she nodded in agreement. Dat remained aloof but finally gave his consent. So they seated themselves around the still form on the couch, her eyes closed, as still as death itself. Just as Sadie was about to ask Anna the first question, a buggy flashed past the window.

Charlie! Reuben had returned. Would he bring Tim along in?

It was Tim all right, dressed in Mark's clothes, sniffing self-consciously, throwing his hair out of his eyes. He was wearing black trousers low on his hips, a beige shirt with the sleeves rolled halfway up his forearms, a black vest hanging open, appearing relaxed, completely at home in his Amish clothes. Reuben was jubilant, proudly producing Tim to his family as if he had discovered him all by himself.

"Look it!" he beamed.

Tim tried to shake it off, but the huge grin on his face gave away his true feelings.

"Does this mean...?" Mark stammered.

Sadie put a hand on his arm, steadying him as Reuben yelped gleefully, "What does it look like?"

Anna's head rolled to one side, and she fixed her large-eyed gaze on Tim, her expression as vague as the thin body under the quilt.

All Tim said was, "Guess I'll try it; see how deep my roots go."

Mark lowered his head as tears rose to the surface, and Sadie slipped her arm through his.

Mam went to set the warmed food on one end of the table, stooping low to talk to Reuben as Tim strained to hear her words. They ate hungrily, bending their heads to the delicious food the way growing young men do when they can't fill themselves up fast enough. After they finished, the family opened the subject of Anna's sickness, confronting her with the sad facts of her slide into the delusional state she was in. Dat and Mam both talked to her, asking her if she was willing to go for help.

Anna shook her head from side to side. "I only have the flu."

She kept insisting. No amount of coaxing would change her. Leah promised her a new rug for her room. Rebekah pleaded with her for Mam and Dat's sake, but nothing changed. Reuben finally became quite frustrated and told her he hoped she was happy now, ruining everyone's Christmas this way. Sadie saw Tim wince. She saw his eyes as he watched her, listened to the family's pleading without comment, shifting uncomfortably in his chair. A few times he looked at Mark, opened his mouth slightly as if to speak, then shut it. Finally he walked over to the couch and placed his hand on Anna's forehead.

"Yeah, you are running a temperature. I think you do have the flu."

Turning, he addressed the family, saying she did have a fever, then looked at Anna and asked if she wanted some chicken soup, a cup of tea? Anna's eyes were fixed on Tim's face, as if a savior had indeed presented himself.

"Soup, I'll have soup."

"I'll get it."

Mam followed him to the kitchen, flitted about like a nervous bird, emptying a can of Campbell's chicken noodle, filling a mug with tea. Anna insisted on coming to the kitchen, the quilt wrapped around her shoulders, then sat at the table, bent her head, lifted the spoon methodically to her mouth, until it was all gone, then started busily slurping the hot, sugary tea. Tim sat with her, saying nothing. The color in her cheeks slowly returned. Sadie wanted to go to her so badly, but Mark shook his head no.

They began to talk. Mam suggested they begin opening gifts, which they did, fully aware of the miracle taking place in the kitchen. Dat was presented with a very expensive fly-fishing rod, the product of everyone chipping in, leaving him wide-eyed, exclaiming over and over about his wonderful gift.

"He'll never go to work now," Reuben chortled, leaning way out of his chair to watch the progress Tim was making in the kitchen. Sadie grabbed his shirt sleeve and hauled him back.

Mam was given a new canner and a cultivator for her garden, both items to make her life easier, which she exclaimed about in great detail, saying she had no idea anyone would spend so much money just for her. For Reuben there was a huge package, containing a brand new black leather saddle with a bridle to match. There was a moon inscribed on both, in memory of his horse named Moon, which he accepted with a quiet, controlled coolness, but Sadie could tell inside he was jumping up and down with pure glee. The girls had their usual dress fabrics, decorative items for their rooms, harmonicas, which Rebekah promptly began to play, getting Tim's and Anna's attention.

Anna smiled weakly, then came in to sit on the couch, Tim following to sit cross-legged on the floor by her side.

Rebekah was good. She played a rendering of "Silent Night," followed by "What Child is This?"

Sadie opened her package, a new bathroom set, the rugs reversible, something she had wanted ever since she had her own bathroom. The rubber-backed bathroom rugs never lasted very long, having to be put through the wringer of the washing machine. They were suitable for awhile, but eventually the rubber backing became pinched between the covers of the wringer, resulting in a tear, then bit by bit the rug deteriorated. These reversible ones would be much more serviceable, much easier to wash.

Mark received a German-English dictionary, which Tim promptly tried out to see if he remembered any German from his school days. Every Amish student learned German but spoke Pennsylvania Dutch, a sort of pidgin language derived from real German with English mixed into it, a product of hundreds of years of being the minority among English-speaking people.

Wunder. Wundfieber. Wundstarrkrampf. Wunsch. Tim rattled off a row of words pronounced correctly, then grinned, his hand going to his mouth unthinking, a motion to hide his decaying teeth. Anna watched him, her eyes slanted downward on his thick blond-streaked hair, then pulled the quilt around her thin shoulders. That began a volley of German words and their meanings, arguments, fists banging on chair arms, resorting to the dictionary many times, accompanied by raised fists and shouts of glee.

Mam spread the afternoon snacks across the table. There were oranges and grapes, coffee and punch, Chex mix, pretzels, a cheese log, and too many cookies to count, besides all the different candy.

Tim and Reuben soon got up to load their plates, then went to the basement to start a game of Ping-Pong. Anna watched Tim go. Sadie sat beside her, putting both arms around her and squeezing, quilt and all.

"How you feeling, Sissie?" she asked lightheartedly.

Anna fixed her gaze on Sadie's face.

"S...Sadie, you know what Tim said?"

"What?"

"A girlfriend of his had to live in a mental place because she was so bad. Wouldn't eat, you know."

"What?"

Anna nodded miserably. "Is that what happens?"

"Anna, yes. Of course it is. I often tried to tell you."

"Yes, but...Tim saw it happen. You never did."

"True."

"I'm not like that though." Sadie watched her face. "Am I?"

"Are you?"

The quilt lifted slightly, then fell as Anna shrugged her shoulders. How it happened, Sadie was never sure, but the remainder of the day, Anna followed Tim and Reuben. First, she shrugged off the quilt, then slyly, quietly, she went to the basement. After that, Sadie found her playing Monopoly at the kitchen table, sipping tea. She stepped back as she watched Tim break a cookie in two, offer Anna the other half. Anna lifted her eyes to his face, held his gaze, then slowly reached out and took it. It was a peanut butter cookie with a Hershey's kiss on top, the chocolate candy staying on Anna's half. Deliberately, she reached out thin fingers, loosened it, and put the whole thing in her mouth, letting it melt, savoring its sweetness, watching Tim's expression. His eyes spoke his encouragement. Anna blushed faintly.

Reuben looked from Tim to Anna, then blurted out, too emotional to stay quiet, "You better eat about two dozen more of them things!"

"Maybe I will!"

Reuben howled with laughter. Tim laughed, his hand going to his mouth.

Chapter 16

THE STORM RAGED. THE WIND BLEW GREAT WHITE whirls of fallen snow into restless, never-ceasing drifts that obscured anything in the line of visibility. Pine trees bent and waved, shaking off any accumulation on their branches. Snow swirled off rooftops, the wind moaned and howled around the eaves, the fire burned high until the wood stove in the living room gave off a tremendous heat, logs being added every few hours. The family popped fresh popcorn, made hot spiced cider and leftover ham sandwiches.

Reuben won the first Monopoly game, then went to check on the horses. He was gasping for breath when he came back, saying this was not a snowstorm, it was a blizzard, like the one in the Laura Ingalls Wilder book called *The Long Winter*.

So they all stayed for the night, Sadie acknowledging happily that it was the smart thing to do. Mark fretted about frozen water pipes at home, but Dat assured him if they filled the stove with wood before they left, it should be all right for a few days. The horses would be hungry and thirsty, but they'd survive till Mark returned.

They sang Christmas songs, then all gathered around the table in the light of the softly hissing gas lamp and drank hot chocolate. For some reason they began talking about cream of wheat, that soft white cereal mixed with brown sugar and creamy milk poured over it until it had the right consistency. Tim's eyes shone. He said Aunt Hannah used to make it for him after his egg sandwich, and he put a slice of shoofly pie in it. Dat said he'd like to try that, so Mam produced a pot of cream of wheat and, of course, a freshly baked shoofly, which was almost a staple in the Miller family. They all tasted it.

Anna watched, swallowed. Sadie urged her to try it, then watched as she looked at Tim. He met her eyes and held them. You can do this. Go ahead. The message was there as plain as day.

She smiled slowly, then scraped the last of the cereal from the pot, added a teaspoon of brown sugar, a dash of milk. Slowly, she cut only a sliver of pie, let it fall into the cream of wheat, then took up her spoon in those pitiable white fingers. Again she looked at Tim. This time Sadie couldn't watch. It was too personal. Almost sacred. Slowly, she lifted the spoon. "Mmm," she whispered, then ducked her head, embarrassed.

During the night, Sadie began coughing, an annoying itch in the throat, and couldn't stop. Mark snored, rolled over, and grabbed all the covers, so she gave up, scooped Leah's flannel robe from its hook, and made her way downstairs to the kitchen. She needed some honey and lemon or some over-the-counter cough medicine, even a lozenge of some kind. She was surprised to find a kerosene lamp on in the living room. Someone forgot to turn it off, she thought, and she walked through the wide doorway to take care of it. No use wasting kerosene.

"Oh!" They scared her.

Tim. Anna. They were sitting on the floor by the fire, both looking up at her. They were clearly at ease, innocent, neither of them offended by her appearance, waiting to hear what she wanted.

"What are you two doing still up?" she asked.

"We're talking." Anna offered shyly. "Reuben just went to bed."

"Oh. Well, I can't stop coughing, so I need some medicine."

There was no answer, so Sadie decided to leave well enough alone, found her medicine, and returned to bed. She shook Mark awake, whispering her concerns about Tim and how good was it that he sat down in the living room with Anna? And how could they know he was sincere? Just because he came to the Christmas dinner with Mark's clothes on didn't mean he wasn't the same lost teenager he'd been when they met him, and he knew how vulnerable Anna was, and how in the world could they ever feel comfortable having those two together? Mark told her to go to sleep, they weren't getting married, and hadn't Anna eaten that shoofly pie?

After Christmas, everyone dug out of the snow and life continued. Tim cut his hair, becoming quite embarrassed when Sadie made a fuss about how neat he looked, how manly, so much older. Mark's praise brought a grin, a punch on the arm, and Sadie knew his eyes smiled the rest of the evening. They paid for his dental work.

He went to church for the first time, making sure no one else knew he was planning to go. Sadie hoped she could see Anna when he walked in and was completely surprised to see how strong Anna's reaction really was. She watched the row of boys file in, then sat up straight, shocked, visibly shaken at the sight of Tim with his hair cut. Just as suddenly, she lowered her head, embarrassed, trying hard to hide the onslaught of feelings.

Ah, Sadie thought. And then she prayed for both of them. The long prayer, after both sermons were over, was extra meaningful. The prayer for a godly life, to be more Christlike. It was all a plea for her own life, the wisdom to deal with Tim as well as Anna. Was it God's will? Would they be able to make it work, in spite of all the adversities in their lives? And what about Neil Hershberger? He always managed to reappear somehow.

✿ ✡ ✿

Erma Keim remained sedate, walking quietly through the kitchen, beaming her happiness, a halo of angelic goodness following her. She praised Dorothy's biscuits, and Dorothy acknowledged her praise with a bowed head, then proceeded to tell her she should never have turned her back on that Dollar General, that their shortening was still the best and cheapest by far.

"Ya see, Erma, I can't drive by the Dollar General, keepin' the grudge against them shoes. They's still good shoes. I'm jus' gittin' old, is all it is. I like my Crocs, don't get me wrong, but I gotta return to the Dollar General. It's muh store, so it is. You know they got toothpaste, Colgate, for a dollar? Now I told you, they're gonna hurt Walmart, you mark my words. And sauerkraut to cook with my pork? Ninety-nine cents!"

Erma nodded her total agreement, buttered a biscuit, and proceeded to tell them both about her first date. She started out humbly enough.

"We went out to eat in his horse and buggy. We could

tie at the hitching rack behind Lowell's in town. He ordered a steak, and I had roast chicken and filling. We talked and talked. He's so easy to talk to. He intends to stay in Montana, asked if I'm happy here. I said I am. So I figure we'll get married. He sees me here at work, knows what a good worker I am. I'm old, though, so likely we won't have a big family. I plan on having fried chicken and dressing at my wedding."

Dorothy snorted. "What's dressing? You mean, like French and ranch and stuff?"

"No, it's filling. Like stuffing, only better. It has chicken and carrots and celery and potatoes."

"Sounds like slop to me."

Erma's halo slid off center a bit before she could catch herself, and she told Dorothy she shouldn't say that before she tasted it. Dorothy said she wasn't about to taste it anytime soon, and what, pray tell, is wrong with plain old stuffing anyhow? The halo disappeared completely when Erma wagged a finger under Dorothy's nose and said that's what set Amish cooking apart, the know-how passed down through the ages that English people knew nothing about. Sadie was seriously afraid Dorothy would pop a blood vessel after that. She became highly agitated, telling Erma it was all a matter of acquired taste, that alcoholics liked the taste of alcohol, too, and it was slop, same as dressing.

Luckily Steven Weaver came in with a box of turnips from the Giant in town, and Dorothy was beside herself with joy, saying she hadn't had a good dish of mashed turnips in a coon's age. Erma smiled sweetly and said she bet they were delicious, although she had never acquired a taste for them, which mixed Dorothy up a bit, unsure how to take that comment, so she let it go.

Sadie decided it was why she came to work, this constant sparring between these two interesting characters whom she loved. Richard Caldwell and his wife were good friends, too, not just employers, and every day at the ranch held some new adventure, argument, or challenge.

After Steven left, Dorothy asked Erma what made her think Steven would ask her to get married. Erma said it was just the way he looked at her when he asked if she was happy here.

"Just such an intimate look," Erma finished, clasping her hands across her stomach, looking reverently at the ceiling.

"That don't say nothing," Dorothy said, not quite loud enough for Erma to hear.

Sadie had to go clean the steam table, so if there was more drama after that, she was blissfully unaware of it.

At home that evening, Mark bent over Paris's hind foot, prodding gently as Sadie came over to look at the swollen tissue inside the hoof. Mark smelled the infected area. His eyes were clouded with concern when he released the foot and straightened to his full height. Sadie stroked Paris's flank, her eyes going to her husband's.

"Should we call the vet again?"

Mark sighed. "I don't know."

No amount of antibiotic, salve, hot water baths, or any other remedy would heal that foot. Sometime Paris had become foundered or eaten too much grain, perhaps made her way out of her stall while unattended and broken into a sack of grain. Whatever the cause, the result was swollen, red, infected tissue, causing severe pain and lameness. Sadie had felt so confident when Paris returned, so glad to be able to nurse her back to health.

But the Paris of old was not to be found ever since.

Her coat still shone after the extended grooming and the minerals on her portion of feed. But the foundering had slowly progressed to a serious case of laminitis.

Now when Sadie entered the barn, she could smell the infection. Paris no longer threw up her proud head, nickering that soft rumbling of her nostrils, her eyes bright, alive, eager to see Sadie, wanting to run down the driveway with Sadie astride her back. The thing was, she was in pain.

"How bad is it?" Sadie asked finally.

"It's pretty serious."

"Isn't there anything you can do? Can't we call another vet? Someone who specializes in horses?"

Mark answered wearily. "We did."

"Someone better?"

Sadie laid her forehead on Paris's, taking both hands to massage each side of her face.

"Good girl, Paris. You're doing great. You're a brave lady," she murmured, her throat swollen with unshed tears.

Mark walked her, but it was too cruel, so Sadie made him stop. "Mark, it's not just one foot anymore. It's both front feet, too. It's like she's walking on eggshells."

"I hoped you wouldn't notice."

He held her securely when she let the tears come, releasing the tightness in her throat. She had to accept this, she knew, but why had God allowed her to return, only to put Sadie through this pain?

"We'll try a different vet," Mark said, kissing the top of her head, stroking her back to console her.

He made the phone call that evening, Sadie by his side as they ran their fingers through the Yellow Pages, looking for the best equine veterinarian available.

Tim returned from his job, cold, his face wind-bitten, his hands blistered and bruised, his beanie lowered so far Sadie had to lift it to find his eyes. Laughing, he said it was warmer that way.

"Doesn't the wind ever stop in Montana?" he asked.

"Never," Sadie answered.

She dished up the barbequed meatballs, fried potatoes, and green beans, adding a side dish of pickled red-beet eggs. She watched as Mark and Tim loaded their plates, slathered homemade ketchup all over the potatoes, bent their heads, and ate without saying a word. They were so much alike, these brothers. Yet so different.

Since Tim had gone to the dentist and had teeth filled, capped, and cleaned, he smiled so much more often, so effortlessly, that it endeared him to her more than ever. He was definitely a work in progress. He had fewer scars from his early childhood years than Mark, but he was still a child adrift, without biological parents, anchored to Aunt Hannah in some ways, yet left to find his own way through the maze of a life divided by two cultures.

He had never stolen from anyone, but he had spent a few weeks in jail for repeated underage drinking arrests. Sometimes he talked of these things. At other times, he would retreat to that dark place, brooding silently for an entire evening for no apparent reason. The next day he would grunt to Sadie's "Good morning," wolf down his breakfast sandwich, and head out the door with his plastic cooler containing vast amounts of food. He'd return in much better spirits. Sadie just never knew. They talked about it, and Tim tried to explain it, saying he wasn't really angry, just tired of trying to be happy, in plain words.

"It's sort of like walking along a narrow road that's

slippery, and for a long time you can keep going, stay out of the ditch. Then you get tired and let go, fall in it, and stay there awhile. You know it's not good, that you can't stay there, but for a while it rests your spirit to remove yourself from everything."

Sadie shook her head. "But why?"

Mark's face was taut with suppressed emotion. "It's the remembering. It's the thinking back to times when life was a battle, when it took every ounce of energy to stay afloat, when circumstances were so overwhelming you will never, ever forget it no matter how hard you try. It's a scab you pull off repeatedly. It heals over, sort of, but sooner or later, you'll pull it off again."

Tim nodded, his eyes moist. "I probably had a much more normal childhood than anyone thinks I did. For one, I went to a one-room Amish school. Even if the children tried to make fun of me in any way, Aunt Hannah would report it, either to the teacher or the parents. So, in a way, I had that protection, which you probably never had."

Mark nodded agreement. "Still, there were good people. I remember the butcher on Second Street. He was a Jew. Had all those kosher meats. Different days they did different things. But he was good to me. He used to call me in if I stayed outside his windows, looking at the cheese and meats, my mouth watering like crazy."

Tim smiled.

Mark continued. "He used to give me a paper bag full of cheese rinds, pieces of little beef sausages, and a stack of dark brown rye crackers. His accent was so different I could barely understand what he said, but we'd communicate somehow. Sometimes he'd throw in a jar of pickled herring, and I'd eat them with mustard. He was a kind man, devoted to his stout wife and all their good-sized children."

Tim laughed. "At least they had enough to eat."

"Right."

Sadie could not begin to fathom the times of hunger, of not having the security of Mam and Dat, her sisters, the loving home. Yes, their family had problems, still had, but not without the foundation of God and good parenting. The path Mark explained was completely foreign to Sadie. That same evening they sat up late discussing the Amish church, the rules of the *ordnung*, the new birth, what was expected of Tim when the time came and he dedicated his life to God, accepted Jesus Christ as his personal Savior, took up instruction class, and was baptized into the church.

It was a long and serious conversation. Tim stumbled as he tried to explain what kept him from committing his life to God. The year of not being good enough, mostly. Mark told Tim how that had been the biggest hurdle for him as well. Grasping the fact that God loved him just as he was. That just blew him away. He explained the years of counseling, the difficulties after he met Sadie, his inadequacies.

Tim kept nodding, understanding. Then, "How's Anna?"

Sadie looked up sharply. "Why?"

Tim shrugged his shoulders. "It's been awhile since I heard anything."

"You think she's pretty bad?"

"Yes, she is. I'm not sure if my girlfriend was any skinnier when they hospitalized her."

A dagger of fear shot through Sadie. "You can't mean it."

Tim nodded. "She desperately needs counseling. Although ... I don't know. I learned a lot with my former girlfriend. If I could see her more, talk to her, I might be able to help her some."

"We can invite her over."

"She wouldn't come if she knew I was here." Tim kicked the table leg self-consciously, resorting to his usual sniffing.

"She might."

Then Tim lifted his head and asked a completely surprising question, "Do I have to change my life completely to be able to date…um…someone?"

"You mean follow the Amish way?"

Tim nodded.

"It's encouraged, but not every couple is a member of the church before they begin dating," Mark answered.

Tim kicked the table leg again, then left abruptly and went to bed.

The new veterinarian came out, prescribed a different antibiotic, and left, leaving a 200-dollar bill before driving off in his new red Hummer. Mark ground his teeth in frustration. Sadie bedded Paris with extra straw to relieve her feet from any hard surface. She felt as if her heart could break into pieces, watching Paris change positions painfully from one foot to the other, over and over, her head bent, her eyelids half closed as she patiently bore the excruciating pain. Wolf would enter the barn with Sadie, then whine and cry outside her stall, as if he wanted to help but was unable.

Mark talked to Steven Weaver, who said he remembered hearing an old remedy for foundering, but he forgot who said it or what it was. He'd write to his grandfather in Indiana. Richard Caldwell got on the Internet, his remedy for everything, but said he couldn't find any information other than what the veterinarians had told them.

Mark said he vaguely remembered the Jewish butcher on Second Street coming up with old remedies for animals, but for the life of him, he couldn't remember what it was.

Sadie brought apples and carrots, bits of cookie crumbs, even a few raisins, which Paris lipped off her extended palm halfheartedly, then turned her head away. Sadie even braided her mane and tail the way she did when she was a single girl at home. She braided a length of pink ribbon into the creamy colored hair, then stood back to admire it.

She would get better, wouldn't she? These antibiotics would work, surely. For awhile, it seemed as if they would. Paris was eating better, her eyes looking only a bit brighter, but definitely not clouded with the same pain as the week before. Sadie was ecstatic.

Anna came to check out Paris's progress, only to be completely struck when she saw this poor, sick horse sagging against the wooden slats of the stall's divider. Anna tried to contain her emotions, but the tears spilled over on to her pale cheeks. She looked over at Sadie beaming proudly through the door.

"She's getting better!" she announced confidently.

"Sadie! She's so sick! I had no idea."

"Oh, no, Anna. She's a lot better than she was."

And now Anna understood. She could not reach Sadie to tell her Paris was dying.

Was Anna the same? Sadie could not reach her to tell her she was starving.

Sadie was blind when it came to relinquishing her desperate hold on her horse.

Was Anna as blind when it came to seeing why she controlled her determination to be stick-thin? For Neil?

For that controlling person who hurt her over and over?

Anna's heart cried out for help, for herself as well as for Paris. I'm so stupid, God. Sadie is so pathetic, God. Humans are all pretty much in the same boat, aren't they?

When Tim came to the barn, he found two sisters holding onto each other as they grappled with the bitter struggles of their lives. He backed away silently, lifted the iron latch, and slowly moved through the door out into the biting cold.

Chapter 17

He turned as the latch clicked again and watched as Sadie stumbled through the door, then bent her head to gain momentum as she started running to the house, her only thought to be with Mark as soon as she possibly could. Tim waited, and when Anna did not appear, he turned back, hesitant at first, then decisively. He found her with Paris, a bewildered look in her eyes as she raised her head to find Tim watching her.

"She's not going to make it."

Tim nodded.

"Sadie will grieve terribly."

"Yeah."

Anna gave Paris a final pat, sighed, then turned, her eyes luminous in the flickering yellow light of the kerosene lantern. She stood, her arms loose inside the too-large sleeves of her heavy, black coat, her thick, dark hair too heavy for her thin, almost translucent face. She shifted her feet self-consciously, bit down on her lower lip, then, as if reaching an agreement, said his name too loudly.

"Tim."

"Yeah?"

"Do you think ... do I ... ?"

There was a long, painful silence as Anna tried to muster all her courage, her low self-esteem putting up a visible battle. She cleared her throat, jammed her thin, white hands into her coat pockets, then raised her head quite suddenly.

"Paris is going to die, right? There is no such thing as a miracle, right?"

Tim gazed at an object over her head. He would not meet those large eyes, so full of hope already lost.

"They're few and far between."

She nodded. She looked behind herself, then lowered her small frame to a bale of fragrant hay. Tim reached down and pulled another bale out, facing her as he sat down, his large hands on the knees of his jeans, as if he was unsure what he should do with them. Neither said anything. Truman scraped his halter across his wooden feedbox with a heavy rumbling sound. Duke snorted, a wet slobbering sound from the automatic water trough built between the two stalls. A black cat slunk along the stable wall, saw them, and quickened her slow creeping pace. The wind rattled a loose piece of spouting in a quick, staccato rhythm, then quieted down. Anna pulled a loose piece of hay out from beneath the baler twine, chewing it reflectively.

"You're eating," Tim observed dryly.

Anna looked startled, then caught the twinkle in his eye, her lips parted as she smiled timidly. "Guess I am."

"Feel free to eat the whole bale."

Anna laughed. The sound was new to Tim. It was the loveliest thing he had ever heard, a gentle, deep-throated, genuinely delightful sound from this frail, captivating girl. He had never heard her laugh.

She paused, tilted her head sideways, and said, unexpectedly, "Am I so thin?"

Tim searched for the right answer, took his time. "You're too thin, yes."

"How much too thin?"

"Hospital thin."

"No."

"Yes."

"You are not serious."

"Yes. I am dead serious."

"Well…"

Anna stopped, looked at her black, fur-lined boots, then lifted her head to find his gaze, kind, patient, and above all, understanding.

"I… sort of… back there with Paris, when Sadie stood there with all that false… believing… hope, whatever it was, making herself believe her horse was getting better, when in reality she's dying. I… Well, Tim, that's me."

She said his name! The most unique way he had ever heard it pronounced. Tee-yum. Oh, say it again, he thought. Please say my name again. But he said nothing.

"That's me," she repeated. "I have to stop forcing myself to throw up. I do it a lot. It's so repetitive, it's like going to the bathroom or washing my hands. Eat enough to suit Mam or Dat or Leah, whoever, feel like I weigh 300 pounds, wash dishes, slip away, and… and… well, it's easy to make your stomach obey after you get the hang of it. Am I out of control, do you think?"

"Sounds like it."

"I don't do it every time I eat something. Just mostly. I was dating Neil and he… he… He's really cute. All the girls wanted him. He likes his… girls thin, he said. I guess it was Neil's fault. I just tried to get too thin."

Tim shook his head. "Wasn't the guy's fault."

"Why not?"

"Your own, more than likely. You were trying to control him, yourself, your whole life, feeling if you were only thin enough, he'd settle down, quit his ways, marry you. Am I right?"

Anna nodded, the pain of hating herself contorting her beautiful mouth.

"He never loved you."

"He said he did!"

Her head came up, her eye's black with rebellion.

Tim shook his head.

Anna spluttered, searched for words, then dropped her head miserably.

"Sorry. Don't mean to hurt you. I had a girlfriend once who was probably about as thin as you. She was hospitalized. We almost lost her. She had to remain hospitalized, went for extensive counseling, nothing helped. She died."

Anna's eyes were very large and dark. Her thin hands came up to cover her mouth. "No!"

"Yes. She died so completely mixed up in her own world of suffering."

"Was she a Christian?"

Tim shrugged. "She was very young."

"Do you still love her?"

Tim said nothing.

"I miss her, I guess," he said finally.

"I won't die. I'll eat."

"You have to stop making yourself throw up first. Go for counseling."

"I'll ask God."

"You feel as if he'll hear you?"

Anna shrugged.

"Did you ever become a Christian, Anna?"

"Amish people are Christians always. From the time that we can sit on our Dat's knee and listen to Bible stories, we're Christians. We know who Jesus is and God and the devil, and the end of the world and hell and heaven. We're just sort of raised with all of it."

"Yeah, Aunt Hannah, the church, the neighbors, all of that, I know what you mean. But sometime, we have to go through that time of taking responsibility. We're lost, need a Savior. I'm about to start... thinking I need something... or somebody."

"You mean, get married?" Anna asked, innocently.

"No, I mean, I'm seriously thinking of giving my life to God. Repenting of my past life, accepting Jesus, that whole bit."

He could feel his face becoming warm. He felt ashamed, lowered his head, his hands hanging loosely between his upturned knees.

"Was your past life very sinful?"

"Yeah. It was bad."

"Then you need to go talk to Jesse Detweiler. He's one of the best ministers for the youth to talk to."

"Will you join the church if I do?" he asked boldly.

"I'm young."

Tim nodded.

"Why are you going Amish?" she asked.

He found her gaze, held it. She lowered her eyes first, a slow blush creeping up her cheeks.

"Anna, I was raised in the Amish church by my Aunt Hannah, a single, maiden lady. As small and round as a barrel, and rolling around her house, gaining momentum as the day wore on. She was a spitfire! Energy to spare. The house was immaculate, her garden a picture of tilled soil producing tons of vegetables. She'd yell at me for tracking mud into the house, for spilling juice, for everything. But she loved me fiercely. She'd fight with parents of kids who made fun of me, protected me. I had no Mam and Dat.

"It's Hannah who makes me want to come back. Everything about her life I want for my own. The peace she had. She'd rock on her front porch, listening for the whip-poor-wills behind the house in the mountain. She loved her birds, as she called them. Could tell the name of every bird she heard.

"She chewed people out when she thought they deserved it, but she'd go to their house with a huckle-berry pie the next day. She loved God, said she couldn't die until I became a born-again Christian."

"How are you going to do that?" Anna asked.

"I don't know. I guess just tell God that I want to be a new person, accept Jesus, then go talk to Jesse Detweiler like you said."

"Some people have a very big experience, as if God is talking to them. Did you?"

Tim could tell that Anna was a very innocent, young Christian, not sure exactly how much she understood.

"No. I just have a sincere feeling about…I don't know, I guess taking care of my soul."

"Good way to say it," Anna said, nodding.

Then, "Well, if you're going to become serious, then I guess I need to pray for help if I'm going to lean on God to help me overcome my…What did you call it?"

"Bulimia."

"No, the other word."

"Anorexia."

"Yeah, that. You said I can't blame Neil. Why not?'

"Because he was not the one rebelling. You were."

"He was, too."

"You were."

She became very quiet then. So quiet, in fact, that he watched her face, afraid he had upset her.

Then, "I want to be like Sadie." It was only a whisper, but he caught it.

She stood up to get away before he saw the tears. He heard the sob that rose in her throat and stood up awkwardly, his arms hanging loosely by his side, watching intently as a tear balanced on her dark lashes, then slid quickly down her pearl-hued cheek, leaving a small wet trail, the most exquisite sight he had ever encountered.

He wasn't going to put his arms around her. He wasn't even going to touch her sleeve. Not even put a finger on the black wool coat. He just wanted to let her know it was all right to want to be like Sadie. It was okay.

What he did say thickly was, "Anna, I..."

When she looked up, another tear shivered on her lower lashes, made another irresistible trail down her shadowed cheek, and he only wanted to feel the beauty of it. He reached out, one large fingertip tracing the wetness on the pearl cheek. He stopped tracing it, his fingers slid to her chin, and without knowing what he would do, lifted her face. Her eyes became dark and wide, her breath quickened. His eyes told her everything. They told her he was attracted to her, she was lovely, he wanted to be with her, protect her, love her to the end of his days.

Had she ever been kissed? Neil? Ah, but the Amish were strict about purity. Some of them. His hand fell away, the spell was broken. The strict rules had spoken. Still, they stood. Suddenly afraid she would go, he could not bear to part with her now or ever. He moved, pulled her close, held her shoulders, lowered his hands, and crushed the too-thin body to his, murmuring things he didn't know he said.

He remembered saying, "Stay with me, Anna, don't go. Please stay with me, here, now."

He wanted to say "forever." Her frail, thin fingers stayed on his coat sleeve, then, like a hovering butterfly and just as lightly, went up his sleeve to clasp his shoulders with a surprising strength.

Tim never understood the meaning of true love until he held Anna in his arms. He was shaken to the core of his being, the huge difference in what he had always thought was love and this tender caring, this passion to be a better person for her sake. He saw with new eyes the scepter of her love being held by the strength with which her arms encircled him.

Who let go first? It wasn't him. When they did, they smiled silly, crooked smiles, and both started talking at once, saying what they had wanted to say weeks ago. How good he looked with his dental work. How beautiful she was. How she couldn't help being attracted to him the first time she saw him. Even if she told him to go brush his teeth? When she became flustered, apologizing, he laughed, a sound so genuine she wasn't sure she had ever heard it before.

They talked most of the night. The kerosene steadily lowered by the small rectangular flame burning steadily inside the chimney, but still they talked. They decided people like Aunt Hannah and Sadie went on with their lives and never really knew the huge influence they had on other people. They were genuine individuals who were not perfect but had a kindness, a sort of goodness about them, like an aura of peace and calm that made you want to be like them. They cared absolutely.

They talked about Paris. They couldn't bear to think of Sadie parting with her beloved horse.

"Couldn't we drench her with some home remedy?" Anna asked, in a desperate voice.

Tim held very still, not even blinking.

Drench?

What was it about that odd word? He remembered it from somewhere? Was it Aunt Hannah? What was "drench"?

When the lantern sputtered, sending sparks up the glass chimney and creating a sort of film around the glass, they knew the kerosene had been used up. The night was over. They walked to the house in the bitter night, the sky black with another approaching storm, the earth still and sharp with the aching cold.

Suddenly shy, they thought of Mark and Sadie lying side by side in their big, cozy bed, creating an intimacy they knew was not theirs to have. They separated quietly, a whispered good-night their only parting.

In the morning the snow was already falling, thinly, but with the same drive that makes real storms start with a vengeance. Sadie was down at the barn trying to lead Paris out into the snow, thinking the soft coldness might reduce the swelling of the *laminae*, that soft tissue so painfully red and swollen, protruding down into the base of the hoof, causing severe pain. Sadie knew Paris was simply buying time. Some horses would already have stopped breathing. She was convinced it was Paris's will, that strong spirit, that kept her alive.

Whoever had stolen her, wherever they had taken her, had not been good, leaving her in poor health. Likely she had had a diet of corn, too much protein, or black walnut shavings as bedding. She may have had access to too much grain, which would have foundered her, then because of exposure and a poor diet had fallen into the dire case of laminitis.

Paris lowered her head, sniffing at the cement floor of the forebay as if to determine whether she had the strength to place her painful feet on top of it. Courageously now, she stuck a foot out, then another, the pain forcing her to place her feet quickly, lightly, as if she was literally walking on eggshells. Her back was bent, her haunches tucked in, as if to touch only the front of the hoof on the unforgiving concrete.

"Good girl," Sadie coaxed.

When they hobbled out to the snowy whiteness, Paris extended her neck, kept going bravely as Sadie led her in circles, something the last veterinarian had told her to try. But when her breathing came in short, shuddering gasps, Sadie could not bear to listen to the sounds of her intense pain.

Circling once more, she slid open the barn door. A lump built steadily in her swollen throat as she struggled to resign herself to Paris's fate. She could no longer dismiss the grim reaper on the horizon who would come to claim Paris. She looked up as the door opened and Tim emerged, poking his arms into his coat sleeves, pulling on his beanie sloppily, as if he had to be somewhere in a great hurry. She was puzzled, this being Saturday.

"Sadie! Sadie!"

It was Anna, racing after Tim. Incredibly, Mark emerged, pulling on his clothes with every bit as much haste.

"Sadie!"

"What is going on?" she asked.

"*Drench*! I remember that word! Aunt Hannah's neighbor—he drenched his horse with mineral oil! He said it purges the bad bacteria that causes laminitis. Cleans the stomach! Sometimes it works. Sometimes it doesn't. He cured Harry, his draft horse. He got laminitis from being too fat!"

Tim was shouting, the veins standing out on his neck.

"What?"

"Mineral oil! Do you have any?" Tim was still shouting.

"No. Oh, my! No, I don't have any. Please, Mark, somebody! Go get some somewhere."

"Call a driver?"

"Fred Ketty's store?"

"Go to town?"

They quickly decided town was the most trustworthy. The driver was called, Anna riding to town to procure it while Sadie rubbed Paris down with clean cloths. Mark paced, unable to watch Sadie as she crooned over her beloved Paris, promising help. It seemed to take forever, but finally the four-wheel drive pickup came through the whirling whiteness, and with a glad cry, Sadie straightened and came toward them.

Together they worked, pouring the oily liquid into a long-necked drenching bottle, deciding Sadie would be the one to open Paris's jaws wide enough to allow the intrusion of the bottle to the back of her throat. Would Paris allow it? Some horses fought violently.

It was heartbreaking to watch Sadie, the intensity with which she massaged the neck, speaking to Paris as if she were human, explaining every step, telling her to be good and let this mineral oil do its work. Her white scarf circled her face, and she had never been more beautiful in the light of the gray, white storm outside. She had eyes only for Paris, unaware of those around her. Paris stood, thin, breathing hard, yet her coat shone from the constant brushing. Slowly Sadie cupped her chin, put gentle pressure on it, enough to lift the face. It would be easier to get the bottle down farther if she lifted her face.

"I need a stool. Or a bale of hay," she said tightly, the only way they could tell she was under stress.

Tim hurried to comply.

"Just hold the bottle, and when I say, 'Okay,' put it in," she said quietly.

Mark nodded, gripped the bottle till his knuckles turned white. Anna looked at Tim. He raised his eyebrows. Up came Paris's head. The horse barely resisted. It was as if she knew Sadie would make everything better. That, or she was so weak, she had no strength to fight against anything.

"Okay," Sadie said, evenly.

Mark held the bottle as Sadie's thumbs remained imbedded in the socket behind the jaw bone, enabling him to slide it into the well-opened mouth. They all watched, holding their breaths as the clear, oily liquid gurgled down the dying horse's throat. They heard the swallows, saw the neck muscles contract, then broke out in triumphant cheers of accomplishment when Mark extracted the empty bottle.

"She did it!" Anna cried, beside herself now.

"We'll try another bottleful if this one doesn't work," Sadie said. Mark looked at her, hiding the doubt he felt.

They all leaned on the stable wall watching Paris. When she groaned, then heaved, her legs folding under her, and she settled down hard, they rushed into her stall. Mark stood helpless.

Tim watched Sadie as she got on her knees beside Paris, stroking her neck, talking to her. Anna hid her eyes in her hands, peeping between her fingers. Sadie decided Paris would relax if they all left her alone for awhile, saying mares would foul best when left alone, so why wouldn't this be the same? That mineral oil could churn around in there by itself. They would go to the house and make waffles for breakfast.

When Mark put a protective arm around Sadie's shoulders on the way to the house, Tim jammed both hands into his coat pockets to keep them from going around Anna to protect her from the cold and snow and to keep her by his side as long as the world revolved on its axis.

Chapter 18

THE WAFFLES TURNED OUT LIGHT, PERFECTLY caramel-colored. They'd be slathered with soft butter and soaked in maple syrup. Anna fried small patties of sausage, swallowing her hunger, dreading the act of pulling up a chair to Sadie's table, inserting a fork into that lard-laden sausage and putting it to her mouth. Couldn't she just have a poached egg? Eliminate the yolk the way she did at home? Mam allowed it.

Mark manned the orange juice pitcher. Tim sat on the recliner, put up his feet, and said there was no use four people tried to make breakfast, three were enough. Mark set down the pitcher of orange juice, made a mad dash for the recliner, grabbed Tim's ankles, and pulled with all his strength. Tim yelled but was pulled across the glossy oak floor at an alarming speed, until they both crashed into the dining room table, dangerously rocking the orange juice pitcher, which brought a resounding "Hey!" from Sadie.

After "patties down," Anna took a small sip of juice, then shifted her fingers between the knife and fork, nervously trying to portray some semblance of normalcy. Sadie helped herself to a large waffle, topped it with an outrageous amount of butter, and called across the table for Tim to please pass the maple syrup.

Anna slanted her eyes in the direction of Sadie, who was swallowing as she lifted a huge forkful of waffle to her mouth, leaning over her plate to avoid the dripping syrup. Anna took a deep breath. Sadie stopped eating, reached over, and calmly picked up Anna's plate. She placed half a waffle on it, then dabbed on a small amount of butter and a drizzle of syrup. She cut a sausage patty in half, added a small amount of scrambled eggs, and plopped the plate back in front of Anna.

"Eat."

Anna looked to Tim for help.

"Go ahead, Anna. I would love to see you put on 20 or 30 pounds."

"Seriously?"

"Of course."

Slowly she inserted the fork and pulled away with a sizable chunk of waffle attached. Anna's hand trembled as she lifted it to her mouth, but she put it in, chewed, swallowed, and closed her eyes as she savored the taste. Tim smiled at her, the corners of his brown eyes crinkling exactly the way Mark's did. She never thought she would be able to do it, but she ate everything on her plate and wanted more. She sipped juice, then pushed back to go to the bathroom and get rid of all the lard-and-calorie-laden waffle. Then she remembered.

Paris was in her stable, struggling to stay alive, the mineral oil slowly churning in her intestines. Without its help, she would die. Without calories, so would she. She needed to talk to someone.

They all acted as if they weren't aware of her eating, talking and laughing as if she wasn't present.

Clearing her throat, she said, "I ate everything, Sadie."

Sadie looked, then put a hand on her shoulder. "Good, Anna. You know you can do this."

Nothing effusive, no big fuss, just sincere encouragement. And when Anna leaned over the commode and purged all of it, she was pleased that some of it stayed in her stomach, but also pleased that she had shown all of them who was the boss. That's what they got for acting as if they didn't care, the way they talked and laughed, ignoring her totally. Tim didn't care nearly as much as he let on. He never loved her. They had only just met.

That evening Sadie walked to the barn, her shoulders drooping wearily. The thing was, the mineral oil wasn't working. She had lost her temper at Mark when he said to wait to administer the other bottle till morning, telling him Paris would be dead by then. What was he thinking?

Tim was upset about something, and Anna had suddenly grabbed her duffel bag and gone home, as if she couldn't get out of there fast enough. So now Mark was pouting, averting his eyes, not going to the barn, and as usual, her whole world had gone black the minute she knew Mark's dark mood had descended.

Why, oh, why could she not learn to keep her mouth shut?

Paris was standing. That was unusual. Just when her hope soared, Paris grunted, heaved, her legs folded, and she rolled into a heap, then stretched out on her side, her breathing coming in hard gasps. Was it fair to allow an animal to suffer this way? In addition to her three infected hooves, her stomach was churning and roiling with the slimy mineral oil. She should be walked, which would help her digestion, but on those feet, it just was not feasible.

Opening the gate, Sadie lowered herself, then slipped Paris's head in her lap. This time she would be strong enough to say good-bye. She would call the vet in the morning, and she'd stay with her as he plunged that needle into her neck. The last thing Paris would feel would be Sadie's touch. She'd have to let go.

Paris heaved, her breathing labored, then relaxed, breathing more shallowly. Sadie stroked her neck, braided her mane. She put pink ribbons in it, then said good-bye.

"I have to go to bed, Paris. Mark is mad at me, which I'll just have the rest of my life, I guess. It's his way. Just so you know, you'll never be replaced. I'm never getting another horse as long as I live. It's only you, Paris. This is good-bye. I won't leave you in this pain after tomorrow. I love you, Paris. Good night."

One final kiss on the sunken eyelid, with tears raining down her face, she struggled to her feet, closed the gate blindly, stumbled out of the barn, slipped and fell into a snowdrift, then just sat there crying. Her whole world had never looked darker. If she hadn't married Mark and all his stupid complexities, she would have been a lot better off. Smarter for sure. She wished the horse thieves would have kept Paris. Why let her come home to put her through all this? She cried on.

Tim was in a foul mood the following morning, which was still pleasant compared to Mark. He drank black coffee and grunted instead of saying good morning, his nose stuck in *Outdoor Life*. Sadie decided she had nothing to lose and told him he'd be better off applying himself to his Bible to find out how to get over something.

She felt completely unpeaceful, her eyes swollen from last night's crying, her mind made up to call the vet, Sunday or not. They would pay the bill when it came in the mail. Crows were wheeling about the pine trees by the barn, which was a bad omen. Crows always gave her the shivers. Big, black with greedy eyes, stealing eggs from pretty birds' nests, they reminded her of harbingers of evil.

"Go away! Shoo! Get on out of here!" she shouted.

They merely settled on the top branches, opened their long, black mouths, and cawed fiercely.

Resigned to her fate, accepting the crow's bad prophesy, she opened the barn door. A repulsive odor, so strong it made her hand go to her mouth and nose, slammed into her senses. Paris would not have decomposed so suddenly in winter. Gasping, she slid back the bolt, her eyes adjusting to the dim light in the stall. An unbelievable amount of excrement lay steaming in the far corner of her stall. The stench was worse than anything Sadie had ever smelled. She looked at Paris. She caught her breath. Paris was up, still in pain, there was no doubt about it. But there was a difference. She was lipping her feed box, making that snuffling noise Sadie loved so much.

"Paris!" she cried.

As if in answer, Paris lifted her tail, hunched her back, and expelled a stream of foul liquid, sending Sadie gasping for air, the latch sticking stubbornly as she struggled to get out of the barn. How could one beautiful horse smell so disgusting?

Racing to the house, she flung open the door and stopped, breathless.

"Mark! Tim! You have to come see! Quick! It's Paris! She's making an awful mess. The mineral oil is working."

For a moment, she thought Mark was going to ignore her, but he dutifully laid down his magazine, shrugged on his coat, and walked to the barn. Tim followed on their heels.

"Sure enough!" Mark said.

"Pee-yoo!" Tim backed out the door, refusing to come back in.

Mark shoveled the odorous mess out the door, spread clean straw, lifted Paris's hooves, shook his head.

"Should we...give her more?" Sadie asked, lifting pleading eyes to Mark's face.

"I don't think so. Let's see how she's doing tomorrow."

Paris was chomping hay on Monday morning. Her ears were pricked forward, and she let out that soft, rumbling nicker when Sadie opened the barn door. Her hooves were still hurting, but not as badly. Mark lifted her feet and said he would put on four new special shoes to aid in the healing process. Sadie threw herself into his arms and kissed him so soundly he had to pick up his straw hat afterward.

"Thank you, Mark. You're too good to me," she called as she went out the door, hearing Jim Sevarr's pickup truck turning into the driveway. Her whole world had turned from a despairing blackness to this vibrant, sunshiny, color-infused day.

"Jim, she's better!" was her way of greeting.

"Aw, no! Ya mean it?"

Jim was so pleased he actually took the toothpick out of his mouth, rolled down his window, and threw it out before thinking what he'd done.

The ride to work was a joy. She prattled on and on, describing the whole emotional roller coaster to Jim, who promptly put on his dark glasses, saying that sun on snow was about more than he could handle, his eyes were getting old. But Sadie knew better. They all loved Paris.

Richard Caldwell said he'd heard about mineral oil.

He just figured it wouldn't work as long as she'd been sick. He warned her that Paris might never be the same; her hooves would always be a little iffy. Sadie said that was all right, she wasn't the young girl who raced around the field of wildflowers anymore either. At least she had Paris.

Dorothy rejoiced with Sadie the way a true friend will do. Erma Keim said her dad had a "Belgiam" draft horse that they had to put down. Foundered, he was.

Dorothy winked at Sadie, said the word was "Belgian," not "Belgiam," and they got in such a fierce argument, Sadie crept into Richard Caldwell's office and looked in his enormous horse book, then had to lug it all the way to the kitchen to show it to them both.

Of course, instead of being a gracious winner, Dorothy's eyes gleamed, and she let out a resounding, "Aha! Told you!"

Erma Keim ducked her head and acknowledged her mistake, leaving Sadie open-mouthed with admiration. My, what a change Steven Weaver had brought about!

Before the day was over, Dorothy told Erma it was a fair mistake, a lot of people said "Belgiam."

Erma smiled such a smarmy grin that Dorothy stayed suspicious all week. Until she found out Steven had proposed. Steven Weaver actually asked Erma Keim to be his wife. The wedding was only six weeks away, so they could move and have everything completed and tucked into their home before spring planting.

If Erma had seemed quiet and reserved before, tiptoeing about in all her righteous goodness, she was elevated to an almost angelic height now. She sang, hummed, and whistled. Her feet slid quietly along the floor, a sort of studied gait that made her appear to float a few inches above the linoleum. She took on every menial task that no one else wanted to do. She scrubbed, cleaned, peeled, chopped, all without complaint, until Dorothy took to calling her Cinderella, which sent her into hysterical giggles, finally saying yes, her prince had arrived. After much eye-rolling and sighing Dorothy told her to go peel some onions, marriage wasn't exactly living happily ever after, so get down off yer high horse. The whole kitchen was a delight.

Sadie helped Erma scrub the dining room floor. Together, on their hands and knees, Erma became very serious. "Sadie, do you think I'm too excited to be married to Steven?"

"No, Erma. I'm so happy for you. Of course not."

"But you're thinking things you're not saying, right?"

Sadie paused, then sat on the floor, throwing her rag into the bucket of warm, soapy water. "Erma, marriage is a good thing. I love Mark with all my heart and soul. But it can be tougher than anything you've ever encountered. Personally, I don't think it's fair to us young girls to read books that portray an unrealistic version of living happily ever after. It just isn't true.

"But then I live with a man who had a very unusual childhood, and he's flawed, although only sometimes. We have many good times, but it's not the way I always imagined it to be. I read so many happily-ever-after books, and I think for some people, it is almost true. But for me...I know we will always have our dark days."

"But..."

Erma lifted miserable eyes to Sadie's. Oh, my. Something personal. She hoped she would have the wisdom to deal with it.

"But...do his feet smell okay when he takes his shoes

off?" Erma whispered this, a bothersome question that had clearly bugged her for some time.

Sadie kept a straight face and told her Mark did not have a foot odor problem, thankfully. Erma rolled her eyes, then launched into a colorful account of Steven's foot odor, until Sadie's eyes were squeezed shut and she was holding her sides laughing.

"The poor guy!" she gasped, finally.

"Well, if it's all right, I plan on doing something about it. He's not going to sit in my living room with his feet propped on a footrest, smelling like a skunk."

"Talk to Steven about it."

"I can't. I'm afraid he won't marry me then. And I do so want to be Steven Weaver's wife."

When Sadie arrived home from work that evening, there was a message on the voice mail, Mam's speech hurried, breathless, saying they were coming over for the evening. She'd bring ingredients to make soft pretzels.

Mam dropped the bomb only five minutes after they arrived, when Dat was still out in the barn with Mark. Kevin and Junior had *both* proposed. But they did not want a double wedding.

"It'll get the best of me!" Mam almost wailed.

"When? When are they planning on getting married? Surely not both of them in one month?"

"No, but just as bad. One in May and one in June. You know Leah had planned on being married last fall, then Kevin's grandmother died and his mother was so sick with her arthritis, so they put it off, and here Junior pops the question. *Siss net chide*!" (It's not right!)

Mam threw her hands up helplessly, then got up and began tossing ingredients into a bowl, soaking yeast in warm water to make soft pretzels, talking as fast as she could. Sadie smiled to herself, knowing Mam would get through this. The way she handled stressful times was to work hard and keep moving constantly, planning, taking notes.

"You'll do well, Mam," she said, reassuringly.

"I'll go mental again," she said, softly.

"Do you ever feel that way?"

"Oh, my, no. I'm so much better. I just have to take my medication."

She said it so humbly, so gratefully, Sadie loved her more than ever.

Dat was full of news from the community. David Troyer was building a huge 40-foot by 100-foot shed and was planning on building storage sheds. He shook his head, wondering if it was wise, but then, you never knew if something would go if you didn't try. And David was a manager. Sam and Clara Bontrager had another little girl named Dorothea, but something was wrong with her heart. She had been flown to Bozeman. Dat asked, what was a young couple to do these days, with medical costs like that? They'd be apt to spend a hundred thousand, depending on the seriousness of the situation.

The Amish community was fairly new, so the alms collected at church would not be any significant amount, although they could always depend on other communities for support. Dat told Mark it was a wondrous thing, this *arma geld* (money for the poor) a blessing, for sure. No one would begrudge this young couple the help that was rightfully theirs. Mark told Dat that was one of the things that brought him back to the Amish. The sense of safety, the love of community, the protection that this love of fellow men really was, coming from the place he had been in his teen years.

The soft pretzels were buttery and salty, everything a soft pretzel should be. Mam flushed with the heat of the oven and Mark's praise. The kitchen was bright and homey, Mam and Dat both in good spirits at the prospect of being held in high esteem, having two daughters getting married in one year. That was really something, in Dat's book, Mam said.

When they smiled at each other, a song started somewhere in Sadie's heart, and she knew 30 years from now her marriage would still survive, become stronger, sweeping them along on the tides of time. God was still on his throne, same as he had been for Mam and Dat, and Mommy and Doddy Miller, and their parents before them. They would have their times of anger, pain, despair, but they were stepping-stones to the good times, when the love and trust were remembered, appreciated.

God had a plan for a man and a woman. A union that was perfect, bringing a blessing on the children, so their lives were sanctified as well. The husband gave his life for his wife (as Christ gave his for the church), doing things to make her happy, giving up his nature to love and cherish his wife. In turn, she was called to give up her own will, submit to her husband's, as the weaker vessel, which really was not hard if the husband stayed in his place, subject to God's will.

The perfect circle of harmony could be ripped apart if the wife rebelled against the will of her husband, or if the husband rebelled against the will of God. That sweet, loving circle of kindness and love could turn into a vicious circle of anger and pain, the husband struggling to be the loving provider he should be, if his wife nagged, complained, and belittled him, or if the wife rebelled against choices her husband made.

It all sounded so doable the day you became husband and wife, but to actually live day by day with another person was something else entirely. When the minister said we will have rainy days and days of sunshine, he was definitely skimming across the top, sort of like spying the top of an iceberg from the crow's nest. In actuality, it was much greater and deeper and darker than anyone knew. The thing was, people were people. They all struggled to be saintly, living for each other, but they couldn't always.

Amish marriages were meant to stay. Divorce was out of the question, a sense of duty deeply imbedded, as it had been for Dat and Mam. Their days were not perfect. Their time together was good, their lives blessed, but not without the occasional air of tension, Mam tight-lipped, Dat pouting, perhaps a major disagreement erupting at the dinner table. They both knew it was wrong, but it happened anyway. Still, the good times far outweighed the bad. With Mark, Sadie had definitely bumped into the iceberg, knew its width and depth, and respected it.

Take Paris's health. Why had Mark become so aloof? Pouting in his chair when he could have supported her so many times. It was as if he tried to turn a knob and make his life go away when a situation arose over which he had no control. The resentment boiled like a pot being carefully watched, but boiling nevertheless. She wanted to shake him, scream at him, make him see the error of his ways. Why sit there like a bump, an obnoxious sort of anger permeating out of his very head, even his socks, when he should have been in the barn with her, supporting, encouraging?

But no, all he could think of was himself, what a poor victim of cruelty he was. Then he blamed her for this laminitis. How could she take the blame, when quite clearly, it was the neglect Paris suffered while the horse thieves had her?

Shouldn't Mark be getting over the fact that he had a rotten childhood as he approached middle age?

Sadie's thoughts spun away as she listened to Dat, watched Mam's flushed face, and kept an eye out for Tim. Where was he? Sadie still wondered what had happened to make Anna leave so suddenly, and Tim looking like a volcano just before eruption.

Chapter 19

As if Tim knew she was thinking of him, he sauntered into the kitchen, sleepy-eyed, his dark, blond-streaked hair tousled, his T-shirt hanging over his Amish broad-fall denims. He was barefoot, something he would not have been when he first arrived.

He had been terribly self-conscious. His feet were always hidden, he had a shirt on, and he had that constant sniff, averted eyes, the hand going to his mouth to guard against anyone seeing his decaying teeth. He had eaten quickly, his eyes downcast, sliding in and out of his chair, very seldom adding to the conversation.

Now he smiled widely, a relaxed greeting, an affirmation of his state of acceptance. He was comfortable among them, which was a God-given miracle.

"How's it going, Tim?" Dat asked jovially as he upended the mustard container on a warm pretzel slick with melted butter.

"Good! Hey, you sure you need all that mustard, man?"

Tim was teasing. Dat accepted it good-naturedly, patted a chair beside him, told him he didn't know what he was missing. Tim lowered himself into it, bringing Mam like a magnet with a plate of pretzels and some cheese sauce. Did he want coffee or tea? Some deer bologna?

Sadie smiled to herself. Mam would always be the same. Her whole life, she had *fer-sarked* (taken care of) others. Bustled about, softly whistling, sweeping, cooking, cleaning, serving, seeing to her family. Everyone must be fed, have clean clothes to wear, a clean bed to sleep in at night, shoes on their feet, coats in the winter-time, the list went on and on. But she was happy doing exactly what she did best. Serving those around her.

Dat was telling Tim about Reuben's mishap at work, tumbling backward 12 feet off an aluminum ladder, landing in a snowdrift so deep he was afraid he'd suffocate instead of breaking limbs from his fall.

Tim's eyes sparkled, then he laughed a deep down, genuine laugh, thinking of Reuben floundering about in the snowdrift. In the short time they had known each other, they had discovered a shared sense of humor that had grown and escalated.

"Why didn't he come along over tonight?" Tim asked.

"Oh, you know. He's his own boss now, too old to ride in Pap's surrey. I think I heard him ask Anna to accompany him over, so I don't know if they'll be here or not."

Tim nodded and stayed quiet. There was a space of silence, not awkward, one of those comfortable silences when slurped coffee, the chewing of soft pretzels, a cleared throat, were only sounds of companionship, an evening inside a snow-covered house surrounded by pine trees, the white moon rising above them, creating light on the snow almost as plain as daylight.

The light hissed softly, then slowly turned darker. When a gas lamp ran out of propane, you weren't sure at first if it was your eyes or if the light was becoming dim. Soon though, you could tell as the light became increasingly insufficient.

Mam swiped a hand over her eyes. "Either I'm passing out, or we need a new propane tank," she announced.

"I'll get it," Mark said as he rose from his chair.

The door burst open, and Reuben and Anna literally spilled into the house.

"Where's the light?"

"We thought no one was here!"

Sadie hurried to light a few candles till Mark got the extra propane tank and the wrench he always used to change it. This was nothing unusual, only an evening enjoying candlelight until the tank was changed.

The candlelight, however, did nothing to stop the flow of words spilling out of Reuben's mouth. Anna stood beside her agitated brother, her eyes large with remembered fright, twisting the tassels of her cashmere scarf in thin, cold hands. Mark stood, the wrench in one hand, the propane tank in the other, forgetting the work he had been about to do.

"I mean it, you guys have no idea what we just saw!"

Dat licked the mustard off his fingers before remembering to use a napkin and said it couldn't be that bad.

Sadie motioned Mark to go ahead with the propane tank exchange, then wished she'd kept quiet when he glowered at her.

"Seriously."

Reuben paused, pulled off his gloves, took a deep breath, then launched into a colorful account of their trip across Atkin's Ridge with Charlie and the buggy.

"What I can't figure out is how could they have done this for so long, right under our noses?"

"What? Who? Done what?" Mark asked, as he squatted to open the oak door of the lamp cabinet.

"We were just driving along, Charlie slowing to a walk up the steepest part of the ridge road, when these two vehicles passed, and I mean, not just passed, but zoomed past, slipping and sliding, zigzagging, fishtailing, whatever you call it. They were flying! We no more than rounded the curve, you know, just before you get to the place where Sadie and … well, you know, where the buggy went down over, that night."

He looked at Sadie apologetically. She gave him a smile of reassurance.

"Just before you get to that steep place, these vehicles slowed and turned sharply into a space I had no idea existed. Their cars, well, one was a pickup, bounced up and down terrible. You'd think they'd have busted a tire. I had a feeling … I don't know. I asked Anna if she wanted to watch Charlie. She didn't. So we pulled off. You know the right side of the road has a big turn-off before that bank goes straight up?"

Sadie nodded.

"We tied Charlie to a tree, put a blanket on him. I told Anna I was going to find out what was going on down there."

Sadie shook her head. Mark told him he had more nerve than common sense. Dat said he was nuts. Mam said that about Anna.

Reuben ignored them all and went on with his story.

"It was rough going. The rocks and ravines, no road to speak of, and it was all covered with snow. There is a road, sort of, though. I don't know why we never noticed it before. Anyway, it goes way down, through the rocks, trees, an open field, then takes a sharp right. You have to cross a creek. It's frozen though."

Sadie was horrified.

"Reuben, what were you thinking? What about Anna? Suppose she would have fallen in? You could have been shot!"

"Oh, you're a good one to warn me!" Reuben shot back.

"Now, now." This was from Dat.

Mam shook her head.

"Am I allowed to continue or not?" Reuben asked, slapping his paired gloves on the table top.

Anna reached out and grabbed them.

"So these vehicles had already gone out of sight. They went the long way out around, but we sort of took a shortcut. We had to climb another ridge, then walk through the snow another, oh, I don't know, quarter of a mile through the trees. We couldn't hear a thing. Then all of a sudden, below us we could see the lights of the vehicles."

"And Sadie...!" Reuben was fairly vibrating with intensity. "You're not going to believe this. I guarantee it's exactly where Paris was! There were vehicles' lights shining, a trail of light, rickety metal gates sort of wired together, a rough shed open on one side, more like a lean-to. Some bales of hay, some rope, some rusted drums, you know, those old oil barrels, drums, whatever.

"We heard horses then. They came crashing through the trees, strained against the metal gates, and pawed the air with their hooves. You can hardly tell they're horses. Their hair is so long they look like donkeys. And skinny! Sadie, you couldn't stand it. They're so skinny they look like walking fossils. Some of them pawed the air, but most of them had already lost their spirit.

"They just stood there, their skinny necks hanging out, barely supporting their heads. Some men got out, pitched in a few bales of hay, and those horses went crazy. They fought, tore at the hay, but a few of them were so far gone they just stood there and…I don't even know what kept them on their feet."

Reuben's voice ended on a note of desperation, and Sadie knew if he was 12 years old, he would have cried. He was crying inside now, but he was too old to allow any emotion to escape.

The usually quiet Anna forgot herself and burst out, "It's awful. Seriously. There are at least 30 or 40 horses, and if nothing's done, they're all going to die. It simply makes no sense."

Tim watched her face and couldn't take his eyes off her.

"Two bales of hay, that was it. The hay disappeared in less than 10 minutes. I was shaking all over. The guys got into their vehicles and left. We just stood there. We didn't know what to do."

Reuben took over. "Finally, we went down. We got to the fence. The horses stand on frozen ground, their unshod hooves are cracked, bleeding. The burrs in their manes and tails, the filth, there's so much disease. If we do decide to help them, where do we start? Who do we call?"

Dat shook his head in disbelief. "We all thought the end of the horse-thieving had come. None of the Amish have had their horses stolen for a long time. Where do they come from and why? If they wanted to make a profit, surely they'd feed them better, care for them, and not hide them away like that."

Mark spoke up. "The first thing would be to call the police. They would know of any organization to rescue the horses."

Tim nodded, his eyes dark. "We have to do something. We can't let those horses starve." His eyes met Anna's, and she lowered hers first.

All talk of wedding plans, community news, or any other subject was dropped, forgotten, as the men planned the following day's activities.

They would call the police in the morning, meet at Dat's house, and proceed from there. They would need direction, not knowing the course that would need to be taken.

After the good-byes were said and the buggy lights turned left onto the main road, Mark came back into the laundry room, kicked off his boots, hung up his coat, and found Sadie washing dishes, Tim beside her with a dish towel, drying. She was telling him about the misadventures of the previous years, more animated than he'd seen her in a long time.

When she heard Mark's approach, she turned, her eyes glad to see him. They clouded over with bewilderment when she received only a scathing look, a back turned, his whole being telling her he disapproved of something. Immediately her voice died, she became intense, her dish-washing taken to a tremendous speed.

When Tim went to bed, he could tell Mark was not in a good mood, and he vowed to treat his own wife better. That guy had his times. Big baby.

But then...

Tim was like a fledgling bird, his wings not used to supporting his weight in flight. God was not an intimate friend; his Christian life had just begun. He stood by his dresser, running his hand over and over across the chest Sadie had given him to keep his deodorant and cologne, his loose change, keys, or whatever.

She was too good for him. He wished he'd met her first.

Ahh … no, he was too young.

But … Mark …

"Okay, God, I don't know for sure if you'll hear me, but you need to watch that Mark."

With that, he climbed into bed.

Sadie swiped viciously at the table top. Now what?

Well, she had had enough. Being submissive was one thing, but Mark was simply acting terribly toward her, and enough was enough. He could be so friendly, the life of the evening when Dat and Mam were around. But the minute they left, he continued his dark mood, which had been hanging around for days now, while she scuttled around like a scared rabbit trying to make his life better. This scenario was not working out.

It was going to take courage, but this would have to be dealt with.

Instead of heading for the bathroom and a long, hot shower she hung up the dishcloth, straightened the mug rack, and almost tripped over the rug as premature fears blinded her. Quickly she swiped at them before kneeling beside Mark's chair, reaching out and taking his magazine away, firmly placing it in the oversized crock with the others.

Mark looked up, surprised.

"Okay. What's wrong?"

"Nothing."

"You know there is."

"Just go away. Leave me alone. I don't want to talk."

"No, Mark."

"What?"

"This is not what I bargained for when I married you.

There are no instructions for your husband treating you with complete disdain. I think it goes beyond what the minister called a rainy day. It's more like a monsoon with hurricane-force winds."

No answer. A log fell in the stove, the sparks pinging against the glass front.

"What did I do wrong now?"

"Nothing."

"Then why do you hate me?"

The word *hate* got his attention. It was a strong word, one he would never have chosen to describe his feelings toward his wife.

"I don't hate you."

What had happened? How had it come to this? That day when Nevaeh lay sick and dying in the snow, the jays screaming in the treetops, hadn't her knees gone weak with...what? His perfect mouth, that cat-like grace with which he jumped down from the cattle truck. Could she ever remember that feeling? Here was this same person, the perfect mouth in a pout of self-pity, slumped dejectedly in his lair, that same recliner he always slouched in when he was in a bad mood.

Was love meant to be this way? Was it truly all her fault? She knew firsthand what it felt like to be heartsick. She was shaken when Mark sat up quite suddenly, slapped down the footrest of the recliner, grabbed the armrests but stayed seated. His face changed color as he spoke. Why did she remember the color of his anger when the words pelted painfully in a hailstorm of hurt?

"It's all about you, Sadie! You and Paris. You and Tim. You and Anna. That's all you care about. I mean tomato soup one evening, Cheerios the next. You don't care how my day went, you don't even ask. Tonight, when you talked to Tim, you were happier than you've been with me in weeks! You don't care that I come home from work with my back aching from shoeing horses, you're too worried about Paris or Anna or Tim. You don't love me; you never did."

Somehow Sadie could picture her spirit being hit by a flying object, blown off course, righting itself, and continuing.

"Mark, that is simply not true. How am I supposed to smile and talk animatedly at length with a person who is always blind to anything or anyone other than himself? You walk around the house like an angry wolf, and in plain words, I'm scared of you. All right, I confess. I have spent too much time with Paris, and I do worry about Anna. But..."

Suddenly she burst out. "How in the world would you ever cope if we had a baby? Babies take much more time than Paris ever did."

"Maybe that's why we don't have one. You don't want a baby as long as you have Paris."

Sadie's mouth literally fell open in disbelief.

"Mark! Are you...jealous of Paris?"

There was no answer as he wrestled visibly with his pride. Sadie sat back, watched Mark's face. When he lowered it into his hands, she held her breath. Muffled now, his words came from beneath his fingers.

"Sadie, I'm jealous of everything and everybody around you."

His words tumbled over each other then, dark muddy waters that crashed around rocks, assaulting her ears. Pain of his past. A mother who chose to leave with a stranger rather than care for her children. Always, he searched for her love. If he found a tiny morsel, it evaporated the minute she left him alone with five hungry siblings, the responsibility a life-sucking parasite he could never get rid of.

Now, if he loved Sadie and she did not return it, the only thing that kept the monster of failure at bay was his anger. Anger slashed through failure and disappointment. It made people do what you wanted them to. If he got no respect or attention, if Sadie didn't act the way he thought she should, anger brought her around. It made her submit. So he lifted his dagger of anger and everyone straightened up, including himself. He didn't have to be afraid of responsibility. Of feeling unloved.

Through his volley of words, Sadie shook her head repeatedly, completely incredulous. How could she explain? She understood, then, a vital part of living with Mark. He did not have the solid foundation of two parents' love for a child. Instead he'd been left alone in a cold, filthy house with his needy, hungry brothers and sisters, watching his mother leave, succumbing to the terror of responsibility and never being enough. Having to put cherry Jell-o in Tim's bottle instead of good, wholesome milk that a loving mother warmed in a saucepan.

When Sadie talked and cared for others around her, he felt left out and wrestled with falling down a deep dark hole of discrepancy. The Cheerios. Cherry Jell-o. How could she be so blind to his unending sense of loss and inadequacy?

But he had been okay with it. Said he wasn't hungry. He had even smiled. She had offered a grilled cheese sandwich. He waved her away, and she was glad, ran to the barn, grateful. But...inside, he was churning with resentment. It was her turn then.

She apologized for any wrong she had done, but warned him that using anger as a means of controlling her would not work. Yes, she was afraid of his pouting, more than she could ever explain. And, yes, it made her submit to him, but more out of fear than anything else, which in the end brought loathing.

"You know, Mark, when you lie in that recliner and pout, what I really want to do is hit you over the head with a broom and seriously knock some sense into you. But I have to realize, you're not normal."

Mark snorted, asked her what she meant by that remark, and she told him. The fat was in the fire now, she said, and kept right on going. A good hard thunderstorm clears the oppressive heat in summertime, and so a good long talk does the same in a relationship. They ended up at the kitchen table, dipping cold soft pretzels in congealed cheese sauce, making sandwiches of deer bologna, mayonnaise, bread and butter pickles, and onion, drinking the rest of the sweet tea, and talking some more.

They talked longer than they ever had. The clock struck midnight, the moon began its descent down the star-studded night sky, casting rectangles of ghostly light across the rugs on the oak floor, and still they talked.

Mark told her the worst part of his life was trying to overcome it, which clicked in Sadie's understanding. Excitedly, she told him maybe that was his whole problem. He couldn't give up. But he *had* to give up and accept his childhood. Stop trying to get away from it.

It had happened, through no fault of his own. Why God chose to single out one small boy to suffer in such a harsh way they could never know. God's ways weren't their ways. He could not blame other people now. Yes, they had done wrong. But it was over, in the past, and they were in God's hands. Not in Mark's hands. The past was over, as soon as he accepted it.

Tomorrow was Saturday, and they could sleep in. Sadie had a long, hot shower sometime after one o'clock, while Mark put logs on the fire, checked on Paris, and locked the doors.

As Sadie covered herself with the heavy quilts, her whole body ached with fatigue. It had been a long day, scrubbing floors with Erma Keim, having her parents visit, but far above all of it, she had the opportunity of taking a giant leap in the journey of understanding her husband.

When he came to bed, she asked him if he thought Tim would ever fall in love with Anna. When he laughed and said Tim had already fallen so hard he'd never get over it, Mark took Sadie in his arms and told her he knew the first time he saw her he couldn't live without her. It was like God's hand came down and used an enormous eraser, obliterating every hurt that had ever been between them. The beauty of a relationship was not in the outward show, but in transforming the dark valleys to new heights of joy and love, brought about by the ability to forgive.

Chapter 20

THEY DROVE TRUMAN TO SADIE'S PARENTS' HOUSE after a late breakfast, their necks craning to find the secret enclosure containing the horses. At one point Sadie thought she saw a pair of tracks but couldn't be sure.

They unhitched the horse, and Sadie slipped and slid along the walkway to the house, scolding Dat for his lack of work shoveling the sidewalk. She could have fallen. Wasn't he ever going to improve? He laughed as Mam welcomed her warmly, reminding her what a treat this was, being with her last evening, and here she was again!

"Can I go along to see the horses?"

"Guess you can ask Dat. Or Mark."

As it was, they all piled into the buggy to drive to the location. Reuben was acting as if he was the town hero until Anna told him to get down off his high horse. He was acting like a banty rooster.

There was no doubt about it—Reuben was on to something. When they followed him down the side of the ridge, over the creek, and up the adjacent hill, Sadie's heart was pounding more from excitement than the strenuous climb.

She watched Anna's face, afraid she would not be able to make it in her weakened condition. But there was a healthy flush in her face, her eyes were bright with excitement, and her gloved hand slid guiltily out of Tim's when Sadie turned to look at her.

And then she saw them. It was a concentration camp for horses. It was a scene of deprivation, heartlessness, and just plain cruelty. The horses stood in their long shaggy coats, pitiful sentries of death, calmly awaiting its arrival. Some of them milled about, snuffling the snow, lipping it as if it were nutritious.

They made their way down slowly. A cloud of disbelief led them over the fallen logs and debris. How long had these horses been here? How many horses had come and gone since this lean-to had been erected?

No one spoke at first as they absorbed the sadness. It was the same as when Nevaeh was sick. What broke Sadie's heart entirely was the calm acceptance of these animals, the way they patiently endured the hardships men inflicted on them. They existed in this squalor and neglect, living in the only way they knew how, to be obedient, grateful for the few bales of hay thrown to them on an irregular basis.

Dat spoke then. "It's enough to make you sick."

Reuben was talking, talking, but the words faded for Sadie. She saw the rib cages, the jutting hipbones, the poor bleeding feet, and then knew she was going to fall into the snow in a completely uncharacteristic faint.

The cold of the snow was a rude awakening. Mark bent over her, calling her name. Dat assured him it was all right, she'd come to. He could believe this was too much for Sadie, the way she loved horses and all.

Tim leaned on the heavy steel gate, extended a hand,

but the horses kept their distance, the whites of their eyes showing their fear.

Anna yelped, pointed with a shaking, gloved finger. "There ... beside the fence," she said softly.

They all turned to look and saw the gory sight of a freshly ravaged carcass, the bones protruding from the mass of unchewed flesh where the carnivores had eaten their fill, leaving the remains for a later snack.

Nausea overtook Sadie, and she stepped aside to deposit her breakfast neatly into the snow. A hand patted her back, and Anna said dryly, "I stopped doing that. Don't you start now."

Sadie wiped her mouth, then smiled. "I wasn't planning on following your example."

Mark was very attentive, searching her eyes, asking her if she was sure she could walk back to the buggy. She assured him everything was fine, but for the remainder of their stay she sat on a bale of hay and refused to look at the horses.

Anna sat beside her. "I quit *cutsing* (throwing up)."

"Really?"

"Yep, I'm eating, too. I ate a whole entire slice of bacon."

"One whole slice?"

"Yep. And one slice of whole-wheat toast."

"When did you decide to change?"

"I didn't. Tim made me. He said if I don't quit doing this, he was going to go back to New York."

"You don't want him to?"

"No."

Sadie closed her eyes as another fresh wave of nausea approached her senses. She just wanted to leave. Get away from this sadness, these poor creatures. It was more than she had bargained for. She should never have come.

Later they called the police and Reuben escorted them to the location. Dat told him it was all right to do that, but he was not supposed to talk to reporters or have his picture taken. The ministers had warned strictly against it. They had hoped all this publicity would stop after the horse thieves had been arrested and sent to prison, so Dat was very stern with Reuben, who, he knew, was much too fond of the limelight to begin with.

So when Reuben's full length picture landed on the front page of the local paper, along with members of the Humane Society and the police officer, he had an awful time explaining it to his father. But, as usual, he talked his way into Dat's good graces, was forgiven, then had the audacity to tell Sadie he thought he looked pretty tall standing beside that officer, and how did she like the way he wore his beanie low like that?

Sadie began waking up at night, crying out, covered in cold sweat. She had never experienced nightmares like this, even following her accident. When her nausea persisted, Mark became extremely concerned, but she assured him it was only the flu and nothing to worry about. She'd just have to get the whole scene of those starving horses out of her head.

How had Paris ever managed to escape? Sadie was convinced she had been there, her emaciated state being a dead giveaway. She would have been close enough to her home that she would have been ferocious in her will to escape. Over and over, Sadie mulled this subject, playing out one scene after another. She imagined Paris running at breakneck speed, and, in desperation, clearing that fence at the last minute. That terrible, rusted, filthy gate.

She shuddered as she leaned on Paris's gate, watching

as she lifted a right front hoof daintily, as if to remind Sadie that she was healing nicely.

"Yes, I know. You're a royal wonder, Paris. All you need is a tiara, and you'll be the princess you think you are."

She turned, her ears tuned. What had she heard? Someone calling her? Quickly, she stepped outside, looked up and down the driveway and toward the house, but the sun shone on the snow with blinding intensity, so she ducked back into the barn, shivering from the cold. She swept the forebay and was reaching up for the small canister of saddle soap, when she heard it again. Voices.

Then a pair of boots hung over the ladder that went to the haymow, followed by denim trousers, which turned and crept down the ladder, followed by black, fur-lined boots.

Tim! Anna!

When Anna completed her descent, she was holding her right arm close to her body.

Tim said, "Hey, Sadie. What's up?"

Anna looked at Sadie completely guileless, as innocent as a child. "Look. I knew your Mama Katz had kittens somewhere."

Sadie was furious. "What were you doing in the haymow? Anna, why are you here this early in the evening, and Tim, why aren't you at work?"

They were completely taken aback, surprised at Sadie's suspicion.

"Come on, Sadie. Grouch. Look at these kittens. Can I keep them after they are weaned?" Anna begged.

"No."

Tim frowned, watching Sadie's face. He couldn't believe the mood she was displaying.

"Hey, just calm down. Anna wanted to look for these kittens last week already, and I promised her the first Tuesday I'd be off early, I'd help her, and today it worked out. Why does that make you so angry?"

"It doesn't."

And then because they just stood and looked at her, she began to cry, slammed the barn door, and went to the house. Someone had better tell that couple what was proper and what was not.

When the nausea worsened, the moodiness increased. Mam figured it all out, telling her she honestly thought they would soon be grandparents. Dat grinned behind his paper, Leah and Rebekah whooped and giggled and ran around the table, hugging each other with sheer excitement.

Reuben grumbled and told her in no uncertain terms that he had been right. What else could she expect, getting married the way she did, just out of the clear blue sky? Now he was peeved at this improper celebration.

When Sadie found Mam's predictions to be true, she was scared, excited, flustered, and caught completely off-guard.

When she told Mark, after Tim had gone upstairs, he took a long, deep breath, tears came to his deep brown eyes, and he said there was no way he could express his feelings just then. He held her in his arms with a new tenderness, almost a sort of reverence, and told her this was the happiest day of his life, besides the day she promised to become his wife.

He got his coat and went outside. He didn't return for a half hour or more, and when he did come in, his eyes were swollen, although he kept them hidden whenever he could. He soon showered and went to bed, which was puzzling to Sadie.

During the night, the bed shook with the force of his sobs till Sadie lit a kerosene lamp and forced him to look at her. She saw all the emotions in his dark eyes, a roiling mass of joy, pain, remembrance, hope, resolve, and she knew he was letting go, bit by bit, of his self-hatred.

"If God lets us have a child, he must think I'll be an okay sort of dad, don't you think?" he asked.

The humility in his voice was unbearably sad. Was this, then, how low his self-esteem really was, as he made his swashbuckling way through life much too often? She assured him this was so true, and it was wonderful of him to think along those terms.

Dorothy was not pleased, making absolutely no effort to hide this fact. She fumed and scolded, asking Sadie what she was thinking, and just who did she figure would take her place helpin' in the ranch kitchen. Huh? Just who?

Erma Keim was taken by surprise at Dorothy's reaction, so she said nothing.

Sadie went to work, slicing the cooked potatoes for home fries, then smelled the raw sausage Dorothy was shaping into patties for frying, gagged, swallowed, and made a desperate dash for the bathroom.

Dorothy brought her a cup of hot ginger tea with two teaspoons of sugar in it, saying, "Drink this. Put some peanut butter on these saltines. Eat 'em."

Sadie knew she'd come around, although grudgingly for awhile yet.

"You won't be able to be table waiter at my wedding!" Erma hissed when they were away from Dorothy.

"Yes. Yes, I will. I won't always be nauseated."

Work in the ranch kitchen became a challenge, then an unbearable drudgery, as her nausea worsened. She only had to smell the dish soap and her day was ruined. She finally told Dorothy if she fixed her one more cup of ginger tea she was going to turn it upside down on her head, and Dorothy became so insulted she didn't speak to Sadie the remainder of the day.

Then they found out about the horses. Richard Caldwell exploded into the kitchen, his face ashen, his mustache bristling with indignation. It took a long time for Sadie, white-faced and trembling, to explain in full detail Reuben's suspicion, his discovery, the resulting visit from the police, the professional individual who knew exactly which steps to take.

There was a huge article in the paper with the news, Richard Caldwell said. Why hadn't he known it was Reuben? The Amish had some strange ways. And he should have known Sadie would be in the thick of it, the way she always was.

He did not say this unkindly, but it hurt Sadie somehow. Richard Caldwell was a good man, devoted to his wife, Barbara, and their young daughter. He had always treated Sadie with respect after he learned to accept the ways of the plain people. Why this frustration now?

He told her, then, that he still worried about her safety. Clearly this ring of horse thieves was not giving up. The jail sentences had been handed down to the guilty individuals, but a remnant of them was bolder than ever. It made no sense whatsoever.

Sadie bit her lower lip and tried desperately to keep from crying. Richard Caldwell eyed her still face, then asked if there was anything at all she found unusual about the gates, the lean-to, the animals themselves.

Sadie shook her head. "But, then, I...don't want to admit it, but I passed out. Fainted. It was...too much.

I don't remember much, besides, perhaps the snow, the carcass."

Richard Caldwell nodded.

"I still think you need to bring Reuben to the ranch. I need to question him and your sister, is it Anna?"

Which was why they accompanied her to work the following week. They were to have an interview with Richard Caldwell, the three of them.

Reuben grumbled the whole way. He was perturbed, having to leave Dat with too much concrete work in the basement of a log home they were building. Anna didn't mind a day off work, and Sadie was feeling too sick to care either way.

Signs of approaching spring were in evidence, the way the snow was creeping away from the fence posts. Patches of gray shingles appeared on roofs where the snow had been blown to a thin layer. Water dripped off the spouting as the sun became a bit warmer each day.

The ranch had grown and added buildings every year. It was still beautiful. Sadie loved the handsome brick ranch house surrounded by well kept shrubs and trees, tended lovingly by Bertie Orthman, the master gardener.

Sadie knew, however, that her work days at the ranch were numbered. In the near future she would spend her days at home doing laundry, cooking, baking, keeping her home clean, making their own clothes on her treadle sewing machine, following the footsteps of Amish mothers all over North America. They did not work outside of the home, unless necessity demanded it. Like Fred Ketty, they might start a dry goods store or a greenhouse, perhaps a small bulk food store, but then when a baby was born, they spent their days at home, caring for the child, making do with the money their husbands provided.

Sadie embraced this future; she was thrilled by it. She loved the ranch, especially Jim and Dorothy, but there was a time for everything, in Dat's words. She was ready to devote her life to Mark and their children, the years coming like gentle waves lapping at the sands of time, living her life the way Mam always had.

There would be quiltings and sisters' days, shopping trips, frolics, and school meetings, all patches of the quilt, sewn securely, forming the essence of the community. The people would rejoice when they became first-time parents, bringing food, visiting, plunking baby gifts in Sadie's lap.

Dorothy would come, too, and Richard Caldwell. They would remain friends, but the ranch and its activities would slide into the distance, a memory to be examined time after time. It was the way of it.

When Richard Caldwell ushered them into his office, Sadie kept close to Anna, who looked as if she was being taken to the gallows, her face pinched with fear.

"It's okay," she whispered at one point.

Reuben, of course, who had reached the maturity of 16 years, walked resolutely into the office, his hands in his pockets, his neck craning as his head swiveled constantly, taking it all in—the massive oak beams, the taxidermy, (a mounted bighorn sheep, Sadie!) the huge flat-screen TV, all things he saw in the ads from Lowe's or Home Depot that fell out of the daily newspaper. But to see a television of those dimensions protruding from the wall like that was truly unbelievable. He'd never imagined them to be that big.

And when Richard Caldwell turned it on to show them the news reports he had recorded, Reuben was glued to his chair, his eyes never leaving the screen.

"Watch closely now. Isn't there anything that seems

unusual to you? I mean, this thing is chewing on my nerves. It can't be just about horses. Why horses? If you're going to steal them, shoot them, mistreat them ... "

His voice trailed off as he shook his head in frustration. He recovered when an image of the carcass flashed on screen, the pitiful bones swelling up from the snow.

"I mean, look at that. How can you make sense of it? Why steal horses if you're not going to make a profit?"

They had no answer. Not Reuben, either.

They watched the different scenes and news reports. Sadie shuddered, wishing it would stop. She felt a thin elbow in her side and turned to find Anna, her eyes huge in her thin face, pointing at the screen with shaking fingers.

"What?" Sadie whispered.

Richard Caldwell was quick to notice the disturbance. "Speak!" he ordered.

Anna obeyed, her voice gathering strength as she spoke. "The ... dead horse? The head, lying in the snow. I noticed the day we were there. The dead horse has no halter. And ... I thought it seemed weird that every horse, no matter how thin and sick, all wore an expensive leather halter, the leather, the straps, extraordinarily wide and thick. But who removed the dead horse's halter? And why?"

Reuben sat upright, his eyes wide with understanding. "Yeah!" he burst out. "I thought about those halters, Anna. But I figured it was people from a wealthy stable. Like the place the horses were taken from was a ranch like this and all their horses wore those halters."

Anna nodded agreement.

"But still, those halters aren't worth that much. Why not remove the halter? Why are they all wearing them?"

Richard Caldwell nodded, his eyes sharp, observing Sadie's face. "What do you think?"

He had respect for Sadie's opinion, having been involved in the episodes that had occurred from the very first.

Sadie shook her head. "Would it be worth trying to find a horse? See if you can examine the halters?"

Instantly Reuben was on his feet, his hands waving, as he told Richard Caldwell he bet anything those halters were made of some expensive substance and were worth a few thousand dollars apiece.

Sadie cringed when Richard Caldwell stroked his gray mustache, his eyes twinkling, hiding the smile that wanted to form.

Sadie knew Reuben was just being Reuben, completely carried away by his own enthusiasm, his guilelessness making him blurt out any nonsense, a man of the world like Richard Caldwell seeing straight through him.

"It would be worth a try."

Sadie exhaled with relief.

"Hey, you know those Chinese? What were they? Japanese? Those people whose horses were shot? You remember? We had a benefit auction for them? They got one!"

Reuben was shouting now, but it was no louder than Richard Caldwell's own booming voice.

Dorothy glared out the kitchen window, washing celery at the sink, wondering where that Sadie was traipsing off to now, riding around in the boss's diesel pickup that way? She told Erma Keim to come look, and Erma said it was likely none of their business. Dorothy said it was, too, her business. Sadie going off like that without her lemongrass tea and peanut butter crackers. She'd fall out of the pickup in a dead faint, and then what? Her well-kept secret would be out, the boss would know and make her quit her job. Then where would they be?

Erma Keim told her she'd be nauseated, too, if she was given a cup of lemongrass tea every morning, and didn't she know Sadie only drank that vile brew to please her? Dorothy said if she didn't know anything about tea it would be better for her to keep her mouth shut, so Erma did, for the remainder of the day, the fear of losing her flesh and blood blessing named Steven Weaver, a very real fear in her life.

Chapter 21

THE DIESEL TRUCK STOPPED AT THE BARN, THE vehicle's occupants spying the small, lithe form in the barnyard—a horse on a long rope loping in a relaxed circle around its owner.

The barn was small, old, but in good repair, the long pieces of sheet metal replaced with a newer variety, shinier, but with the appearance that someone cared about the place. The small ranch house was covered with new gray siding, the shutters black, a new oak-paneled door on the front. There were curtains in the windows, a tidy front porch containing only a snow shovel and a stack of firewood, neatly piled along the left side of the door.

An older pickup truck was parked beside a four-wheel-drive SUV that was also not a recent model, but it was clean and well kept. Two dogs came loping out of the barn, their tails wagging, their barking friendly.

The girl in the barnyard pulled the horse, a lean appaloosa, to a stop, then turned to lead him into the barn as they all stepped out of the truck. Effortlessly, she climbed over the fence, a weather-beaten one but in good repair, her hair tied back in a ponytail, hatless, her ears red with the cold. Her flat, dark eyes in the flawless face shone a welcome as she reached down to hush the dogs.

"Hello!" Richard Caldwell's voice never failed to take strangers by surprise. It was just so strong, so powerful. He put out a huge hand, swallowing the small gloved one. "Richard Caldwell from Aspendale East."

The girl nodded, recognizing him.

He turned. "Jacob Miller's kids," including them all with a wave of his arm.

They smiled their acknowledgment, voiced their greetings politely. Richard Caldwell told her their mission, and was it true that her family had been given one of the stolen horses?

"Doo!" Proudly, she held up two fingers.

"You got two?"

She nodded and motioned for them to follow her. The barn was well lit, smelling of fresh shavings and the molasses in the horse feed. Sadie never tired of that good, pungent odor. There was no one else at the barn, she informed them. Her parents had gone to work at their restaurant in town, but her brother was at home, coming to exercise the horses as soon as he finished his schoolwork.

"Home-schooled?" Sadie asked.

"No, no. Medical studies. Home for short time."

Sadie nodded. Hardworking, so industrious. An admiration for this family made her heart glad. Many immigrants, people seeking better lives generations before, were what made this country so good. An undeserved blessing, she thought.

The horse was brought out. Still undernourished, his neck so thin, the hairs long, every rib visible. He snorted, the whites of his eyes showing as he tossed his head in fear. Sadie had to hold her hands behind her back to keep from reaching out and stroking that thin neck, to try and calm this animal that remembered too much.

The halter was not there. Reuben caught Sadie's eye. She shook her head. The horse was wearing a blue nylon halter, a typical, ordinary one bought at any animal supply store.

Anna could not be patient.

"Was ... Is this the halter the horse was wearing when you received him?" she blurted out much too eagerly.

Innocently, the girl shook her head. "Oh, no! Leather. Much doo 'eavy!"

She walked to a cupboard, opened it, and took down a brown leather one, which she handed over for them to examine.

Richard Caldwell lifted it up, turned it around to the light. His fingers felt along the leather, the side panels, the chin strap. He rolled the thick leather between his thumb and forefinger, his shaggy eyebrows drawn down in concentration. Suddenly, with urgency, he asked for a knife.

The girl ran to the adjoining shop, returning with a retractable utility knife, which Richard Caldwell grasped firmly. His eyes intense, he lowered the halter to the floor, grunting as he got down on his knees. Instantly, Reuben and Anna followed, as Sadie's eyes met those of the girl's.

"Your name? I forget," Sadie offered.

"Kimberly See. Kim," she said, smiling.

Richard Caldwell was slicing expertly along the seam, severing the heavy thread that held both pieces of leather together. A strangled cry emerged from his throat, followed by words Sadie had never heard him use. Reuben whistled. Anna gasped. Sadie bent to see.

A small trickle of ... what was it?

"If these ain't diamonds, I'll eat my hat," he ground out, a visible tremor in his hands now.

Sadie could feel her heartbeat in her temples as she saw the trickle of whitish-blue objects hitting the concrete floor of the barn. Reuben whistled, then looked over his shoulder, as if already the thieves knew they had stumbled on their secret. Anna remained quiet, which was her way, keeping strong emotions to herself. Sadie had to know why.

They all began talking at once. Kim See was genuinely alarmed, asking them to call someone, anyone, immediately. She would not be going to prison, would she? Reuben must have felt such a genuine sympathy that he assured her no one was going to prison, everything would be all right, obviously savoring his moment of being a hero in her eyes.

Kim gave the second halter to Richard Caldwell. It contained a dark red jewel, spilling out like fractured frozen blood clumping on the hard barn floor.

"We need a bag. A pouch." Richard Caldwell said, urgently.

Kim ran off as lightly as a deer, returning with a Ziploc bag. Carefully they scooped the glistening jewels into the plastic bag and handed it to Richard Caldwell, who ran his fingers thoughtfully along the closure.

Sadie stood back, deep in thought, remembering a time in the Caldwell's bathroom when she was depositing the ragged garments into the laundry chute. Marcellus and Louis. Those dear children who had shown up at the kitchen door dressed in filthy clothes, carrying a bag from a designer shop, a bag with a small drawstring pouch of jewels. Why jewels? Was there a connection?

"It was too far out," she said aloud.

When they all turned to listen, Sadie realized she had spoken out loud, then told them about the blue drawstring bag.

Richard Caldwell nodded, then shook his head. "It does seem crazy, but … "

He seemed to connect his train of thought, then, saying they'd take these to the police station, assuring Kim that everything would be fine. Her family may be questioned, and of course, they'd have the media to deal with, but she was not to fear anything. She nodded soberly, her eyes wide, waving as they made their way to the truck.

Richard Caldwell took them all home for the day, telling them he had a feeling this was the beginning of the end. Justice took awhile, he said, but there was far more to this than horse thieving.

Lots of questions rolled through Sadie's mind. Why didn't the horse thieves take better care of the horses they had stolen? Maybe they were thrown off track when they discovered jewel-packed harnesses, Sadie reasoned. Greed makes people do crazy things, she thought, trying to imagine the mind of a horse thief.

She wondered if maybe they had a disagreement among themselves, remembering how panicked the fat man became while he was guarding her in the mansion. Maybe some thought the horses were more valuable and others got carried away by the glittering jewels. Dumb stuff happened when people grabbed things that weren't theirs.

Sadie could not face the day at home alone, so she got off with Reuben and Anna, exploding into the kitchen the way they had done as children, all three of them talking at once.

Mam had just put on her glasses, thankfully sinking

into the soft, brown recliner with *The Budget*, the Amish newspaper she hadn't had time to read all week. She had planned on a long wonderful nap, covered with the blue fleece throw Sadie had given her for Christmas. She hadn't even opened the newspaper when the diesel truck wound its way up the drive, three of the children (as she still thought of them) tumbling out and crashing her peace and tranquility. It was motherhood, she thought, as she reluctantly laid down the paper, folded the throw, and stood to face whatever had them all in a dither now.

They ate hot dogs slathered in ketchup and mustard, piled chopped onions on top, drank tall glasses of orange soda, and munched piles of potato chips. They all agreed it was the best, most unhealthy meal you could think of, especially rounded out with a huge slice of Mam's fresh chocolate cake spread with caramel icing, a small river of fresh creamy milk poured over it.

Mam said she had eaten after doing laundry, and Anna ate mostly ketchup, mustard, and onions on half a roll. But it was home, where you could say anything and everything you wanted, and you didn't need to worry about offending anyone or being responsible for black moods. Everyone laughed about the same thing, and you could punch someone if they said something wrong. They could punch you back the moment they felt like it.

They talked endlessly about the horses, the jewels, the what-ifs, the might-have-beens, adding, embellishing, but always coming back to the basic truth. It was a ring of horse thieves to begin with. It was bigger, now, as Richard Caldwell always knew it was. Reuben said he was a smart man. Anyone that owned a ranch that size was plain down brilliant. Or lucky. Maybe both.

Sadie told him Amish people wouldn't be allowed

to have a ranch that big, which Reuben corrected, saying they'd likely be allowed, they just wouldn't have the brains to do it.

"Fred Ketty would," Anna observed dryly.

"She'd be way too lazy," Reuben said, stuffing another potato chip in his mouth.

"Now," Mam warned.

Being called lazy was not allowed within Mam's earshot. Folks were relaxed about their work, which was not always a bad thing, being talented in other areas of life, and no one was to judge. Some of them who hurried and scurried their way through their work, living in immaculate homes, may be missing the roses along the way.

"But, Mam, Fred Ketty's store is a mess. She needs a *maud*," (maid) Anna said.

"Why don't you apply?" Reuben broke in, wagging a finger.

"Oh, no, I think Richard Caldwell will be asking for Anna to take my job this summer," Sadie spoke up. "She'd be perfect, working with Dorothy and Erma Keim."

Turning to Anna, she said, "You'd listen to them and never say a word."

"I won't work at that ranch. It's much too scary. Richard Caldwell reminds me of the giant I was always so afraid of in Jack and the Beanstalk. He even looks like him."

Sadie burst out laughing, then related a vivid account of the Pledge furniture polish bottle flying out of her hands when she started her job at the ranch.

Reuben said he was going to start shoeing horses with Mark, and Mam said, oh, no, he wasn't. Who would help Dat? And Reuben said that was the whole trouble with being Amish, so much emphasis on being obedient, and if you were English you were allowed all kinds of choices. Mam snorted and told him quite forcefully that English children were obedient, too, that they just naturally had more choices in their world.

Reuben went upstairs to his room. Sadie remembered the exact same feeling. At 16 you were pretty sure the whole world was full of people telling you what to do, and you were a pitiful victim of abuse, which was laughable now.

At home that evening they lingered around the table, discussing the day's events. Mark and Tim were incredulous. Tim said it was like a television show; Mark said they wouldn't know.

"It's not a part of our lives, remember?' he said sternly.

Sadie looked up from her plate of green beans and ham, surprised to see her young husband display such harsh judgment. His face was inscrutable, so she shook off the feeling of consternation, changed the subject, and let it go.

Her life with Mark was full of uncertainties. She was often left guessing what he meant, and to dig for answers was not always the best, often resulting in frustration and a sense of being left outside a barred door and being too dumb to know where the key had been left the last time.

Sometimes, trying to figure out his feelings, she discovered things about herself in the process. She did not always have to know. Just forget it, you can't understand, she'd tell herself. Until the next time.

The news swept across Montana and way beyond. The Amish community stayed out of it as much as possible, except for Reuben's picture on the front page, his beanie lowered thankfully almost to his nose, eluding Richard Caldwell even. Sadie read articles in the paper, the half-truths as well as genuine ones.

The law was busy, the way it sounded, but events of this scale took time and patience, so life went on. People lived their lives the way they do, going about their work and events, putting the horse thieves in the background until another article was printed in the paper.

Erma Keim's wedding was only two weeks away now. Sadie was eagerly looking forward to being a table waiter with Mark, her handsome, complicated husband.

She made a new dusty purple dress, the color and fabric Erma had chosen for her table waiters. She spent many hours at the sewing machine, getting the dress just right, using a wet handkerchief placed on the fabric, pressing it with the sad iron heated on the front burner of the gas stove in the kitchen.

She traveled to the town of Butte to buy Erma an expensive sheet set and bought a drip coffeepot from Fred Ketty, who informed Sadie it was the single most brilliant non-electric appliance anyone had ever come up with, saying she never had a bad cup of coffee since she owned one. Sadie laughingly told Fred Ketty she was going to miss Erma Keim terribly and planned on having coffee with her on a regular basis, before realizing she had almost given away her secret.

Her eyes narrowing shrewdly, Fred Ketty asked, "Why?"

"Oh, I…I…She'll likely be quitting at the ranch," Sadie answered, completely flustered.

"But you don't know."

The eyes behind the plain glasses bore into hers, until Sadie was every bit as uncomfortable as a guilty person at a cross-examination. She exited the store as soon as she possibly could and vowed never to go back until the news was out.

No doubt about it, that woman was one shrewd person. If you forgot Mam's words about judging someone, her store could be much better if she put more physical labor into it, which sounded better than the word "lazy."

Jim and Dorothy were invited.

Dorothy was in a stew, buying a new dress at Sears for herself and one for March, as she had taken to calling Marcellus. Dorothy was never able to pronounce the name properly, often saying Marcelona. Jim had a good Sunday suit, and Louis was fitted into one last fall for Sunday school, so he could wear that.

She was worried about the seating arrangement, saying there was no way she was going to sit on a hard wooden bench for three hours listening to a minister talking in German, unable to understand a word he said. Sadie assured her there were always folding chairs for the English people, and they wouldn't need to arrive until the service was half over. And no, she would not have to get on her knees. Sadie said she could sit while the congregation knelt for prayers, fervently hoping she would have the humility to keep her eyes downcast, instead of checking everyone out with her bright, bird-like eyes.

And then, because she knew how much she would miss Dorothy when her time at the ranch was over, her nose burned and quick tears sprang to her eyes, and she had to turn her head away so Dorothy wouldn't see.

The day of the wedding arrived, the morning frosty, the sun bursting over the mountaintop as if it shone for Steven and Erma alone. Spring was on the sun's rays, warming Mark and Sadie through the windows of the buggy, Truman trotting briskly, his coat shining from Mark's careful brushing.

The lap robe felt cozy on her lap. Mark looked so handsome in his white shirt and black suit, his beard neatly washed and trimmed, his black felt hat just right. The back seat held the wedding gifts wrapped in silver-and-white-striped paper, with white ribbon and bows, a large wedding card attached with Scotch tape.

As they approached the home of the Detweilers, the family who had kindly offered to host the wedding service, teams were arriving from both directions, the occupants dressed in their wedding best, smiling happily, everyone glad to participate in Erma's special day.

The wedding dinner was to be at the Yoder home about a half-mile away, so that was their destination, being table waiters, helping with the preparations in the morning, then sitting in the congregation to see them being joined together as man and wife by the minister.

Sam Yoder had a large shop that was painted and cleaned to perfection for the wedding. Long tables were set up along each wall, with tables in the middle of the room as well, seating as many as 150 to 200 people at a time. White tablecloths covered the tables, with white Corelle dishes at each place. It all looked so clean, white, and elegant.

When Sadie spied Steven and Erma's corner, the table where the bride and groom would be seated, she put a hand to her mouth, reducing the gasp to a mere intake of breath. Oh, my goodness, she thought. Fiesta-ware! Typical of Erma Keim. The dishes were every color of the rainbow, brilliant colors meant for a very modern, young kitchen or dining room. The plates were fire-engine red, the dessert plates an electric lime-green. The serving bowls were about the color of a cloudless summer sky, the water pitcher a Crayola yellow. The tablecloth, thankfully, was off-white, with orange napkins. But would it have made any difference if it was a lilac purple?

When she heard a girlish whisper behind her, followed by a genuine snicker, she turned on her heel and frowned at Lavina and Emma Nissley.

"Hey, it's her day, her choice. If she likes these colors, then we need to respect it."

She marched off, her thoughts tumbling over each other. There had been a time when she may have been those girls. No more. Erma Keim was as close to a saint as she could imagine anyone to be. She may be short with her temper at times, but she would do anything for anyone, uncomplaining, happy to be of assistance to the lowest of people. So what if her hair was never combed quite right or her covering was wrinkled? So she was over 30, marrying a man of questionable appearance. They would be happier than most other couples, of this she was positive.

And when she sat amid the congregation and listened to the minister pronounce them man and wife, she cried. When they stood to pray for them, Sadie added a fervent prayer of thanks for providing a husband for this deserving girl.

Surprisingly, Erma's hair looked decent on this day of her wedding, as did her covering. Steven was smiling all day, his small blue eyes radiating joy alongside his glowing bride. And when they sat down to enjoy their wedding dinner together, the glow of the brilliant dishes could not have matched better.

With Mark beside her, Sadie served dish after dish of fried chicken, mashed potatoes mounded high in serving bowls, a river of browned butter dripping down the sides, bright peas and carrots steaming in separate dishes, piles of thick, buttered noodles, stuffing, and salads arranged on oblong platters. They filled and refilled hundreds of water glasses, took away empty serving bowls, passed gravy and homemade dinner rolls.

The air was festive and joyous, the community celebrating this day of love and happiness for Steven and Erma.

When they saw the piles of wedding gifts, Erma let out such an unladylike roar of surprise. A few babies began crying. She clapped both hands to her mouth, then apologized and just stood there, rocking back and forth from heel to toe, her eyes protruding scarily, her hair completely gone awry.

Erma's day had come. She was the center of attention. Her mother and the dear relatives all knew what this day meant to her, and they had given lavishly. Sixteen-quart stainless steel kettles, more than one! Large wooden racks to dry their laundry! A laundry cart to put the clothes basket on so she wouldn't have to bend over, which Sadie knew she would never use, as bending over came easily to Erma, her tall sturdy form fluid in its movement. There were clothes hampers, a canister set, a mountain of Tupperware products, lanterns, shovels, hoes, a wheelbarrow, a gas grill.

After the initial shock, Erma seemed to remember to preserve her blessing, becoming quite sedate, a murmured word of joy in Steven's ear, a humble thank you to a special cousin, her manners completely restored, a sense of the angelic settling over her.

Sadie could only remember to thank the good Lord that Dorothy had already gone home, saying she couldn't stand one more minute in these ridiculous shoes, knowing it was more the crowd of people that drove her crazy.

When Erma opened the large gift and found the plastic flowers covering the Styrofoam cross, she spluttered and struggled, her smile becoming lopsided until she read the wedding card from the Dollar General and found Dorothy's signature. As Sadie smiled at her reassuringly, her smile returned, her day restored.

It was a few weeks after the wedding that she confided in Sadie that she thought it was someone's crude joke about their age.

"Sadie, they're graveyard flowers," she whispered.

"I have some exactly like it in the attic with the same card," Sadie whispered back.

Dorothy was so glad they liked their wedding gift, saying you just couldn't beat that Dollar General.

Chapter 22

Sᴀᴅɪᴇ ᴡᴀs ʜᴜᴍᴍɪɴɢ ᴜɴᴅᴇʀ ʜᴇʀ ʙʀᴇᴀᴛʜ ᴀs ꜱʜᴇ shoved the heavy scoop into the feed bin, coming up with a tad too much, giving it a vigorous shake, a small shower of grain sliding back into the bin. Paris tossed her head, stamped her front feet against the concrete, whinnied, and just made a big fuss in general.

"Paris, you're getting fat! You're only getting one block of hay."

Paris buried her nose in the sweet-smelling grain, chewing happily, her long eyelashes quivering with the rhythm of her teeth. Sadie threw one block of good hay into her rack, then opened the door, putting both arms around her neck for a long, solid hug. She laid her head against the stiff hairs of her mane and told Paris how glad she was they had beaten back the evil laminitis.

"We'll have many years together, Paris—you and I. Someday, you can give my children a ride, and they can feed you apples and carrots. You're still my favorite, most bestest horse."

She stopped to scratch Truman's face, then hurried out when she heard Jim Sevarr's pickup grinding its way up the driveway.

Spring had finally come, the warm breezes tugging at her covering strings and lapping at her skirt as Jim opened the door of the pickup. She took a deep breath, the odor of the pines reminding her of the field of wildflowers on the ridge in the spring. There was just something about wet pine needles that left a sweet, spicy odor in the air, as if the cold and snow had preserved the scent to make everyone happy when the warm breezes melted it.

Her usual "Good morning" was met with a grunt, a toothpick shifted, then no attempt at conversation. Sadie tried, failed, then gave up, enjoying the lovely air. The green spring emerged out of bare brown nothingness, as new life was pulled up and out of the ground by the sun's rays.

Sadie knew her days at the ranch were numbered, so each day was special. Her friendship with Dorothy had grown after she accepted the fact that Sadie was leaving her job in September, making them closer than ever. Sadie knew Erma (now Weaver, since the wedding) would take her place after Dorothy learned to accept her.

This morning, however, she met a glum Dorothy, her face drooping, her eyes red-rimmed, heavy-lidded, her mouth set in a straight line of disapproval, the very hairs on her head electric with displeasure. So Sadie swallowed the greeting on the tip of her tongue, hung up her light sweater, and tied on her apron. Dorothy was beating the biscuit dough with so much vehemence that Sadie looked for what there was to do rather than ask. Bacon done. Sausage gravy not started.

She still had the same song on her lips but hummed very quietly. Life was good. Truly. The nausea was past, leaving her energized, ravenously hungry, enjoying her food more than ever. She read cookbooks, tried new recipes, offered to bake pies wherever church services were held, always appreciating the fact that she was no longer sick to her stomach.

She was crumbling the sausage into the brown butter, the steam rising to her face, when Erma breezed in, her hair looking worse than ever, her covering sliding off the back of her head, her face pink with the pleasure of being alive.

"Good morning, my ladies!" she yelled, stopping to receive their returned well wishes.

Sadie lifted a finger to her lips, drew her eyebrows down, and rolled her eyes in Dorothy's direction. Erma raised her eyebrows, lifted her shoulders, then lowered them. Sadie shook her head.

"Sorry I'm late. We got up a bit later than usual. I told Steven we're starting to make it a habit."

She said it with so much happiness that Dorothy told her abruptly they didn't need to know they got up later than normal, in a voice that left no doubt to her objection.

There were no breaks, no coffee, just quiet, efficient work. Sadie cleaned bathrooms until lunchtime, a pleasure to scrub and polish, the bathroom cleaner's scent no longer making her ill.

At lunchtime she was ravenous, returning to the kitchen to fix herself some food. She remembered last night's pot roast, planning the sandwich she would build. She stopped short when she found Dorothy, her face buried in her hands, her plump shoulders shaking.

"Dorothy!"

Immediately, Sadie was on her knees beside her.

"Don't cry. Dorothy. What's wrong?"

"They're takin' my children," was all Sadie could fathom between the loud honks into her handkerchief.

"What? Who? Who's taking the children?"

"They. The people. Their mother."

Sadie got to her feet, sat down heavily, disbelief in her eyes as she met Dorothy's swollen tear-filled ones.

"But... how can they? We weren't sure they... their mother was alive." "Oh, she's alive all right."

This was said with so much bitterness, so much dejection, it was hard for Sadie to grasp the depth of this great-hearted person's disappointment.

"Sid down!" Dorothy commanded, so Sadie sat.

With a sigh Dorothy got up, bringing a cherry pie and a gallon of whole milk. Heavily, she went to the refrigerator, rummaging, searching, finding cheese, ham, a container of onions, then slid them onto the table.

"Git yerself a plate."

Again Sadie obeyed, grabbing the whole wheat rolls sitting on the counter. As they ate, the whole miserable story unfolded. It had all started with a phone call, the foreign-sounding voice saying she was Louis's and Marcellus's birth mother—and how soon could she come for a visit?

"I knowed it would happen. I had a feelin'. Somepin' about that there bag o' jewelry. It jus' seemed to run alongside them other ones, sewn in them horses' halters. I pushed it back, thought it was ridiculous, or tried to.

"Well, she came. Yesterday. It'll be all over the news. This woman, she's a beautiful lady, looks like Louis. She was a victim. Her husband's the brains, the whole mastermind, Jim said, behind all the thievin' and goings on. Her and the children knew too much. The husband threatened them.

"Oh, Sadie, the evil! Like the devil himself. She feared

for her life and those children's, so she did what she thought was best. She knows Richard and Barbara. She figured if no one knew where they came from, they'd never be found, and Richard Caldwell would never turn anyone away.

"She left the country, went to Spain or someplace Spanish. I ain't certain. It all worked out for her. They caught the … forget what Jim calls him. Anyway, the husband. They got him. They's a bunch of 'em. They brought her back to reunite with the children.

"The costly diamonds in that blue sack? They were to keep the children from harm. Some strange belief. I think she figured it would help provide for them, if you sold them anyhow. She don't seem pertickler religious to me.

"So, think about it. The whole horse-thievin' thing was right under our noses. Kin' you think about it, Sadie? My children's daddy! He was the one gittin' rich. Stolen horses, jewels, cars, anything he could get away with, dozens of people working for him. Livin' in a mansion. Like a king. Livin' off stolen goods. These poor innocent children."

Dorothy's voice drifted off as grief overwhelmed her. Sadie's mind raced. Was it the mansion where she had been held? Could it be?

"Them children, though. It was a sight."

She cut a wide slice of cherry pie, slid it carefully onto her plate. Taking the knife, she cut a sizable chunk off the point, lifting it carefully to her mouth, expertly sliding the knife away. She chewed methodically, then swallowed.

"Needs sugar," she stated dryly.

"Them children. The joy of the angels came straight down and settled over 'em. They jus' stood there against my couch. I'll never forget. The mother came through that door. She's beautiful. Did I tell you? Black hair, dark skin, her dark eyes. She was dressed nice. She couldn't talk. She couldn't move.

"Them children knew her. Right away, so they did. You could see it in their eyes. Louis didn't say anything. But that Marcelona, ya know how she is. Quick. She said as plain as day, 'My mama.'

"That's when it all broke loose. They just crashed together and hugged and kissed and carried on. It was a sight. I may as well not even been in the room. Ol' Dorothy was forgotten."

Sadie nodded, understood.

"We talked then. Understood. Said she'll owe me for the rest of her life. The little blue sack? They ain't stolen. They…"

Here Dorothy looked away. When her gaze returned, her eyes meeting Sadie's, her blue eyes were clouded with guilt.

"They're mine now," she said, her voice barely more than a whisper.

"What?"

Erma chose to make her entrance at that moment, announcing in her booming voice that she couldn't get the gardener to believe those pine needles were killing the hostas. Too much acid.

"Sid down!" Dorothy commanded.

Erma sat.

"Eat your lunch."

"Thank you, I will. I'm starved. That Bertie, he doesn't listen to anything I say. He thinks he knows everything. He needs to transplant those hostas. Otherwise, they'll die."

"You said that before. Get on with your lunch. We

have matters to discuss much more important than Bertie's hostas."

Sadie nodded soberly. Erma picked up a slice of Swiss cheese, turned the mustard bottle upside down and squeezed, pushing the whole slice into her mouth, chewing a few times before she swallowed.

"Like a frog eatin' a minny," Dorothy told Sadie later.

Sadie told Erma Dorothy's story as briefly as she could, then Dorothy resumed quietly.

"It's hard. It's jes' terrible hard. They stayed till evening to make things easier for me. She brought boxes. We packed up their things. But in the end, I had to let them go.

"They're going to live with her mother and dad, in New Mexico. She's gettin' a divorce. Well, an annulment. They're strict Catholics. He'll be in jail for a long time. Maybe always. She cried, said he was a good man till greed, pride, got in the way. She says he fell in with the wrong people. A horrible, bad influence. They preyed on his weakness. I think, in a way, she still loved him but knew she had to get away from him.

"I kissed them good-bye, told them to be good. We all cried, all of us. Even the children, bless their hearts. Now I'm left with them jewels. I feel so guilty. Jim says I shouldn't. I don't know how much they're worth. Jim says I can retire. I'd rather have my children. My angels, I always said. It'll break my heart at this age. I can't take it."

She cut herself another slice of pie, shaking her head.

"I'm gonna give the money to the church. Go right on workin' here till I die."

"Dorothy, why? I'm quitting here in September. It might be a good time for you to retire."

"Retire? What would I do? Crochet? No, that's not fer me. Where would I get my paycheck? Money don't grow on trees, ya know."

"The jewels."

"I'm givin' 'em to the church."

"Dorothy, the Bible says to tithe a tenth. Just a tenth would be perfectly honorable."

Dorothy ate more cherry pie, drank milk, wiped her face, then said she was in no shape to make decisions. She taped pictures of Louis and Marcellus on the refrigerator and on the bathroom mirror. She put other pictures in frames and set them on countertops. She asked Richard Caldwell if he wanted one for his office.

Jim came in for a sandwich, nodding his head as Dorothy spoke of her plans for the future. Jim's voice was so kind, so rough with emotion when he told her it was her choice, that he'd be here for her no matter what she decided to do. When he laid his large, gnarled, work-worn hand on her shoulder, calling her "Ma dear," and she lifted her weeping, red-rimmed eyes to his, the beauty of it brought a tightening to Sadie's throat.

Oh, Dorothy would work on, saying she needed the paycheck. She'd feel guilty about the money, the jewels. In September, though, she wouldn't last long. She'd sputter, falter, then say her sciatica was flaring up, and the doctor gave her orders to stop working.

She'd be happy, making many trips to the Dollar General for her necessities, enjoying herself thoroughly, tooling that old car all over the Montana countryside, visiting Sadie, taking her places, finally freed from the pressures of her job, wondering why she hadn't done this a long time ago. That was just Dorothy.

It was all over the news, then. Dat read his paper and

whistled, low. Reuben almost popped a blood vessel in excitement, saying he should be given a large reward for tracking those vehicles through the snow that night. Mark and Tim bent over the paper, reading out loud to each other, exclaiming, talking until their supper was completely over-baked.

"Dumb! I mean, what were these guys thinking?" Tim asked.

"I think they actually got to the place where they felt invincible," Mark answered. "Like, well, we're big horse thieves and got away with it all these years, so who would care about a few million-dollars' worth of jewelry heisted here and there. You know? Don't they say something like this is usually found out because of their brashness, the longer it goes on, the bolder they become? That's their undoing in the end."

Tim nodded.

Sadie sat at the kitchen table, her head in her hands, feeling tired and drained after the day's emotional toll.

Dorothy developed a headache after lunch, but Sadie knew it was more a heartache, mourning the loss of her "angels." Yet the way she had described the children's mother, how could you not be happy for them? To be returned to their rightful place, with the mother they had never forgotten, was, after all, a tremendous gift of God. It would take awhile before Dorothy could accept this, but Sadie knew she would.

Dorothy had gone home early leaving Erma and Sadie scrambling to prepare the huge evening meal. Erma made meat loaf with green peppers and bacon, a lavish sauce spread thickly on top, served with fried potatoes, cole-slaw, green beans, and onions cooked in a cheese sauce.

Sadie told her the grease and calories were stacked to

the ceiling. Erma hooted and chortled, saying nothing would be left, that all men loved meat loaf and just wait till the compliments came rolling in.

Sure enough, one by one, friendly, grizzled, weather-beaten faces appeared at the kitchen door with grins of appreciation. "Great meal!" "Thanks!" all of which Erma answered without the slightest trace of humility. She was the perfect replacement for Dorothy. No one could handle it better. She had self-confidence to spare, was a fast worker, and clean-up time was cut in half when she was there to help.

Sadie's head sank lower into her cupped hands, her eyes became heavy lidded as Tim and Mark exchanged remarks about the article. It was the talk of the community for quite some time. The elderly among them shook their heads in the wise way older people do, saying surely the world was encroaching into their way of life. They had to be more careful.

Well, that Jacob Miller's Sadie was married, at least, and the way it looked, she wouldn't be going on with too many shenanigans anymore, which was a good thing. She was the one that started the whole thing, taming those wild horses, now wasn't she?

Fred Ketty told them sharply that Sadie was as innocent as the day was long, she was just a victim of circumstance. But then old Henry "Ernie" said "God chasteneth those he loveth," and with Sadie riding around like that against people's advice, he definitely took her in hand. That shut Fred Ketty up.

The minister spoke a stirring sermon that Sunday, setting right any misplaced blame. As was their way, he was thankful. Thankful for the *obrichkeit* (government). Thankful for rulers who still enforced the law. A

community of caring English people who worked together to eschew evil.

On this Sunday, the usual thanksgiving for being
allowed their freedom of religion held deeper meaning.
To live among the English people, preserving their way of
life as much as possible, was something, wasn't it?

Change would come, but slowly. The adherence to
the old ways seemed worthless to some, but they had
structure, tradition, order, all the things that kept the
people together, dwelling in the Montana countryside.
He thanked God for the people of the community, wishing the blessing from above for them all.

It was a moving sermon, the main topic being thankfulness. Hearts were full of gratitude as they assembled at
the dinner table. The old practice of having a light lunch
after services was more meaningful that day.

The steaming coffee poured from silver coffeepots, the
pungent aroma of small green pickles, spicy red beets,
platters of meat and cheese—it was all home. It was a
place on earth where you belonged, and it belonged to
you in return. A safe place to grow, to mature, to learn,
to stay.

Being Amish, you knew there were boundaries. If you
overstepped these boundaries, you got in trouble. Was
not that the way of the English, as well? Of course it is
for every person. Here on earth, because human nature
is our burden, we all need boundaries. It was when the
fear of those boundaries is replaced with audacity, boldness, lack of respect for authority, that's when people get
themselves into trouble, just like the horse thieves, Sadie
thought. So our boundaries are a bit stricter, tighter, but
if it's a way of life, it becomes a culture, she knew.

She loved her people, from Dat and Mam to Fred

Ketty. She loved Dorothy and Richard Caldwell the same. It was the way God intended, to be friendly, share God's love, and dwell among the English in peace.

Mark was in a pensive mood driving Truman home from church, the reins loose in his hands, the warm breeze stirring the short, black hair surrounding his tanned face.

"What would you like to do this afternoon?" he asked Sadie.

"Could we pack a picnic lunch and go riding?" she asked.

"I don't know. Is it okay for you?"

"Certainly. As long as we take it slow. But let's stay off the road. No use getting anyone all riled up."

Mark laughed. "You already did rile up a lot of people with your riding."

"No more," Sadie said, soberly.

And so they did go riding. It was the most memorable ride in Sadie's life. The sheer beauty of the country, the gratitude in her heart for Paris's health, for her husband, her church, the minister's message, the sun's warmth, the waving of the wildflowers, was almost more than Sadie could bear.

And when Mark rode Truman close to Paris, reached out and held Sadie's hand in his strong one, she burst into tears of joy she could not contain. When Mark's eyes teared up as well, and he told her he loved her today more than ever, that he was thankful for having her as his wife, she sniffled and had to wipe her eyes with her sleeve. She cried and laughed at the same time and said she guessed she was a little crazy, being in the family way, but he was not to worry when she got like this.

They stopped their horses on a high rise, the valley

spreading before them in colors of green, blue, brown, and purple, the hills undulating, the colors interwoven, a tapestry no one could duplicate. The wind sighed in the pines, that sweet, mournful sound that was so achingly beautiful. It stirred Paris's mane, and Sadie reached down to grab a handful, which she held in her hand, loving the feel of the long, coarse hair.

Mark grinned at her. "You'll always love horses, Sadie."

"Just Paris. I usually have only one. Like husbands."

Mark's eyes darkened with the love he felt, and then he came close and kissed her, sending her heart into a lovely little flutter filled with rainbows of promise.

Chapter 23

Tim was nervous. He paced the floor, wishing Mark and Sadie were home. At least Sadie could tell him what to do. A huge question lay heavily on his mind, and it was driving him crazy. How did one go about asking a girl for a date? The real thing? Not just hanging out with a bunch of his friends, Anna among them. He wanted to ask her for a date, the beginning of a serious relationship. He knew in his heart he loved her. He cared about her very deeply and worried about her battle with anorexia.

He had started instruction class, his heart yearning for God, wanting a personal relationship with Jesus Christ, his Savior. He felt at home now, knowing this way of life was what he wanted. So with all the peace he felt, why was his heart banging around somewhere in the region of his ribs? He was short of breath, his head hurt, the palms of his hands were perspiring, and he couldn't hold still. He was completely miserable.

He sat on the couch, punched a green pillow, then sent it flying across the room. He wished Reuben would show up, just to take his mind off this looming mountain labeled "a date with Anna."

Finally he went upstairs, leafed through the shirts in his closet.

Brown? Nah. Blue. Not that blue. And on and on. Indecision is a terrible thing, he decided.

When blessedly, Reuben did show up, driving Charlie to the hitching rack and then jumping out and yelling, Tim began laughing before he opened the window and stuck his head out.

"Come on up!"

"Right!"

In a minute, Reuben was clattering up the stairs.

"Where are Mark and Sadie?"

"Went riding. They left a note."

Reuben was hungry and couldn't believe Tim wanted nothing to eat, insisting that he had eaten, which wasn't strictly a lie. He had choked down a slice of bread and peanut butter after church.

When had this conviction started? This steady pulverizing of his insides, this nervous churning of his thoughts? When he saw Anna sitting in church? Dressed in that dark royal blue with her snow-white cape and apron, her hair as smooth and dark as the night sky? Her eyes downcast, perfect dark half-moons framed with eyelashes. Her complexion was like pearls. Her mouth so perfect. Her innocence, the way she lacked confidence, made him want to stand tall by her side the remainder of her days.

But he was only who he was. That was the scary part. He checked his appearance in the mirror. Bad skin. Flat, nondescript eyes. Hair nothing that would turn heads. He was a nobody, really. What made him think he would ever be good enough? He knew that when a youth asked a girl for a date, it was supposed to be prayed about. He was supposed to seek guidance and obtain God's leading and wisdom. But whenever he prayed about it, he got the same bunch of butterflies he had today.

He would just go ahead and ask and get it over with.

"What's eating you?" Reuben wondered, opening a bag of potato chips with his teeth.

"Nothing. Why?"

Reuben shrugged.

✿ ✡ ✿

The supper crowd was a nightmare. Neil Hershberger was there, looking better than ever, the most confident youth in attendance. Anna stood beside him to play volleyball, the whole game making Tim so miserable he left his place for someone else to take.

The hymn singing was no better. Anna sat across from Neil, her eyes alight with happiness, Tim watching the two of them from his vantage point at the end of the table. Finally when the singing came to a close, he knew he couldn't take one more week of this. He was going to jump off this cliff of uncertainty. A flat no would be better than living like this.

Outside the night was almost heavenly. Every star in the sky twinkled and shone, spreading enough light with the help of the white half-moon, to be able to discern faces. Would she be out soon? He figured his best chance was to detain her as she went to Reuben's buggy. He had brought his own team, which took some heavy explaining to Reuben. He needed the experience, his horse needed exercise, he wanted to get home earlier, they had a big roofing project to start in the morning. He could tell Reuben didn't believe any of it.

Suddenly she was there. Straight across from him.

"Hey, Tee-yum!"

He thought he would crumble away in a dead faint, his heart's rhythm being so severely taxed the way it was. Steady, now. In his mind, he felt like the captain of a ship, using every keen sense to guide it safely through uncharted waters.

"How are you, Anna?"

"I'm good."

"Really?"

"Yes. Getting better."

"Good."

He kicked at the grass at his feet, already wet with the night's dew.

"Can we ... would you ... "

He stopped. This was all wrong. His ship had hit a sandbar.

"Anna, I'm too nervous to make any sense, okay? Would you allow me to take you home tonight?"

When her head went a bit sideways and she caught her breath, her hands going to her mouth, then a slow shaking of her head back and forth, his ship settled into the sandbar, broke apart, and sank to the bottom. His hope was gone. Maybe he hadn't worded that right.

"Anna ... "

She was whispering something. He stepped forward, lowered his head.

"I said ... I thought you would never ask."

The ship became buoyant; all the pieces miraculously slammed together. It burst out of the water and went full steam ahead with every light on and all the music playing as the stars danced and sang a chorus of their own.

He wanted to grab her and crush her in his arms. What he did, his voice shaking now, was say, "Thank you, Anna. I'll get my horse."

In the barn his knees shook so badly he could barely walk. His hands trembled so severely he couldn't get the bit in Reno's mouth. Neil Hershberger swaggered over and offered assistance, but Tim told him he could get it, he had a new horse, not used to the bit.

"That's your excuse," Neil snickered.

"Yeah, well, looks like I have it under control," Tim answered, as the bit slipped between Reno's teeth.

Looks like I do, he thought happily to himself, his teeth chattering.

Anna helped him hitch up, lifting the shafts so he could back his horse between them. They fastened the harness to the buggy, the britchment to the snaps attached to the shafts, the long, heavy straps fastened to the collar, which they slipped on to the short metal bars at the end of the shafts. Anna hopped lightly into the buggy, when Reuben called.

"Hey, what's up, Anna?"

She put her head out of the side of the buggy, saying Tim was taking her home.

Reuben came running up to Tim, slapped him hard across the back, crowing, "So that's what was wrong with you today!"

Tim climbed into the buggy and Reno was off with a flying leap, leaving Reuben grinning in the dark.

The trip to Anna's house was a dream, the kind where you never want to wake up, but just stay in that pleasant state forever. He couldn't remember what she said or what he said. He came down to earth after they were settled on the porch swing, slowly rocking, the chain creaking in time to the constant movement. His knees had stopped shaking, his teeth no longer chattered. This was, after all, his Anna. The girl he had spent hours with. How could be have gotten so crazy?

It was the leap from an ordinary, everyday friendship to a serious relationship, in which you had to let the girl know your intentions were completely purposeful, pursuing her in the way that suggested you may want to have her for your wife someday. That was a big hurdle.

But she was so light. So fragile. He really needed to know how she felt about her bulimia.

"Are you doing better, the way you said?" he asked.

She nodded.

"I am." She said it firmly.

"You're still thin. How much do you weigh?"

"I won't say."

"Come on, Anna."

"No."

"I'll carry you in and set you on the scales."

"You don't know where they are."

"The bathroom?"

She hesitated.

He jumped up, turned, found her hands, tugged.

"Okay. But, Tim, this is huge. I haven't weighed myself since you got mad. At least a few months ago."

He still held her hands. He loved holding those thin, delicate hands.

"Quiet," Anna warned.

They tiptoed across the kitchen. He noticed the orange glow of a kerosene lamp.

Good.

They both entered the bathroom. She picked up the scales, the large black letters behind the domed plastic lid, the elongated metal covered with black treads.

"Tee-yum?"

"What?"

They were whispering now, aware of the sleeping parents in the adjacent room.

"This takes a lot of courage for me."

"It's okay."

"You won't tell anyone?"

"Only if it's below 100 pounds. Then I will."

She stepped up, then put a hand on his arm, lifting her eyes to his.

"I can't."

She had never been more beautiful. The light of the kerosene lamp obliterated any shadows, casting her perfect face in a soft yellow light, her eyes luminous, pleading with him to help her.

How could he let her know his feelings for her? His emotions crashing and banging, the cymbals of love clashed their high sounds in his heart. He only wanted to convey his love. Slowly he lifted her hand and brought it to his lips. He kissed the tips of her fingers, then released her hand.

Her eyes were so large. What was the light in them? Did she actually feel the way he did?

Slowly his arms went to hers, his fingers encasing her elbows. Slowly he moved his hands to her shoulders, brought her small form against his chest, then searched her eyes.

"Anna?"

It was a question. A permission? In answer, her arms came up, stopped. He bent his head, his lips found hers, lightly. A feather touch.

"Tee-yum?"

He was strangling with feelings and couldn't answer.

"Let's not. I have to talk to you about..."

"It's alright, Anna. Sure."

She sighed and looked down at the scales.

"Up you go," Tim whispered.

She stepped up, brought her hands to her face, covered her eyes. Tim bent, stared at the number.

"One-oh-eight!" he hissed.

A sharp intake of breath, followed by Anna bending over to see for herself.

"I...gained a lot of weight," she said, incredulous now. "My lowest was 93 pounds."

"It makes me happy, Anna, and relieved. You're doing an awesome job."

"Am I?"

Firmly, he led her back to the porch swing and told her many things. She told him many things.

Reuben came home and sat on the porch rocker, his grin wide, his eyes glistening in the starlight. He told Anna he knew Tim was going to take her home, as strange as he had been acting. When he finally went to bed, they were both relieved, resuming their conversation.

She told him about Neil. He told her of his "lost" years. She told him about going out with Neil, the times she had let him kiss her, the convictions she had now.

"Tim, I need something better. I don't want to be hurt again. At first, being touched, being close to Neil made me feel loved, wanted, and for a girl like me, I depend so much on that physical touch. But I do want something better, I just have to have enough courage to think someone...you...you like me."

Tim grinned. "Well, Anna, it looks like I'm the luckiest guy in the world. The rest of my life, I want to let you know how much I love you."

Anna gasped. "Tee-yum! Those are strong words!"

"And we're not even dating, are we?" he said, laughing. "I plan on starting next weekend, if this girl will say yes."

Anna laughed with him, then very soft and low said, "Yes."

So they spent the evening on the same wooden porch swing where Mark and Sadie had sat. The same stars and moon hung low in the night sky over the same low buildings nestled on the side of the hill overlooking the Aspendale Valley.

Dat and Mam lay in the same bed, feigning sleep, wondering who was spending the evening with Anna, but in traditional Amish fashion, would not venture out to ask. This was all in secret. Parents were people to be ashamed of, respected, and definitely kept in the background until a couple had been dating for awhile, at least.

Leah's and Rebekah's weddings were scheduled in a few weeks, and now Anna was dating. Mam sighed. Dat thought girls left the house really fast after they finally got started.

Across Atkin's Ridge, in the house snuggled under the pines, Sadie woke with a start, opened one eye to look at the face of her alarm clock—1:23.

Where was Tim? Leaping out of bed, she hurried across the kitchen, her bare feet sliding across the sleek hardwood floor. The barn was dark. No buggy. Her breath came in dry gasps now. Where was Tim? She woke Mark, grasping his shoulder, shaking him hard.

"Mark! Mark!"

He groaned, turned on his back.

"It's 1:25. Where is Tim?"

"I dunno."

Clearly concerned, he threw back the covers, stuck his legs into his denim trousers, buttoning them as he moved across the floor.

"Where could he be?"

"He may have had trouble with his horse. That Reno. He's a spirited one."

Sadie put an arm around Mark's waist, needing comfort. His arm came around hers, his love and concern warm in his touch.

Headlights? They held their breath as the bluish LED lights turned in the drive. They both exhaled, then decided to stay up, see what had happened. The washhouse door opened, shoes were kicked off, and Tim charged through the door.

"Hey!" Mark said, from the darkened living room.

"Whoa! You scared me!" Tim said.

"Why don't you light the propane lamp?"

Mark and Sadie blinked in the bluish light. Mark pointed to the clock and Tim grinned sheepishly.

"We thought you may have had an accident," Mark said sternly.

"Nothing like that."

Tim grinned again, self-consciously this time. Then, as if there were no words to tell them how happy he was, he moved across the floor, gathering them both into a bear hug, one on each arm.

"I have a date with Anna."

His words were so full of happiness, they were like music. Mark clapped Tim's shoulder, congratulating him warmly. Sadie hugged him back and said she was glad.

They made hot chocolate, Tim got the shoo-fly pie, soaking it with the warm sweet liquid, and Sadie asked if Anna hadn't offered him a snack. He said she hadn't, and they all laughed when Mark said that was what Sadie used to do, too. No snack.

And then, because there was so much happiness that the house could barely contain it all, they sat in companionable silence as little swirls of contentment permeated the air.

Sadie knew their future held trials, dark valleys, days of despair, but that was God's way. He supplied the strength and courage to face each dawning day.

In the barn, Paris whooshed her nose in the feedbox, then crumpled to the clean straw, resting, content, the happiness from the house including her.

The End

The Glossary

Arma geld—A Pennsylvania Dutch dialect phrase meaning "money for the poor."

Bupp-lich—A Pennsylvania Dutch dialect word meaning "childish."

Chide—A Pennsylvania Dutch dialect word meaning "nice or normal."

Covering—A fine mesh headpiece worn by Amish females in an effort to follow the Amish interpretation of a New Testament teaching in 1 Corinthians 11.

Cutsing—A Pennsylvania Dutch dialect word meaning "throwing up."

Dichly—A Pennsylvania Dutch dialect word meaning "head scarf" or "bandanna." A *dichly* is a triangle of cotton fabric, usually a men's handkerchief cut in half and hemmed, worn by Amish women and girls when they do yard work or anything strenuous.

Dat—A Pennsylvania Dutch dialect word used to address or refer to one's father.

Driver—When the Amish need to go somewhere too distant to travel by horse and buggy, they may hire someone to drive them in a car or van.

Fer-sarked—A Pennsylvania Dutch dialect phrase meaning "taken care of."

Gaul's gnipp—A Pennsylvania Dutch dialect phrase meaning "the horse's knot."

Goot-manich—A Pennsylvania Dutch dialect phrase meaning "kind."

Grosfeelich—A Pennsylvania Dutch dialect word meaning "proud" or "conceited."

In Gottes Hent—A Pennsylvania Dutch dialect phrase meaning "in God's hands."

Kannsht doo Amish schwetsa?—A Pennsylvania Dutch dialect question meaning "Can you speak Dutch?"

Kalte sup—A cold refreshing snack served in very hot weather as an alternative to cookies. Made with fresh fruit, served in a bowl, it contains a liberal amount of sugar, a few slices of heavy homemade bread broken on top, and ice cold milk poured over everything.

Loddveig—A Pennsylvania Dutch dialect word meaning "pear butter."

Mam—A Pennsylvania Dutch dialect word used to address or refer to one's mother.

Maud—A Pennsylvania Dutch dialect word meaning "maid."

Obrichkeit—A Pennsylvania Dutch dialect word meaning "government."

Ordnung—The Amish community's agreed-upon rules for living based on their understanding of the Bible, particularly the New Testament. The *ordnung* varies from community to community, often reflecting the leaders' preferences, local traditions, and traditional practices.

Opp-Gott—A Pennsylvania Dutch dialect word meaning "almost a god," or "idol."

Patties down—Putting one's hands on one's lap before praying, as a sign of respect. Usually includes bowing one's head and closing one's eyes. The phrase is spoken to children who are learning the practice of silent prayer.

Phone shanty—Most Old Order Amish do not have telephone landlines in their homes so that incoming calls do not overtake their lives and so that they are not physically connected to the larger world. Many Amish build a small, fully enclosed structure, much like a commercial phone booth, somewhere outside the house where they can make calls and retrieve phone messages.

Rumspringa—A Pennsylvania Dutch dialect word meaning "running around." It is the time in an Amish person's life between age 16 and marriage. Includes structured social activities for groups, as well as dating. Usually takes place on the weekend.

Schadenfreude—The feeling of gladness at seeing your enemy suffer a defeat or setback.

Shtrubles—A Pennsylvania Dutch dialect word meaning "messy, fly-away hair."

Siss kenn fa-shtandt—A Pennsylvania Dutch dialect sentence meaning "That's unbelievable!" or "That's not right!"

Siss net chide—A Pennsylvania Dutch dialect sentence meaning "It's not right."

Toste brode, millich und oya—A Pennsylvania Dutch dialect phrase meaning "toast, hot milk, and a soft-boiled egg."

Verboten—A Pennsylvania Dutch dialect word meaning "forbidden."

Voss iss letts mitt ess?—A Pennsylvania Dutch dialect question meaning "what is wrong with her?"

Ya—A Pennsylvania Dutch dialect word meaning "yes."

About the Author

Linda Byler was raised in an Amish family and is an active member of the Amish church today. Growing up, Linda loved to read and write. In fact, she still does. Linda is well-known within the Amish community as a columnist for a weekly Amish newspaper.

Linda is the author of three series of novels, all set among the Amish communities of North America: Lizzie Searches for Love, Sadie's Montana, Lancaster Burning, and Hester's Hunt for Home.

Linda has also written four Christmas romances set among the Amish: *Mary's Christmas Goodbye*, *The Christmas Visitor*, *The Little Amish Matchmaker*, and *Becky Meets Her Match*. Linda has co-authored *Lizzie's Amish Cookbook: Favorite Recipes from Three Generations of Amish Cooks!*

More Books by Linda Byler

Available from your favorite
bookstore or online retailer.

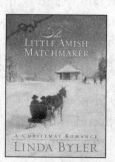

THE LITTLE AMISH MATCHMAKER
A Christmas Romance

THE CHRISTMAS VISITOR
An Amish Romance

MARY'S CHRISTMAS GOODBYE
An Amish Romance

BECKY MEETS HER MATCH
An Amish Christmas Romance

LIZZIE SEARCHES FOR LOVE SERIES

BOOK ONE   BOOK TWO   BOOK THREE   TRILOGY

SADIE'S MONTANA SERIES

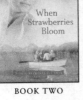

BOOK ONE   BOOK TWO   BOOK THREE   TRILOGY

LANCASTER BURNING SERIES

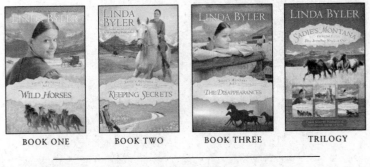

BOOK ONE   BOOK TWO   BOOK THREE   TRILOGY

HESTER'S HUNT FOR HOME

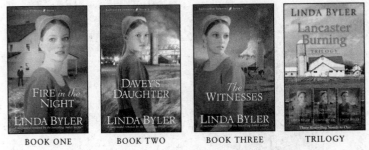

BOOK ONE   BOOK TWO   BOOK THREE